TWO KINGDOMS

DC MOORE

Two Kingdoms

ISBN 978-0-578-70928-4

Published by:
TK Publishing
Frederickson, Washington 98387

CONTENTS

Castrum Regis

Regnvm Altissimi

High Rock

Pevensey
Bridge

Bartscastle

Southwick

Sir John

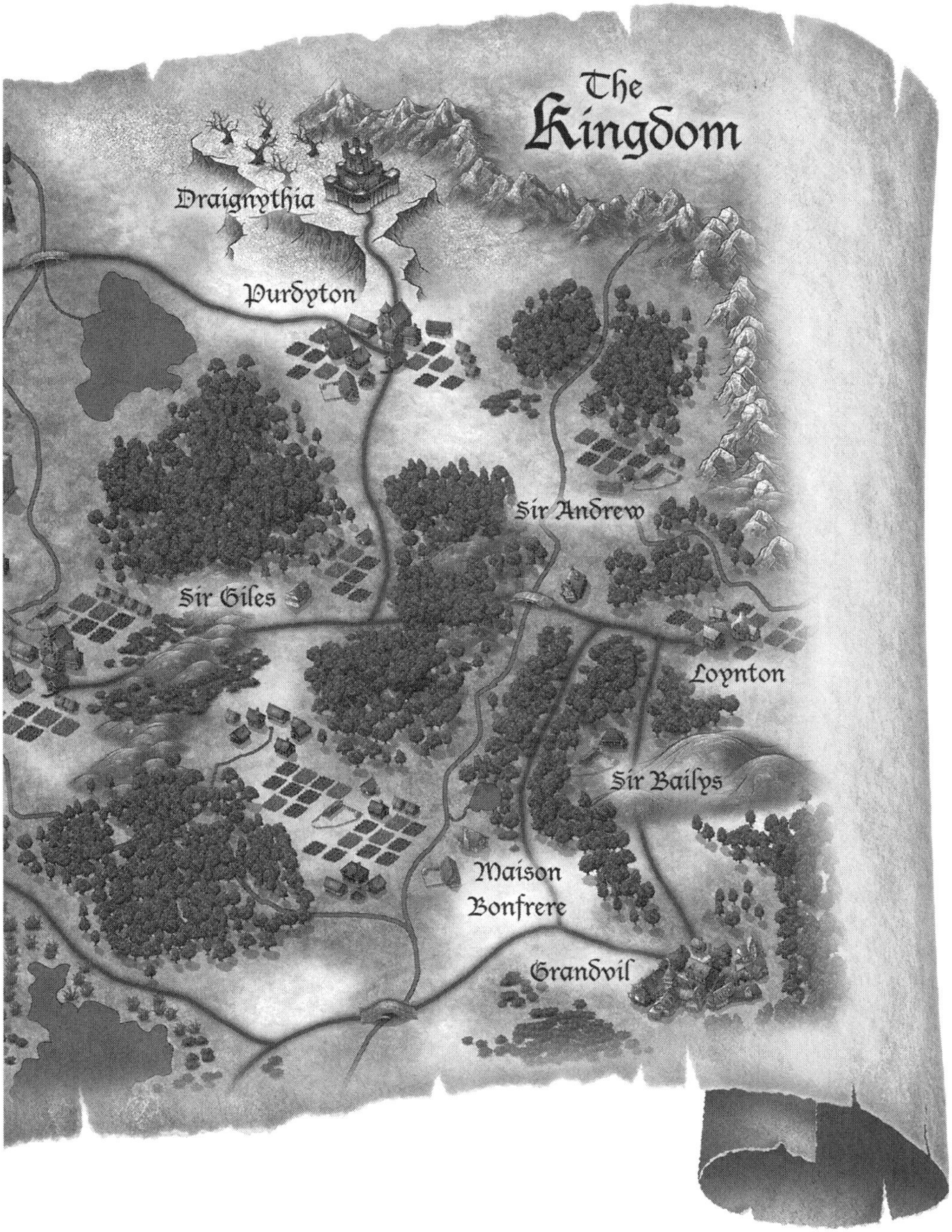

The
Kingdom

Draignythia

Purdyton

Sir Andrew

Sir Giles

Loynton

Sir Bailys

Maison
Bonfrere

Grandvil

PROLOGUE

THE MESSAGE

"T HE KING IS coming! The King is coming!"

An urgent clatter of horse hoofs on cobblestones rose above the bustle of the weekly market in the crowded town square. The throng of sellers and bargain-seekers hurried to part and make way, gathering into whispering knots among the market stalls as the breathless horseman reined in his frothing mount by the public fountain and shouted his message.

Then, as quickly as he had come, he spurred his horse and galloped away, affording no explanation.

Murmurs became excited conversations. Suspicion was replaced by wonderment.

"The King? Here?"

"We are so far from his castle. Why would he come here?"

A fair-haired, well-muscled young man loitering on the periphery of the market had also heard the message. Having finished his morning's work in the smithy, Henry had walked into the town center to buy bread and cheese. He felt equally puzzled by the announcement. The small town, Purdyton, lay on the outermost borders of the kingdom as far as he knew, and certainly could not be of much interest to the King. The unassuming cluster of buildings and houses had slumbered in its hill-rimmed bowl undisturbed for centuries. Its surrounding lands belonged to the fief of the High Lord of Purdyton, and even he did not come to the town in person, nor had he ever revealed his name to his subjects, preferring to be known only as "High Lord," though his castle, with its crenellated walls and towers, hunched on its hill like a dark beast, brooding over the town and its inhabitants. Henry supposed the High Lord owed allegiance to the King, but the townsfolk and peasants were beholden primarily to the High Lord and they paid their annual hearth tax of money and lord's share of the harvest to him in return for his protection and the privilege of farming the land.

Henry had become the town's blacksmith only in the previous year, after his father, to whom he had apprenticed, died unexpectedly from an injury—poorly managed by the High Lord's surgeon, some said. In all his twenty-five years Henry had not seen such excitement about the King, and though the King's emblem was prominently displayed inside the town inn—the Rose and Crowne—identifying Purdyton as belonging to his kingdom, the King was seldom spoken of. So after Henry bought his supplies, with a burgeoning curiosity he ducked into the two-story, half-timbered inn that fronted the square to seek out the innkeeper, James. Although he had never stayed overnight at the inn, Henry considered James a friend. James's ready smile nestled in a white beard and mustache, and the twinkle in his eyes when he smiled had a way of pulling one into his confidence. As the innkeeper James knew the business of every traveler who came through and therefore served as an invaluable source of information to those whom he trusted, Henry among them.

Henry entered and strode up to the small window where all travelers were to report upon entry to the inn. "James, have you received word that some of the King's entourage will stay with you?"

Seated behind the window at a small table lit by a rushlight, James appeared to be tallying figures on a piece of parchment. He raised his head to acknowledge Henry, the wrinkles around his eyes relaxing as he recognized his friend.

"I have not," James said. Tapping his quill on the table, he mused, "Hmm... Though it is told that the King travels throughout his realm from time to time, the announcement is as much a surprise to me as to you, but perhaps he intends only to visit the High Lord."

"That would make sense," Henry said, nodding, "but why would the messenger announce it to the town as well?"

James's eyes narrowed, his brow becoming wrinkled as if he were about to share confidential information. "You know, there are some in this town who do not believe the King is real and care little about him since they have never seen him. Perhaps he wishes his subjects to see him with their own eyes. The mayor has called a meeting at dusk in the alehouse next door to discuss how the town should welcome the King. Have you not heard?"

Henry had not heard, but he would certainly attend, if for no other reason than to seek answers to the many questions that had begun to gnaw at him.

He had never seen the King either, but he always had assumed he was real. Throughout Henry's childhood his parents had certainly spoken as if the King were real. They had described him as majestic and benevolent, one who would be well worth meeting, though perhaps with some trepidation. So, yes, Henry would welcome a chance to see this King.

After returning to the smithy, he pondered the meaning of the messenger's visit while finishing his day's work making nails for one of the carpenters. At the end of his workday, he hung his worn leather apron on a hook and placed his tools neatly back on the smithy bench as usual. He then stepped out into the rutted lane amid the sound of thunder and the hiss of rain to seek out his friend William, the tanner, to accompany him to the Thirsty Hound next to the inn. Henry soon recognized William by his shorter stature, dark hair, and closely cropped beard as he stood waiting for him at the edge of the square near where the cobblestones began. William was leaning against the stone wall of a merchant's townhouse, taking shelter under its eaves while scraping mud from the bottom and sides of his shoes with his knife. Henry announced his arrival with a clap on the shoulder, William responding with a friendly arm tugging Henry to his side.

The alehouse was usually the busiest place in the square each evening, as townsfolk gathered to drink away the drudgery of their days and soak up tidbits of gossip that floated through the fetid air, heavy with the aroma of sweat and alcohol. By the time Henry and William had reached the cobblestones that surrounded the fountain and identified the alehouse by its painted wooden plaque sporting an overly joyful, obviously inebriated hound holding a sloshing mug in one paw, the hubbub of excited and drunken townsfolk had already spilled out of the tavern into the evening shadows, echoing off the cobblestones and stone buildings fronting the square.

Stepping carefully over the bodies of two blissfully unconscious drunks on the doorstep, oblivious to the raindrops pelting their cheeks, Henry and William entered a room filled to overflowing, warmed to excess by closely packed, exuberant, ale-swilling men and women, energetically haranguing one another with questions and ideas. In front of everyone stood the mayor, straining to make sense of the commotion of suggestions. The oblong tables flanked by benches that usually sat in the center of the common room had all been piled against one wall for the meeting, all the revelers standing, rosy-cheeked, garrulously bumping into one another or jockeying for space at the front near the mayor.

"We should send someone to tell the High Lord first, shouldn't we?" one said.

"Surely he was told before we were," another added.

The insistent banging of a mug on the counter turned heads toward the mayor, who climbed with a grunt onto the counter to be more easily seen, his arms raised to gather the attention of all and bring calm to the meeting.

"We must have a feast and present the King with a gift from his subjects," he announced in a loud voice above the diminishing din of damp revelers.

"I will donate a sheep," a farmer said.

"And I will provide ale," the alehouse owner said, clearly ecstatic at the huge profit this meeting was bringing to his pockets.

"Henry!" the mayor called. "You must craft a fine gift—a sword perhaps."

"Yes, I will give it some thought." Henry offered his reply as he forced his way through the press of sticky, sweaty bodies, carefully dodging careless spills of ale onto the wood-plank floor from tipsy mug-wielding townsfolk, still somewhat in disbelief himself that the King was really coming. "But how will we know when he is coming?" Henry asked.

"The High Lord will surely know," the mayor answered. "We will ask him to send us a messenger when the King is near. And, William, since you own a horse, I appoint you to be the one to ride to the High Lord's castle to learn more."

Eventually the mayor, having restored sufficient order to hear individual suggestions and having given instructions to the eager townsfolk, called an end to the meeting. The atmosphere was the most joyous Henry had ever experienced as the crowd stumbled out into the square, backslapping and singing, each parting in a drunken daze to return home. Having themselves been carried through the door like flotsam, William and Henry parted, Henry bidding William good night, returning soberly to his smithy, still intrigued by the horseman's announcement and the unrestrained reaction of the townsfolk. He looked back in the direction of the High Lord's castle. What did the High Lord already know and what was he keeping from his subjects? The sky held no moon, nor were there stars; the blackness of the night rendered the castle invisible, but strangely Henry could feel its presence, as if it were pressing into the space above the town on tensed haunches—probing the alleyways with cat eyes, listening with bat ears.

Why had the message seemed so urgent that the messenger had to depart in such haste? Was the King already near? Henry thought about the meeting just dismissed. He could indeed fashion a fine sword, he thought, but surely the King would have a far better one, and there might not be enough time anyway. What else? He had made a mace for the High Lord recently. Or perhaps spurs. It was good to have extra spurs, and they were easier to make, but could he truly make anything worthy of a king? He would have to leave the decision until the morrow.

The next day, after completing a set of knives for one of the merchants' wives, Henry was drawn back to the square. He always tried to spend some time there at the end of each day because it was the one place where he could find out the news of the day. In addition to what he could learn from James, he could often find in the alehouse travelers who were staying at the inn and who were also eager to share news of other parts of the kingdom over a mug of ale. On this day, however, booths were noisily being erected around the square by the same hung-over citizens who had thronged the alehouse the night before. Someone had already tacked written signs proclaiming the King's coming at various sites around the square. Colorful banners were flying from the inn. It seemed as though a carnival atmosphere had seized the town. A local peasant even practiced juggling in the square. Henry sought out his friend William again for conversation over a mug at the alehouse, knowing that William had probably been to see the High Lord that day and returned with useful information.

"Have we had any message from the High Lord?" Henry asked after greeting his friend at their usual meeting place at the corner of the square.

"Shh," whispered William. "Walk with me."

Raising an eyebrow, Henry followed William out of the square down a narrow, muddy lane, overhung by crowded houses, skirting slippery trash heaps full of putrid, rotting food buzzing with flies, attempting not to breathe the foul air too deeply.

"I was not admitted to see the High Lord, but his chamberlain told me they knew nothing of the King's visit and we should not expect one," William said once they were out of earshot. "He added that they would certainly be on the watch for his entourage. He seemed somewhat caught off guard and upset by the news."

"Why?" Henry said. *How could he not know? He is the lord of the fief!* It made no sense. "Then who was the rider?" Henry continued. "His horse bore the emblem of the King. And why would our lord be upset by a visit from the King? It would be a distinct honor, would it not?"

"I do not know what to think," William answered, shrugging. Pausing to look around for eavesdroppers, he added, "I believe we should still prepare.

Remember the stories passed down in our families of the King's coming? They said he would come with little warning and we should always be prepared because he would reward those who were prepared for him."

Henry did recall from his childhood the stories of the King coming to be with his people. He had not fully understood what this meant, though his parents seemed to be looking forward to such an event with great hope. Likewise he was not sure what it meant to be prepared, nor had he any idea what a reward for those prepared was all about, but it had sounded good enough.

The following day two armored riders from the castle arrived in the square. After posting notices at the alehouse, on the pillory and stocks, on some of the booths, and at the inn, they returned to the castle. The message, written on parchment, read:

Proclamation

A rumor has been spread
about a visit from the King.
There is no truth to this rumor.
If the King is to come,
you will hear of it first from me.
There is no cause to plan
a feast of welcome.
Return to your normal work.

High Lord of Purdyton

Having read the announcement, Henry was troubled. He found William again later that afternoon in the town square among the gaily festooned booths and gossiping groups of townsfolk. "Come and see this," he said to William, tugging him to one of parchments announcing the King's coming. A large 'X' in smeared mud defaced the parchment, obscuring the hand-drawn King's emblem and the words.

"Who would do this?" William asked.

"Remember what you told me yesterday? The High Lord's soldiers were here in the square earlier today. Have you talked to the mayor yet?"

William nodded. "I told him of my experience, and he did not believe me, but now he will. I think he will call off the celebration."

"What about the gift you were going to make for the King?" Henry asked.

William paused as if to consider the implications of the High Lord's proclamation and the vandalized announcement. "I am disturbed by the reaction of the chamberlain and the attempt to cross out this sign. It seems that he and the High Lord do not want the King to come, as if it were an unwelcome intrusion. But what he is responding to is not a rumor. There was definitely a messenger and he came from the King. Why would the King send a messenger if he did not intend to come? The question in my mind is, when?"

William jumped back against the wall of a house to dodge the splash of a chamber pot being emptied above him into the street. "An additional question I have is why the High Lord would want us to ignore what we have seen with our own eyes and heard with our own ears. I think I will still make my gift."

The High Lord's proclamation was the news of the day in the Thirsty Hound as Henry and William took a smaller square table in the corner, each sitting on an empty barrel that served as a stool, eavesdropping over their mugs of ale. They found nothing new to be learned, except there now seemed to be a division among the townsfolk—those who still believed the King would come and those who believed the High Lord's announcement. After parting company with William, Henry pondered the events of the past two days as he returned to the smithy. Why would the High Lord not know of the King's coming? He would undoubtedly be required to host the King. Was it possible that he did know but did not want his subjects to know? Henry could not dismiss William's answer. A messenger would not come without a reason. Henry decided he would still make his gift as well.

The next day, as William had predicted the night before, the booths came down and the banners disappeared. The atmosphere in the town changed overnight from one of celebration to one of gloom. Henry sat with William in a nearly empty alehouse that evening, listening to an alcohol-tinged drone of disappointment and dissatisfaction from the few regulars who still came.

"I told you the King would never come here," the miller said to his companions.

"Who are we to the King, anyway?" the apothecary asked.

"Who would play such a mean trick on us?" the carter said.

And that was that. After a week had passed and no more news of the King came, Henry heard no more talk of the King, as if he were a figment of one's imagination and the whole event involving the message a cruel joke.

Some days later Henry heard someone enter his smithy while he was working. "Can you make a key?" asked a deep male voice.

"Of course," Henry answered. He did not bother to look up, giving his fire another puff from the bellows, then continuing to hammer the blade of an axe. "There are some examples on the wall," he said, motioning behind him.

"No, I would like you to make one like this."

Henry glanced up to see the man—a stranger, cloaked and hooded so that his face could not be seen—pulling from beneath his cloak a small piece of parchment displaying a drawing with dimensions. There was nothing special about it, Henry thought after looking at it.

"I can have it ready tomorrow," he replied, focusing again on the axe blade.

"Excellent," the man said. "Bring it to me at the inn."

"Certainly," Henry answered as he looked up. "And who are—"

But the stranger was gone. Henry rushed out into the lane. The man had vanished.

The next day Henry finished the key as requested and strolled to the inn, whistling an old folk tune, wishing he had taken more time to engage the stranger in conversation to learn his identity and the purpose of the key, though in fact it was none of his business. As he stood beneath the weathered sign, its faded long-stem red rose resting within an equally faded golden circlet, his hand on the door ready to enter, he paused. How could he find the stranger if he did not know his name? Nor could he even describe his face, for he had not seen it.

Henry entered and, as best he could, described the man and his mission to James, who nodded even as his kindly face assumed a puzzled expression.

"He departed this morning," James replied. "But he told me to give this to you." The innkeeper lifted a wooden box from the floor and set it on the rough-hewn ledge of the window where Henry stood. "He said that you would have the key for it."

Henry was equally baffled why the stranger would not stay to receive the key, as well as why he would leave a box for him without explaining its purpose. He picked the box up, thanked James, then took a seat on a bench in the foyer of the inn. Examining the box, he turned it over from one side to the other. It was about a foot long and half that wide but made of an unusual wood that Henry did not recognize, its sides fitted with remarkable precision. Strips of iron crossed the rounded top and continued around underneath. He saw no apparent keyhole, but where the keyhole should have been he discovered a metal medallion adorned with a bird of some kind. Henry had seen this sort of hidden keyhole before; he had even made this kind of device for boxes. He pushed laterally with his thumb and the medallion snapped to the side, revealing the keyhole. Henry fitted the key into the lock and turned it. A click sounded, and the lid lifted easily.

Inside lay a parchment scroll with a wax seal bearing the image of the same bird as on the medallion. *Who would send something like this to me? And why?* After breaking the seal and taking care in unrolling the scroll, he gazed at what appeared to be a map. His eyes scanned the details, noting roads, rivers, villages, orchards, and pastures. He looked around the edges of the map for the town of Purdyton, assuming it would be on the boundary somewhere, but, surprisingly, almost nothing was labeled, and the few written names were in a tongue strange to him. At the bottom were the words *Regnum Altissimi.* In the center was a castle, labeled *Castrum Regis.* All the roads and rivers seemed to fan out from it. Henry found no castle of Purdyton either.

Henry showed it to William later that day. "What does it mean?" he asked William. "And why would it come to me?"

"I do not know," William said, pursing his lips. "Come to think of it, I never imagined our kingdom having a name. I know we have a king and he has a kingdom, and our lord is the High Lord of Purdyton. I don't know if that map is our kingdom or not. Purdyton is not on it."

"Then what does it represent? And who was the stranger who gave it to me?"

Like Henry, William had no answer.

"I will keep it and ask the traveler if he comes through again," Henry concluded.

Henry sat alone by the forge after leaving William, unable to banish from his mind the strange events of the past few days. He was puzzled still by the inscrutable map, the mysterious stranger, and the news of the King's visit. Were they somehow connected? He could make no sense of it. But he had decided what to make for the King: he would fashion a fine steel battle-axe that bore his emblem on the blade. William had confided that he would craft a covering for a shield made by a carpenter friend that would display the King's emblem in different colors of leather. And they would present their gifts to him together—if he ever came.

MISGIVINGS

AS DAYS AND weeks passed, with neither news of the King, a return of the messenger, nor even the return of the stranger, Henry and William no longer talked about the King, or the map. They remained merely mysterious events for which there was no explanation. One evening as they sat in the alehouse nursing mugs of ale and discussing their day, they noticed a cluster of townsfolk around the table of a new traveler.

"He is a teacher," replied the alehouse owner to Henry's query.

Just as Henry and William had maneuvered close enough to eavesdrop, the door to the alehouse flew open with a bang. One of the High Lord's soldiers marched straight to the teacher's table, scattering the stunned listeners, and grabbed the teacher by his cloak before brusquely ushering him out without a word from either him or the soldier. The startled crowd reacted in shock and fear, some scurrying right out of the alehouse.

Henry caught one of the remaining listeners by the arm as he too was hurrying out. "Why was he taken?" he asked.

"He was telling us things about the High Lord," answered the trembling man, struggling to break free.

"What things?" Henry said, more curious than ever about the High Lord by now, having read the notices posted around the square and having discussed the implications with William.

"Dangerous things," whispered the man.

"Such as? Don't be evasive, man!" Henry barked, grabbing the man with both hands, giving him a shake.

"Such as, the High Lord does not give his allegiance to the King, but to himself. He does not give a portion of our taxes to the King as he should but uses it to build his army and improve his castle. He says that our lord does not tell us the truth about the King. Now let go of me! I have told you enough!"

"What truth about the King?" Henry inquired, relaxing his grip.

"He was about to tell us when the soldier came in." The frightened man broke free and bolted for the door.

Henry and William left the alehouse soon after, deeply troubled by the event. In all the years they had been going to the alehouse, they had never seen someone seized and dragged away. In their minds they began to question the benevolence of their lord. It seemed as if their lord's attitude had changed to one of hostility toward the King since the visit by the messenger.

The next day new notices were posted in the town square:

Proclamation

All travelers who pass
the night in Purdyton
must register at the inn
and state their purpose.

High Lord of Purdyton

The townsfolk became even gloomier, if that were possible. The innkeeper, James, seemed especially morose. Many of the interesting travelers who used to stay there no longer came, as if Purdyton had been marked as a town to avoid. It became difficult to hear news of the kingdom outside Purdyton. Moreover the High Lord stationed an armed guard in the town square next to the pillory, and the guard seemed to be watching everyone who came through.

Nevertheless Henry still came to the alehouse to meet William for their habitual mug of ale, but they often found the alehouse nearly empty except for them. The alehouse owner remained mum about the new announcement and the behavior of the High Lord, and even people in the town were less willing to talk—about anything. Henry sensed an amorphous undercurrent of anxiety and fear in the town, causing people to distrust each other. Fortunately the ale at the alehouse still loosened tongues. A rumor began to circulate about one of the merchants who had sold everything he had, closed his shop, and left the town. He gave no explanation, except to say that it was "for the kingdom." A few weeks later Henry heard another rumor about one of the wealthier merchants who had abandoned his business and departed abruptly. It was said that he had found land outside of Purdyton that he bought. He would not tell where the land was, or why he bought it, but also said he was leaving "for the kingdom."

The news of the King's coming, the map, the reaction of the High Lord, and the departure of important townsfolk weighed on Henry. Try as he might, he could not relate these things to one another. He began to feel uneasy about the intentions of the High Lord and anxious to share his misgivings with William. They met again at the alehouse, taking their usual table in a corner where they could observe the activity and overhear gossip but not be overheard themselves.

Henry swirled the ale in his mug as he voiced his thoughts. "I am beginning to wonder if we are even part of the kingdom," he said to William softly. "Weeks have passed. The King has not come, Purdyton wasn't on the map, and important people are leaving the town 'for the kingdom.' It sounds as if the kingdom is somewhere else."

"I have spoken to the mayor," William answered. "He has been to see the High Lord himself now and has been assured that we are in the kingdom. He says the High Lord is placing soldiers in the town to protect us from dangerous influences and misinformation. He also has sent soldiers to look for the townsfolk who have disappeared. Apparently he is very concerned about what has been happening."

"But … what do you think?" Henry asked.

"I wonder too," William replied, glancing around the room, speaking now in a lower voice. "I wonder if the High Lord is really the King's enemy and he is impeding us from hearing the truth. Maybe that is why he was upset by the messenger, why he snatched the teacher from us, and why he seems to be trying to influence us to forget about the King's coming."

Henry's eyes grew wide. "The King's enemy?" He caught himself and looked around quickly to see if anyone heard his outburst.

The barkeep was looking straight at him.

He leaned in and continued in an urgent whisper, "If you are right, he could call on us to fight the King, could he not? Then we would have to choose sides!"

"I do not know," William sighed. "But it seems as if the High Lord does not trust his own people—placing guards in the square to watch us, and keeping track of who stays at the inn. If he is rebelling against the King, who is our sovereign, I think I would have to side with the King."

Henry spoke the realization as it dawned on him: "That could mean abandoning our livelihoods and becoming fugitives, for we could not safely remain in Purdyton."

"I hope I am wrong," William answered, "but for generations my family has always been loyal to the King, as has yours."

Within a week, as if to confirm Henry's and William's doubts, new notices appeared in the town square:

Proclamation

No person is permitted to leave Purdyton
without the consent of the High Lord.
Furthermore it is forbidden to display
the emblem of the king.
The king has no dominion
over these lands.
Only the emblem of the High Lord
is permitted for display.

High Lord of Purdyton

A few days later James, the kindly innkeeper, was led away by soldiers of the High Lord and placed in the pillory. Rumor had it that he refused to take down the King's emblem in the inn. The High Lord provided a new innkeeper the next day, and the name of the inn was changed to the Black Swan. Henry hurried to the square that evening to find William, coming instead upon a jeering crowd tossing rotten food at James, whose sad face projecting from the pillory was covered with a mixture of pulp from rotten fruit and vegetables and the dripping residue of broken eggs.

Henry waited out of sight until the crowd had emptied its bags of rotting food before carefully stepping through the slippery mess up to James, who was still wincing from some of the direct hits on his face, his nose bloodied, his lips swollen, bruises already evident on his cheeks from the more solid projectiles.

"What led to this, James?" Henry asked, wiping the juicy mess from James's face with his sleeve.

"The guard told me to take down the King's emblem," James said. He cleared his throat and spit out a loose tooth. "I refused, saying that doing so would dishonor the King. He said, 'Didn't you read the notice, man? The king does not rule here!' I told him I would not commit such an act of disloyalty. He came back with another guard and they dragged me here!"

Already alarmed by the turn of events, Henry started when William walked up beside him and clapped him on the shoulder, his face registering surprise and dismay at James's appearance.

"What will happen to you now, James?" William asked after he had heard James repeat his sorry story.

"I do not know," James answered, his eyes mere slits due to the swelling and the pain of moving his face to talk. "They told me I was placed here to reconsider my loyalty. But I will not. Could I be banished? Or worse?"

"That is our fear as well," Henry said. "But you will be our brother wherever you go."

Knowing they were powerless to release him, the two gave James's shoulder a firm squeeze while they bade him a reluctant farewell.

As they walked away, Henry glanced up at the hill behind James, where the gray towers of the castle reached toward a gloomy sky, forming an impenetrable barrier between him and his lord. He stiffened and set his jaw. "You are not *my* lord," he murmured.

William followed Henry to their table in the alehouse. Speaking in low voices, they discussed the new announcement and what had befallen James.

"You were right, William," Henry said. He gulped his ale and calmed himself, realizing how anxious he felt. "The High Lord is the King's enemy! This new announcement leaves no doubt. He has become a rebel lord, which means we are in danger as well if we remain loyal to the King. Anyone could turn us in."

"And we would face the same fate as James," William replied. "I think it is clear to whom we must be loyal now. We must not let anyone know of the gifts we are making because they identify us as followers of the King."

"Or the map," Henry added. "It may be connected somehow to the King. And it is no longer safe to meet in the alehouse now. The guard has taken note where we meet in the corner of the square. He watches when we enter and exit the alehouse, and his eyes were on us the whole time as we spoke to James. We should meet at the smithy henceforth."

Some days later, when he arrived at the smithy to meet Henry, William stopped short at seeing a stranger outside, cloaked and hooded in dark blue. William paused at some distance, not wishing to give himself away. Should he just turn and walk away? The stranger glanced his way and motioned for him to come. William approached with hesitant steps, and the stranger whispered to him quickly as he opened his cloak to reveal the king's emblem sewn inside. At almost the same time, William noticed Henry poking his head out of the smithy, Henry's face taking on an expression of shock as his eyes found the stranger.

"William, whom do you have with you?" he whispered. "No one is supposed to know—"

"He was standing outside and said he came from the King," William said, his eyebrows raised. "He says he has a message for someone who possesses a certain key and map."

"Can we trust him?" Henry asked.

"I think we should," William said. "He bears the King's emblem."

With that Henry disappeared into the smithy and reappeared shortly, brandishing the key and map, eyeing the stranger. William watched as Henry handed the stranger both articles, wondering if this man could possibly be the one who first visited Henry.

"Yes, those are the items I spoke of," the stranger replied, examining them, his face still obscured by his hood. "And here is the message: a representative of the King's court will be in town tomorrow to meet with you and William."

"With us only? No," Henry replied. "That would be extremely risky for all three of us!" he exclaimed. "Have you not read the announcements in the square? Do you not know what befell the innkeeper? A royal representative could be arrested immediately by the High Lord, and so could we!"

As Henry spoke the words, William continued to size up the stranger, disturbed that he kept his face hidden. "Why the two of us?" William asked. "And who are you? Show us your face!"

"The representative is aware of the danger," the man said, his deep voice rumbling from the shrouded darkness of his hood. "He is seeking you because you have steadfastly and loyally expected the coming of the King—and because you have been given a key. Who I am is not important." He glanced from side to side as if to detect if he had been discovered. "Now I—"

Henry interrupted, "I do not know if you are the one who brought me the design for this key, but I must ask you about the key and the map it unlocks. They were given to me by someone dressed like you. What do they mean?"

"I must go now," the stranger answered. "Word has reached the High Lord that I am here."

He turned in a whir and hurried down the lane away from the smithy, soon obscured by a trail of dust, leaving Henry and William alarmed and puzzled as they went inside.

The encounter was both heartening and worrisome. The stranger's visit seemed to be evidence that the King had not forgotten about Purdyton, so maybe they were still in his kingdom and he would yet come, but their possession of the key and map, as well as their meeting the King's representative, would certainly mark them as enemies of the High Lord.

They kicked aside the iron tailings on the floor, each sitting on a barrel by the forge, discussing in anxious voices what they should do. The King's representative would certainly be obvious from his royal clothing and could be arrested the moment he arrived. And if they were seen with him, they would surely be arrested as well. But they both agreed that they needed to see him if only to ask what he knew about the map, and perhaps to learn if the King was really coming.

"We need to find a way to bring him to the smithy," William said. "Perhaps we could tell him his horse needs a new shoe."

"And if we are stopped, we can say we are there to lead his horse to the smithy," Henry added.

William nodded. "That should work—hopefully."

The next day they took turns lurking at the edge of the square in one of the narrow alleys, watching for visitors. What had once been the major meeting place for townsfolk was empty the whole day except for an occasional peasant, cloaked and hooded, scurrying across. The town had become a place of secrecy and suspicion, no one able to trust another for fear of who might inform the High Lord and what he might do next.

Moreover James had disappeared from the pillory, his fate unknown. Around dusk, as lights began to glow in the inn and alehouse, and shadows stole across the square, both had just agreed to go back to the smithy to discuss their disappointment over another false message when they heard a cacophony of bleating. While they looked in the direction of the sounds, a shepherd emerged from a cloud of dust, leading his flock into the cobblestoned square straight to the fountain, which was no more than a circular stone basin that caught the water as it came from a pipe in the central stone post.

"A brazen act for a shepherd, bringing his animals to drink from the public fountain," Henry whispered, looking about for the guard, expecting him to chase the shepherd away.

Fortunately it seemed the guard had slipped into the Thirsty Hound for a mug of ale. The shepherd took a seat at the fountain as if it were his watering hole, while the sheep milled about and drank, but he seemed to be staring at Henry and William.

Feeling the pressure of the shepherd's gaze, Henry looked at William, who also seemed undecided what to do. Why would a shepherd be watching them? He did not appear to be afraid of them. Perhaps they should just caution him about the guard and tell him to move on.

They stared back for a few moments before saying a few words to each other and deciding to leave the shepherd alone and return to the smithy. What was a shepherd to them? It was best not to cause any commotion and attract the guard from the alehouse, Henry thought.

But then the shepherd, his gaze unwavering, raised his hand and pointed in their direction.

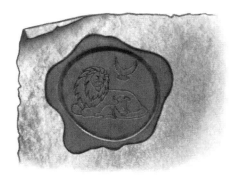

THE SHEPHERD

"**D**ID HE MOTION to us?" Henry asked.

"I think he did," William said.

The two looked around for anyone who might be watching, then took tentative steps out to the fountain, shooing sheep out of the way. Like any shepherd, the man had a scraggly beard and unkempt hair, his face lined and tanned from hours in the sun, his tunic dirt-covered and torn from who knew what adventures in the fields. But he smiled a welcoming, yellow-toothed smile as the two approached.

"Did you beckon to us?" Henry asked.

"Yes," the shepherd said. "I have something to show you."

From his rough tunic he pulled a faded piece of parchment displaying an emblem. Henry immediately recognized it as the emblem of the King—a lamb lying beside a lion, and a white dove with outstretched wings hovering over both.

"You are the King's...?" Henry said, letting his question hang.

"Son," the shepherd replied.

"Son—you mean the Prince?" Henry gasped. "Milord, you are in grave danger!" He gulped audibly while sinking to a knee. "Our lord is your enemy! Why did you not come with your bodyguard?"

"It was my father's wish that I come alone because his Kingdom is not as people imagine," the Prince answered.

Henry shook his head as his eyes explored the shepherd's bronzed face, his ruffled hair and untrimmed beard, which portrayed a radically different appearance than Henry expected of such a royal personage.

"Not as people imagine?" William repeated.

Henry glanced at William, seeing in his friend the same confusion and anxiety he felt as he remembered the conversations and doubts they'd had. "Sire," Henry said urgently, "it is not safe for you here! Many in the town are already hostile to the King. The guard will return at any moment. Please come with us to the smithy. We have many questions to ask you."

"My time here is short, but, yes, I will come," the Prince replied, seemingly unaware of the danger surrounding him. He stood, his woolen tunic casting off a wisp of dust and animal smell.

Henry and William led their unexpected guest up the uneven lane to the smithy, his sheep following with only a soft word and a prod of his staff now and then. Henry and William walked ahead, sharing their questions with each other. The Prince himself had come to see them? Why? Was this the visit announced by the horseman weeks ago? The Prince, not the King? And why was he not dressed as a prince? And where was his royal entourage? What if they had been seen? Was this instead a ruse of the High Lord to entrap them?

They had settled nothing by the time the smithy came into view in the failing light, except to agree that it was worth taking the risk if they could obtain answers to their questions. They led the Prince into the smithy in a moving cloud of dust raised by the bleating sheep, both men aware they were in great danger if discovered.

Upon arrival at the smithy – the soft glow of embers from the forge casting their shadows on the wall as they entered – Henry dashed into the adjoining cottage to bring a stool for the Prince to sit on, he and William each finding a keg. Henry continued to struggle with a mixture of puzzlement and disbelief as he arranged the stool and barrels in front of the forge and they sat before the Prince, their faces dimly lit by the dying coals of the hearth.

"Milord, I trust you are the Prince because you have said so, but you do not appear to be so," Henry began. "Forgive me, but there is nothing royal about you, dressed as you are in a shepherd's clothing."

The Prince's eyes moved from William to Henry. "Perhaps this will ease your doubts." He lifted his right hand to display a gold ring engraved with the emblem of the King.

The sheep in the lane outside the smithy rustled and began to bleat as if disturbed, but Henry scarcely took note of it as he studied the gold ring.

"Surely you have heard the stories about the coming of the King as they have been handed down through your families and are still told by traveling teachers even now," the Prince said. "There was one in your town recently, was there not?"

"Yes, that is true," Henry recalled, "but he was immediately arrested before he could say anything of consequence."

"And the stories—" William said, then stopped midsentence.

Henry glanced at William, noting that his eyes were fixed on the wall above the Prince's head, apparently unwilling to look directly at him.

"The stories are so old," William went on, "they have become legends. The King never came. Almost no one takes them seriously anymore."

"Yes, I am aware," the Prince replied. "It has saddened the King to see his messages ignored and his teachers torn from the people they are to teach. As a final resort he decided to send me, his son, thinking surely the people will listen to me."

Despite having seen the royal ring, Henry still struggled to accept what his eyes and ears were telling him. "But why have you come in such humble fashion?" he asked. "Surely if you were to come with the King's army, our lord would bow to you, and people would know the stories are true."

"Your lord is a rebel," the Prince said. "He would not bow even to my father, the King. Besides, my father's Kingdom is not one of armies and lords, but of the humble and powerless."

Other questions churning in his mind, Henry hardly took note of the Prince's words as he rose and disappeared into the cottage again to retrieve his key and the map. "Does it have anything to do with these, then?" he asked, showing them to the Prince.

"I see that you have your key," the Prince said.

"You know about the key?" Henry asked, still trying to shake the notion that he was talking to a shepherd who should know nothing of it.

"Yes, my father said that he sent a key to all whom I was to meet."

"Then maybe you will also know about this map." Henry unrolled the parchment. "It has nothing on it except the name *Regnum Altissimi*."

"That is my father's Kingdom," the Prince said, "but it is not a map of the land."

"What do you mean?" William asked. "There are fields and roads and rivers."

The Prince looked at Henry and William in turn, as if assessing their ability to understand what he was about to tell them. Finally he answered, "It is a map of the true Kingdom, with the King's castle at the center."

Henry stared blankly at the Prince, then at William, whose expression told of his own confusion. After a moment of silence, Henry said, "A map of the true Kingdom? I don't understand. Why are there no labels of places? Where is our town?"

"My father's seal is on the map," the Prince continued. "It is his pledge to those who receive it that they are under his authority and protection. Its features will be revealed to you after I have left you. I came to tell you and others about the nature of his Kingdom."

"We don't think we are in this kingdom," Henry said, glancing at William.

William nodded, adding, "Yes, Purdyton is not even on the map."

"The Kingdom is not a place," the Prince said. "My father's Kingdom is people's hearts."

He shifted his gaze from Henry to William and back, his eyes alight as if seeking the slightest spark of understanding. Apparently seeing none, he continued, "It is the hearts of those who trust and are loyal to the King and who desire to follow and obey his rule. Each is given a key."

Focusing on Henry, he said, "Henry, both you and William have trusted the King as your ruler and attempted to live by his Kingdom Rules, and you have steadfastly believed the stories passed down in your families. He has chosen to give you a key to his Kingdom, not because of anything you have done to deserve it, but because it pleases him to do so."

Henry's jaw dropped. "How do you know our names?"

An evanescent smile stole over the Prince's lips. "How do you think the messenger who brought you the key knew whom to give it to?" he asked. "The King knows the names of all to whom he gives a key, as do I."

"But I do not know why I have received the key," Henry said. "The messenger disappeared without telling me."

The Prince leaned in, fixing his eyes on Henry. "The key affirms your inclusion in the Kingdom and gives you access to its mysteries, Henry," he said. "Your legends have always pointed to a time when the King will gather his true subjects to live among them. Only those who have been given a key will be invited."

"And the map?" William asked. "It seems to be related to the key somehow."

"Yes, it is," the Prince said, shifting his eyes to William. "The key unlocks the map, and the map of the Kingdom displays the features of the Kingdom for those whose hearts are ruled by the King. Moreover, at the time the features of the map are revealed to you, you will receive a mark of the King's authority over you—an assurance that you are a member of his Kingdom."

The whole explanation left Henry totally baffled, understanding little by the time the Prince had finished. There were features yet to be revealed? And there was a mark of some kind? At least he now knew that the map was connected to the King somehow, and so was the key. But the two had more to talk about with the Prince. William had brought his shield, as both he and Henry hoped to show their gifts to whoever came, though they had certainly not expected it to be the Prince.

William looked at Henry and then down at the covered shield.

Henry gave him a nod.

"Because we thought he was coming soon, we made gifts for the King," William said.

Feeling a swell of pride, Henry brought forth the battle-axe as William hefted the shield.

"Do you think he will accept them?" William asked. "They carry his emblem."

"They are beautiful pieces of work," the Prince said, examining each, "and I am sure you are proud of them. But keep the shield and battle-axe for yourselves for your own protection. He does not seek, nor does he need gifts from his people; he desires naught but your loyalty and obedience. The key and the map are his gifts to you. Moreover, each of his subjects has also been gifted in different skills that he desires you to use in his service as well."

"Gifted in skills?" William asked. "By the King?"

The Prince leaned forward, looking each in the eye, then settling on Henry before he spoke. "Henry, you are gifted in fashioning objects of metal. You shall henceforth be a keymaker for the King and his Kingdom. First you may begin by making one like yours for William so that he can receive a map. You will receive messengers from time to time from the King, to whom you will give keys you have made."

Henry raised his eyes, studying the ceiling, wondering what it all meant. Was the man who told them of the Prince's coming one of those messengers?

Next the Prince looked at William. "And, William, you are gifted in working with animal hides. You will be a mapmaker for the King. You may begin making fine parchments to bear maps of the Kingdom that will last forever so that the knowledge of the true Kingdom will never be lost."

"But the map was brought to Henry and I am not skilled in drawing," William replied. "How can I possibly make one like it?"

Their conversation was suddenly interrupted by a shuffling outside the smithy and the bleating of sheep again, followed by the rapid footsteps of someone running. William jumped from his barrel and ran into the lane, seeing no one in the darkness.

"We were followed!" William cried. "Quickly, you must go, milord!"

"And do you think my sheep will become invisible?" the Prince asked. "I have done what I was sent here to do. I will remain here until they come for me."

"No, sire, you must not!" Henry said, knowing full well that he and William would suffer the same fate. "If he finds that you are the Prince, the High Lord could torture and kill you!"

The Prince merely smiled again, as if unconcerned about any danger he might be in. "A good shepherd does not abandon his sheep," he said. "Nor does your King abandon his people. A good shepherd risks his life for his sheep if he must. I have come as a shepherd for that reason, at the risk of my life—so you may know that your King will not abandon you, his sheep. That is why I wear this." He extended his hand again to reveal the ring with the King's emblem, then fixed them with an inscrutable gaze.

"And unless I go with them, your map will remain blank."

"Blank?" Henry said. He still did not understand the Prince's meaning, but realizing that the Prince would not depart, Henry gulped.

"We will be found with him and they will take us as well," William whispered to Henry.

The Prince leaned forward again and gave a reassuring smile. "When they learn whom they have caught, they will leave you alone. But you would be well advised to depart tonight for another village that will welcome you in order to begin anew your trades for the Kingdom."

No sooner had he finished speaking than the sound of many footsteps reverberated from the road as a noisy crowd approached the smithy. Henry and William gripped each other's arm, trembling.

Followed by an unruly mob, a guard burst into the smithy, surveyed the room, and barked, "Take them all!"

"I am the only one you want," the Prince said calmly, turning to face them while lifting his hand to show the ring.

A gasp arose from the crowd as it shrank back a step. "It is the royal Prince!" someone exclaimed.

"Take him!" the guard snarled. "The High Lord will be greatly pleased. We will come back for the other two."

Henry watched as the Prince stood without speaking and, with bowed head, allowed himself to be jerked from the smithy by two soldiers and then pushed down the road toward the square amidst the jostling crowd, who hurled jeers and threats as they shoved him. Some of the sheep outside tried to follow him, while others began to bleat and mill around as if lost, finally scattering into the countryside with no one to guide them.

Henry and William immediately bundled up some meager food and supplies, a few tools, the box with the map, the key, and their gifts. So frightened were they at the turn of events, they set out that very night, telling no one, leaving only a note for family members that they were on a mission "for the Kingdom," much as the merchants had done earlier.

The two walked for days until the road ended in a village far away from Purdyton and the castle, where they cast themselves on the mercy of the villagers. The people of the village of Loynton accepted them readily because each plied a trade that would be a boon to the village.

As instructed, Henry made a key for William. Not long after, a traveler, cloaked and hooded as before, came through and dropped off a box containing the map for William. Less than two months later they heard sad news concerning the Prince. He had died at the hand of the High Lord, just as they had feared. Although they recalled how amazed they had been to be visited by the Prince, they remembered little of what he had told them, and now assumed it had all been for naught.

A few more days had passed when another traveler, cloaked and hooded in the same blue color as the King's messengers, appeared as evening fell at Henry's new smithy, where he worked with the other village blacksmith.

"Henry, do you and William still have your maps?" the traveler asked after showing them the King's emblem.

Even though they were now far away from Purdyton and the High Lord, Henry and William, uncertain of the reach of the High Lord, had continued to be cautious after what had happened to the Prince. Even the blue cloak and emblem were not enough to allay their suspicions this time.

"Who wants to know?" Henry queried, folding his arms. "And how do you know our names?"

"I come from the King," the stranger replied. "You have seen that I carry his emblem."

Henry was not convinced. "Show me more proof," he said.

The stranger drew back his hood. Henry dropped his tongs, jumping back as the glowing horseshoe he had been hammering crashed to the stone floor in a shower of sparks.

It couldn't be. But there was a resemblance, he thought. "You look like—"

"The shepherd Prince?" the visitor replied.

"Milord! How did you know what I was thinking? But you were killed, were you not?" Henry said just above a whisper, now kneeling in obeisance.

"I am on my way back to the King's castle," the Prince said, "but I want to remind you of what I told you before. The map is ready to be revealed to you. And after it has been revealed, I will be with you in spirit henceforth."

Though he had not thought of or remembered much about what the Prince had said since he and William left Purdyton, Henry recalled now the Prince's words about the map.

"But, milord, how can it be? What happened?" Henry asked. "We heard that you had died at the hand of the High Lord. And yet you are alive!"

"It is as you say," the Prince answered. "The full truth will be revealed in time. But you are witness to a part of it."

Henry's heart jumped with excitement. "I must go and bring William! He will want to see you too."

The Prince smiled. "Of course."

Henry dashed out of the smithy exulting, soon returning breathless with William in tow. But the Prince had vanished.

"He is gone. But it was him, as surely as I am standing before you!" Henry said with earnest eyes. "Do you not remember he said it would not be the end of him, but we did not understand what he meant?"

"Mm, yes, there were many things we did not understand," William said, stroking his chin, "but that couldn't have been him. We know he was put to death."

"It really was him!" Henry said, and then paused to think. "Wait—William, do you remember what he told us about the map? We dismissed it when we heard he was slain, but perhaps we should take it seriously now. He told me he came back just to remind us. Go and get your box."

William returned quickly with his box and they sat in the light cast by glowing embers in the forge, each holding his box with trembling hands, preparing to take out their maps and look at them again, having neither expectation nor hope of seeing anything different.

Henry lifted his box and pushed his thumb against the medallion to reveal the keyhole. Something caught his eye as he did. "William, did you ever notice the bird that is on the medallion?"

"No. Why?"

"Remember when you made the shield for the King?"

"Yes. I still have it."

"It's the same bird as the one in his emblem, and the one on the seal of the map is the same too."

"So, perhaps that is how we can know it is from the King," William said.

As Henry inserted his key into the keyhole, he noticed William examining his own key.

"Henry, there is writing on my key. What did you write?"

"I wrote nothing," replied Henry. "It is just the key I was told to make."

"Look at it closely. Does yours have words?"

Henry took out his key and squinted at it. On the shaft of the key in small letters were the words, *Fides clavis regnum est.*

"It is in a foreign tongue. I did not put it there. Nor do I know what it means." Henry shrugged. "It must have appeared later."

"The same as happened with my first map copy! I told you then," William said. "Remember?"

Henry shook his head.

"When I made a parchment in the shape of the map and attempted to make a copy of yours and mine, I knew that I was not skilled enough to draw in the same fashion. But as I put my quill to it, the map began to appear on the parchment as if drawn by an invisible hand."

Yes," Henry recalled, now ready to believe there was more to the key and the map than he and William imagined. Henry lifted his map out of the box and unrolled it. All the roads, rivers, villages, orchards, and pastures were there as before, but as the two looked on, names began to appear on the map, once again as if written by the same unseen hand. The rivers bore names like *River of Life, Eternal Spring,* and *Living Water.* The orchards displayed names like *Love, Joy, Peace, Patience, Kindness,* and *Goodness, Faithfulness, Gentleness,* and *Self-control.* The villages and pastures had names like *Shepherd's Sheepfold* and *Field of Harvest.* The castle was named *King's Castle.* And the title on the bottom read *Kingdom of the Most High.*

As they pondered the meaning of the names on the map, the words of the Prince returned to Henry, and he said them aloud: "'It is a map of the true Kingdom, with the King's castle at the center... My Kingdom is not a place; it is people's hearts—hearts that are ruled by the King." And—yeow!" Henry yelled. He jumped up and backed away from the forge.

"What?" William shouted, jumping back as well.

"It must have been a spark from the forge." Henry bent over, his hand to his chest.

"Let me look," William said. He lifted Henry's hand and then his tunic. He gasped. "You have a mark on your chest, over your heart. It looks just like the bird!"

"What?" Henry said. He looked down. "What do you—"

"Ahhhh!" William's hand flew to his chest.

The two stood in silence, each gingerly rubbing their skin where the image of the bird had appeared, both struggling to understand the event that had just taken place.

Recovering his composure, Henry placed his hand on William's shoulder, looking him in the eye. "William, it all makes sense now. Everything has happened as the Prince said. He said we would receive a mark of the King's authority. He said the map would reveal the features of the Kingdom—the characteristics of the hearts of those who belong to the King. We *are* in the true Kingdom, and we can recognize others by those same characteristics!"

At that moment Henry also realized they had been given access to a mystery of immense importance, one that could make them hunted men, yet without a full understanding of why they had been chosen to receive it.

PART ONE

THE SMITH, THE SQUIRE, AND THE MAIDEN

Chapter 1

THE BLACKSMITH

A SANDY-HAIRED, WELL-CHISELED YOUTH stood patiently at the bellows of the forge as his father shaped a key on the anvil, his face dripping sweat from the blazing fire within. As often occurred while he performed the mindless task of working the bellows for his father, Hugh's thoughts took flight. He had vivid childhood memories of peering over the edge of the rough-hewn boards of the trestle table in his family's one-room cottage attached to the smithy, watching candlelight flicker on the faces of two men, one his father, as they used a similar key to unlock a box, speaking in whispers to each other in the soft glow that seemed to emanate from the tabletop. He remembered the excitement and earnestness in their hushed voices as they examined a piece of parchment rolled out before them. And even now he could sense the aura of mystery that seemed to hover over their conversations together about the parchment. Curious-looking strangers would also come, cloaked and hooded, and then depart silently after receiving such a key from his father. Throughout his childhood Hugh had wondered what it was all about, because his father cautioned him not to tell anyone about the keys, or the parchment.

Twenty-five years had passed since Hugh's father, Henry, and his friend Brian's father, William, had arrived in Loynton. There, both men, fugitives at the time, found wives and settled down to raise families. Unlike Purdyton, the town from which they had fled, Loynton was a forgettable collection of mostly thatched, wattle-and-daub cottages and farmsteads scattered beside a dusty road that led into the center of the village and stopped there. There was nowhere else to go. The ground beyond was stony and unsuitable for farming. A small stream tumbled down from the highlands and paralleled the road on the other side of some of the houses, providing water for a mill. Hugh had grown up in Loynton and apprenticed to his father. Likewise his friend Brian had joined the leatherworking trade alongside William.

Hugh knew the events of Henry and William's flight to Loynton to escape the oppression of the rebel High Lord over Purdyton. Since childhood he had listened to the stories told by his father of a benevolent and loving King who promised to come and gather his people someday. The King had never come, yet his parents both spoke as if they held a steadfast hope, even an assurance, that he would come. He'd also many times heard the curious tale of a shepherd who visited his father and Brian's father—who turned out to be the Prince in disguise—and how the map on the parchment changed, and how that was connected somehow to the keys his father made and the parchments Brian's father made.

The village of Loynton, Hugh knew, sat in a fief of one of the knights loyal to the High Lord, whom his parents now called "the Dragon" because he had forbidden the display of the King's emblem in the fiefs over which he had influence and had replaced it with his own dragon emblem. The knight, Sir Bailys, though he was lord over Loynton and several other villages, showed little interest in the villagers beyond what he could gain from them in produce and money. Hugh supposed that, like most knights, Sir Bailys lived for war and loot. Sometimes he would stop in the village alehouse with his two ruffian bodyguards after a successful hunt and get roaring drunk before riding away to his manor house.

Hugh also understood that everyone, supposedly even the Dragon, was subject to a king. He had seen how his mother and father openly discussed their loyalty to a king they had never seen, even though they had seen their immediate lord, Sir Bailys. Hugh perceived as well that he and his parents lived in a time fraught with danger because the Dragon was a rebel lord who opposed the true King. That was why everything to do with the keys and maps had to be secretive. His father had told him that the map was of a different kingdom, which had only confused Hugh, because when he had looked it over himself, there seemed to be nothing of interest on it.

Once he was old enough to apprentice, Hugh had learned from his father how to forge axe blades, hand tools, utensils, horseshoes, even plowshares, but his father had never taught him to make the key. Although a simple task, it was apparently a family secret that could not even be divulged to his son. Hugh had wondered why and even felt a little frustrated by now that his father seemed to be withholding this last piece of the trade from him.

Having turned eighteen and become a journeyman, Hugh now already stood taller than his father—strong of body, with dark, mischievous eyes that peered from beneath a shock of unruly fair hair, though he kept his face shaven, as did his father. He was a man now, so he could think of no reason why he should not be allowed to make the keys and know the secret. Since the keys seemed important enough for special visitors to come to their smithy to procure them, Hugh wanted one, even if he had to make it himself—and thus he shared this desire with his father.

"These keys are only for those for whom I am told to make them," Henry said to Hugh's request, mopping his brow with a sweat-stained tunic sleeve. "I hope someday you will have one."

Someday? Why could not he have one now? He was determined to know why his father continued withholding the instruction. What could possibly be so special about a mere key that he could not be included in the secret?

"I am a journeyman now, Father," he said, holding his father in a focused stare with his intense brown eyes. "You can make me one or teach me to make them. It is not a difficult task. What must I do to merit one or at least join you in making them?"

Henry shook his head. "There is nothing you can do to deserve one, son," he replied. "Though I fashion them, they are only given by the King to those whom he chooses. No one knows how the King chooses, but he selects those whom he wishes to be recipients of keys that unlock the mysteries of the Kingdom map. The night visitors deliver them."

Hugh rolled his eyes. He knew his father was still withholding information from him.

"Look, Father," he said. "I have looked at the key and you have shown me the map more than once. There is nothing special about the key, the box or the map."

Henry put down his hammer and caught Hugh's eye. "That is because it is not your key and not your map. Your mother and I have told you about the Kingdom ever since you were small, and we have told you that we hoped you would be included someday. Perhaps now that you are eighteen, it is time for you to decide for yourself if you believe what we have told you about the King and his Kingdom."

Hugh had indeed been told, though not fully understood, that the Kingdom his father referred to was, as he said, a "kingdom of the heart," not of lords and knights. His father had eventually shown him the map and explained that what Hugh could see was not all that was there, that only those in the Kingdom could see the full secrets of the map, and that they must receive a key first. He had seen the map from time to time when Henry and William were together and had attempted to find anything different on it that would show he was in the Kingdom. It was always the same, with roads and fields and a castle in the middle and a few words he could not read. He was puzzled now by his father's statement that he did not deserve a key, but remembered being told it was a matter of entrusting his heart to the King, whom he had not seen and might never see, as far as he knew.

Over the years the stories his parents told had become real to Hugh, and though he could not understand how it all worked and why he was not already in this Kingdom, he decided he would entrust his heart to the King, whatever that meant—partially because it seemed his father and mother expected him to, and partially because he had become tired of being excluded and felt more than a little curious about what secrets the map held. He told his father of his decision, as well as his uncertainty understanding the meaning of a "kingdom of the heart" and his misgivings about not having seen or met the King whom he was deciding to trust with his heart.

A few days later they received another visit from one of the mysterious strangers, whom his father had explained were messengers from the King. The next day his father made a key. He seemed to be in a cheerful mood, whistling as he hammered and shaped the iron.

"You always seem happy when you make keys," Hugh said, working the bellows as usual.

"This is a special one, for someone you know," Henry replied.

"Who? Brian?"

"You'll see," he answered with a chuckle.

That very evening around suppertime, Brian, his parents, and his younger sisters arrived, as their families often shared meals together. Elizabeth, Hugh's mother, had made enough squirrel-and-vegetable pottage for all, and they sat down on wooden benches around the plank table in the cottage, devouring the pottage as well as the round bread trencher it was served on.

After everyone had finished their meager meals, Henry pushed back from the table, beaming. "Thank you for coming, William and Charis—and you too, Brian, Mary, and Emma." Then Hugh's father turned to Elizabeth. "Mother, bring out the box."

Hugh shot Brian a grin. He had seen the key his father had made and assumed the box went with it. Elizabeth reached into a burlap bag at her feet, a broad smile on her face, and lifted out a small wooden box enclosed in strips of iron. It was like his father's; Hugh had seen the messengers slip a map in one like it and hastily depart. He knew that his friend Thomas's father made the boxes, but he never sold them. Elizabeth set the box in Hugh's lap.

Surprised at first, Hugh figured his mother had given it to him to pass on, so he began to hand it to Brian.

"No, Hugh, it is for you," Henry said. Then, to all, he announced, "Today my son is given a key to the Kingdom!"

Everyone clapped as Henry handed Hugh the very key he had just made. Hugh's eyes widened and went from the box to his father and back again. He not taken the time to inspect one of these boxes closely before now. He turned it over and over in his hands, examining it. It did not seem to have a keyhole. He did see a sort of medallion where a keyhole should be.

Hugh realized he must have looked flustered, because his father bent over him and said, "Watch." As Hugh looked on, his father used his thumb to slide the medallion aside to reveal the keyhole.

"So that's how," Hugh said. He slid the key in and turned it.

The lid lifted to reveal a roll of parchment with a seal. Hugh cautiously broke the seal and unrolled the parchment, revealing the map with the castle at the center. It looked the same as his father's, but as usual he saw none of the words and names his father and William would speak as they studied it together. So why was this night special, then?

Hugh's look of confusion changed slowly to an expression of awe as the names of features appeared before his astonished eyes, and the name *Regnum Altissimi* at the bottom was replaced with *Kingdom of the Most High*.

"It is the full map of the Kingdom you showed me and told me so much about!" Hugh said. "And the names are there, the same ones that you and William would say to each other. But why could I not see all of the names before?"

"Remember what I told you?" Henry said. "The true contents of the map are only seen when one enters the Kingdom, and the key is what unlocks access to it." Henry clapped his hand on Hugh's shoulder. "Now I can teach you to make the keys," his father said, and Hugh could see the pride in his eyes. "You will serve the King as I do."

Hugh was no longer listening. For the past few moments he had been aware of a pain in his chest that was now growing more intense. "Yeeow!" he shouted, standing up with a jerk, then falling backward over the bench and landing on the dirt floor in a cloud of dust, his hand clutching his chest.

His father stooped to grab him, holding him tightly in both arms. "Don't be afraid, son," he said. "That was the confirmation. Pull up your tunic."

Hugh was still wincing from the searing pain. It burned as if he had been branded with an iron straight from the forge. Edging up his tunic, he found a mark on his left breast above his heart. "What is it?" he asked, rubbing it gently.

"It is the mark of the dove," Henry said. "Look," he continued, going to the corner of the room and retrieving a shield. "This is the shield William made for the King, and gave to me. It bears the King's emblem. The bird on the shield is the same as your mark. It is your assurance that you are under the authority of the King and are a member of his Kingdom. The seal on the parchment scroll bears the same image, as does the medallion you pushed aside."

"Why did you not warn me it was going to hurt like this?" Hugh asked, still rubbing his chest.

"We did not want to influence you in any way," Elizabeth answered. "Your father and I have known some who have claimed to have the burning in their heart, but have not received the mark."

Hugh gave a grunt of acknowledgement as he slowly stood, then resumed his place at the table, examining the box and the key. Something about the key caught his eye. "Father, there are words on the key. What do they say?"

"I do not know," Henry said. "When I make a key, they are not on there. They seem to appear after the key is given."

Less than two weeks later Hugh and his parents were invited to Brian's house to witness Brian receive his key and map. Brian knew what to expect and did not even let out a yelp when he received his mark. Then Thomas—the carpenter's son and a friend of Hugh and Brian—received his mark a month later. In time the three learned from their fathers how to make the boxes, with maps and keys, to be delivered to the King's messengers as they came through. The disguised messengers always came by night, stayed a short time, placed the seal on the map, and left with their filled boxes.

One night thereafter a messenger came with a different purpose. Although clothed as usual in a cloak and hood, his face hidden by the hood's shadow, he had brought something with him that he wanted to show everyone. Along with the families of Brian and Thomas, who had been invited for a communal meal, Hugh and his parents gathered around the table by candlelight as the messenger unrolled a scroll containing many sheets. Hugh's father had been taught to read by the apothecary in Purdyton and had taught both his mother and him how to read. Together they read the title—*A Chronicle of the Prince.*

The messenger seemed excited as he spoke. "It tells about the Prince and the Kingdom. You have received a copy because you can read and teach others what it says."

Hugh watched as his father grabbed the scrolls, fumbling through them with shaking hands to the last parchment, following his finger as he read each line.

"It is true!" Henry said, tears bursting from his eyes.

"What, Father?" Hugh asked, stunned by his father's abrupt action. How could he know what would be there?

"It says that the Prince came to some disguised as a shepherd, and after he was killed, he appeared to those same followers before he went back to the castle of the King!" Henry said.

Hugh had never seen his father sob so profoundly. Even his mother was silently weeping. William rose to look over Henry's shoulder at the passage marked by Henry's shaking finger.

"It validates one of the stories I have always told you, son," Henry said, blotting his eyes with a sleeve. "My commission to make keys for the Kingdom was given to me by the Prince himself. He came to Purdyton dressed as a shepherd for that purpose, and to commission William as well. He was snatched from my smithy and taken by soldiers of the Dragon."

"We felt powerless to do anything because he seemed as if he wanted it that way," added William.

Henry continued, "And then, after we had fled to Loynton, and after the Prince had been killed, a man visited me. He looked just like the shepherd, but he said he was on his way back to the King's castle. I knew it must be him, but I knew he had been killed. How could it be? Just after that, we received the mark and the features of our maps appeared to us."

The messenger's deep voice issued from the shadow of his hood. "Yes, the Prince did return to his father. But he did not die in the Dragon's castle that night as you may have thought. He eluded his captors and rejoined his inner circle of knights. Later he fell in battle against the Dragon, but before he died, he commissioned his inner circle to carry on his work of building the Kingdom, just as he commissioned you—Henry and William—to do your parts. One of his knights wrote this chronicle. It is the King's desire that a copy of the *Chronicle* should be made available to any who will read it. This is the Loynton copy, which you may pass around to those who can read until there are more copies.

Furthermore, as the true Kingdom grows, the King will need more members of the Kingdom to serve as messengers and witnesses to the truth of the *Chronicle*."

"I will do it gladly," Hugh replied, "though I do not yet know what it says."

"I am perhaps too old to ride about the countryside now, having passed my fiftieth year," Henry said, "but I will also faithfully be a witness to what I have seen and heard if people come to me."

"Excellent," the messenger said. "You must all strive to read and know what it says. As darkness grows in the land, people will ask where they can find others who are loyal to the true King and who can explain the *Chronicle* to them. I will spread the word that people in this and surrounding villages can come to your smithy, Henry."

A few weeks had passed when Hugh and Henry were interrupted by the sound of horses' hoofs approaching the smithy. The sound stopped outside. Hugh heard some gruff voices and then Sir Bailys strode in, followed by his two ruffians. Hugh had never seen the knight this close before. The sight was not a pleasant one—limp, oily black hair hanging in strands around a sallow face framed by a stubbled chin and jaw. Yellowed teeth crowded behind chapped lips, and although he had broad shoulders from wielding weapons of war, his bowed legs made him a ludicrous figure. The torn, smudged black and yellow surcoat[1] that covered his mail shirt bore witness to the fact that he was a bachelor knight who spent his income on things other than his personal appearance.

"Where is Henry Smith?" Sir Bailys said, his eyes surveying the inside of the smithy and its two occupants.

Hugh tensed as his father said, "I am he," while turning to face the knight.

"There have been rumors of strangers visiting your house at night," the knight said, plopping himself down onto the anvil. "I have ignored them because it is beneath me to be involved in the affairs of peasants. However, I have heard of a new rumor that a scroll—which is disrespectful of the High Lord—is being circulated from your smithy. You will give me that scroll." He extended his hand.

Hugh exchanged glances with his father.

"It is true that we have guests from time to time," Henry responded. "We have many friends in the village."

---

[1] A calf-length outer garment usually in the colors of the knight, worn over chain mail.

"The scroll, man! Give me the scroll!" Sir Bailys jumped up, standing chest to chest with Henry.

"I am unaware of any scroll that is untruthful or disrespectful of your High Lord," Henry answered.

Hugh remained motionless, impressed by his father's carefully chosen words. At the same time, he realized that whatever the scroll said about the Dragon, if anything, must be true then.

"Very well," Sir Bailys said, his posture clearly betraying his doubt of Henry's veracity. "It is also said that some who oppose the High Lord bear a mark on their left breast. Lift your tunic and show me!"

Henry lifted his tunic with no apparent concern over what Sir Bailys might see. Hugh knew well what would be there. He held his breath with unblinking eyes, gripping the bellows with trembling hands as he watched his father calmly expose his chest. There, over his father's heart, was the same mark he had received. What if the knight told Hugh to lift his shirt too?

"It is not there, sire," spoke one of the men-at-arms.

"No matter! Take him!" the knight shouted. "Perhaps the Rat or the High Lord himself can loosen his tongue."

The two men-at-arms grabbed Henry and dragged him out of the smithy as Hugh looked on in helpless anguish. Henry did not struggle, but did call to Hugh over his shoulder, "Remember to whom you belong and look after Mother, son."

Hugh stood in stunned silence, his mouth gaping. As soon as the sound of horses' hoofs had receded, he ran into the adjoining cottage.

As he burst through the doorway, he shouted, "Mother! They have taken Father!"

"Sit down, Hugh, and catch your breath. Who? Where? I heard some voices."

"Sir Bailys and his men. They are taking him to the Dragon! It is about the new scroll."

Elizabeth dropped the wooden spoon with which she was stirring a pot hanging over the fire and then slumped onto a stool. "It has finally happened here!" She sighed, stifling a sob. Her eyes glistening, she said, "We talked about this, your father and I. We knew it could happen. Your father thought we were far enough away from the Dragon now that he would not be interested in us. But the Prince told your father that anyone who wished to serve the King should be willing to follow in his footsteps and suffer as he did. Hugh, your father was taken in exactly the same way the Prince was taken."

Hugh listened, but refused to dismiss the plan he'd already come up with. "And I am going to rescue him before they reach Purdyton!" he said. He ran to the wall and snatched Henry's shield from its hook with a jerk.

"No, son!" Elizabeth said. "Sit down. We both knew we could suffer for the King. What is important is that we continue to serve him where we are. You must stay here to make the keys and deliver to the messengers the boxes and maps that Thomas and Brian and their fathers make. I will go and plead with the Dragon."

Ignoring her, Hugh yanked his father's sword from the wall as well, then stood tall before his mother, sword at the ready. "He will not grant an audience to a woman villager! And it is dangerous for a woman to travel alone. I cannot allow you to go, Mother!"

"I cannot manage the smithy, my son," she replied. "You must stay. I will ask William to go with me. Brian can handle the leather work and make the parchments."

Heaving a sigh, Hugh knew she was right. Only he could fulfill the villagers' demand for a blacksmith. He collapsed onto a stool, defeated. There was nothing else to say. There was no use in arguing when his mother had made a decision.

"Mother?"

"Yes, son."

"There is one thing I do not understand. They asked Father to show his mark, and he did, but they acted as if they could not see it."

She gave him a knowing look. "That is one of the ways the King protects us, Hugh. Only those who have the mark can see it on others—just as the map remains blank until someone has received a key."

Hugh recalled then that as a child he had indeed seen his father bare-chested many times and had never noticed the mark. He would certainly have asked about it if he had seen it. But that was not going to protect his father now. And his mother was going to put herself in the same danger. The rest of the day, try as he might, Hugh could not dissuade his mother from her plan.

In the morning she departed with William, each on horseback. Hugh gathered a small amount of money in a bag that she could wear around her neck and gave it to her.

"Be careful, Mother."

Hugh pressed a stoic kiss on her cheek, and stood stonily as her hand slid from his, perhaps for the last time. After watching them until they rode out of sight, he ran down to the streamside tannery to see Brian, a fist of nausea lodged in his throat, fearing the worst. Every time he went to visit Brian, he was secretly thankful that he was a blacksmith and not a tanner. The tannery always reeked of foul odors, not only from the dead animal skins but also the chemicals Brian and William used in the vats for tanning the skins.

He knew when he was near from the smell, and by the pits near the house where the skins were cured and packed with oak bark for tanning. He found Brian calmly scraping a sheepskin stretched on a wooden frame. Brian was a few inches shorter than Hugh, with dark hair and a well-groomed beard and mustache like his father. Unlike Hugh he always appeared to be easygoing and relaxed. Nothing seemed to faze him. How would he react to the departure of his father?

"Brian, what do you think will happen? Are you not afraid for your father?" Hugh asked.

Hugh, who at six feet stood above even the tallest of the villagers, gazed down at Brian, waiting for a reply. The unruly mop of curly, apparently untamable, sandy hair, locks of it sprouting in random directions above Hugh's fierce brown eyes, made him seem even taller. But it was his intense stare, peering from the darkness of his prominent brow that demanded an immediate response. Brian had once told Hugh that if his brow began to furrow and heap up like a thundercloud, lightning flashed in his eyes.

"I begged him not to go," Brian answered matter-of-factly, "but he said he must. He said he was with your father when the Prince was taken and they both had dedicated their lives to each other and to the mission he gave them. I know that he wants more than anything to see your father freed, but I am aware that he too may not return."

Hugh furrowed his brow and glared at Brian. "How can you be so calm about it, then? It is most unfair! Why does the King not protect us from unjust knights like this?" The thundercloud was beginning to form, the eyes to flicker.

"I do not know, Hugh, but Mother says we must trust that the King knows when we suffer and that he has a purpose even so."

"How can he know? Does he even care?" Hugh shouted, gesticulating with his arms, his loose curls bobbing with each outburst as if to emphasize his point. "He is sitting safely in his castle, wherever that is, and he did not even bother to protect his own son!"

"I do not understand it either, Hugh," Brian said softly, "but I want to be loyal to the King and trust him."

"My mother acted the same way," Hugh said, then huffed, beginning to pace back and forth, his dander still up. "But I wanted to mount up and ride after them to give them a taste of my sword!"

"Which would have been foolish against three armed men, don't you think?" Brian observed, not looking at Hugh but continuing to scrape the sheepskin.

Hugh halted and fixed smoldering eyes again on Brian—even-tempered Brian. Why didn't he share Hugh's passion for justice? A huge injustice had occurred, and now Hugh's mother and Brian's father were caught up in the consequences. What was going to happen to them? What could Hugh do about it? Nothing. He was the village blacksmith now.

Hugh stomped out of the cottage and returned to the smithy with heavy steps, more certain than ever that he would never see either of his parents again. He decided to hunt some rabbits to augment the stew that was always simmering over the fire. Maybe that would take his mind off the dire outcomes his mind was inventing. Retrieving his bow and some arrows from the now silent house, he was flooded with memories of childhood: his father teaching him how to hold the bow, nock[2] the arrow, and steady his aim; his father's pride when he shot his first rabbit; and how much he missed having him there now.

The hunt was not a satisfying diversion, despite his success in bringing back two rabbits. It mattered not that the rabbits were the property of his lord, Sir Bailys, since the lands were all his. He ate his pottage in a solitude that fell heavily on his shoulders that night, the house seemingly cold despite the flames in the central fire pit, empty without his mother's hearty laughter and his father's fascinating stories. Scarcely a day had passed since his father had been ripped from him, but Hugh's mind was becoming captive to a single thought—vengeance. He knew not where the Dragon lived or how to get past his guards, but he resolved then and there that somehow he would exact a price, or die in the attempt.

A few nights later Hugh received an unexpected visitor. Hooded and cloaked in dark blue like a King's messenger, the man was sitting at the table of Hugh's cottage when Hugh walked in from the smithy.

"You are the keymaker of Loynton now?"

Hugh almost jumped at the sight and the words that startled him, then said in an even voice, "Who wants to know?" He'd grown more suspicious than ever now that his father had been taken. Even though he was familiar with the dark blue cloak of the King's messengers, he had become wary of anyone whose face he could not see.

The visitor opened his cloak; the low candlelight revealed the King's emblem sewn to the inside.

---

[2] To set the notch of the arrow onto the bowstring.

"I come from the King."

Still cautious, Hugh demanded, "Show me your mark and your face! Anyone could carry one of those emblems nowadays."

"Messengers of the King do not bear a mark," the man answered, "and my identity is not important. However, I assure you that I can both see your mark if you choose to reveal it. or describe your mark if you do not."

The answer was not satisfying, troubled as Hugh was by the absence of his parents, but the authority in the man's voice immediately stilled his suspicions. Hugh took a seat on the bench at the table opposite the messenger. "Yes, I am now the local keymaker. What is your purpose?"

The visitor did not ask for a key, as Hugh expected, but said, "A person hereabouts is to receive a key and map," he said. "You are to take him the key and map. It is a dangerous mission. Will you accept?"

"Dangerous? How?" Hugh inquired, his curiosity piqued.

"It is a member of the household of Sir Bailys—his stable master."

The irony did not escape Hugh. *The Dragon takes my father and the King takes one of his.* Then a thought came to him: *If I do this, maybe word will reach the King and he will somehow get my father released.* "Of course," Hugh answered. "I will be loyal to the King, whatever he asks. But why are you not delivering it yourself?"

"You may recall when a messenger came some time ago with a copy of the *Chronicle*, he said the King desires his subjects to be messengers now, and you volunteered," the visitor said, hunching over the table, his face still unseen. "It is a part of your service to the King. You had best go under cover of night and meet the stable master at dawn before the knight has need of his horse. Bring me a map so that I may apply the seal to it before I go."

Hugh rose from the table and disappeared into the smithy, returning with a parchment map from the supply William and Brian kept stocked. He watched as the messenger brought a stick of wax from under his cloak, melted a drop onto the scroll, and pressed the ring on his right hand into the soft wax, leaving the imprint of the dove before placing the map in one of the boxes Thomas also kept stocked at the smithy.

"How will I know this stable master?" Hugh asked.

"He will be in the stable tending the knight's horses. You will say the word I tell you. He will answer with the second word I tell you. It is the way you will identify followers of the King without needing to expose your marks."

Although the words he heard next meant nothing to him, Hugh listened, studying the stranger's darkened face, almost indiscernible except for two glowing blue eyes that pierced him from the shadows.

"From your voice I think you are the same one who brought the *Chronicle* to my father, are you not?" Hugh asked.

"Yes, I am the same."

"I would like to know your name."

"You may call me Clyffe." With that he rose from the table and vanished into the darkness.

"Will I see you again?" Hugh called after him.

There was no answer save the sighing of the wind.

Chapter 2

THE SQUIRE

SEVEN YEARS STEPHEN had eagerly hoped for this day. It was his fourteenth birthday, but more importantly he would become a squire today. Splashing his face with water and running his fingers through his shoulder-length dark hair, he caught his reflection in the basin as the water stilled. Dark brown eyes peered from beneath a lock of hair that fell from his forehead. How should he present himself to the lord of the castle? Today would be a big step in his quest to become a knight. After practicing several expressions so that he knew how his face felt in each, he adopted a serious but confident one. He then donned his best tunic and secured it with his dagger belt. Next, he tied on his leather shoes and hurried down the spiral tower stairs two at a time to the great hall, where he would attend the knight at breakfast. Old Sir Bartholomew, or Sir Bart, as everyone called him, was one of the King's trusted knights—a member of his inner circle, they said. To be his squire meant that you were serving one of the King's best.

Ordinarily a squire came from a family of nobility or some wealth because there were expenses involved—a sword, a chain mail shirt for protection, a horse and saddle eventually—and not everyone was suited by their upbringing to the expectations of knighthood. But Stephen had been taken into the castle at age seven to be a page to Sir Bart. His father, the knight's bailiff, had fallen in battle defending a wounded Sir Bart from almost certain capture. In gratitude the knight had promised Stephen's mother to take him in at his own expense to be trained as a page, and then a squire if he had the aptitude. Now that he was to become a squire, perhaps even knighthood would be in store for him when he reached his eighteenth year. He could only hope.

Stephen had found that castle life agreed with him—it was all he was used to now. As a Knight of the Chalice, Sir Bart had sufficient wealth to be able to build a stone castle. It was still simple enough—a four-floored square keep near the north and east walls, with an attached round staircase tower, the keep surrounded by a roughly rectangular enclosure with eight round towers, and a gateway on the western side with twin entrance towers. Against the longer south wall were two floors of rooms used by Sir Bart's elderly unmarried sister, Lady Anne, who educated noble girls in the ways of ladyhood, and next to them a barracks for the castle garrison. Surrounding the walls—except to the east, where a cliff dropped away—was a dry moat spanned by a single drawbridge on the west side, and outside on the west, a cluster of wattle-and-daub houses inhabited by some of Sir Bart's soldiers and merchants who served the castle.

The castle stood on a rise overlooking the fertile farmland that belonged to the knight; a stream curled around the base of the rise, passing beneath the rocky cliff on the east side. At the bridge where the road from the castle spanned the stream, a village had sprung up, initially on the same side as the castle, but now houses had spread to the other side as well. Beyond the town stretched the fields farmed by peasants to produce food for the fief.

Stephen had spent many hours both inside and outside the castle in the past seven years, under the tutelage of Owen, the castle steward. In addition to his rare duties of attending to Sir Bart's lesser guests along with castle servants in the castle during feasts, Stephen had received training to determine if he had the aptitude to become a squire. He'd had lessons with Lady Anne to learn how to read, and the knight had assigned various trainers to teach him the rudiments of combat and horsemanship. Of course he was only allowed to use a wooden sword and shield, and the "horsemanship" had more to do with learning how to be around horses, groom them, and clean up after them. Nevertheless he had learned to ride a pony, and in the past two years he had ridden one of the horses into town on errands for the knight.

But he would sit sometimes at his tower window, watching the knight's men practice with real swords, dreaming of what it would be like to someday hold his own sword and fight with it. He loved to hear the clang of metal on metal and imagined seeing sparks fly as the men grunted with each thrust and parry. It never occurred to him that there might be some danger involved. He had been told that he showed promise, and after his twelfth birthday he was given a program to strengthen his body as he approached adolescence.

That was when he went outside the castle. In the quarry where the stones for the castle had been hewn, a rocky face now stood, and Stephen climbed it from bottom to top. He had done it so many times now that he was certain he could do it with his eyes closed. He knew every crack and every handhold. He learned to swim, and when he had free time, he would go down to the stream and swim upstream against the current. His body was strong now; he could feel it.

As he descended the circular staircase to the great hall, where Sir Bart ate his meals and conducted his business as lord of the surrounding lands, Stephen held his head high, certain he was a little taller than the day before, his mind reviewing all that he had accomplished to prepare for this day. He thought about his father, now a distant memory, remembering how he had encouraged, even pushed him, to be the best he could be. What if he could see Stephen now? Would he be proud, or would he pull Stephen aside and counsel him to excel at whatever tasks lay before him? It would probably be the latter, but still, Stephen half-wished his father could be present to see what he had achieved.

Stephen entered the great hall, reminding himself it was the most important room in the castle, the place where the lord received visitors and held court, where many of the castle staff would sleep on the floor at night, and where great banquets were sometimes held. Its high ceiling was supported by great carved beams, from which hung banners in both Sir Bart's colors of green and gold, and the King's colors of dark blue, gold, and white.

A great chandelier was suspended overhead, anchored to the ceiling by a chain in the center of the hall, its large candles filling the circular base. Along the length of the stone-walled hall at intervals, torches jutted from the walls in their holders, the quiet flickering of their flames providing a constant background crackle. In between the torches hung tapestries, both for decoration and to help warm the hall. It was still a cool room, even though wooden planks formed a floor over the cold stones beneath, because the small arched windows high in the south-facing walls, which admitted some light, also let in the cold air of winter and impeded the warm air of summer.

As soon as Stephen had entered the hall, Sir Bart came in as well, heading to the lord's table, which sat on a platform at the head of the hall.

Catching Stephen's eye, Sir Bart winked. "It is your big day, lad."

"Yes, sire," Stephen responded, suppressing a grin.

"We will go to the chapel after breakfast. I have asked one of my men to bring your mother from town to the castle."

Sir Bart ate alone except when he had guests. He had no wife—he was too old for one now, his short beard speckled with gray, his shiny dome bearing evidence of long-lost hair. Breakfast was a simple affair: a basket of bread, a block of cheese, a bowl of dried fruit or preserves, and water from the well. Stephen stood behind his lord's right shoulder patiently as Sir Bart ate, hoping there would be some left for him.

"There you go, boy," Sir Bart said, pushing away from the table with a grunt. "Finish it up and come down to the chapel."

Stephen unsheathed his dagger, cut a slice of cheese, and spread some preserves on a piece of bread, devouring it. Usually there was more than even he could eat, and he was careful to leave a little for the kitchen staff to enjoy after him.

Licking his dagger clean, Stephen left the great hall and half-ran down the stone steps into the courtyard. The castle was beginning to awaken. Already a peasant was coming up from the gate beside his cart, which was laden with produce for the kitchen. Some yeomen were setting up targets for archery practice along one of the walls. Silhouetted against the eastern sky, a sentry hunched over the battlements of the wall, his spear piercing the rose-tinted clouds of dawn.

The chapel was a crude one-room stone structure built into the north wall of the keep, meant to be used only by castle residents. Perhaps twenty people could stand in front of the stone altar. There was a single window on the north side that provided dim light, the chapel being in the shade all day due to its position on the north side of the keep. As he entered, Stephen saw only three people. A friar was standing behind the altar, fussing with things like friars were wont to do, Stephen supposed. A single candlestick with a large candle gave a glow to the area around the altar. Sir Bart was standing to one side, talking to Stephen's mother. They looked up, smiling, as Stephen walked in.

Because of his duties as a page, Stephen had not been able to see his mother as often as he would have liked. Whenever Stephen had a birthday, Owen would bring her up from Bartstown to share a meal with Stephen and Lady Anne in her quarters, where the events of the previous year were reviewed. Sometimes, during festival and feast occasions, when town folk mingled with castle folk, Stephen would be able to spend time with her. Seeing her smiling face now, he was reminded what an encouragement she had been to him. Though barely literate, she would scratch out simple letters to him in her limited writing vocabulary, telling him how happy she was that he was being educated by a knight and how impressed his father would have been at his progress.

"Oh, Stephen, I am so proud!" his mother said as he strode toward them.

Tossing a tuft of his dark hair away from his eyes, he paused to allow her to embrace him and to give her a welcoming hug.

"You are going to be a knight!"

"No, Mother," Stephen said. "Just a squire."

She knit her brows as she held him. "But squires become knights, don't they?"

"They do—and I hope he will," Sir Bart interjected. "But there is much to be done before that day. Come to the altar, lad."

Approaching the altar, Stephen could see what the friar had been busy with. In the center, reflecting the candle's light, stood a silver chalice. Stephen reminded himself that Sir Bart was a knight of some means, even though he led a simple life. On the friar's left was a sword belt made of leather, and beside it—a sword! On his right was a pair of silver spurs.

The friar spoke: "Kneel before the altar, my son."

Stephen lowered himself to his knees, studying the dirt floor with his eyes, wondering what would come next.

"Today you will be made squire to Sir Bartholomew," the friar said. "As a squire you will serve him as his second in war and in peace, performing whatever duty is required. Do you affirm this?"

"Yes," Stephen replied, his eyes still focused on the floor.

"You will owe him your utmost loyalty, even to the point of death. Do you affirm this?"

A shiver passed through Stephen's body. Death? He had not thought about that part. "Yes."

The friar went on, "Sir Bartholomew. For your part you will undertake to train Stephen in the ways of knighthood, so that he will be able to present himself fully prepared to serve the King by the time he is eighteen. Do you affirm this?"

"With pleasure," Sir Bart answered.

"You may give the boy his spurs."

Sir Bart approached the altar and took the spurs. Stephen heard the knight kneel behind him with a muffled grunt. He soon felt the pressure of Sir Bart pushing the spurs onto the heels of his leather boots.

"Arise, Squire Stephen," the friar said.

Stephen stood, facing the friar across the altar. Sir Bart then took the sword belt and fastened it around Stephen's hips. Last Sir Bart took the sword, and

Stephen turned toward him. The knight presented the sword with both hands, and Stephen accepted it in the same fashion, supporting it with his fingers at chin level.

"With this sword," the friar said, "you will defend the life of your lord to your last breath. Do you affirm this?"

"I will," Stephen answered, surprised at how light the sword felt compared with the heavy wooden ones he had trained with.

"You may kiss and sheath the sword."

Stephen pressed his lips to the sword, almost recoiling in response to the chill of the cold steel.

Next the friar lifted the chalice. "Sir Bart and Squire Stephen, come forward."

They stood side by side—almost shoulder to shoulder, Stephen noticed.

"By sharing the wine from this cup, you affirm the commitment of your lives to each other as if you were of the same blood, for the next four years or the duration of the training."

Sir Bart drank first, then passed the cup to Stephen. Stephen followed suit, handing the cup back to the friar, who gave them both a blessing, completing the ceremony. As Stephen turned to leave, he was met with Sir Bart's outstretched hand. Sir Bart was smiling, something Stephen had rarely seen him do, having not been alone in his presence much as a page. They grasped each other's wrists. *His grip is still strong,* Stephen thought.

"My son," Sir Bart said, looking Stephen in the eye.

Stephen glanced at his mother, who appeared equally as surprised as Stephen.

"My father," Stephen answered, wondering at the significance of what he had just said.

As they walked out together, his mother on his other side, Stephen was mindful that Sir Bart had indeed been the closest thing to a father he'd had for the past seven years. Sir Bart had provided food, shelter, and training for him, and although his time around Sir Bart had been limited to occasional feasts in the great hall and encounters in the castle, he always had the feeling that Sir Bart cared about him and looked out for him. Walking back across the courtyard to the keep, they came to a stop near a guard holding two horses.

"Good-bye, son," said his mother, embracing him once again. "Do your best. Your father would be so proud that you have come so far."

Stephen watched as she mounted and rode away with the guard. She had a good heart, always thinking and hoping for the best. He sometimes regretted that he was not able to go home to help her more. Did she feel lonely with his father gone and him at the castle? Did she wonder what he was doing each day? He knew that Sir Bart was looking after her too, having given her a stipend after his father's death.

Sir Bart's voice broke through his musing. "Starting tomorrow, you will begin a new program. You will have breakfast with me rather than after me, and I will begin to teach you what you must know to become a knight. You will also meet the trainer of squires and learn your new schedule. In the evening, after supper together, you will have another time of instruction with me in the great hall. Tonight we will have supper together to celebrate this day. In the meantime you will read this and begin to prepare yourself." Sir Bart handed him a parchment scroll.

After bidding Sir Bart farewell for the moment, Stephen climbed the tower stairs to his cramped outside room on the third floor of the castle keep, above the great hall. Sitting on the straw-filled mattress that served as his bed, he slowly unsheathed his sword, drawing his fingers carefully down the metal blade, grinning. Imaginary enemies soon filled his room as he leaped from side to side, thrusting and parrying. He envisioned himself back to back with the old knight, defending his standard on a high hill, victorious over all—that is, until an errant swing sent a candle flying from his table onto his bed. Fortunately the candle was not lit.

Surprisingly, Stephen had no other requirements this day, except to read what Sir Bart had given him. He sat by the small window in the room and carefully unrolled the scroll. At the top were the words *Duties of a Squire.* The list was quite long, but Stephen recognized most of the duties because he had already prepared for some of them, like developing climbing and swimming skills. Others, like attending to the knight, he had been prepared for by Owen, trainer of pages. After a cursory glance and wondering if he should seek out Owen to practice with him as he usually did, he decided to reward himself with a guilty day of leisure.

The hours dragged like laden peasants while he sat at the window, his head propped on his arms, watching the shadows of the wall towers grow longer in the courtyard, attempting to imagine what it would be like to actually sit at the table with Sir Bart for supper and ask the many questions he had longed to ask. He would finally be able to find out what it was like to be a knight, what it was like to be in a real battle, and more importantly what it would take to become a knight. His imagination stirred at the excitement of stepping out into a new adventure that would lead he knew not where.

Below, archers were busy at target practice. He saw his former trainer, Owen, teaching swordplay to a new page with wooden swords. Had he once been as small as that child? He reflected on his seven years, some of them spent with Lady Anne, learning table manners and proper behavior around adults, the arduous process of learning to read, the thrill of first wielding a sword, albeit a wooden one, and of overcoming his initial fear of being around horses.

Stephen resolved to try and find time to befriend this young boy he now watched and teach him some of what he had learned on his own—even though Sir Bart's previous squire, who had departed a month ago, had not done so with Stephen, knowing he was not of noble blood. It was not as though he'd had a right to expect anything of the previous squire, but his haughty manner around Stephen had resulted in Stephen feeling belittled, an experience he would not wish on anyone, especially a young child.

Finally word came that it was time for supper. Stephen sheathed his sword and descended the stairs proudly, one at a time, to the great hall, his head held high, rehearsing to himself his new name—"Squire Stephen." Sir Bart was already at the head of the lord's table, dressed in his green dinner jacket.

He smiled as Stephen entered, shaking his head. "We do not wear our weapons to supper, lad." He chuckled as he glanced at Stephen's feet. "Nor our spurs."

Feeling his face flush, Stephen unfastened his sword belt and slipped off the spurs with shaky hands.

"Forgive me, sire," Stephen mumbled. *I have begun badly,* he thought.

"No matter. Come, you will sit at my right hand when I have no guests."

Stephen pulled out the carved wooden chair and sat, not daring to look at Sir Bart now.

"But when I have guests, you will stand at my right hand and serve in whatever fashion is needed." He clapped his hands. "Bring our food now," he called to a servant standing in the doorway behind them.

Soon platters of food were placed on the table and the aroma seemed to fill the hall. Stephen surveyed a repast of a roast goose with leeks and herbs, a platter of bread, and platters of cabbage and beans, his stomach rumbling. A servant held containers of a dark beverage and water. Stephen presumed the dark liquid was wine but wasn't sure if it was for him too.

Apparently noting Stephen's confused expression, Sir Bart waved a hand, saying, "You may have wine if you like, but water would be better for you."

Stephen chose water.

Cutting off a goose leg with his knife, Sir Bart began. "Knighthood is about many things, not just about learning combat. Becoming a knight involves developing character and wisdom. It is about loyalty, obedience, commitment, knowledge, and service to your King."

Having served himself, Stephen glanced up from his plate, nodding.

Sir Bart went on and on, Stephen retaining little while attempting to appreciate the privilege of sitting at Sir Bart's right side and eat with him instead of afterward, though his earlier gaffe weighed heavily on his mind.

"I serve a great King, and someday I hope you will serve the same King," Sir Bart concluded, placing his knife beside his plate. "Is there anything you would like to ask me?"

Stephen was caught by surprise, unable to recall most of what Sir Bart had said, so buried had he been in his own thoughts. Yes, Stephen wanted to know many things about Sir Bart, but he did not feel free to ask now, having already been chastised by the knight and not wanting to reveal that he had retained almost nothing Sir Bart just said. What should he ask? Was Sir Bart expecting a question about something he had said?

It was the first time Stephen had ever been alone with Sir Bart in the great hall with time to look around, though he remembered serving at the great feasts when long tables were set up and laden with food, and the hall was filled with the garrulous shouting and laughing of many guests, and music of minstrels. Then Stephen's mind had been busy with helping servants bring food to the tables without spilling it. His eyes had been exploring the great hall again, reliving those memories, when Sir Bart asked his question. At that moment Stephen was gazing absently at some writing on the far wall facing Sir Bart.

"Uh, what is that writing?" Stephen asked, having nothing better to voice.

"You are a good observer," Sir Bart replied. "Those are the Kingdom Rules. I had them put there as a constant reminder to myself and others of what the King requires of us. You can read, can you not? Go closer and read the ones on the right to me."

Stephen slipped out of his chair and approached the wall. On two fields of blue with arched tops, there appeared to be written in large fanciful gold letters two lists. The one on the right displayed two statements.

"The first says, 'I am the King. There is no other King but me.'"

"And the second?"

"'You shall love your King with all your heart and mind and strength, and you shall love others as you love your King.'"

"You must believe and practice those rules if you would serve the King perfectly," Sir Bart said.

Stephen thought a moment. "That seems impossible. I do believe the King is the only king, but—how do you love the King? And I don't think I can love everybody."

"Then you have something to learn about love," the knight replied. "First you must understand what it means that the King loves you. But that will be a subject for the future. Do you have any more questions?"

"What about the writing on the left?"

"Those are the original Kingdom Rules, ten in number. Read the first two."

"'I am the King. There is no other king but me,'" Stephen said. He looked at Sir Bart. "It is the same."

"Indeed. Now read the second."

"'You shall not bow down to any false king, nor serve anyone or anything but me.'"

"Therein lies our problem," Sir Bart said, "for there is now a false king who claims the crown, whom we call the Dragon, to whom many have pledged their allegiance, and who holds sway over even more who pledge allegiance to no one but themselves. Now read the rest of the ten and tell me, if you are able, the difference between the two sets of rules."

Taking his time, Stephen read the last eight rules, shaking his head as he finished.

"Well?" Sir Bart said.

Stephen could see the expectancy in the knight's eyes. "Well, all but two of the last eight are things we should not do." Stephen swallowed hard. "And I have already done some of them."

He did not want to voice his next thought: *Does that mean I am disqualified to be a squire?* Feeling his heart race, he looked at Sir Bart, as if expecting to be banished from the castle immediately.

He was not prepared for Sir Bart's reply: "As have I. What is different about the two rules on the right?"

Stephen glanced back at the first rules he had read. "They are both things we should do. But I—"

Sir Bart interrupted, "The Prince himself told those of us in his inner circle that the two on the right summarize those on the left. If you can fulfill the two, you will have fulfilled the ten."

He heard Sir Bart's explanation, yet Stephen could only think, *But I haven't fulfilled the two either.* Ashamed of the poor impression he was making, and unwilling to admit he had heard almost nothing of what Sir Bart had told him, much less understood anything, Stephen became quiet. It was his first day as a squire, and he had already broken the rules. This was going to be much more difficult than being a page, and though he recognized that Owen had taught him some of the rules in a different form as "proper behavior," never had he imagined that they were the King's rules! How could he ever hope to become a knight? Should he just admit he was unqualified right now and leave the castle in disgrace? His mother would be disappointed, of course, but no more disappointed than he felt in himself at his moment.

"I cannot think of any more questions, milord, but perhaps another time…" he added, his voice trailing off into silence.

They ate the rest of the meal without words, Stephen not daring to speak, feeling he was undeserving of even being there. His father's face appeared before him, his voice accusing, *"How could you fail so spectacularly?"* Stephen stole a furtive glance at the knight from time to time, attempting to read his expression, half-expecting Sir Bart to order him to surrender his sword and spurs on the spot and leave the castle at once.

A cheese course and some wafers, with ypocras, ended the supper. Stephen knew that ypocras was a spiced wine, and though he was curious how it tasted, Sir Bart did not offer any, and Stephen did not dare pour his own. After draining his own mug of ypocras, Sir Bart pushed back his chair with a scrape, stood up, and walked out. Stephen sat in stunned silence, listening to Sir Bart's footsteps echo off the cold walls until they faded. He was alone.

Realizing that his appetite had deserted him, Stephen picked up his sword belt and spurs and trudged back upstairs to his room, anxious and confused, plagued by self-reproach. He flung himself on his mattress and lay motionless, gazing at the stone ceiling of his room, reviewing the sequence of events he had just experienced. There seemed to be rules for everything—what to wear to supper, how to be a knight, what to do, what not to do. Too many rules!

He thought back to only the previous week, when his days had seemed carefree, his life an exciting adventure. No longer. The dream of knighthood was probably beyond his reach now. He drifted into sub-consciousness, hearing the impatient voice of his father demanding, *"Just get up and brush off the dirt, son! You are going to keep doing this until you succeed!"* and seeing the face of his patient mother, saying, *"You can do anything you can dream, Stephen."*

Then came an onrush of questions, each pricking like a biting gnat. What did it mean that the King loved him? How could he love someone he did not know? And what hope had he if he could not follow the rules? He fell into a restless sleep fraught with dreams, in which he was dressed in full plate armor like Sir Bart wore. It seemed he was to be knighted. In the distance sat the King on his throne; behind him on the wall were written the Kingdom Rules. The King was pointing at them and wore an angry expression. Stephen attempted to walk forward and bow before the King, but his legs would not move, nor could he lift his arms due to the weight of the armor. His visor slammed down with a clank and he was in darkness, trapped in armor so heavy he could not budge.

Stephen awoke in a sweat, feeling momentarily paralyzed, his heart pounding, his breathing rapid. The room was totally dark. He shook his arms free from the grip of the dream and lay wide-eyed, daring not fall asleep again. Throughout the rest of the night, he tossed from side to side, thoughts of what he could have done better marching through his mind, preparing himself to face on the morrow his worst fear—that it would be his last in the castle.

Chapter 3

THE MAIDEN

A SMALL BROOK GURGLED and curled around stones behind the house, continued down the hill, and settled briefly into a pond before frolicking its way into the countryside. When she wanted to be alone, Marie would come to its edge, flop onto the bank, gaze into the forest, and release her thoughts like butterflies to flit wherever they would. She wasn't really alone, she knew, for her nurse, Henriette, was usually behind the rough, half-timbered manor house that she called home, watching her in order to be sure she did not stray into the forest. The forest belonged to Marie's father, Sir Guy de Bonfrere. Marie had watched him ride into the forest with his sergeant-at-arms from time to time to hunt, but she was forbidden. Her mother, Lady Clare, had warned her that it was a dangerous place. Why then did her father always seem in a happy mood when he rode forth? Her mother always spoke of the forest in hushed tones, as if it had ears and could hear what she said. "There are wild animals in that forest—and other things." She would never tell Marie about the "other things."

To Marie, her place by the stream was a personal refuge where sunlight would dance over the rocks and sparkle in the water as breezes ruffled the leaves of the trees that stood sentinel at the forest edge. She would shut her eyes and allow her thoughts to chase the songs of the birds into the forest, imagining where they perched and what they were saying. In the evenings she would listen to frogs at the water's edge, the small ones with their treble *briiink!* and the large ones with their hoarse *rerrk!* But when darkness neared, Henriette always called Marie inside. There was work to do.

It wasn't that Marie was forced to work. In fact she was vaguely aware that she was privileged. Her mother never failed to remind her that she was the daughter of a knight, as if that were something important. True, they had a servant who prepared meals and kept the house clean, and her clothing seemed simpler than Marie's. Her nurse was also lady-in-waiting to her mother. The duties that Marie called "work" were not difficult or tiring, just boring, and since her twelfth birthday just days ago, they seemed to be taking over far too much of the time she could be spending in her imagination.

As Marie lay on her back in the grass, watching the clouds above her begin to change color in the waning sunlight, the call of Henriette shattered her reverie: "Come, child! It grows late. Milady has need of you in the kitchen."

Marie pulled herself away from the cool shadows of the darkening forest with a groan and trudged back to the house. Unlike most of the modest houses in the countryside, it was a four-bay design with two levels. Coming in through the door, she entered the spacious main room, the hall, which filled the central two bays and whose timbered ceiling arched the full two levels above a stone floor covered by simple rugs for warmth in winter. In the center stood the large rectangular wooden table at which the family ate meals—flanked by four sturdy chairs, one at each end for her father and mother, and one on either side for herself and her younger brother, Edouard. Tapestries adorned the walls opposite the entrance between two windows. To the right stood an open fireplace with a chimney stretching upward, and in the bay beyond, a smaller room bustling with the noise of meal preparation—the kitchen, with its buttery and pantry. To the other side in the fourth bay was her mother's sitting room, where Lady Clare did her embroidery, played her music, or read. A narrow staircase against the back wall led to the upper level, where a small open balcony overlooked the hall, spanning the space between the upper bedrooms: the one above the kitchen where her mother and father slept, with its own fireplace; and the one on the other side for her and Edouard, also shared with Henriette.

Marie's ears were assaulted by her mother's urgent voice as she entered the hall: "Where is that child? She is always somewhere else! These are things she must learn."

Heaving a sigh, Marie emerged into the heat and light of the kitchen, where a roaring fire silhouetted Ginette, their cook and house servant, as she chopped carrots and turnips on a small table. Marie noted a roast pheasant on a spit in front of the fire, the bird's golden skin announcing it was ready to eat, its aroma reminding Marie that she was ready to eat as well.

"Marie!" Lady Clare said. "You have missed most of the meal preparation. You must know about this."

"Why, Mother? You already know all about it."

"Because now you are twelve!" Lady Clare huffed. "It is time to begin learning the duties of a wife."

"A wife?" Marie half coughed, choking as much on the idea as the word. "But I am a child. You call me 'child.' Henriette calls me 'child.'"

Lady Clare turned to confront her, hands on hips. Though her face remained in shadow, backlit by the fire, Marie recognized the look of exasperation.

"No longer," Lady Clare said. "You are now of age. At twelve you must begin to learn how to manage a household, for you will be a wife. Now watch what Ginette is doing. Even if you do not prepare meals yourself, you will supervise someone like her."

Marie slumped against the wall of the kitchen, exhaling another sigh, and watched as Ginette removed the pheasant from the spit and began to cut off small pieces of the roasted bird, gathering them in a pile. Finally the bones were clean and Ginette gathered the bits of pheasant, dropping them into a pot hanging over the fire. Next she collected the cut turnips and carrots and pitched them in. After stirring it together, she took an open bottle of red wine and poured some into the pot, continuing to stir. Last came some peppercorns and cloves.

Frowning, Marie continued to lean against the wall, watching the stew bubble and steam. The aroma seemed more than she could bear.

"When will it be ready, Ginette?" she asked.

Ginette smiled at her. "It's almost—"

"Come, Marie!" Lady Clare called from the hall. "Your father is here."

Marie shrugged at Ginette, then slid into the hall to see her father standing near the door. He grinned when he saw her.

"My fair daughter!" he said, his eyes smiling. "Mother says you have been busy learning how to supervise the kitchen. That is good."

"When I can get her in there," Lady Clare muttered.

"Yes, Father, I have," Marie replied, averting her eyes. She always seemed to herself very small in the presence of her father, especially in moments like these when he was attired in his chain mail hauberk[3] and his surcoat, whose

---

[3] A thigh-length shirt of armor made of metal rings.

emblem bore witness to his service to the King. Sir Guy de Bonfrere had just returned from such a mission.

"Give your father a smile," Sir Guy said, placing a finger under Marie's chin to lift it.

Marie did not like to smile, especially if her teeth showed. She knew that her two front teeth overlapped slightly, an imperfection she did not like to show anyone, even her father. Even though her mother told her that her brown eyes and cascading brown curls were beautiful, she did not feel beautiful. Her eyes seemed too big also. Nevertheless she managed a polite but evanescent curl of her lips, then looked away.

"You must be hungry, milord," Lady Clare said, pulling a sturdy wooden chair from the head of the table. "Sit, and tell us about your journey while Ginette brings you a savory stew."

After placing his sword and sword belt on a bench, Sir Guy heaved himself into the chair with a grunt. "I come from Bartscastle, where I and some others gathered to hear from Sir John as he rode through with tidings of the Kingdom." He paused and looked at Marie. "Run along and play with your brother. This news is for your mother."

Lady Clare raised her hand to stop Marie. "Milord, you know she has passed her twelfth birthday. She should begin to hear about these things."

Sir Guy's eyes regarded Lady Clare momentarily, as if weighing the implications, then settled on Marie. "Very well, my daughter, remain and learn." He turned his attention back to Lady Clare. "Sir John told us that the Dragon is growing restless. His scouts have been seen here and there, as though they were looking for weaknesses to exploit. We are to be ready to join Sir John at a moment's notice with as many men as we have."

Marie shivered, as if a chill had crept into the room. *The dragon?* She glanced at her mother, whose face was lined with concern.

"That is unwelcome news, milord," Lady Clare said. "If such a need arises, who will manage the land?"

Sir Guy frowned. "If we must go to battle, the women must make do. Richard, as he is our steward, would also stay to help you manage. But Daniel will train as many of the peasants as he can in the skills of archery and use of the spear, the sturdier ones in swordsmanship."

Visions of men brandishing bows, swords, and spears began to fill Marie's imagination. She was looking into these men's dimly lit faces, which wore expressions not of determination but of fear. Of what? The scene widened. She was among the soldiers now, facing a giant scaly dragon, flames licking from the corners of its mouth as its angry eyes searched the crowd that blocked its way. She was unarmed. Where was her father? What could she do?

"Father?" Marie blurted, ready to voice a long-held wish. "Would Daniel teach me archery too?"

"Shush!" Lady Clare glared at her. "The skills of war are for men."

"But what if the men are gone and the dragon comes?" Marie stared at her mother. "You have a bow. I have seen it!"

"Ladies!" Sir Guy said, raising his hands.

But even as he said it, Marie could tell that he seemed amused by her bold request.

"Your mother is right, Marie. Archery is a skill of war. Daniel is my sergeant-at-arms. He only trains men for war. Your mother's bow is for shooting at targets with other women. You must let the men worry about the Dragon."

Marie said nothing in reply, aware that she could not share her frightening vision, nor did her parents know of her fantasies while she sat by the stream— fantasies of riding like the wind on her horse, bow in hand, shooting magic arrows at imaginary beasts to tame them, of conversing with them about their lives, of being the ruler of a magical kingdom where people and animals were friends. That world had no dragon.

Unwilling to back down, she sat up to her full diminutive height, saying, "Mother said I am twelve, and I am ready for these things. Why may I not learn to shoot her bow?"

Lady Clare narrowed her eyes, shaking her head, opening her mouth to speak. She was halted by a hearty laugh from Sir Guy. *"Alors, ma petite fille!* You were easier to manage when you were a child." Winking at Marie's mother, he continued, "But I see no reason why you should not learn to shoot at targets while you are learning all of the other duties of a lady."

Lady Clare's glare dissolved into an attitude of surrender. "Yes, milord. As you wish."

A clatter from the kitchen announced the arrival of Ginette with a steaming pot of pheasant stew.

"Marie, go and fetch your brother for supper," Lady Clare said.

Marie gave a curt "Yes, Mother," then disappeared up the stairs, returning with Edouard and Henriette. Edouard took his seat across from Marie as Sir Guy spooned stew into each of their wooden bowls.

"A welcome repast," he said, smacking his lips after the first taste as he regarded Edouard. "And what did you do today, my son?"

Speaking through a mouthful, Edouard answered, "Daniel is fashioning a wooden sword for me. Will you show me how to fight with it, Father?"

Bellowing another throaty laugh, Sir Guy said, "My son, already a warrior! Soon it will be time to send you Bartscastle where you will be a page to Sir Bart and learn the ways of a knight."

"But he is only a child, milord," Lady Clare protested. "It is enough that your daughter has come of age this week."

Sir Guy winked at Edouard. "Your day will come, son." Then he turned to Lady Clare. "And you, milady. What will you do tomorrow?"

"I go to Grandvil to purchase supplies and sell produce. Marie will accompany me this time. Now that she is twelve, she is to watch and begin to learn the duties of a lady."

Despite her apprehension about what the "duties of a lady" might be, Marie suppressed a grin, trying to imagine the adventure that awaited her. She would be leaving their lands for the first time, seeing the countryside and experiencing the sights and sounds of a town, all new to her.

"As always, take Richard with you," Sir Guy said. "The fief in which Grandvil lies has come into the hands of a knight favored by the Dragon. He has not been hostile toward us, but be careful."

As the meal and talk continued, a shadow of fear began to darken Marie's excitement about her impending journey the next day. By bedtime, though, excitement had won out and she could barely fall asleep while imagining the adventure that awaited her.

As morning dawned, Lady Clare and Marie broke fast with bread and dried fruit, then stepped out into the summer sunshine to meet Richard, who held their horses at the ready. For reasons she could not fully explain, Marie had been coming to feel that a chasm had opened between her and her mother. They were not alike, she sensed. There seemed always to be an urgency in her mother's behavior, as if it were her duty to see that everything turned out as it should—or as she thought it should. In contrast Marie was a dreamer, preferring to allow her imagination to take her where it wished, and to just experience her life as it opened before her like a blossoming flower. There were no "shoulds" in her world. Her mother would never understand this, though. She had never tried. Did she even care about Marie's thoughts and dreams?

Although she was not looking forward to the prospect of spending the entire day with her mother doing whatever wives do, Marie was always excited to mount her horse for a ride. Only the previous year she had been given her own horse and learned how to ride. She had taken short rides in the countryside with her mother and with Richard, her instructor, but was never allowed to ride alone. Today was no exception. A sword prominently buckled to his waist, Richard accompanied them as they turned their horses toward the road that led six miles to Grandvil. A cart loaded with produce to sell, guided by a peasant, followed behind.

They rode at a slow pace, Richard in the lead, passing fields where peasants worked at pulling weeds and doing summer plowing. In other fields the flax harvest had begun. The cool morning air was laden with a breath of the heat that would follow as the sun rose to its zenith. The road remained muddy from recent rain, their horses' hoofs splattering mud to either side as they rode. Though the road was largely deserted, they would occasionally be overtaken by a peasant's cart, at which time Richard would lead them off the road momentarily so that their clothes would not be spattered with the ubiquitous mud.

Once out of sight of the house, Marie began to yield herself to the excitement and curiosity stimulated by a new adventure. She discovered many new sights and smells of the countryside—a distant view of sheep in a pasture and the sweet aroma of flowers and grasses by the road. She felt a peace, a sense that everything was in its place. She was about to see Grandvil for the first time. What would the large market town be like? Many people lived there, she knew, but what did they do? Would she be fascinated by the spectacle?

An exclamation from Richard interrupted her thoughts. She saw a beggar scurry off to the side of the road as Richard brandished his sword at the man.

"What did he want, Mother?" Marie asked.

"They all want our money!" Lady Clare hissed. "Sometimes they are brigands in disguise, seeking to rob."

"He looks hungry, Mother," Marie said, glancing over her shoulder at the beggar. "Can we give him something to eat on the way back?"

"I am sure he is hungry, but if he would work in the fields, he would have enough to eat."

"But maybe he can't work. You don't know—"

"Do not tell me what I do not know, Marie! Remember your place. We take good care of our peasants. They have plenty to eat. It is not our responsibility to feed the masses."

That was the end of any conversation until the buildings of Grandvil came into sight. Marie had already fallen into a dark mood, her sense of adventure now squashed. On the outskirts of the town, they passed a smithy, noticeable by the smoke coming from a chimney and the clanging of hammer on anvil within. Then a most awful smell assaulted Marie's nose. She had grown accustomed to the smell of horse manure, but this was far worse.

She soon noticed piles of garbage in and beside the muddy streets. Pigs and dogs roamed freely, snorting and snuffling amidst the rubbish and heaps of rotting food. Then came the noise—not only the slopping sound of horses pulling carts through puddles, but people shouting to each other, along with screaming, barefoot children chasing each other through the muck and filth. Marie thought back to her quiet spot next to the brook. Was coming to a place like this part of being a wife? Repulsed by what she saw and smelled, she decided that she already did not like towns.

As they approached the center of town, the mud gave way to cobblestones, the clattering of their horses' hoofs echoing off the stone and wood buildings. Marie recognized the shops of merchants by the wrought-iron signs that hung above the doors. She could smell the bakery before they even reached it, and a vision of freshly baked bread formed in her mind. Soon she saw a symbol of twisted bread hung outside the bakery. Then came a large bronze quill dangled above the door of a scrivener, a pair of real boots above the door of a cobbler, giant scissors outside the shop of a tailor. Finally they reached the town square, where a bustling market was in sway.

The scene that unfolded before Marie's eyes went beyond even her imagination. Extending from the center of the town square stood rows of wooden tables and open booths, each manned by a seller. Some order likely existed to it all, but Marie's senses were overwhelmed by the sights and sounds. More people than she had ever seen in her life milled through the passageways among shouts of men and women attempting to attract a buyer. Over it all, a cacophony of animal voices rose—the bleating of sheep and goats, quacking of ducks, honking of geese, and barking of dogs. The sound of music from unseen minstrels added a festive air.

As their party dismounted and gave their horses to the care of a horse minder, Lady Clare tugged Marie aside.

"Stay with me, Marie. We do not mingle with the masses. Richard will deliver our produce to be sold, then tend to the list of supplies for the kitchen. Most of our food comes from our fields and forest, so we do not need to buy animals or food here. Richard will visit the spicer to buy sugar, salt, pepper, cloves, and cinnamon for cooking. We are going to the foreigners' quarter."

Marie nodded, glancing back at the market as her mother led the way to a quieter section with neater booths, somewhat apart from the garrulous crowd jostling among the tables laden with food and crafts, and the stalls confining the complaining animals.

"The best of the market is what comes from abroad," Lady Clare said, pausing before a stall with stacks of fabric.

"Good morning, milady," the merchant said, then smiled. "I bring you the best cloth from Flanders."

"Good day, sir," Lady Clare replied. She fingered the fabric, then turned toward Marie. "We are going to buy some cloth today to have some new gowns made for you. You must look your age now."

"And a fine young lady she is," the merchant said, displaying a gold tooth nestled in his smile.

Her mother said nothing in reply. Marie did have to admit that she enjoyed new clothes, but she did not always agree with her mother's choice of colors. Nonetheless her eyes grew wide at the spectrum of colors now displayed before her.

"We will take five ells of the light blue ," Lady Clare said. "You look so pretty in blue, Marie."

After the morning conversation, or lack of it, Marie could only bite her lip. *Red! I like the red!* Next they bought some lace and came finally to the wine merchant, who, seeing them approaching, poured a sample into a tasting cup.

While sampling several vintages, Lady Clare told Marie, "Your father prefers wine made by the monks of Burgundy. We will buy a barrel and leave it for Richard to pick up."

"Yes, Mother," Marie said. Then she noticed a roving pie-seller. "Oh, Mother, could we buy some meat pies to eat on the way back?"

Lady Clare smiled at her. "Of course, dear."

Marie replied with a quick "Thank you," surprised at her mother's sudden good mood, but surmised that it came from visiting the foreign merchants and making her purchases.

"I will mention it to Richard," Lady Clare said. "We should go back to our horses now and separate ourselves from the crowds."

On the way back through the market, Marie tried to take in all the activity her eyes could find. "Mother, there is a group of people over there watching something and laughing! Can we stop and listen?" She gestured toward a booth on the edge of the commoners' market and looked up at her mother.

Lady Clare's good mood disappeared in an instant. "Absolutely not!" she snapped. "That is a common puppet show. The stories they tell are not fit for your ears!"

"But—" Marie paused. *You buy cloth to dress me as an adult and now you treat me as if I am a child!* That thought was best not spoken, though, so she held her tongue.

By the time they had completed their tour of the merchants' stalls, Richard had gathered all the supplies and went next to fetch the barrel of wine and roll it into the cart with the help of the peasant driver. The three mounted their horses and began their journey home, the din of the marketplace fading with the unforgettable stench of the town. Marie welcomed the fresh air of the countryside as they began to pass fields again. A peace descended on her, which she recognized had been missing in the town. She wished they were already home so that she could run out to her restful place by the stream and listen to the sounds of the forest.

A familiar sight soon interrupted her daydream. Ahead by the road sat the same beggar they had passed on the way to town that morning. He rose to his feet and bowed as they drew near.

Marie heard a *schreesh* as she saw Richard begin to unsheathe his sword. "Wait!" Marie called.

Richard paused, looking back at her quizzically as the party came to a stop.

"Mother, I would like to give him my meat pie. He looks so hungry."

Lady Clare's face twisted into an expression of annoyance. The beggar now stood by Marie, looking up at her. She turned away from her mother and gazed down at the man, his mud-encrusted hands outstretched and trembling, his lean face shadowed with gray stubble, his eyes pleading above hollowed cheeks.

"Ladies," he said, his voice raspy, "would you show a pitiful man some mercy? Have you a farthing or perhaps some food for one who has not eaten this day?"

With a heavy sigh Lady Clare said "Richard!" and motioned to the cart with her head.

Richard trotted back to the cart, dismounted, and brought a meat pie to Marie.

"Thank you, Mother," Marie said, ignoring her mother's expression. She handed the pie to the beggar, who snatched it with unsteady hands as if someone might steal it away, then shoved it into his mouth as if he would eat the whole thing in a single gulp.

"Bless you, milady. You have allowed a poor man to live another day," he said, his voice muffled by the enormous mouthful of pie, crumbs dropping from the corner of his mouth.

Marie felt a surge of compassion. "What is your name, sir?" she asked.

"Piers." He took a final swallow and said clearly, "My name is Piers."

Marie smiled. "Go then, Piers, and live another day."

After he offered his thanks again, Marie nudged her horse forward and the journey resumed in silence. Though she had drawn her mother's ire once again, Marie felt pleased with herself. She had helped this pitiful man. Maybe it would help him live a few days longer. She saw no use in talking to her mother now—and yet a thought had been growing in Marie's mind all day. Finally, after more minutes of silent travel, she could no longer contain it.

"Mother?"

"Are you regretting now that you gave your dinner away?" Lady Clare replied.

Marie shook her head. "No. I am glad. But I just wanted to know—when will I be a wife?"

"That is your father's choice," Lady Clare answered. "My father betrothed me to your father when I was fifteen."

Marie rode in silence for a moment, considering the reply. Something about her mother's answer did not seem right. "Why does Father decide?" Marie asked. "Do I not have a choice?"

A pained expression appeared on her mother's face. "Your father will make the best choice for the family. He will find the son of a lord who owns many lands so that your son will have more lands than we."

Her suspicions now having been confirmed, Marie's breath caught. Was marriage only about gaining more lands and wealth? She spoke her next thought without further reflection.

"But what if I do not love the one he chooses? Or what if I do not want to marry at all?"

Marie watched her mother's lips settle into a familiar grim line. "You will do the best thing for the family and you will obey your father," Lady Clare answered, stiffening in her saddle.

Though Marie could easily read her mother's body language and tone of voice, she would not let the matter rest. "Did you love Father when you were given to him?"

"I obeyed my father," Lady Clare responded. Marie saw her jaw tighten while she kept her gaze fixed straight ahead. "Your father is a good man. He has provided well for us. Do not cross him." She glanced at Marie. "We are through talking about this!"

Duty and obedience. That is my mother—not me.

Biting back a sigh, Marie thought about her mother's words. If those were the requirements of a wife, Marie felt certain she could not be one. She would be no more than a servant to the knight to whom she was wed! Where was the freedom for her to be herself?

The group had no more conversation until they came into sight of Maison Bonfrere. Smoke curling from the chimney gave promise that Ginette was already busy preparing a tasty supper, which brought some warmth back to Marie's heart. The forest beyond beckoned, warming her heart even more.

"We will leave Richard to bring the supplies into the house," Lady Clare said. "Marie, you will come with me to the kitchen to observe."

No! she thought, but kept her voice steady as she said, "May I first go to the brook and sit awhile, Mother? I have so looked forward to it all day."

"You may not!" Lady Clare answered. "It is time to put childhood play behind you."

"Yes, Mother," Marie sighed through nearly clenched teeth.

They dismounted, a gloomy Marie moping along behind her mother into the kitchen, her mind churning. *It is not childhood play you are telling me to give up. It is my whole life!*

She came to a halt behind her mother and saw that Ginette had filleted fish from the pond, rubbed salt and pepper on them, sprinkled some dried herbs on, and was now letting them cook over the fire while she sliced vegetables.

"We bought more salt and spices for you at the market, Ginette," Lady Clare said. "Richard will bring them in. Have you seen your master today?"

"I saw them ride into the forest to hunt, milady—he and Daniel."

At that Lady Clare gave a nod and then began narrating to Marie everything that Ginette was doing in the kitchen. The waning afternoon seemed to drag on until the sound of neighing from the stable announced the return of Sir Guy from the hunt. Soon his heavy tread was at the door and he strode into the kitchen, grasping two rabbits by the ears.

Lady Clare and Ginette greeted him in turn with "Milord," and then Marie gave a forced smile before saying, "Father! You are back—and with game for us!"

"Yes, though not much for a day in the forest," he said, then sighed. "We saw the great stag, but he eluded us." His eyes narrowed. "But we saw something else. We discovered evidence of an encampment in the woods—in my forest! There were signs of at least one horse, so I do not think it was any of our people."

Lady Clare gasped. "Milord! What does it mean?"

"I believe it is as Sir John said. Scouts of the Dragon are on the move. We must be vigilant. I have entrusted Daniel with the task of riding the woods daily to report back to me what he has seen." He handed the rabbits to Ginette, then said, "Bring our supper, Ginette. Come to the table, milady, and Marie."

They followed him into the dining area, where he pulled a chair out from the table and collapsed into it. "Now, let us eat," he said.

Marie and her mother both sat down. A moment later Sir Guy called for Edouard, who bounced down the stairs and seated himself just as Ginette brought a platter of fish surrounded by vegetables. She then placed a bottle of decanted wine next to Sir Guy.

"Now tell me about your journey to Grandvil, my daughter," he said, eyeing Marie.

Marie's first thought—*I don't ever want to go again!*—would undoubtedly draw more of her mother's ire. She chose her words carefully. "We bought some more wine for you—from the monks, Father."

"Ah, yes—good!" he said, smiling. "Even though my blood is Norman, the best wine comes from the monks in Burgundy! What else?"

"We bought spices for Ginette."

"Yes! She makes such belly-pleasing suppers. Do you hear me, Ginette?" he called over his shoulder.

"Yes, milord. Thank you, milord," Ginette answered from the kitchen.

Sir Guy laughed and looked at Marie again. "And what did you think of Grandvil?"

Marie could not restrain herself. Her memory of the smell and filth of Grandvil engulfed her senses like a noxious cloud. "I never want to go again, Father!" she cried, unable to stop herself bursting into tears.

Lady Clare leaned in and said, "We had a nasty encounter with a beggar."

"No!" Marie said between sobs. "No, that's not it! He was hungry. I gave him my pie."

Sir Guy sat up to his full height. "Did he threaten you?"

"He was very bold," Lady Clare said. "He came right up to Marie's horse. Richard was about to give him the tip of the sword—"

"But I stopped him," Marie interrupted. "I wanted to give him my pie."

Sir Guy settled back into his seat. "That was kind of you, Marie, but you must be careful. It is good that Richard was with you. Sometimes the beggars carry a knife and will rob you."

Lady Clare nodded. "It was her first time away from the house. I think it all was a bit overwhelming for her. It will be better next time."

"Please don't make me go again, Father!" Marie cried, her voice growing higher pitched and panicked.

At this Sir Guy leaned forward, his elbows on the table, his hands folded, engaging her eyes with his. "Marie," he said, his voice a calm monotone, "you must learn to be a lady. There will be things in life that are difficult. You must learn to manage them."

Marie could not stop crying. Embarrassed now by the spectacle she was causing, she shoved back her chair and ran up the stairs to her bedroom, wiping her cheeks, flopping headfirst onto her bed, angry at her mother for making her go to Grandvil, angry at herself for losing her composure in front of her father.

Soon after, Edouard came in.

"Go away!" she shouted.

"I can't," Edouard answered in a small voice. "Mother and Father told me to go to bed."

Marie could hear her mother and father talking in loud voices as if there were some disagreement. She held her breath to listen.

Her mother spoke in an exasperated tone: "She is as stubborn as a mule, milord! I cannot train her. She does not respect me."

The conversation continued in low voices—sometimes her mother's, sometimes her father's—with Marie lying as still as she could, straining to hear.

A chair scraped on the floor. Her father cleared his throat, and the words Marie heard next set her heart pounding: "Very well. I will send Daniel to Bartscastle tomorrow. Maybe they will take her."

Her eyes wide, Marie swallowed, feeling she could hardly breathe. She was to be sent away? Did her parents no longer want her? What had she done that they would cast her away so casually and so cruelly?

Chapter 4

MICHAEL

THE MORNING AFTER his inauspicious debut as Sir Bart's squire, Stephen descended the stairs to the great hall with slow steps, head down, fully expecting to have his last breakfast with the knight. How his fortune had changed! He had nothing to look forward to now. He would probably be given even more rules he could not master. At least he had remembered to leave his sword and spurs in his room—as if that would make any difference. But as he entered the great hall, he noted that Sir Bart was not alone. Sitting to Sir Bart's right was a tall, partially balding, middle-aged man, his hair closely cropped, garbed in chain mail and surcoat as for battle. Stephen slunk his way to the chair on Sir Bart's left.

"Good morning, Stephen," Sir Bart said, giving no notice of any displeasure with him. "This is Michael."

Stephen realized that he had seen this man before from a distance, with the squire who had recently departed. Because of the man's size, Stephen had felt intimidated just looking at him, believing him to be a great warrior who served the knight. Now he was face to face with the same! Michael seemed amply muscled beneath his tunic and mail hauberk, with a serious, well-weathered face devoid of any evidence that he had ever smiled. Moreover it was marked by a scar that began beside his right eye and extended to his ear, the top of which was missing. But his most striking feature was his eyes—deep blue, with an unwavering gaze that pierced Stephen as if he were a mere shadow.

"Good day, master," Michael said to Stephen, his expression unchanged.

"G-Good day, sir," Stephen said, assuming now that Michael was there only to escort him out of the castle in disgrace.

"After we break our fast, Stephen," Sir Bart said, "you will go down to the courtyard and Michael will explain your daily training schedule to you." He turned toward Michael. "You may go now, Michael."

Rising, Michael excused himself and departed, leaving Stephen wondering what would happen next. Sir Bart took a piece of bread and fruit from a platter in front of Stephen and himself, then cleared his throat to speak, giving no evidence that any of the events of the previous day were on his mind. Stephen listened expectantly, a wave of relief flowing over him as he allowed himself to hope that perhaps he had been given another chance. He determined that he must make the best of it.

"Now, we will start with the King," Sir Bart began. "As you know, I serve the King. He gave me the lands that constitute my fief, and in turn I pledge him my sword when it is needed, along with a portion of the income from my lands. In times of war he can count on me not only for my sword but also for at least twenty men-at-arms and as many archers. Other knights in the vicinity will also gather to my banner. In times of peace I serve the King by being a steward of what he has given me and by training new members for his Kingdom."

"Like me?" Stephen asked, reaching for a piece of bread himself.

"Like you."

Feeling bolder now that he apparently was not going to be dismissed, Stephen continued, "Have you ever met the King, milord?"

"Not face to face, but, yes, I have seen him many times."

Sir Bart seemed to have a far-off gaze, as if he were studying the Kingdom Rules on the wall opposite him.

"Years ago," he went on, "I was a member of the Prince's personal guard. Those were turbulent times. There was a rebellion, with much warfare and strife. We would ride with the Prince as his bodyguard, but after he was killed in battle, the King scattered us to the outermost parts of his lands to train others and to build his Kingdom."

Recalling bits of conversation he had overheard, Stephen ventured, "It is said that you are one of an inner circle called Knights of the Chalice."

Sir Bart popped a dried fig into his mouth. "That is true. There were twelve of us. We would sup with the Prince at a table in the King's castle. But, alas, one of our members betrayed the Prince in battle. He took his own life afterward, so then there were eleven, and sadly one of those has already fallen in battle, so we are now ten."

"Why are you called 'Knights of the Chalice'?" Stephen asked. Even as he uttered the query, he realized he felt more and more comfortable now in the knight's presence, long-held questions stifled by his embarrassment the day before tumbling forth.

Sir Bart fingered his cup slowly in a circular motion as he answered, "At our last meal before the battle in which the Prince was slain, he passed his cup around to each of us and we drank from it. It has since become a symbol of the brotherhood we shared with him."

"Since then, do you ever come together and meet with each other?"

"As I said, we have been scattered across the King's lands, but if a time of danger should arise, the King could call us back together to defend what is his. Occasionally one of the ten will come through and stay the night; in that case you might meet some of the others."

Sir Bart continued, relating stories of each of the other Knights of the Chalice, then concluded, "So, above all, you must be mindful that I am preparing you to be a servant of the King, not of Sir Bart."

Finishing his bread and fruit, the knight waved his hand, saying, "Now off you go. Michael is waiting for you in the courtyard."

"Yes, milord," Stephen said.

After gulping some water, he stood and hurried out of the great hall and down the steps into the courtyard, swallowing the last of the bread he had taken, relieved that Sir Bart apparently bore no ill will regarding his performance the night before, but apprehensive at what would come next while in the hands of his imposing trainer. Michael was waiting for him in the shadow of the east wall in an area where straw had been strewn over the dirt, his sword unsheathed, his dark form seemingly growing in size as Stephen approached. He still was not smiling.

"Alright," Michael said, scowling as Stephen came to a nervous halt, his eyes on Michael's scar. "You cannot be a squire to Sir Bart if you are not prepared. Where is your sword?"

Stephen patted his hip and felt his stomach sink. "I.... I'll go get it."

"No, you won't. You will use a wooden one today. In the future you must come prepared! Now show me what you have learned."

Michael tossed a wooden sword at Stephen. Catching it, Stephen looked up to face Michael—and the cutting edge of a real sword!

"Now come at me, boy. Don't waste my time!"

Stephen took a two-handed swing at his trainer. Michael parried and easily pushed Stephen's sword aside. Stephen tried again, this time swinging at Michael's knees. Again his blow was knocked away, and suddenly the point of a sword was resting on his chest.

"You have much to learn," Michael muttered, sheathing his sword. "You must learn to wield your sword with one hand, without showing your opponent where you will strike. Now follow me to the archery butts."

They walked to a section of the east wall where several targets had been placed with their backs to the wall.

"Take a bow and three arrows," Michael instructed.

Stephen was feeling better about this part. He had usually been able to hit the target with his previous trainer, Owen.

"Fifty paces," Michael barked.

Now Stephen felt a twinge of anxiety. That was a greater distance than he had ever shot as a page with his training bow—twice as far. The shortbow felt good in his hands, and his draw was as steady as it could be with Michael staring at him, but the first arrow missed above the target. Stephen lowered his aim. The next one struck the target at the bottom of the outer circle. Stephen raised his aim slightly. The third struck the target as well, on the right in the outside circle. Two out of three—not bad for the first time.

Michael grunted, then said, "Your enemy is untouched. You must learn to place three arrows in a tight pattern in the center before I count to fifteen. Now, each morning will be divided into two parts: sword practice and archery practice. You will work with me on cutting and thrusting, and then parrying and counterthrusts. You will practice with the bow until you can place three arrows within inches of each other. Now come with me to the stables."

The stables were located outside the castle on the west side. Although Sir Bart had a small stable inside the castle for his charger, the castle stables housed the horses of his men-at-arms and those of visiting guests. Stephen was very familiar with these stalls and horses, having cleaned and groomed them all as a page. Approaching the stables, Michael pointed out a diminutive man who was saddling a horse. Stephen recognized the man—Jacky—who had always greeted him kindly in the past but never conversed beyond that.

"That, as you know, is Jacky," Michael said. "In the afternoons he will teach you how to saddle and ride a horse. Once you have satisfied him, he will work with you on the use of a horse in battle. When he is finished with you each day, you will work on improving your strength. Come with me."

Michael led Stephen back across the drawbridge to a pile of stones next to the north wall, each stone the size of a large melon, the stones rising to his waist.

"You will move this pile of stones fifty paces to a new position each day and rebuild it anew. I will time you. When you have finished, you will then run the perimeter of the moat. I will also time you in that. Do you understand?"

Feeling totally overwhelmed and cowed by Michael's size and aura of authority, Stephen answered softly, "Yes, sir."

"You will not call me 'sir,'" Michael said, unsmiling. "I am Michael."

"Yes, Michael."

"Now go and fetch your sword. Meet me where we began."

By the time Stephen returned, the morning was nearly gone. Michael had him practice one-handed sword strokes. Stephen was no less clumsy than before. He clearly needed to strengthen his sword arm, as he failed time after time to touch Michael, his swing knocked away by Michael's sword. Moreover Michael had the annoying practice of placing the point of his sword on Stephen's chest every time he missed. Stephen felt humiliated. In his eyes he seemed like a page with a wooden sword fighting shadows. Michael probably viewed him that way as well. How could he ever meet Sir Bart's expectations? Michael mercifully released him for a midday meal.

Stephen munched on a piece of bread and a chunk of cheese as he headed out to the stables. As he walked in, Stephen found Jacky feeding one of the horses.

"Aye, master, it's you for horsemanship, isn' it?"

"Yes, Jacky."

"The lord told me ye would ride this one," Jacky said, rubbing the horse's snout. "He used to ride it himself. Name's 'Gascon.' He knows how t' handle an armed rider and isn' afraid t' charge. Here, give him some of these, so he gets to know ye." Jacky handed Stephen a basket full of oats. "Just hold 'em up to him. First thing t'day is ye'll put on the saddle and bridle so he gets the feel of how ye handle him."

Stephen liked Jacky already. When Stephen had been in the stables as a page, cleaning and grooming, Jacky—though he was not in charge of Stephen—would always give him a greeting and a ready smile. Stephen also liked that he seemed as if he wanted to help, not criticize, like Michael.

Stephen had no problem saddling and bridling the horse, so Jacky went on, "First few days ye'll just ride him around the castle grounds. Once ye feel like he's responding t' ye, then we'll begin to work on how t' handle him in combat. Yer other task will be t' care for the lord's warhorse, 'Minotaur.' Ye'll groom him as ye've done the others in the castle stables an' ye'll prepare him fer the lord whenever he goes out. Ye'll learn how t' fasten his armor fer battle when the lord rides for the King. When ye finish here each day, ye'll go t' the lord's stable an' tend to his horse. We'll ride over there now."

Stephen, already sensing that he and Gascon would get along well, followed Jacky across the drawbridge to the small stable attached to the keep, where they dismounted and walked in. The stable had only two stalls. Sir Bart's horse gave them a nod and a snort as they approached. He was a quite a large horse, a destrier, probably half again as large in mass as the others and a third taller. Stephen recalled that he had seen Sir Bart once in full armor for a festival, cantering across the drawbridge. The sight had stirred his imagination. How could anyone stand up to such a magnificent knight on such a powerful beast?

"T'morrow we'll look at Minotaur's battle armor and ye'll begin t' learn how t' place it on. That'll be all for t'day. Ye should just ride yer horse around the castle for a while before goin' back to the stables."

That wasn't really all for today. As Stephen rode back to the stables, he could see Michael standing by the stone pile, his beefy arms folded, watching him. He wasn't smiling. The thought of what would come next weighed on Stephen like an armful of those stones as he rode down into Bartstown and back. Gascon was easy to handle, probably because Stephen had cleaned his stall and groomed him in the past. After returning to the stables, he unsaddled and unbridled Gascon, leaving him in his stall, then walked slowly back through the gate to the waiting Michael.

"Let's get to it, master," Michael said as he set a rapid pace to the stone pile. "You haven't all day. I am timing you—now."

Stephen lifted a stone and balanced it on his shoulder, counted off fifty paces and dropped it. He dashed back and bent to lift another. That wasn't too difficult.

"I counted to thirty going and to twenty-five back. This is not a stroll. You must move faster!"

Stephen lifted another stone to his shoulder, hurried to the new location and dropped it.

"Twenty-five there and twenty back. You must rebuild the pile as it was. Move faster!"

After the first twenty stones the new pile was beginning to rise, but Stephen's arms already ached. He struggled to lift the stones with his arms only. He had to crouch now and lift them first onto his knee, then to his shoulder. Sweat was forming on his brow, trickling into his eyes, and dropping onto his tunic.

"Thirty and thirty," Michael shouted. "You are slowing!"

It was no use. Stephen could not move faster. He was down to the bottom layer of stones, and his arms screamed for rest, his back ached, his face streamed with sweat. He struggled through the final stones.

"Forty-five and forty." Michael ended his final count with a shake of his head as Stephen trudged back to the start, feeling the strain in every muscle. Michael grimaced. "In battle you will be wearing armor. You cannot allow yourself to slow like this, or you will be overcome by the enemy."

Stephen didn't care. He wanted to sit down and rest—immediately. More than that, he wanted Michael to shut his mouth.

"One circuit around the moat. Start now!"

Stephen did not move, blotting the sweat from his face with his sleeve.

"Now!" Michael pointed at the gate and shook his finger.

There was no way out of this. Stephen broke into a trot. At least it would put distance between him and Michael. He could hear the count fade as he headed toward the gate towers: "Four...five...six...seven ...."

Across the drawbridge he turned to the right past the stables, and right again along the north wall of the castle. To his left now was the knight's forest. Timber for construction still came from the forest and he recalled that Sir Bart hunted there as well. He could tell already that his count was not going to be good for the run. Even his legs ached from the lifting and hurrying back and forth to the stones, but at least he was away from Michael's disapproving stare. Except he wasn't. In the back of his head he could hear Michael's voice, counting. Michael might as well have been trotting behind Stephen, his impatient eyes marking every labored step.

As Stephen rounded the northeast corner tower of the castle, the long shadows and slanting golden rays of the sun informed him that it would soon set. He would be late for supper with Sir Bart, who would undoubtedly be disappointed with him once again. But Stephen could not will his legs to go any faster. Leaping carefully over the ditch that channeled the contents of the castle latrine over the cliff to the stream below, he struggled along the east and south walls back toward the gate, totally exhausted.

Michael was standing at the drawbridge, his arms folded, unsmiling as usual. But was there a hint of disgust in the never-changing expression?

"Much too long," Michael said. "I stopped counting. Did you tarry and watch the sunset?" Michael grunted as Stephen came to a breathless halt. "My lord is waiting for you in the hall."

Bent over and grabbing his knees to keep from collapsing, and gasping for breath, sweat dripping from his hair, Stephen did not look at Michael, nor respond to his comment. Glad to leave him behind and just walk again, Stephen labored up the steps into the great hall. Sir Bart appeared to already be halfway through supper.

"Did you forget you are to sup with me?" he asked, not looking up.

"No, sire, I was just—"

"I know what you were doing," the knight answered, smiling. "You've had quite a day, haven't you? And there will be many more like it. Come, sit with me. What did you think of Michael?"

Stephen sat heavily, seizing and gulping an entire cup of water. Michael was the last thing he wanted to think about. "Uh, he's not very friendly, sire," was all that he could manage.

Sir Bart chuckled. "No, he is not. That is not his purpose, although he can be a friend. His purpose is to teach you to survive on the battlefield and to be victorious. Michael is the one man I would have stand with me in battle. He has taken wounds for me, and he would defend me to his last breath. He does not ask you to do anything he does not do himself. When you return to the stone pile tomorrow, you will see that he has moved it back to where it was. Now eat your fill and we will talk of other things."

Stephen was definitely hungry this night, and thirsty as well. More than that, he was glad that his body was finally at rest. Tonight they had mutton with bread and vegetables. He did not leave any for the kitchen staff.

"Now," Sir Bart said as they finished eating, "this morning we talked about the King. Tonight we will talk about knighthood. You will spend each day in training for combat, but knighthood also involves a code of conduct. Michael will train you to fight as a knight. I will teach you to behave as a knight. Once you are a knight, you will have responsibilities—to your lord the King, but also to the lands and the people in your domain. To the King I owe loyalty and obedience; to the people, benevolence, justice, and mercy. The peasants work the land to support me and in times of emergency can be called upon to fight beside me. In return I and my men protect them and provide them a place of refuge if needed. You should care for them as you would want them to care for you if the situation were reversed. The same is true for the merchants in the town." Sir Bart paused and looked at Stephen, as if giving Stephen time to assimilate what he had said. Then he asked, "Can you see that this is a reflection of the second Kingdom Rule?"

Stephen had not made the connection, but he was aware that he benefited from the knight's benevolence too. If it had not been for his taking on Stephen as a page at his own expense, Stephen would not be in this position now.

He nodded and said, "Yes, milord," as if he had understood. But now some questions he had not asked the previous night or earlier at breakfast still lingered in his mind, so he went on, "How did you become a knight, milord?"

Sir Bart rested his eyes on Stephen a moment as if recollecting a distant memory. "I was chosen by the King himself, trained by the Prince, and knighted by the King."

"You must have been very worthy," Stephen replied, somewhat awed, and mindful of his less than praiseworthy day with Michael.

"On the contrary—I was not worthy of anything. The King chose me and made me worthy. The longer I rode with the Prince, the more I learned about the Kingdom and how to behave as a knight of the Kingdom. It was not only what he taught me, but the example he set as well."

"So, do you still ride with the Prince sometimes? Will I meet him?"

Sir Bart grimaced. "Perhaps you did not need to know this when you were a page, but I am training you to play a role in the Kingdom, so you must know the full truth. The Prince was killed in battle by the Dragon some years ago."

What? The Prince was no longer alive? Stephen sat back in shock, his eyes wide, feeling a jab of fear. If the Dragon was able to kill the Prince he must be very powerful indeed.

"Were you with him? How did you escape?"

"We scattered. The Dragon was not interested in us." Sir Bart stroked his beard, wearing an expression of puzzlement. "I still do not fully understand it. The Prince was more powerful than any of us twelve, and I am convinced he could have avoided it if he wished to; in fact he desired peace. The most remarkable thing was what he told us before the battle—he preferred that there be no battle, but if there was, he said that he would fall. It seemed as if he knew something we did not know. We did not believe him and even joked that we would fall with him. And at our last meal before the battle, he said that one of us would betray him."

Stephen nodded. "And you told me that really happened."

"Yes, it was such a shock, and totally unexpected. We were behind the lines of battle, and the one who betrayed him rode up from behind with a group of enemy knights. We were taken by surprise. One of our number managed to wound an enemy knight but the Prince told us to sheath our swords. He rode away with them. We thought he intended to parley with them or even slay them all himself—he could have. But once they were safely away from us, they knocked him to the ground and killed him on the spot. He did not resist."

Stephen realized his mouth had fallen open. "He allowed himself to be killed? Why?"

"We did not understand until some time had passed." Sir Bart studied Stephen's face as if to determine whether he was ready for him to proceed. "It is a lengthy tale," he said finally, "but it is one you must know and understand yourself. Long ago those who went before us became disloyal to the King and were banished from his Kingdom because they did not obey the Kingdom Rules, for which the penalty was death."

"In fact," the knight continued, "it is in our nature to disregard his Kingdom Rules, as you discovered last night, so even now we deserve death."

Only yesterday Stephen had left Sir Bart fearing banishment, and now he deserved death?

From his own King? Until this moment Stephen had believed the King was a benevolent and caring monarch. This revelation made no sense; it was contrary to all he had been taught thus far.

"Then why are you serving a King who wants to kill us? Is that why you are here—to hide from him?" Stephen asked.

"No, no," Sir Bart said. "Though we currently have a strained relationship with our King and we cannot enter his throne room or see him face to face, he does not want to kill us. He is a patient King who loves us and wants to restore us to his favor. The death sentence still stands but he is being merciful in withholding it until the right time to carry it out."

Stephen was becoming uneasy. He knew he had not kept the Kingdom Rules. It wasn't just Sir Bart he had to worry about; he was in serious trouble with the King now.

"Is the right time coming soon?" he asked.

Sir Bart smiled. "That is where the full story of the Prince comes in. The King himself provided the solution. Only if someone served as a substitute for us could the death penalty be lifted from us. The substitute would have to be one who was by nature loyal to the King and not under the death sentence. The Prince, who had never broken the Kingdom Rules, was our substitute."

"So the King executed his own son? That makes no sense," Stephen said shaking his head. "Nobody would do that."

"No, he did not. The King sent him from his castle to live among us and teach us about the Kingdom, knowing he would become a target for the Dragon.

He knew that if the Dragon killed his son, it would seem to the Dragon like a victory, but we came to understand that there was more to his plan than that."

"What more?" Stephen asked, listening intently now unlike the previous evening, despite his exhaustion. "It sounds like the Dragon won."

"That battle, yes, but the King's plan was much larger than one battle. The Prince sacrificed himself to lift the King's death sentence on those who were under the death penalty so that he could extend mercy and bring us back." Sir Bart paused, as if he had no more to say, his eyes resting expectantly on Stephen.

"And that is what it means that the King loves you."

Stephen could only shake his head again. "You mean the Prince took their place in the death sentence? And did so willingly?"

"He took your place too, though you were not present when he died," Sir Bart said. "If he had not, there could be no Kingdom. He told us before he died that he would always be with us in spirit, and by his spirit we would continue to build the Kingdom."

Stephen, now completely baffled by the story, leaned back, closed his eyes and tried to link together the various pieces he had been given. There was a death penalty for anyone who did not keep the Kingdom rules. He was one of those. But the Prince took his place because the King wanted him to and now Stephen was safe? And that meant the King loved him?

Sir Bart had paused again, as if aware that he had been dispensing far more information than Stephen could possibly grasp. "So I believe it is by the death of the Prince that we are made loyal and acceptable to the King again and through the spirit of the Prince that we remain loyal."

Stephen exhaled, aware that he had hardly been breathing as he listened. "Although I have heard parts of this story as a page, it was more about the Prince being an example to me of how to live. I have no memory of being told there was a death penalty or that he was already dead. This story is so immense and deep, and beyond my understanding."

"As I said, it is lengthy, and it is ongoing. And you must understand it. Even you may have a part to play in it someday."

"Me?" Stephen questioned. "I am only a bailiff's son, not even of noble blood. I do not even deserve to be here."

"No, you do not," the knight said. "But it is sometimes the King's pleasure to use the least, not the greatest, for his purposes."

Stephen allowed his thoughts to turn inward. "I hope someday I will be worthy," he said quietly.

"It is not a matter of making yourself worthy, son," Sir Bart said. "It is a matter of trust, obedience, and readiness. You have already been chosen. You must be ready to trust the spirit of the Prince when the time comes."

Sir Bart's last statement would stay with Stephen from that time forward. He did not fully understand what it meant to be chosen, unless it meant that Sir Bart chose him to be a page, but he understood that he needed to be ready—whatever that meant. And he was most certainly not ready. He determined to try his best, Michael or no Michael, to become as prepared as he could be.

With supper over, Stephen half-limped, half-walked up to his tower room, every muscle aching for respite. He soon collapsed on the mattress, lying there senseless until he heard a rap on the door and then a voice: "Breakfast, master."

Morning already?

Stephen urged his still-aching, stiff body out of bed, alarmed to think that Sir Bart probably sat at the table already, wondering where he was.

As he descended to the great hall once again, this time neither proud nor humiliated, Stephen's head was filled with confusing ideas of what the King must be like, what it would have been like to know the Prince and why the Prince did what he did. He still wasn't sure what it meant to be chosen, nor what it meant that the King loved him, or how to love the King either. But he was grateful that Sir Bart seemingly had overlooked his shortcomings and the King was not going to put him to death. Now...how could he prove he deserved to continue as a squire? Michael's face materialized before him. It wasn't going to be easy.

Chapter 5

A DANGEROUS MISSION

AFTER CLYFFE DEPARTED, Hugh sat slumped at his table, the pitiful flame of the lonely candle scarcely pushing back the darkness that surrounded him. The room that usually reverberated with the voices of his parents seemed as silent as death. It had been mere days since his father had been so violently torn from him, and his mother had followed. What was their fate? Would he ever know? He'd had plenty of time for his anger to simmer over the injustice of the situation in which he found himself. Though he had yet to concoct a plan to avenge the taking of his father, Clyffe had given him something to hang on to. It did not replace striking at the Dragon, but Sir Bailys was an accomplice in the deed and Hugh felt a glimmer of satisfaction that he now had a way to strike back at Sir Bailys and the Dragon for leaving him bereft of parents. He began to plot.

He would first need to request a map and box from Brian and Thomas. The following night there would be a secret meeting of villagers loyal to the King, which had been inaugurated by his father and Brian's father, both now absent. Hugh had offered the smithy as a continuing meeting place for the Servants of the King, as they called themselves, to gather until his father and William returned, or a new leader was chosen.

A spirit of sadness and anxiety pervaded the meeting, which included Charis, Brian and his siblings, Thomas and his parents, and a scattering of peasant farmers. The lingering aroma of wood smoke hung in the air over the small gathering huddled around the central fire pit as Hugh, now the host, took charge, though he knew he was in no way prepared to lead the group. His preferred role at this point would have been to be a foot soldier in an army of the King advancing on the Dragon's castle.

"We have suffered a grievous loss," Hugh began, suppressing a mixture of sorrow and anger. "Both of our leaders are gone. I know that my father would always begin with a reading of the *Chronicle*, but I confess that I do not know what to read, so I would like to repeat to you something my mother said to me before she departed."

Hugh cast his eyes over the upturned faces, lit softly by flickering coals in the fire pit, each looking to him for some kind of encouragement. He had none.

"Most of you know the story told by my father and William about how the Prince was taken. My mother reminded me that my father was taken in the same way—standing firm in his loyalty to the King and willing to suffer the consequences. She told me the Prince said that all who were loyal to him and the King could expect to suffer similar hardship."

After only a moment's silence, Hugh heard a trembling voice, "So do you mean they will come back for the rest of us?" It was a farmer asking, his voice betraying his fear.

"I do not know," Hugh answered. "I am still struggling to understand in my own mind how to view all of this. I do not understand why the King would allow it, but I do not believe our meetings have been discovered yet."

"Maybe we should just disband for a while," another suggested.

"No, I think not," Hugh said. "My father always said there was strength in meeting together."

"Hmph, well, look around," Thomas said. "I don't think we are strong enough to stand up to anyone."

"Perhaps," Charis said, "but don't you think he meant our strength is found in the one we are loyal to?"

Thomas shook his head in response. "You mean the one who is nowhere near and probably doesn't even know what has happened? Do you really think the King cares about what occurs in villages like ours?"

Always soft of speech and gentle in her manner, Charis replied, "William has steadfastly told us that our strength now is in the spirit of the Prince and in his words found in the *Chronicle*. That is why he and Henry always read to us from the *Chronicle*. Isn't that right, Hugh?" she said, turning toward him.

Put on the spot, with all eyes now on him, Hugh felt his own doubt confronting him. He did not wish to discourage Charis but the pressure of their gaze forced him to respond. He shifted his weight as he searched for an answer.

"I must admit that I do not understand how the spirit of the Prince gives us strength, nor can I gainsay Charis's words either."

It was neither a satisfactory nor an encouraging response, Hugh knew, but he was uncertain in the role thrust upon him, feeling as if the refuge in which everyone had assumed they were safe had been set afire and they were looking to him to rescue them while he was still trying to assess the danger and survive himself. The meeting was brief, without a reading and discussion of the *Chronicle*, the participants agreeing only to continue meeting and supporting one other however they could. As one after another departed, Hugh pulled Brian and Thomas aside to tell them of his mission and of the need of a box and map.

"I have a dangerous delivery to make. Will you go with me?" Hugh said, and then explained his plan.

"Absolutely," Brian replied. "It will be like striking a blow without Sir Bailys knowing it."

Thomas, though, hesitated. About Brian's height, with a mop of thick brown shoulder-length hair, and a bushy, almost unruly, full beard that his friends joked could easily shelter small animals, he seemed always to have a different opinion. When he finally answered, he sounded less enthusiastic than Brian: "I will come along for the adventure, though I judge it to be a futile enterprise. Sir Bailys will learn quickly of his stable master's new allegiance and put him to the sword."

"Perhaps," Hugh answered, "but our duty is only to carry out our mission. Come back to the smithy when the moon begins to fall from its height."

When Thomas arrived with his bow and a quiver of arrows, Hugh realized he had not thought the plan through. What if they were discovered before he delivered the box? Should they go armed? He grabbed his sword as well. When Brian arrived, unarmed, he greeted the others with raised eyebrows but said nothing. The three set out along the five-mile road that passed by the knight's manor house on its way to the market town, Grandvil, their way lit only by the full moon. The road led them past fields alive with the chirp of crickets until it neared the manor house, where it skirted a dark wood whose shadows protected the party as they crept in among the trees.

"It's really dark in here," Brian whispered. "Unhh—"

Hugh heard him trip over an unseen root but saw him catch himself before he went down.

"What if we come across someone unexpected?" Brian asked.

Before Hugh could answer, Thomas exclaimed, "I brought my bow!" There was too much excitement in his voice for Hugh's liking. Hugh stopped and faced them.

"I also brought my sword, but only for protection. We will not be the ones to start a fight," he said, feeling a puff of pride that he had been chosen for this task, and eager that it end well. "We are on a mission for the King. We must accomplish it carefully ... and safely." He held to his hope that the King would hear of it and take action to release his father, though he had no idea how it could happen.

Thomas only gave a muted grunt of assent in reply.

Approaching the manor house through the forest, Hugh could make out the silhouette of the stable in the moonlight of the chill autumn night. He chose a spot in the woods within view and sat. "We'll wait here until dawn," he whispered.

"Did anyone bring food?" Brian asked, rubbing his arms to keep warm. "I am hungry—and cold."

"We can share my bread," Hugh whispered.

He unwrapped a loaf from the bundle containing the box. They each pulled off a piece and munched, listening to an occasional stamp of horse hoof and snort of horse breath, each taking turns massaging each other's shivering backs. Faced with nothing else to do, Hugh took stock of his situation. Scarcely eighteen, he was already on his own. He had obediently followed his parents into the Kingdom, but so far this Kingdom was not what he had imagined. Instead of sitting around a warm fire discussing the *Chronicle* with his parents, he sat in a strange forest, shaking with cold while risking his young life. He had agreed to this mission for the King primarily because it gave him a way to strike back, but now his original doubts about the trustworthiness of a King he might never see stirred anew. Was the risk worth it for such a King?

Finally the light of dawn began to bring details out of the shadows. At Hugh's lead they rose and crept closer to the stable.

"Shhh! I hear someone inside," Hugh whispered.

"Well, it has to be the stable master," Thomas said.

"Not necessarily," Hugh said in a low voice. "I will go closer, alone, to see who is there. Do not come with the box, Brian, until I signal. Watch for the bodyguards, Thomas, but do not shoot, unless it is to save us from capture."

"How will you know him?" Thomas asked. "You have never seen him."

"I have been given a word, as has he."

Hunched and creeping as softly as possible, and hoping the messenger had told him the truth, Hugh approached the stable stealthily and looked inside. A man stood grooming one of the three horses. Almost as if he had heard something, the man turned and looked straight at Hugh.

Hugh knew that he was unexpected, and prepared himself to flee if he had found the wrong man. "*Columba*," Hugh whispered. He tensed as the man walked toward him. Almost involuntarily, Hugh began to back away, whereupon the man stooped, looked him in the eyes, and spoke.

"*Alba*," he answered softly. "You are the one I was to expect?"

"Yes, I am Hugh, one of the Loynton blacksmiths."

"And I am Gerald."

"You are in a dangerous position," Hugh said, standing fully from his half crouch.

"As are you," Gerald replied, now standing face to face with Hugh. "You are only footsteps from the knight's manor house, where he is no doubt breaking fast with his bodyguards as we speak."

Hugh gave a quick nod, then stepped out and signaled Brian, who came at a trot down to the stable. Retrieving the box, Hugh handed it to Gerald along with a key, then showed him how to insert it to reveal the map.

"Now," Hugh whispered, "you're going to feel—"

"Yeeow!" Gerald cried, clutching his chest.

The horses snorted and stamped in their stalls; Hugh felt his heart race.

"We will be discovered!" Gerald said. "Quickly, you must go!"

Behind him the door of the manor house opened and then closed with a slam.

"Hide the box until later," Hugh said over his shoulder as he hurried into the shadow cast by the stable in the morning light. "And come to the Loynton smithy in the evening six days hence."

Hugh and Brian had scarcely reached the denser shadows of the forest when he saw Gerald, who had ducked into the stable momentarily, re-emerge without the box and the scroll, only to be accosted by an armored man-at-arms. There were words, the guard pointing in the direction where Hugh and his co-conspirators hunched, breathless, in the woods. Gerald shook his head, pointing out at the road. There were more words and gestures. The guard walked out to the road and looked both ways, then back at the forest, straight at Hugh and Brian. Hugh heard movement behind him.

"I can take him down," whispered Thomas, standing with his bow fully drawn.

"No!" Hugh exhaled, pulling Thomas's bow down. "He hasn't seen us. This is not the time."

The guard looked back at the stable and then walked slowly back to the house. Hugh and his companions breathed a sigh of relief.

"That was a near disaster," Brian muttered.

"But we have claimed another for the Kingdom," Hugh said. Even though still trembling from the rush of adrenaline occasioned by their narrow brush with capture or worse, he couldn't keep himself from grinning.

They took a different route back to the village, avoiding the road and then parting company before they came within sight of any houses. Though Hugh knew it probably would not bring his father back, he felt his spirits lifted by the success of their mission.

"We have struck a blow for the King, and for our fathers!" he said before they parted.

A day later Hugh's mother, Elizabeth, returned alone. Though glad to see her return, Hugh's heart sank at the absence of his father. Deflated, he sat at the plank table across from his mother in their one-room cottage as she related her adventure.

"We were approaching the outskirts of Purdyton when we were met by two of the Dragon's horsemen. We could see the dark castle on its hill, and we pointed to it and tried to explain our purpose, but they would not listen. They robbed us and tried to take our horses too. Only when I begged that it was dangerous for a woman to be walking the roads alone did they relent. But, Hugh, they took William and his horse! How will I tell Charis and Brian?"

Hugh breathed a heavy sigh. "I do not know, Mother," he said, "but at least you have returned."

"Yes, but barely," Elizabeth replied. "Alone, I despaired of successfully returning home without harm, but at a crossroads I fell in with a friar who was headed to Grandvil. He said I could accompany him for safety. He fed me and gave me his cloak to cover me at night."

Hugh could only look on as his mother rocked back and forth, stifling a low moan before she went on, "But, Hugh, I asked Charis if William could go. It is my fault!"

"Mother—no," Hugh said. "You mustn't think that. You did what you could."

She could not be consoled, her body now heaving with great sobs as she sat hunched over the table. Hugh stood and went to her side, his hand on her shoulder to comfort her as best he knew how, knowing not what else to say, his mind now on his father, already searching for an alternate plan to secure his release.

"I will go to the King, Mother," Hugh said finally. "Only he can put a stop to this. I will go tomorrow."

She sniffled and wiped at her eyes. "You do not know where he lives, Hugh. And you are now the village blacksmith. The village cannot function without you, my son."

Hugh knew she was right, as always. If he left, no one would be there to make or repair tools for the farmers, fashion knives or pots for their wives, or even craft carpentry tools for Thomas. What was he to do? Disappointment became anger—at the Dragon for taking his father, and at the King for not protecting his subjects. Though Hugh instinctively knew that somehow the King was his only hope if he were ever to see his father again, he wondered if Thomas was right. Did the King really know or care about what happened to mere villagers?

"You are right, Mother, but the King must hear of this! The next time a messenger comes, I will tell him."

She sniffed again and spoke words that left him a flicker of hope: "I know your father is in danger, but the King knows the length of our days. Our only purpose here is to serve our King as long as we are able. Your father has done that and will continue to do it as long as he has breath."

From that day on, Hugh's mother wore black and would not leave the smithy cottage. Over the succeeding days Hugh willingly took on the extra responsibility of hunting, buying food, and preparing meals. As the time for the next village meeting of the Servants drew near, Hugh's heart grew heavy. By then he had already told Brian and Charis about William's fate. Although both Henry and William had been absent at the previous meeting, and Hugh had reluctantly taken the lead, he knew he could not provide the leadership they had exercised. Both had been among the last to see the Prince alive and had actually learned from his words. Though his mother had returned, the cost of serving the Kingdom had become dearer with the capture of William. It no longer seemed like the Kingdom they had taught him about. But Hugh determined that he would attempt to be better prepared for the meeting this time. He also decided he would read to them from the *Chronicle*, continuing with the theme of the previous meeting.

The Servants committed to each other to meet rain or shine. Today they were greeted by steady rain. Villagers began to filter in as soon as darkness fell. They met only at night, and they were to come at staggered times so that no suspicion would be aroused by so many people going to the same place. When it was time to begin, Hugh looked around the room and greeted the damp and subdued group as they sat shivering in their wet clothing on the dirt floor of the cottage around the central fire pit. He counted twelve tonight: Brian and his mother, Charis, with the two other children in tow; Thomas and his parents; a peasant farmer with his wife and child; and two teenage farmhands. Everyone had now had a few days to assimilate the news that William had not returned, and all sat silently at first, the flickering flames revealing their expressions of sorrow and concern. Hugh's mother, meanwhile, lay in the dark on a pallet behind the group.

"Hugh, Brian," the farmer said, breaking the silence. "We are troubled by what has befallen your fathers. The members of our group have always shared what they have when others have had needs. So we have brought fresh vegetables from our gardens for both your families."

"You are more than generous," Hugh said, accepting the bags of produce, then waiting to continue while Brian did the same. "Now let us begin."

By the light of the crackling and popping fire, Hugh painstakingly read a portion of the *Chronicle* to those in attendance, most of whom were unable to read it themselves.

"In light of what has happened, the *Chronicle* is very instructive," Hugh said. "As you know, the Prince's words are written here, along with stories about him. He says very clearly that after he is gone, those who follow him will face difficult times. The hostility that he faced will come to us also. These past weeks we have seen that prediction come true. We should all prepare ourselves to encounter harsh treatment at the hands of the Dragon and his followers."

"Which our King apparently cannot prevent," Thomas said, his voice colored with sarcasm.

Hugh watched Thomas's father open his mouth to say something to his son, but he stopped at the sound of a hard knock on the door. As one, the group shrank back with wide eyes and a scattering of gasps.

"Are we discovered? Already?" Charis whispered.

"Shh," Hugh said. "I will not let them in."

Slowly he rose, grabbed his sword, and then went to the door, opening it a crack. A moment later Hugh stepped back into the light of the dying fire, smiling.

"Friends," Hugh said, "this is Gerald Stabler, of the household of Sir Bailys. He is truly here at his peril, but he is one of us."

Gerald entered the circle, dripping wet and shaking from the cold, and gave a nod to everyone before taking a seat on the floor amongst the others. Each of the group welcomed him in turn as they made room around the fire.

"Since this is Gerald's first time with us," Hugh said, "I should explain that we try to meet weekly in order to encourage each other in our loyalty to the King and to study the *Chronicle* and what it tells us about the King and the Kingdom. We want to encourage you, Gerald, to be steadfast in your trust in the King even while in the difficult position of being obligated to serve a knight who is loyal to the Dragon."

Gerald, warming his hands over the fire, cleared his throat and glanced around at the members of the group. "Thank you, friends," he said. Looking somewhat ashamed, he continued, "I confess that I cannot read the *Chronicle*, or the map either, so I hoped that in coming I could learn from you."

"That is exactly why you should come," the farmer said. "Many of us cannot read, but Hugh's father explained the map to us, and each time we meet, we talk about something the *Chronicle* says."

Hugh went on to explain how the events they had experienced and would experience were told in the *Chronicle*.

At one point Gerald spoke up, "There is a castle on my map. Is it not the King's castle? Why don't we take our problems to him?"

A spark of anger at the absent King jabbed Hugh as he opened his mouth to reply.

But Charis answered first. "I believe the King is aware of what happens to his followers. However, that castle is not one made of stone. He does not live in buildings made by men, though he may visit them. It says so in the *Chronicle*."

Gerald shook his head. "Then where does he live? Is he not real?"

"Yes," Charis said, "he is real, but he lives primarily in the hearts of those who trust him. Come, I will explain your map to you."

She gave a glance to Hugh as if to seek his permission, and Hugh nodded, thankful for her assistance. As Charis took Gerald aside began and in low tones to explain the nature of the map and the names on it, the rest of the group listened to Hugh continue to speak from the *Chronicle*. The meeting lasted until the fire had become glowing embers, Hugh ending this one the way he had seen his father always do it before: "Remember that all lands and our hearts belong to the true King, and however difficult it may be to work for the Dragon and his knight, Sir Bailys, do your work as for the King."

Once the cottage had emptied, Hugh found himself alone again in the darkness, listening to the rise and fall of his mother's breathing, and the drip of rain from the eaves, ruminating. His mother had failed to bring his father back; she was lying on her bed unspeaking, as if she had given up, and now William was gone as well. Furthermore, Hugh knew he could not go after them—and he had been thrust into a role for which he did not feel prepared. The small cottage might as well have been a coffin for all the good he could do. How could he encourage others and right an injustice when he was trapped in Loynton and angry at his King?

Chapter 6

THE MESSENGER RETURNS

AUTUMN FADED, AND the red and gold leaves of the stately oaks and elms floated listlessly to the ground, laying their colorful carpet as they died. As the chill winds of winter began gusting through the smithy and blowing into the cottage, Hugh became more worried about his mother. Though he kept a fire going day and night, he could not convince her to do more than to lie on her pallet day after day beneath piles of covers, shivering, refusing to eat, becoming ever more pale and thin. Periodically he would find her weeping. She would not even talk to him, other than to say, "Your father is gone. It is time for me to go, too." Hovering between youth and manhood, Hugh felt unprepared to first lose his father and now to watch his mother slip away. He longed for someone who could tell him what to do. The silence in the cottage hung over him like a heavy shroud, threatening to descend and entomb him in hopelessness and loneliness. His father was gone, but might he not still be alive? His father was the strength of the family; he would surely find a way back to lead the Servants. His mother's attitude seemed to deny that hope, but Hugh clung to it.

A few days later Hugh entered the cottage from the smithy to check on his mother and came to an abrupt halt upon seeing another messenger sitting quietly at the table. The messenger drew back his hood as Hugh entered.

Drawing closer, Hugh realized who it was. "Clyffe, it is you again!" he said. "There is much I need to tell you. The King must know that my father is still captive. And William is there too. Can he send troops to free them?"

Clyffe looked up at Hugh but his expression did not change. "He knows, Hugh. I have come for a different reason—to give you a message. Do you have your copy of the *Chronicle*?"

"Oh—yes, of course," Hugh replied.

He fetched it, taking a furtive glance at his sleeping mother as he did so, and then returned to the table to spread the sheets of the scroll before Clyffe.

"Is the message in the *Chronicle*?" Hugh asked as he sat down.

Clyffe pointed toward the scroll. "I want you to read the last paragraph."

"I know what it says there," Hugh answered. "The Prince is speaking to his inner circle."

"Yes, and it applies to you, too, and to all in your group—but especially to you, since you own a horse. Now that the *Chronicle* is being disseminated, the King's messengers will no longer deliver keys and maps; you are to be a messenger to the villages in Sir Bailys's fief. You will deliver keys and maps, and copies of the *Chronicle* when it is necessary. It is the King's desire that every village, and eventually every person who can read, have a copy of the *Chronicle*."

Hugh just stared at the scroll sheets, and then shook his head. "But how will I know for whom to make a key?"

"Everyone knows instinctively that there is a true King, but not all will acknowledge him," Clyffe replied. "Those for whom you are to make a key will be revealed to you as you sleep. When you present their key and map, you will tell those who affirm allegiance to the true King that the *Chronicle* brings a message of freedom from bondage to the ways of the Dragon and—"

"Oh, really?" Hugh stood abruptly. "And is the King coming with his army to free us from that bondage, then?" he asked, with no attempt to hide his sarcasm. "He can start with my father and Brian's father."

Clyffe said nothing for a moment, keeping his unblinking blue eyes fixed on Hugh, then he replied, "I am speaking of freedom of the heart and mind. Remember what the true Kingdom is, Hugh. The hearts of those who are not Kingdom-minded are in bondage to self-service, power, greed, and lust of life—the ways of the Dragon. Those who are prepared to follow the King will affirm what the *Chronicle* says about the truth of the Prince's words and the Kingdom; those who prefer to reject that knowledge and follow the Dragon will not. You are only a messenger to those who are ready to enter the true Kingdom."

Hugh exhaled a clipped breath, sat again and said, "Yes, yes, yes, I know all that. But the King should pay attention to the kingdom we live in too." Hugh felt his body tense as he thought of discussions in prior meetings of the Servants.

"Besides, speaking of that kind of freedom in this fief now is tantamount to rebellion and presents extreme danger to us all. My father was taken based on mere rumor! You speak as if you and the King do not care that the Dragon and his knight own our lands and the villagers' bodies are also in bondage to him."

In a deeper voice than usual, Clyffe said, "Careful, my son. I know better than you what is happening throughout the land and what the King intends. Remember what you have been taught and what you yourself have said to end your meetings. The ownership of the lands still belongs to the King, though the Dragon and his knights may control them. Physically you will remain in bondage, and serve them with your labor as they direct, but—."

"We are to work as for the King," Hugh said, completing the sentence with a sigh.

"So you must remain faithful to that calling. And, again, the freedom you will be speaking of is freedom of the heart and mind. What did your father teach you about the map?"

Hugh had heard it many times. Painfully he recalled the earnest face of his father, so recently torn from him. "He said it was a map of the heart, with the King's castle at the center."

"Yes," Clyffe replied. "And those who have the King's castle at the center of their heart are under his authority. They are free from the Dragon and his power. And do you remember what your father told you about the Kingdom?"

Hugh knew he could not argue with the truth, even though he was feeling no freedom at this moment. "The Kingdom is those whose hearts are ruled by the King. So that is why the map is given with the key. It documents our freedom," he said, knowing his voice carried little enthusiasm.

"And shows the characteristics of those in the Kingdom as well as the road they follow."

Clyffe stopped speaking, his eyes still on Hugh as he studied his face silently.

Just as Hugh was about to look away, Clyffe said, "You are worried about your mother, aren't you?"

Hugh's thoughts were jerked back to the present. "How did you know?" Hugh whispered, aware that she lay on her pallet behind him. "She grows weaker every day. I am afraid she is dying."

Clyffe's lips drew into a tight line, but his eyes showed only compassion. "Her time has almost come," he whispered back.

"What?" Hugh exhaled. He felt his heart pound in his chest, and a surge of anger ripped through his body. He stared at Clyffe and tried to control his voice as he said, "You must go—now! I have heard enough." He stood up from the table, intending to usher Clyffe out.

But Clyffe did not move. Instead he continued to regard Hugh with eyes of compassion. Softly he continued, "Sit down, Hugh. The King knows the days of his people. When they have accomplished what he wishes they do for him, they may go. Your mother knows this—and so did your father."

Now Hugh felt his brow furrow and his eyes begin to burn. He gulped to swallow a cry of agony and rage. Taking a deep breath, he blurted his next thought aloud: "So *did* my father? My father is dead?"

"I am sorry," Clyffe replied. "He was faced with the choice of giving his allegiance to the Dragon and denying the King, or remaining loyal. He refused to bow to the Dragon, declaring that the King is the rightful ruler."

A storm of uncontrollable proportions exploded within Hugh. He became deaf to Clyffe's words and oblivious to all about him as he gripped a plank of the table with trembling hands and lifted it above his head to hurl it at Clyffe.

"Peace! Be still!" Clyffe's sonorous voice rose like rumbling thunder, filling the room until the walls of the cottage shook.

As quickly as the storm arose, it abated. Hugh allowed the plank to drop from his hands, watching it hit the dirt floor with a loud *thunk*. He collapsed onto the bench, empty, an unbearable sorrow and fatigue descending upon him like a heavy cloak. In her soft voice, his mother's words after she had returned from the futile attempt to find his father came to him: "The King knows the length of our days. Our only purpose here is to serve our King as long as we are able. Your father has done that." He heard her sobbing quietly behind him. She must have known the truth already.

"I know what you say is true," Hugh said. He slumped over the remaining plank of the table, his anger gone, the hollow, bottomless, pit of loss remaining. "But I was unprepared to hear it. I will still serve the King—no matter what happens, though I do not understand his ways."

His King had let him down, again. What possible purpose could the King have that he would allow both Hugh's father and mother to be taken from him— one by death and the other by grief? There was no use speculating. He probably would never know. And now this same King expected something of him, again.

Hugh thought a moment. The map required a seal. "Who will apply the seal to the map now?"

"As the messenger of Loynton, you will." Clyffe produced a signet ring. "You must handle this with extreme caution. It identifies the holder as a follower of the King. You must not allow it to fall into the hands of the Dragon."

Clyffe placed his hand on Hugh's shoulder, giving it an empathetic squeeze, then rose and departed. Hugh sat stoically, wrestling with mixed emotions—a smoldering anger and burgeoning grief over his father's death at the hand of the Dragon, and the helpless feeling that his mother would continue to slip away, both tempered ever so slightly by a spark of pride that he had been entrusted with the signet ring. Perhaps he was someone special to the King. It was all he had to cling to now. The siren song of vengeance was stilled—for now.

Within the month Elizabeth had passed. Hugh truly was alone. But he had a new mission, and he again felt some measure of pride to be the one chosen for it, as if he had gained the King's favor. But he approached the next meeting of the Servants with a heavy heart yet again. At his mother's burial he had shared the news about his father with all who had not heard. The members of the group again came with condolences and offerings of produce. They sat in silence as Hugh solemnly voiced his gratitude. Despite his urge to walk away from it all to be alone for a while, Hugh realized that solitude would only rouse the demons of anger and sadness. So, mindful of his new mission, he picked up the last parchment of the *Chronicle* and read the last paragraph aloud.

Then he said, "What it means is that we are all to go about in the village now and even to strangers to find those who are prepared to be new followers of the King. The King knows who they are. We are to find them by telling them the stories and words of the Prince we have learned from the *Chronicle*. If they desire the freedom the Kingdom promises, and desire to declare their loyalty to the King, they will respond positively to what they hear. You are to tell me so that I can make a key, and Brian and Thomas can make a map and box for those who are to be added to the Kingdom."

Upon hearing this, a farmer gasped. "Our meetings have been secret. If we publicly admit we are followers of the King, could not our land could be taken and given to someone else—or worse, I and my family be brutalized or executed by the knight?"

"And my smithy could be taken and I could suffer a similar fate," Hugh said. "I am aware of that."

"If my own father knew I belonged to this group, he would disown me," one of the youths said with a shaky voice. "He thinks I am helping a neighbor widow."

Hugh knew he could offer no encouragement to his fearful listeners, nor was he willing to soften the words of the *Chronicle*. It would be like denying the King, which his father had refused to do. The Servants had been struck a heavy blow, and there could—likely *would*—be more to come. But as hopeless and dangerous as it seemed, Hugh determined he would not forsake the mission entrusted him by Clyffe. Bereft of his father and mother, he now viewed himself as standing alone against a force he did not understand, as if a great tempest were blowing down houses and uprooting trees and he had been told to venture out into it and stand firm. Despite his doubts and disappointment, he could not and would not disavow the King for whom his father had died, even though this King seemed distant and uninvolved. But he also sensed a new freedom in his aloneness, a freedom to forge his own way without regard to others' expectations. He was now the Servants' de facto leader.

"This is not a time for timidity," Hugh finally said while rummaging through the sheets of the *Chronicle* with a newfound urgency. "Look, here are the Prince's own words: 'If you value your family or possessions more than me, you are not worthy of me.' He said there would be risks. Look at what has already happened—my father, killed by the Dragon; my mother, dead from grief; Brian's father, captive, feared dead. Each of us has to decide whether we will stand for the King."

"Or die for the King," Thomas added in a somber voice, echoing everyone's thoughts.

A spirit of uneasiness and anxiety hung over everyone as the group broke up that night. After the others had departed, Brian came up to Hugh, bearing a quizzical expression on his face.

"Hugh, if we are not to receive messengers anymore, where will we get copies of the *Chronicle*? None of us are able to write in that fashion. Even the maps I make assume their features after I make the parchment. Am I to make parchments and hope the *Chronicle* will write itself?"

"A good question, Brian, and I do not know the answer," Hugh said, having not thought that far ahead. "The messenger did not tell me, and I did not think to ask. But if it is our duty to find new followers, there must be a solution. I will go into Grandvil, beyond where Sir Bailys's manor house stands. Merchants are there, and I may find an accountant or a scrivener who can write."

The next morning Hugh mounted his horse for the ride into Grandvil. Being the only town in Sir Bailys's fief, Grandvil drew its importance from the fact that it grew up around an important crossroads near the manor of the knight. It was also a free town, with a charter of liberties granted by the King, and therefore did not belong to Sir Bailys, although as the largest landowner, he was treated by all with the deference and respect due a noble.

Hugh took the same road he and his companions had walked the night they brought a map and key to the knight's stable master, Gerald. The dirt road, no more than a path worn by the passage of peasant animals and carts over time, passed by fields and orchards that belonged to the knight and were farmed by his peasants. The land lay fallow in the chill of winter, frost sparkling in the slanting rays of early-morning sunlight. Hugh passed the area of uncleared land marked by white, frost-laden trees behind the knight's manor house, which was known as the knight's forest, in the fringes of which he had crouched not long before. He knew that the knight also hunted there with his ruffian bodyguards, and it was rumored to shelter brigands as well. Hugh passed the knight's house and continued to follow the road. He had not taken notice before, but the house was more substantial than any in Loynton, with stone walls enclosing a lower floor, above which a half-timbered second story perched. The enclosure was contained by a low wall, with some small outbuildings, and gated in front and on one side, where a path led to the stable outside the walls.

The road bore few travelers, all wrapped in layers of cloaks against the cold, and by now Hugh was also shivering beneath his cloak. Before long the outskirts of Grandvil came into view. As he began to pass the jumble of houses built haphazardly abutting one another and approached the town square, the clatter of his horse's hoofs gave notice that he was nearing the center of town, where cobblestones replaced the rutted and frozen muddy lanes that led in from the countryside. Merchant and trade houses began to line the road as he neared the square, their trade announced by a wrought-iron sign in front, hanging above the door. One of them caught his eye—an emblem of a quill pen hanging from a pole above a door. He reined in his horse. After dismounting and tying it to a post, he went inside.

The large room was lined with floor-to-ceiling shelves, packed with rolls of dust-covered parchment and bound books. Cobwebs were strung from the ceiling and corners of the room. An odd aroma of dust mixed with something else hung in the air. Maybe it was the parchments and books. Hunched over a table in the light of the single window sat a cloaked, gray-bearded man, making careful strokes with a quill, his eyes close to the surface of the table. *A scrivener,* Hugh thought. Apparently he had not heard Hugh enter.

Hugh cleared his throat.

With a jerk of his head, the man looked up. "Yes?" he said, squinting at Hugh.

How do I do this? Hugh had brought both the map and the *Chronicle* with him, but he was aware it could be dangerous to show them to someone who might be an enemy. *I will try the word. If he doesn't respond, nothing is lost.*

"*Columba,*" he ventured.

The man's gaze now became intense, his squint unwavering. "What did you say?" he asked suspiciously.

Suspecting he'd been found out, Hugh tensed under a surge of fear and anxiety, his heartbeat accelerating and pounding in his chest, his throat beginning to close. He would have to say it again—or maybe he should just run now before the man sounded an alarm.

"*Columba*?" he croaked.

"That is a Latin word, and you appear to be a peasant. How do you come to know such a word?"

Hugh began to back toward the doorway, his eyes shifting to make sure his horse was still there. "I...I heard it from someone," he answered. "I thought you might know it. But, um, maybe I should just leave now."

The man's face broke into a smile, his squint melting into a welcoming expression. "*Alba,*" he said. "One must be careful, you know. It is the first time I have had to use the word, and I did not expect to hear the first word from a peasant. Have a seat, my boy. My name is Joseph. What brings you here?"

Trembling from the fear of possibly being discovered, Hugh was overtaken by sudden fatigue, collapsing onto a stool. "You know the words!" he exclaimed almost involuntarily. "I confess I don't even know what they mean—but that means you are a follower of the King!"

"They mean 'white dove,'" Joseph said. "It is the symbol on the box and the seal of the map. The same appears on the King's emblem."

"Then you have been given a key and map and—"

"Received the mark? Yes, two weeks ago a messenger came to me with them and told me that I was to receive a mission for the King that would require writing. But two weeks have passed and I have had no further messenger. How can I help you?"

Hugh was momentarily speechless as he considered Joseph's words and their ramifications. The realization fell on him like a heavy weight. He must be the one with the mission. Already it was happening as Clyffe said.

Feeling his strength return, Hugh straightened on the stool. "I am the bearer of your mission," he said.

"Oh? And what does a peasant know about writing?"

"I am no peasant, but a tradesman—the village blacksmith of Loynton," Hugh answered. "My parents taught me to read, though I cannot write." He pulled his copy of the *Chronicle* from the cloth bag that hung from his neck, concealed beneath his tunic. "You received this, did you not?"

"I did," Joseph said. He reached down into a pile of scrolls, pulling out his copy. "Fifty sheets—a weighty tome indeed. I am still reading it and trying to understand all of it."

"I believe that you are to make copies of it for the King, to be given to any who will read it," Hugh said. "Did your messenger not tell you that yours is the Grandvil copy?"

The old man rested his chin on his knuckles, stroking his beard with one finger as if considering the authenticity of Hugh's announcement. "Yes, he did. But fifty pages a copy—that is much work. He did not tell me to copy it."

"There will be others to share the work," Hugh said, certain that he must be right. "You will be the copyist for the fief of Sir Bailys: Grandvil and the surrounding villages."

The old man continued to regard Hugh cautiously. Then, casting his eyes on his copy, he replied, "An interesting thought, my boy, but the *Chronicle* was delivered to me by a messenger of the King. Was it not the same for you? Why would the messenger not have told me he would need copies?"

Hugh began to doubt his purpose now that Joseph was questioning it. "Yes, it was," he said. "Has not a messenger spoken to your group of the King's followers? Surely such a group exists in Grandvil."

Joseph's eyebrows raised as he eyed Hugh and said, "I know of no such group."

Hugh was at a loss for words. He could not seem to convince Joseph to accept the mission he felt certain he was bearing. Then he recalled how his encounter with Clyffe had ended.

"My mission is to deliver the maps and keys. Sometimes if it is a new village or someone able to read, I deliver the *Chronicle* as well. You were told to expect a messenger. I believe I am the messenger you were expecting." Hugh fumbled in his tunic and brought out the signet ring. "This is the ring that imprinted the seal on your map, is it not? It authenticates my words."

Joseph examined the ring with his near-sighted squint. "It is indeed. It bears the same imprint of the dove."

"So you must find the group that meets in this town," Hugh said, feeling a sense of growing assurance. "If there is no group, you must find others who are loyal to the King and form one. There is no power in serving the King unless you are part of such a group, each person fulfilling his function. You undoubtedly have a keymaker and mapmaker here; they will need your services as well. And you will need to bring your copy of the *Chronicle* to your group, for therein is found the truth about the Kingdom and the words of the Prince, and you may be the only one who can read it."

As he recounted to Joseph his last visit with Clyffe and the mission he and his companions had been given, Hugh pulled out the last sheet of the *Chronicle* and showed the concluding words to Joseph.

"No more such messengers will come from the King. The spread of the news of the Kingdom is in our hands now. We are the messengers. You must find the followers of the King in Grandvil, and you, like I, must begin to look for new followers ourselves."

Hugh knew he was speaking with much more authority than he possessed, but the words poured forth as they entered his mind. Even he was surprised that the first messenger had not given Joseph his mission, but he concluded that perhaps this was the way it was supposed to work now. *We are to labor together, help each other, carry out our missions for the King, even if we do not feel prepared to do so—or are not sure why they were given to us, just as my father said he felt upon leaving Purdyton.*

The old man looked pensive again. "The messenger did not say it was he who would return to give me my mission." He paused, again stroking his beard. "Yes, I think you must be right. That is my mission. I had already asked myself how the *Chronicle* was reproduced for others and whether I should make a copy. I assumed a messenger of the King would always deliver it." He nodded to Hugh. "Very well, I will begin tonight."

Hugh nodded in return. "Both I and other messengers from the town or villages will come to you from time to time for a copy when there is a need." He rose to leave, saying, "We and others will keep you supplied with parchments."

At the door Hugh paused, another unanswered question on his mind. "You understand other tongues. Do you have your key?"

"Of course. We are always to have it, are we not?"

"There are words on it that appear after I make the key. I have never understood them."

"Yes. And important ones they are," Joseph said.

"What do they mean?" Hugh inquired.

"*Fides clavis regnum est*," Joseph said, as if from memory. "Trust is the key to the Kingdom."

Chapter 7

JOURNEY TO BARTSCASTLE

E VERYTHING HAD BEEN decided without consulting Marie. The previous summer, a month after Marie's realization that she would be sent
away, Daniel had returned with the tidings that a place would not be
available at Bartscastle until the next year. Now, on a bright spring morning, Sir
Guy and Marie mounted their horses to set out for the castle. Richard and Lady
Clare would stay behind with Edouard and manage the household. Daniel would
accompany Marie and her father as added protection on the two-day journey.

Marie had spent the fall and winter ruminating about the fate that had befallen
her. She blamed the decision on her mother, who seemed determined to see her
married off. The intervening months had brought them no closer. They had taken
additional trips to Grandvil, with more moments of tension—and no apparent
attempt by her mother to understand Marie's point of view. Marie had tried to
share her thoughts and feelings with Lady Clare, but it always seemed to come
across as an unwelcome jab at her mother's authority, as if Marie were like Ginette:
not a person with hopes and fears, but a servant to implement her mother's wishes.

Compounding Marie's misery, she also resented her father's complicity. He
doted on her, did he not? So why did he not come to her defense? Was he not
the head of the family? It seemed as if he had delegated all decisions about the
children to her mother. The winter had been difficult, Marie cooped up with
nothing to do but the tasks her mother gave her under the guise of "learning to
be a lady." And worse, now she was forced to make her journey in the pale blue
riding gown that she hated.

At this point she was of two minds about the event. She had concluded that freedom from the chores and her mother would be a relief, and hopefully she would soon outgrow the gown, or discard it as soon as she could get another at the castle. But she also felt the bitter sting of leaving home. Spring was Marie's favorite time of year. She thought back to glorious moments sitting by the stream, the warmth of the sun playing over her, listening to birds singing in the forest, accompanied by the burbling of water trickling over moss-clad stones, ruling over her fantasy world. Though she had tried to make herself believe that her parents wished the best for her, she couldn't shake the undeniable feeling that they were casting her away, perhaps because she no longer fit in. From the stable, with tear-moistened eyes, she gave a longing glance back at the house she knew as home, wistful for the childhood innocence upon which this journey would close the gate forever.

"Come, Marie," her father said. "We must go. Did you kiss your mother farewell?"

She had not, although her mother had kissed her. A kiss spoke of love, did it not? At this moment she did not love her mother. Did her mother even love her? They were different people. They would always be so.

"We had our farewell," Marie mumbled, ambling to her father's side.

He looked quite handsome dressed in his mail hauberk, which was covered by a fresh, light blue surcoat, his shield fastened to his horse, a sword hanging from his belt, clanking gently as they moved. Daniel followed on horseback behind, also in mail and a dark blue and white gold-hemmed surcoat, with shield and sword, leading a packhorse with Marie's clothing and meager possessions. The road was puddle-filled from recent rains, but today the radiant blue sky, with its many large puffy clouds, lifted Marie's spirits—a little. Their direction was away from Grandvil, between fields already populated with peasants plowing and planting, the scent of freshly turned earth hanging in the air. Marie bade a bittersweet farewell to the bucolic setting of her heretofore peaceful life, yet found herself somewhat surprised by the spark of excitement that rose as she turned her face toward the adventure of an unknown future.

Marie rode silently, though full of questions, beside her father, who, oblivious to the surroundings, seemed lost in thought. Curious by nature, she always wondered about things she did not understand. Her mother was no longer someone she could ask, but to Marie, her father was one who not only could do anything but one who knew everything. Still, she hesitated to interrupt his thoughts, because they might be important ones.

Eventually, though, she could not hold back her questions any longer: "Father, you have been to Bartscastle," she said. "What is it like? Will I like it?"

"It is like a large stone house with many rooms. Many people live there. Strong walls surround it and it is protected by a moat—a large ditch. Sir Bart is an important knight of the King."

"But will I like it?"

"You will learn to like it, Marie."

Marie had grown to almost despise the word "learn" in the past year because it denoted difficult and unpleasant things. *You will learn to be a lady. You will learn to be a wife. You will learn to like this or that.* But she remained undeterred in her quest for understanding. The opportunity to be alone with her father was a rare one that she did not want to squander. Though always intimidated in his presence, she had stored up many questions since the previous spring, and she was determined to have them answered.

"Father?"

They were riding side by side now, Marie looking into the distance, unwilling to confront her father face to face.

"Yes, my daughter?"

"Mother says this is to teach me to be a wife."

"Yes. She is right."

"What if I do not want to be a wife?"

Her father turned in his saddle, his attention finally focused on her. "That is your destiny, Marie. You will be wife to a knight as your mother is wife to a knight. You will bear him a son so that the family will continue."

Marie turned away to hide the frustration that rose within her, squeezing her eyes shut to prevent the inevitable tears. The sights and scents of Grandvil lingered in her memory; the forever lost moments by the stream tugged at her heart. She could not contain the raw emotion that surged up.

"Father, the duties of a wife repel me! There is nothing about it that I desire," she blurted, allowing her tears to flow.

Sir Guy stared back at her, unmoved. "Life brings many things we do not desire. Yet we must do them. You have an independent spirit, Marie. It must be trained in obedience."

You mean it must be stifled. Marie fell silent again, sniffling, wishing to expose every thought she had, to ask every question she had thought of over the past year, knowing that if she did, it would spoil this special moment with her father. Perhaps she already had. She hated to cry, especially in front of her father. She looked down at her tear-spotted blue gown, and began to sob again. *They don't know me. They don't want to know me.*

At length the party came to an intersection of roads, the road they were entering bearing evidence of considerably more use. Sir Guy turned his horse to the left, stretching his arm in a gesture to the right. "That is the road to Loynton. We are turning left toward Bartscastle."

By then Marie had regained her composure and began anew. "Mother says you will choose the man I marry."

Sir Guy nodded. "That is right. I choose for the good of the family."

"Not for the good of me?"

"I did not say that, Marie. You must trust me to do what is best for you and for the family."

"But what if I do not agree with the one you choose? I mean, what if I do not love him or he does not love me?"

Sir Guy came to a halt, looking Marie in the eye, his face breaking into a smile. "And what do you know about love, my daughter?"

Marie lowered her head in embarrassment, fully aware of the warmth in her cheeks and the truth that she was talking about something she did not understand. "I...I don't know." Her voice trailed off. She could feel the heat of her reddening face. Didn't love have something to do with marriage? What was love anyway?

"I have heard you say you love Mother."

"And I do, but it is not what you might think. When we are young, we think love is a feeling, and if the feeling is not present, there can be no love. The truth is, we learn to love."

There is that hateful word again. "There is too much to learn!" Marie huffed.

Her father laughed softly, then continued, "Arriving at love is a process, Marie. It begins with learning about another; next come feelings toward the person. But even that is not all. Then come trust and commitment. Like one of the flowers by your stream, love must be nurtured and grown during a lifetime, before it blooms in its fullness and beauty. It is the same whether loving another or loving the King."

"Loving the King? What does that have to do—"

"You know that is one of the Kingdom Rules, Marie."

Marie did not wish to be reminded about the Kingdom Rules at this moment. Rules were like learning—things she was supposed to do but did not want to do. And why did he have to bring up the King who was responsible for the rules? This was supposed to be about her. After all, they were talking about her future.

She remained focused on her train of thought. "But how can I learn to love someone you have chosen?" she continued, beside herself with frustration, the pitch of her voice rising. "Someone I have never even seen?"

"That is where you must trust me," Sir Guy replied, resuming the pace. "I must think of the future of our family and good stewardship of the King's lands. What I learn about the man you will wed must fit what I know about you—and I know you better than you think."

"Really? You don't know me at all, Father! Mother doesn't know me!"

Apparently disregarding her words, her father continued, "And I am advised by the King as well."

Marie sighed. *The King again.* "How can the King care whom I wed? He doesn't know me either, nor do I know him. And what does he know about love?"

Sir Guy again came to a halt, catching Marie's eyes with his. "He loves you enough to want the best for you, Marie, and that includes the man you wed."

He reached out and placed his hand on Marie's shoulder as they sat side by side. She lowered her eyes, unable to look at him. How had they come so far from her original question— about loving and being loved by the one she would be forced to marry? It had been like talking to the wind, for all the good it had done her.

"You must trust me to find a man whom you will want to love. But this is not the time to figure out love. You must learn many other things first; that is why we are going to Bartscastle."

They rode on and again Marie lapsed into silence, pondering her father's words. Love was a process? It was more than feelings? She certainly did not have any feelings toward her mother that she could call love. And the King loved her? What did that mean? She felt as if she had just opened a large chest and found it full of objects that were strange to her, ones she might never comprehend.

This uninvited direction of her life had all started with her twelfth birthday. She wished she had never turned twelve! Then her world would not have been torn apart. There was seemingly no escape from the future that had been thrust upon her. They continued onward without speaking, Marie consumed by her thoughts, until Sir Guy reined in his horse. Marie looked up to see two armored horsemen stopped in the road ahead.

Daniel was soon beside her, fastening the packhorse to her bridle. "Just stay here and be calm," he whispered.

He joined Sir Guy, both slowly advancing to meet the horsemen who now rode toward them. The four men stopped, facing each other. Marie, sitting alone at some distance behind them, could not hear any words, but the strangers gesticulated with their arms. Both her father and Daniel kept their hands on the hilts of their swords but did not draw them. After a period of time, the two horsemen backed away from Sir Guy and Daniel, and began to ride toward her, accompanied by her father and Daniel. Marie tensed as they drew near. Unshaven and dirty, both horsemen looked her up and down as they passed, one cracking a yellow-toothed grin. Instinctively Marie backed her horse away. They continued slowly past her in the direction of the crossroads that led to Maison Bonfrere and, farther on, to Loynton and Grandvil.

Daniel untied the packhorse as Sir Guy resumed his way.

"Father, were they robbers?" Marie asked, relieved now that they had passed.

"No, they were Sir Bailys's men. Did you notice their red shields? They bear the emblem of the Dragon."

Marie nodded. "Yes, they were a different color than yours."

Her father frowned. "Proof that Sir Bailys professes loyalty to the Dragon."

A clammy chill crept over Marie's body, the same chill she had experienced when her father first mentioned a dragon after returning from Bartscastle the previous year. She had forgotten until now the frightful vision she'd had then.

"Did they want to harm us, Father?"

"Perhaps, but they were all bluster. When I told them they were trespassing on our land and were no match for Daniel and me, they backed down like the cowards they are." Sir Guy chuckled. "I do not know Sir Bailys, but these men look like the kind who would do their mischief under the cover of darkness when they are not opposed. They will slink home to their master now."

The three continued down the road, Marie troubled by the unseen dragon and an amorphous danger that seemed to be gathering around her. Who, or what, was this dragon? Why had her mother reacted with anxiety? Her father had not seemed concerned. Why not? It was useless to speculate about something she did not understand. Soon the heat of the day gave notice that the sun was high in the sky.

"Here is a grassy spot," Sir Guy said, then motioned with a hand. "Let us stop and eat."

The three dismounted and Daniel tied their horses to a tree, and then placed a cloth on the grass for Marie to sit on. Out of one of the packhorse bags Daniel brought bread, cheese, and wine.

"You may drink watered wine if you like, Marie, but drink sparingly," her father said. "We will rest awhile before continuing to the house of Sir Giles, where we will stay the night."

Marie had been wondering what they would do when darkness came. She was relieved to hear that they had a place to stay.

"Is he a friend?" she asked.

"He is a fellow knight of the King. We offer hospitality to our brothers-in-arms. Daniel made arrangements before we set out."

Marie sat on the cloth, basking in the warmth of the sun and examining her surroundings. They rested at the edge of a meadow that appeared as if it had been sprinkled with wildflowers, which nodded lazily in the intermittent breezes. Drifting clouds scattered moving shadows over the meadow, abuzz with the sound of bees. But soon her mind drew itself back to her flowered refuge by the brook at home, a prick of sadness deflating her reverie as she wondered when, if ever, she would see it again. Then her thoughts turned to the encounter with the two men and the mention of the dragon, her sense of adventure now tempered by a jab of fear.

"Father, are we in danger from a dragon on this journey?" she asked, attempting to hide a growing anxiety.

Sir Guy regarded her, then, seemingly aware she was troubled, stood up and sat beside her. "You are safe with us, Marie," he said, placing his arm around her shoulder. "While it is true that the Dragon wishes to conquer us, he will not attack a knight unless he has a larger force than you saw today. He knows that we fight with the power of the King, and he will slink away as those men did when we resist him, unless he greatly outnumbers us or he finds us at a time of weakness."

"He sounds so ferocious." Marie's throat began to tighten. "But...dragons are not real, are they, Father?" She gulped.

"No, they are not real animals, but he is real enough," Sir Guy said. "Though he is a rebel lord whom we call the Dragon, he is like a mythical dragon—he has been known to burn villages and extend no mercy. He is also greedy like a dragon, seeking to own all of the King's lands and his people. And he is clever like a dragon, often using deceit to get his way. But the name by which we call him comes primarily from the emblem he has chosen for his coat of arms—a gold dragon on a red shield."

Her father's denial notwithstanding, Marie's worst fears would be embodied henceforth by a scaly, fire-spewing dragon, flapping about the countryside, his eyes blazing hatred, incinerating all who followed the true King. Her original vision of facing such a dragon unarmed, alone and hopeless conjured itself again in her mind.

"Father, I felt helpless back there," Marie said. "Wouldn't it be better if I could defend myself?"

Sir Guy smiled. "Daniel and I are with you to defend you. Your duty will be to bear strong sons who will become knights of the King and defend you."

Marie bit back a frustrated sigh. Father did not understand. She did not want to depend on anyone else. Her mind continued to churn, her fantasies now including real threats instead of magical beasts. "But what if I was alone with Edouard and someone came?"

"Richard is always there. He would summon some of my armed men."

Marie would not back down. "But what if there wasn't time?"

Sir Guy grew silent, as if thinking the unthinkable. "Then, I guess you would have to defend yourself, wouldn't you? Is that what you wanted me to say?"

"No," Marie answered, ashamed at having manipulated her father so brazenly. "I didn't want you to say it, but I just want to be able to defend myself. I want to be able to shoot a bow and use a sword."

"I understand what you want, Marie, but that is not how ladies are taught at Bartscastle," Sir Guy replied, "nor does it have anything to do with being a lady. Some noble ladies play at archery, shooting at targets. Perhaps they will allow you to do that. But there are more important things to learn."

Marie scowled. "Like how to be a wife."

"Yes. That is your destiny."

Daniel stood and brought the horses. "It is time to proceed, sire."

As the journey continued, the countryside began to change. The fields of vegetables, flax, and barley gave way to forest and hills. Occasionally they would pass a traveler heading the opposite direction. Before long Marie became conscious of a steady, roaring sound that gradually grew louder as they approached it. Eventually they rounded a bend to see a solitary two-story, half-timbered building with a courtyard, and beyond it, where the road forked, a wooden bridge. A painted sign hanging above the door identified the building as the Wolf's Den Inn. Just beyond, by the bridge, a roughly dressed man was leaning on the railing next to a sign that read *Purdyton*. Sir Guy reined in his horse as the man approached him.

"Three pence t' cross," the man said, holding out his hand.

"Out of the way, man!" Sir Guy ordered. "This is the King's bridge. He does not collect tolls."

"It does b'long to the king alright," The shaggy man smirked, looking at Sir Guy's shield. "But not *your* king."

A sword screeched as it left its sheath; Daniel rode slowly past Marie. He placed the tip of his sword at the man's throat. "You will allow us to pass," he said.

The grizzled toll collector carefully placed two fingers on the sword and stepped back from its blade. "Day's comin' when ye'll be at the other end o' the point," he said, wagging a finger.

Sir Guy led the way onto the bridge, Marie following, clenching her reins, her eyes on the boisterous water leaping over great rocks, throwing spray onto the slick planks of the bridge. She made her way cautiously, falling behind her father, reflexively tightening her legs around the saddle each time the bridge jolted in response to a surge in the current. Finally across, she paused by her father as Daniel brought the packhorse across.

"Ill tidings," Sir Guy said above the roar of the torrent as Daniel approached.

"Indeed," Daniel replied. "You saw that the name of the inn has changed?"

"Something has also happened to Sir Andrew. This was his fief. The sign pointing to his manor is gone. The Dragon is clawing closer to us. We must tell Sir Bart."

"I suspect he knows," Daniel said. "Nevertheless we should be careful from here to the next crossroads."

Marie watched her father give a grim nod in reply. She attempted to suppress her mounting anxiety, sensing that she was riding into an unknown danger, one that even Sir Guy might not be able to protect her from. The road ahead led into a dense stand of trees, flanked by forested hills. Even though her father and Daniel stayed near her, she felt even their presence might not be sufficient to prevent whatever was out there from harming her. Almost immediately the road disappeared into darkness, leafy branches above forming a dark, gloomy canopy. Only the clop-clop of the horses' hoofs could be heard, echoing from one tree to another. No birds sang in this forest. Undergrowth crowded the sides of the road, which had narrowed considerably into a path.

Try as she might, Marie could not free herself from the grip of her imagination, glancing nervously from side to side for moving shapes or the glow of a dragon's breath. At last the comforting sound of a trickling brook joined them, and soon after, the way ahead began to give promise of light. An occasional sunbeam reached the forest floor, and far ahead, as if the end of a tunnel, a bright archway appeared. They emerged into sunshine. Before them, not more than five hundred paces away, lay another crossroads. Where the road forked, a post stood, with a shield nailed to it.

Sir Guy stopped as Daniel joined him to look at the shield, red in color, with a gold dragon rampant.[4]

"The sign pointing to Bartscastle has been taken down," Daniel said.

"The Dragon appears to be claiming the crossroads," Sir Guy replied. "Unless you know where you are going, you would not know which road to take."

"Which road *do* we take, Father?" Marie asked, momentarily relieved that they were out of the forest now, but unnerved by the ongoing references to the mysterious Dragon.

"One would have a tendency to take the road to the right," Sir Guy said, gesturing in that direction, "because it appears straighter and more traveled now. But that road leads to Purdyton and the castle of the Dragon. The road to the left leads to Bartscastle. There used to be a sign pointing in that direction."

"What about the weathered sign farther down?" Marie asked.

Sir Guy squinted. "Terra Media," he read aloud. "A land shrouded in mystery, in which we would be strangers—but that is another story."

They turned their horses to the left and started down the lightly traveled, overgrown road, dust from their horses' hoofs hanging in the still air. In less than three miles, they were again among fields where a substantial house with outbuildings loomed ahead.

"Our abode for the night," Sir Guy said. "This is the manor house of Sir Giles and Lady Margaret."

The party came to a halt before the house as a youth ran up to them. "Welcome, sirs and milady. My master desires that I take your horses to the stable."

No sooner had they dismounted than Sir Giles and Lady Margaret burst from the house with wide smiles.

"Welcome, Sir Guy and Daniel—and this must be Lady Marie," Sir Giles said, glancing at Marie. "Come inside and quench your thirst; rest your bones. Your arrival is timely. We will sup together shortly."

"Yes, come, Marie," Lady Margaret said. "Allow me to show you where you will sleep tonight."

"Gladly, milady," Marie said as she dismounted.

---

[4] Rearing to attack.

They entered a large room with an elevated, beamed ceiling and a table in the center, much like the hall of Maison Bonfrere. Lady Margaret led the way up a stairway to the top floor, where Marie saw two rooms facing each other above the expanse of the hall, as in her house.

"You will sleep in the children's room," Lady Margaret said.

She took Marie into a room with two beds and a trunk. Small windows pierced three of the walls, one admitting a bright shaft of sunlight. A table with a rushlight sat by one window, and there were hooks on the walls for clothing.

"The children are gone now, so we are able to house travelers." Turning back to the stairs, Lady Margaret said, "Now, you must be thirsty, my dear. Come down to the table and we will have something to drink."

Downstairs, Sir Guy, Sir Giles, and Daniel were already seated, grasping mugs of ale, exchanging news.

"Sometime during the winter," Sir Giles was saying, "I was riding out that direction and I noticed the sign was gone. There are fewer travelers our way now."

Sir Guy remarked, "The Lion and the Lamb has changed hands. It is now the Wolf's Den. And the Dragon is attempting to collect toll at the bridge. Have you heard from Sir Andrew lately?"

"I have not," Sir Giles replied, his brow darkening. "Perhaps we are next."

"But you are less than a day's ride from Bartscastle," Daniel said. "That would be a bold move."

Sitting quietly on a chair against the wall, Marie could not suppress a growing sense of impending doom. Ever since they had left home, she had heard nothing but talk about the spreading reach of the Dragon. She imagined herself being slowly surrounded by a creeping, formless mass of sinister proportions that she could neither feel nor see until suddenly she would find herself in its grip, unable to escape.

"Father?" she said.

The men turned and stared at her, seemingly unaware that she had entered the room and been listening.

"Yes, Marie?" Sir Guy replied.

"Can't anyone stop the Dragon?"

"He will be stopped," Sir Guy said. "The King will stop him."

"Then why are all these things happening? Why does everyone seem worried?"

"They are signs of the times," Sir Guy replied. "Do you remember sometimes Mother and I would take out the *Chronicle* and read to you and Edouard?

"I was a child then," Marie said, although it had been only in the past year. "I … wasn't listening," she said, feeling her face flush.

"I know you weren't." Her father smiled. "The *Chronicle* tells us to read the signs of the times. The things we are noticing tell us that the Dragon is growing bolder and more powerful. It means that the time may be close when we are called to join with the King to defeat the Dragon once and for all."

Marie found no comfort whatsoever in her father's answer. There might be a fight? The King might as well have been in a different world as far as Marie was concerned. She had only heard about him from her parents but had certainly never seen him. Despite what her father had said about the King loving her, she wasn't totally convinced that he was even real.

"Well," Marie said, "why doesn't the King just bring his army and put an end to it? Why does he let the Dragon grow stronger?"

"No one knows when the King will act," Sir Guy answered, "but what I do know is that the King will prevail, in his own time. Our role is to serve him now however he wishes. When we travel, our shield reminds people of him. When we show kindness, they are reminded that we represent the King. But if he calls us to fight, we owe him our swords—and our lives."

These last words stirred Marie's anxiety such that it grew into a whirlwind by the time she went to bed. *So we are to just let the Dragon have what he wants until the King does something about it? Even let him kill us?* Sleep, when it finally came, was fitful, Marie tormented by thoughts of stealthy forms creeping up to the house by night, bursting through the door and dragging everyone away to the feet of a ferocious dragon. And who knew what would happen next? Or maybe the dragon of her imagination would descend upon the house as she slept and, with flaming breath, incinerate her there—tonight!

She descended the stairs in a state of agitated resignation the next morning to find the three men huddled around the table in the hall again, talking in low voices. A block of cheese, a bowl of dried fruit, and a partially eaten loaf of bread sat at the other end.

"Marie!" Lady Margaret called from the kitchen. "Sit down and break your fast. Everyone was waiting until you had gotten enough sleep."

"I did not," Marie said, recognizing the gloom in her own voice, "but I guess I am ready to go."

Marie lowered herself into a chair, listlessly pulled off some bread, and held it in her hand, uneaten. Her hand trembled; her mouth felt excessively dry. She thought about home—the last place she had felt safe. She missed her bed at home and her quiet, secure place by the brook, her excitement for adventure now totally extinguished.

"Marie, you must take some nourishment for your ride," Lady Margaret said as she sat down next to her. "Perhaps some dried fruit?"

"I had a horrible dream last night," Marie said, gazing at the piece of bread between her fingers as if it were an unidentifiable object.

Lady Margaret smiled faintly. "I know this is a strange place and we are perhaps not whom you expected. You have never been away from home over-night, have you?"

"No! No, that is not it," Marie said. "I awoke suddenly in the night, feeling something was wrong. There was a red glow outside the windows." She bit hard into her lip as she re-experienced the terror. "And then a black dragon with scales and horns raised its head, looking straight through the window at me with its angry red eyes as if it knew who I was! I tried to scream but no sound came out. Then it loosed a blast of fiery breath that blew into the room and everything burst into flame. I opened my eyes, more frightened than I have ever been. My heart was pounding. I could hardly breathe—but then I realized it had been a dream."

Lady Margaret leaned in and placed a hand on Marie's shoulder. "I fear we have spoken too much of the Dragon for your tender heart." She again offered Marie some fruit. "But it was a dream. And though the Dragon may visit us in dreams to discourage us, rest assured that if we know the truth about the King and trust him, the Dragon has no power over us, even in dreams."

Marie chewed unenthusiastically on a piece of dried fruit until the neighing of a horse outside signaled it was already time to depart. She said her good-bye to Lady Margaret and went out to Daniel and her father, who stood by their horses with Sir Giles, talking. Downcast, she pulled herself onto her horse; in her mind it would be another day of running from the Dragon. Soon all were mounted and on their way.

Immediately she rode up to join her father. "Father, what did you talk about with Sir Giles? What will happen to him and Lady Margaret?" She could not voice the questions that actually gnawed at her: *What will happen to me? Will I ever see home again?*

"We agreed to discuss everything we have seen with Sir Bart," her father said. "He may have a better understanding of what the King's intention is."

It was not the answer Marie wanted. He was avoiding answering her ques-tions with the full truth. Did he not appreciate the degree to which talk of the

Dragon frightened her? The Dragon could be stalking them even now, and all her father planned to do was talk to some other knight? In resignation she fell back, alone with her troubled imagination. But soon the warmth of sunshine and the distant sound of birds in the trees took Marie's mind off the Dragon, freeing it to return to her storehouse of other questions.

She rejoined her father and asked, "Will I stay at Bartscastle for a season and then come home?"

"Not quite," Sir Guy replied. "It takes at least two years for a girl to become a lady."

Two YEARS? I will not see home for two YEARS? Marie's throat began to close, and her vision blurred as tears welled up, then traced their silent course down her cheeks. She drew a deep breath, then realized that she had nothing else to say. What could she say? It had all been decided without asking her, as if she were an object on her packhorse to be dropped off at Bartscastle and forgotten.

She lagged back behind her father again, riding in silence, imagining that she, not the packhorse, was the one on a tether, being led into a dark cloud where all was obscured, where eventually her father would sunder the tether and ride away, leaving her alone in the midst of invisible and unknowable dangers, perhaps to be snared in the claws of the stealthy and ferocious Dragon.

Chapter 8

LADY ANNE

MARIE WAS DEEP into her thoughts about her exile to Bartscastle, as she termed it, when her senses awakened to familiar sounds and smells—but not pleasant ones. A cluster of low, thatched houses lined the road, and a stray pig snorted as it nosed through some rubbish heaped between the houses. The contour of the land dipped out of sight. Beyond stood the outline of a town, smoke curling from a jumble of chimneys and rooftops, creating a hazy screen behind which stood the faint towers of Bartscastle. The three travelers topped the rise, following the road as it sloped down to a stone bridge across a small stream, then up again on cobblestones to the market square, which spread from a central fountain where women were washing clothes. So familiar did the townsfolk seem with armed horsemen that only an occasional head lifted to acknowledge their passing. As the party continued through the square, the road became dirt again and wound up to the Bartscastle drawbridge, which was lowered as the group of three stopped at the moat. They were expected and recognized, at least.

Marie scanned the walls and towers with awestruck eyes as they neared the gate, craning her neck to examine the portcullis when they passed beneath. A youth ran to meet them once they were in the courtyard, followed by a tall, muscular man wearing a mail hauberk and sword belt.

"I will see to your horses, sires," the youth said, grasping the reins of Sir Guy's horse.

The armed man approached, clad in the blue, white, and gold surcoat of the King's men, the hint of a smile threatening to break his stern countenance. "Good morrow, Sir Guy—and Daniel. I did not expect both of you."

Dismounting, Daniel replied, "Good morrow to you, Michael. We were transporting precious cargo." He nodded toward Marie. "The utmost protection was necessary. I will return home tomorrow."

Cargo, Marie thought. *That is all I am?*

"And I will stay a day to confer with Sir Bart about recent events," Sir Guy said. "Would someone show Marie to her quarters?"

Michael looked over his shoulder. "Yes, she is coming now. She saw you from her window."

A slender, frail-appearing woman with gray-streaked hair bundled into a crespine[5] now hurried up to the group, her kind brown eyes focused on Marie as she caught her breath before speaking.

"And you must be Marie, dressed in Bonfrere blue! I am Lady Anne, Sir Bart's sister and educator of noble girls. Come and allow me to show you where you will live."

Marie was still assimilating the sights and sounds of the castle, alive with the noise of men shouting as they trained with swords and of archers at the butts, shooting their arrows, the tall multistory keep towering over all. She looked from Lady Anne to her father. Was this it? Wasn't there going to be a farewell? Sir Guy was already deep in conversation with Michael and Daniel. He made a motion with his hand as if to shoo her away. Or was it a wave good-bye? She suppressed the urge to run to him and hug him tightly. Perhaps it would embarrass him. Worse, maybe she would not be able to let go. Blinking away a tear, she obediently followed Lady Anne, fighting a mixture of feelings—of abandonment by her parents, of fear that she might never see her father again, of losing the joy of her childhood forever.

Lady Anne led Marie across the courtyard to a two-story building, telling her it was the women's quarters, then pushed open the sturdy wooden door to reveal a spacious room with a beamed ceiling.

"This is our common room," she said, spreading her arms. "Since you are the only young lady I will be educating the next two years, we will do everything together in this room." She showed Marie around the room, introducing her to its contents. "We will eat together at the table, read and write, and play games. By the window—" she pointed toward a horizontal loom, "I will teach you to weave

---

[5] A jeweled hairnet that held coiled hair in place on either side of the head.

tapestries like those on the walls. By the fireplace there are musical instruments," she lifted a tambourine and tapped it, "which you will learn to play. We will take trips together to learn other aspects of administering a household." She smiled at Marie. "I think you will enjoy yourself here."

Two years? Marie could not banish the thought from her mind. She could not deny that some of what Lady Anne was telling her sounded interesting, but what did they have to do with why she was here?

"My father says that I am here to learn to be a wife," Marie said flatly. "How does learning these things prepare me to be a wife?"

Marie's eyes remained on Lady Anne as the older woman folded her hands and stood patiently a moment before speaking. It seemed as if she had heard such questions before. "You will be a wife someday. We do not know to whom. That is a choice for your father and the King. But I will be educating you as if you were a daughter of the King or as if you were to be a wife to the Prince. You will someday spend time in the company of noblewomen and host noble families in your own home. What if the King or the Prince were to stay with you? What if the King desired music? You must know how to conduct yourself in a way that pleases the King."

The King?

The one who had made all the rules? Why would the King want to stay with her? Who was she to the King? She would probably be scared speechless were she to be in the presence of this King whom she was still having difficulty regarding as a real person.

Lady Anne led Marie up some stairs to a small room containing a bed and table with a cushioned chair, next to a window. Though the room was smaller than Marie's room at home, which was shared with Edouard and Henriette, it seemed nicer. A small chest for clothes sat in a corner, and a soft rug lay on the floor. A candle sat on the table, which sported an embroidered tablecloth and a vase of freshly cut flowers.

On the wall opposite the window hung a tapestry depicting what appeared to be a hunting scene—lords and ladies on horseback, with eager hounds leading the way through a forest strewn with wildflowers. A forest … and flowers! Marie's thoughts drifted momentarily to her refuge by the stream. How she missed it already! The sound of shouts and the clash of arms in the courtyard banished that thought and drew her to the window. She walked to the table and peeked out, hoping perhaps to see her father gazing up at her, bidding her a silent fare-well. But no, there were just men-at-arms practicing at swordplay. She had so wished to hold her father tightly in her arms and be held in his before parting. Would he even miss her on the way home?

"You will sleep and study here," Lady Anne said. "We will begin your instruction this evening over supper. You may rest until then."

Marie turned to the bed, which was covered by a beautiful green and gold quilt—the colors of Sir Bart, Lady Anne told her just before she left. Marie pulled back the quilt and plopped herself onto the mattress. Filled with feathers, it was much softer than hers at home … but it wasn't home. Realizing now that she was indeed tired, she lay back, lowering her head into the feather pillow, covering herself with the quilt, and sank immediately into a fatigued sleep.

"Marie. Marie," Lady Anne whispered.

Marie's eyes fluttered open. She saw Lady Anne bending over her bed.

Lady Anne smiled down at her. "It is time to sup with me."

Marie sat up, confused by her surroundings, and then remembered she was in a room in a castle. Rubbing the sleep from her eyes, she followed Lady Anne downstairs to the table in the common room, where there were two chairs, an earthenware plate and cup on the table in front of each, and a steaming platter in the center.

"We will enjoy some herbed trout with fresh vegetables from the castle kitchen while we talk," said Lady Anne, taking her seat. "Tell me about your family."

Marie grimaced. She might as well have had no family. "What can I say? They dumped me here."

"I see," Lady Anne replied, pursing her lips. "I can tell you are not happy to be here. Perhaps we could begin with something about your childhood and the things you liked to do."

With a mixture of longing and sadness, Marie related what she could, mostly facts about the family home and her place by the stream, which seemingly lay forever beyond her grasp.

"Hm, you like to dream, then?" Lady Anne said. "Tell me about some of the places your imagination takes you." Lady Anne's eyes seemed relaxed, not inquisitive, as if she were talking to a friend.

Surprised, Marie sat up and leaned in toward Lady Anne. How did Lady Anne know? And why did she want to know more?

"I-I thought about the animals and birds and what they were doing and imagined I could talk to them, but what does that have to do with being a wife?" Marie said, amazed that she was revealing her secret world to a stranger, yet yielding to the impulse that it wanted to be revealed to this unassuming lady who exuded a warmth and acceptance that seemed to tug her close, like embracing arms.

Lady Anne smiled; even the wrinkles around her eyes smiled. "Before I can teach you, Marie, I want to know who you are. Based on what you have told me, I believe that you care about others, regardless of who they are or what they are—and you want to be cared about in the same way you care about them."

Marie now felt completely disarmed. Within the first day this lady whom she had just met had searched her heart and knew what was there.

"And I believe there are stories inside you that want to be heard," Lady Anne continued. "Has your mother taught you to read and write?"

"I can read, but not write," Marie said. "At least not as well as she thinks I should. It was too hard to do it perfectly, so my mind wandered."

"So I heard," Lady Anne said, smiling again. She pushed a book toward Marie. "Have you read this?"

"It says *A Chronicle of the Prince,* but it does not look like the one we have at home."

"It is written on paper. Yours may be on pieces of parchment bound together. How much of it have you read?"

Embarrassed, Marie looked down at her lap. "Not much. My mother and father would read it to my brother and me. It was too hard to understand on my own."

"Never mind that," Lady Anne said. "We must all start somewhere. Your daily study when you are on your own, for as long as it takes, is to read a portion of the *Chronicle* until you have read it all." She pushed a stack of paper and an inkwell with a quill next to the book. "While you are reading through the *Chronicle,* I will be helping you to improve your writing—but it does not have to be perfect. You will attempt, as best you can, to write on a piece of paper what you think the *Chronicle* has spoken to you. I will help you form the letters and words as you learn to write them. We will then discuss what you have written and what it means. If you do not know some of the words you are reading, you may point them out and I will explain them to you. We will do this after supper every day."

Marie already felt overwhelmed by the size of the book and the length of the task. "Why must I read and write about the whole thing? If I am able to satisfy you with the first few pages, isn't that enough?"

Lady Anne responded evenly, "It is not just about reading and writing, Marie. It is about gaining knowledge of and understanding the King and his

Kingdom. You may never meet the King in person, but he wishes you to know what he is like and what he expects of his people. This book tells you what he desires that you know of him; of his son, the Prince; and of his Kingdom. The man who takes you as his wife will expect you to know this as well."

Marie had no answer to this, nor did she have any way out of it. She was a prisoner here at the castle, as she saw it. She could rebel against it and perhaps be sent home, but she could not bring herself to dishonor her father in that way, despite her parting feeling that he had just dropped her here like tiresome baggage. From that moment she decided that she would make the best of it and attempt to do all she was asked. If she did everything well, perhaps she could go home sooner.

Each day thereafter she spent several hours painstakingly reading the *Chronicle* and writing about what she had read as best as she could. Her ability to write the words improved with time, and she began to understand, with Lady Anne's help, some of what she had read. She began to comprehend that she was part of something far larger than herself or even her family—a vast Kingdom ruled by a benevolent King who loved her, just as her father had said. There was no talk about her becoming a wife. Lady Anne instead filled her head with ideas about the Kingdom, and about finding her purpose in it.

The days became weeks, and weeks lengthened into months until it was midsummer. It had been almost a year since that ill-fated night when she first overheard the words that sealed her fate. It seemed like a year had passed since she had come to Bartscastle, though it had been but four months. In the beginning she had thought about home almost daily, especially when she and Lady Anne would ride into town to visit the merchants and the market, and Lady Anne would teach her how to shop and bargain wisely, handle money responsibly, and interact graciously with the people. Then she would smell the freshness of spring, hear distant birds, and feel the warmth of the sun on her shoulders.

And although suppers with Lady Anne were certainly educational, she still missed the feeling of belonging to a family, of her father asking about her day, even of talking with Edouard sometimes after dark when they lay in bed, listening to the soft murmur of their parents' voices below. But her fantasy world seemed as if it were slipping irretrievably from her memory, crowded from her thoughts by the need to master the necessities of the real world that faced her each day.

As Marie's thirteenth birthday drew near, Lady Anne said, "On your birthday you and I will sup with Sir Bart. He desires to meet and converse with the girls I educate when each has a birthday."

On the day itself Lady Anne surprised Marie with a new gown she had commissioned for her—forest green with gold collar and cuffs, the colors of Sir Bart. Marie had to admit that she liked it very much.

"Sir Bart will be pleased," Lady Anne told Marie, tying some gold ribbons in her hair.

As they stepped out to walk across the courtyard to the keep and the great hall, Lady Anne said, "Remember to curtsey when you are introduced. He is the lord of the castle, so you must address him as 'sire,' or 'milord.'"

Marie felt conspicuous as she accompanied Lady Anne, conscious of the examining eyes of everyone they passed on the short walk to the keep in the waning summer sunlight. Peasants stopped to stare, and even the soldiers stopped their practice to watch the spectacle of two well-dressed noble ladies crossing the courtyard. The two climbed the circular tower staircase to the second floor, where they paused outside the great hall as a servant announced them, Marie's heart thumping wildly.

At the far end of the hall was an older man Marie presumed was Sir Bart, wearing a green jacket with gold trim and seated at the end of his lord's table, which was set with a white tablecloth and three silver plates and cups. A basket of bread sat before him. Smiling, he rose as Marie approached.

"Sir Bart, I present Lady Marie de Bonfrere," Lady Anne said, motioning Marie to the left of the knight.

Marie curtseyed as instructed, which the knight acknowledged with a nod.

"Marie of the Bonfreres," Sir Bart said as he seated himself. "Your father is a good man. I am honored that he chose to have you educated in my castle."

Aware that she was in the presence of someone important, Marie found herself at a loss for words. She curtseyed again and mumbled, "Yes, milord."

Sir Bart clapped his hands. "Please sit."

As Marie did so, a youth brought steaming bowls of vegetables and a platter of carved venison.

"Thank you, Stephen," Sir Bart said to the lad. "You may wait in the doorway by the fireplace."

Lady Anne took her place to Sir Bart's right as he pushed a bowl toward Marie.

"Please, serve yourself. Now tell me about your education. Lady Anne tells me you have read the *Chronicle* and become knowledgeable about the King and his Kingdom."

"Yes, sire. I have, but I am hardly knowledgeable about it," Marie responded, beginning to feel more relaxed now that Sir Bart had offered her food.

He seemed like a kind man, his eyes smiling as he conversed with her. She glanced around the hall. Tapestries hung on the side walls between the high windows. Above them at regular intervals were torches that cast a flickering light over their meal. Behind Sir Bart sat a large fireplace, which would no doubt hold a crackling fire in the winter. The serving youth stood dimly silhouetted in a doorway near the fireplace. On the wall where they entered was some writing that Marie could not make out in the low light.

Sir Bart went on, "Lady Anne has told me how diligent you are in your studies. And she has taken you into town to teach you about provisioning a household. What have you learned?"

This was a familiar question. Marie's mind fleeted to an image of her father's face, asking the very same question. But she did not resent the reference to "learning" anymore. She knew that Lady Anne understood what she needed to hear and presented it to her in a way that reflected her care about Marie and about her future. Marie considered her weekly ride into Bartstown with Lady Anne. In some ways it was like her trips to Grandvil with her mother, but oddly she felt more comfortable with Lady Anne. She still did not like the smell and chaos of towns, but Lady Anne always remained patient with her, explaining what she was doing and why, with no requirement that she be able to do it immediately ... or perfectly. And the townsfolk seemed to know and like Lady Anne. After a while they had recognized and welcomed Marie as well.

"She has taught me about buying and selling and how to handle money, how to recognize the quality of merchandise, how to determine the value, and how to bargain without offense. She is also teaching me weaving, writing, and music."

"Very good," Sir Bart replied. "And what do you do for amusement?"

Amusement? When did she have time for that? True, she sometimes sat at her window and watched people go to and fro in the courtyard, wondering what their lives were like, the way she wondered about the animals in the forest, and she enjoyed watching the men training with swords and at archery.

"I don't think I have had time for amusement, sire," Marie said with a frown.

The knight chuckled. "Well do I know that! As a teacher of the mind and heart, Lady Anne is among the very best. As for amusement—"

"Sire!" Lady Anne whispered.

Sir Bart looked at Marie and smiled. "She knows what I am going to do." He laughed again and clapped his hands.

The youth scurried from behind him, bearing an object on both out-stretched hands.

"It is time for you to begin to play at targets, Marie. My gift to you is this bow."

Marie's eyes widened as she watched Sir Bart take the bow and hand it to her. It was beautiful, fashioned of a shiny wood with carving above and below the grip. She could not hide a grin as she held it her hand.

"Oh, thank you, sire! I will become the best at targets. I hope you will be proud," she said.

"Your father told me of your desire. It is not to take the place of your other studies, though," the knight said. "But Lady Anne will begin to allow you time with my steward, Owen, to practice." His voice changed to a serious tone as he spoke to Lady Anne. "She is ready, is she not?"

"I believe she is," Lady Anne said.

Sir Bart turned back to Marie, who was still admiring the bow, stroking the shiny wood with her fingers.

"Lady Anne has told you about the nature of the King's Kingdom and shown you the map, has she not?"

"The one with the castle in the middle? Yes. And that it will only speak to me and help me develop qualities desired by the King if I declare loyalty to him and trust him," Marie answered, repeating Lady Anne's words to her, as if she understood what they meant, though she was aware she did not.

"She also tells me that you are often full of questions." He smiled again.

Marie thought a moment, uncertain where Sir Bart's comment was leading, but it was certainly true. There were many questions on her tongue now. "I guess I am, sire," she said, looking up.

"That is good," the knight replied, "unless they come from an unruly heart."

The eyes that seemed to smile before now pierced her. Marie imagined herself suddenly pinned to her chair with two spikes, wanting to squirm but unable to budge. Nothing she had studied had prepared her for this moment. She opened her mouth, but no words came forth, only thoughts boiling up inside. Her mind began to fill with scenes of hurtful words she had said to her mother and to her father, of unkind thoughts she'd had toward them, of times she had resisted their authority. *I do have an unruly heart,* she concluded, somewhat surprised at having the thought. *I need help to rule my heart.* Where were these accusing thoughts coming from?

"I-I don't know what to say," she said, attempting to evade the answer that seemed to be required.

The steady eyes still held her fast, as if waiting for an answer before they would release their grip.

She could no longer look at Sir Bart, instead studying her trembling hands as she attempted to master the tumult within. With a heavy sigh Marie finally looked up. "I do want to trust the King," she said just above a whisper. "And I need help in trusting him."

"You want the King to rule in your heart," Sir Bart said.

"Yes … I do," Marie said after a pause, not exactly certain what she was affirming, but yielding to the powerful conviction welling up inside that she needed to say it.

Sir Bart clapped again. The youth returned with an ornately carved wooden box enclosed in strips of silver. It was a beautiful box, but what was it for?

"This box contains your own map, and as a knight of the King, who invites only those whom he chooses into his Kingdom, I am now presenting you with the key he gives to all whom he chooses. When you return to your room tonight, you must open the box and look at your map. You may want to do it with Lady Anne at your side. She will explain to you more fully the significance of what has happened. Now, I am ready to hear your questions." Sir Bart smiled again.

Holding the box in her lap, with her shiny silver key in one hand, uncertain of the ramifications of what had just transpired, but glad to see Sir Bart smiling again, Marie slowly recovered her composure. "Sire, I have learned much about the King, and I do feel safe here, but I would like to know more about the Dragon. It seemed as if he was all around me on my journey here, and my parents would speak of him as if he was very dangerous."

Marie noticed Sir Bart exchange a glance with Lady Anne, who shook her head. But the knight turned toward her, folding his hands, his brow furrowing. "You perhaps did not need to know this when you were under the protection of your family, but I believe your education should include the unpleasant truth as well as the pleasant." He cleared his throat and leaned toward her. "Milady, the Dragon has been at war with the King as long as I can remember. He is both powerful and dangerous, and he is always seeking to win allegiance to himself, sometimes by trickery, sometimes by force. We are in a period of time now, since the death of the Prince in battle, when he is growing bolder, because he believes the King is weak."

The death of the Prince? A cold shiver rippled through Marie's body as she looked back at Lady Anne in confusion. *You told me you were training me as if*

I was to be a wife to the Prince. And he is dead? Her eyes explored Lady Anne's, seeking some sign of an answer but finding none.

Sir Bart continued, "But I assure you, the King is powerful enough, and he will defeat the Dragon, at a time and place of his choosing."

Marie felt no reassurance, any more than when her father had said the same thing. In her mind, if there was danger, and you were strong enough, you eliminated it immediately. Why wait?

Questions began to well up in profusion and she offered the first: "If the King is so powerful, how could he allow his son to die in battle?" Left unspoken was an additional and more frightening question: *"Why should I believe he will not allow the Dragon to capture and kill me too?"*

Sir Bart sat back and sighed, as if he had answered this question many times. "It is difficult to understand, I know, milady. It was even for me, and I was on the same battlefield," he said softly. "I do not comprehend everything about our King either, but I have come to realize that the victory is not won on the battlefield of the countryside, but the battlefield of the heart. The Prince did lose his life in a battle, but he lives on in spirit. It is his spirit that readies and captures our hearts for the kingdom. The same spirit will lead you to an answer to your questions."

The hall suddenly seemed to grow cold; it wasn't the chill of fear that had seized Marie before but a pervasive and lingering chill, a damp chill, as if she had been doused with the truths of coming of age only hinted at by her father and mother. Her mind tumbled with new realities: *We are at war. Our enemy is dangerous and powerful. He killed the Prince. —I just gave my allegiance to a king who allowed it to happen. My heart is a battlefield?*

Marie's troubled expression seemed to stir Sir Bart, for he said, "You are wondering if you can really trust the spirit of the Prince. You have never seen him or the King, but you have read about them in the *Chronicle*. Consider your thoughts before you gave control of your heart to the King. Where do you think they came from?"

Marie recalled her surprise at having those thoughts. They were not thoughts she had ever had before. And with them a powerful urgency had overcome her. Following Sir Bart's lead, she ventured a guess: "The spirit of the Prince?"

"Indeed," Sir Bart said. "And once he captures our hearts for the Kingdom, he does not let go of them." He slid his chair back and rose. "You will of course need time to assimilate the events of this evening, and Lady Anne will help you."

By the time Marie had returned to the common room with Lady Anne, she was exhausted, her mind so stuffed with unresolved questions that it was threatening to burst.

"Sit with me and open your box," Lady Anne said, taking her place beside Marie. "After you unroll your map and look at it, you are going to feel a pain in your heart. Do not be frightened."

Marie nodded, not understanding, but did as she was told. While she watched the map reveal its secrets, her puzzled expression turned to amazement.

"All of the names, they—Oww!" she shouted, her hand flying to her heart even as Lady Anne held her tightly. "What—is happening?"

"An event you will always remember," Lady Anne replied. "When you enter the true Kingdom, you receive a mark of the King's authority over you. Did you notice that your map was sealed with an imprint of a dove? The King's seal signifies his authority and rule. When next you look, you will find the design of the same dove over your heart, a sign that your heart is safely sealed for the King, that you are under his authority, and that the spirit of the Prince will guide you henceforth."

As the pain disappeared, Marie realized that she understood little of what Lady Anne had said, but her eyes went back to the map. "There are so many things on it that were not on the one at home, or the one you showed me earlier."

"Yes," Lady Anne said. "They are not visible until you are in the Kingdom. The roads show the many ways to the king's castle. Each of us takes a different road, and only you can see which road you are on. There are some orchards and towns you must pass through, and rivers you must cross, and hills you must climb on the way, whose names will not appear until you reach them."

Lady Anne stood and glanced toward the loom by the window. "You have watched me weave and had time to practice with your loom. Tomorrow you will begin a new project—a tapestry of your map which you will hang on the wall of the house or castle you will eventually live in after you are wed."

The whole evening had been both unexpected and overwhelming for Marie, but she understood that something important had happened. What she had been learning about the King and his Kingdom suddenly seemed more real and personal to her. She laid her head on her pillow that night with a thrill of excitement, her mind abuzz. *The spirit of the Prince was with me tonight! And I am a member of the true Kingdom now. Was this part of why I came here?*

The first winter snow had fallen before Marie finished her tapestry. Passing the shuttle back and forth on the loom had been clumsy for her in the beginning, but with Lady Anne's help she progressed, and the outline of the map gradually became visible. Even though to her eyes it was in reverse, Marie took pride in her evolving work. The fact that her tapestry was in color, unlike the map, gave her much pleasure. When she finally took it off the loom and turned it over, she was proud of her accomplishment. The blue castle in the middle, though a darker blue, reminded her of her mother's delight in "Bonfrere blue," a color she had come to dislike, but the rich greens of forests and orchards, the gold roads, and the dark blue rivers and ponds made a striking picture. Now all that remained to do was embroider the names that appeared on her map. Lady Anne was pleased with the result as well.

As Marie neared the end of her project, Lady Anne had a surprise for her: "A master weaver will be visiting the castle to bring a tapestry for Sir Bart's great hall. I will ask him to stop and look at your work. Maybe he will give you some ideas for your next one—a gift for your mother, perhaps?"

A master weaver? Marie accepted the news with a mixture of pride and trepidation. She considered herself a novice at weaving, and though she felt proud of her finished piece, surely a master weaver would find fault with it. But it was finished now, and she resolved to try and learn whatever she could.

On the appointed night of the master weaver's visit, Marie was seated by the fireplace reading when she heard a knock at the door. Lady Anne hurried to the door to invite the guest in. Stamping snow off his feet, he entered, giving a courteous greeting to Lady Anne. Marie did not know what to expect—maybe someone with long, supple fingers? When he emerged into the firelight, she beheld a balding middle-aged man with a kind face, one that had not been weathered by work in the fields. A well-groomed mustache graced his upper lip. Marie offered her hand as he bowed and extended his. No, the fingers were not long, but his flesh was soft, his hand warm, and his grasp gentle.

"Lady Anne asked me to comment on your tapestry, milady," he said softly. "It would be my pleasure to do so."

Marie had hung it on an easel by the fireplace with a large candle stand in front to light it.

"Yes, sir," Marie replied, accompanying him for a closer look. "It is nothing original, just based on a map that everyone has."

He glanced at her, then back at the tapestry. "Actually it is original, because it is your map, and not everyone has a map."

"Oh, I meant I didn't think it up," Marie added, now abashed by her false attempt at humility.

"And it is good that you did not think it up, because then you would be on the wrong road." He crouched and put his face close to the tapestry as if examining it with a critical eye.

Marie held her breath. She knew she had made mistakes and had to redo parts.

He pointed to a lower corner. "This is your road, and there you are on it."

Marie craned her neck to see. Just above his finger on one of the gold roads was a light blue heart she had not noticed before. "You are about to pass through an orchard, but there is no name on it. Your tapestry is unfinished."

Marie's expectant confidence was crushed. *He has found fault with me.* She had no explanation. "It-It wasn't on my map," she said. "Everything isn't named."

"You are exactly right," he said. "Let's see—" He began to brush his finger over the image of the orchard.

To Marie's astonished, unblinking eyes, letters began to appear behind his moving finger, as if embroidered in red. When he had finished, the word *Obedience* clearly marked the orchard in front of Marie's heart. His finger touched the orchard on the other side of the road and began to trace its course again. Beneath his moving fingertip the word *Trust* emerged. Marie could hardly breathe. His eyes met hers in silent communication. She understood immediately what had happened. The map was speaking to her, just as Lady Anne had said.

The master weaver stood and faced Marie. "These are the fruits you must cultivate before you progress farther on your road, milady."

He turned and bowed to Lady Anne, then silently made his way to the door as Marie collapsed onto a stool.

After the door closed behind him, Marie realized that she was trembling. "Wh-Who is he? How did he know about my heart and where it was on the road?"

Lady Anne knelt beside her and slipped an arm around her to draw her close. "He is the King's master weaver. It is he who created the map and knows every road."

Chapter 9

BECOMING

S TEPHEN'S FIRST YEAR as a squire passed quickly, Stephen sitting with Sir Bart at meals every morning and evening, listening to the knight's instruction about the Kingdom and the Prince. He now understood that his training would prepare him for a role in the Kingdom, though he did not know what that would be, or even if he would ever be worthy to become a knight.

He continued to work with Michael each morning after breakfast as well. By the end of the first summer he had learned one-handed swordsmanship well enough that he could occasionally strike Michael, who now had to wear armor during their training. Stephen could place three arrows in the center of the target by a count of fifteen, though not always close enough together to avoid a caustic mumble from Michael. With Jacky he had learned to manage his horse with one hand while wielding a sword. He still could not move the stone pile without slowing toward the end, but his running time around the castle had improved.

As fall progressed into winter, he spent less time outside, particularly when cold winds howled around the keep and through the open windows, and snow blew in gusts. But Michael took him out into the courtyard for short periods, snow or no snow, so that he would not become "soft." Other times they would practice their swordplay in the armory underneath the great hall. He took on new duties such as learning to oil and polish Sir Bart's armor, as well as his horse's armor, and he practiced helping Sir Bart on with his armor. He sat and listened when Sir Bart granted audiences to peasants in his realm and settled disputes, as well as when Owen, his steward, reported on the affairs of the fief. Having served Sir Bart for single guests, Stephen learned next how to set the table and serve the knight and his guests of honor at the lord's table when it stood at the head of the banquet hall.

Spring brought Stephen's fifteenth birthday, Stephen having now lived in the castle for eight years, seven as a page, and although he would visit his mother in town as he had time, he viewed Bartscastle as home, and had come to realize the truth of Sir Bart's calling him "son" when he became a squire. Sir Bart was mentoring him as a father would, but without the unrelenting pressure of expectation he remembered from his own father. Michael now occupied that role.

Nonetheless Stephen still fondly remembered his own father as someone who would play with him and hug him and pull his blanket up over him at night, giving him a gentle kiss on the head. And though he thought his father loved him, his father had been a different man, an important one who accomplished things and expected the same of his son. After his father was killed, Stephen remembered at age six feeling an unspoken responsibility to take his place as the "man" in the home, but without anyone to teach him how. From that point on his approach to any task was tempered by the fear that he might not measure up, that he would not have what it took, that he would never be as good at anything as his father was or expected him to be.

Stephen knew also that he would never experience a familial relationship with Sir Bart, yet something about Sir Bart allowed Stephen to see himself as being like a son to the knight. Perhaps it was the great fund of knowledge and wisdom that he possessed, and seemed eager to impart to Stephen. Perhaps it was his sincere assurance that he was training Stephen to become a leader in the Kingdom, though Stephen hardly thought himself capable of leading anyone now. The hardest part for Stephen was his constant struggle to understand the nature of the Kingdom and the King. He always felt stupid when the dinner conversation turned to these subjects, yet Sir Bart never seemed frustrated with him when he failed to grasp the truths he was presenting. "It will come in time, as long as you are diligent," he always said.

For Stephen's fifteenth birthday Sir Bart presented him with his own chain mail hauberk. That same day Stephen began training with sword and shield. Michael had already taught him how to anticipate a blow by watching subtleties of his opponent's movements. It wasn't too difficult to learn to block the blow with a shield and still leave enough opening to counter with his own strike, the only problem being that Michael was now using a shield too. Stephen noted also that the weight of the shield on his arm and the weight of the mail shirt slowed him down. He did not touch Michael once. As always Stephen berated himself on his poor performance, and once again he began to question his ability to master the newest challenge. But, with the determination engendered by his father, he resolved to try harder and make himself yet stronger.

Jacky began to work with him on the lance and quintain. Though Stephen had seen previous squires practice when he was a page, the quintain seemed an odd thing. It looked to him like a scarecrow in armor with a shield on one side of the wooden T-bar that represented its arms. On the other "arm" hung a sack full of dirt. The whole thing swiveled when one hit the shield with the lance. The first few times he rode too slowly. He hit the shield all right, but the bag swung around and smacked him off the horse before he rode free of its range. Once he began riding faster, the shock of hitting the shield jerked the lance completely out of his grasp. Jacky taught him how to lock his elbow over the lance after he had seated it against his chest, whereupon he was knocked completely off the horse, still holding the lance. Next he learned the importance of centering his feet in the stirrups and gripping the saddle with his thighs to absorb the blow.

By the end of summer Stephen could move the stone pile without slowing. He thought Michael actually smiled at him the first time he did it. But a few days later Stephen found a new pile of stones—larger ones. Again he struggled to move them as fast as Michael desired. Through the next fall and winter, he practiced sword-and-shield combat either in the courtyard or in the armory with Michael, who continued to instruct him on his footwork.

"When you are wearing full armor with a visored helmet, you will not be able to see your feet," Michael told him. "You must know where your feet are and how to move them instinctively so that you can concentrate on your adversary's movements."

It seemed to Stephen as if he would never master everything. There was always more.

Another spring arrived, bringing gentle breezes and fair skies, and with it, Stephen's sixteenth birthday. Sir Bart presented him with a charger to replace Gascon—not a true warhorse like the knight's, but a courser, and a sturdy one at that. Jacky had already trained the horse to face an adversary in combat and to charge the quintain. He responded well to Stephen's touch, and Stephen thought that they moved as one when he rode. Stephen named him "Centaur."

Michael began to teach Stephen the use of two new weapons—the axe and the mace. For this, they both had to wear plate armor, and for the first time Michael had to tell Stephen to be careful. They were to strike only where there was plate armor—the torso and thighs. The full armor slowed Stephen again, and he got the worst of it. He could tell that Michael was holding back, but the clangs on his armor where Michael struck still left him bruised.

Stephen now rode Centaur armored, and he began to ride with a helmet. He had only a narrow slit for his eyes to see, and he had to lower his head in order to see the quintain well enough to strike it. Once, he lost sight of the quintain's shield until he smacked into it with his head, waking up on the ground with Jacky standing over him, extending a hand.

He was also still struggling with the larger stones. He had improved his time but now Michael had him carrying each stone with both hands above his head rather than resting it on his shoulder. His arms tired much quicker bearing all the weight on extended arms, but his running time around the castle continued to improve, even wearing the mail shirt. He supposed that he'd only have a pile of even bigger stones awaiting him if he conquered these.

Spring had already given way to summer when one morning at breakfast Sir Bart greeted Stephen with unexpected news: "Tonight we will have a guest. Sir John, one of the Brethren, will stay and sup with us."

"The Brethren?" Stephen asked, for he had not heard this word before.

"Knights of the Chalice," Sir Bart was quick to say. "We call ourselves 'the Brethren.' He has news from the King."

The prospect of meeting another of the King's great knights excited Stephen the entire day. He surprised even Michael with the energy he put into his mace training, and he moved the stones the fastest yet. He came to the great hall early, as he was to set the table for the two knights and serve them. At the appointed time the two came in together, chatting as long-lost friends. Sir John definitely looked younger, and kept himself clean-shaven, unlike Sir Bart. They seated themselves, Sir Bart at the head of the table, Sir John at his right. Stephen took his place, standing at the right of Sir Bart's chair.

Sir Bart made the introduction: "Sir John, this is my squire, Stephen."

Stephen bowed. "A pleasure, sire."

"Mine as well," Sir John answered with a nod of his head. "Sir Bart has told me how enthusiastically you are training, and what thoughtful questions you ask. You may have need of both your skill and your learning soon."

"Soon, sire?" Stephen said.

"Sir John has told me that war clouds are gathering again," Sir Bart said. "The Dragon has been emboldened by the lack of any campaign against him in the past few years. He has imprisoned some of the King's knights and taken their fiefs. Now his forces are gathering on our borders. He has already sent spies throughout the King's lands to gather information and spread lies."

"Yes," Sir John said. "The King has sent me to warn all of his knights to prepare for battle." Turning to Sir Bart, he said, "The castle must be stocked for siege as well and the people warned to prepare for such a possibility."

Sir Bart clapped his hands. "We are forgetting to eat." He chuckled.

Stephen hurried out to bring in the dishes. *Roast boar tonight!* A basket of fresh bread, platters of vegetables, and a flagon of wine completed the meal. The two knights attacked the boar eagerly with their daggers, carving off great steaming slices. Stephen stood quietly, his stomach rumbling, refilling their cups as necessary, comforted by the knowledge that there would be plenty left for him and castle staff.

"You know, Sir John," Sir Bart said, his voice muffled by the large hunk of boar meat he was chewing, "things haven't sounded this dangerous since the Prince was killed. We have had some serious skirmishes, such as the one where I was wounded, but it sounds as if our enemy will be coming from all sides now."

"Do not overlook that our army is also larger now," Sir John replied, "and we are led by the Prince in spirit. We will prevail, but we must trust in the King's plan."

"Yes, but it is not what I expected," Sir Bart said. "Instead of uniting us all at his castle, the King is asking us each to defend our own lands."

Sir John nodded. "Thereby inviting our enemy to divide his forces, because he does not know where or when the King will strike. The Dragon may try to take us one castle at a time, without committing his entire force, but he will try to do so by deception, because commencing a siege will tie up his forces and may bring a quick response from the King."

Sir Bart turned to Stephen. "Speak up, lad. Do you have any questions for Sir John?"

Stephen had not taken his eyes off Sir John the entire time. "I...I—Sir Bart has told me so much about you. He said you were the one the Prince loved best."

Sir John shot a glance at Sir Bart. "Well, I often rode by his side, and perhaps he told me more than some others about his father, the King, and the Kingdom, but we are all equally Knights of the Chalice."

"You have fought the Dragon. What is he like?" Stephen asked.

"I'm sure Sir Bart has told you this," Sir John said, his eyes focused on Stephen. "He appears to be very strong, even invincible. He will try to deceive you into thinking he is stronger than you, but before a knight who fights with the spirit of the Prince, he is weak, and he will run. He preys on those who do not trust in the power of King and the spirit of the Prince to protect them, but who try to rely on their own strength."

"Yes, he has told me that," Stephen said, nodding. "But I worry that I will not be able to discern the deception, and I will be the one who runs."

Sir John offered a reassuring smile. "That is why you are squire to Sir Bart. He fights with the power of the King, led by the Prince's spirit. As long as you are by his side, that same spirit will guide you."

The answer did not comfort Stephen. Sir Bart was obviously older than Sir John. Even though Sir Bart had stressed to him that he depended on the spirit of the Prince, Stephen himself had experienced none of this. And though he had not seen Sir Bart in combat, he was not certain that Sir Bart could even better him now.

Reacting to the expression of doubt that had crept over Stephen's face, Sir John continued, "Rest assured." He chuckled. "The spirit of the Prince stands with us when we need it. Even 'old' Sir Bart here can fight like a lion when he is empowered."

Sir Bart laughed. "But it has been awhile. Michael keeps me on my toes every night after supper. There are perhaps a few more battles in me."

Stephen's eyes widened. Sir Bart still trained with Michael! So he wasn't just a kind, old father figure—he could still fight!

Sir John departed the next day. Almost immediately the castle was caught up in preparation for Summer Tourney, which rotated among the castles of the region. This year was Sir Bart's turn to host. Outside the castle walls the jousting lists[6] were refurbished, seats were constructed, and booths for the judges and special guests were built. Extra stalls were added to the stables, and the rest of the land between the castle and town was cleared for the pavilions[7] of visiting knights.

Stephen continued to work with Michael in the mornings. He had improved his mastery of the mace, but wielding the heavier axe was still awkward for him.

---

[6] The field divided by a low wall where jousting knights clash.
[7] The circular tent in which a knight kept his belongings and slept when traveling.

He had achieved the goal of three arrows in a tight pattern by a count of fifteen, whereupon Michael had changed everything again. Now it was seventy-five paces—half as far again! Stephen was glad that Jacky had worked so hard with him on the quintain. He was confident about his jousting skills now—at least with the quintain. Sir Bart had given him permission to enter the squires' joust, even promising to do a few practice jousts with him on the lists before the tourney to familiarize him with the grounds. Though at the end of each day Stephen sometimes wondered if the grind would go on forever, the goal of knighthood enticed him on, and he resolved each new day to attempt to conquer whatever was thrown at him.

The same summer, Marie observed her fourteenth birthday. Over the previous year she had completed reading and writing out her interpretation of the *Chronicle* to improve her handwriting, along with learning about provisioning and running a household, and handling money; she had produced another tapestry, this one for her mother—a weaving of home, as best as she could remember it, with the forest behind and the stable to the side. She had learned to play the recorder and the tambourine, and she had spent time with Owen shooting arrows at targets with her bow.

Lady Anne now had a new project for her: "It is time to begin French lessons," she told Marie one day. "Noblewomen must be able to understand and speak French."

Marie concealed a laugh. "Have you forgotten? My father is Norman. *Je parle francais tres bien, n'est-ce pas?*"

A bemused expression stole across Lady Anne's face. "Well, yes, I suppose you do."

"Instead of French lessons I would like to substitute something else," Marie was quick to say.

"And what might that be?" Lady Anne inquired.

"I have mastered shooting at targets with my ladies' bow. I would like to learn the shortbow."

Lady Anne face looked aghast. "You know how I feel about that, Marie. It is a man's skill and a weapon of war."

Marie set her jaw. "My birthday supper with Sir Bart is near. I would like to ask him to allow it."

Lady Anne exhaled a heavy sigh. "I will not forbid you. You have so far done everything I have asked, and done it well. But do not press him. He has many concerns more urgent than whether young ladies can shoot arrows."

On the day itself, Marie again wore her green and gold gown, which no longer touched the ground but now came to her ankles. It had been a year since she had been in the knight's presence, but this time she took her seat at the table with confidence.

As he had the previous year, Sir Bart immediately focused his attention on her. "Ah, you have grown in understanding and beauty, haven't you, milady." He smiled.

Marie beamed back. She thought so herself—well, maybe not beauty—but she was pleased to hear herself addressed as "milady."

"You are halfway through your sojourn with us," Sir Bart said. "What think you?"

Scenes of the previous year passed before Marie as she chose her words. Although she had enjoyed learning to shoot at targets, the novelty wore off quickly, and she had bridled inwardly at the prospect of being limited only to target practice with a ladies' bow. The structured life of being "educated" also had at times become wearisome, there being no refuge to run to and allow her imagination to take flight as it once did. But she had come to value the long conversations with Lady Anne, when she could ask anything and feel that Lady Anne cared enough about her to answer without reservation.

Two events, however, had changed Marie's outlook and attitude forever. Exactly one year ago she had sat in the same chair and experienced the movement of the spirit of the Prince in her thoughts and then received the affirmation of her entry into the Kingdom. And six months later had come the visit of the master weaver. In her mind she could still see his finger passing over her first tapestry, revealing the words *Obedience* and *Trust*. She knew then that, somehow, her "independent spirit" must be tempered by those two words, and she had made a decided effort to trust the spirit of the Prince thereafter, even though she did not understand completely what it meant to do so. And from that day on, she viewed everything Lady Anne asked her to learn as something she should do for the King.

"Milord, thanks to you and Lady Anne, I have learned many things that will be useful to me as a wife and, more importantly, will enable me to be of service to the King."

"Well said, well said," the knight answered. "And there is more to come. What would you like to converse about tonight?"

As before, the list was long. Though she had felt safe in the castle and Lady Anne had been careful never to mention the Dragon, Marie could never completely dismiss the reality that there was a Dragon. He no longer took the form of a scaly, fire-spewing beast in her dreams, but watching men-at-arms and archers in training reminded her constantly that an enemy existed and that he was dangerous.

"Sire, I have seen in the past few months much coming and going of carts with provisions and more men training in the courtyard. Is something about to happen? Is it the Dragon?"

Sir Bart's expression changed to one of seriousness. He leaned forward as if to speak in confidence. "Milady, there is no reason to be concerned, but I will tell you so that you will not worry. We are readying the men for battle and the castle for siege by the Dragon. But we have a strong position; this castle has never fallen to the enemy."

This castle? Besieged? Suddenly the hall grew colder, her hands clammy. "Why then do people speak of him as if he is more powerful than we are and able to defeat us?"

Sir Bart kept his eyes on Marie as he seemed to consider his answer. "He is powerful, and a worthy adversary, and he is able to defeat us if we try to rely on our own strength."

Without reflecting on her next words, Marie's immediate response was, "What other strength do we have?" As she said it, the image of her standing empty-handed before the fierce dragon of her dreams flashed before her eyes.

The knight's eyes widened and his eyebrows raised, then he said, "After a year with Lady Anne you should know the answer to that by now, milady."

Reading a hint of disappointment in Lady Anne's eyes, Marie remembered. "Oh, of course," she said quickly, "you mean the spirit of the Prince."

He nodded. "Never forget, milady. That is your only strength. Someday you may have need of it. Though the Dragon grows stronger, I and my knights can and will rely on the spirit of the Prince for victory over the Dragon."

Sir Bart and his knights. With that comment the image of her father's smiling face materialized in Marie's mind. She no longer harbored resentment that he had dropped her off like a useless object; Lady Anne had made sure of that. But how she missed him! Did he think about her? Did he miss her too?

"My father is one of your knights, is he not? Do you have news of him? Is he well?"

"He is well. He will be here for the summer tournament. I am sure you will see him."

Aware that her body had tensed over her concern about the Dragon, Marie now relaxed and leaned back in her chair, Sir Bart sitting back in turn.

"Now that the tournament is almost upon us," he said, "I have a request of you as well, milady."

What could she possibly do for the great knight? "I am at your service, sire," she replied.

"It is traditional that the prize for the squires' joust be presented by a maiden. I would like you to perform the duty. You will sit in the esteemed guest box with Lady Anne."

Marie felt both honored and excited. Sir Bart was entrusting her with an important assignment—and she would be able to watch the jousting as well!

"And I have commissioned a new gown for you to wear for the occasion," Lady Anne said.

Smiling at Lady Anne, Marie realized that she was so delighted she'd almost forgotten the last item on her mental list. "Sire, I have a final request of you."

"Yes, milady?"

"I have become proficient with the ladies' bow you generously gave me last year. Owen will attest to it. I would now like to learn to defend myself so that I will not be helpless. Would you permit Owen to train me with the shortbow?"

Sir Bart's brow furrowed, his fingers stroking his beard as he considered the request. "No lady has ever asked this of me."

Sensing that her opportunity was fleeting, Marie pressed on: "You have said that the Dragon grows stronger and bolder. If the castle comes under attack, you will need all your soldiers to defend it, not to guard the women. I do not wish to be the cause of any soldier being unavailable to you."

"Well argued, milady," Sir Bart answered, the hint of a smile tugging the corners of his mouth. "It is true that all soldiers would be needed on the walls if we were attacked," he said, nodding, "however unlikely that might be." He paused, resting his bearded chin on folded hands, a contemplative expression on his face. "Lady Anne has told me that you have completed all of the tasks she has given you thus far."

"Did she also say that I have time to learn the shortbow since I do not need to learn French?"

Sir Bart wore the struggle of the decision on his face. At the same time, Marie noted Lady Anne's expression of anxious horror. She hoped it would not sway the knight's decision.

Finally his face relaxed. "These are not normal times," he said, gazing into the distance as if weighing the uncertainties of the future. "The time when the King gathers his people and fights the final battle against the Dragon could come soon." Looking a breathless Marie in the eye, he said, "As your birthday gift, I will grant your request. However, you must train only with Owen and at times when the archery butts are unoccupied. You may not mingle with the soldiers."

Marie could not restrain herself from grinning. "Oh, yes, sire! I will do as you say. Thank you, milord!"

Lady Anne and Marie had no conversation on the way back to the common room, Marie sensing Lady Anne's disappointment at the outcome of her request. Marie remained secretly ebullient—until Lady Anne brought out the new gown she had commissioned for her birthday. *Ugh! Blue!*

Attempting to appear grateful, Marie forced a smile. "These are different colors from Sir Bart's colors."

"Yes," Lady Anne said proudly. "Since the tournament will attract many knights who, along with Sir Bart, pledge their swords to the King, you will wear the colors of the King—blue, white, and gold!"

The King's colors? Marie now began to look at the gown with different eyes. Although the bodice was dark blue, the long, flowing sleeves were white with gold cuffs. A gold collar graced the upper gown and a gold border hemmed the lower part. A gold chain was draped around the waist. Marie pictured herself descending from the viewing box at the tourney to present the prize, all eyes following her as if she represented the King. Maybe a handsome squire would notice. The color blue now held a different meaning for her. No longer would she associate the color blue with only her family. It was a color of the King!

"I will be honored to wear it, milady," she answered.

But Marie's mind was really on something else—the shortbow.

Chapter 10

SUMMER TOURNEY

STEPHEN GAZED OUT of his tower window with a mixture of excitement and anxiety. Today was tourney day. Colorful green and gold banners paired with the King's blue, white, and gold banners fluttered everywhere—at the entrance to the lists, on the stables, the castle gate, and flying from the castle towers. A half-dozen knights' pavilions dotted the open field. Many wooden booths had been erected around the lists and the combat fields, where enterprising merchants were selling food, ale, souvenirs, and wagers. Traveling buskers and jugglers who had stopped by for the day circulated among the crowd. It was a holiday for the peasants, and free entertainment for them as well.

Stephen had been meticulous in oiling Sir Bart's armor and grooming his horse. Sir Bart would lead the procession for the joust, though the knight himself would not participate. Stephen had also checked the balance of the wooden lances to be sure that they were fair before climbing the stairs to attend Sir Bart, who was in the great hall receiving visitors, all of them friends from the region. Stephen stood at Sir Bart's side to do whatever might be needed until the audience was nearly finished. The foot combat for men-at-arms was already underway. He could hear the clank of swords as pairs of men squared off in the castle courtyard. For the purpose of competition, they were using unsharpened swords, but a well-aimed blow could still break a bone or cause a major bruise. With Sir Bart's permission Stephen excused himself to watch the sword competition, which was almost over. The two finalists were about to step onto the straw-strewn venue.

As Stephen drew near, his jaw dropped. In the center was Michael, his sword and shield at the ready, facing another opponent equally as tall as he. Both were covered with grime and sweat from previous combats. They wore no helmet; blows above the neck were not allowed. The goal was to make one's opponent resign or to force him to fall to the ground. It did not matter whether it was your blow that brought him down or he tripped on his own feet, as long as he went down. The fight began. Stephen recognized many of the techniques Michael had taught him as Michael thrusted and parried. He watched Michael's feet, marveling at how quickly he moved, keeping his balance even when forced back. His opponent was equally adept, though.

Eventually it seemed that even Michael was tiring, still blocking his opponent's blows but not attacking as vigorously himself. His antagonist unleashed a mighty strike that knocked Michael to one side. He staggered backward and crouched, the tip of his blade resting on the ground in front of him, as if he were not able to rise, whereupon his opponent rushed forward, his sword raised to give a final blow to force him to the ground. Quickly, Michael flicked his blade from the dirt and thrust it between the legs of the oncoming adversary, catching one foot above the ankle. Down he went in a cloud of straw and dust, next to Michael. The crowd of mostly local peasants cheered as Michael reached down to help him up with a word of encouragement: "Well fought, Daniel."

Stephen was awed by the skill displayed by both, but impressed by Michael's winning strategy. *Masterfully done! Not by power but by deftness of hand. I will remember this.* He wanted to walk up and congratulate Michael but hesitated. It might look as if he thought Michael would not win. Instead he decided to stroll among the booths surrounding the lists and buy a meat pie for a snack. The squires' joust would be just after lunch, and already he was beginning to feel a little queasy. He knew that five squires had entered, including last year's champion, and most were older than he. Opponents were chosen by lot. The previous champion would receive a bye until the final joust, with the two winners of the initial round facing off to see who would meet the champion.

Before Stephen was settled and ready, trumpets sounded, announcing the opening of the lists for the squires' joust. Struggling to calm his anxiety, he walked to the stables to find Centaur. Jacky had agreed to groom and saddle him so that Stephen would be fresh.

As Stephen led Centaur away, Jacky clapped him on the shoulder. "Remember, keep yer head down, lock yer elbow, protec' yer front an' aim for the shoulder."

Stephen was second in sequence. He struggled into his borrowed plate armor with the help of an attendant, and at the trumpet sound he cantered to his end of the lists and waited. Scenes of the months of practice with the quintain and the patient instruction of Jacky flashed through his mind. His father's face materialized, telling him to just go out there and win, to make him proud. Even though he had practiced with Sir Bart, they did not gallop at full tilt, so he had no idea what the full force of the crash would do to him. Would he be up to the challenge, or would he shame Sir Bart by being unhorsed on the first pass?

Stephen knew there would be up to five passes, during which he would attempt to unhorse his opponent, which would give him an immediate victory, provided he was not unhorsed as well. Failing that, his goal was to register a solid hit on his opponent or his shield that broke his own lance even if it did not unhorse the rider. If no one was unhorsed, the one with the most splintered lances would be declared the winner. He tried to size up his opponent, to no avail. His opponent's horse seemed somewhat frisky, though; he was having some difficulty reining him in. Stephen reached down to receive his lance from the lance bearer. It was none other than Sir Bart!

"Milord! I am honored!" Stephen said.

"He has a young mount," Sir Bart said, nodding. "Therein may lie an opportunity. Jacky has taught you well. Trust his advice."

Stephen nodded, accepted the lance, then moved to the start and lowered his weapon, his heart pounding. At the signal he spurred Centaur forward with a leap. Then he seemed to glide, the thunder of hoofs filling his helmet. His foe came in a blur, hurtling into a loud crash. Stephen experienced a mighty jolt, feeling himself lifting out of the saddle. When he recovered his senses, he was still astride his mount, gripping Centaur's mane, heading for the far end of the list, his lance splintered. He felt a pain in his left thigh near his groin, but he had survived his first clash. Turning for another run, he received a new lance, seated it, and caught his breath. *Have to remember all that Jacky taught me. I must keep my mind clear—must focus better!*

At the signal they were off again. This time seemed more awkward, as Stephen rode the opposite side of the barrier, his mind distracted by the throbbing pain in his thigh. *Must keep my lance steady.* His eyes fixed on his oncoming foe; this time it seemed like slow motion. He noticed that his opponent's horse tended to veer away from the low wall that divided them and that he was aiming low again, but keeping his body well covered. Stephen's lance glanced off his shield, as did his opponent's off Stephen's.

Coming back to Sir Bart, Stephen lifted his visor.

"Good, good," Sir Bart said, patting Centaur. "I don't think he has found a weakness yet. That first one was a low blow at your thigh that almost unhorsed you. He should have been disqualified."

Slamming down his visor, Stephen said, "I have found a weakness. It is just as Jacky said."

The signal sent the two careening toward each other a third time. Stephen kept his eyes on his opponent's left shoulder. As his foe's horse turned its head to its right, his left shoulder became more exposed. Stephen braced himself and aimed just above his opponent's shield. The crash almost unhorsed Stephen again as he was twisted backward. But he stayed in the saddle, holding his splintered lance, now conscious of cheers on all sides. Turning at the end of the list, he saw his vanquished opponent on the ground, struggling up from his knees. Trotting back to Sir Bart's end, flushed with the elation of his first victory, Stephen dismounted.

"Excellent, lad!" Sir Bart said, beaming. "He allowed his shield to dip, giving you the advantage."

Aware that he was shaking all over from the violence of the clashes and the extreme concentration required, Stephen led his horse out to a grassy spot and sat, speechless, his head throbbing.

Sir Bart followed and crouched beside him. "It is as much mental as it is physical, son."

Nodding, Stephen knew Sir Bart was right. He had to have confidence in himself and his horse. He had to have confidence in what Jacky had taught him. And he had to concentrate on his opponent's weakness.

By the time his turn came again, Stephen had calmed. He led Centaur back into the lists and mounted. At the signal he spurred forward, keeping his head down and his left shoulder protected. Once more he focused on his opponent's left shoulder. At the crash he was again partly lifted and jolted back in his saddle, his lance splintered and knocked from his hand by the force of his strike. But he heard cheers. Turning back, he was astonished to see his opponent flat on his back. He returned to Sir Bart with an air of confidence. *I am getting good at this!*

Stephen's self-congratulation was sobered by the sight of his last opponent, the previous year's champion, entering the lists. The cheers were now for this young squire. Both he and his horse seemed quite large, Stephen noted. His horse moved slowly and deliberately. *I just have to remember what I was taught,* Stephen reminded himself, seating his lance. At the signal they charged. *He is protecting himself well,* Stephen thought as they galloped toward each other. *But there is still a small space.* The crash felt so violent that it threw him into the air, still holding his lance. Losing the splintered lance halfway down, he landed on top of it on his left side, so stunned that for a moment he could not move. Slowly rising to his knees, he stood to the sound of cheers that were not for him. Suddenly feeling weak and ashamed, Stephen trudged back to Sir Bart, his head sagging.

Helping him off with his helmet, Sir Bart clapped his shoulder. "You almost unhorsed him, lad! That was a good strike. He lost his lance also and had to hang on to make it to the end."

"What happened to me?" Stephen asked, still dazed.

"He had a good strike too. He just hit you harder; that is all."

I must make myself stronger, then, Stephen concluded. *Whatever it takes.* His head still hanging, his whole body aching from the fall, Stephen led Centaur back to the stables, where Jacky welcomed him.

"Not bad for yer first time, master," he said. "Ye bested last year's second-place finalis' in the firs' joust."

Offering a weak nod, Stephen did not want to be encouraged now; he just wanted to be alone. Going straight up to his tower room, he plopped on his mattress, not bothering to take off his armor, painfully replaying each second of the final joust in his head. He had disappointed himself, and not only himself. He could see his father shaking his head as if to say, "You were not prepared, son. You have shamed your family." Even his mother would be ashamed…what if she was there and saw it? No, she probably would have wanted to run to his side to see if he was hurt. Only Sir Bart seemed to not be disappointed, even though Stephen had brought dishonor on his green and gold. What was it going to take to be the best?

Having never seen a joust before, Marie sat with an air of importance in the guest box among the many well-dressed ladies, wives of knights who were competing, seated with their families. From her vantage point the whole tournament was a feast for the eyes and ears. Colorful banners rippled in the breeze. Onlookers shouted encouragement to the rider they preferred or had placed a wager on. The riders themselves were a spectacle, each with a different color surcoat, some with feathered crests on their helmets, their horses adorned with colorful caparisons[8]. She kept her eye on one in particular who was garbed in a green and gold surcoat, the colors of Sir Bart. He made it through to the finals, but alas, was ignominiously knocked flat on his back in the final joust.

Now it was her turn to take the stage. Though Marie had been enjoying the pageantry, she had been wondering about squires and knights. *Why would they do something like this that could knock the sense out of them?* Following Lady Anne's reasoning, they did not have that much sense to begin with. She had also been wondering how she would meet the one she was to marry. Maybe this was the way it worked. Perhaps the winner would notice her and things would progress from there.

All eyes followed the victor as he slowly rode to the box where Marie stood, then the eyes were on her, in her gown of the King's colors, with a garland in her hair. She did not feel nervous, as she feared, but instead was enveloped in a warm glow because she was representing the King. The squire stopped, facing Marie, and then removed his helmet, revealing a head of dark hair almost obscuring his deep brown eyes, balanced by a neat beard and mustache. An unexpected thrill coursed over her body as Marie stood before the handsome squire. Their eyes briefly met, whereupon he shook a lock of hair from his eyes and looked away with a nonchalant, almost condescending, expression. Did he find her that unattractive?

"He is supposed to acknowledge you with a nod of his head," Lady Anne whispered.

He did not.

Staring over Marie's head as if pained by the whole procedure, the squire slowly lowered his lance within Marie's reach. As she had been instructed, Marie dutifully lifted a small bag of coins attached to a ring and placed it carefully over the tip of his lance. He raised the lance, turned, and cantered away. Marie had not known what to expect but as she followed Lady Anne out of the box she felt somewhat deflated by the whole experience.

"I thought he would show some appreciation at receiving the prize," Marie said to Lady Anne while they walked through the booths back toward the castle. "And he acted as if he could not bear to look at me."

"Squires, knights … they are only interested in the combat. Winning the joust was his prize," Lady Anne replied. "He merely suffered the ceremony because it is required."

---

[8] A decorative cloth covering showing patterns or elements of the knight's coat of arms in the knight's colors

Though she had enjoyed the spectacle of the joust and was energized by the merriment of the tourney, Marie knew she still had much to learn about squires and knights. As she and Lady Anne approached the drawbridge to the castle, she heard a familiar voice behind them.

"Well done, milady!"

Marie turned to see her father in full armor, grinning at her. "Father!" she said, running to him. "You have come!"

Her composure as a "lady" crumbling, she enveloped him in the hug of an adoring child, holding him tightly, resting her head on his shoulder, unwilling to release him, feeling secure in the firm arms that enwrapped her.

"How you have grown, my daughter!" he said in a low voice, stroking her hair gently, as if to be careful not to displace the garland she wore. "You looked so beautiful in your gown and you played your part perfectly. Has she been a good pupil, Lady Anne?"

"Aside from her independent spirit, she has, Sir Guy. She has in fact excelled."

"Father, are Edouard and Mother well?" Marie asked, looking up at him, still unwilling to release her grasp. "Has anything changed at home?"

"They are well," Sir Guy replied, engaging Marie's eyes with his. "Edouard asks when you will return. I think he is wondering when he will have to share his room again. And how are you enjoying your stay at Bartscastle? What have you learned?"

The last question brought Marie's thoughts back to those times as a child at the table over supper with her family, when her father would ask the same question of her. She would be so eager each day to tell him something new from her world, even if it was just about how a butterfly seemed to sun its wings on a flower, or how her horse had pressed its nose against her cheek after she had brushed it. She had always felt cared about when she was a child. Then she had turned twelve and everything had changed. How she had missed that feeling thereafter! But now that she had been away over a year, she felt some surprise at realizing she had not been having the bittersweet longings lately at all—until her father's question brought them back.

She wasn't sure how to respond this time, knowing her father probably expected her to be as excited about things she had learned at Bartscastle as she used to be at home. Marie glanced at Lady Anne. She would be expecting the same. Trying to ignore the tug of fond memories by the stream at home, she straightened herself, dropped her hands to her side, lifted her chin, and assumed as dignified an expression as she could muster.

"Father, I am fourteen now," she said. "Lady Anne has taught me many things about being a lady. I have seen how she treats the less fortunate with dignity and respect, and have learned the importance of behaving as if I am representing the King. I can write and weave and play a recorder. I know how to handle money and bargain, and I am ready to—"

"Good, good," Sir Guy interrupted. "Your time has been well spent. Your mother will be pleased." He turned as if to leave.

Marie bit her lip, her last request having been interrupted—*I am ready to come home now.* Surely she had been at Bartscastle long enough. Surely her father had come to the tourney to take her home.

"How long can you stay, Father? Can we sup together?" Marie asked, looking at Lady Anne.

"The knights will be having supper with Sir Bart tonight to share news of the Kingdom," Sir Guy answered. "And I must return home in the morning. But I will return for you in a year. Mother will be pleased to hear you are well."

The encounter was all too brief for Marie, her father's presence having reawakened in her the joys of her childhood. Though she knew she was already a different person than the twelve-year-old who had departed Maison Bonfrere more than a year ago, she could not imagine what she needed another year to learn. And though she understood that it was probably important for the knights to sup together, she could not suppress the all too familiar, helpless sensation of being excluded again as her father turned his back to her and walked away, conversing with another knight.

Another year? How can I endure another year?

Chapter 11

DIVIDED LOYALTIES

ALMOST TWO YEARS had passed since Hugh's father was taken. Hugh had become hardened, like the objects he made of iron and steel, and though he dutifully plied his trade as the village blacksmith—furnishing the needs of the village, such as plowshares, horseshoes, and various utensils—he kept to himself, brooding over the injustice that had thrust him into his present position. The loss of both their fathers had strengthened his bond with Brian, even though Brian seemed to have taken the events somewhat fatalistically, in Hugh's opinion. Hugh's lonely nights in the cottage were relieved by frequent invitations to share supper with Brian and his family, and his loyalty to the King had remained, hanging by a filamentous strand, a testament to Charis's and Brian's simple trust in the King and his own resolution not to stain the steadfast belief of his parents in a benevolent King. But on the darkest nights the lurking specter of vengeance steadfastly stalked his thoughts.

His life, though not the one he expected, had assumed a certain rhythm now. With Charis's encouragement he continued to lead the meetings of the Servants. Though he read and tried to interpret the *Chronicle* to his listeners, his heart was not in the process, and it remained, for the most part, a stack of writings he did not fully comprehend. When he attempted to make applications to their present situation, he felt lost, as if the words he read were as dead as the distant King seemed to him. He had had no personal experience with the Prince as his father had, and though he had made that decision in the past to trust the

King, he seemed no closer to understanding the King than he had been then. Often it was Charis who asked a question that sparked discussion and insight into the readings. He was grateful for her contributions, though he could not grasp how something that was so clear to her could be so obscure to him.

Periodically, in his role as messenger, he would deliver parchments to Joseph, and maps and keys to new members of the Kingdom, always by night lest he be discovered. One night after he returned to Loynton from such a mission, he found Brian waiting for him in the smithy. He seemed excited.

"Hugh, my father has returned! He is anxious to see you and talk to us about the Dragon—and about your father."

Hugh had thought little of his father the past few months and had assumed that William was dead as well. It was a sad chapter of his life that he had resignedly closed. The news came as a thunderbolt, awakening emotions he thought he had buried with his determination to lower his head and push forward alone against the winds of fate that had left him bereft of family.

"That is wonderful news, Brian," he forced himself to say.

But as they walked through the darkness down to the tannery, Hugh's emotions began to stir, long-suppressed rage over his father's death rising again. With it came resentment—that Brian's father had returned and his had not. He bit hard on his lip and kept silent until they reached the tannery, which was empty except for William; Charis had taken the girls into the village to visit friends.

Brian stepped aside as a gaunt William greeted Hugh with a hug, holding him in his grip for an unbearably long time without speaking. Hugh allowed it until angry tears began to form. Attempting to deny them, he jerked away and sat on a stool in the central room of the cottage, his shoulders slumped.

"Tell me about my father," Hugh said, exhaling a sigh, wishing he did not have to hear confirmed what his imagination had invented, yet knowing that he must in order to close the door on it and move on.

"I only saw him once," William said, his eyes glistening. "He had been beaten almost beyond recognition. They lashed him daily. I could hear his groans from my cell. I flinched with every blow; it felt almost as if they were beating me. They demanded names of those in Loynton who belonged to the so-called subversive group. He would not tell. I believe that he eventually died from the lashings."

A vision appeared before Hugh of his father tied to a post, with weeping ribbons of crimson scarring his back, staggering from each blow. Though he dug his fists into his eyes, Hugh could not restrain his tears, both anger and sorrow wrestling to be expressed. William's hand on his shoulder broke through his tangle of emotions.

"He was like a brother to me, Hugh."

William's gesture could not stop Hugh's weeping. His body now shook with great moans as the wound once nearly healed was torn open again.

"I will miss him terribly," William said, his own voice choking. "But he was loyal to the King."

Lifting his tunic to blot his eyes, Hugh pushed William's hand away. He did not want sympathy; the time for that had passed. He wanted vengeance.

"Who did it?" Hugh said. "I will see him dead!"

"I do not know the names of anyone," replied William. "There did seem to be a knight in charge of his torture. They called him 'the Rat.' But you could never get close enough to harm him; the castle is too well defended. And, besides, what happens to him is not your decision anyway. It is the King's, is it not?"

"Do not tell me what my decision is!" Hugh shouted, standing abruptly and stalking away from William to a corner of the cottage.

The King had already had his chance. In Hugh's mind, if he was ever given the opportunity to right this wrong, he would take it. He stood there in silence, digging his nails into the wooden corner post, pressing his head into the splinters, attempting to restrain himself from destroying something. Finally the internal storm began to dissipate.

Hugh changed the subject: "And you? How did you escape the same fate?"

"Your father was an example for all of us," William said. "Although they lashed me a few times as well, I think they decided that if he would not tell, neither would I. And I am not sure they thought I was a member of the group, since I told them I was only a villager accompanying your mother and they could not find the mark on me. At the time they seemed to be in need of workers, so I became one of their slave laborers."

Hugh said nothing, so William continued, "It sounded from my cell as if the Dragon was making preparations for battle. Over the two years they would bring us prisoners out from time to time to do manual labor. We spread straw in the courtyard, helped to dig a deeper moat, and hauled stone to build a new barbican[9] for the castle. Many archers and men-at-arms practiced their skills in the courtyard, and they were constructing great engines of war as if preparing to lay siege to the King's castles. They must have decided they would need all their subjects, even their prisoners, working for them to prepare for the next battle.

[9] A gate tower to protect the drawbridge.

"But then the work parties became less frequent, and one day they marched all of the prisoners out into a field. There seemed to be no work for us to do. I sensed what was going to happen when I saw a group of archers form a line. We were going to be their target practice. Someone shouted, 'Run!' and the arrows began to fly. I knew we could not outrun the arrows, so when the man next to me was hit, I fell beneath him as he fell and lay still. I could hear the archers laughing, calling us 'vermin.' Finally I heard no sounds but the groans of the dying. Having had their fun, the soldiers did not bother to verify that all of us were dead. I lay still until nightfall, when I struggled free of the body lying on top of me and began to make my way back, avoiding the roads."

Hugh's anger surged anew, imagining the agony and terror that William and the others must have experienced with the archers. He looked up at William, who seemed so emaciated that he could hardly stand.

"That is what is wrong with our King!" Hugh shouted, resentment mixed now with compassion for the man who had been like an uncle to him. "Where was he? Why did he allow this? Someone must pay!"

"There were times when I despaired of life," William said, "but I hung on, hoping someday to see you and my family again. I believe the Dragon is nearly ready to march to battle and he decided we were extra mouths to feed, so we were to be eliminated."

Brian spoke up. "It makes sense. The bailiff was here today to tell us that the hearth tax has been doubled throughout the fief, no doubt to help Sir Bailys buy more soldiers and equip them. Perhaps the Dragon will call Sir Bailys to fight alongside him."

"The Dragon must be raising money to equip his army and buy more soldiers as well," William said.

Though he truly was pleased that William had returned, in part because it would relieve him of the task of leading the Servants, Hugh's thoughts were quickly drawn to the Dragon. Would he really attack the King himself? On further reflection it made sense to him as well. The King certainly had not shown his power anywhere near Loynton. His son, the Prince, was dead, and the King had apparently lost control. Perhaps he was so weak he could no longer resist the Dragon.

"I have tried my best to think of the King as someone great and powerful," Hugh said aloud to no one in particular, now pacing the room. "But every time he has had a chance to prove himself to me, he has not. Does anyone believe the King can defeat the Dragon? It sounds as if the Dragon can take anything he wishes, including all that belongs to the King."

"I do not know," William answered. "I am sure that in his heart, the Dragon is always at war with the King ... but some knights in the land are still loyal to the King. Perhaps the Dragon is merely going to enlarge his domain by taking their fiefs rather than attack the King himself."

Hugh kicked the table, and then almost shouted, "That is exactly what I mean! Why would the King permit that? It just encourages the Dragon to take more!"

Again Hugh sat, hands on knees, breathing heavily, attempting to collect his thoughts. What did all this mean for him? Should he just abandon his smithy, seek out the nearest knight of the King, and join him? At least he would feel that he was doing something for his father. What if he stayed? If the Dragon were equipping an army, he would require Sir Bailys to furnish his quota of soldiers. The need for armor and weapons would be distributed among the blacksmiths, and he would perhaps be paid more for fashioning them. On the other hand a levy of soldiers could be placed upon the village, and he could be forced to fight with the knight against the King.

"On the whole this is not good news," Hugh said finally. "Although the King has greatly disappointed me, he is still my King, and I cannot fight against my King on the side of him who is responsible for my father's death."

Without another word Hugh stamped out of the cottage and stumbled through the darkness back to the smithy, his mind awhirl with emotions—anger at the Dragon and all who followed him, anger at the King for allowing the Dragon to flourish, fear that perhaps the King was not powerful enough or did not have the will to stop the Dragon, and anxiety that his loyalty might waver if he were called upon to fight the King—or die for the King—who had done nothing for him.

He knew he had caused an ugly scene in William's house, and that he and Brian were too polite to confront him about it. He regretted pushing William away from him—William, who loved him like he loved his own son. Hugh hated the tidal ferocity of his emotions. He never knew what would trigger them, and he could not control them when they erupted. By the time he reached the smithy, the dark cloud had lifted, but he could still feel the anger seething beneath the surface.

A few weeks later their suspicions were confirmed. The bailiff rode from house to house, informing villagers that Sir Bailys had placed a levy of ten archers and ten spearmen on the village for an eventual campaign. Those willing to volunteer were to assemble in the village square in two days' time, the bailiff to select ten of each to form his company.

The next evening at the smithy, the tax and levy were the only subjects of conversation in the meeting of the Servants.

"We are already taxed enough!" the farmer said. "We can scarcely feed our children."

Since he was one of the founders, William, though still weakened, had resumed leadership of the Servants, much to Hugh's relief.

"If none of us appears in the town square," William said, "it may arouse suspicion, especially if all able-bodied men do not report, as the bailiff expects. Besides, the words of the Prince tell us that we are to be subject to our authorities."

"But not if it means taking up arms against our King!" Thomas said.

"No, not if it means fighting the King," William said. "There must be a way out if we are forced to go with Sir Bailys."

"I have a way," said a voice from the shadows

"Gerald Stabler, speak up," Hugh said. "William has not met you."

"It is only for your ears," Gerald answered, standing and leaning to whisper to William.

"I believe that is a possible solution, Gerald," William replied, "if you can do it successfully. So, is it agreed that we will all report tomorrow? I, for one, will volunteer, as I have a fine longbow crafted by Thomas."

"As will I," Thomas added, "though I will not fight the King."

"I will bring my sword and bow—but I may use them on Sir Bailys," Hugh said sourly, wondering why Gerald's plan was a secret.

"And I will bring my bow," Brian said.

The next day the square was crowded with nearly fifty villagers, mostly farmers, mixed with a few tradesmen. The bailiff looked pleased.

"Men of Loynton!" he began. "You have answered your call of duty. We have much to do. Hugh, you will be tasked with arms and armor; William and Brian, you will use some of your hides to make leather jerkins for the archers; Thomas, you will make longbows of yew for the archers and spear shafts for the spearmen. In three days' time we will have a contest to select the best archers."

"My son and I have bows already. We will volunteer," William said.

"Praiseworthy," the bailiff replied. "Nevertheless Sir Bailys desires to have the best. There will still be a competition."

"We *are* the best," Brian said. "And we will prove it!"

On the appointed day five targets were set up in a field on the outskirts of the village. Because it had rained the night before, straw was scattered over the area where the contestants would stand to cover the mud and give better footing. Groups of five would shoot a pattern of five arrows at fifty paces and again at one hundred paces. Most villagers possessed bows for hunting, and some of the older farmers had even been in battle, but few had one of Thomas's longbows that, unbent, stood the height of a man.

The bailiff said, "It is well known that Thomas's bows shoot farther and with more force than other bows. Therefore each man may use one of Thomas's bows for his shot."

"Well, that evens the competition," Hugh whispered to Thomas.

"No, it does not!" Thomas said. "They will not be able to control it without practice."

"Any man who wishes to use the longbow may take as many practice shots as he wishes before competing," the bailiff added.

"And what say you now?" Hugh asked, giving Thomas a nudge.

"We'll see."

The first group of five included William and Brian. Both placed all five arrows in the first target. At one hundred paces both placed four arrows, the best of their group. Thomas was in the next group, placing five arrows in each target. A farmer's son placed four. Hugh was in the fifth group. He repeated Thomas's feat. By the end of the competition, the ten best had placed four or five arrows in each target. William, Brian, Thomas, and Hugh were all chosen as members of the company.

"See? I told you it would be easy," Thomas said to Hugh as they returned to their homes.

"I just hope William is right that we will not have to use our bows against the King's men," Hugh replied.

Hugh soon got caught up in the preparation for battle, with orders from Sir Bailys for swords, spearheads, and armor. He realized that he would need an apprentice. Sir Bailys consented that he could train one of the farm youth. Hugh asked George, one of the field laborers in the Servants, if he would make himself available, and then put him to work making small items for the village while Hugh worked on the implements of war. William and Brian stayed busy making leather jerkins, and Thomas crafted longbows for the other archers who would make up the ten, as well as ten spear shafts for Hugh's spearheads. It was backbreaking work, but they were well paid for a change.

By the end of the winter months, all bows and a few jerkins had been made. Hugh, on the other hand, had been able to make only one mail shirt for Sir Bailys's soldiers, as well as a few swords. The archery company practiced daily when the weather permitted. The six others who had never drawn a longbow were progressing. Already they had grown strong enough to perform a full draw because of their work in the fields, but their accuracy was not as good as it had been in the competition with their own bows.

Throughout, the Servants continued to meet. Brian was excited as they began one of their meetings.

"I was talking to John, one of the farmers' sons in our company. He asked whom we were to fight. I told him I thought it was to be the King's men. He seemed to be very disturbed when I said this, saying he thought it wrong to fight against the King. When I said that there were others who believed the same, he became very interested and began asking questions. I told him about the true Kingdom. He says he wants to become one of us!"

"Wonderful!" William said. "We will bring a map tomorrow if you will make a key, Hugh."

"And I have similar news about the baker's wife," Charis added. "We will need one of each for her as well."

"I must wait for the confirmations," Hugh said, "but will proceed to make two keys, and I will need to make a visit to the scrivener soon as well."

White clouds of vapor issuing from him and his horse as they exhaled, Hugh rode into Grandvil the next week, following the well-worn path past Sir Bailys's manor house, the ruts now frozen. Passing the knight's house, Hugh noted something new—a banner hung above the door. He supposed it was the banner of the Dragon—a gold dragon rampant on a sea of red. Could it mean that the Dragon was coming to Grandvil? For what reason?

Entering the scrivener's shop in Grandvil, he found Joseph in his usual position, hunched over his table, this time with a young man opposite, armed with a quill also.

In no mood for niceties, Hugh plopped himself down on a stool and nudged a pile of blank parchments toward Joseph, ignoring the young man who now stared at him. "Joseph, I have need of a copy of the *Chronicle*," Hugh said. "I try to have at least one extra on hand at all times."

Joseph looked up with his familiar squint. "And good day to you as well." He sighed, then said, "It has been a busy time, preparing copies of the *Chronicle*. As you see, I have had to hire help. James here is a member of our local group of Servants. Most of the villages and some merchants in town have a copy of the *Chronicle* now. You will have our last copy."

Hugh gave James an absentminded acknowledgement. "Joseph, do you know why Sir Bailys is flying the banner of the Dragon?"

Joseph looked surprised and a little fearful. "Have you not heard? Sir Bailys is to have a visit from one of the Dragon's most infamous knights."

"Who? And why would he come here?"

"They call him 'the Rat' because he is both sneaky and vicious. He is one of the Dragon's top commanders and his chief weapon against subversion." Joseph then lowered his voice as he said, "The Dragon is apparently concerned about the spread of our secret groups loyal to the true King. The Rat is being sent to root them out. It is said that he has burned entire villages to the ground when they have resisted him. A rumor is spreading that he has targeted your village, ever since a peasant captured there resisted his attempts to gain information about the groups."

At the mention of the Rat, Hugh jumped to his feet, his entire body tense, his simmering anger beginning to boil. William was right. *This "Rat" killed my father!*

With a surge of rage he said aloud, "Then we must kill him!"

"What?" Joseph said. "Kill him? That is a certain way to bring retribution upon our town. We have even decided that our group will not meet while he is here."

Hugh shook his head. "Cowards! You are allowing fear to make you disloyal!" he huffed. "No! I and some of the Loynton archers will ambush him then. When is he to arrive?"

"In the spring," Joseph said. "But he will not come alone. He will undoubtedly be accompanied by an escort of armed horsemen, and Sir Bailys's soldiers will ride with him as well. Your attempt will be futile."

"It will be worth my life just to have a shot at him!" Hugh shouted.

Finally he noticed that both Joseph and James sat motionless, staring at him, their eyes wide and unblinking, their mouths agape.

"That does not sound like a member of the King's followers," Joseph said. "Does not the *Chronicle* have something to say about how to treat your enemies?"

Hugh slumped in his chair, letting his chin fall to his chest. Once again he had lost control. Though it did not change his conviction that the Rat must die, he felt shame at his outburst. He, who had once led the Loynton Servants, was not being a good example. Joseph was a new follower and already he was bringing up the *Chronicle*. Of course he was right.

"I apologize—to you, Joseph, and to you, James. It is not the way a follower of the King should behave," Hugh said. "But I cannot accept the prospect of going meekly into captivity, nor of seeing my village torched and my friends murdered! I must think of something."

"We have thought of finding a reason to be away from Grandvil," Joseph said.

Hugh thought on it, then replied, "That would arouse suspicion, and it would not spare our village."

There seemed to be no answer, so he bade farewell and departed, wrestling with conflicting thoughts all the way back to his smithy. As usual the King seemed to have no regard for him or for Loynton. And *Chronicle* or no *Chronicle*, in Hugh's estimation the fate of Loynton rested in his hands now. He resolved to bring up the impending visit at the next Servants meeting.

That night Gerald surprised everyone by bearing the most interesting news: "I have overheard Sir Bailys's men discussing the arrival of the Rat. They say that even Sir Bailys is afraid. He thinks the Dragon is sending the knight to discipline him for not stamping out the groups himself."

"Maybe that is all it is about, then," Charis said. "Why would he burn our village? We supply the food of the realm."

"Yes," the farmer said, "and we pay the taxes that build their castles and buy their horses and soldiers."

"Possibly, but I am not so sure," Hugh said. "It is said he has no regard for a peasant." He paused. Then, exhaling a heavy breath, he stood and faced everyone. "And it is he who killed my father! He must die!"

Silence descended as all eyes were fixed on Hugh, who stood with his muscles tensed, his teeth clenched, his face hot.

"Revenge is not the answer, Hugh," William finally said, "and you do not know that he personally killed your father." He stood to face Hugh, reaching out to place a hand on his shoulder. "Let us consider the *Chronicle*. What did the Prince do? He did not resist his enemies. I was with him. So was your father. What are the Prince's words? 'Love your enemy.'"

Hugh twisted out of William's grip, shoving his hand away. "Do not throw the *Chronicle* at me!" he shouted. "Our enemy does not love us. We cannot meekly allow ourselves to be exterminated like vermin. You yourself have witnessed their callous brutality, William." Hugh stared him down and shook his head.

"How can you accept this? It cannot be what the King wants. He wants us to grow his Kingdom, not go like lambs to slaughter."

"But, Hugh, it is *his* Kingdom," William said gently, "and he knows how he wants it to be grown. Surely he will provide an answer."

Though he felt no vindication, Hugh knew William was right, and the *Chronicle* was right. It was always right. But he did not want to hear what was right—he wanted justice, even if he had to administer it himself. He had nothing but disgust for everyone's fatalistic platitudes; this was a time for action. Every blow he and his family had taken had brought no response from the King. He wanted a King that would stand up for him, one who would fight for him. As far as he was concerned, all talk about the King was useless speculation.

Hugh had never sensed more clarity than he possessed right now about what should be done. But it would be up to him alone to devise a strategy to assassinate the Rat. He resolved to talk to the others privately, and so ended the meeting without further discussion.

Having thought through his plan since waking, Hugh found Thomas the next morning fashioning an axe handle.

"If the three of us each stood behind a separate window along the Rat's route into the village, we would have three, maybe more shots before we were discovered," Hugh said.

Thomas looked dubious. "That is not the way I wish to die for my King, and I am not sure Brian would agree either. You heard his father. You know that I have my doubts about the King too, but I do not think throwing our lives away furthers any plan, including whatever solution the King might have."

"Well, he hasn't told me his solution," Hugh retorted. "And he has done nothing to avenge my father!"

Thomas laughed. "And you are his trusted advisor, that he should tell you his plans? The *Chronicle* does not say anything about us attacking the Dragon and his knights by ourselves. It says that it is the King's prerogative. Vengeance belongs to him. Although, like you, I admit I just wish he would act on it."

Hugh shook his head. "I will do it alone, then!" he said, turning and stomping out.

But how could a solo assailant eliminate a great knight surrounded by bodyguards?

Chapter 12

OF DANCES AND SPIES

A WEEK AFTER MARIE'S father had departed for home, she still felt dispirited. She thought of her family suppers around the table, of her mother and father reading the *Chronicle* aloud to her and Edouard, of her mother encouraging her to read it on her own, though 'encourage' would not be the word she would have chosen at the time. What if she had listened more attentively or tried to read it herself instead of running out to her spot by the stream? Would she still be here now? Would her father have supported her against her mother? They were useless questions. She was condemned to Bartscastle for another year and nothing she could do would change it now.

Lady Anne sat with her after supper as she usually did, this time to introduce a new pursuit. "You have learned all of the business of managing a household. Now it is time to experience the pastimes of a noblewoman. You will be alone at times and you will enjoy yourself in activities such as reading and weaving, but sometimes you will be with other noblewomen. You can share various pastimes together with them, some even with your lord and husband. Come with me to the small table and take a seat."

On a table near the fireplace lay a stone slab engraved with lines to form squares, with rows of small stone figures facing each other. *A chess set,* Marie noted as she sat down, having seen one in her mother's sitting room.

Lady Anne sat opposite her and said, "Our men believe this is a game of combat, but it is really a game of strategy—and the mind—something we use more than they." An evanescent smile stole across Lady Anne's face; Marie could not restrain herself from smiling as well.

"All of the pieces are men, save one," Lady Anne said as she picked up the queen. "But the sole woman is the most powerful piece. The king is helpless without his queen and his army around him." She then began to explain the movements of the various pieces, finishing with, "Like the other pieces the queen has two functions—to defend her own king and to put the other king in danger."

Lady Anne rearranged the pieces to demonstrate the moves open to the queen. "But the queen must use her power carefully. Sometimes it is even necessary for her to sacrifice herself to save her king or to give her king's army an advantage. Likewise, when you play against your lord and husband, you may desire to sacrifice your queen and your advantage to allow him to win."

"Are you serious?" Marie recoiled as if affronted by the idea. "If I have the advantage, why would I?"

"Though it is a game to us, he sees it as a combat to win. If he is using his mind, he will recognize your sacrifice and cherish you all the more. It may be a better strategy to lose the game and gain his affection than to diminish his manhood by winning."

Marie thought on this for a moment. Men certainly seemed to be curious creatures. Why would one like her more when she showed weakness by sacrificing an advantage? Shouldn't he be more impressed if she showed strength?

She looked back at Lady Anne. "But it would be acceptable for me to win against you."

A startled expression fleeted across Lady Anne's face. "Well ... of course, if you are able."

"If you teach me well, I shall," Marie replied.

Within a few months Marie had gained her first victory—without sacrificing her queen. Lady Anne was quick to introduce a new pastime.

"Music is a delight in the home," Lady Anne said. "I will next teach you to play the harp and sing, for a wife who plays the harp and sings for her husband can soothe the savage heart within him and ensure peace in the home."

Marie again proved herself a rapid learner, finding that she enjoyed making music because it soothed her own heart as well, though she felt less enthusiastic about singing. After hearing Marie sing, Lady Anne never again mentioned it.

Intermingled with the pastimes Marie met with Owen for archery instruction. The first time together, Owen had given her a shortbow, allowing her to draw the bowstring and handle it until she became comfortable with it. It was somewhat heavier and harder to draw than the ladies' bow but she was able.

Then he showed her an arrow. "Before, you shot target arrows," he said, running his fingers along the sharpened tip. "This bodkin is a weapon of war. It can pierce mail and can take a life."

"Or save one," Marie said.

"Yes—if you are defending yourself. Once you have nocked your arrow, you must always have it pointed toward the ground unless you are facing a target. You may shoot now."

Marie let fly an arrow. It flew more swiftly than the target arrows, landing above the target, clacking off the stone wall of the castle. She adjusted her aim. After a few shots she placed one in the target.

"Good," Owen said. "We will do this daily until you can place five arrows consecutively in the target."

"In the *center* of the target," Marie said. "This is not a game for me."

"Of course, milady," Owen said with a bow of his head.

Soon enough Lady Anne announced a new project: "We are going to have a guest daily for a while. It is required that squires learn to dance and behave properly around women. Sir Bart's squire is to join us for this teaching."

Though Marie felt intrigued at the prospect of meeting the squire, whom she had seen from a distance at the joust, she was definitely not looking forward to doing it this way.

"I know nothing about dancing," she said. "I will be awkward and clumsy, and I will embarrass myself in the presence of the squire."

"Nor does the squire know anything about dance," Lady Anne replied. "You both are to learn. We begin tomorrow."

The next day Marie prepared herself by dressing in her King's colors gown, with gold ribbons in her cascading brown hair. She was sitting by the fireplace, struggling with one of her assignments—writing a poem—when she heard two knocks on the door. Lady Anne rustled to the door, admitting four people into the room. Marie quickly fluffed her hair and rose to meet them, recognizing one as Owen, her archery tutor. In addition she saw a woman, a man carrying a small drum, and a man carrying a recorder. Marie was puzzled. Which one was the squire? All of the men looked too old, much older than the squires at the joust.

Lady Anne began the introductions: "Marie, here is Owen, whom you know, and his wife, Mary, who will demonstrate the dance steps for you. Geoffrey and Colin are Sir Bart's musicians. They will play the music."

Marie curtseyed.

The musicians offered a greeting, then took their position by the fireplace.

"And the young man?" Owen asked.

Lady Anne pursed her lips and shook her head. "He is late. I hope he has been taught to read a sundial."

The musicians occupied themselves by playing some music to warm up. Soon Marie heard an urgent knock.

"The door is open," Lady Anne called above the music.

Through the doorway stumbled a breathless youth, his tousled dark hair askew, a sheen of sweat on his face, his lively dark brown eyes darting around the room at all the onlookers. Marie bit her lip to stifle a laugh. She had seen this face before—it belonged to the youth who served at her birthday suppers with Sir Bart and who practiced swordsmanship in the courtyard with other soldiers. The shadow of manhood spread over his chin and strong jaw, beneath his ruddy cheeks. Overall it was not an unpleasing sight, despite his boisterous entry.

"You are late, Stephen," Lady Anne said.

"Forgive me, milady. I-I forgot. I was—"

"And you are inappropriately dressed as well," Lady Anne added, gesturing toward his rough, sweat-soaked tunic.

An expression of embarrassment stole across his face. "I was practicing swordsmanship with Michael and the time eluded me. I thought I should come immediately rather than take the time to change."

"Mm, well, at least you *thought*," Lady Anne said. "There is not time now for you to change, but next time you will wear your best tunic."

Still catching his breath, he shifted his feet and nodded. "Yes. Yes, milady, I will."

Lady Anne turned to Marie and said, "Marie, this is Squire Stephen. You will address him as 'sir' during the lesson." She turned back to Stephen. "And this is Lady Marie. You will address her as 'milady.'"

Marie curtseyed and said, "Sir."

Stephen in turn bowed and replied, "Milady."

Lady Anne nodded approval, then said, "Now, Owen and Lady Mary will demonstrate the first dance. Observe them closely."

Marie watched as Owen extended his left arm and Lady Mary placed her right arm on top of his forearm, her hand on the back of his. When the music began, they turned to each other and nodded a greeting, after which each took a step forward, bringing the second foot slowly forward beside the first, repeating it three times, then rose on their toes. Afterward they stopped and gave a nod of acknowledgment to each other. The dance continued in this fashion until they had completed a circle, whereupon Owen grasped Lady Mary's hand and raised it, allowing her to make a complete turn. They then faced each other and Owen bowed while Lady Mary curtseyed.

This doesn't look too difficult. Marie was grateful that she had asked Lady Anne to show her some of the steps the night before. She had practiced balancing on tiptoe until she was steady.

"Now, Stephen and Marie, you will follow," Lady Anne said.

When Marie lay her arm on Stephen's outstretched arm, her hand on the back of his, it seemed as if she had rested her arm on the bough of a tree, so firm did the arm beneath hers feel. A whiff of body sweat assaulted Marie's nose, but oddly she did not find it entirely offensive, intrigued as she was by the unassuming nature of this future knight. The music began and they lurched forward, Marie almost stumbling to keep up.

"No, Stephen!" Lady Anne said. "Your lady does not have the legs of a man. Your steps must be small. Now begin again."

The next few steps went well until they were to rise on their toes. Marie went up slowly, as she had practiced. Suddenly she was pulled off balance as Stephen careened to the side.

"I am sorry," he mumbled. "I have never had to stand on my toes before."

"Perhaps you should stop and practice, then," Lady Anne said.

Marie stepped aside and watched with amusement as Stephen, an expression of excruciating self-conscious misery on his face, attempted to rise and balance on his toes several times, teetering to one side or the other, until he was able to maintain his balance at least once.

Lady Anne said, "Now try it with Lady Marie."

The music began again. Around the circle they went, sometimes taking steps together, sometimes not, always rising on their toes at different times, Marie having to grab Stephen's arm occasionally for balance, Stephen regarding his feet intensely as if trying to control with his eyes two objects not connected to him.

"Stop!" Lady Anne said with a huff. "Stephen, raise your arm and allow her to turn."

Almost as an afterthought, Stephen's arm flew up, flinging Marie's hand into her face.

Lady Anne rolled her eyes and snapped, "You must grasp her hand first! Now ... bow and curtsey."

Their eyes met for the first time, unexpected compassion rising in Marie as she peered into eyes that seemed to her as those of a frightened animal.

"We are done for the day," Lady Anne said.

Stephen lowered his head and bolted for the door, disappearing in a flash. Marie continued to rub her nose, which was still smarting from its violent collision with her hand.

With a cluck of her tongue, Lady Anne said, "I have not seen a squire yet for whom this was not the worst aspect and least enjoyed of their training."

The next two weeks bore this out. Stephen arrived on time and appropriately dressed, but went through the motions dutifully, acting as if he could hardly wait for his agony to cease. Even Marie was glad for it to end, sorry as she was for being a part of Stephen's misery.

Still stung by his ignominious defeat in the joust, Stephen threw himself almost angrily into his training with Michael for the rest of the summer and into fall. He no longer resented Michael's no-nonsense approach, actively seeking his criticism. By autumn's end he had mastered the battle-axe and Michael had begun to work with him on group combat. First Michael brought one of his men-at-arms to work with one-on-two combat, and then another joined in for two-on-two combat. Stephen learned to always be aware where his companion's back was, and to position himself to defend it.

He mastered the archery shoot at seventy-five paces and asked Michael to set it up at a hundred paces. At the stone pile he practiced the two-arm outstretched carry and then the one-armed outstretched carry. He increased his run to twice around the castle. During the winter he continued to do sword, mace, and axe work with Michael, going out every day, freezing or not, snowing or not, to lift and carry the stones.

Winter melted into spring, Stephen still supping with Sir Bart, their conversations centering on the Kingdom and the looming conflict. He knew by now all the stories about the Prince and the King and the Knights of the Chalice. Through them he had learned the meaning of loyalty, courage, obedience, and sacrifice. He had finished reading *A Chronicle of the Prince*, which he knew had been written by one of the eleven, and was being circulated throughout the Kingdom. He had learned music, courtly dance, and proper behavior around women. Sir Bart had taught him about justice and mercy for the weak and benevolence to the poor.

Now Sir Bart was teaching him how to play chess. "As a knight you will lead men in battle," Sir Bart told Stephen. "You must know their strengths and weaknesses, and how to employ them effectively. Just as each of these pieces has strengths and weaknesses and you must develop a mental strategy to use them together to win, so you must have a mental strategy to lead your men to victory. You can fight a good battle with strong, brave men, but you must have mental superiority and know how to use them effectively to win a victory."

Nodding, Stephen thought back to the way Michael had won the sword competition in the tourney the previous summer—not with physical power, but with mental superiority.

His seventeenth birthday approaching, Stephen found himself caught up in preparations for imminent battle. Grain was being brought into the castle to be stored in case of a siege. A new well was being dug. Michael was training new men-at-arms. Sir Bart had increased their number to thirty and had named Michael, his sergeant-at-arms, their commander. Moreover Stephen was in charge of his own training now. Sometimes he convinced Sir Bart to participate in the group combat so that he could see how Sir Bart fought and understand his moves. He lengthened his archery practice to one hundred twenty-five paces. He carried two stones at a time, one in each outstretched hand. He circled the castle three times.

During one of these circuits, Stephen was surprised to come across a peasant between the north wall and the forest. He had never seen a peasant on this side of the castle before. The man was walking parallel to the wall and looking up at it, his mouth moving as if he were counting.

Curious, Stephen stopped to address him. "Ho, man! Are you lost?"

The peasant looked surprised. "Er, yes, maybe so."

"Where do you live? In the town?"

"Um, yes."

"Well, come with me. I'll point you in the right direction."

"Oh, no," said the peasant. "I know the way."

Stephen studied the peasant, whose eyes now darted back and forth as he began to walk away.

"You weren't really lost, were you?" Stephen asked, his eyes narrowing.

"N-No," the peasant said, walking faster. "I was just out … for a walk."

Moving toward the man, Stephen said, "Peasants do not have time for walks. You were spying, weren't you?"

At that the peasant took off. Stephen was on him in an instant, bringing him to the ground with a thud. "You will answer to Sir Bart for this treason!"

"Please, sir, I just did as I was asked," the cowed peasant answered. "A man paid me to measure the length and height of the walls."

"Where is this man?" Stephen said.

"He was in the alehouse next to the inn last night."

"You will take me to him—now. It is almost dusk."

The peasant gave a weak nod. "And then you will let me go?"

"Yes, provided he is the man about whom you speak."

They walked together into Bartstown, Stephen keeping his hand on the peasant's collar so that he would not bolt.

When they reached the alehouse, Stephen gave the peasant a shove. "You go in first. I will stay in the doorway. If you see him, go to him."

"But I do not have the information he wants," the peasant said.

"I will take care of that," Stephen answered. "Go. Now!"

The peasant walked in, looked around, and vanished out of sight. Stephen followed, noting the peasant was heading to a corner table, where a single cloaked figure sat, drinking a tankard of ale.

As the peasant approached, Stephen joined them and said, "I understand from this man that you want the dimensions of the castle. I know the castle well. I can give you more than that."

The stranger eyed him. "And who are you?"

"I am the forest warden," Stephen said. "I make a circuit of the castle every day." *That is partially truthful.* "I encountered this man while near the forest. He told me of your need."

"And why should I trust you?"

"The lord of the castle does not pay me en—"

"He will not be lord much longer," the stranger growled.

"How do you know this?" Stephen inquired.

"A force is advancing toward his castle this very hour. They are waiting only for my information."

"How many are they?"

"At least fifty horse and foot. They will be joined by others."

"Fifty men cannot take a castle like Sir Bart's," Stephen answered.

The stranger's eyes narrowed. "There are ways. Now, if you could tell us how to pass through the gate without the drawbridge being lifted, there'd be some money in that."

"I will return tomorrow with information about the gate guard," Stephen said.

"And I will be in the same place," the stranger responded.

Stephen hurried out of the tavern, mindful that he had missed supper with Sir Bart, but he felt that the information he had obtained would excuse him. When he arrived in the great hall, Sir Bart still sat at the head of his table, conferring with Michael, the food having been cleared.

"Sire, I have important news!" Stephen said as he ran to Sir Bart's side.

Sir Bart raised his hand to silence him, continuing to talk to Michael. "And they were sure he was sent by our enemy?" Sir Bart asked.

"Who else would want to know such information about the castle?" Michael asked.

"How long will he be staying?"

"Difficult to know. During the day he wanders around the town talking to people. At night he sits in the alehouse. He appears unafraid of being discovered. I have detailed one of my men to dress as a peasant and lurk around the alehouse to see where he goes."

"Good. Keep me informed."

"Milord!" Stephen said. "I can tell you more!"

"How is that? You are even late for supper," the knight said.

"I was at the alehouse, meeting with the very man of whom you speak," Stephen said. Then he told Sir Bart the details of the meeting and of his promise to go back. "You should send several soldiers with me to capture him," Stephen concluded.

"Yes," Sir Bart replied. "He must not be allowed to escape with the information. And, Michael, you must send out scouts to find the force of which he spoke."

"At once, sire," Michael answered, taking his leave.

Sir Bart turned to Stephen. "So you actually went into town to meet this man? That was bold. He was probably armed. Had he found you out, it could have gone badly for you."

"I am sorry, milord," Stephen replied. "My only concern was the safety of your castle."

"Yes, and well done. As the enemy grows stronger, we must be watchful."

The next day Stephen did his usual training. After his run he reported to Michael in the courtyard after strapping on his belt, patting his dagger to be sure it was reachable in case there was trouble. Two other men were there, dressed in cloaks to cover their swords.

"They will follow you at a distance and wait outside the alehouse," Michael said. "If the person in question is there, come to the door and signal. They will run in and apprehend him."

Stephen approached the alehouse cautiously, aware that there could be a fight this time. He opened the door with a trembling hand, his heartbeat accelerating, drumming in his ears. Entering the alehouse, he looked to the corner table, then around the room. The stranger was not there. Walking to the rough-hewn counter, Stephen caught the eye of the alehouse owner, describing the stranger to him.

"Yes, I remember him," the owner said. "He paid his stay at the inn and his bill here, and departed this morning."

"Where to?" Stephen asked, relieved that there would be no fight.

"He wasn't saying."

Disappointed, Stephen left the inn and walked back to the castle with the soldiers. At supper he told Sir Bart what had happened.

"It does not surprise me," Sir Bart replied. "Our enemy is sly and deceptive. Michael's scouts will no doubt bring some information soon. Now, how about a game of chess?"

Chess? Now? When our castle is in danger? Stephen kept his thoughts to himself as he obediently took a seat and Sir Bart pulled a chessboard toward them. Still flushed with adrenaline from the near encounter with the enemy spy, Stephen fidgeted with a sense of urgency that Sir Bart apparently did not share.

Sir Bart advanced a pawn. "Your move, son."

Stephen went through the motions of moving his pieces, having no particular strategy until Sir Bart spoke again.

"See, I have castled. Do you understand my reason for making this move?"

Stephen remembered that it was a good move to make, but the reason escaped him, occupied as his thoughts were with the present danger to Bartscastle. Sir Bart's nonchalance seemed troubling. Was he losing his ability to see and react to real threats?

"Um, no," Stephen mumbled.

"By putting my pieces in this position, I am protecting my king with the castle and at the same time freeing my castle to attack or defend," Sir Bart said.

The realization hit Stephen like a bolt of lightning: *That is it! He is counting on Bartscastle to protect him! But can it? Will it?*

Chapter 13

FOOD FOR THOUGHT

A S DAYS PASSED with no more reports of spies nor of enemy forces descending upon Bartscastle, Stephen concluded that Sir Bart must have been right. There was no need to worry. Sir Bart had always assured him that the castle had never fallen to the enemy and never would. He would have to trust the old man at his word. It was not Stephen's responsibility anyway.

Stephen observed his seventeenth birthday soon thereafter. Sir Bart arranged a multicourse feast in recognition of his completing his formal training, presenting him with a helmet, a full suit of plate armor, and a battle-axe. The knight's generosity overwhelmed Stephen.

"I am most unworthy of such gifts," he said, imagining the impressive appearance he would present in his shining armor astride Centaur.

"Worthiness has nothing to do with it," Sir Bart answered. "You must be properly equipped to fight alongside me. I have been equipping your mind in our conversations, but you also must be well protected in combat. You have yet to be tested. If such an occasion arises, and you master it, the King may wish to bestow knighthood upon you."

Knighthood. That had always been the goal, though Stephen was still uncertain what he had to do in order to receive the coveted recommendation. He decided now was an opportune time to bring up an unfinished conversation.

"Sire, when I first became your squire, you told me about the Kingdom Rules. I was not sure at the time that I could follow them. I still am not sure. What test must I pass for the King to confer knighthood?"

"A worthy question," Sir Bart replied. "Which rule can you not follow?"

"I believe that he is the true King, but I still am not certain what it means to love him, nor can I love everyone. I do not love the Dragon, who is my King's enemy."

Sir Bart leaned forward, his eyes studying Stephen's. "Yes, those are among the most difficult rules to keep, even to understand. Perhaps it is time to tell you what they mean to me." He drew a deep breath. "As for loving," he began, "I believe that to love someone, anyone, is to desire what is best for them and to commit oneself to achieving that best even to the point of self-sacrifice. You must first understand what this means regarding the King."

"That is it," Stephen was quick to say. "I am not sure I understand."

"Three years ago, at this table, I told you that to understand loving the King, you must first understand what it means that the King loves you," Sir Bart said. "So let us start with that. The King has a plan for his Kingdom that is beyond our understanding, but since he loves us, he desires that we trust him to seek the best for us and trust that he will do all that we allow him to do in order to bring it about."

"So his love for me means he is seeking the best for me?" Stephen said.

"Yes. The King desires that both your heart and your mind be ruled by him – that is the best for you. But there is a problem. Since the Great Rebellion long ago when the Dragon and his followers were cast out of the King's castle, there has been a struggle between the King and the Dragon for the hearts and minds of his subjects."

"You have told me that," Stephen answered, "but what does that have to do with—"

"Allow me to finish. Our natural inclination, instead of seeking to follow the King's desires for our lives, is to follow our own desires, which is the way of the Dragon, and which earned us a death sentence from the King because it breaks his Kingdom Rules, as I have told you before. Part of the King's plan, as I have also told you, is to link hearts back together in his Kingdom."

Once again, Stephen felt himself losing his grasp on this train of thought, as if the horse he was trying to mount was galloping away with him hanging onto its mane, struggling to swing his body into the saddle.

Nonetheless Sir Bart forged ahead with his explanation. "So the King gave us an example. Knowing that our hearts would not seek what was best for us, but steadfast in his love for us, he sent the Prince from his castle to show us the life he desired of us and to die the death that we all deserved for failing to observe his rules and put his desires first."

"Wait," Stephen interrupted. "You are saying that the King *wanted* his son to die?"

"Most certainly," Sir Bart answered, "because it was his son's self-sacrifice that removed our death penalty, which satisfied the King's justice, and made it possible for him to mercifully accept us back so that our hearts could be recaptured for his Kingdom. As I told you then, this is what it means that the King loves you."

Stephen shook his head in disbelief. "What kind of king would allow his own son to be sacrificed because I broke his rules?"

"A great one," the knight said, barely above a whisper.

Stephen became silent, the ramifications of Sir Bart's words churning in his mind. "So the King's love means he allowed his own son to endure the death I deserve so that he could give me what is best for me?"

"Exactly," Sir Bart replied. "And that brings us to the next part of the rules—loving the King, seeking what is best for him. I believe, and the *Chronicle* affirms, that the best for the King—what the King desires—is that we trust, honor, and obey him, which includes accepting his love and seeking what he desires for us. Unfortunately our hearts, influenced by the ways of the Dragon, seek instead what *we* think is best for us. For example, you want to become a knight, do you not?"

"More than anything, sire," Stephen said. In fact he was trying his hardest to figure out what more he needed to accomplish to achieve that goal.

Sir Bart fixed unblinking eyes on Stephen. "You cannot truly love your King if you love yourself above him. Can you see that if you place the goal of knighthood above trusting and honoring the King and seeking what he desires, you are following the ways of the Dragon?"

Stephen's skin began to prickle, heat spreading over his body like a wave as he squirmed in his chair. That was exactly what he was doing! Ever since that day in the chapel three years ago when he became a squire, all his thoughts, dreams, and efforts had been directed to becoming a knight. He had been viewing all that Sir Bart had said about the King merely as interesting information for a knight to know, but not vital to becoming a knight. He was following the ways of the Dragon!

Stephen sat in stunned silence, stung with reproach and shame, unable to muster a reply to Sir Bart's question. He dared not. He would be exposed as a fraud. After three years of training, it would end now with his admission that he had not truly been seeking the King's desires for him.

After a moment of watching Stephen struggle with his realization, Sir Bart continued, "What is best for you is to seek what is best for the King—not only to honor, obey, and trust him, but to understand what he desires for you and others, and to do it."

"Then, it has nothing to do with knighthood and all you have been teaching me?" Stephen asked, furrowing his brow.

"Not quite." Sir Bart smiled. "A knight is a leader, one who has responsibility for others. I have been teaching you how to exercise that responsibility. Whether or not you become a knight depends on the King, and whether you believe what I have told you about him and decide to trust him and the spirit of his son, the Prince, to guide you in seeking his way rather than the way of the Dragon."

Stephen shook his head again as if attempting to fling the fog of bafflement from his brain. "It is too confusing for me," he said, then exhaled. "Why does understanding this have to be so difficult?"

"The deep truths of the Kingdom are not apprehended by those who do not seek them diligently," Sir Bart replied. "One does not cast pearls before swine."

Running his fingers through his hair, Stephen tilted his head back, closed his eyes, and took a deep breath. "Start again. I want to understand it. I need to. Help me understand."

"We instinctively seek what we think is best for us," Sir Bart repeated. "The rule says that we should put the King in that place instead of ourselves."

"So the rule means that we should desire what the King desires, being willing to sacrifice everything for it … even if it costs us our life?"

"Yes, that is the essence of love, and the mark of a heart captured for the King."

Stephen paused to reflect. "And it is the same with other people—that we should desire what is best for them—I mean, what the King desires for them?"

"Yes. To love them as we love the King is to desire the King's best for them, not what we or they think is best. What is best for them is what the King desires for them."

"And even if it requires sacrifice for them?"

Sir Bart nodded. "Indeed, because what did the King's love for us require?"

Stephen pictured the King in his mind, as best he could, speaking to the Prince as a father to a son, the Prince bowing and nodding, then turning to leave, knowing he was being sent a on mission that would end in his death. The whole scene seemed improbable, almost unbelievable, yet Stephen understood somehow that it was an event fueled by love—the love of the King for his people, the love of a son for his father, a kind of love about which he knew nothing.

"But what about our enemies, like the Dragon?" Stephen asked. "Even the King must be against his enemy."

"The Dragon has made himself an enemy of the King in the same way we have—by failing to honor and obey him," Sir Bart said. "If we love our enemies as we love the King, we will desire for them what he desires for them. That is how you can love your enemy, even the Dragon."

Stephen knew one thing now—he did not truly know the King. Even a lifetime might not be enough to comprehend the full significance of what he had just heard. He wanted to love his King, but he did not understand how he could love someone like the Dragon, who seemed maleficent toward all who belonged to the King, and intent on taking the King's lands.

As Stephen attempted to make sense of the jumble of thoughts in his mind, a new question posed itself: "If I am supposed to love the Dragon—who plots to kill and steal what is not his—why then am I being trained to fight him?"

"Well considered," Sir Bart answered. "As knights, all that we think we possess—our castles, our fiefs, and the people in them—has been given us by the King. We in turn must answer to him for how we manage them. If the King's lands or people are attacked, our duty is to defend them, because though we oversee them, they belong to the King. It does not change what the King desires for the Dragon or how we should view him."

"Whew!" Stephen exhaled. "You have rightfully called these 'deep truths.' I think they may be *too* deep for me."

"And that is not all. Listen carefully," Sir Bart said quietly, "Here is the deepest truth, and few ever understand it. You can do none of what I have told you on your own, as I believe you have realized. The true mystery is that the ability to follow the Kingdom Rules, to love the King and others, is given only to one who is guided by the spirit of the Prince."

Stephen's head spun. He sensed he had almost grasped something of immense importance. He imagined he had just been shown a jewel of rare value and exquisite artistry that he could not hold in his hand and possess, or even fully examine all at once to understand it in the fullness of its beauty. Yet perhaps he could come to appreciate it over time, as light shone on it in different ways, causing individual facets to sparkle and reveal its secrets, one facet at a time.

After supper Stephen climbed to his tower room with more questions than answers swirling in his mind. He thought he understood what it meant that the King loved him, but why? What kind of love would prompt him to do what he did? He thought he had heard correctly what it meant to love the King, and he wanted to. But how could he put the King's desires above his? How could he even know them?

As summer and her fifteenth birthday approached, Marie began to take stock of her time at Bartscastle, knowing that it would soon be time to return home. She realized she was a different person now, no longer the carefree girl who daydreamed by the stream, but a young lady confident in her abilities and able to take care of herself. She no longer even thought of her place by the stream at home, or her imaginary magical world, her eyes having been opened to a much larger and complex world that she was eager to learn to negotiate successfully.

Although she partially understood what it meant to be wife to a knight, she still could not accept the idea of marrying someone selected by her father, someone she had no chance to even become acquainted with beforehand. Then again, if he loved her and treated her with respect, that would make all the difference. She caught herself, picturing her conversation with her father on the way to Bartscastle two years before, and the embarrassment she had experienced when her father had chided her for asking questions about love. *"If"* he loves me? *What am I thinking? What do I know about love?*

Marie had never mentioned to Lady Anne her struggle with understanding love. It was only a matter of time before the subject came up one evening over dinner.

"Lady Anne, I know you are educating me to be a wife, but my father will choose whom I marry. What about love? Isn't that part of it?"

Unaccountably, Lady Anne appeared unprepared for the question, remaining quiet for awhile as if touched in a way she had not expected. Finally she spoke.

"I loved once," she said. Her voice was scarcely audible, her eyes seemingly focused on something unseen.

"You did?" Marie sat in stunned silence at the revelation. Never had she had such a thought about Lady Anne.

"Yes," Lady Anne continued. "We were both so young. Our lives lay before us, full of promise. He was a Knight of the Chalice, a companion to my brother. He was the first of them to fall to the Dragon."

Looking into Lady Anne's glistening eyes, Marie felt she was peering into a deep well of sadness, a sadness that still remained over a loss that could never be replaced, a sadness that could be hidden but not erased. "I am sorry, milady. I did not mean to cause you grief," she said.

"No, don't be," Lady Anne replied in a soft voice. "I want to talk about it. You need to know." She breathed deeply and then continued in a wistful tone. "Though our time together was short, our love burned like the brightest flame—a flame that even death could not quench. It was a love that was stronger than death, for I love him still." She lifted a finger to catch a tear.

Marie realized she had hardly breathed as she listened. *A love stronger than death?*

"It was a love like the King's that was given to my beloved and me—the kind of love I wish for you and your future husband someday."

This kind of love sounded wonderful to Marie, but what was it, and what did the King have to do with it?

"The King gave it to you?" Marie said. 'But how does it happen?"

"It is one of the mysteries of the Kingdom," Lady Anne replied. "The truest love for another is like the King's love for us. It is given freely, it is given forever, and it is only awakened in us at the right time by the King's love."

Marie was captivated by the brief glimpse into Lady Anne's heart. She knew then and there the love of which Lady Anne spoke was the love she wanted.

As the end of her time at Bartscastle grew near, Marie assessed the value of her stay. She had come to appreciate all that Lady Anne had taught her, and especially what Owen had taught her, but one goal remained unattained. She mustered the boldness to ask Lady Anne to relay to Sir Bart a suggestion for his final birthday gift to her. She wasn't sure, but she thought that Lady Anne, despite her comments about Marie's "independent spirit," had developed a certain respect for her, as she had excelled in all tasks that Lady Anne had given to her.

On Marie's birthday Lady Anne presented her with another gown, this one deep burgundy, with a fur collar. Marie was pleased since it was a color she liked, and, as her mother always said, "A noblewoman cannot have too many gowns." It was a winter gown, though, and too warm to wear for supper, so she wore her blue and white King's colors gown, her very first green and gold gown having already become too short, now coming several inches above her ankles and therefore no longer befitting a lady. Although she knew the castle had been preparing for war, and that Sir Bart was undoubtedly preoccupied with many things, she found him as hospitable as always, anxious to welcome her and spend this evening with her. Stephen served as usual, but her birthday supper with Sir Bart being a private affair, he was relegated to the back of the hall except when serving.

"Your long exile soon comes to an end, milady," Sir Bart said, smiling, as she took her seat at the lord's table.

How did he know that was how she felt in the beginning? "It hasn't really been an exile, milord," she responded.

"Many young ladies feel that way at first," he continued, "but Lady Anne has a way with them."

Sir Bart was right. From the first night, when Lady Anne's manner had totally disarmed her, until now, Lady Anne had been at her side skillfully and gently nudging her from childhood to adulthood. She knew that her duty was to tutor girls and turn them into ladies. Despite her no-nonsense approach, she was single-minded and successful. For Marie it felt like the first time anyone had attempted to know who she was and to help her become who she could be.

She glanced at Lady Anne and nodded in acknowledgment, then turned back to Sir Bart. "Milord, I did feel like that in the beginning because I missed my home and family, but I see now that she had a larger vision for me than I had for myself."

"Well spoken, milady," Sir Bart answered. "That is because she serves the King, who has a larger vision for us in his Kingdom than we can imagine. What she has been teaching you these past two years is not just how to serve your future husband but how to serve your King."

Marie thought back to the reason she had been given for coming to Bartscastle—to prepare to be a wife. She still did not know how that would happen or when, but she understood now that she had a part to play not just in a household, but in the Kingdom. Though she did not know what that part would be, she also understood that loyalty to the King demanded she be ready play her part, trusting him and the spirit of the Prince.

"Yes, milord," Marie replied. "And I am grateful for the experience."

"Now for my gift to you." Sir Bart clapped his hands. "I have never given such a gift to a lady before," he said, "but I have decided to honor your request."

Stephen came to his side, holding a tray bearing a magnificent shortbow and a quiver of arrows. Marie's eyes momentarily met Stephen's, finding not an expression of familiarity, but one of astonishment, as Sir Bart picked up the bow and handed it to her. Touching it, Marie gasped. *I cannot use this. It is too beautiful.* On either side of the grip, above and below, was an inlay of ivory in the shape of a dove. Next Sir Bart handed her the quiver, which was fashioned of fine leather, with a gold medallion in the shape of a lion at the top on one side, an ivory one of a lamb on the other.

"The quiver will hang on your horse or your belt. There is one arrow for each month you have spent at Bartscastle."

Marie finally found her tongue. "Sire, they are works of art. I am loath to use them."

Sir Bart chuckled. "I confess, milady, that you have discovered my motive. I hope you never have to."

A few weeks later Marie's father was to arrive to escort her home. Lady Anne had a final gift to give her—a riding dress in the colors of Sir Bart. Marie had rarely seen Lady Anne in such a tender mood.

Blinking a tear onto her cheek, Lady Anne said, "I always behave this way when one of my ladies departs. It is like releasing the daughter I never had."

Marie began to feel a similar emotion. Although she had never admitted it to herself, she had come to view Lady Anne as like a mother, one who accepted her as she was, but who wisely and gently guided her in the right direction. Though still excited to return home, Marie now thought of Bartscastle almost as a second home.

While Marie was admiring her riding dress, Lady Anne brought out a second gift, one which Marie had long desired, but never thought Lady Anne would ever be the one to give her.

"A leather jerkin!" Marie said, surprised at her own outburst.

The soft leather garment was in the style of a long vest that extended below her waist, secured by laces in the front. It came with a wide belt for her waist. She would be able to wear it over her riding dress.

"There is a ring on the left of the belt to attach your quiver while you ride," Lady Anne said.

"You spoil me, Lady Anne," Marie replied. "I will not wear it without being reminded of your generosity."

"And I would be remiss now, as you journey home, not to remind you that you are also on a journey of the heart—a journey to find your purpose in the Kingdom. Allow your map to speak to you and the spirit of the Prince to guide you henceforth."

Marie nodded, then retrieved and unrolled her map. The blue heart had progressed beyond the orchards named *Obedience* and *Trust*. In front of it now lay a river and a bridge. She wondered about their significance. What lay ahead on her road? How would the spirit of the Prince guide her?

Chapter 14

FAREWELL TO BARTSCASTLE

WHILE MARIE SAT with her map pondering her future, Lady Anne had gone to the window.

"Your father is here," Lady Anne called. "He is in the courtyard."

Marie rolled up her map and hurried to her room to change clothes and gather her belongings. A knock on the door soon announced Sir Guy, who strode in to find Marie already in her riding dress and jerkin.

As a year before, Marie could not restrain herself, running to her father with open arms, hugging him and resting her head on his shoulder, as if he were rescuing her from years of bondage, though she knew in her heart it was not the case. In reality Marie felt torn about her imminent departure as she glanced back at Lady Anne, who was forcing a smile while dabbing her eyes with a kerchief.

"Father, I have so looked forward to this day," she said softly, feeling the warmth and strength of his arms around her.

"As have I," he answered, catching her eyes with his. "Now you are a lady."

Uplifted by her father's words, Marie turned to embrace Lady Anne and whispered *"Au revoir."* Then she walked out into the sunlight with Sir Guy. Marie's belongings were loaded onto a packhorse tethered to her mount and she swung herself into the saddle, placing her bow in its case. As they started for the gate, Marie took a last look at her home of the past two years; at Lady Anne in her doorway, kerchief still to her eyes; at the keep, where she had conversed with Sir Bart; and at the archery butts where she had learned to wield a bow. The experiences she had had here, which had propelled her from childhood to ladyhood and started her on her road in the Kingdom, would be a treasure of great value. She imagined herself riding forth on a wondrous new adventure, one in which she would be serving her King. She did not know how or when, but she believed she was ready.

As they passed through the gate, her father smiled at her and said, "I see that you are armed. I thought I was coming to take home a lady."

"Father, do you not remember it was you who first gave me permission to shoot a bow?"

Sir Guy laughed. "That was for targets with a ladies' bow. And look what it has led to!"

"Sir Bart gave me permission and he gave me the bow and arrows," Marie said, straightening in her saddle.

"I see. And now I must find a husband who wishes to wed a warrior."

"It is only for self-defense, Father, and Sir Bart said he hoped I would never have to use it."

"Nor do I, my daughter."

As they walked their horses toward the gate, Sir Guy leading, Marie sensed someone was missing. "Father, where is Daniel?"

"It was necessary for him to remain at the house," replied Sir Guy. "I could not leave it unprotected."

Marie had not thought about the Dragon in some time, but as they passed beneath the portcullis and left the castle behind, the old apprehensions began to surface.

"Has the Dragon threatened us, Father?"

"No, but Sir Bailys has become bolder. He rides the roads of our lands in the daytime with his bodyguards and sends his peasants to harvest our crops by night."

"What? And you allow it? Why do you and Daniel not stop him?"

"I do not want war with him. He has not harmed anyone yet."

Marie trotted her horse up next to her father's. "But is he not exploiting you, thinking you are showing weakness?"

"Perhaps, but if there is to be fighting, I do not wish to be the one who starts it."

She shook her head. "Father, I do not understand. Do you want him to take our lands as the Dragon took those of Sir Andrew?"

"I do not believe he is strong enough. He is merely using the time-worn methods of the Dragon—intimidation and deceit," Sir Guy answered, looking at Marie. "Why don't you just allow me to worry about Sir Bailys?"

Silenced and put in her place, Marie began to look around her. They crossed the bridge in Bartstown and soon were on the outskirts of the town, entering the open country. Marie had almost forgotten what it was like to be among the fields, to smell the aroma of freshly turned earth, to hear the songs of birds and the bleating of sheep, having become used only to the neighing of horses in the castle courtyard and the simple twitter of the swallows that nested on the castle walls. A soft breeze played in her hair as the sun warmed her face. She released her concerns to the glory of a summer day. By midafternoon they arrived at the manor house of Sir Giles. Sir Giles and Lady Margaret greeted them warmly.

"Lady Marie, you are a woman now," Sir Giles said. "Please, both of you join us for some refreshment."

The four of them sat around the table in the hall over mugs of ale, catching up on each other's news. Inevitably the conversation turned to the Dragon.

"His men ride the roads in twos and threes," Sir Giles said. "It is said that he is raising an army to fight the King himself."

"We are prepared to leave on a moment's notice and flee to Bartscastle," Lady Margaret added, a tone of anxiety in her voice.

Marie remained silent, a mounting frustration building within since the conversation had begun. Finally, as she heard Lady Margaret's words, she could no longer contain herself: "Why does no one stand up and unite to defend their lands?"

Sir Guy turned to face Marie. "It is not the King's desire, Marie. Did you not learn to desire what the King desires?"

Her father's words stung as if she had been slapped. Of course she had learned that. Now was not the time she wished to be reminded of it.

"I just don't understand why the King would allow his lands to be taken one by one."

Lady Margaret spoke again: "It is not our lands or even our lives that we are to hold dear to us. The King sustains them both and he can allow them to be taken away. It is our hearts that he holds dear. These he will protect."

Marie could not gainsay those words, though they did not answer her question. She lapsed back into silence, brooding over her thoughts, which she continued to do the remainder of the evening. The next morning, however, she awoke refreshed. There had been no frightening dreams as there had been when she spent the night here more than two years prior. The men were outside talking as she descended to the hall to have breakfast with Lady Margaret.

"Good morning," Lady Margaret said. "You must be joyful to be returning to your family."

It was true. Marie was feeling a certain happiness and anticipation of being home again. But she remained aware that she was now a different person from the child who had left the manor with the gurgling stream. And those she left would be different too. How would her mother react to her now? Would Edouard still look up to her or would he resent having to share his room?

"Yes," Marie said. "I have been away a long time. Everything will be different."

"That is so true," Lady Margaret replied. "In this world all we can depend on is that things will change—but the King never changes."

Although she had only been with Lady Margaret twice now, Marie decided that she liked her. She had a way of lifting Marie's thoughts higher, above herself. Though it was time to depart, she hoped she would see Lady Margaret again.

Marie mounted her horse and followed her father's slow pace toward home. The sun was high when they reached the crossroads. The road they traveled had been blocked there by downed trees as if it were in disuse. As they detoured around the trees, Marie noticed that the red shield was gone. In its place was a sign pointing in the direction opposite from whence they had come. The sign read *Purdyton*. The road in that direction appeared now to be the main road from the direction of their home.

"Father, what does the sign mean?" Marie asked.

"It is the name of the town near the Dragon's castle," Sir Guy replied. "He has erected signs at all crossroads. He wants all roads to lead to his castle."

Marie's thoughts were transported to the map she guarded inside her jerkin. *How ironic. On the King's map all the roads lead to his castle. I am traveling a different road.*

Soon the dark forest that had so unnerved Marie before came into view. As they passed through the tunnel-like entrance beneath the spreading branches, the gloom she had experienced before was absent. There were no shifting forms to be wary of. She was conscious only of the softly swaying boughs and twittering birds. The shade was a welcome relief from the warm sun. Surrounded by the sights and sounds of nature she so loved as a child, she felt energized and fully alive—alive to enjoy the world around her, alive to what lay in front of her.

All too soon the shade of the forest came to an end. Her father reined in his horse, Marie coming to a halt behind him. A hundred yards ahead stood the rickety bridge, two horsemen halted beside the entrance.

"It may be Sir Bailys's ruffians. Wait here in the forest where they cannot see you," her father said. "I will go and see what they want."

Marie watched as he slowly trotted toward the bridge.

"It is risky to ride alone in the forest, milady," spoke a voice from behind her.

Marie turned her mount to behold a lone mail-clad horseman in a yellow and black surcoat beside the packhorse, his hand on the tether. Strands of unkempt dark hair framed an unshaven face with an uneven grin. She had not seen this face before.

"I am not alone," she replied, her heart pounding.

"Yes, you are," he said, then smirked, swinging his sword in a wide arc, sundering the tether. "He is too far away to help you."

Marie began to back her horse away, glancing toward the bridge. Her father had stopped in front of the two at the bridge, his sword drawn.

"Go ahead, take your prize. It is nothing but clothing," she said, continuing to back up.

"Oh, that is not my prize. *You* are my prize," the horseman answered, grinning.

Marie could no longer back away, realizing too late that he was not holding the tether to the packhorse, but to her horse.

"We're just going for a ride in the forest," he said, giving her horse a yank and leading it slowly off the road.

Heart still racing, Marie looked back at her father. Though she knew his purpose in riding ahead, a panic began to grip her as the dark, suffocating grasp of abandonment closed around her. And there was more. She knew what this horseman wanted from her and she did not want to give it. Why hadn't her father included her? She would have been safe with him. Should she call for help? No, he would be distracted and they might strike him down. *What can I do?* Overcome by the same sense of helplessness she had once experienced in dreams, she knew full well that she could not overpower an armed swordsman. Her father could not rescue her either. He would not know how to find her once they left the road. Should she scream, or would that invite injury from her abductor? Her mind swirled with turmoil. They had left the path now. No one could see her.

"Call upon me and I will deliver you." The words came like a thought, though they were not.

Marie hesitated. *Was that a thought—or a voice?* Attempting to focus her whirring mind, Marie looked around her for a source of the voice. She saw no one else, and they were going deeper into the forest. The soft click of arrows in her quiver drew her attention. Silently, she lifted her bow and drew an arrow from her quiver.

"Stop!" she shouted, trembling, as she aimed the arrow at her captor.

The horseman turned to face her. "Your puny arrows cannot pierce my mail." He laughed. "Drop your bow now and I will not harm you."

He was right. Owen had taught her nothing about how to fight an armed and armored opponent. But she kept her bow drawn and pointed at her adversary.

"Release me!' Marie shouted, hoping her voice was not quavering.

The horseman's expression changed from nonchalance to determination, his eyes burning, his hand reaching for his sword. "Drop your bow now, or I will strike it from your hands!" he said, brandishing his blade.

Marie was conscious of an ache building in her muscles. She had never held a bow drawn this long before. She knew she could not keep her abductor at a distance much longer. She would have to give in and lower her bow. Her thoughts continued to tumble.

More words came to her: "My strength is made perfect in weakness. Trust me."

The horseman dropped the tether, raised his sword, and began to move toward her. In an instant Marie adjusted her aim and let her arrow fly, striking her adversary's arm below the elbow where there was no mail.

"Aaagh, wench! You have wounded me!" he snarled, dropping his sword, then clutching the arrow with his other hand and yanking it out.

Though her captor was disarmed and her horse free, Marie sat frozen in place, unable to decide what to do, her mind totally blank. Then she became aware of a thundering of hoofs behind her, coming closer. Was it one horse, or two? She dared not look.

"You will pay for this!" Her opponent glared at her, clasping his bleeding arm.

"Marie! Are you hurt?" Sir Guy shouted, riding up behind her.

"No, Father, just terribly frightened!" Another arrow nocked and ready, she exhaled a heavy breath, almost a groan, unaware that she had not taken a breath since hearing the sound of horses' hoofs.

Sir Guy looked at the stranger, nudging the tip of his sword against his chest. "Sir Bailys … I should have known you would resort to trickery! Now take your filthy companions back to your rat's nest and count yourself fortunate that you have not been more seriously wounded."

Sir Bailys spat in their direction and, lowering his head, spurred his horse, trotting back to the road and toward the bridge, his teeth clenched, grasping his bleeding wound.

"The two horsemen were just a ruse to distract me," Sir Guy said, grabbing the tether of Marie's horse. "They must have been watching us. When they pointed in your direction and laughed, I saw him lead you off the road. He intended to capture you. And he almost succeeded."

Still trembling, Marie replayed the whole event in her mind. "Father, I-I did not know what to do!"

"I am sorry," Sir Guy said. "I did not foresee the deception."

"But something happened. I—"

"You took care of yourself. That is what happened. Sir Bart was wise to teach—"

"No, Father!" Marie interrupted. "I was about to give up, and in my thoughts, I heard, 'I will deliver you' and 'trust me.' And then I thought about my bow and arrows. Everything happened so fast. I felt I was not in control."

Sir Guy grew silent. "It was the spirit of the Prince," he said softly. "He is strong when we are weak. He protected you when I could not."

The words of Lady Anne formed themselves in Marie's mind as her father spoke. *"Allow... the spirit of the Prince to guide you henceforth."* Once again, Lady Anne had been proven wise and trustworthy.

"Father, Lady Anne told me to trust the spirit of the Prince, just before we departed Bartscastle. I just did not know how it would happen. He used the sound of the arrows in my quiver to remind me of what I could do."

"And I am grateful for it," Sir Guy replied. "Never forget that his spirit is always with you, even when I am not."

They rode together back to the road. Sir Guy re-tied the tether to the pack-horse and they resumed their journey. "Come, let us continue, Marie. I will not leave your side."

The rickety bridge was empty when they reached it. Sir Guy followed Marie across, keeping his eyes on her and on the other side. The jolts of the current did not bother Marie this time, her mind still reviewing the preceding events. They passed the Wolf's Den Inn, which was devoid of activity except for a drunkard sleeping outside the door. Marie lagged back so that they were riding side by side now.

"Father, have you ever been afraid?" Marie asked.

Sir Guy hesitated as if considering how to best answer his so recently ter-rified daughter. "Yes, I have. In battle every knight knows fear, if not of death, then of dishonoring his King."

"I felt so alone, so helpless. I never want to feel that way again," Marie con-fided, attempting to keep her voice from trembling.

Sir Guy leaned in to give her a hug. "I am sorry. I failed in my duty to protect you. It will not happen again. I will instruct Daniel to place an armed guard with you at all times."

They rode in silence until the road forked and led into their lands. Sensing the nearness of home, Marie began to think of how her journey had begun. She was to learn to be a wife.

"Father, you sent me to Bartscastle to be educated to be a wife, did you not?" she asked.

"Yes, and I believe Lady Anne has prepared you very well," he answered.

"When will that happen and how do you find someone?"

"The King knows who are the eligible knights and ladies. I will make my decision with his guidance."

The question that had always burned in Marie's heart was still there, unan-swered. Her experience with the condescending squire at the joust materialized fleetingly.

"The one you choose—what if he doesn't desire me?"

"He will desire you after you are married," Sir Guy replied.

"No, Father, I want him to desire me before I am his wife!" Marie said. "I want to know before that I am desired and loved."

Sir Guy stopped, reaching over to lift her chin with his hand, his eyes cap-turing Marie's, which had already filled with tears of frustration that she felt coursing down each of her cheeks.

"Marie, you will both learn to love each other. Few are those who understand the true nature of love before vows are given, but you must first love the King and trust him to know your heart. When you truly love your King and desire what he desires, he will give you the desires of your heart."

The two rode on, again in silence, Marie sniffling, pondering the words of her father and the inscrutable "desires of the King." How could she love a King she had never seen? What if he wasn't loveable? What if *she* wasn't loveable? She thought about the love Lady Anne had told her of. She wanted to be loved like that, but it seemed now like a hopeless wish. One thing was clear, however: she understood neither love nor men. And she might never understand them.

Soon the stable, then the manor house, came into view.

A taller Edouard ran up to them from the stable. "Father! Sister! Welcome home!"

He was followed by Lady Clare, running from the house with her arms out, then stopping halfway to examine Marie. "Look at you, Marie! You are a lady now!" She paused, her eyes on Marie's jerkin. "But you are dressed as a peasant."

Marie exhaled a forbearing sigh. "Yes, Mother, but my good gowns are packed on the horse. I will wear them for you. You will like them." *Even if you still are not satisfied with me.*

Everything had changed—and nothing had changed.

Months had passed since Hugh had resolved to eliminate the Rat single-handedly. But he did not come in the spring, and now it was summer. Nevertheless Hugh had honed his archery skills by sneaking into Sir Bailys's forest to hunt larger game than squirrel and rabbit. There was no other way to train to bring down a moving target like a man on horseback. He had begun to enter the forest with impunity whenever he had little to do in the smithy. He knew that brigands sometimes camped in the forest, and though he was stalking game, he welcomed the opportunity to send an arrow through one of them if the opportunity arose, preferably if they were running.

Brian and Thomas had not agreed to join his plot. In desperation Hugh had hatched another plan. If the Rat would not come to him on his own, he would lure the Rat to him. In Hugh's view, though Sir Bailys had not killed his father, he was complicit in the death of his father. If he could wound or kill Sir Bailys, perhaps that would be enough to attract the attention of the Rat. He could not be seen in the attempt, or he would be hunted down and squander his chance to kill the Rat. He figured he would have to kill the two bodyguards as well, and quickly. If even one saw him and got away, his life was worth nothing. He took to walking the knight's forest armed on a regular basis.

On this day he was striding down a forest path when he heard the sound of voices and horses' hoofs. He hurried into the brush up the hillside to a point that overlooked the path. Three horsemen were moving slowly, looking to either side, the one in front gripping a sword in his left hand, his right arm bandaged. Hugh recognized Sir Bailys immediately.

Hugh shoved three arrows into the ground in front of him and nocked an arrow. *I have a shot. It must all happen rapidly.* He stood and released, then crouched again and grabbed another arrow.

Sir Bailys dropped his head to inspect the ground just as the arrow whizzed behind his head. Jerking his head up to look at the hillside, he shouted, "Brigands! Follow me, men!"

Hugh dropped to a crouch and hurried farther up the hillside, ready to shoot again. The three men were making their way toward him in a row, slashing the underbrush. From his crouched position, Hugh sent an arrow to his left, shredding some leaves as it hit the ground.

"This way!" Sir Bailys barked, turning his horse toward the sound.

Hugh crept in the opposite direction, berating himself over his errant shot. His opportunity was lost. He continued farther into the forest and waited until he heard the sound of horses' hoofs disappear. Then he retraced his steps and retrieved the arrow still stuck in the ground near where he'd taken his first shot. Finally he trudged back to Loynton. He would have to be patient. Surely there would be other opportunities if he remained steadfast in his determination.

The next day the bailiff appeared at his smithy. Dismounting, he approached Hugh with a grim expression. "Hugh, you are a valued member of our village. But I must ask you a question."

"Go ahead," Hugh responded, wiping his brow and taking a seat on a barrel, wondering what would bring the bailiff. Was he suspicious about the meetings of the Servants? Had someone observed the comings and goings?

"Some villagers have observed you walking out the road with your bow as if you were going hunting. You are aware that hunting on the knight's lands is forbidden, are you not?"

"They have not seen me return with anything have they?" Hugh answered. "It was for target practice. You want your archers to be proficient, do you not?"

"Yes, I do," the bailiff replied. "And I do not think you would do something so foolish. But only yesterday Sir Bailys was targeted in his forest by someone wielding a bow. Fortunately they missed. And you were seen returning from that direction later in the day. He demanded that I find out who was hunting in his forest, and I intend to." The bailiff's stare was unwavering.

I have been discovered! Hugh looked the bailiff squarely in the eye. "A coincidence," he said, standing to his full height, unblinking, looking down at the bailiff. "If I had taken the shot, I would not have missed. Good luck finding the miscreant."

The stare-down continued until the bailiff blinked and turned away with a sidelong glance.

"The knight's penalty for poaching is hanging; for attempted murder, it is far worse," he muttered, taking his leave.

Chapter 15

BATTLE

S EVERAL DAYS AFTER Marie and Sir Guy departed, a horseman galloped into the courtyard of Bartscastle, his horse frothing at the mouth,
its flanks wet with sweat. Seeing Stephen, the horseman said, "I have an
urgent message for Sir Bart!"

Stephen hurried him to the keep, where Owen, the steward, took him to
Sir Bart. After a few minutes Stephen saw the rider come back out, followed
by Owen. Owen headed to Michael, who was practicing swordsmanship with
some of his new men, and then came back to Stephen.

"My lord wishes to see you immediately."

Stephen followed behind Michael, finding Sir Bart leaning over the message
that he had laid out flat on the table in the great hall. He nodded his head in
greeting as they gathered around the table.

"It is from Sir John. The Dragon is moving to cut the road to our west, which
would deny us access to the King's nearest castle. The King desires that I gather
the local knights to my banner and join Sir John at the field by Pevensey Bridge.
We must defend the bridge to keep the road open." To Michael he added, "Send
messengers immediately to the knights in my domain. They must ride day and
night to join me as soon as possible. Bid them report with as many men-at-
arms and archers as they can by the end of the week." He turned to Stephen.
"Stephen, ready my horse, my weapons, and my armor. As soon as the knights
have gathered, we will march."

Stephen spent the rest of the day inspecting and oiling Sir Bart's and Minotaur's armor, then his own. He sharpened both of their swords, as well as his and Sir Bart's battle-axes. It seemed that Stephen would finally have the opportunity to put his training into practice. But the next few nights, as he awaited the arrival of the other forces, Stephen's sleep was troubled, visited by visions of himself and Sir Bart on the battlefield, not victorious this time, as in his imagination when he first became a squire, but outnumbered and surrounded by the Dragon and his army, Stephen feeling panicked, wanting to run. The enemy soldiers were too many and too strong; each time the soldiers closed around him and Sir Bart, he awoke in a sweat, trembling, his throat choked with fear. He did not share his forebodings with Sir Bart, though he wrestled with mounting anxiety as the day when the army would venture forth drew near.

On the morning of departure, he armored Sir Bart's charger and helped Sir Bart on with his plate armor, the gold trim identifying him as a knight of some importance. Stephen then donned his own armor, fetched Centaur, and rode to the courtyard, holding Sir Bart's green and gold banner. Michael joined him, clad in the blue, white, and gold colors of the King and bearing the King's banner with its emblem. Sir Bart looked an impressive sight on his warhorse, the golden highlights of his armor gleaming in the sunlight. How could they not be victorious? Why then was Stephen still troubled?

Most of the knights near Sir Bart's domain had joined him, but he could delay no longer. Stephen could tell the other knights by the royal blue and white surcoats they wore instead of their own colors when they were riding for the King, and by their shields, which bore the king's emblem—a lamb lying beside a lion, and a white dove with outstretched wings hovering over both. Sir Bart's shield had one additional feature: a chalice above the dove's wings.

Finally the force was assembled in the castle courtyard—Sir Bart and his six knights with their squires or sergeants-at-arms, and fifty men-at-arms, led by Michael on horseback. Ten stayed behind to oversee the castle. On foot were thirty archers and about seventy peasants, mostly sons of farmers, some in leather jerkins, others in quilted tunics, armed with swords, spears, and bows. Stephen rode by Sir Bart's side in front, holding the knight's green and gold banner as they slowly made their procession out of the castle and down to the bridge in the village.

The knights followed them, then Michael with the men-at-arms, several carts holding supplies, including lances, arrows, food for the horses and soldiers, and pavilions and food for the knights and then the remaining men. Some of the townsfolk had turned out to gawk and cheer as they rode to battle. Stephen's chest surged with pride as he rode beside Sir Bart down the narrow streets of the town, his banner rippling proudly with each breeze. A young girl spontaneously ran up to him with a handful of flowers, which he accepted gladly with a smile.

The small force followed roads west most of two days until they spotted an encampment of pavilions near a bridge over a rushing, high-banked stream. Stephen directed the positioning and provisioning of Sir Bart's pavilion. He himself would sleep outside the entrance on a straw pallet. A post was placed next to the pavilion, to which their horses were then tied and Sir Bart's banner placed beside it. Once all was prepared, Sir Bart invited Stephen to ride back with him to the ridgeline over which they had just come. As they crested the ridge, Stephen was aware of a bustle of activity on the forward slope. Men were cutting saplings and sharpening the tips, then embedding them in a row at the bottom of the ridge. Some hurried themselves in using supple boughs to braid wicker shields large enough to hide behind.

"Those are our archers," Sir Bart said. "They are erecting a barrier across the road on which the enemy will advance, in order to halt their knights. Some, especially those with crossbows, which take longer to crank the bowstring, will use the wicker shields to hide behind as they reload. Behind them our dismounted men-at-arms will stand with sword and shield, and our spearmen with them, to engage any knights that get past the barrier. The enemy knights will have to dismount to do so, lest they wound their horses on the stakes. Then they will be on equal footing with the swordsmen and spearmen. Sir John has chosen this field to our advantage."

Sir Bart gestured with his left hand. "To our left is a forest too dense for a large mounted force, and to our right is the stream, which curls around behind us to the bridge. The enemy must come at us on the road and up this slope. They will tire coming up the slope in their armor and our archers will have a greater range from halfway up the slope."

Stephen marveled at all the planning that had already gone into preparing for battle. He was reminded of Sir Bart teaching him chess: *"You must have mental superiority to win."* As they sat on their horses observing the activity, another horseman approached, his shield identifying him as a Knight of the Chalice. Stephen recognized Sir John as he greeted them.

"Sir Bart, you have arrived!" Sir John said, smiling. "The enemy approaches. There will be a battle on the morrow, but we are outnumbered, as I suspected. As you are the senior knight on the field, I yield command to you. With my ten knights and their squires, we have a score plus two mounted lances and swords to add to yours. I have also brought threescore men-at-arms and an equal number of archers, as you can see. My men will join yours."

"How many are the enemy?" Sir Bart asked.

"At least three times our number, but poorly equipped in my judgment, except for the knights. And I would guess the morale of the rank and file is lower than that of ours. Do you approve of my choice of battlefield?"

"Excellent," Sir Bart responded. "The Prince trained us well. But still, our small number must fight as three of theirs. We will place all our archers and men-at-arms athwart the road to pin them, and you will keep your mounted force behind the ridge out of sight. The sight of my small mounted force atop the ridge will embolden them to charge. When they are engaged, you will ride quickly with your mounted men and strike them in the flank. Everyone should be in place before dawn."

"One more thing," Sir John said. "They are led by the Rat. So we dare not fail."

The archers and swordsmen slept in place with their weapons, the squires taking turns mounting watch on the ridge crest. Stephen's time came just prior to dawn. It made no difference anyway; he hadn't been able to sleep, a mixture of anxiety and anticipation plaguing him. When he relieved his predecessor on the ridge crest, he already felt uneasy. Would he stand or run? And who was the Rat? What would happen if they lost? Sir Bart had pointed out where he would stand on the ridge to manage the battle. Stephen relocated Sir Bart's banner there and sat down.

A cool night breeze deepened the chill of his armor, accentuating the clamminess of his hands as he tried to envision how the battle would unfold. The enemy would charge, the barrier would slow them, and then the foot soldiers, led by Michael, would stop them. No one would be able to overcome Michael and his men. Then why did Sir John seem concerned about the Rat? Stephen shook off a shiver. It was still dark, but he could see lighted torches moving in the far distance and he heard the distant clank of armor mixed with the soft hoofbeat of horses moving into position.

Sir Bart joined Stephen just before dawn as the landscape was beginning to lighten, his presence doing nothing to dispel the alarm that crept over Stephen as he watched what began to emerge from the morning fog that clung to the field at the bottom of the ridge. Not just one, but many rows of dark shapes were ranged across the road, their heads emerging and disappearing in the shifting fog. Larger shapes, men on horseback, were ranged behind in several rows; he counted far more than the twelve that now stood mounted on the hill with Sir Bart, the largest mass of soldiers Stephen had ever seen, eclipsing even the numbers he had envisioned in his worst dreams.

As the sun rose, the lines on each side remained impassive. Stephen could see the enemy commander riding back and forth, his standard bearer beside him, red and gold banner fluttering. The longer they waited, the more Stephen began to succumb to despair. The thin line of archers and swordsmen below him surely could not defeat the horde now facing them, even with Michael leading them. Why didn't someone attack?

"Why do they delay?" Stephen asked Sir Bart.

"The Rat is hoping we will attack first, thus nullifying our defensive advantage. He has underestimated us. Eventually he will tire of waiting, like you, and he will charge. When we are engaged, you will signal Sir John by dipping my banner."

Stephen glanced behind and to his right. Sir John and his twenty-one men were already mounted and waiting behind the brow of the ridge.

A single horseman rode forward from the enemy lines, bearing a flag of truce. A horseman from Sir Bart's side rode out to meet him. After a short parley both horsemen parted, galloping back to their respective commanders.

"Michael!" Stephen exclaimed as the horseman from their side approached.

Michael reined in his horse. "The Rat wishes to discuss a truce with you," he said to Sir Bart. "I believe it is a ruse. You should not go."

"Look!" Sir Bart answered. "He approaches the middle of the field alone. If there is a way to avoid bloodshed, we should take advantage of it. I must go and hear him out. Stephen, in the event Michael is correct, remember what I told you about the banner."

Sir Bart trotted down the slope to meet the enemy leader between the armies. Stephen could see them gesticulating with their arms. He, too, hoped they could reach some kind of agreement that would allow them to go home in peace. As he watched, the enemy leader abruptly turned and galloped back to his lines; Sir Bart likewise turned and began to trot back. Stephen watched in horror as the enemy archers nocked arrows and raised their bows. Sir Bart was not yet back to his lines when the first volley filled the air.

"Sir Bart! No!" Stephen shouted.

He spurred his horse, thundering down the slope even as the arrows found their mark, clattering off Sir Bart's armor as his horse went down, pitching him to the side, Minotaur coming down on top of him, then rolling and trying to stand. But Sir Bart did not move. In an instant Stephen dismounted and was by his side, as the first volley of arrows from Sir Bart's lines now filled the air overhead. He snapped open Sir Bart's visor.

"My leg!" Sir Bart cried.

Michael had already run forward and grabbed Sir Bart's shield. "Help him up and back to the lines!" he shouted. "I will shield you from arrows."

Stephen pulled Sir Bart up, and with the knight's arm around his neck, he helped him hop to the line of archers as another volley of arrows crashed off Michael's shield and around them.

Then the ground began to shake. As they reached the line of swordsmen, Stephen paused to look back. At least fifty armored knights thundered toward them, lances down, already more than halfway across the field. The archers prepared to retreat behind Sir Bart's swordsmen and spearmen, who were bracing for the collision.

"Aim for their mounts, then withdraw," Michael shouted to the archers.

Another volley of arrows crashed into Sir Bart's archers and swordsmen, dropping many where they stood.

"We are too slow!" Sir Bart gasped to Stephen. "You must leave me here and run up to dip the banner, or we will lose our chance for victory."

"I cannot leave you unprotected, sire!" Stephen said, now lifting Sir Bart partly onto his back and continuing to struggle up the hill.

The collision of forces was marked by audible groans from horses as some of the knights, overlooking the sharpened stakes, drove their horses painfully into them. The clash of steel on steel and the cries of battle resounded as the oncoming knights dismounted and waded into the line of swordsmen and spearmen.

"Now is the time!" Sir Bart shouted. "Put me down. The line cannot hold long!"

Stephen labored to the top, and set Sir Bart down as gently as possible near his banner, despite his moans of pain. Stephen dipped the standard and looked back to the battlefield. Stray mounts ran aimlessly; others were being led by squires back to enemy lines. Sir Bart's thin line of swordsmen, led by Michael, was backing its way up the hill, grudgingly giving ground to the enemy knights. Just behind the knights now came a mass of enemy swordsmen and a peasant rabble on foot with spears, so dense that Stephen could not count them all. Michael would surely be overwhelmed. To Stephen's right the small mounted force of Sir John was beginning to move up the reverse slope of the hill, still out of sight of the enemy. Sir Bart's archers, in a line behind their swordsmen now, began to target the oncoming swordsmen, but there were too many. Michael's line gave way under the push of the enemy, and some of the enemy knights hacked through the archers, starting up the hill to Sir Bart.

Sir Bart, sitting propped against his standard, yelled to Stephen, "Bid Sir Giles charge with my other knights and squires to blunt the advance of the enemy. They must stall the attack until Sir John arrives, or all is lost!"

Stephen passed on the order, watching fearfully as the small force of six knights and their six attendants charged into the armored mass struggling up the hill. He heard a thunderous crash and cry as the oncoming knights were momentarily stopped, after which Sir Bart's knights and squires dismounted and lay to with sword and battle-axe. Sir John's force, now at full gallop, was driving for the flank and rear of the disorganized mass of enemy swordsmen and spearmen.

From Stephen's left came the sounds of another mounted force galloping up the hill. Turning, he could make out five armored riders coming from the direction of the forest. *Just in time. Even five can make a difference.* They were riding straight toward Sir Bart. Stephen's heart leaped into his throat—their red shields bore the golden dragon of the enemy!

"Sire, we are lost," Stephen said to Sir Bart. "The enemy is upon us!"

"Help me to my feet!" Sir Bart cried, unsheathing his sword. "I will not die sitting like a beggar. Let me use the standard for support. Remember all you have been taught!"

The five horsemen reined in and dismounted. "Stand aside, boy!" their leader barked. "Take the old man alive," he shouted to his men.

Two of them rushed forward. Everything happened so fast that Stephen did not have time to think. Instinctively he stepped in front of Sir Bart, gripping his sword. With a single swing he sent the sword flying from one man's hand, and with a twisting slash he sent the other to the ground with a wound in the knee.

"The pup has teeth!" the leader growled. "Eliminate him first! The old man can wait."

The remaining three advanced toward Stephen, while the fourth picked up his sword and the fifth still lay on the ground clutching his knee. In the moment Stephen had time to reflect, he knew he was outmatched. The urge to run, just as he had dreamed, gripped him. He turned to see Sir Bart, sword in hand, standing helplessly on one leg, holding onto the standard, unable to come to his aid. Then he pictured Michael, crouched on the ground in his tourney combat. What had he thought then as he watched Michael snatch victory from defeat?

The words formed in his mind: "Not by your power, but by my power."

No, that wasn't it.

"Not by your might, but by my spirit."

No. What was it? No matter. Stephen looked back at the approaching attackers. What followed was to Stephen as a dream.

Pointing his sword at the leader, he shouted, "Throw down your swords! You are my prisoners." He knew they were not his words, yet it was his voice speaking them.

All the enemies but the leader hesitated and began to back up.

"Cowards!" the leader shouted at his men. "I will kill the boy myself!"

He unleashed a mighty blow that caught Stephen's breastplate and left a furrow. So great was the force that Stephen staggered backward, nearly falling. As the assailant lifted his sword to strike again, Stephen, seeing an opportunity, lunged in, plunging his sword into the enemy's armpit. Howling with pain, the man dropped his sword.

"Look around you," Stephen shouted to the others. "The battle goes against you. If you do not throw down your swords, you will all die at my hand."

The enemy swordsmen looked to the battlefield, Stephen stealing a glance as well. Sir John's charge had driven a wedge into the massed swordsmen and spearmen from the side and rear. Even though they greatly outnumbered Sir John's force, many were already running back to their lines in panic. The enemy knights now had Sir Bart's knights in front of them and Sir John's behind them. And closer still, scrambling up the hill toward them was a sweat-smeared Michael with two men-at-arms. The three remaining enemy swordsmen dropped their swords, the leader still gripping his armpit to stanch the flow of blood as Michael ran up to Sir Bart.

"Sire, we are victorious, but only by the narrowest of margins. Your men have suffered grievously for the King."

The enemy swordsmen and peasants below were in full retreat, and now the enemy knights were giving way to the onslaught from both sides.

"The spirit of the Prince was surely with us today," Sir Bart replied, limping to Stephen's side. "And with this young man," he said, motioning to Stephen. "I was unable to defend myself. He disarmed five enemies."

Stephen looked at his trainer in disbelief. Was Michael smiling?

"You earned your spurs today, lad," Michael said, clapping him on the shoulder. "One against five, eh? Even I have not faced such odds. Those are exploits worthy of a knight."

Still speechless, Stephen knew he had done something good. He also knew that he had not done it alone.

Finally he found his tongue. "It was the Prince," he said.

"What are you saying?" Sir Bart asked.

"In my thoughts—it must have been the voice of the Prince that I heard. It said, 'Not by your power, but by my power.' And all that happened after that, even the words I spoke, was his doing, not mine."

"Spoken like a true knight of the King," Sir Bart said, smiling, then grimacing as he shifted his weight. "You recognized the inadequacy of your own strength and chose to trust the power of the Prince. I owe a double debt to your family now. First your father, and now you, have saved my life."

The knight's eyes surveyed the battlefield, where the enemy knights were now retreating to the red banner of the Rat, and came back to rest on Stephen. "And a knight you shall be. As soon as my leg has healed, we will join the King as he stays at one of his castles. It is my desire that you be knighted by the King before a convocation of his knights. Sir John will relay my request to the King."

Stephen shook his head. Had he heard Sir Bart correctly? *Knighted by the King?* "But, I am not yet eighteen, the age at which you said you would recommend it."

"Forget about traditions," Sir Bart answered. "Today you have proven on the field of battle that you have the knowledge, skill, and character to be a knight. Do you remember I told you once that you had not yet been tested? Today you met that test, and you allowed the spirit of the Prince to guide you. With courage, bravery, and humility, you rescued me from certain captivity, or worse."

As Michael led the four prisoners away, their leader having remounted and fled, Stephen helped Sir Bart back to his pavilion and out of his armor. His ankle and lower leg were badly bruised and swollen. Stephen was helping Sir Bart prop his leg on a cushion when Sir John poked his head into the tent.

"It was a brilliant plan, Sir Bart. When we hit their flank, they scattered like the vermin they are. We have taken more than fifty prisoners, and their army is on the run."

"But the Rat lives to fight again," Sir Bart noted.

"You sound as if the Rat is someone to be feared, but we defeated him," Stephen said.

"He is feared because of his ruthlessness," Sir John replied. "He is one of the Dragon's most trusted knights. He used one of his lord's methods today— deception—but he has torched villages and he takes no prisoners. Even his men are afraid of him, though they served him poorly today."

"We will undoubtedly see him again," Sir Bart said. "He will not accept this defeat kindly."

Upon their return to Bartscastle, Stephen became the full-time caretaker of Sir Bart, helping him dress each morning, serving as his support as he hopped about on one foot wherever he went, even helping him to his private garderobe[10] and back.

A few nights later, as they sat together at the lord's table in the great hall enjoying a meal of venison, Sir Bart, his injured leg propped on a stool, said, "Tonight will be a memorable night for you, son."

"Why?" a puzzled Stephen asked.

"Remember, once I told you that someday I hoped you would serve the King as I do?"

"Yes, sire," Stephen replied, "and I have tried my best to be worthy of the King's trust."

"And I told you it was not a matter of being worthy but of being ready."

Stephen had heard that also, but what was being "ready" compared to being "worthy"?

"Yes, but—"

"Word of your actions in the battle while trusting in the spirit of the Prince rather than in yourself has reached the King, and he has declared you ready."

"I don't understand, sire," Stephen said. "Ready for what? Knighthood?"

"That will come, too," Sir Bart answered, "but first things first." Gingerly repositioning his bruised leg, he continued, "The past three years I have taught you what it is to be a knight, but I have also told you about the true Kingdom—the Kingdom that binds hearts in loyalty to the King. The King has declared you ready to be brought into his Kingdom, and he has sent you a gift."

Stephen could only shake his head. "You mean I was not already in his Kingdom?" The very thought baffled him. How could he have spent all this time with Sir Bart and not be in the Kingdom? Then his mind drifted back to his first evening with Bart and the writing on the wall. He thought of the deep discussion they had just had on his birthday. Now he understood what Sir Bart had told him—that the rules had been there not as something to be obeyed but to remind him that they could not be obeyed. How then was it possible to enter the Kingdom?

---

[10] A private latrine that was adjoined to the lord's bedroom.

"There is so much that I do not understand, and the Kingdom Rules—I cannot completely observe them," he said, "so how—"

"It is not a matter of knowledge or observing rules," Sir Bart said, "as much as both might be desirable. It is a matter of loyalty of the heart and of whom you trust. Up until now, you have steadfastly attempted to make yourself worthy through your training and actions, but in battle you were placed in a position where those were inadequate and you had to trust in a strength greater than yours."

"The spirit of the Prince," Stephen murmured.

"That trust is the manifestation of a heart captured for the Kingdom."

Sir Bart clapped. An attendant arrived at the table bearing a tray, placing it before Stephen. On the tray sat a wooden round-topped box with strips of gold wrapped around it. On the front of the box was a medallion with an image of the same dove on the King's emblem. Beside it lay a gold key.

Stephen still felt puzzled. From the look of the shiny wood and polished gold, it seemed as if he were being given some kind of treasure box. The poor bailiff's son inside him strained to imagine what he would see when he opened it. Was it a reward for rescuing Sir Bart? Would it be filled with gold coins? Or rare gems?

"This box and its contents are a gift from the King. Likewise the key, which is like mine," Sir Bart said. "The key unlocks the mysteries of the Kingdom. A gold key is given to those who will be leaders in the Kingdom, as knights are expected to be, and as I have trained you to be."

Stephen was speechless, and elated as well, for this signified to him that somehow he had pleased the King, though he had yet to understand how he had, nor did he truly comprehend the significance of this gift. He reached for the key and examined it, noting that there was writing in small letters on both sides.

"I-I don't know what this is for or what the writing means," he said, showing his puzzlement.

"On one side it says *Fides clavis Regnum est* —'Trust is the key to the Kingdom'— and on the other, *Potentiam tuam, non meum*—'Your strength, not mine.' The second is only on keys given to those who are to lead, because they, of all people, must remember this," Sir Bart said. "You trusted the spirit of the Prince and relied on his strength in battle. The key is always to be a reminder of whom you trust. Now slide the medallion aside and unlock the box."

Stephen did as directed, and lifted out a sealed scroll, chuckling self-consciously as he did so. "From the looks of the box, I half-thought there would be treasure inside."

"Indeed there is," Sir Bart replied. "And many are those who fail to find it. The key unlocks not only the mysteries of the kingdom but the treasures also."

"You mean this scroll is a treasure?" Stephen asked, rolling it back and forth in his fingers, for it appeared to be naught but a piece of parchment to him.

"Unroll the scroll," Sir Bart said.

Stephen broke the seal and unrolled the parchment, watching in wonder as the map began to reveal itself. "Is it a treasure map?" he asked.

"The Kingdom is the treasure," Sir Bart said. "The map will show you the content of that treasure … as well as the cost."

Stephen began to examine the map in more detail as the features became clear. "It is the map you showed me and told me about, but there is so much more on it now!" As names wrote themselves across the map, it seemed as if the fog that had encircled Stephen's brain like a persistent cloud suddenly began to lift. The meaning of the Kingdom was coming into focus—it was and had always been a kingdom of the heart, and the treasures displayed, such as peace, joy, and love, were likewise treasures of the heart.

"The map is your guide to the Kingdom, and one of the roads is the one you follow," Sir Bart continued.

Stephen was again perplexed as he read the names to himself. "These names all sound like good things, but you said that map also shows the cost. What did you mean? I thought it was a gift from the King,"

"The gift is the Kingdom," Sir Bart replied. "But there is a cost, both for the King and for you. Both have already been paid."

Stephen cocked his head, trying to decipher Sir Bart's comment. The fog was descending again. "Did you not tell me that the King owns everything? How could it cost him?"

Sir Bart placed his finger on the map. "What does this say?"

Stephen peered at the spot where Sir Bart's finger rested. There was an X marked on the map. Beneath it appeared the words, *Here fell the Prince.* Stephen's thoughts returned to the evening not so long ago when Sir Bart had patiently explained the meaning of the King's love. He realized immediately that the map was a piece of the puzzle he had been trying to assemble ever since Sir Bart had begun to tell him about the Kingdom. Clarity returned as he fixed his eyes on the words. Although he remembered Sir Bart telling him how the Prince sacrificed himself for his father's Kingdom, he understood for the first time, seeing these words in their finality on the map, that one of the facets of the gem he had pictured then was now revealing its beauty. There had been a cost to the King, a cost borne out of love. But that did not answer the entire question.

"You said there was a cost to me. I didn't pay anything for this," Stephen said, confused yet again. "It was a gift. You told me so."

Sir Bart smiled. "It may not be apparent now, but your initial cost was paid when you accepted the gift, because in so doing you transferred authority over your life henceforth to the King and the spirit of the Prince. As you follow your road, you will learn of other costs, which you will accept because of whom you trust and the treasures that are yours in the Kingdom."

"Oww!" Stephen cried, placing his hand over his heart. "What was that?" he said, rubbing his chest.

"One of the things that make this event so memorable," Sir Bart said. "The confirmation."

"Confirmation of what? That I can feel pain?" Stephen winced.

"Confirmation that your heart is now ruled by the King. If you look, you will find over your heart a mark in the shape of the same dove that is on the medallion and the seal of your map."

Wiping beads of perspiration from his forehead, Stephen said, "You are right. I am not going to forget this pain!" He edged up his tunic to examine the mark. "What else have you not told me?"

"The key and map must be with you at all times, and though you still have much to learn, they are assurance that the spirit of the Prince will be with you to guide you as he does me."

After the pain subsided, Stephen became introspective. "All these years I have thought my goal was to please you and the King with my ability to understand and fulfill the Kingdom Rules and all you have taught me, yet this event had nothing to do with any of that, did it?"

"No, it did not. You are not admitted to the Kingdom because you have somehow pleased the King; rather the King is pleased to admit you into his Kingdom, for his own purpose. You must discover that purpose," Sir Bart replied. "Admittedly, there is much to learn before one becomes a knight, for knights are leaders. But to be a knight of the Kingdom, or to be in the Kingdom at all for that matter, it is a question of whom you trust, for it is only by trusting the spirit of the Prince that we can do anything worthy in the Kingdom."

"Yes ... Yes, I must remember that," Stephen said.

Sir Bart placed a firm hand on Stephen's shoulder and looked him in the eye as if to emphasize his point. "Your future may well depend upon it, son."

PART TWO

THE RAT AND THE KNIGHT

Chapter 16

A RAT IN THE DRAGON'S NEST

PURDYTON ALWAYS SEEMED like a gloomy place, even to those who lived there. Perhaps it was the way the castle had spread its ever-growing bulk like a creeping fungus over the hill behind it over the years, its towers and curtain wall blotting out the light as the day wore on, threatening to engulf the town itself. The castle dominated the western skyline with its mute and intimidating presence, a testament to the one who lived within it. As the Rat led his sodden, defeated army through the streets and up the road to the walls, lashed by gusts of wind and rain, the towers seemed to grow in size and proportion, as if rising up to rebuke him. Under gray, growling skies, the Rat's dejected survivors splashed through puddles, drenched to the skin by the steady downpour, which seemed to punctuate their unexpected repulse. The Rat had been given a chance to eliminate one, perhaps two, of the enemy King's closest knights and had failed. Oblivious to the rivulets running down his face and back, and angry that his men had failed him, he brooded over the events of the battle.

He had almost finished off Sir Bart with his ruse to bring him out in front of both armies where his archers would have an easy target. But then that horseman had galloped out to drag him to safety while a soldier protected them with his shield. Even his clandestine raiding party had been foiled by a mere youth from snatching the wounded Sir Bart. All those raiders had been captured by the enemy but one who managed to flee and tell the story. He had been immediately executed of course, as were some of the others who had fled the field.

The Rat's king would not be pleased with him. A third of his knights had fallen, as had many more men-at-arms and archers, not counting those who were rounded up and captured. He was returning to his king's castle with half his force and a tarnished reputation.

As he trotted across the drawbridge ahead of his demoralized band, the Rat pondered his situation. A mercenary—or "soldier of fortune" as he preferred to think—he had been lured to his king's side from his native principality only by the promise of personal gain, and his king paid him well, not to mention that he looked the other way when the Rat looted the villages he raided. He was not altogether displeased with the epithet he had acquired—the Rat. If it frightened villagers into fleeing their villages, all the better; the villages were that much easier to plunder and burn. His ruthlessness had endeared him to his lord, who, though not above taking to the battlefield himself, preferred to achieve his gains through deceit and guile, and through those who pledged loyalty to him. The Rat had only been in his lord's service a few years, but in that time he had grown close enough to learn more about him than many who served him.

His lord had already declared himself king of the realm when the Rat joined him, but he was aware that some called his lord "the Prince of Darkness." He supposed it was because his king preferred the castle to be dimly lit and because he usually wore black while within his castle. But he had other names as well. As the ruthless and pitiless rebel leader of a war on the enemy King's realm, who thought nothing of burning villages to ashes if they resisted him, he was known by his enemies as "the Dragon," a name clearly affirmed by his fearsome emblem and the shape of his throne, although he did not allow his followers to speak that name in his presence. Certainly his power was undeniable, as he seemed to be able to loot and burn the weak enemy King's villages with impunity. It was no surprise his enemies would bestow such a name on him, nor that he would privately relish it.

Rumors circulated that he had once been the commander of the enemy King's bodyguard, but had been disgraced and banished following an attempted palace coup. Many of the enemy King's knights had joined him in exile. His realm and that of the enemy King had been at war ever since. It was common knowledge among his followers that he had taken his present name, King Oen Llofrudd, after orchestrating the murder of the enemy Prince, but there were also rumors that he had served the enemy King under a different name.

As the Rat entered the inner gate, the king's chamberlain was waiting for him.

"The king would see you now for details of your battle," he said.

"I am sure he already knows," the Rat said, dismounting. "He could easily tell by the pace of our return and the size of the remaining army."

The Rat slowly entered the massive keep and mounted the stairs to the great hall that contained the king's throne, shivering from the chill of his wet armor, considering how he would reply to the certain displeasure of his lord. The great hall always seemed cold and dark, even though torches hung along the walls, with tapestries between them to retain warmth. As if to emphasize the natural darkness, there were no windows, and the tapestries were all black in color with a red dragon emblazoned on them—save one. Behind the king's throne hung a magnificent colored tapestry of the king seated triumphantly on his throne, with what appeared to be princes and kings bowing before him, laying their crowns at his feet.

As the Rat expected, the king was seated alone on his throne at the end of the hall, scarcely visible in the dim light, wearing his self-bestowed crown, dressed entirely in black, his black surcoat bearing the image of a red dragon couchant.[11] The throne itself was fashioned of iron as if to last for ages, but its shape alone was enough to forbid approach, even when unoccupied. Forged in the image of a seated dragon, its muscled, clawed forelegs gripping the floor, its haunches supporting the seat, its ruby-inlaid eyes glaring down from its fringed open-mouthed head, it threatened to envelop the king in its darkness with its partially spread wings that reached forward to enclose the seat on each side. To the king's left rested a lamb fashioned of iron, head down, lying on its side with a slit in it which served as a holder for the king's sword when he was seated..

The Rat approached the throne, leaving a trail of drops from his wet surcoat, his footsteps echoing off the stone floor. Despite his reputation for greed and his ambition for power, the king was not of unpleasant countenance. Flowing shoulder-length black hair and a meticulously groomed mustache and beard framed startling blue eyes. His smile, though rare, was said to be quite disarming. Today he wore a scowl.

"You have embarrassed me, Rat," the king said, straightening to his considerable height, glowering down at the Rat as he kneeled.

"Give me better men, and I will give you better results, milord," the Rat replied, rising to give his report. "Your battle strategy did not work either. We waited for them to charge, but they did not. Your ruse to expose their leader almost worked, but he was only wounded, and two of his soldiers rescued him before we could capture him. Then I was forced to begin the battle and charge

---

[11] At rest.

a well-positioned defense that bogged us down. I thought of your strategy in eliminating the Prince and sent a raiding party from the flank to capture Sir Bart, but they were defeated by a mere youth. And then we were struck by surprise in the flank by another of the enemy King's inner circle. The army disintegrated. It seemed that nothing we were going to attempt would succeed."

"There was no one on that battlefield more powerful than I!" the king snapped. "You failed as a leader to ensure that my men felt that power behind them as they rode to battle."

"Oh, they looked for their king—but he was not there, milord," the Rat replied with no attempt to hide his sarcasm.

"Do not deign to bite the hand that pays you!" the king answered, his voice reverberating throughout the hall. "You did nothing worthy of your retainer in this debacle. You knew well that a conclave of knights of my realm is a week hence. I was to bestow the fief of Sir Bart upon one of my Immortals. And now it appears there could have been two fiefs to bestow if you had done your duty!"

"Their army fought with more spirit than ours. Perhaps you should lead your men yourself," the Rat retorted.

"Perhaps I will if you fail me again," the king said. "Now begone! Train more soldiers. There will be more opportunities."

The Rat climbed the stairs to his quarters in disgust. He had been out-generalled. It would not happen again.

The week before the conclave passed with no change in the king's attitude toward the Rat, although the lost battle had been little more than a skirmish in the Rat's mind. The king had to have more on his mind to allow this minor setback to bother him so, the Rat reasoned. The conclave brought knights from all over the king's realm, its purpose being an annual opportunity, or perhaps require-ment, for all to pledge loyalty in person to their king and to plot strategy in the ongoing war against the enemy king. According to custom, attendees came in their battle dress. Much clanking and scraping of metal filled the air as the Rat, along with other knights, made his way up the tower stairs from the courtyard where they had first gathered and into the great hall, the king's throne room, in which long benches had been placed so that knights could face their king.

At the far end stood the king's imposing throne, tensed as if ready to rise to battle with the king on it, the king sitting upon it clad in his own battle dress—a red surcoat with a gold dragon rampant, a gold crown on his head, and holding instead of a scepter, a gold mace. The Immortals had already arrived, the ten of them dressed, as always, in black, standing mutely in a row behind the throne, visors down, both hands resting on the hilts of their swords, which stood in front of them unsheathed, tip resting on the floor. The Immortals, every bit as imposing in size as the king, answered only to him, remaining silent in his presence, arrayed behind him like a menacing and impenetrable wall. Everyone but the Dragon referred to them as Companions or Black Knights, perhaps because the name 'Immortal' conjured visions of powers no one wished to contemplate, much less face.

The Rat knew that there had once been twelve, the two most vicious having been captured by the enemy King and confined in chains in a deep dungeon. The knights filed in and began to take their places on the benches. As one of the king's trusted knights, the Rat sat on the front row. Before taking his seat, the Rat glanced at the wall opposite the throne, which held a map of the realm, showing in red the growing extent of his king's advance into the territory of the enemy King. From Draignytha, his castle, red fingers spread in all directions, indicating lands that had been claimed.

Once seated, the Rat tried to prepare himself for the king's address, fully expecting to be humiliated publicly for his recent defeat, as he had seen happen before. Though the hall was filled with warm bodies, about two hundred by his estimate, and the torches projecting from the walls on either side were crackling, the great hall seemed unusually cold this time.

Trumpets sounded, announcing the beginning of the conclave. The hall's occupants stood as required. The obligatory greeting—"All honor to the king, and death to those who oppose him!"—having been shouted by all, the knights remained standing until the king acknowledged the greeting by raising a hand. As if choreographed, all sank to a knee in obeisance.

"You may rise," the king said.

He stood and began to pace as if in an unsettled mood, his black cape ruffling behind him, the stone walls echoing the determined pace of his heavy boots. He stopped several times to survey the sea of faces before him, slapping the shaft of his mace into his gloved right hand each time, as if searching for the correct words to begin his address.

"Men of destiny!' he said finally, motioning to the back of the hall. "I welcome those of you who are new. Our dominion steadily expands! More and more villages and people have fallen under our sway. Our enemy weakens as our efforts are crowned with success, save a few temporary setbacks."

The king was now looking straight at the Rat, his icy blue eyes fixed in a stare.

"Our final victory draws near," the king went on. "The enemy King is now too weak to resist us. His son was his principal weapon; he has not dared show himself outside his castles with what little army he has since we claimed the life of the Prince. We must continue to wipe out pockets of loyalty to him. Whether by force or by deceit, it matters little." He stopped pacing and looked slowly across the faces of his minions as if to engage the eyes of each. "Now it is time for the final push!" He gave the mace an emphatic slam into his hand.

The king strode down the aisle to the map on the opposite wall, a chill breeze following him, causing even the torches above to gutter, then he turned to face the knights. A rumble of scuffing and scraping ensued as the knights changed position to face the map.

"This is the year to complete our victory!" the king continued. "Those who are not yet with us are confused because the enemy King has not ventured from his castle to defend them. Some now doubt even if he is still alive or has sufficient power to help them. Our strategy will be to take advantage of this weakness."

"We shall strike those who would resist at times and in places they do not expect. Among those who doubt, we will encourage their doubt. More than anything we will seek to convince all that they are more advantaged under our rule than under the enemy King. We will seek to know their desires and reward their greed, lust, and ambition. Where there is hesitation, we will sow fear!" The king stopped, looking over the audience to assess the effect of his exhortation. "Whose is the victory?" he asked.

"The victory is yours, O King!" chorused the crowd, drowning out the Rat's less than enthusiastic contribution.

"Yes!" the king said, spreading his arms wide. "It is I, even I, who have accomplished this...for my glory. I *will* be lord over all. I *will* sit on the throne of the Most High."

He looked to the other end of the hall and lifted a hand toward the Immortals. "Behold, the time has come to release my Black Knights, the Immortals, upon the land."

A muffled murmur spread through the hall as the seated listeners turned to regard the ten knights in black, who shuffled mutely in their places like caged beasts awaiting the removal of their leashes before bursting forth to kill and destroy.

"Each has been given a domain to conquer for me." The king turned to the map. "The remainder of the enemy King's land has been divided into ten regions, each marked by a symbol. You will find on the map the region you have come from and gather around the Immortal who bears that symbol above the dragon on his surcoat. You will take orders from him and cooperate with him however he directs."

As the king announced the name of each Black Knight, the Immortals strode heavily down the aisle between the benches and reformed their wall of silence behind the king. The knights rose en masse, examined the map, each halting at a safe distance from the Immortal who wore his symbol, forming a queue. Since the Rat resided in the king's castle and received his orders directly from the king, he found some relief in having no Immortal to approach.

The Immortals dispersed and ten groups formed, the Black Knights gesturing at the map and haranguing their men in deep, rasping voices that caused the men to shrink back. The Rat was reminded that he had not liked the Immortals from the moment he first saw them. It wasn't necessarily because they were both larger and taller than him or every other knight, or that they spoke to no one. It wasn't even envy that they seemed to be closer to the king than he. Rather, something about them seemed almost bestial, otherworldly. Part of it was their gruff voices and their size, to be sure. The Rat knew also they were powerful enough to best any man, including him, in solo combat. They were single-minded in their loyalty to the king, and it was said that they were used only for special missions of great importance. The Rat considered this unexpected move by his king. *That must be why the king seems out of sorts. He has decided to throw the dice and risk all!*

The insistent voice of the king shattered the Rat's musings: "Rat!"

"Milord," the Rat answered, bowing his head.

"Remain behind after the others leave. I have more words for you."

The king's tone sounded worrisome. He had just made a triumphant speech about releasing his Black Knights to consummate his victory over the enemy King, yet he still seemed troubled. The Rat returned to his bench, and sat with elbows resting on his knees, attempting to discern what lay in store for him. Had the king grown tired of him? Was he to be cast out, now that the Black Knights seemed to be in charge?

Sitting alone as the Black Knights finished exhorting their followers and the convocation ended with the dismissal of those who had come, the Rat felt his anger rise. The more he thought about it, the tenser his body became. He had served his king well. Everyone fell a little short sometimes. He did not deserve to be shoved aside. He held his tongue as the ten Immortals returned to the platform one by one, reforming their inscrutable wall—save one, who halted beside the throne, which had been re-occupied by the king.

"You may now approach, Rat," said the king.

The Rat stood and knelt before his king.

"Rise and face me."

The Rat complied, but he had made a decision that could well seal his fate. *This is it. I will not yield, even to a Black Knight.*

"Behind me stands Gythreul," the king said.

The black form gave a guttural growl from within his closed helmet.

"I have given him authority over the lands from Grandvil to Bartscastle. The two of you will work together now. You two have one of the most restive regions to overcome. Even though one of my knights has the fief that borders Grandvil, for the past three years there have been rumors of clandestine groups loyal to our enemy, and it is said they are growing in number. Furthermore, they make copies of a scroll that is said to be uncomplimentary of me, and some pass them on to others in order to foment rebellion."

"Yes, milord," the Rat replied, his anger abating, though still not pleased to hear his work would be shared with a Black Knight. It would most certainly mean less sport and loot for him.

The king went on, "The knight, Sir Bailys, failed to come to the convocation, a most grievous affront to me. I am now reinstating your previous mission that was interrupted by the opportunity to lure Sir Bart into battle, in order to allow you to redeem yourself—and not require you to lose so many of my men." The Rat could feel the chill of the icy eyes.

"I am at your command, my king," the Rat replied, hoping it would not be a shared mission with the Black Knight who towered over him.

"You are to take some trusted men and pay Sir Bailys a visit. Find out why he did not come, and whether the reason he did not—and the reason his fief is out of control—is active disloyalty. If you discern even a whiff of disloyalty, you are to execute him on the spot. If not, you will give him a mission by which he can prove his loyalty."

"And will Gythreul be accompanying me?" the Rat asked, glancing up at the silent figure.

The king shook his head. "He has more important issues to attend to, such as how to bring Bartscastle under my control. Sir Bart is weakened now that he is recovering from his wound, so this is an ideal time for you to strike villages and knights that look to him for protection. On your way to see Sir Bailys, you will pass near the fief of Sir Giles, who is loyal to the enemy King and who has been protected by Sir Bart. You must make a detour to claim it for me while Sir Bart is unable to respond. Take enough men to defeat him quickly, then burn the manor house and capture him if you can. After you have dealt with Sir Bailys, you are free to loot and burn whatever villages you wish, including Loynton, the source of one of the villagers Sir Bailys passed on to you for torture and interrogation. It is time to ratchet up the terror!"

"As I recall, the villager did not reveal any useful information," the Rat said, allowing himself a smile now that he was not to be paired with a Black Knight. "But perhaps my methods will be more fruitful when I have the whole village in my grip."

"Whatever it takes, there must be an end to the spreading of lies about me, and loyalty to the enemy King must be extinguished. Your purse will be fattened accordingly." The king's eyes narrowed. "Do not fail me this time, Rat!"

"It will be my pleasure to carry out this mission, milord," the Rat replied, relieved that he was being trusted for another mission and delighted that he had his usual freedom to pillage and plunder. "May I loot Grandvil as well?"

"I think not," the king said, his eyes now turning to the map as if debating the question. "It is an important market town. Taxes on its wealth support our effort."

"And if I might ask, milord, how am I to cooperate with Gythreul?"

"He will have his own missions. You are not to interfere with him but you will render him service anytime he requires it of you."

The Rat looked back up at the Black Knight, who had not moved during the entire conversation. Heavy, muffled breaths emanated from the closed helmet. The Rat could just see the glint of two blue eyes holding him in a steady emotionless gaze, as a predator would observe its prey before pouncing. It was the closest he had been to a Black Knight and the first time he had looked one in the eye. The Rat was not one to be easily intimidated, but he found himself looking away from the penetrating eyes behind the black visor. He did not wish to be commanded by, or even in the presence of, this Gythreul.

"Is that all, milord?" the Rat asked, looking back to his king, who, even when irascible, seemed more personable than any of his Black Knights.

"You are dismissed. Inform me when you depart on your mission."

The Rat bowed and made his way out of the great hall, down the stairs, and into the courtyard. Darkness had fallen. The courtyard was empty, the faint glow of torches outlining the walls of the castle and the slow-moving sentries.

He climbed the stone steps onto one of the walls and leaned on the parapet, overlooking the huddled buildings of Purdyton that groveled below, pondering what had just transpired. He understood that a major step had been taken in the war on the enemy King. But what was the full significance of the release of the Black Knights? What would they do? What were they capable of? He turned to look back at the keep, which reared above him like a giant dark beast. Its narrow, arched windows, lit within by flickering torchlight, gazed back at him like unblinking eyes, yielding no answer.

Chapter 17

THE RAT BITES

HUGH SUSPENDED HIS forays into Sir Bailys's forest until rumors of an attempt on the knight's life had died down. A known brigand was run down and captured, then publicly drawn and quartered on the Grandvil town square. Hugh felt no contrition over his role in the innocent man's death, nor over his failed attempt to eliminate Sir Bailys. Though his plan to lure the Rat to Loynton was dashed, he would have to be more careful henceforth. He had been fortunate to escape arrest, but he knew that if he made another attempt on Sir Bailys, the bailiff, who might suspect him still, could turn him in and he would suffer the same fate.

Several more weeks had passed when, on the way back to the smithy one day, Hugh ran into the bailiff. He seemed to have dismissed the confrontation with Hugh from his mind.

"Hugh, how is the armor fabrication coming?" he asked.

"Well enough," Hugh said. "I am working on a fourth mail shirt."

The bailiff leaned closer to whisper. "Listen, Sir Bailys will be coming with an important visitor within the week. It is said they are looking for a secret group disloyal to the king. They thought your father might have known about it—of course they were wrong, I am sure. Sir Bailys will be making a surprise visit tomorrow to flush them out. It will bring him honor from the visitor if he does. I want you to ride with us and alert me to suspicious people."

Hugh found himself at a loss for words. How could he ride with his enemy seeking out his friends? What would they think, seeing him beside Sir Bailys? What if he refused? He had to think quickly.

"I know to ride with Sir Bailys may seem like a high honor," the bailiff continued, "but as the village blacksmith, you are an important member of the fief, as am I."

"Yes, it is an honor," Hugh said, attempting to hide his contempt for Sir Bailys, his mind still racing. "But surely he would not want to take me from the work he has given me. As the village blacksmith I will be hard pressed to make all of the armor and weapons he tasked me with if I take the time to do this."

"Yes, I understand," the bailiff replied. "Do your work. But be on the look-out for suspicious people. We will stop by your smithy to ask if you have seen anyone to tell us about."

After the bailiff departed, Hugh went straight to Thomas to warn him, and then down to see Brian and William.

"Do you think Sir Bailys knows the truth about you and my father?" Hugh asked William.

"The bailiff almost certainly would have told him what he suspects," William replied. "Not that he knows."

Hugh shook his head. "No, what I mean is, if he knew you went with my mother, are you in danger from him?"

"He did know that—but I do not intend to run away," William said.

"I have an idea," Brian said. "Tell the bailiff to assemble the archer company to show Sir Bailys. He will not suspect any of his own soldiers. We can safely walk with them and avoid questioning."

"Excellent!" Hugh replied. "He asked me to ride with them. I will offer that possibility instead. Would you tell the others in the group, Brian?"

The next morning the bailiff and the ten archers waited in the road leading into the village as Sir Bailys and four soldiers approached on horseback.

"Sire, I present the Loynton Company for your review," the bailiff announced.

"Fine," the knight replied, waving his hand in acknowledgment, scarcely giving them a glance. "Have them fall in behind us. Who are we visiting?"

"The baker, the miller, the carter, and several of the farmers, sire," the bailiff said.

"And the blacksmith," Sir Bailys added. "That was where the whole problem began!"

The bailiff glanced at Hugh. "The blacksmith is one of your archers, sire," he replied.

"Then find me someone who is one of the secret group!" Sir Bailys barked.

At the bakery both the baker and his wife were busy making loaves to be used as trenchers for meals. The baker's wife, Alis, exchanged an uneasy glance with Hugh as Sir Bailys swaggered in. Fortunately his questions were all directed to her husband, who claimed to know nothing of the group. So it went with all of those questioned until they came to the last farmer, who also said he knew of no such group.

By now Sir Bailys was visibly agitated. "We cannot have wasted a morning for nothing! Take him for further questioning."

"Sire, have mercy! My family—"

"Take him!"

Hugh's hand instinctively reached for an arrow. But he withdrew his hand and clasped his shoulder, watching as the farmer's hands were bound with rope and he was jerked away by one of the horsemen. Who was this visitor Sir Bailys was trying to impress?

The Rat was no closer to an answer to his concern about the Black Knights. A week passed between the conclave and the day the Rat's men had recovered their morale and healed sufficiently from wounds. Choosing ten men-at-arms and five archers who had not fled in the previous battle, he set out for the crossroads, a day's journey away, with his small force and a provision cart.

Instructing his sergeant-at-arms, he said, "We will camp near the manor house of Sir Giles and strike at dawn."

Early the next morning before sunrise, he arranged his men in a circle around the house of Sir Giles, out of sight, several armed with unlit torches. At his command they began to approach the house, slowly closing the circle to prevent any escape. The house was dark as they approached in the dim light of dawn, the Rat following on horseback. Soon the soldiers were tightly grouped around the house, awaiting the Rat's next order.

Gathering five of his men-at-arms, he whispered, "Break the door and bring them out alive."

With a loud grunt the men heaved themselves against the door, breaking it open and rushing inside. Within minutes they reappeared.

"There is no one here, sire."

"The coward has fled," the Rat growled. "Take all of the food to provision us, keep whatever else you want, then light a torch and burn it down!"

His men jostled as they all forced themselves at once through the doorway, each to seek his reward, the Rat remaining on his horse to review in his mind what had gone wrong. *They must have seen our campfires last night and fled to Bartscastle. Or perhaps they were warned. By whom? Never mind.* Loynton would pay. He would bring back more captives to amuse himself with.

Light began to flicker on his face as flames licked out of windows in the house, his men carrying out sacks of loot they would either use or sell. He instructed the men to place their sacks in the provision cart. But he knew that men caring for their ill-gotten gains would fight poorly if the need arose.

"Men, there is an inn ahead a few hours' ride," he said. "You will leave your sacks there for the innkeeper to guard on pain of his death."

The men began to grumble about returning to Purdyton to deposit their plunder before continuing. Discipline threatened to dissolve.

The Rat drew his sword. "He who does not follow my instructions will forfeit not only his prize but his life as well."

The men fell grudgingly into line and followed as he led the way back, dissatisfaction still rumbling through the band as they trudged behind the horses of the Rat and his sergeant-at-arms through the forest beyond the crossroads. As the force crossed the old bridge over Roaring Fork, the few men outside Wolf's Den Inn hurried inside, open shutters soon slamming shut. The Rat dismounted and went inside, emerging shortly, his hand on the collar of the trembling innkeeper.

"He will keep your sacks of loot in his own bedroom until we return," the Rat said, giving the innkeeper a jerk. "Will you not?"

"Y-Yes, sire," the cowed innkeeper replied.

More murmuring rippled through the band as the men deposited their burdens, each sack tied with a piece of cloth to identify its owner, in front of the innkeeper.

"Now let us enjoy a mug of ale, eh?" one suggested.

"We have an unfinished mission," the Rat said. "There will be both loot and ale enough for all after we accomplish it."

The Rat remounted and turned his horse toward Loynton and Grandvil, his grumbling band kicking up a cloud of dust behind him. The light was failing as they reached the fork that led to either Loynton or Grandvil.

"We will overnight here," the Rat said, dismounting.

"Milord," one of the men said, pointing at the sign for Loynton, "we are near the village you are seeking. Why do we not attack and burn it tonight?"

"We will, in time," the Rat replied, "but on the morrow I must speak with Sir Bailys about what has been happening in his fief, and we must re-provision in Grandvil."

The next morning the chill of oncoming autumn energized the soldiers as they threw off their cloaks and rose from their makeshift beds of leaves. They warmed themselves by a fire while having some bread, dried fruit, and drink before trudging the last miles to Sir Bailys's manor house. They were not expected.

As the Rat stopped in front of the house and dismounted, a man ran from the stable. "Good morrow, milord," the man said, surveying the group. "I am Gerald, Sir Bailys's stable master, at your service. You bring a great army to this small place. What may I tell my lord of your purpose?"

"I would speak with Sir Bailys if this be his house," the Rat replied.

Gerald took a look at the Rat's face, then his shield and surcoat, which bore a toothsome gold rat above the dragon, and turned to hurry into the house.

The Rat followed him to the front door and listened, hearing the urgent conversation within.

"Sire!" Gerald said. "It is the Rat! He is outside at this moment wishing to speak to you!"

"What? Who?" The voice sounded confused, as if just awakened from sleep.

"The Rat! He is at your door!"

"Already?" A grunt followed, then, "Delay him! I must be dressed to see him."

Hearing Sir Bailys's words, the Rat frowned, then hammered impatiently with his fist.

A moment later the door opened to reveal Gerald.

"Where is your master, man?" the Rat asked. "Does he know who awaits him?"

"Yes, yes, he is coming, milord. Please sit at the table. May I offer you some ale?"

"I do not drink ale in the morning," the Rat replied, a tone of disgust in his voice. He entered and heaved his body onto a chair.

An unshaven Sir Bailys soon stumbled out of his bedroom, his hair and red surcoat askew. "Greetings, milord. You have finally come."

"At a most inauspicious time it would appear, considering your condition," the Rat remarked. "Do you manage your fief the same way you manage yourself? It is no wonder I was sent here by the king."

Eyes now wide open, Sir Bailys sat in a chair opposite the Rat, swaying as if he would fall to one side or the other. "W-We are so far from his castle," he said. "I thought we were of no import to him."

"And that is why your fief is the most restless in his realm!" the Rat said.

"Wh-What are you going to do?"

"First you are going to answer some questions," the Rat replied. "You were absent at the recent conclave. Do you have any idea what the consequences of ignoring the directives of the king are?"

The Rat noticed Sir Bailys's hands trembling atop the table as he spoke: "I-I was ill, milord. I was t-too ill to travel."

The Rat glared at him. "And yet you did not bother to send a message to the king to that effect—a message that should only take two or three days to reach him. Why not?"

Sir Bailys's breathing now sounded labored, each breath accompanied by a long wheeze. He opened his mouth, but no words came out.

Recoiling from the heavy aroma of alcohol, the Rat continued, "I think it is obvious what happened. You took ill the night before you were to leave in the same way you took ill last night—drowning in a barrel of ale!"

Sir Bailys began to sob with great groans. "Have mercy on me, sire! I am a simple man. Wh-What do you want me to do?"

"You will tell me to which king you are loyal!" the Rat shouted.

"Y-Your king," Sir Bailys said, sniffling. "His banner is outside my door."

"The banner means nothing. And why did you say he is *my* king? Is he not *your* king?"

"Yes, yes, he is my king too," Sir Bailys said, his whole body shaking visibly.

"Then you will follow my directions," the Rat said. "We—you and I—are going to root out the followers of the enemy King. Word has reached our king that one of your villages, Loynton, is a hotbed of subversion. There are secret meetings, a scroll of writings treasonous to our king is passed about, and the disease has spread to Grandvil. Is this true?"

"I sent you one of the peasants several years ago," Sir Bailys said. "He was the ringleader."

"He gave us no information, nor did the other one we captured when he came for the first one," the Rat said. "And that was three years ago. What have you done since?"

"I-I have raised a company of archers and men-at-arms as I was told," Sir Bailys responded. "I do not know what for—"

"What have you done about the subversive activity, man?" the Rat said, raising his voice.

"I-I was in the village yesterday. They don't know any—"

"And that is the problem!" the Rat interrupted, jabbing a finger at the trembling Sir Bailys. "You have lost control of your fief. If Loynton does not hand over the culprits, I will burn the whole village to a heap of ashes. And if that does not bring me satisfaction, I will torch this house as well. Do you understand me?" He slammed his fist on the table for emphasis.

"Y-Yes, milord," Sir Bailys wheezed.

The Rat stood, knocking his chair over. "Now get yourself and your men ready for battle. We are going first into Grandvil to provision. On the morrow we bring judgment to Loynton!"

For what seemed like an interminable period of time, the Rat paced, emitting an occasional impatient huff, shouting commands to "hurry up" through the bedroom door. Once in his armor and outside, Sir Bailys staggered to the stable to find his four men-at-arms. The Rat listened impatiently as Sir Bailys roused the men from sleep, and then all five men brought out their horses. The Rat sat on his horse in front of the house, fidgeting, totally disgusted with the entire process. His own men had filed into a pasture where they sat, playing games and grumbling to each other.

Finally Sir Bailys and his four men were mounted and as ready as they could be. The Rat decided that he had correctly diagnosed the problem: Sir Bailys was not disloyal, just a dissolute drunkard. Though he would have given little thought to executing all five of the hopeless examples of humanity before him, he restrained himself. He was, after all, a man of principle.

"Now lead us to Grandvil," the Rat ordered.

"Yes, milord," Sir Bailys mumbled. Then he took the lead, slumped on his horse—gripping its mane to keep from falling off, it seemed. The Rat and his men fell in behind. The pace was slow, Sir Bailys's men having to ride beside him to keep him propped in his saddle, lest he slide to the side and tumble from his horse.

Toward nightfall the procession reached the outskirts of Grandvil, continuing into the market square where the Silver Coin Inn was located. By this time Sir Bailys was asleep in his saddle, the Rat having to go inside to arrange rooms for the two knights, stable room for their horses, and sleeping space in the courtyard for his men.

The Rat was now in a foul mood, likewise his men. Instead of encountering a knight eager to help him in his task, he had found more of a liability than an asset. Moreover he was disappointed that he was not allowed to harm Grandvil, for he could tell it was a wealthy town, which held much of value for the discerning looter. It had been a long day in which little had been accomplished. He released his men to do as they wished for the next few hours. He would have a few drinks and a meal at the inn.

Not wishing to be in the company of Sir Bailys, he ate alone, planning his actions for the next few days. He would visit each village near Grandvil, beginning with Loynton, which seemed to be the source of all the trouble. He hoped there would be sufficient plunder to make it worthwhile for him and his men. His meal was soon interrupted by the approach of a well-dressed gentleman, who stopped at his table to introduce himself.

"Good evening, milord. My name is Nicholas. I am mayor of Grandvil. Might I sit with you and learn your purpose in bringing such an unexpected armed force into our town?"

Taking a sip of wine, the Rat motioned him to sit. "My purpose is for me alone to know," the Rat replied, "but perhaps you can provide me with some information."

"Gladly, milord," Nicholas replied, "as long as you bear no ill intent against our town."

"I do not," the Rat said. "We are here to stay the night and re-provision. But I would know how your people view the king."

"You would of course mean the Dragon," Nicholas said, his eyes on the Rat's surcoat.

"He does not like to be called by that name," the Rat said with a scowl. "It is the name used by his enemies. Which are you?"

"We are a free town that depends on trade for our livelihood," Nicholas answered. "It matters not to us who is king as long as we are unhindered in our pursuit of wealth."

"A praiseworthy position," the Rat said, "but you would certainly want the king's protection if you were attacked, would you not?"

"Of course, though we have a town militia."

"So it matters to whom you are loyal" the Rat continued, "because neither I nor my king will protect you if you are loyal to our enemy."

The mayor smiled. "Well then, of course we are loyal to *your* king—today."

The Rat smiled back. "Then perhaps you can tell me if there are any groups meeting in your town that are loyal to the enemy King—today. They meet privately after dark and pass around a scroll of parchments that spreads lies about my—and your—king."

The mayor pursed his lips as if thinking. "No, I am not aware of such a group or groups … though it is said that one hand does not know what the other is doing in the shadows of darkness, is it not?"

The Rat nodded. "It is indeed, and for your sake and your town's sake, I hope you have spoken truthfully. We will depart tomorrow. I hope we do not have to come back to reexamine your loyalty. Now, if you will permit, I would finish my meal alone."

"Of course, milord. Grandvil always welcomes those who come with goodwill."

The mayor rose and departed, leaving the Rat to continue his plotting. Once finished with his meal, he went across the square to the alehouse and rousted out his and Sir Bailys's men—finding Sir Bailys among them—then herded them into the inn's courtyard to collapse until morning, finally directing Sir Bailys to follow him to the rooms he had reserved for them. The Rat bedded down, heartened, as his usual feeling of excitement before looting and plundering began to rise, visualizing the terror he would sow on the morrow, wondering if he would find any of the culprits he was seeking.

The same morning that the Rat departed for Grandvil, Hugh received a visitor.

"Gerald!" Hugh said. "It is midmorning. Why are you here?"

"I bring ill tidings. You must warn the village."

"The Rat?" Hugh guessed.

Gerald nodded grimly.

"He has come, then," Hugh said. "The bailiff told us Sir Bailys was expecting an important visitor."

"Yes. And I heard him say to Sir Bailys that he would put Loynton to the torch if the true King's followers were not found."

Armed with news of the Rat's imminent arrival, Hugh passed on the word, even as he began to plot. Terrified villagers piled their belongings on carts and headed for the countryside. Nor was the bailiff anywhere to be found. A few villagers who did not believe such a calamity could befall them stayed to protect their cottages. Hugh knew now that there would be around twenty soldiers accompanying the knight, but he remained undeterred in his intent to execute his plan, even though it would be certain suicide. At least he would go to his grave avenged. He hardly slept that night, imagining how he would identify the Rat, take careful aim, and send an arrow straight through his eye. The entire night was a restless rehearsal of this one act.

The next morning Hugh left the smithy in the care of his apprentice, George, and went to his place of ambush. None of the villagers would allow him to use their houses for such a plan for fear of reprisal, even after he had explained what the Rat might do to them. He found a copse of trees two miles from the village along the road to Grandvil where it ascended a hill, and there he crouched in wait. As the Rat crested the hill from the other side, the morning sun would be in his eyes and the eyes of those with him. They would not see Hugh rise and take aim. At fifty paces he could split the Rat's head like a ripe melon.

The morning was already too warm—it would be unusually hot for an early autumn day. Even now Hugh could feel rivulets of sweat creeping down his back and beading on his forehead. He could not relax, endlessly reviewing in his mind his planned act of revenge. Three years he had waited for the King to right the injustice. Three years he had struggled with loyalty to his King. Now the opportunity was being given him to do what the King would not do. It had come down to this—a life for a life, his life for the Rat's life. Hugh viewed the end of his life calmly, without regret or sorrow. What was it worth in a Kingdom without justice, where both of his parents were already dead?

The sound of horses' hoofs sent his hand to an arrow. Straining to glimpse any movement at the top of the hill, he waited, crouching behind his tree, his hands sweaty, his heart pounding. Revenge was almost within his grasp. He could feel it! A single horseman appeared in silhouette. He took a deep breath and nocked his arrow.

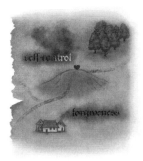

Chapter 18

THE RAT TURNS

HE RAT ROSE early, riding around Grandvil with his sergeant-at-arms, directing him where to buy food to restock the provision cart. He had left Sir Bailys with the task of assembling the men in the square after they had eaten. Surprisingly Sir Bailys was there with all the men when the Rat and his sergeant-at-arms returned with the provision cart. The Rat chuckled. Perhaps the previous day's encounter had scared some backbone into Sir Bailys.

With a soberer but still anxious Sir Bailys beside him to show the way, the Rat led his soldiers out of Grandvil, the mayor looking on, no doubt to be certain they departed. The entourage wound along the road to Loynton in the late-morning sunlight, an unseasonal heat already beginning to rise from the muddy road. The men were in good spirits, having filled their stomachs with food and ale the night before, eager for the loot they would add to their haul later in the day. But by the time they were passing by Sir Bailys's manor house, it had become a steamy day, the men complaining of thirst, the effort of carrying their weapons, and the weight of their mail shirts.

As they rode, the Rat attempted to question Sir Bailys about the village they were to visit first. They would not be expected. Who should be questioned? Which houses should be ransacked? The blacksmith, of course. But who else? Sir Bailys was too intimidated to be of any help. The Rat decided he would just collect everyone in the center of the village and question them as a group. Those who acted as if they had something to hide would have their houses searched and plundered. Then, if he still had no answers, he would apply the final solution: burn the village to the ground.

It soon became unbearably hot. Sweat rolled down the Rat's face and stung his eyes. He had heard that a stream ran next to the village. Perhaps he would halt his men there to freshen themselves before they undertook the serious business of rooting out traitors. His plan complete in his mind, he felt content. This was the kind of thing he was born to do. He could not explain why it gave him such a rush of pleasure when surrounded by screaming peasants dashing from burning houses, but somehow it just quickened his spirit to know he had such power over people.

They were moving up a hill now. Everyone was laboring in the heat. Perhaps they would catch a breeze on the other side. Perhaps he should stop sooner and let his men rest. He was feeling inexplicably fatigued. The sun seemed insufferably bright. Perhaps he—

The Rat swayed in his saddle and tumbled from his horse, hitting the ground with a thud, motionless.

Hugh stood to take aim as more horsemen crested the hill, apparently in a hurry. But something was not right. One of the horses bore a man's body, slung like a sack over the saddle. The others were guiding it quickly down the hill toward the village. Unable to identify the Rat among the silhouetted figures, he lowered his bow and placed it over his shoulder, intending to follow at a distance. The party—around twenty in all, as Hugh had expected—rode toward the village, foot soldiers and archers trailing, down toward the stream below where William and Brian did their tanning.

As Hugh watched from afar, the group stopped, lifted the body from the horse, and laid it by the stream. The soldiers began to splash water on the man's face. Out of the corner of his eye, Hugh saw William and Brian striding along the shore downstream to where the men were. His plan once again foiled, Hugh broke into a run down to the stream. It would be impossible to kill the Rat now with so many people milling around, but perhaps he could at least identify him for a future opportunity.

A man with shoulder-length auburn hair, wearing a chain mail hauberk and a red surcoat, lay on the shore of the stream. William was bending over him, patting his cheek. A golden dragon was emblazoned prominently on the surcoat. From the agitation of the men around him and the appearance of his face, Hugh knew immediately who it was. A long, pointed nose jutted from between two closely spaced eyes, underlined by a bristly mustache. He was looking down at the body of the Rat.

His victory stolen, Hugh's fury erupted. *It was mine to avenge!* His whole purpose, to which he had subordinated everything else in his life, had been squashed in a moment. He stood over the body, fists clenched, rigid with indignation and bitter satisfaction.

"He is not dead," William said, removing the knight's chain mail cowl, drawing back a bloody hand.

Hugh looked on as William looked up at Sir Bailys and asked, "What happened?"

Sir Bailys appeared to be visibly horrified, his face a shade of grayish white. "We…We were coming up the hill before Loynton, when he cried out and fell from his horse. The only word I remember he said was something like 'Who?' We drank much ale last night, and we did not drink any water yet today. We were all feeling oppressively hot in our armor. We thought it must be the heat. That is why we rushed him to the stream."

"He is unconscious; he has sustained an injury to his head," William said. "He may also be overheated; his lips are dry. He must be brought out of the sun, but moved properly. Leave him still until I return. You may continue to splash his face, but do not move his head. Brian, come with me." He rose and his eyes fell on Hugh—and then Hugh's bow. "Hugh, where did you come from? You come with us, too."

Hugh nodded, then he, William, and Brian hurried to William's house upstream.

Once there, William said, "Find me one of our bows, Hugh, while Brian and I fetch some sheepskins."

Hugh ran into the cottage and took a bow off one of the walls, returning as William and Brian secured two sheepskins. William laid his and Hugh's bows parallel, then punched holes in the sheepskins and tied two of them transversely between the bows with leather strips. He was making a litter, Hugh figured, and Hugh was not at all in agreement.

"That will do," William said when he had finished. "Let's take it to the knight."

With Hugh trailing along, breathing measured breaths and attempting to maintain his composure, William and Brian carried the litter back downstream and laid it beside the knight as the others looked on.

"Now," William said to all, "we will lift him, without changing the position of his head, onto the litter. Brian, help me hold his head steady."

Carefully four of the soldiers lifted the knight's body, keeping it level as they were instructed, while William and Brian prevented his head from moving.

Hugh wanted nothing to do with it, wishing that he could end the Rat's life here and now, but something held him back.

Once the Rat was on the litter, William said, "Carry him to my house—slowly—while Brian and I steady his head."

Again Hugh followed along to William's house, where the Rat was lowered onto a straw pallet. A moment later Charis appeared and began to look over the wounded knight.

"He must stay here for now," William said. "We will take care of him. He cannot be moved until he either awakens or dies. The next few hours are critical."

"I-I will ride to Grandvil to find a physician," Sir Bailys said, still a shade of pale.

"That will be unnecessary," said Charis, who was already dabbing the Rat's head wound with what Hugh knew to be a mixture of salted water and ale. "The last thing he needs is a physician to bleed him. This will be decided before a physician can arrive anyway."

"We will stay with him, then," one of his soldiers said.

Hugh watched as Charis looked to William, who nodded.

"You may sleep on our floor and around our cottage," Charis said, now dribbling water onto the Rat's tongue a drop at a time.

"You should give him more water," another soldier said.

"He can neither eat nor drink until he regains consciousness," Charis replied. "It would be too dangerous. He cannot swallow; the food and water might pass with the air he breathes and kill him. He is breathing now as if asleep. That is good. All that can be done now is what I am doing." Charis continued to drip water onto the knight's tongue. "If the injury to his head was not severe, he will survive. Let us hope that is the case."

Hugh did not hope that was the case. The Rat had fallen into his hands without having to be lured. A precious opportunity to settle the score had been lost. Still seething, he backed out of the cottage and walked slowly back to the smithy, attempting to formulate a new plan. Maybe the Rat would just die and save him the trouble. Hugh would lose the satisfaction of administering the blow, but at least his father would be avenged.

The next morning Hugh's curiosity took him back to the tannery. Little had changed. The Rat still lay on the pallet; an exhausted Charis crouched beside him, dripping water onto his tongue as before.

"She has been there all night," William said to Hugh. "She would not let me spell her. The good news is that the knight has not died. The bad news is that he has not awakened."

Hugh felt agitated. The good news was not good news at all. "Why didn't you just leave him and let him die?" he said bitterly. "If he recovers, he will still exact retribution on us as he had planned!"

"Perhaps. Perhaps not," William said. "Hugh, do you remember a story in the *Chronicle* about a peasant who came across a noble who had been beaten and robbed by brigands?"

Hugh huffed. "The *Chronicle* again. You always have to bring it up, don't you?"

"Calm down, Hugh," William said. "I simply asked you a question."

"Of course I know the story. A party of nobles had passed him by, but the peasant stopped and gave him water and bound his wounds."

"Whose behavior was applauded by the Prince?"

"The peasant, naturally," Hugh answered.

"Need I say more?"

"No—and don't!"

Hugh strode out, frustrated by William's refusal to acknowledge the potential danger they faced if the knight survived. William always seemed to know how to set Hugh off by quoting the *Chronicle*. William simply did not understand justice. Thankfully neither he nor Brian had said anything about Hugh "coincidentally" showing up—with his bow, no less—as they had come upon the wounded Rat.

All day Hugh worked on a shirt of chain mail, methodically crimping rings, his heart simmering with bitterness. That evening he tramped back to the tannery, hoping the knight would finally be dead and his father's death avenged.

Brian stood outside. "Hugh, the knight is improving. He has opened his eyes, though he still cannot talk."

More unwelcome news. Just when Hugh thought this quest was about to end, justice had been snatched from his grasp. He could not allow the Rat to escape. Hugh looked past Brian without speaking; then he stepped inside, considering what to do next. Charis had seemingly not left the knight's side. Hugh looked down upon the Rat. His hazel eyes roved slowly from side to side; he blinked occasionally and even exhaled a deep sigh. How could so much evil lurk behind that face?

William spoke from behind Hugh. "Sir Bailys paid a visit earlier. He was relieved to know that the knight was improving. Charis and I both believe he will recover."

Hugh tensed. Time was short. He could just grab a knife and plunge it into the Rat's heart now while he was still helpless. William and Charis would be horrified, and he would be immediately cut down by the Rat's soldiers, but then it would be finished!

"Mmmm-ff."

"Look!" Charis said. "He is trying to speak. And I saw him swallow."

Hugh felt of two minds now. He knew that William and Charis were doing what they thought was right, but he also knew that this knight would have no regard for them when he was healed. In Hugh's mind they were nursing back to health their own executioner. He noticed one of William's scraping knives, but something restrained him, as if his mind were being pulled in different directions. He visualized himself standing over the knight, the knife raised to plunge it into the knight's chest. Then the faces of William and Charis appeared before him with expressions of hurt and betrayal. He opened and closed his hand several times as if to seize the knife, but could not will himself to pick it up.

Finally he stumbled out of the cottage holding his head. Why couldn't he do what he had waited three years for? He returned to the smithy in turmoil. What was wrong with him?

By morning Hugh had gotten no closer to an answer. He had rolled to and fro on his pallet, his head filled with visions of the Rat, torch in hand, laughing, setting fire to his smithy. In spite of his indecision, Hugh was drawn back to the tannery once more. Things had changed dramatically. The Rat was sitting propped against a wall, his head bandaged, a cup of water in his hand.

Much to Hugh's chagrin, Charis looked pleased. "He is talking now," she said. "Not always making sense, but he is talking. He does not know where he is or why he is here. Sometimes he talks about feeling very hot, seeing a great light, feeling as if he were sliding from his horse and then things going black. He seems to understand some of what we say."

Though Hugh admired Charis for the care she had given the Rat, he knew it would not change the knight's mission. He looked for the knife he'd seen yesterday. It had been moved out of sight. As much as he had wished it to be so, perhaps this was not the time. Perhaps once he was away from Charis and William, things would be different. Watching Charis's selfless care for her enemy was the one thing that had stayed his hand.

His curiosity aroused, Hugh stooped beside her. "Charis, how did you and William know what to do? I mean, with the bows and not feeding him and giving him drops of water?"

"William knew," she replied. "When he lived in Purdyton, a man was thrown from his horse and hit his head in a similar way. The townspeople tried to sit him up to splash water on his face. He immediately went limp and died the same day. The apothecary told William later that they should not have moved him like that. It broke his neck. They should have done what we did. William remembered."

Impressed, but still troubled by visions of the Rat torturing his father and torching the village, Hugh left and returned to the smithy to continue his work. His mind was not on it, but crimping the small rings of the chain mail was mostly mindless work anyway. By the time daylight dimmed, he had decided he would ambush the Rat in the village from a vantage point near the smithy. The Rat would certainly come there when he was well. He placed his tools on his bench and went into the cottage to have a bowl of the rabbit stew he kept simmering in the pot. From time to time, he would add cabbage or turnips, and more rabbit or squirrel as he caught them.

As he entered, Hugh jerked to a halt upon seeing a dark form seated at his table. As he approached, the stranger removed his hood.

"Clyffe!" Hugh said. "You said you would never come again."

"It is no longer my mission to bring word of new followers, but this is a special case. The message is specifically for you, and it has two parts."

Feeling a mix of conflicting emotions, Hugh nodded and sat at the table. "Go ahead."

"There is a wounded knight at the home of William and Charis who is to become a follower. You are to take him a key and the map."

Hugh exploded up from his seat, kicking his chair against the wall behind him. He turned and pounded his fists on the table, causing the board to jump into the air.

"Impossible!" he shouted. "You do not know who this man is!"

"Sit down, Hugh," Clyffe said, his deep voice calm and controlled as always. "Remember, I am a messenger of the King. Do you think the King does not know who he is?"

"You are mistaken! This man is the Rat. He killed my father. He burns villages. He came to Loynton specifically to root out and murder our group of Servants." Hugh felt his hands shaking with rage, his face burning. "I will not do this—I cannot!" Hands clenched now, Hugh began to pace, kicking up dust, hammering the walls with his fists. "No! Do not tell me to do this!"

Clyffe still did not raise his voice: "Sit down, Hugh," he repeated. "Calm yourself."

As before, the authority in Clyffe's sonorous voice filled the room, sweeping over Hugh, draining away his fury like a receding tide. The pressure of Clyffe's quiet gaze brought him to a stop. His anger replaced by emptiness, Hugh leaned his head against the wall in silence.

Clyffe continued, "The second part of the message is related to the first. It is necessary before you can fulfill the first. Do you know where your map is?"

Offering no reply, Hugh went to his pallet, lifted, it and slid out his map.

"Open it."

Hugh unrolled the map on the table in the flickering flame of the candle, which gave the room a dim light, casting shifting shadows on the walls.

"What do you see?"

Hugh leaned in, his eyes scanning the map. He knew what would be there—the King's castle, roads, rivers, pastures, orchards. What was the point?

"Show me where your heart is on the map."

Hugh traced a road with this finger, stopping before a hill. "At the bottom of this hill."

"That is correct. Now what do you see?"

A thin wisp of smoke began to rise from the map where the hill stood. Hugh snatched the map back, fearing it had gotten too close to the candle. In the place where the smoke had begun, a word began to form over the hill, becoming darker and darker, smoke rising from it as if it were being burned into the parchment. The word said *Self-control*. Hugh threw down the map.

"Wait, there is another," Clyffe said.

On the other side of the hill, smoke began to rise again. Burned into the parchment now was the word *Forgiveness*.

Hugh became conscious of a growing pain in his heart. It wasn't the same sharp pain as when he had received the mark. This pain was more like an ache, as if his heart had been stabbed, the dagger turned and the wound left open. While he gazed at the word *Forgiveness*, a heavy cloak of sorrow descended on him. Tears filled his eyes, blurring the word, streaming down his cheeks, leaving shiny drops on the map. He did not try to stop them. He sat, bent over the table in silence. The ache began to ease until it finally disappeared, leaving him slumped, drained of strength and energy.

Sensing Clyffe's eyes still on him, Hugh said, "You knew what I would see, didn't you?"

"Yes, I did," Clyffe answered softly.

There was more silence, as if Clyffe were allowing Hugh time to struggle with the event that had just occurred and the emotions it engendered.

"Do you understand what has happened?" Clyffe asked. "The map has spoken to you."

Hugh knew what Clyffe meant. He could not control the outbursts of anger, and he could not forgive. He had seen the shock and dismay of those around him when he lost control. He hated who he had become.

"It—" Hugh began, "It comes without warning, overpowers me, and makes me a different person. I have almost hurt people. I am sorry." He dabbed at his eyes with his sleeve.

"In order to accomplish the first, you must also accomplish the second," Clyffe continued. "Without forgiveness you can have no self-control. You have yielded control to those who have wronged you because you believe they have incurred a debt you must make them pay. The mere thought of them drives your rage as a master drives his slave. But when you forgive, both of you are freed— one from the debt, the other from the rage and bitterness over the wrong. The rage will dissipate and self-control then becomes possible."

Hugh took a deep breath, understanding Clyffe's words but not accepting them. "All I wanted was the justice that my King did not give me," Hugh said. "I can't forgive. I can't—until I have justice."

"You can forgive, Hugh, but first you must understand the King's justice. If the King gave you justice, you would face death for violating his Kingdom Rules. Instead of justice, with the key the King offered you mercy and forgiveness, though perhaps you did not understand it at the time."

It had been years now, but Hugh could hear his father's voice explaining that no one could perfectly keep the Kingdom Rules and therefore were as rebels to the King, though he did indeed not see it then. He did not see it now. He had not let the King down; the King had let him down. If justice and vengeance belonged to the King, why didn't he act?

"No," Hugh replied. "Nothing was said about forgiveness. It was just about trusting the King. I did then, though with misgiving, but now I am not sure I can."

"And by trusting the King then, you gave him authority and control over your heart. But you have tried to take it back, and in so doing you have lost control over yourself."

Hugh remembered his father's statement that trusting the King was giving the King authority over him, but he had been too focused on obtaining a key to comprehend what his father meant. Now, enslaved by his mercurial rage, he had already attempted to murder Sir Bailys, and he had nearly killed the Rat. He had lost control. But why should he yield control back to the King? How could he trust the King to deliver justice for his father?

"I want to trust the King. Something must change," Hugh said. "But how can I forgive?"

"Do you understand why you need forgiveness?" Clyffe asked, his eyes searching Hugh's. "Though you had not attempted to kill anyone or even thought of it at the time you were given the key, the seeds of who you have become were there even then. The King has already given you forgiveness with the key; accepting his forgiveness frees you to forgive."

The events of the last three years passed before Hugh's mind as he considered Clyffe's words. He had always taken pride in being in control of his life. The mission to make keys and deliver the maps and being entrusted with the ring had fed that pride and given him a sense of control over even the King's affairs while nurturing a belief that he was above others. The news of his father's death had been the event that shattered his world and propelled him onto his current path. His thoughts and actions had become captive to one goal—revenge—and he had totally discounted and ignored his King. Yet this same King upon whom he had turned his back was willing to set aside those slights and forgive him. Perhaps this King was someone different than he imagined. Perhaps this King could do what he himself could not. Perhaps Hugh could trust him again.

"I want to find again the person I once was," Hugh said, then sighed. "If accepting forgiveness will help me forgive, I need to."

"Will you fulfill your mission?" Clyffe asked.

"Yes, I will," Hugh replied.

The map had spoken to him, as his father said it would. His quest had ended, though not the way he imagined. The wound remained, and also the sorrow—sorrow not over losing his father, but of realizing what he himself had become and of knowing that he could not be the one to execute justice. That still belonged to his King.

"You will not have time to go to the scrivener, as the knight is to leave tomorrow. I have brought you a copy of the *Chronicle* to give him. Farewell, Hugh." Clyffe laid the scrolled parchments on the table, pulled up his hood, and stepped into the night.

Hugh sat in the dim candlelight, broken and listless, his mind re-envisioning the words as they formed on his map. Only recently plotting to kill, his mind still rebelled at the thought of what he had agreed to do, but his aching heart told him he must. He lay down on his pallet without eating, enduring another restless night. He tried to visualize himself presenting the map and key to a grateful Rat. Hugh could not imagine such a thing, for the Rat would be incapable of gratitude.

Hugh faced the next morning as if going to a funeral, dragging himself out of the smithy and stopping by to pick up a box from Thomas. He did not intend to tell Thomas who it was for, but Thomas asked.

Hugh could hardly make himself answer: "It is for ... the Rat," he said, nearly choking on the words.

"What? He is the last I would imagine!" Thomas said, then exhaled a heavy breath. "But ... just like William said, I guess the King did have a plan."

Hugh frowned. "I'll believe it when I see it," he muttered, then clomped out of Thomas's workshop.

Still skeptical, Hugh struggled to suppress his latent bitterness as he approached the tannery. First he stopped in the house to get a map from Brian and seal it.

"He is out there by the stream," Brian said, handing him a map. "Once he was our enemy, but now he is a follower of the King—and a friend." Brian smiled as he handed Hugh a map.

Not my friend. Saying nothing to Brian, Hugh sealed the scrolled map, slipped it into the box and clicked it shut, sliding the dove medallion over the keyhole, then placed it in his bag with the *Chronicle*. He walked out, finding the knight on his feet, his head still bandaged, standing by the stream gazing at the water as if in deep thought. Strangely, as he walked up behind him, Hugh realized he was devoid of anger, though a little apprehensive. How would he react when he looked his father's murderer in the eye? In his mind he saw Clyffe's eyes, fixed on him expectantly, willing him forward on a mission he knew was from his King.

"Sire?" Hugh said.

The knight turned to see who had spoken. He was perhaps a head taller than Hugh. To Hugh's surprise he smiled when he saw Hugh.

"You are the one I was to expect?"

"Yes, sire," Hugh mumbled, avoiding eye contact.

"Walk with me to my horse. My soldiers do not yet know what has happened."

As they began walking, Hugh asked, "Sire, if I may ask, what has happened?"

"What is your name, son?" the knight asked.

"I am Hugh, smith of Loynton."

The Rat chuckled. "It was my intention to torch your smithy, with you in it ... and you are the one the King sends. He is not without a sense of irony." He paused.

Hugh could feel the Rat's eyes on him, but he could not look up.

"I understand that I am known hereabouts by an insulting name, the—"

"Rat!" Hugh said, perhaps more forcefully than even he'd intended.

The knight laughed. "And I bore that name with a certain pride as the counselor and enforcer of my former lord—you call him the Dragon, don't you?"

Hugh could only look at his feet and furrow his brow, wondering why the Rat was telling him this.

"You can probably tell by my speech that I am not one of your countrymen," the Rat went on. "The Dragon employs many mercenaries, and I was one. In my country, because of my hair and Teutonic ancestry, I was called the *Roten Ritter*, or 'Red Knight,' and I was hired to be the Dragon's counselor, his *ratgeber* in my native language. You can see how one could twist those into an insulting name like—"

"The Rat." Hugh coughed as if trying to dislodge a foreign object from his throat.

The knight seemed amused at Hugh's lack of discretion. "In fact that is the name by which I am known in the Dragon's army as well. The name was well-deserved and I bore it proudly. I was on my way here to flush out the secret followers of the true King and burn the village to the ground if necessary when it happened."

Hugh nodded, then thought on the past several days. "If I may ask, what did happen on the road?"

The Rat took a deep breath. "We were about to crest the rise of the hill that leads down into Loynton. I was feeling overheated in my armor in the direct sunlight. A feeling of sudden weakness came over me, and a blinding light seemed to envelop me. I sensed that someone of great authority was beside me, but I could not see him. I thought, *Who are you?* But I must have spoken it aloud because my soldiers tell me I cried out as I began to slide from my horse. The next memory I have will remain with me forever—the gentle face of Charis bent over me, dripping water on my parched tongue."

"But, you seem to have changed," Hugh said. "What caused the change?"

"As I regained my faculties, before I could speak, Charis was saying things to me, perhaps even before I opened my eyes to see her. But in my semi-conscious state, I fought them. It seemed as if a struggle went on in my mind over what was true. By the time I could think clearly, the answers to my questions were already forming in my mind, and by the time I could relate what I remembered, Charis confirmed the answer with an authority that I could not doubt."

"What did she tell you?" Hugh asked. What authority could Charis have over a knight?

"She kept saying to me that the presence I felt was that of the Prince, or the King himself, and my struggle was with the Dragon, who was trying to keep control of me. During that struggle my attitude toward all I had been doing for the Dragon, all that I thought praiseworthy, began to change, so that I viewed it with shame and disgrace. Charis confirmed that my life was saved so that I could serve the true King rather than attack him. It seemed to ring true because I no longer harbored any hatred for the enemies of the Dragon. In fact I was inexplicably drawn to the true King."

They reached the knight's horse and stopped.

The story rang false to Hugh. People didn't just change like that. It wasn't possible. "Why would a knight believe the words of an uneducated woman?" he asked.

"It seems unlikely, doesn't it?" The knight chuckled. "Ordinarily I would skewer a peasant like her without a second thought. But this morning it was confirmed by another person with greater authority."

Hugh shook his head. "There are only peasants and tradesmen in this village. Who?"

"A man who said he was a messenger of the true King stopped to talk to me. He bore the emblem of the King inside his cloak. He is the one who told me about you, to wait for your coming before I left. He confirmed that I was to serve the King by giving me a mission. I was ready to hear this, because when I awakened this morning, I no longer held any allegiance to the Dragon."

"Was his name Clyffe?" Hugh asked.

"He did not say, but he was taller than me and had deep blue eyes. He said I should use a different name now."

"That was Clyffe. He sent me as well. Well, here are the key and the box with the map." Hugh pulled them out of a bag, holding them in his hands with astonished eyes, as if he would not part with them. "Th-The key!" he said. "It is gold! And the box is not the same!"

"You speak as if you have not done this before, yet I was told to expect you."

Hugh could only stare at the key and box. "Every key I have given until now has been of iron. I cannot explain this. And moments ago when I put the box into the bag, the strips were iron, I am certain!" he added as he handed the key and the box to the Rat.

"You will receive no explanation from me, since I knew not what to expect."

"Oh, you will also feel a pain in your heart after you open the box," Hugh said.

"Of that I am aware," the knight replied, taking the box and key.

Hugh watched as he opened the box, removed the map, then clenched his teeth and went rigid for a moment, but he did not cry out. He stuffed the box, map, and key into a saddlebag.

Next Hugh gave him the *Chronicle*. "And this tells what you need to know about the Prince and the King."

The Rat accepted it with a nod. "Yes, Charis has told me about it. I think she was even quoting from it while I was still stuporous."

Having delivered the key and map, Hugh had completed his mission. He had felt neither relief nor joy in doing so. The impulse to turn and walk away overwhelmed him, but the image of his map and the words of Clyffe formed in his mind. He knew he had more to say.

"Sire?" Hugh asked

"Yes, son? And you may call me 'Sir Ralf' now, for that is my true name."

"Sir Ralf." Hugh gave a heavy sigh, then said, "There are some things I have to tell you before we go back. The day that you fell from your horse, I was waiting just over the hill to kill you with an arrow."

"That does not surprise me," Sir Ralf answered calmly. "I am sure that many wish to, and some have tried."

Hugh's emotions now began to overwhelm his resolve. He clenched his jaw, bit hard on his lower lip, and became quiet.

"What is it, son?" the knight inquired. "You want to say something."

Hugh could feel blood beginning to trickle down his chin. He could hold it no longer. "You killed my father!" he blurted.

"I have killed many men," Sir Ralf replied matter-of-factly. He hesitated as if searching his memory. "Was he the blacksmith from Loynton who was captured some years ago?"

The moment his father was taken appeared in Hugh's mind—as freshly as if it had happened yesterday. But instead of rage, he felt only sadness, and the ache of the wound that would never close.

"Yes," Hugh said, his head sagging, eyes fixed on his feet.

The knight's hand grasped his shoulder. "Hugh Smith, your father was a great man, and loyal to his King to the end. I have not seen such courage as he showed. Knights like me who may appear to be courageous are usually motivated only by hatred or greed, but he had real courage. I remember marveling at the time how he could endure such punishment and not break."

The next thing Hugh had to say was even more difficult. He shifted his feet and took a deep breath. "I…I want you to know that I forgive you." Hugh forced the words out, then gave another heavy sigh. "I have to." He wanted to look Sir Ralf in the eye when he said it, but he could not.

"Thank you, son," the knight replied. "There are many things I have done that I now regret and recall with shame. And although the messenger assured me that the King forgives me for them, I cannot forget them. It is a burden I will always carry, but you have made it a little lighter."

"And I want you to forgive me for wanting to kill you," Hugh added.

"Me—forgive you?" Sir Ralf said, raising an eyebrow. "I hardly know what you mean. Clyffe spoke to me about it and I understand that no one deserves forgiveness. But, I also understand now that I have been forgiven for far worse. So, yes, I forgive you."

Having completed however imperfectly the task laid on his heart, Hugh finally felt peace, but he could not dismiss the thought that it had all been pointless, that somehow he would never see Sir Ralf again after the Dragon learned what had happened. Considering Sir Ralf's reputation as "the Rat," he could be a great soldier for the King, but he would probably never get the chance. Nevertheless, Hugh found himself wondering what it would be like to be one of Sir Ralf's soldiers and to ride with him for the King.

In parting Hugh said, "I am sure the King will be pleased to have you fighting for him instead of against him."

"Not nearly as pleased as I am," Sir Ralf answered.

He clapped Hugh on the shoulder before he mounted his horse and began his ride back to his waiting men. He was an imposing figure astride his charger in his armor and red surcoat. Hugh stood quietly, looking on as Sir Ralf reached the tannery, where William, Brian, and Charis awaited him. Sir Ralf signaled to his men to mount their horses and start up to the road. Once their backs were to him, he reached down to clasp arms with William and Brian, and then gave Charis a kiss on the back of her hand. With a final wave Sir Ralf spurred his horse, his auburn hair flying, and galloped to the head of his men.

Hugh watched until he vanished from sight, no longer harboring any anger but rather a feeling of anxiety, wondering what now lay in store for Sir Ralf at the hands of the Dragon.

Chapter 19

THE RAT'S POISON

SIR RALF'S MEN were already grumbling again as he took his place at the head of the column.

"Why didn't we burn the village as you said?" one asked.

"You have denied us the loot you promised!" another said.

Reassuming his former Rat persona, Sir Ralf scowled. "They saved my life. I have decided to reward them by sparing them—temporarily. We will have other opportunities after I have fully recovered. You will get your booty."

The journey back to Draignytha took three days, the men stopping at the Wolf's Den Inn to retrieve their sacks of loot, their spirits much improving afterward. As the horsemen clattered across the cobblestones of Purdyton town square, peasants disappeared down side streets, windows were quickly shut, and doors slammed. Everyone knew the Rat. The guard at the entrance gate to the castle recognized him from a distance, and the drawbridge was already down before he reached it.

As he entered the courtyard, his shadow long from the setting sun, Sir Ralf could hear tongues already wagging: "Here comes the Rat! What village has he burned this time?"

Once again he was returning having failed to accomplish the mission he'd been given. His life would be worth little when the truth was known. But he was not going to slink out of the castle by night. He had always done things with flair. Plundering villages was easy; incinerating them afterward had become his signature. He knew he would be summoned before his king in the morning to give a report of his mission, but he had already hatched a surprise on the way back. He would make his departure memorable.

Using his authority as one of the king's top commanders, he went to the stable first. "Have twenty mounts ready for my men at the gate at dawn."

Then he entered the keep and went to the armory. "You will prepare swords and shields, enough for twenty men," he told the armorer. "We will have a test of arms outside the castle tomorrow. Have the weapons laid out and ready at dawn."

"Yes, milord," the armorer answered.

Sir Ralf then went down the dark stairs to the dungeon. "I am here to interrogate one of the prisoners," he said to the guard, who obediently opened the heavy wooden door, as he had for the Rat on many occasions before. "Give me the keys and a torch. I do not need to be accompanied. I will give them back when I return."

As the king's inquisitor, as well as his counselor and enforcer, Sir Ralf knew well who was in the dungeon at all times. The most important prisoners were kept near the front, where the occupants could be heard through the square, barred window in the dungeon door. He took the torch from the guardroom and plunged into the blackness of the dungeon, placing the torch in a holder on the wall.

At the first cell he whispered, "Sir Andrew!"

"I know it's you, Rat! You can't disguise your voice by whispering. Begone!"

"Shh! I have something to tell you, but it must be done quietly."

"You have nothing to tell me! I am a dead man," the voice spoke from the darkness.

"Sir Andrew, I am alone. You are not to be tortured tonight."

A dirt-caked, bearded face appeared in the barred window of the cell door, highlighted by the dim light of the torch on the wall behind Sir Ralf, its eyes distrustfully searching his face.

"Stay," Sir Ralf said. "I must speak with you."

"I will not speak with the man who is to watch my execution in two days' time!" Sir Andrew spat. "Go back to your Dragon and leave me be."

Exhaling a heavy breath in frustration, Sir Ralf unbuckled his sword belt, gathered up his surcoat, and lifted his mail shirt and tunic to reveal his chest. "What do you see?"

"Nothing," Sir Andrew answered. "Now leave me. I have no more to say to you."

Sir Ralf turned so that the light of the torch played on his chest. "Come closer."

Sir Andrew's face pressed against the bars, his eyes widening with astonishment as he gasped. "Aye, that'd be the mark!"

"I am one of you now," Sir Ralf said

The distrustful look reappeared. "How do I know it's not just painted on, or maybe a tattoo?"

"How would I know what it looks like?" Sir Ralf replied. "And you know that those without it cannot see it on those who have it. I am unlocking your cell. Pull up your tunic. I will find your mark with my finger."

Sir Ralf opened the wooden door and faced the disheveled knight. Still looking dubious, Sir Andrew reached down and grabbed the bottom of his torn and soiled tunic, pulling it slowly to his neck. Sir Ralf stretched out his hand and placed it on Sir Andrew's chest, tracing his mark with a finger.

"There. I see it and have traced its outline. And do you recognize this?" He held up his gold key to the box containing the map.

Sir Andrew, again wide-eyed, whispered, "Yes. That's the key. Who did you steal it from?"

"No one. Now will you listen to me?"

Sir Andrew lowered his eyes and sighed, then slid to the dirt floor by the door, leaning against the wall. "All right. Say what you came to say."

Sir Ralf sat down beside him. "You are not going to be executed."

"You forget that I made an attempt on the life of the Dragon when he entered my domain," Sir Andrew said. "Even you cannot stay his revenge for that, as you have told me yourself."

"I serve a different master now, Sir Andrew. Your King is now my King."

"If that is true, you will occupy this dungeon with me tomorrow—that is, if you are not executed beforehand, as you should be," Sir Andrew replied scornfully.

"I have not spoken with the Dragon. He does not know, and he will not know until my plan is completed."

Sir Andrew shook his head. "What is your plan then, and why are you telling me?"

"You know which of the prisoners have the mark and are of us, do you not?"

"I do. There are twenty including myself."

"The exact number that was put in my mind!" Sir Ralf said. "Tonight you must convince them that I am a follower of the King. I am leaving your door unlocked. When the guard has fallen asleep, you must go their cells and talk to them. I will return at dawn before breakfast is brought to you. There will be twenty horses and sets of arms waiting for you. You will take the keys from me and unlock the doors you have marked and we will escape together."

Sir Andrew lifted tired, doubtful eyes to study Sir Ralf's face. "No one ever escapes from here. You told me that yourself."

"The Rat goes where he wishes," Sir Ralf said, the corners of his mouth forming a half-smile.

Sir Andrew continued to study Sir Ralf's face, still giving evidence of his suspicion about what he was being asked to do. His eyes drifted to Sir Ralf's chest, now covered, and back to his face. "Something is telling me I should trust you, much against my own inclination."

"You must call on that same something when you talk to the others," Sir Ralf said. "I am offering you, and them, freedom."

"Very well, we have nothing to lose," Sir Andrew said. "It may be just another way to die, but I have been in this stinking cell long enough."

"You must be ready before dawn, with the men at their doors. It will happen quickly."

"We will be as ready as men you have broken can be," Sir Andrew replied, with no attempt to hide his sarcasm.

Sir Ralf did not begrudge Sir Andrew's reply, giving him only a nod of understanding. Then he stood and closed the knight's cell door, leaving it unlocked. He gave the keys to the guard, who locked the dungeon door, and made his way up to his quarters overlooking the courtyard. Night had fallen; the courtyard was quiet as usual. Torches on the battlements outlined the sentries as they walked their courses on the walls. Sir Ralf sat on his bed, reviewing in his mind the sequence of events for the morrow. A heavy sense of oppression settled around him as he reviewed his strategy. He knew that his plan was fraught with extreme danger for both him and those he would lead, his only weapon being the trust he had gained from those in the castle who knew him, a trust that he would soon betray.

He spent the night sleepless and was still at his single window as the first light appeared to the east. The clop of horses' hoofs informed him that the stabler was bringing his horses to the gate. He took a deep breath and headed toward the dungeon, passing the chamberlain on the way.

"Sire!" the chamberlain said.

"Later. I can't stop," Sir Ralf said, brushing past him.

"But, sire, the king wishes you to join him as he breaks fast. He is anxious to hear how you eliminated the subversive activity in Loynton."

"Certainly. I am on the way to see an important prisoner. I will join him shortly."

"Sire, I remind you that the king does not brook delay, even from you."

"You must tell him that after I have seen the prisoner, he will hear of an unimaginable success," Sir Ralf said over his shoulder as he continued down the stairs.

Entering the dungeon, Sir Ralf found the guard asleep, as he had expected.

"Quickly, man," he shouted. "The king is waiting on me."

The guard woke with a start, jumped to the dungeon door, and unlocked it. Sir Ralf grabbed the torch and entered.

"Come in with me," Sir Ralf ordered. Once inside, he barked, "Give me the keys!"

Cowering, the guard complied.

"Sir Andrew!" Sir Ralf whispered into the darkness.

Sir Andrew's cell door swung open to reveal the haggard figure.

"Take the keys and gather your men!"

"But, sire!" the guard said. "These are the worst of the king's prisoners. They will escape!"

"Not another word from you, if you value your life!" Sir Ralf hissed, the point of his now unsheathed sword nudging the guard's throat.

Keys in hand, Sir Andrew went from cell to cell, unlocking doors and sending unkempt, filth-caked men into a group by Sir Ralf.

After a matter of minutes, a breathless Sir Andrew rejoined the group. "We are twenty—as you desired."

Sir Ralf shoved the guard into Sir Andrew's cell, locking it. The crowd then stumbled out of the dungeon into the dim light of the guardroom, blinking, some steadying others as they waited to see what would happen next.

"When I return, be ready to move," Sir Ralf said before disappearing up the stairs.

Reaching the entrance to the courtyard, he looked toward the gate, noting that the portcullis was up and the drawbridge down to allow the horses to be taken to the outer gatehouse. He glanced back in the direction of the armory. The door was open. Hurrying back down to the dungeon, he motioned to the prisoners. "Follow me! No words or noise."

The din of shuffling footsteps filled the curving staircase as the jostling mob labored to the surface. Sir Ralf sprinted to the armory and burst inside, sword drawn, followed shortly by the mob, the stronger helping the weaker.

Backing the armorer to a wall with his sword, Sir Ralf pointed to the shields and swords laid out on tables, then said to the group, "Arm yourselves and remain here until I signal. Sir Andrew, come to the keep entrance and watch the gate tower. When you see a torch moving in the window, it means I have disarmed the portcullis guard. Run to the gate with your men."

Sir Andrew laughed. "Run? We can hardly walk!"

"Then move as fast as you can."

Sir Ralf poked his head out to assure himself the guards on the battlements were still patrolling, looking outward as usual. No one had raised an alarm yet. Then he raced across the courtyard to the gate tower, and up the stairs to the room housing the winch for the portcullis.

"You are to relieve the gatehouse guard," he told the portcullis guard. "I will remain here until your relief comes."

The man rose, said "Yes, sire," and headed down the stairs.

As soon as he had vanished, Sir Ralf jerked a torch from the wall and flashed it back and forth near the window overlooking the courtyard. Within seconds a dark crowd stumbled out of the armory and began to struggle toward the drawbridge, followed by the armorer, shouting, "Escape! To arms! Close the gate!"

"Escape!" echoed from the walls as footsteps of soldiers began to pound along the walls and down the stone steps.

Sir Ralf met the portcullis guard coming back up. He kicked him down the stairs and kept running, leaving him in an unconscious heap. Sir Andrew and his men were halfway across the courtyard to the drawbridge, but straggling as weaker prisoners fell behind. Already a guard was beginning to crank the winch to raise the drawbridge. Sir Ralf emerged from the guard tower and administered a heavy blow, knocking the guard to the ground. As the front of Sir Andrew's mob reached the gate, numerous forms poured from the keep and the battlements, racing toward the gate, swords drawn. The escapees were not moving fast enough! Sir Ralf's plan was beginning to unravel. An awful decision confronted him.

"Run!" he bellowed. "You must leave the stragglers!"

The strongest of the group panted through the entry, across the drawbridge to the outer gatehouse, where a puzzled guard stood, his sword drawn, clearly frightened by the size of the armed and desperate force coming upon him. He dropped his sword and fled. The four stable hands, each holding five horses, were equally perplexed, as if trying to decide whether to remain or release the horses and run as well. Sir Ralf cast a glance back at the courtyard. Already some of the stragglers had been brought to ground and were being dragged away.

"Hold the horses!" Sir Ralf commanded from the front of the mass of emaciated men.

Recognizing the Rat and the shields with the dragon emblem, the stable hands complied until Sir Andrew, with Sir Ralf, had brought his men to them.

"Mount up, men!" Sir Ralf shouted above the din of mailed feet behind them on the drawbridge.

Already arrows were sailing over them and thudding into the ground near them. Another fugitive went down with an arrow in the back.

"Follow me to the true King!" Sir Ralf said, spurring his horse onto the road.

They sped away at a gallop, maintaining their pace as long as they could. By the time the crossroads came into view, the day was waning and their horses were spent. Sir Ralf counted only fifteen men, all clinging to their mounts and gasping for breath, some having dropped their shields and swords along the away. They were not a group fit for combat.

"We will go to Bartscastle!" Sir Ralf shouted, mindful that a horde of the Dragon's soldiers was surely close behind. "If your horse gives out, mount with another. We must reach Bartscastle or die trying!"

Sir Ralf found the road to Bartscastle amidst the downed trees, the others following. Ahead on the road stood a solitary armed figure, his visor down, beckoning Sir Ralf to stop.

"Out of the way, man, lest we trample you!" Sir Ralf said hurriedly.

"Sir Ralf!" the other shouted, raising his visor. "I would have a word with you."

Sir Ralf reined in his frothing horse. "How do you know my name? Be quick! We are pursued!"

"I am here to help you. You are in the King's domain and under his protection now."

Sir Ralf looked the stranger over. He was tall, well-muscled, and clad in mail, wearing the blue and white surcoat of the King. He looked to be a worthy fighter, but he was only one.

"Who are you? And what can one person do to help us?"

"I am Michael, Guardian of Bartscastle," the man replied. "The King has sent me to protect you."

Sir Ralf laughed. "Protect me? How? There are fifty to a hundred men behind us!"

"Remain with me and watch. You may send the others on to Bartscastle. They are safe. Walk with me to the crossroads."

"Dismount?" Sir Ralf shook his head. "Get out of my way! I am going to lead my men to Bartscastle. You can try to do what you came to do on your own. The consequence of my being captured is certain death. You do not know the Dragon."

"Actually I do know the Dragon, and very well," Michael said. "As you are new to the Kingdom, it is the King's desire that you remain with me as a witness to his protection of those who are his."

"Protection of those who are his? What does that mean? It is going to take a lot more than one of his men to protect us from what is coming. What I need is distance from our pursuers, and you are impeding me. Good luck." Sir Ralf turned his horse to continue on the road.

"Wait, Sir Ralf!" Michael called out. "When the King's messenger told you that you were to receive the key and map, did he not also tell you that the same Prince whom you encountered on the road would henceforth be with you in spirit and power?"

"Just words. What do they mean at a time like this? I have never trusted any power but my own, and it has been sufficient. Rescuing these men was entirely my doing."

"Perhaps it was, and perhaps it was not," Michael answered. "Nevertheless you are about to face power that you cannot overcome on your own. And you will not escape unless you remain with me and trust the power of the Prince."

Sir Ralf was unsure of Michael's meaning, but he knew well that a large force was certainly in pursuit, more men than he could overcome alone, and he was more than a little curious to see what this Michael would do with the "power of the Prince."

"Very well, though it is against my better judgment," Sir Ralf said, dismounting. "But I would yield to the King's wishes. You had better have some more men close by. You're going to need them."

Having instructed Sir Andrew to lead the survivors toward Bartscastle, on foot if necessary, Sir Ralf accompanied Michael on foot to the crossroads where the sign pointed to Purdyton, arriving just as the pursuers came into sight, led by an imposing knight clad entirely in black save for his red shield with the gold dragon.

"It is one of the Dragon's Immortals!" Sir Ralf said. "We are outmatched already."

"I know who it is," Michael answered, showing no sign of fear as he lowered his visor.

"Then you know also that even two of us cannot prevail against him," Sir Ralf added, looking quickly behind him for Michael's reinforcements.

The Black Knight came to a halt, nothing visible through his visor but two ruthless blue eyes focused on Sir Ralf with the same predatory stare that had made his skin crawl in the Dragon's throne room.

"Well, well, it looks like we have cornered a Rat!" the Black Knight roared in his ragged voice.

"A cornered rat can be a vicious animal," Sir Ralf snarled, drawing his sword. "You will have to fight me!"

"Ha! Those are foolish words from one who does not have the power to defeat me."

"But *I* do," Michael said, stepping out from behind Sir Ralf and raising his visor.

The horseman lifted his gaze from Sir Ralf. "Michael? It has been awhile," he rasped.

"Yes, it has, Gythreul," Michael said.

"You know well that we are of the same ilk, and that you are no more powerful than I," Gythreul said. "This is not your fight. Step aside!"

"Therein you are mistaken, Gythreul. It is the King's fight, and I stand against you with the spirit of the Prince and the might of the King before and behind me. You know as well as I that you cannot prevail against them, nor can your rebel lord!"

Clearly taken aback, Gythreul paused, as if restrained by the truth of Michael's words. Sir Ralf watched in amazement to see what would happen next as the Black Knight refocused his gaze back to him.

"You have been fortunate this time, Rat," Gythreul said, giving no hint of what had changed his mind. "Note well that my king does not forgive such betrayal. From this moment I and my Companions will hunt you until your last breath! If ever we catch you without your so-called 'protection,' rest assured that our king himself will be the one administering your torture before he butchers you!"

Looking back at Michael, Gythreul said, "My king does not take lightly such interference, Michael. Look well to your castle!"

Then Gythreul spurred his horse, barking orders to the soldiers who had formed up behind him: "Follow me. We return to the castle. There will be other opportunities to trap a Rat."

Sir Ralf stood motionless, still holding his sword, and watched them ride off, his face displaying an expression of shock.

"What you have just witnessed," Michael said, "is the power of the King when one trusts the spirit of the Prince. The same power is yours if you claim it. Let us go to Bartscastle now. I want you to meet Sir Bart and tell him your story."

Gathering his wits, Sir Ralf nodded. "Gladly, Michael, but I have a request." He sheathed his sword, still reviewing in his mind the remarkable event that had occurred. "There is some unfinished business I must attend to."

"You may present that request to Sir Bart," Michael replied.

"Then perhaps you can tell me more about yourself as well on the way there, Michael. You said you were a guardian of Bartscastle? What does that mean? I have never seen anyone stand down one of the Immortals as you just did."

Chapter 20

THE KNIGHT

OVER A MONTH passed before Sir Bart had healed sufficiently from his wound to travel. By that time summer had slipped into fall, and they had welcomed Sir Ralf—formerly the infamous Rat—into the castle after Michael himself brought the knight to Sir Bart. Stephen could hardly believe the turn of events, but was learning to expect the unexpected as a new member of the Kingdom himself.

Not long afterward, Stephen and Sir Bart set out on the four-day journey to the closest of the King's castles. Sir Bart invited Stephen's mother to accompany them, providing a cart for her. The morning air was crisp, the leaves beginning to turn scarlet and gold in the forests along the road when they set out. Stephen rode with a sense of excitement mixed with anxiety. He was going to become a knight! People would address him as "Sir Stephen." What if his father could see him now?

As the party neared the castle, his thoughts flew back to times as a child when he had wondered if the King were actually real, and now he was going to actually see him! Then he began to wonder if the King really knew everything about him. What if a mistake had been made and he would not be knighted after all when the King found out his shortcomings? Or maybe the King already knew and he would be stopped at the gate, then be told to turn around and leave. After four days of uneventful travel, still feeling a mix of anticipation and apprehension, Stephen topped a rise to behold in the distance in faint silhouette a series of towers, more than he had ever seen before. It seemed as if rings of towers surrounded a great keep that itself was as large as and much taller than Sir Bart's entire castle. Another hour passed before they finally arrived at the gate of the first curtain wall.

"Is this where the King lives?" Stephen asked in a hushed tone.

"It is one of his castles," Sir Bart answered, "one of the places he stays when he travels his lands. No one is allowed to visit the castle where he lives unless they are invited."

When they crossed the first drawbridge, the King's banner with its emblem—a lion, a lamb, and a dove on a sea of blue—was draped prominently above the gate. As they entered through the second gate, Stephen noted that hardly any soldiers patrolled atop the walls—and no one among the castle staff they met seemed afraid of anything. Both Stephen and his mother were given rooms on one of the guest floors of the keep. They had never seen such luxury. Not only the floors, but also the walls were wooden—polished wood—adorned with colorful tapestries, and they slept in actual beds with canopies, feather pillows, and feather mattresses. Fresh flowers in each room gave off the sweetest aroma, and the rooms also contained a standing chest with drawers for clothing and a table with cushioned chairs. On the table was a copy of the *Chronicle* in book form, with colorful illustrations, gold lettering and gilt-edged pages, and beside it a stack of paper and inkwell with a quill.

That first night, Stephen received a visitor from the King's court who told him, "Sir Bart has informed the court of your training and your character, as well as your conduct on the battlefield, and your trust in the spirit of the Prince, all of which have been relayed to the King. He is greatly pleased with you. I will explain to you now the sequence of events."

Early the next morning before the ceremony, Stephen went as instructed to the chapel to prepare himself to be in the King's presence. The chapel extended out of one end of the keep and had a height of several floors itself, but it was completely open inside to the vaulted ceiling. Stephen had never seen one of the King's chapels before, but as he entered, he recalled travelers' stories describing great and magnificent buildings of the King. The stone pillars that supported the roof had ribs that met in the peak of the ceiling to form majestic pointed arches, and the upper walls of the chapel were filled with great windows of colored glass that illustrated stories from the *Chronicle*. Sunlight cast dazzling patterns on the stone floor as he approached the altar. He imagined himself being washed with the colors of the *Chronicle* as he walked toward the apse.

No one was in the chapel as he knelt at the altar. He searched his heart for all the ways that he had fallen short of the Kingdom Rules and confessed them as he had been instructed to do.

After returning to his room, he waited for Sir Bart, who took him to another room next to the chapel reserved for the purification ritual. Inside sat a circular stone vat, into which Sir Bart poured hot water. Stephen discarded his travel clothes and plunged his whole body under the water, lathering up as he never had before. The water held his body in such a warm and soothing embrace he did not want to emerge. If this was truly to purify him, he wanted to be spotless!

After spending more time in the bath than he should have, Stephen emerged and began to dry himself off, finally sitting on the steps to dry his feet.

From where he had been standing at the edge of the room, Sir Bart called out, "Stop! That is my job."

"What? Drying my feet?" Stephen asked.

"It is part of the ritual that I serve you," Sir Bart said. "I put your water in the bath and prepared your clothing for the ceremony. It also includes my washing and drying your feet."

Stephen shook his head. "I don't understand why you are serving me. You are a great knight of the King. And especially why wash my feet? They are the dirtiest part."

"It is something the Prince did for each of us twelve before we went into the last battle. We did not understand either, but he said he did it as an example of how we knights are to serve others. We are not to put ourselves above the lowest form of service—something you would do well to remember."

Sir Bart re-washed and dried Stephen's feet, then brought him a new set of clothes to wear, all pure white—white leggings, white braies[12] to attach them to, and a white tunic. Over that came a white surcoat with the King's emblem emblazoned on the chest, and for his feet, soft leather boots. Last, Sir Bart brought out a hooded cloak that was deep scarlet in color.

"These are the garments you will wear before the King," said Sir Bart. "Even though you have undergone the purification ritual, the King knows that you are not totally pure. However, he desires to see you as pure when you come before him."

"But the cloak is scarlet," Stephen said. "How does that speak of purity?"

"The white clothing is a gift from the King for you to keep, but this," he said, holding up the cloak, "belonged to the Prince himself. After the Prince died,

---

[12] Underwear.

the King established a new order of knighthood to perpetuate the character and memory of his beloved son. He named its members 'Knights of the Blood' to honor the blood that was shed by his son. All new knights are inducted into this order. By wearing the cloak in the King's presence, you declare your loyalty to the King, showing by the scarlet color of the cloak that you are covered by the blood of the Prince and therefore through his death acceptable to the King. This pleases the King and honors his son."

"The Kingdom Rules...the clothing. The King seems very particular," Stephen answered. "I am not sure he will like me."

"To be sure, he is very clear about what he wishes," Sir Bart said, nodding. "The purification and the clothing allow him to accept you into his presence even though you have not kept his Rules. He is who he is, but that does not mean he is unfriendly."

"He must be very old by now too," Stephen said.

"Yes." Sir Bart chuckled. "It is said that he has always been King and always will be. Now come, it is almost time. He is probably in the chapel by now. Are you ready?"

"Not really," Stephen said, adjusting the cloak with trembling hands. "I always dreamt about this, but knowing the order was established to perpetuate his son's character and wearing his son's cloak, now I feel most unworthy." Stephen paused, not certain if he should say what he was thinking. "Sir Bart, I have a confession to make."

"Yes?"

"You are right. I have not satisfied the Kingdom Rules. In the battle I wanted to run away. I did not want to sacrifice myself for the King."

The old knight looked Stephen in the eye. "Son, the King does not expect us to be without error, doubts, or fear. Regardless of how you felt at the time, you did put yourself in front of me in a position that could have cost you your life. Moreover he is not knighting you for your worthiness. Do you remember when you were first a squire, I told you that you had been chosen by the King?"

Stephen scratched his head. That seemed like an eternity ago. "Yes, and it bothered me because I could not understand what you meant."

Sir Bart nodded and continued, "The king chooses those he uses. He had already chosen you for his Kingdom long before the battle, though you were not ready. Remember the voice that spoke to you in battle. Your knighthood is merely the recognition that you are now ready to be used as a leader in his Kingdom."

"I do not feel at all ready to lead," Stephen said, slumping a bit as he felt the full weight of the cloak on his shoulders. "What if I am asked why I am appearing to be knighted, or if I cannot even remember the things you told me to say during the ceremony?"

Sir Bart placed a hand on Stephen's shoulder, gripping it. "The Prince himself told us that we should not worry about how to defend ourselves or what to say, but to say or do what is given to us at the time because it is given by his spirit and we lead by his spirit. You are here now instead of a year from now because you chose to trust the spirit of the Prince to guide you in battle. Regardless of how you feel about yourself now, you must trust that what we have rehearsed will be sufficient, and trust the same spirit that led you before."

After they left the purification room and were walking toward the chapel, Stephen felt more uneasy, his throat began to close, and his breaths became more frequent and shallow. By the time they approached the entrance to the chapel, he had almost become ill, imagining he was about to come face to face with an almost mythical figure, larger than life, indescribable, maybe even unapproachable. When they entered, light and noise flooded Stephen's senses—the light from an undetectable source, the noise a hum of voices emanating from a great assembly of people which echoed off the stone walls. Instead of only three other people as in Sir Bart's castle chapel three years prior, rows of knights clad in surcoats of the King's blue and white colors filled this chapel, all facing the altar. Instead of the near darkness of Sir Bart's chapel, the nave seemed lit from within and without, though Stephen saw no torches. The colors of the stained-glass windows blazed with a brightness that far exceeded his experience of them earlier that morning.

Stephen squinted to detect details of the scene before him. Some distance behind the altar, in the apse, stood a marble dais with steps leading up to a golden throne occupied by a solitary figure, clad in white. Brilliant light flooding through the chancel windows behind rendered the figure in partial shadow, but Stephen could make out a crown on his head, and a golden mask covering his face. The rays of sunlight created a scintillating glow around the seated King which caused the golden highlights of the throne to gleam and the sapphires encrusted in it to sparkle. Even the King's white clothing seemed to glow, as if it were a source of light. *The blue, gold and white of the King's colors,* Stephen realized. The top of the throne was surmounted by the golden head of a lion, its sapphire eyes blazing; to the right of the throne lay a life-size marble lamb, or was it a real one? On either side of the apse, facing each other and forming an aisle leading to the altar, stood a row of magnificent knights in white surcoats facing each other, their hands grasping great broadswords by the hilt, the tips resting on the floor. Trumpeters arrayed behind them on either side raised their instruments to sound a glorious fanfare. Shading his eyes from the intense light, Stephen noted a priest behind the long altar, which displayed the many items laid out for the ceremony.

"We will approach the altar and kneel before the King," Sir Bart said. "Remember, you may not regard the King's face. The priest will conduct the ceremony."

"Why are there so many people here?" Stephen whispered.

They moved toward the altar, which rested in the transept crossing, down an aisle lined by knights wearing the colors of the King, facing the altar. Stephen hoped he would not embarrass himself before such a crowd.

"All of the members of the order rejoice when a new one is added," Sir Bart said, "and as many as possible try to attend."

Stephen and Sir Bart reached the altar, sank to their knees, and lowered their heads, Stephen's heart pounding so hard that he imagined his whole head must be visibly pulsating.

"Why does the King wear a mask?" Stephen whispered.

"It is to protect us," Sir Bart replied. "Those who have broken his rules and once been rebels cannot look upon his face."

"Who comes before the King to become a Knight of the Blood?" the priest asked.

"Stephen, squire to Sir Bartholomew," Stephen squeaked, as he'd been told to say.

"And who presents him to the King?"

"Sir Bartholomew, Knight of the Chalice," Sir Bart answered.

"What are his qualifications?" the priest intoned.

"None," Sir Bart and Stephen answered together.

Sir Bart continued, "Save loyalty to the King and trust in the spirit of his son, the Prince."

"Do you affirm this, Squire Stephen?" the priest asked.

"Yes," Stephen answered, more firmly this time, still keeping his head bowed.

Stephen waited, eyes closed. The silence was palpable, as if time had stopped and he had been left weighing in the scales. Was there a problem? He wanted desperately to open his eyes to see why nothing was happening, but then he remembered what Sir Bart said about looking at the King. He waited, until he felt embraced by an inexplicable warmth.

Finally a voice spoke—the voice of the King, who had joined the priest at the altar, so close now that Stephen could probably reach out and touch him.

His voice did not thunder, as Stephen expected; rather it was soft, kind and gentle, as if he were talking to a friend: "Sir Bartholomew, you have prepared him well. Only seventeen, and he would have given his life for you and for me."

"Yes, my King," Sir Bart said.

Stephen kept his eyes shut, imagining what the King must look like. Was his hair white? Did he have a long beard? Was he as tall as Michael? Taller? What would happen if he saw the King's face? Next he heard the priest's voice: "Squire Stephen, by your voluntary presence before the King, you pledge eternal loyalty to him and him only. Do you affirm this?"

"Yes."

"You place yourself irrevocably under his lordship and pledge your whole self to him, whether it mean living for him or dying for him. Do you affirm this?"

"I do."

The voice of the King spoke again: "You may take your place in the ranks, Sir Bart." Then, in a voice as soothing as the gentle touch of a summer breeze, he said, "Squire Stephen, you pledge to trust the spirit of my son to guide you in all things, to exemplify his character before the world to the best of your ability, and to seek others to be brought into my Kingdom. Do you affirm this?"

"Yes, my Lord."

Stephen felt the tap of a blade on each shoulder.

"Rise, Sir Stephen, Knight of the Blood, and brother to my son. In you I am well pleased. You may stand."

Stephen opened his eyes and stood, to see only the back of the king's white cloak outlined in blinding light as he returned to his throne. The white knights lining his path kneeled as one with heads bowed.

"You will remain standing as we begin the equipping," the priest said.

Only then did Stephen examine the items on the altar—many more than when he had become a squire. The center was dominated by an exquisite gold chalice. At the bottom of the cup was the head of a dove, its head facing him, its two outstretched wings curving up to touch the rim. To either side of the chalice lay a pair of gilded spurs, a fine leather sword belt, a beautiful sword with gilded hilt and leather grip inlaid with a white stone, a blue shield with the King's emblem, a breastplate, a helmet, and some folded blue clothing.

"Sir Bartholomew, come forward. Sir Stephen, kneel to receive your spurs," the priest said.

Stephen watched Sir Bart take the pair of gilt spurs from the altar, and again Stephen felt him push them onto his heels as he had done before.

"These spurs are recognition that you are ready to ride into battle as a knight of the King, to fight for peace in his Kingdom, and to uphold his honor," the priest said. "Stand."

Stephen stood again. Sir Bart lifted the sword belt and fastened it around Stephen's hips. The word *Veritas* was beautifully tooled in the leather. As before, Sir Bart took the sword with both hands and presented it to Stephen. Having noted earlier an inscription of some kind on the blade, Stephen tilted it until he could see that it said *Spiritus Sanctus* on one side and *Logos Theos* on the other. The white stone embedded in the grip was a piece of ivory carved in the form of a dove; on the other side of the grip was a piece of ivory in the shape of a lamb. The bronze pommel was in the shape of a lion's head.

"This belt signifies that you bear the truth of the Kingdom wherever you go," the priest said, "and the sword is your weapon to defend the Kingdom as you are led by the words and the spirit of the Prince. You may kiss and sheathe the sword."

Next Sir Bart lifted the shield and presented it to Stephen. He recognized immediately that it was the same that the knights of Sir Bart and Sir John had carried in battle, with its emblem of lion, lamb, and dove, without the chalice. He could hardly believe he was holding it now. Sir Bart then gave him the helmet, whose crest was in the form of a recumbent lion, its head resting on the ground. Stephen tucked it under his right arm as Sir Bart fastened on the breastplate, which also bore a relief of the lion, lamb, and dove. Finally he handed Stephen the folded clothes, which he supposed was the blue surcoat of Knights of the Blood.

"Trust this shield to faithfully deflect the arrows and blows of the enemy," said the priest.

Stephen's mind wandered to the battle just past when Michael had used Sir Bart's shield to protect him from the enemy's arrows.

"The helmet is a reminder that the King has claimed you as his own and will keep you safely in the Kingdom against all threats; the breastplate proclaims your right relationship to the King while at the same time it defends your heart from the enemy's blows. So equipped, you will be able to stand firm for the King. You may now turn to face your brothers-in-arms."

Stephen turned and faced the crowded nave to a chorus of cheers erupting among the observing knights. The last time Stephen had heard cheers like these occurred when he had won a victory in the squires' joust. A rush of pride energized him, even though he hadn't done anything to deserve it this time.

"The cheers are not for you, son," the priest said, ushering him back to reality. "They are for the King and his Kingdom. Now turn to face me. We will share the cup of consecration."

Humbled, Stephen turned back to face the priest, who was now lifting the chalice by the stem, the dove facing Stephen. Taking a sip, he handed it to Stephen and motioned for him to do the same. Stephen deposited his items on the altar and grasped the stem, turning the chalice to drink, noting that the side now facing him was embossed with the very same lion and lamb that appeared on the King's emblem. Bringing the chalice to his lips, and inhaling the sweet aroma, he recognized that he was drinking very fine wine.

"In this we remember the blood of the Prince, shed for the Kingdom. May his spirit rest on you powerfully."

With that benediction, the ceremony ended. Stephen was now a knight.

Sir Bart was the first to offer his hand. "Until now I treated you as a son. Now I call you 'brother,'" he said, grasping Stephen's forearm.

Many of the other knights filed by to do the same, the last being Sir John, who stayed to walk out with Stephen and Sir Bart.

"I have seen this many times, as have you, Sir Bart," he said, "and it still brings tears to my eyes."

"It brought me a dry mouth, shortness of breath, and a pounding headache," Stephen said, relieved that it was over.

As they exited the chapel, Stephen was still trying to get used to the idea that Sir Bart and Sir John were his "brothers." And other thoughts nagged him. They stopped briefly outside the chapel, Sir John having to depart in a different direction.

Glancing at the two knights in turn, Stephen asked, "That chalice. Was it the one—"

"The one that the Prince shared with us before the battle?" Sir Bart said. "Yes, it is the same. It is said that to be a true Knight of the Blood, you must drink from the Prince's cup."

"The light was almost unbearable," Stephen said. "I wanted to look at the King when he spoke to me, but you told me not to. Why?"

"Our inclusion in the Kingdom does not change the fact that we are by nature still rebels, restored at a price," Sir Bart replied. "The King's royal person cannot be violated by the eyes of one who was once a rebel unless he first permits it. That is why he wears a mask when he is with his people and why when he descends from his throne to be among us, we all kneel and bow our heads.

He is the source of the light—but it is a burning fire to those who disregard his desire and dare to look him in the eye."

"Whew! I am glad I did look not, then, but someday I wish I could. He seemed so kind."

"He *is* kind," Sir Bart said. "And someday you will see him face to face."

The sequence of events flowed through Stephen's mind afresh. *Someday* he would? He was already looking forward to that day. But he had one more question: "The priest," Stephen continued. "Something seemed familiar about him. Maybe it was his voice? I have never seen him before, but I am almost certain I have heard that voice somewhere else."

Sir Bart smiled at Stephen and then winked. "Yes, perhaps. He bears a striking resemblance to the Prince, doesn't he, Sir John?"

Chapter 21

GATHERING AT GRANDVIL

THE MOOD WAS joyous at the next meeting of the Servants. The village had narrowly avoided disaster. Everyone agreed that Charis was the heroine. Both William and Brian were the first to admit that if Charis had not sat with Sir Ralf the entire time she was nursing him back to health and filled his mind with truths of the Kingdom even before he awakened, the outcome could have been different, but all were equally aware that Sir Ralf's transformation had involved more than just Charis. At the same time Hugh had himself undergone somewhat of a transformation. Though he was not proud of how he had performed his task of delivering the key and box to Sir Ralf, he had done that which had been laid on his heart by Clyffe. The simmering quest for vengeance was gone now, though he still wondered sometimes what had become of Sir Ralf. He now looked to each day with a new freedom to devote himself to his mission as a messenger for the King. Another farmer had joined the Servants with his wife and son.

They still faced the threat of imminent battle if Sir Bailys called on them, but the event with Sir Ralf had consumed the attention of the village. Grateful villagers had come to pay their respects to Charis upon their return from hiding in the countryside, but few were interested in hearing Charis's explanation of the reason for the Rat's change of heart, assuming it was merely gratitude for her role in his recovery. Thomas finished the six longbows for the new archers and resumed his normal carpentry duties. Likewise William and Brian completed the leather jerkins for the archers. Hugh and his apprentice were making the last of four shirts of mail and four swords for Sir Bailys's bodyguards.

Because Hugh owned both a horse and a sword, the bailiff had asked him to be lieutenant of the archers, with himself as captain. Hugh was given primary responsibility as well for the training of the six archers who had not used the longbow before. With Thomas's help, he had been able to improve their technique enough that they were passable, though not as accurate as William, Brian and Thomas.

Not long after, the bailiff poked his head into the smithy with a new request: "Hugh, you must assemble the archers and bring them with me into Grandvil tomorrow. Sir Bailys wishes to review all his soldiers. Targets will be set up in the town square so that they may demonstrate their prowess." The bailiff turned and departed without waiting for Hugh's reply.

Hugh stood there, wanting to question the bailiff further. Was Sir Bailys recruiting an army? If so, what for? Was there to be a battle against the King? If that were the case, Hugh knew that he could not be a part of it. He also knew refusal could mean certain reprisal at the hand of Sir Bailys. His anxiety mounting, Hugh rode to each member of the archery company's homes to inform them to assemble in Loynton village square on the morrow.

The next day Hugh arrived in the square early to welcome each archer as he appeared. They all wore their leather jerkins proudly. Thomas circulated to each of the novices to make sure they were comfortable with their new bows, having each do a full draw without an arrow to check their form. Hugh had asked his apprentice to bring his horse, laden with the four mail shirts and the swords that he would present to Sir Bailys. As soon as all were present, the bailiff led them out of the village and up the road to Grandvil, their feet kicking up puffs of dust as they passed the knight's forest, Hugh and the bailiff mounted in front. All seemed quiet as they marched past the knight's manor house and approached the town; no one was about. *An unusual occurrence,* Hugh thought.

As they neared the town square in the afternoon, the sounds of horse hoofs stamping and the guttural shouts of men rose in the still air, and there were a few barking dogs, but where was the hustle and bustle? Where were the children who usually ran in the streets? Upon entering the square, Hugh's eyes took in the largest collection of soldiers he had ever seen. Sir Bailys, on horseback, followed by four mounted bodyguards, was moving slowly back and forth on the cobblestoned surface, which held several separate bands of men. In the middle of the town square stood a small group of armored men-at-arms wearing mail shirts—some sharpening their swords, others carefully practicing their swordsmanship. Another group of about a dozen archers clustered nearby, leaning on their bows, laughing and talking. By far the largest group was one of roughly dressed peasants armed with a smattering of weapons—axes, pitchforks, spears—standing in a dense crowd, looking half-bored, half-annoyed at having to leave their fields.

Hugh surveyed the square. No townspeople were to be seen, but as the group moved into the square, something caught his eye. To one side of the square, swaying gently, a body hung on the gibbet, the rope creaking rhythmically in the wind. A peasant had paid the price. *For what?*

"There's been a hanging!" Hugh whispered to Brian.

"Ah, Gilbert, your fine company of archers," exclaimed Sir Bailys, riding up to the bailiff. "I have been bragging about them. I have bet a hunting dog that they can best the mayor's twelve."

"And so they shall," the bailiff said, glancing back at Hugh with raised eyebrows. "And Hugh, here, has the mail shirts you requested."

"Fine, he can give them to one of my men."

Hugh could tell by looking at the other group of archers that they were undisciplined. Some just slouched on their bows and joked even as another sent an arrow skipping over the cobblestones after a stray dog.

The contest was not even competitive. Each of the Loynton men bested his counterpart in both range and accuracy.

Sir Bailys seemed pleased as he rode up to the group afterward. "You have not let me down, Gilbert," he said. "The Loynton Company is my best unit. Now I want you to prepare them to fire flaming arrows. There will soon be a need."

Hugh pricked up his ears. So they were going to battle! But when? And where? And why flaming arrows? The bailiff brought the company together with the mayor's archers, who had received the same order.

"Men!" the mayor said, "You will find a barrel of pitch and piles of wool fabric, flax fiber, and leather scraps over by the gibbet. My lieutenant, Peter, will demonstrate how it is done."

The men ambled as a loose group to the barrel, trying to avoid looking at the twisting body just above them. A grizzled man already showing the wrinkles and gray streaks of age on his face and in his ruffled hair, Peter stood before them.

"Sit yourselves down, lads, and watch what I do."

With grunts, groans, and complaints, everyone complied. Peter selected a scrap of wool fabric, took out his knife and cut a piece approximately a foot square. Then he gathered some greasy flax fibers from a pile next to him and began to roll it into a ball with his rough hands.

"This flax tow[13] has been soaked in mutton fat so that it will burn," he said.

Next he placed the ball in the middle of the wool and grabbed a piece of leather. Again using his knife, he cut a narrow foot-long strip off the edge and tossed it onto the wool. Sitting heavily with a grunt, he drew an arrow and placed its tip into the ball of flax tow, then grasped the edges of the wool scrap and drew them over the flax ball, twisting them tightly around the arrow shaft. Grasping the twisted wool, he took the leather strip in his teeth and, with his other hand, made the first knot around the neck of the woolen ball. With the ball securely in place, he continued to wrap the strip around the shaft a few more times, tying it again several times. Then he stood and dipped the tip, ball and all, into the pitch until it was fully coated.

"There you have it, lads!" he said, holding the still-dripping arrow up for all to see. "A little fire, and off it goes."

Hugh was fascinated. He had never even heard of such a weapon before. "How did you learn this?" he asked.

Peter looked down at Hugh. "It has been awhile since the likes of these have been used hereabouts. I learned from my father, who fought with the High Lord of Purdyton, now our king."

A murmur rippled through the group.

"You must remember a few things," Peter continued. "You must be sure it is well lit before you shoot so that the flame will not go out as it flies. The extra weight will affect your accuracy, and you will not be able to shoot as far. You should know your range by now. Be sure you are close enough to the target to hit it." He chuckled and added, "Of course if it is large enough, it may not matter. Also be aware of the wind direction. It may drip fiery pitch when lit. Shoot with the wind if possible. And you will not be able to make a full draw without getting burned; this will also affect your range. Each of you should make five arrows. We will practice with two and keep the rest."

The men set to work. There was the usual fumbling, some flax balls came apart, others were too big or too small, and some men could not get their balls to stay on the arrow tip while trying to tie it, but after several hours, with Peter's supervision, most men had five serviceable arrows. Only then did Hugh glance up to notice what else was happening in the square. The clank of swords gave notice that the swordsmen were engaging in mock combat. In another corner

---

[13] Short flax fibers left over after passing flax through a fine comb.

of the square, several straw effigies had been set up. One of Sir Bailys's men was supervising the peasant rabble, which was taking turns jabbing the effigies with their pitchforks and spears.

Brian sat down beside Hugh. "This looks pretty serious, doesn't it? I wonder if we are going to be part of a large army, maybe even one led by the Dragon?"

"I hope not," Hugh answered. "How could we bear arms against the King? I would almost rather be a deserter."

"And face certain hanging?" Brian added, nodding toward the gibbet.

Their conversation ceased with an announcement from the mayor: "Men, we will move out into a field to practice so that we will not endanger the town. You will find targets already set up for you."

They arrived to find four wooden posts in a row. A square piece of wood had been hammered to each. At the firing line a burning torch sat in a holder. Several peasants stood nearby with buckets of water.

Peter addressed the two companies: "I suggest you use a three-quarter draw. The firing line is fifty paces from the targets. Assess now where you will need to stand to hit the target, taking into account the tendency of the heavier head of the arrow to drop in flight. Then proceed to the torch and light your arrow, keeping the head down until you reach your spot. Aim and shoot quickly."

The men milled about while judging their correct shooting positions, then began to file to the torch. Peter went first, demonstrating how to light the tip and carry the nocked arrow with its tip down to let it drip its pitch before drawing his bow and letting it fly.

The ensuing chaos proved inevitable. Even Hugh almost dropped his arrow once it burst into flame. Other men did drop their arrows in fright, and still others whose pitch balls were not secure dropped the flaming balls on the ground, having to jump backward to avoid being burned.

Soon multiple small fires surrounded the torch and the targets, which the peasants scurried around trying to douse. Two men received burns—one a severe injury on the hand when he forgot to do a three-quarter draw, the other on the leg from the dripping pitch. Of those who did get off shots, the accuracy was appalling. Burning arrows littered the field. A few were noted to hit a target and bounce off. No target was set aflame.

Peter gathered the men afterward. Although Hugh had hit a target with his second arrow, it was clear to him that this was insufficient practice if they were to be effective.

"You should not be surprised that no target burned," Peter said. "The targets were there only for you to practice your aim and range. The arrow tip may or may not pierce, but the burning pitch and flax will ignite whatever the arrow comes to rest on, such as a roof."

Standing beside Hugh, Thomas whispered, "Maybe we are to attack a town or a castle, and we won't have to fight an army."

Hugh frowned. "That would be just as bad if it belongs to the King."

The mayor then addressed the archers: "We will sleep in this field tonight. Sir Bailys's tent is in yonder field. Be sure that you carry food for at least two or three days. Tomorrow we march."

"We march? Where?" a chorus of voices said.

"He will tell us when it is time," the mayor replied, ignoring the grumbling that ensued.

The men munched their meager supplies of bread and cheese or dried game, and began to bed down. Hugh and Brian bought some food in town and did the same, waiting until dark, when they met William and Thomas and crept out of the field. Tonight was the night of the weekly meeting of the Servants of Grandvil. Hugh had stolen away to the scrivener's shop while they had been in the square to find where the Grandvil Servants' group met. The town seemed equally deserted at night as it had been in the day. They found the scrivener's shop, entering while the meeting was already underway.

A woman was saying, "It clearly says that if we do not love our brothers, then we do not love the King."

"But who is really our brother?" another asked. "Is it anyone, or just one who is loyal to our King?"

As William's contingent filed in, a voice called out, "*Columba*?"

"It is all right. They are of us," the scrivener said, recognizing Hugh.

William nodded at the group. "We are from your neighboring village, Loynton. We have just spent the day preparing to go to battle. We may in fact be asked to fight against the King or his possessions. Your discussion has particular meaning for us. To whom should we be loyal? Should we be loyal to our commander, Sir Bailys? What if he leads us against the King or one of his towns? Should we love our brothers in the town more and be disloyal to our commander?"

Hugh snorted. "I for one will not fight against my King or his people!"

"In the *Chronicle*," said one of the men in the group, "the Prince says that we must render unto our master what is his."

"But he is referring to our money," another said, "and we already pay Sir Bailys a steep hearth tax."

"Yes," William said. "I believe that is true. We are obligated to pay the tax, but we are not obligated to be loyal when asked to oppose our King. I agree with Hugh. We cannot fight against the King or his people."

"And Sir Bailys will have us swinging on the gibbet the next day," Thomas said. "Surely there must be a way to appear to support Sir Bailys without risking arrest and execution for disloyalty."

"Well, our arrows don't have to hit the target," said Brian, his face breaking into a grin.

"That goes without saying," William said, "but it cannot be too obvious. And we still risk being identified with Sir Bailys and being killed by whomever he is attacking."

"You will remember, William, that I have a plan," a voice said from the shadows.

A moment later Hugh saw Gerald emerge.

"Yes, Gerald," William said. "Perhaps now it is time to tell the others. Gerald is the stable master for Sir Bailys. Some of you in Grandvil may already know him."

Looking around the room, Gerald smiled. "Yes, I know some of you from Grandvil as well. You have sneaked away from the encampment as have I. I have overheard Sir Bailys's plans. Before he left Sir Bailys, the Rat gave him a mission. Tomorrow he marches to strike the domain of a neighboring knight who is loyal to our King. The knight is away, having journeyed to see the King to request more resources to defend his domain. Sir Bailys plans to steal his horses and burn his outbuildings while he is away."

"And your plan, Gerald?" Hugh asked.

"I have notched the girth strap of Sir Bailys's mount. If I have done it correctly, it will hold as long as he walks his horse, but if, in the heat of battle, he gallops, the stress on it will cause it to snap. He will go down, saddle and all."

Hugh laughed. "And his army will panic and run, as peasants are expected to do."

"We of course will be among them," Brian added, smirking.

"But this is a risky thing you have done," William said. "He will know who has done it."

"Yes, he will," Gerald said. "That is why I must flee afterward and make my way to your village where I can live in anonymity, depending on the goodness of your people. I have been assigned to bring out the knight's horses once his stable is aflame. Then I will release them and steal away."

"You will be welcome in our house, Gerald," William said.

"And mine as well," Hugh added.

"We should return to the encampment before we are missed," William said. "Return to your units with the utmost silence."

"May the spirit of the Prince go before you," the group chorused as they departed.

Hugh was the first to speak as the four followed the road back to the field: "Gerald mentioned bringing horses out of a stable. Did he tell you where we are going?"

"That was the first I heard of it," answered William. "He said we were raiding the domain of a knight who is away. But why would we need such a large force?"

"All knights keep men-at-arms," Thomas said. "Sir Bailys has four. Perhaps this knight has more."

"Hm," Brian said. "The bailiff knows our abilities. What if he suspects treason when our arrows go awry?"

"After the practice," Hugh said, "I told him that no one had used flaming arrows before and that our practice was insufficient to guarantee accuracy. I think he understood. Remember, he missed the target both times!"

By the time they regained the field where the army slept, Hugh could not lie down to sleep. He paced back and forth in the darkness fighting conflicting thoughts. What was the right thing to do? He clearly was on the wrong side. Since the encounter with Clyffe, he had no longer thought of wounding or killing Sir Bailys. Although his original reason for doing it was gone, another reason now presented itself: they were being led on an attack against the property of a knight of the King. Only moments before, Hugh had vowed never to fight against any of the King's people. If Sir Bailys were eliminated, surely everyone would retreat and abandon this dastardly enterprise, and they would escape the danger of being wounded or killed by the enemy, whoever they were. Surely the King would agree with that reasoning.

Hugh settled down to a brief sleep, anxious and troubled about what the morning would bring, the rasping noise of a multitude of snores surrounding him like a field of crickets.

Chapter 22

THE RAID

AT DAWN EACH unit marched to the town square and assembled in formation. Sir Bailys rode slowly to and fro in front of the groups, addressing his makeshift army.

"Soldiers of the king! This day will cover us with honor. Today we will strike a blow for our king, and if we are successful, we will be rewarded by our king."

"I think he means *he* will be rewarded," Thomas whispered, leaning on his bow.

Hugh caught his eye and smirked.

"Follow me, men!" Sir Bailys led his horse out of the square at a slow walk.

The knots of men untangled into a single snake that pursued the sinuous road to the west, Sir Bailys in the lead alongside one of his bodyguards who bore his yellow and black banner, followed by his other three mounted bodyguards. Next came ten men-at-arms, their swords clanking softly against their mail hauberks. The archers followed, the Loynton company first, led by the bailiff, then the Grandvil company, led by old Peter. Behind them came the reluctant peasant rabble, pitchforks, axes, and spears in hand or balanced carelessly on their shoulders. A curtain of dust hovered over their path as nearly a hundred pairs of feet cast it up in clouds. The day was waning when they came to a final stop in a field. A fire was built and torches lit.

During the march Hugh had become increasingly disturbed about the coming conflict. Except for William, Brian, and Thomas, he viewed himself as a stranger pressed into service for a foreign army, being taken he knew not where. Those around him might as well have been faceless. It seemed as if he was being carried downstream by a river toward a waterfall with no way to exit. What would happen when he reached the waterfall? Would there be a way out or would he just go over and be killed? Could he make himself take up arms against anyone or anything belonging to the King? Should he just run into the woods now? No, he would be caught immediately. There seemed to be no outcome but death whatever he did—killed by those they attacked or executed by Sir Bailys.

Once everyone had assembled in the field, Sir Bailys rode back and forth in front of his army. "Men! Now is the time to be courageous. Glory awaits you. Archers! You will stop before the stable and set it afire. Gerald, at the first sign of flames, you will free the horses and lead them out. Men-at-arms! You will follow me to the house to overpower its guards. They will be unable to resist us. Whatever you find there is yours." To one of his bodyguards, he said, "Geoffrey, you will follow with the peasants to support us if necessary."

"He is not just stealing horses; he is going to loot the knight's house as well. This is a mean and cowardly act," Hugh said to Brian under his breath. "Should we refuse?"

"I don't know what to do," Brian replied somberly. "I wish someone would tell us."

The soldiers filed back onto the road, a torch-bearer at the front of each group. Soon Hugh saw the knight's house, silhouetted against the failing light. Two guards sat outside the front door; a light already shone from an upper floor. Out of the corner of his eye, Hugh caught a glimpse of a rider galloping from the stable behind it down the road in the opposite direction.

"We have been discovered!" he whispered to Brian.

"We have been seen!" the bailiff shouted. "Hurry to the stable!"

The archers deviated off in a trot toward the stable, carrying Hugh and the others with them as Sir Bailys and his group approached the house. Hugh looked on as the two guards jumped to their feet.

"Halt!" one shouted. "What is your purpose this time of day?"

Sir Bailys reined in his horse and leaned down as another man-at-arms emerged from the house. "You will stand aside," Sir Bailys said. "I am here on a mission from the king."

"What mission? What king?" the third guard said.

"My words are only for your lord," Sir Bailys said.

"He is away. You must leave at once and take your rabble with you," the guard replied.

"Well then." Sir Bailys laughed. "It appears we are free to do as we wish. You are outnumbered."

"Therein you are wrongly advised," the guard answered. "We have already sent for help."

"What help have you, fool?" Sir Bailys nearly snarled. "I see only three pitiful guards. What is your name, man?"

"I am Richard, steward of Sir Guy, lord of Bonfrere."

"On peril of your life, steward, I repeat—stand aside!" Sir Bailys said. "The king has given this domain to me."

"I know no such king!" Richard said, brandishing his sword. "This domain belongs to the true King, not your Dragon."

"No longer!" Sir Bailys turned to his followers. "Men-at-arms! Forward!"

Hugh watched Sir Bailys's surly crowd of swordsmen begin to approach the three guards. But now the archers had arrived within shooting range of the stable and were arranging themselves into a firing line, so Hugh had to focus his attention forward. He watched Peter bring a torch to each archer in turn to light an arrow.

"Remember your training yesterday, men," Peter said. "You need only place your arrow on the roof. It will do the rest. Shoot at will!"

"Gerald's ruse has not worked!" Hugh whispered to Brian. "Sir Bailys sits there on his horse, watching us."

"We must join in, then," Brian answered, "lest he mark us as disloyal."

In his mind Hugh had reached the waterfall. There seemed to be nothing to grab on to. Perhaps he could slip away as night fell, but that would mean abandoning the others. He decided he would adopt the plan they discussed the previous night and deliberately miss the target. Hugh drew his bow as fully as he could without burning himself and watched with satisfaction as his arrow sailed over the stable. Just as he had expected, arrows went everywhere, some over the stable, some wide, some short, setting fire to straw on the ground. But two found their mark, lying on the stable roof as pinpoints of flame.

"I saw that!" Brian whispered to Hugh. "Mine followed yours over the stable."

Peter approached, and they lit another arrow.

From Hugh's other side William said, "Do you see Gerald?"

"No," Hugh answered. "I hope someone did not hit him with their errant shot."

Another volley of arrows scattered around the stable, a few more coming to rest on the roof. The pinpoints of the first had widened into circular spots of flame.

"There he is!" Brian whispered.

A small figure could be seen running into the stable. Hugh hoped Gerald's plan would work—for all their sakes.

From her room on the upper floor, Marie had witnessed with shock and apprehension the approach of the small army. She grabbed her bow and quiver, and ran to her mother's room, where Lady Clare was reading to Edouard.

"Mother, we are in danger! Take Edouard into the forest and hide."

Lady Clare peeked out of her window in alarm. Then, noting Marie's bow, she said, "Marie, you must let the men fight! And then we must surrender. I do not want either you or Edouard to be harmed. They must release us when they see there are women and children."

"No, Mother!" Marie said. "I am fifteen. I will defend us. I can shoot many arrows safely from my window."

"Even if your father were here, we could not resist this force," Lady Clare said. "We do not have a choice. We must surrender and save our own lives. You must not risk yourself!"

Shaking her head, Marie almost shouted, "It is Sir Bailys, Mother! Do you not remember it was he who tried to take me? I will not surrender to him. I heard someone gallop away from the stable. Maybe he went for help. Surely the King does not want this to happen. I must do my part!"

Marie ran back into her bedroom, stationed herself at the window and took aim first at Sir Bailys's men-at-arms. Then she saw Sir Bailys, sitting on his horse. He looked up and stared at her, then pointed at his wounded arm and finally jabbed his finger at her. Two of his bodyguards immediately made a rush for the house. Marie swallowed and let loose an arrow.

Hugh glanced back at the house. A fight had already begun. The three guards, their backs to the door, took up positions against Sir Bailys's men-at-arms while the knight himself sat on his horse at a distance watching. Already one of Sir

Bailys's men had fallen with an arrow in the neck. Someone in the house was shooting arrows!

"An unequal contest," Hugh said to William. "I am ashamed to be part of something so evil."

"I as well," William said. "Perhaps we should just turn against Sir Bailys now and die here for the King."

The stable was aflame now, the archers standing by as if waiting for another order.

"My thought exactly," replied Hugh, recalling his conclusion the night before as they returned to Grandvil. "We should not just stand here and watch!"

Gerald entered the stable as the first holes began to burn through the roof. The horses were already restive, stamping in their stalls. He hurried to unfasten the ropes across their stalls, then led them out, pointing them to the doorway, and gave each a slap. They could be found later. Fiery embers were now falling on the straw, setting it ablaze. He raced for the doorway and turned to make a run for the woods behind the stable, where he would hide. A scream from the house interrupted his dash; he stopped to take in the scene before him.

Though still battling, the two remaining guards had been forced away from the door by seven men-at-arms, and a pair of Sir Bailys's bodyguards were heaving their bodies against the wooden door, which then gave way. Three bodies now lay on the ground next to the manor house. Another soldier stood by, holding a limp arm. Gerald heard another scream. Through the door came Sir Bailys's bodyguards, one carrying a struggling young girl over his shoulder.

Without further thought of his plan of escape, Gerald drew his sword and rushed to the manor house. The two bodyguards took little notice of him until he was behind them. With one swing of his blade, Gerald brought one down from behind. The other turned and regarded him with a puzzled look as if trying to decide whether to drop his load and defend himself or keep going. In that moment of hesitation, Gerald staggered him with a blow to the arm, forcing him to drop his sword, and then the girl.

Pulling her from the ground as peasants began to flood past into the manor, Gerald shouted, "Run to the woods! I will find you later!"

"I can't!" she cried, her eyes wide. "My little brother! He is inside with my mother!"

"You have a brother? We were not told there were children!"

"Please, save them! They are in the bedroom upstairs."

Gerald nodded. "Go behind the house. I will hand your brother out a window, then help your mother out. What is your brother's name?"

"Edouard," she said, then ran off toward the forest.

Gerald turned and saw the still-conscious bodyguard pick up his sword and look for the girl. Beyond, Sir Bailys pointed right at Gerald and shouted, "Grab that man!"

Thrusting himself among the crowd of peasants, Gerald was swept into the house along with them, seeing a peasant drop his torch in his lust to pillage.

Amidst the din of shouts and grabbing hands, Gerald leaped up the stairs to the bedrooms, calling "Edouard?" The house was already beginning to fill with smoke from the dropped torch and burning tapestries. Gerald kicked open the closed door to one of the bedrooms. "Edouard?"

"Yes?" a small voice came from beneath the bed.

"Your sister sent me to help you and your mother escape," Gerald said. "Where is she?"

A head poked out from underneath the bed. "I am his mother. Take him first!" she cried. "Go with this man, Edouard!"

"Come!" Gerald said.

After the boy emerged, Gerald gathered him under one arm like a sack of grain and pushed through the smoke-filled air to the back wall of the house above the stairs, where he smashed a window. As a figure silhouetted against the blazing stable rushed forward in near darkness, Gerald lowered Edouard as far as he could toward his sister.

"Take him!" Gerald said as she grabbed Edouard's hand. "I will meet you in the forest after I bring your mother."

Gerald turned to retrace his steps to the bedroom amidst the thickening smoke, but as he did, he felt a searing pain slash across his neck. Grabbing at the wound, he toppled out of the window down to the ground.

Uncertain what to do next, Hugh and the others remained in their group of archers, their work finished, watching the assault on the house. Another of the guards had fallen. Someone had rescued a young girl from the bodyguards and run into the house with the mob of peasants.

"Could it have been Gerald?" Hugh asked.

"At the peril of his life," William responded. "He told me as we left Grandvil this morning that he had a premonition he would die today. He seemed so calm about it, believing that he would be dying for the King, following the example of the Prince."

"And look at us!" Hugh said. "Shameful bystanders! Now is the time for us stop our idle talk and to stand for our King too. I will eliminate Sir Bailys myself."

Hugh nocked an arrow and took aim at Sir Bailys, who yet sat motionless on his horse, his smiling face lit by the angry flames flickering from the windows of the burning manor house.

But the sound of hoofs restrained Hugh's shot. The noise came not from close to the house, but from behind them, on the road that the escaping rider had taken. Some of the other archers had already begun to walk back to the house. Now they began to run, Thomas with them, leaving Hugh and William with the remainder, glancing in both directions.

Hugh relaxed his aim until they could determine what was happening. He saw that Sir Bailys had also taken notice of the sound of approaching horsemen and was frantically trying to reorganize his unruly mob. His wounded bodyguards remounted and his five remaining men-at-arms gathered around him. The other five lay strewn around the front of the house, mingled with the three fallen guards.

"Geoffrey!" Sir Bailys cried. "Get your peasants out of the house and behind me. Archers! Form a firing line!"

The oncoming horsemen had halted as if to size up their foe. By the light of the blazing stable, Hugh could count maybe seven mounted men, but more on foot undoubtedly followed. Would it help them if he took out Sir Bailys? No, to them he was just one of Sir Bailys's men. A thud next to him brought down an archer with an arrow in the chest.

"They have mounted archers!" Brian shouted.

Another archer near Brian went down with a groan.

"And they are expert shots! We are outlined like perfect targets!" Hugh said, turning his drawn bow in the direction of the strangers.

"Wait!" William said. "What if they are the King's men?"

"Then we are in extreme danger either way!" Hugh shouted, beginning to back away. "If they capture us and find our marks, we will face immediate execution for treason."

The three turned and followed the rest in a dash to the safety of the crowd gathering behind Sir Bailys.

Watching his men fall one by one, Sir Bailys could himself wait no longer. "Men!" he shouted. "Charge! Eliminate the archers!"

He and his bodyguards put spurs to their mounts and bolted forward. The swordsmen ran behind them. Some of Sir Bailys's archers were sending arrows aimlessly in the general direction of the unidentified adversaries. Hugh was momentarily fixated by the spectacle, unable to decide whether to run or fight—to shoot at the new arrivals or at Sir Bailys.

Almost as soon as his horse attained a gallop, Sir Bailys jerked in his saddle, slid to the side, and fell off in a heap, his legs still straddling the saddle.

Gerald's plan! Hugh thought. It had worked!

The knight's bodyguards reined in and stood around their fallen commander, seemingly uncertain about what to do. The swordsmen, who had caught up to the others, also stood in a group looking at the stunned Sir Bailys, as if waiting for an order.

Hugh could see that, behind the archers, Geoffrey was slowly gathering the peasants into a crowd, some holding food, others household items in their hands. Flames had begun to lick from the windows of the house, carrying billows of smoke. The roof of the stable had already collapsed, sending showers of sparks into the night sky.

"Look!" Hugh shouted. "They are charging us!"

Everyone's eyes were riveted on Sir Bailys and the strangers, wondering what would happen next. Sir Bailys's swordsmen turned and began to run back to the house. The murmurs of the peasants turned to panic. One by one they took off in the direction of the field where they had stopped earlier. The archers also began to melt away.

"I'm going too!" Brian said, breaking into a trot.

Hugh could see the recently arrived force now beginning to encircle Sir Bailys and his men.

"You are right, Hugh," William said. "Even if they are the King's men, we must not be captured. Let's go! Head for the forest!"

Hugh only had time to see several horsemen stop by Sir Bailys, before he dashed to the back of the house toward the forest. But they had waited too long. The continued sound of horses' hoofs told them that all of the attackers had not stopped. Hugh looked back to see a single horseman bearing down on him.

He had no hope of escape. *I will give myself up to save the others.* Stopping, he threw down his bow and raised his arms high.

The rider came to a halt, reached down and grabbed Hugh by the collar. "You are my prisoner," he said. "Pick up your bow and walk slowly ahead of me. If you attempt to run, I will strike you down."

Hugh retrieved his bow and did as he was told, walking slowly back to the house where a group of captives had been assembled by the strangers in the light of the flames. All of Sir Bailys's swordsmen had been run down and a few of the archers as well. Hugh did not see Sir Bailys and his bodyguards among them. Had he somehow escaped?

One of the wounded manor guards had been helped to his feet and brought to the group. Hugh was puzzled. Had the knight they were raiding returned in the nick of time with his retainers?

Recognizing him from observing the fight at the house, Hugh leaned in toward the wounded guard. "Do you know who these strangers are?"

"They are soldiers of the King," the guard replied. "And who are you?"

"A friend," Hugh ventured. "How can you tell they are from the King?"

"We know who our friends are, and you are not among them," the guard replied in a brusque voice. He motioned to an archer who stood to the side, an arrow pointed at the group of prisoners "But if you must know, he told me. He says their leader will come shortly."

"How did they know to come?"

"We knew they were near, but we did not know Sir Bailys would strike tonight. We sent a messenger to find them and alert them to Sir Bailys's arrival. And you were with Sir Bailys, were you not?"

"Hmph! They are a little late," Hugh said, looking at the blazing manor house, ignoring the guard's accusation.

The guard glanced at the burning structure and back at Hugh. "Don't try to act like you are one of us. You are part of the cause of this." He grunted and clasped his limp sword arm with a bloodied hand to stanch the flow from his wound, then continued in a low voice as if he were talking to himself.

"At least, they came. We did not know Sir Bailys would attack with so many men or that he would torch all the buildings, as the Rat certainly would have done. I told Sir Bailys that help was on its way, but instead of him being deterred until our friends could arrive, he saw something that seemed to enrage him. That is when things got out of hand." He paused to exhale a heavy breath. "Still,

I must remember that the King's timing is not necessarily our timing. Sir Bailys will no longer be a threat to us now."

Unfazed by the guard's animosity, Hugh interrupted, "You have a rather callous attitude for one who is watching his lord's home burn down. How will your lord receive this?"

Unaware that his musing had been overheard, the guard jerked his head up and looked at Hugh.

"You are calling *me* callous? Look at what *you* have done!"

"I am sorry for my part in it," Hugh said, changing his tone. "We are all members of Sir Bailys's fief. I am here involuntarily. Who are you?"

"I am Richard, his steward. It was my responsibility to look after his house and family. I have failed, but I hope he will consider that I did the best I could to defend against an unexpected and overwhelming attack. I understand, as my lord does, that we may have to undergo difficult circumstances in these times, but we must remember that our King's understanding and purposes are larger than ours."

"Well, that's a pretty fatalistic attitude toward what has happened," Hugh remarked, but then he caught himself. Hugh recalled that he had certainly experienced difficult times himself but on no occasion had he contemplated them being part of a larger plan. And while he thought he had reassessed his picture of the King after the event with Clyffe, he was surprised to experience a jab of resentment, not at the Dragon or Sir Bailys, but at the King again.

"If they were nearby," Hugh said, pointing at the flaming buildings, "do you not think the King could have prevented this by sending his soldiers a little sooner?"

"Perhaps," Richard replied, the light of the flames revealing glistening eyes as he watched the roof of the house collapse, sending a cloud of flaming debris in all directions. "My lord may have lost his home, but I saw someone rescue his daughter, and I must believe that the rest of his family will be found safe. Moreover Sir Bailys was caught in a heinous act of violence against our King. He almost certainly will be imprisoned now and his domain taken away." Richard brushed away a tear with his bloodstained hand.

Hugh clenched his jaw, allowing himself to give in to the tug of resentment. "Well," he said, "I am having difficulty understanding how the King's purposes could permit this. He should protect his people. I think even *I* could be a better king than he has been.

"You don't know what you are saying. He is not even your King."

Richard lifted his good arm and pointed toward the blazing house. "Look! I believe our rescuers' leader is coming."

Hugh whispered, "He *is* my King. I am a follower of the true King, though Sir Bailys is my master. I am one of you."

Richard stepped back, a look of surprise on his face. "Your actions would not convince anyone. But I am not to be your judge. Perhaps the leader will be lenient with you in spite of what you have done."

A tall, lean silhouette, flanked by two smaller ones, approached the group from the direction of the forest, between the burning house and the flames licking the fallen timbers of the stable. As the silhouettes became visible, Hugh recognized the two smaller ones were the girl he had seen before and a smaller boy. A helmet under one arm, the leader strode forward to survey his prisoners. He was backlit by the fires, but Hugh thought he could make out the king's emblem on his surcoat. Although the leader's face was still darkened by the brightness of the flames behind him, auburn highlights glanced from his hair.

"We have ten prisoners, sire," one of his men said.

The leader's head moved as if he were studying each of the prisoners in turn. Then he stopped. He seemed to be staring at Hugh.

Hugh tensed. *This is the time to declare to whom I am loyal.* "Sire, might I have a word with you in private?" he asked, stepping forward.

The leader approached him. "There is no need for that, Hugh Smith of Loynton."

Hugh stopped, his mouth agape. "Sir Ralf?"

"You may join my men, Hugh. I harbor no ill will toward you. You and your Servant archers are now soldiers of the King."

Hugh stood in stunned silence. Instead of death he had been given life.

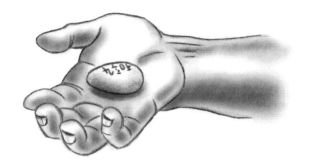

Chapter 23

GERALD

WHEN GERALD OPENED his eyes, he was confused. His last memory was of standing at a window in Sir Guy's manor house. He had been inside for some reason—but what? Moving his eyes slowly, he could not see anything resembling a house. Instead a pair of compassionate blue eyes gazed down at him. He tried to raise his head, emitting a yowl as pain flashed across the back of his neck.

"There," a soothing voice said. "You should rest. You are gravely wounded." The face and voice were connected to hands that softly brushed his face with a cool, damp cloth.

"Where am I?" Gerald asked. "And who are you?"

"You are in a camp for the seriously wounded, and we are sisters of healing. My name is Adele. You must not move. We will take care of you."

Gerald was conscious now of movement and low moans around him. "How did I get here?"

"You were found near the burning house by one of the gatherers and brought here."

"The gatherers? I have not heard of them."

"They gather the fallen after battles and bring them to the healer."

"The healer? I have not heard of him either."

"He is in charge of the camp. You will meet him. He has already applied salve to your wound."

Gerald cautiously reached a hand to the back of his neck, touching the tender gash, bringing back greasy, bloodstained fingers.

"You must give it time to work. Here, drink some water."

The woman held a goatskin flask to Gerald's lips, allowing the cool fluid to dribble onto his tongue. Gerald swallowed. He admitted to himself that indeed he did not feel like moving, remaining content to gaze upward at the sky, following clouds with his eyes as they drifted into and out of his view until the light began to dim. He did not move all day, conscious only of the throbbing pain in his neck and the periodic visits of Adele.

The next morning Gerald awoke surprised by how much better he felt. Adele was soon by his side with some water and bread.

"I feel much better," Gerald said, struggling to sit up.

"Good! And your wound has healed," Adele answered. "Do you feel like eating?"

"I think so," Gerald replied, taking a piece of the proffered bread; then he realized what Adele had said. *My wound is healed?* He reached up and felt no gash on his neck when he ran his fingers over it. "How can that be? You told me yesterday that I was seriously wounded."

"And so you were," Adele answered. "You have been healed. The healer says we are moving camp today. Do you see the tent yonder?" She nodded to the right.

He looked that way, then back at her. "Yes, but I don't understand how—"

"When you finish your bread, come to the tent." And without another word she left.

Gerald could see that some men had already assembled in front. Another group of men sat in a circle nearby with some women, eating and drinking; they seemed to be in a good mood. Gerald finished the last of his bread and walked toward the first group. He counted six men, including him. One of them looked familiar.

"You were at the house, weren't you?" Gerald asked.

"One of the guards, yes. I am Ian."

Gerald still did not have a complete picture of the events of the evening. Perhaps this Ian could be of some help. "Can you tell me what happened?" he asked. "I remember freeing some horses and entering the house. I think I saw you to the side, fighting some swordsmen."

"Yes," Ian answered. "The swordsmen prevailed, and I fell defending my lord's house from an attack by Sir Bailys and his men."

"Sir Bailys? Was I with him?"

"Most certainly," Ian replied. "You were not with us. And frankly I am surprised to find you and some of the others here."

"I am surprised as well because I do not know where I am," Gerald said.

"We are in the healer's camp, I have been told, and they say that generally his gatherers only bring those who have fallen in service of the true King."

Gerald's memory was returning to him in snatches—the flaming arrows resting on the stable roof, him rushing inside and freeing the horses, a scream, a girl, a fight with swordsmen, a dark house, shouts, a small boy, smoke.

"I went inside the house for something, I think," Gerald said. "But in spite of what you say, I do serve the true King." Gerald yanked up his tunic to show his mark.

"Apparently you do," Ian said while glancing at Gerald's bared chest, "yet you were attacking a knight of the King. It is not for me to judge who does and who does not serve the King. But evidently the healer knows."

Their conversation was interrupted by the sound of a tent flap snapping. A figure emerged from the tent and stopped to survey the small group gathered before him. Gerald was astonished. He was expecting to see an old man whose years of wisdom would have creased his face with deep furrows. Instead he was facing a young, clean-shaven man with cropped hair, who nevertheless had an aura of confidence about himself. He was dressed in the rough woolen tunic of a peasant, yet Gerald recognized the emblem of the true King sewn over his left breast.

"Good morning, men," he said. "I trust you are feeling well enough to travel. As you may have discovered by now, I and my companions serve the true King. We will begin our journey back to his castle today. If you are to accompany me, you will be in possession of a white stone."

Gerald looked at Ian, who was tossing his stone in his hand. Unwittingly speaking his thoughts aloud, Gerald blurted, "I don't have a stone!"

The healer looked at him. "In fact you do, Gerald. I gave it to you. Check your purse."

Gerald pulled up the small leather bag that hung around his neck, rummaged through it, his hands finally grasping a round, flat object. Withdrawing his hand, he found himself holding a white stone, just as the healer had said. There seemed to be some characters on it; he would examine them later.

"Good." The healer then addressed the group: "You will leave your stained and torn clothing here. The sisters will provide you with fresh clothes to change into before we leave."

Immediately the sisters were among them, bearing the folded items and handing them out. Gerald received his from Adele and withdrew to a place of privacy in the forest before unfolding his bundle. First was underclothing of fine linen, better than he had ever possessed. He was somewhat ashamed to put it on his unwashed body. Next in the stack came trousers of fine, soft wool and sturdy sandals. On the bottom lay a beautiful tunic of dark blue wool, with the king's emblem sewn over the left breast. Once dressed, Gerald was embarrassed to return to the tent, because he knew he was now better dressed than the healer. And for the first time, Gerald realized that he was missing something important—his sword.

Returning to the tent, Gerald noted that all of the men were dressed alike, each somewhat surprised at the quality of their new clothes. The women stood to the side in a group, grinning. Even the men in the healer's team, whom Gerald assumed to be the gatherers, were smiling.

"This is quite nice," said one of the men, whom Gerald recognized as an archer who had been present at the Servants meeting in Grandvil.

"And unexpected," another added.

"Better than anything I had before," Ian chimed in, speaking Gerald's thoughts.

The healer stood in front of his tent, smiling. "I want you to lack in nothing," he said.

Gerald was already thinking ahead. In their rich clothing they would likely be targets for robbery. Again his thoughts unexpectedly became his words: "I do not have my sword. How will we defend ourselves from bandits?"

"You will not need a sword," the healer said.

"But dressed in such finery, we will surely be targets for thieves and brigands," Gerald insisted.

"Trust me. No one will need a sword."

He had such authority in his voice that Gerald thought it best to drop the subject.

"Now, once the tent is packed into the wagon, we will depart," the healer said.

The gatherers assembled and, with the healer, struck the tent and folded it, placing it in a wagon that Gerald had not noticed before. The group then formed up, the healer in the lead, then the sisters, the healed men, the wagon drawn by two horses, and the gatherers behind.

Gerald found his place by Ian as the group set out on a path through the forest westward. "Have you wondered why you are not going back to serve your lord?" Gerald asked.

"Yes, I have, but why would I pass up a chance to see the king's castle?" Ian said. "It is something I have only heard about. I never thought I would actually see it. Imagine the story I will have to tell when I return."

"That is a valid point," Gerald said. "Still, although I cannot and do not wish to return to Sir Bailys, I thought at least I would return to a village in this area."

Gerald soon found himself examining the sisters and the gatherers. All of the sisters were dressed alike as well, in ankle-length gowns of a lighter blue, their faces partially hidden by hoods. The gatherers, behind, wore tunics of earthen colors, but curiously no one seemed dressed as roughly as the healer, and no one carried a weapon.

Still feeling some anxiety, Gerald said to Ian, "This is certainly an odd procession. We resemble a group of unarmed pilgrims—favorite targets of bandits. What do you think is carried in the wagon besides the tent?"

"Well, there must be some food and water, plus the healer's medicines. What do you think?"

"I hope a group this size has some weapons in the wagon, just in case they need them," Gerald replied, his eyes glancing back and forth to either side of the road.

Soon enough Ian was proven correct. The healer stopped and led the group off the road onto a grassy bank. Out of the wagon he brought a basket of bread, some dried fish, and a large water bag, all of which were passed around. Each group seemed to keep to themselves, the healer eating with the gatherers. Although the healer appeared friendly enough, the aura of authority that surrounded him seemed to keep the others from approaching him.

Gerald sat with Ian, fidgeting. "I would like to know more about the healer," Gerald said. "But I have already been rebuked once. What would happen if I were to inquire of him again?"

"I for one am grateful that he healed me. That is enough."

"To be sure, I am as well. But … why did he heal me? I could have died from my wound. How did the gatherers find me? How did he know where to look?"

Ian had no answer, nor did he seem interested in thinking about the subject. The group soon took to the road again. This was new territory for Gerald—they must be out of Sir Guy's domain now. They were approaching a large forest. As they disappeared beneath the trees, the dense canopy dimmed the bright sunlight. Gerald tensed. It looked like a good place for an ambush. Within minutes the group came to a halt.

Ahead, Gerald could see shadowy horsemen, perhaps as many as ten, blocking the road. They began to approach the group. Almost if it had been rehearsed, the women withdrew to the wagon, standing next to it, and the gatherers expanded into a ring encircling the wagon, the women, and Gerald's group. No one seemed to be panicking. But no one was getting arms out of the wagon either. Suppressing an urge to run to the wagon and check for weapons, Gerald watched as the horsemen continued to approach, swords drawn. The healer stood his ground.

"Bringin' us some gifts, are ye, young man?" said the apparent leader of the brigands.

"It would be a mistake for you to continue," the healer replied quietly.

Some of the horsemen dismounted and approached the wagon. "And ye've brought us some fair damsels and finely clothed gentlemen as well," one said.

"Do not touch anyone in my group," the healer said, unmoving.

"We'll just have a quick look in yer wagon, then," the leader answered. "Go ahead, men."

One of the outlaws approached the gatherer next to Gerald, shoving him aside. No sooner had his hand touched the man's shoulder than the outlaw went rigid and fell to the ground unconscious.

"Ye're goin' to resist us now, are ye?" growled the leader, raising his sword.

At that moment the healer raised his hands, palms outward as if in surrender, and spoke some words that Gerald could not understand. The outlaw leader's gaze seemed riveted on the healer's hands, whereupon he turned pale, dropped his sword, and immediately spurred his horse in the opposite direction. His men dragged their fallen companion to his horse, mounted, and, just as quickly, vanished in a cloud of dust.

"Impressive!" Gerald whispered to Ian. "Did you understand what the healer said?"

Ian shook his head. "No. It sounded like a foreign tongue to me."

"To me as well. There is something strange about this healer and his whole group. I must find out more."

"I would be careful if I were you," Ian said. "Remember what happened to the outlaw who touched one of the gatherers. You don't want to make any of them angry at you."

"Yes ... but the odd thing is, neither the healer nor the gatherer who was touched seemed angry," Gerald said.

The groups resumed their usual locations and continued through the forest without incident. As the sun grew low, they filed into a field where the group built a fire and pitched the healer's tent. Some of the gatherers hung a pot from a tripod of branches and soon they were preparing an aromatic stew. The sisters served Gerald's group, handing each a steaming bowl with a wooden spoon. Adele brought Gerald his food, the gatherers and the healer waiting in their group until the others were served.

"Adele?" Gerald asked as she handed him the bowl.

"Yes?"

"I have so many questions," Gerald continued. "May I ask you?"

"Of course. You were not expecting this journey, were you?"

"That is the least of it," Gerald said. "I do not know where we are. I do not know who you are or where you come from."

"We are in the service of the true King."

"I do understand that, but..."

"And we are from the King's castle, where you are going."

"Yes, but I do not understand why I am going there or how you found me."

"The healer knows that. He sends out the gatherers to bring him those who need healing."

"But how do they find us?"

"Why don't you ask him?" Adele stood to walk away.

"I-I have already been rebuked once," Gerald said, "and he seems to stay with the gatherers."

"Actually he is waiting for you to approach him. You will find that he will receive you gladly."

His questions continuing to burn within, Gerald rose and walked cautiously to the group of gatherers, now being served by the sisters. They were rolling with laughter as Gerald drew near.

"Have a seat and join us, Gerald," the healer called out. "Adele says you have some questions for me."

"Many questions, sir," Gerald replied, taking a seat, his bowl in hand.

"I was wondering how long it would take you to get around to asking them," the healer said, smiling.

"Why do you say that?"

"Since the beginning you have had the look of one who ponders," the healer replied.

Despite his initial reluctance to approach the healer, this time Gerald was beginning to feel more comfortable in his presence. He took a seat facing the healer.

"Adele said to ask you how your group found me since we have never met and you do not know me."

"Ah, that is one of the mysteries," the healer answered, a murmur of assent rumbling among the gatherers. "Pull out your white stone and look at it."

Gerald fumbled in his purse and produced the stone, holding it up to the light of the fire in front of him. He saw characters etched on both sides of its shiny surface. "I don't know what this writing means," he said.

The healer smiled. "Exactly. It is a language you do not understand. There are two sets of characters on the stone. Those on the side you are looking at mean 'friend.' You are a member of a group that calls itself 'Servants of the King,' are you not?"

"Yes, but how did you know?"

"The King, who sent us, knows. Those who are servants of the King are also called friends of his son, the Prince. The characters on the other side spell the name by which the King and those from his court know you."

"It is not 'Gerald,' then?"

"It is your name in the King's royal language. You would not answer to it if we were to use it now."

"But I still do not understand how I was found," Gerald said.

"When someone needs healing, I send a gatherer with his stone. If you are to be brought to me, they will find my name, and yours, engraved on your forehead. The stone goes into your purse and you are brought to me."

Gerald's hand went to his forehead, his fingers searching for evidence of a scar or the unevenness of a symbol. There was none.

The healer smiled. "You can neither see nor feel it, but it has always been there. It is how we know who is ours."

Gerald was puzzled. "But what about the mark on our chest?"

"The mark is given for your benefit so that you can know each other and know that you belong to the King."

Gerald's head was already spinning with the new revelations. How did this healer know so many things? He was glad he was found and glad that he was healed, he supposed. Nevertheless, he plunged ahead with more questions: "What happened on the road today? No one in your group seemed afraid. We were in danger of being robbed or worse, yet you vanquished the outlaws without a weapon."

The healer nodded as if he knew that question would come. "You remember that I told you no one would need a sword."

"Yes," Gerald said, looking down to study his food. "I am sorry that I doubted you."

"These things are difficult to understand," the healer continued. "But I will try to tell you as much as you can receive." He hesitated, seeming to wait for Gerald to assimilate what he had heard. Looking Gerald in the eye, he said, "My tongue is my sword."

Gerald just stared blankly at him.

"When I spoke to the outlaw leader, you did not understand what I said, did you?"

"No, I did not," Gerald said, remembering his amazement at the incident.

"I spoke to him in the King's language."

"Whatever you said certainly frightened him." Gerald chuckled. "And the others as well."

"Those who serve our enemy, including our enemy himself, cannot stand before the King's words."

"If I might be so curious, what did you say to him?"

"Among other things, I said that he could not hinder our journey because we were under the protection of the King. He chose to ignore that warning and told his men to advance. When one of his men fell, I cautioned him that the King was very near and that he and his men would be overwhelmed, captured, and chained forever in a dark dungeon if he persisted."

Revisiting the episode in his head, Gerald asked, "So when his man touched the gatherer and fell...?"

"That was the King's protection. That is why you will be safe until we reach his castle."

That question answered, though not fully understood, Gerald went on to the next: "I do not know why I am going to the King's castle. I know that I should be happy about it, and I guess I am, but ..."

"The King delights in rewarding those who serve and obey him," the healer replied. "Your memory is still clouded by your injury, but you saved the life of the daughter and son of Sir Guy, whose family is dear to the King."

The healer was right. Gerald still could not clearly remember the events leading to his injury. *So that must be why I was in the dark house. I do remember a young girl screaming.*

"Are they both safe?"

"Yes, they are with one of the King's soldiers even now."

Attempting to sort out his jumbled memory, Gerald replied, "I have been reminded that I was involved in the attack on Sir Guy. Certainly I do not deserve a reward for that."

"You are right," the healer answered. "No one deserves a reward from the King. He rewards whom he pleases. But you were a member of the household of Sir Bailys and sworn to be loyal to him, yet you placed your loyalty to the King above that when you notched his girth strap so that he would fall and be captured."

"So he was captured?"

"Yes, and his domain will now be given to a knight of the King."

Pieces of the puzzle began to come together. But it was not complete.

"I do have one last question," Gerald said.

"Finally!" The healer smiled, leaning back on his hands, a ripple of chuckles echoing among the gatherers.

"My wound. Adele told me I was gravely wounded, yet the next day I was healed. I have never known of anyone recovering from such a wound so quickly."

"Ah, yes ... the wound," the healer said. "It is the most common question, and the answer is the most difficult to comprehend. You are perhaps wondering also why we did not allow the sisters to nurse you back to health where you lay and release you to return to your companions."

"Yes! Yes, that is exactly what I was wondering," Gerald said, smiling now.

"Some we do release to return, but others are to be brought to the King. Those are the ones who receive the white stones."

A troubling thought now began to build within Gerald's mind. "So ... it sounds as if there are two kinds of wounded: those who go to the King's castle and those who go back to their villages. How is it decided?"

"The King decides."

The disturbing thought continued to grow until it filled Gerald's mind, eclipsing all that was there. He could not allow himself to acknowledge it yet, but it would not be dismissed. He chose instead to skirt around it.

"Ian, the guard, told me he was excited about visiting the king's castle, because of the stories he could tell when he returned. But—" Gerald swallowed hard and audibly. "But maybe...we're not coming back?"

The expression on the healer's face was so filled with compassion that Gerald, for the first time in many years, could not hold back the tears that began to rise.

"No, you are not," the healer said.

"Then I am really—?"

"Dead," the healer said softly.

Gerald began to rock back and forth, his face buried in his hands, unable to speak.

The healer leaned in and placed his hand on Gerald's shoulder, waiting until he was calm before continuing, "You place such finality on that word. It conjures up a sea of regrets, of lost opportunities, of faces you may never see again, of wrongs unrighted, of dreams unfulfilled. When you pass through that gate, you are always looking backward, as if there is nothing desirable on the other side."

"I just...was not ready," Gerald said, feeling a swell of sadness.

"Few are truly ready because they do not know the mind of the King. But you know now that it is not the end, but merely a healing, the final healing of all that is wrong in you."

"It is just not what I thought," Gerald said, exhaling heavily.

The healer nodded. "I know. But now you are facing a new beginning. The *Chronicle* speaks of having life more abundantly. Few understand the full meaning, believing it refers to prosperity and riches. The abundant life is nothing less than experiencing life in the presence of your King, whether it begins before you pass through the gate or after. In the King's castle, rather than lost opportunities, you will have new opportunities. Rather than faces never seen again, you will see new faces, and perhaps faces long unseen, and there will be no regrets or wrongs to right."

Gerald cleared his throat, trying to compose himself. "Do the others know?"

"Some do because their wound was obviously fatal. Some have already talked with me. Your friend, Ian, does not yet know, but he will soon enough when we reach the castle."

Gerald sat in the low light of the fire, still holding his bowl, his uneaten stew now cold. It had not been the answer he wanted or even expected, but he found himself beginning to experience a nascent curiosity about what was to come.

"I guess I have another last question," he said.

"Yes?"

"Who are you? I mean, where do you fit in the King's Kingdom? You seem to know so much about everyone's business, including the King's."

"I am very close to the King. You know me as the healer. I am also your guide and protector on this journey. You will learn more as you live in the King's castle."

"I meant," Gerald said, "do you have a name?"

"I have many names, including one known only to the King. You will have time to learn them as you live in the castle. You may begin with this one."

The healer held out his hands and opened his palms. On one was the symbol A; on the other the symbol Ω. Gerald did not know their exact meaning, but he remembered seeing them written on a piece of parchment and had heard them spoken in a meeting of the Servants.

"You are alpha...and omega?" he recalled as if seeing the parchment again. "I am."

Chapter 24

SIR RALF

A S SLANTING RAYS of morning sun began to banish the chill of the autumn night, Hugh awoke shivering from an uncomfortable sleep on the ground in Sir Ralf's camp. Looking around, he could tell that there were groups of men bedded down, some with no covering, others under their cloaks. He had been led to his location in the dark and told to sleep there on the ground. Everyone in his area was still asleep, but the clothing of one sleeping form caught his eye.

He rose and tiptoed over several bodies, then gave the sleeping man a shake. "Brian! What are you doing here?"

Brian rolled over, rubbing his eyes and yawning. "Leave me be! I'm tired."

"Brian! It's Hugh!" He shook him again.

Brian's eyes popped open, and he sat up with a start. "Hugh! They caught you too!"

"I was trying to escape with your father," Hugh said. "One of the soldiers rode me down."

"Me too. I was with the rest of the company, running back toward camp with the peasants. They took in a crowd of us, but they released all those who were unarmed. I didn't know what they would do, so I tore my tunic and showed my mark. My captor did not seem to believe me but he shoved me aside and I was led here and told to lie down and wait until morning. I wondered if I should try to escape, but there were guards all around the perimeter, so I decided I would just accept my fate. They took the others over there."

Hugh's eyes followed Brian's gesture. A group of men—some dressed as archers, some wearing mail, probably swordsmen—sat morosely in a group. In front was a glum Sir Bailys, legs splayed, his hands tied with a rope that led to a stake. Several guards were posted around the men.

"Sir Bailys and some of his soldiers were captured," Brian continued. "Two of us with the mark were left unguarded, but I do not know what will happen to us since we were caught in an attack on a knight of the King."

Hugh replied, "I think you will be safe. Sir Ralf himself is their leader. I encountered him last night. He told me we would be soldiers of the King now."

"Sir Ralf? So he escaped the clutches of the Dragon?" Brian paused. "But we cannot follow him as soldiers. You must return to your smithy and I to the tannery."

"Perhaps he will allow us to return. But I have to confess that I have wondered what it would be like to ride with him in service of the King. We will undoubtedly learn more today."

Marie awoke as if from one of her terrifying dreams. In her mind was a vision of her home, burning, of being carried screaming down the stairs and then dropped on the ground before fleeing into the forest. But it had not been a dream. She looked up at the roof of a tent she had been led to in the darkness by an unknown, but kind, knight. Most of the night she had lain awake, stunned by the violence that had ripped her world apart, before exhaustion brought intermittent sleep near dawn. The terror of her near abduction and the horror of watching from the forest as her home went up in flames had seared her mind of coherent thoughts. She hoped she was still safe as she propped herself on her elbows and looked around. Edouard was already awake, tearing at a piece of bread, sniffling.

But someone was missing—her mother. Marie rose, greeted Edouard, and gave him a hug. She then brushed the tent flap aside, poked her head out, and scanned the scene around her. Close by, a group of men sat around a smoking fire, some rubbing their arms to get warm in the cold morning air, others using their daggers to scrape something out of a bowl they held in their hands. One of them pointed at her. A tall one dressed in mail and the same kind of blue surcoat her father often wore rose, smiled, and began to walk her way.

"Good morning, Lady Marie," he said, coming to a halt.

She recognized the voice of the knight who had given her his horse, brought her back to camp the night before, and encouraged her to sleep in his tent. He had introduced himself then as Sir Ralf.

"Sir Ralf, good morning," she said. "Where is my mother?"

Sir Ralf leaned toward her, an expression of sadness on his face. "Your mother was overcome by the smoke and flames, milady. I am sorry."

Marie knew that sorrow was the appropriate response on her part, but she did not feel it. Instead there came a simple thought unattached to any emotion—*Mother is gone.* Though she understood that she would never again see her mother, no tears came. The feeling that rose was more like numbness and disbelief. How could the King have allowed this? Marie did not look at Sir Ralf, instead gazing vacantly at the smoke from the fire, wondering what it would mean to have no mother, wondering too how her father would react to the news when he returned.

Perhaps noticing her absence of emotion, Sir Ralf said, "Milady, in her death your mother performed the highest act of love. She sacrificed herself for her son, and she would have done the same for you, had you been trapped in the house."

Now the tears came, Marie pondering the meaning of Sir Ralf's words. Sacrifice was something she associated only with the game of chess. But it was also linked with love?

Hugh continued to look around the encampment. A fire smoldered in the center beneath a kettle hung between two forked branches. Several soldiers sat around eating what he assumed to be their breakfast. Behind stood a knight's pavilion, undoubtedly Sir Ralf's. Further in the distance a group of horses grazed under the watchful eye of two soldiers. Among them Hugh recognized his horse, which he had left tied to a branch when the archers headed for the stable. An empty wagon stood nearby. He and Brian were in a field, beyond which Hugh could see the road that probably led to Sir Guy's destroyed house. On the horizon a wisp of smoke rose above the tree line, no doubt marking the smoldering ruins of Maison Bonfrere. Low fog lay in the hollows and clung to the trees of the forest on the other side of the field.

Gradually men began to stir and look around. As Hugh and Brian watched, some figures emerged from Sir Ralf's tent. Hugh recognized them as the young girl and the small boy, both sobbing. Wearing the royal blue surcoat of the King's knights with the King's emblem in the center, Sir Ralf led them to the fire, where a soldier scooped out bowls of porridge for each of them. While they sat and ate, Sir Ralf walked away, approaching Hugh and Brian.

"I am sorry I could not offer you a more comfortable sleeping arrangement," he said, then smiled. "You men are welcome to come to the fire for some porridge."

"Thank you, sire," Hugh replied, standing and following.

As Hugh and Brian took their places by the fire, they looked at who else was there. Sir Ralf said, "I would like to introduce you to Lady Marie and Master Edouard, daughter and son of Sir Guy de Bonfrere, and here with them, Richard, his steward."

Nodding to each of them in turn, Hugh recognized Richard, although he was now out of his mail armor and wore bandages on his right shoulder and left hand. Hugh had only seen the children in the darkness. He judged Marie, the girl he had seen screaming, to be about fifteen, with sad brown eyes and light brown hair that rested in curls on her shoulders. *A striking beauty*, he thought momentarily. And Edouard was a handsome young boy of maybe seven or eight, he estimated.

"Lady Marie and Master Edouard were rescued by one of your companions," Sir Ralf said.

Gerald? Hugh looked around the encampment. Where was he?

"Sadly he gave his life for theirs," Sir Ralf continued.

"Father warned him, didn't he?" Brian whispered to Hugh.

"He did," Hugh answered, "but he told me last night that Gerald had a premonition he would die. It seems as if Gerald, by rescuing the two children, voluntarily put himself in a position to be killed."

"Once we have fed the prisoners, we will break camp," Sir Ralf said. "First we will escort Sir Guy's party to the road to Sir Bailys's manor house, where they will find shelter until Sir Guy's return. Then those of you who wish to return home may do so. We will continue to Bartscastle to place Sir Bailys and his men in chains to await justice." With that Sir Ralf departed, leaving all to their breakfast.

Hugh leaned over to Richard. "Can you tell me about Gerald?" he asked.

"I do not know Gerald," Richard replied, "but as I was defending my lord's house, one of Sir Bailys's soldiers came out with Lady Marie over his shoulder. A brave man disarmed him and released her, then rushed into the house with the peasants. I did not see him come out."

Marie spoke next: "I was at my window shooting arrows when Sir Bailys spotted me. He looked furious and he pointed to his arm where I had wounded him not long ago. He sent two of his men rushing up the stairs to my room. I could not resist them. One threw me over his shoulder and carried me outside. Then this man I had never seen—Gerald, you call him—appeared out of the darkness and rescued me. I panicked and told him about Edouard." She paused, her chin quivering. "I sent him to his death," she said, burying her face in her hands at the thought. "This man, whom I did not even know, gave his life to save me—and Edouard."

"He died for his King," Hugh said. "He knew that he would."

"He did what we all should be willing to do, though we do not think it will come to that," Richard said in a contemplative voice. "Yet I and one of the guards were spared, and one was not. It is difficult to make sense of it."

"Gerald was a very brave man," Marie went on. "I could not have escaped the grip of the one who held me. Gerald not only disarmed my captor but another with him. He told me to run to a safe place and then he rushed into the house to save Edouard. He lowered him down to me from a back window and said he would meet us in the forest with my mother. He never came."

As he gazed into Marie's glistening eyes, Hugh was momentarily transported, wishing for an instant that he was a bachelor knight rather than a blacksmith. What was the use of such thoughts? Noble daughters were only given to noble sons. She would be the wife of a knight someday.

The group finished their porridge in silence, some returning to their own places until it was time to leave, Hugh and Brian remaining by the fire with Marie and Edouard. As the groups formed up to depart, Sir Ralf came back to the fire accompanied by a soldier carrying a bow.

"Daniel!" Marie exclaimed. "Where were you? We needed you!"

"I am sorry, milady," Daniel replied, his head bowed. "It was I who rode to alert Sir Ralf. Perhaps if I had stayed, your mother—"

"No," Sir Ralf interrupted. "We could not have arrived in time to rescue you without Daniel's warning. You, Edouard, and your mother might all have been abducted."

"And both Henriette and Ginette are safe," Daniel said. He looked at Sir Ralf and explained, "The lady-in-waiting and house servant." Turning his eyes back to Marie, Daniel went on, "They ran out the back into the woods. I could not convince your mother to do the same with you and Edouard." Holding up the bow and a quiver with arrows, Daniel said, "Milady, I found these on the ground outside your window. They are undamaged."

Marie's eyes widened. "Oh thank you, Daniel! When I heard Sir Bailys's men coming up the stairs, I threw them out the window. I did not want Sir Bailys to be further enraged by seeing them."

"A beautiful lady—who fights?" Hugh whispered to Brian, raising an eyebrow.

As Marie took her bow and quiver from Daniel, Sir Ralf came to Hugh. "All of Sir Guy's horses have been found, Hugh. There are two extra. Would you and Brian like to accompany us in front as we ride?"

"Yes, sire!" Brian and Hugh said in near unison.

"One of them is my horse, anyway," Hugh added.

After everyone had assembled, Sir Ralf led the procession with two armed guards, followed by Marie, Edouard, and Richard, then Hugh and Brian, with Sir Guy's other wounded guard. Next came the wagon, flanked by two mounted archers. Behind them followed a subdued Sir Bailys on foot, the rope binding his hands tied to the wagon, plus his ragged entourage of captive archers and swordsmen, guarded by armed horsemen on each side, trailed by a group of foot soldiers and archers. They had not gone far before the smell of smoke gave evidence that they were nearing the remains of Sir Guy's buildings. The stable was a pile of charred embers, small flames still licking the blackened beams. Miraculously a shell of the half-timbered manor still stood, absent its roof, smoke curling upward from inside and through soot-stained windows. The entire group halted while Sir Ralf rode back to the wagon, dismounted, grabbed Sir Bailys by the back of his hair, then jerked his head up and forced him to gaze upon the result of his deeds. No words were spoken.

As Sir Ralf passed Hugh on his way back to the front of the group, Hugh called out, "Sire, might I ride with you?"

"Certainly," he answered, glancing Hugh's way. "Come."

The two separated themselves to the head of the column as it returned back the way it had come, toward their camp and heading to the road junction that led to Bartscastle or Loynton.

"Sire," Hugh said, "if I might be so bold, could I ask you some questions?"

"Of course, Hugh. Perhaps it would occupy my mind with more pleasant things than what we have just witnessed."

"I have been wondering how you happened to be near enough to Sir Guy's manor house to arrive in time. Surely Sir Bailys thought he had taken those at the house by surprise by attacking when Sir Guy was away."

"He did indeed, but I was aware of his plan because it was I who gave him the mission on the way to Grandvil before the events you know of."

"No offense meant, sire, but if you gave him the mission why then did you not arrive in time to stop the attack?"

Sir Ralf frowned. "I expected to. But I was delayed. After I left Loynton, I returned to the Dragon's castle and released all of his prisoners who were loyal to the King. He pursued us until our horses were exhausted. We went to Bartscastle for protection, where Sir Bart offered us refuge. I told him of Sir Bailys's mission and he allowed me to come back with some of his men. It was my intention to send spies into Sir Bailys's fief to learn of his plans. We were nearby, making camp when Daniel found us."

"But, you could have prevented the loss of their home and the life of the knight's wife, as well as one of their guards, if you had come straight to the house, could you not?"

"Yes, I could have, had I known when Sir Bailys would strike when he did and do what did."

"How then could that loss please the King?"

"It pleases neither me nor the King," Sir Ralf replied, "but you are over-looking the fact that the King has purposes you and I do not see. Though I felt responsible to prevent the attack that I had ordered, I must believe it was the King's desire that I capture Sir Bailys in the act of attacking the King's subjects. That may be why he did not send Daniel to me sooner or why I did not sense an urgency to press on to the house by nightfall."

Sir Ralf looked Hugh in the eye. "I have not been in the Kingdom long, but I understand that those who follow the King know that as long as the Dragon has freedom of action in this realm, evil things happen to those that live in evil times, even to those loyal to the King. You of all people should know that, having experienced it at my hand. Your father's death is one of many that I now contemplate with shame."

Hugh's mind flashed to his first encounter with Sir Ralf as the Rat. He had truly forgiven the knight, but the emotions churned anew as he thought about his father. He remained quiet for a time, composing himself, then said, "Yes, I do know that. But I do not understand it. Why does the King allow the Dragon such freedom of action? Is the King no longer powerful enough to defeat the Dragon?"

An almost imperceptible smile flashed across Sir Ralf's face. "Oh, he is powerful enough, and he will defeat the Dragon in a final battle once and for all.

Why he delays is beyond my understanding as well. But the Dragon has exerted his power over this realm for many years and most have little regard for the true King now. I was one of those. Perhaps it is in order to give a few more like me the chance to turn to him. And I need not remind you, the Kingdom is the hearts of those who belong to the King, not the buildings on his lands or the bodies of those who live in them."

Nodding, Hugh said, "Yes, I know that too, but Sir Guy's manor house has been destroyed, and his family is homeless."

"That is true, and I am sorry for them, and sorry I could not prevent it, but his peasants and lands are unharmed," Sir Ralf said. "He will receive a grant from the King, and his peasants will help him rebuild. Moreover, in capturing Sir Bailys, we have snatched an important domain and town back for the King."

At the thought of Sir Bailys, Hugh's former obsession with justice bubbled to the surface, and with it a pang of bitterness. "So will Sir Bailys be executed as my father was?" he asked.

Sir Ralf did not respond immediately, perhaps to allow Hugh the chance to consider his own words. Hugh, though, remained unfazed, ignoring the surprised stare Sir Ralf now gave him.

Finally Sir Ralf said, "Though I am still a student of the King and his purposes, I know from personal experience that is not the King's way, Hugh. He does not follow the methods of the Dragon. He does not exact immediate retribution, preferring instead to show great patience with those who oppose him. Would you not agree that was the case with me, though I have committed far worse acts than Sir Bailys?"

Hugh could not deny that Sir Ralf's journey from enemy to brother had been remarkable. "Yes, more patient than he should have been, I think," he said. "I just wish the King would act differently and spare us the suffering."

"A sensible wish, but I believe it is his desire that all have an opportunity to swear loyalty to him, even those who are his avowed enemies, as I was," Sir Ralf continued. "Sir Bailys does not understand yet why I am treating him like a criminal, but he will be given time to think about what he has done while he sits in a dungeon. In fact, I will be talking to him about the Kingdom on the way. And as for your father, he was not executed. Regrettably he died from the severity of the floggings."

Hugh knit his brows. What was the difference between execution and dying from torture? He was not mollified by Sir Ralf's words, his imagination conjuring the unbearable spectacle of his father crying out in pain under the strokes of the flail, its flesh-tearing leather strips leaving deep crimson furrows on his back. Hugh's breaths became more rapid, long-suppressed anger beginning again to rise. Then the kind face of Clyffe appeared in his mind, his compassionate blue eyes regarding Hugh. The anger began to subside.

"The way you treated him was tantamount to an execution," Hugh said in a soft but controlled voice. "Either way it does not seem fair that my father should die for doing nothing wrong and Sir Bailys be spared."

"And you would probably agree that it was not fair that I survived my fall as well."

"Yes!—no." Hugh blurted. "I mean, I did think that, but I can see now that some good has come of it, with you becoming a knight of the King."

"That is right," Sir Ralf replied. "The King does not concern himself with our ideas of fairness, but with his justice and mercy. His justice demands that he punish us both: me for the act of killing, you for desiring to do so in your anger. He judges both our actions and our thoughts. They are the same in his mind. Yet he has shown us both patience and mercy. I for one am grateful."

The King's justice—Clyffe had said something about that as well. Hugh had understood then that it was a different thing than his own idea of justice and that the King's mercy stayed that justice in favor of forgiveness.

"I guess I should be grateful too," he said. "There is too much I do not understand about the King."

Hugh lapsed into silence as the group plodded past the field in which Sir Ralf's force had camped after the attack. But soon he had more to say: "I thought I would never see you again. Once you departed Loynton, I thought the Dragon would kill you, as he killed the Prince."

"He tried, but the King protected me, though I have no home now. I go where the King sends me," Sir Ralf replied. "While I was at Bartscastle, I was approached by a visitor—the same one who found me in Loynton and told me about you."

"Clyffe," Hugh said.

"Yes, that was his name. He told me to remain there until the King sent for me. In the meantime the prisoners were one by one repatriated to their towns and villages, except for those whose lands are still under the Dragon's control, like Sir Andrew."

"What will happen to him?"

"He will remain at Bartscastle with me until I am summoned by the King."

"You will actually see the King?"

"I cannot say, but Clyffe told me the King would give me a new mission after this one. You will return now to your village and continue your mission, will you not?"

Hugh shrugged. "That is what I thought, but last night when you captured me, you told me I was a soldier of the King. I confess that I am curious to know what you meant."

Sir Ralf looked sideways at Hugh. "Just as Sir Bailys called on you to help him attack Sir Guy, so the next lord of your domain will call on you to fight with him, except that you will now fight as a soldier of the King."

"The next lord …when will he come?" Hugh asked, feeling a spark of excitement that he would now be a soldier of the King, his loyalty no longer divided.

"I do not know," Sir Ralf answered. "That is a decision for the King. But whoever he is, he will serve both you and the King better than Sir Bailys did."

"I hope so, and soon," Hugh replied. "In the meantime, once you depart, we are vulnerable to reprisal from the Dragon. Surely he will not accept this defeat without attempting to regain what he has lost. What if he sends someone more ruthless than the Rat?"

Sir Ralf rode on, keeping his own counsel. He knew too well the answer to Hugh's question and shuddered at the thought. The only thing worse than the Rat would be a Black Knight—Gythreul!

Chapter 25

A New Beginning

T HE STRAGGLING GROUP reached the road junction leading to either
Bartscastle or Loynton, where it paused, Sir Ralf pointing to the right.
"Lady Marie, you and your party will take this road, which leads to the
manor house of Sir Bailys, where you will find shelter until your father returns.
Daniel will show you the way. Hugh, you and Brian will accompany them as a
guard until you reach your fork to Loynton. The rest of us will journey to the
inn near Roaring Fork where we will overnight."

"Thank you, Sir Ralf," Marie replied, mindful that she was now the lady
of the household, but unsure how she would exercise that responsibility until
her father returned. "Though I am saddened by what my father will find, I am
grateful to the King for sending you."

The groups parted, Daniel leading, followed by Marie and Edouard, then
the rest. Marie cast a parting glance at Sir Ralf and his entourage. She was alone
again—alone like she had been in the forest when Sir Bailys accosted her, alone
like she was when her father left her at Bartscastle. She had not been abandoned
by her father this time, but by her King. How excited she had been when she
was admitted to the Kingdom and when she left Bartscastle eager to serve her
King! But now she faced a future clouded by uncertainty and danger. Her home
by the brook was gone, and her bucolic childhood with it. There was no one to
tell her what to do next. Her mother always knew what to do; she missed her
now. Scenes of the previous day had seared themselves into her memory, but she

had too many pieces to fit together. How could she make sense of the upheaval that still engulfed her?

She rode to the front. "Daniel," she said, coming alongside him. "I realize now that your actions saved us from an even worse fate. But how did you know Sir Ralf was near?"

Daniel gave her a sidelong glance. "Milady, perhaps your father has not told you this, but since you are mistress of Bonfrere now, I shall. I am Guardian of Bonfrere. I cannot explain this to you fully in a way that you can understand, but the King sent me from his castle to watch over the lands he gave to your father. The King also communicates with me, telling me how he wishes me to guard the lands he entrusted to your father and to serve him by watching over those who live on them."

Marie pondered this revelation, then asked, "So did the King know everything that would happen?"

"Yes, milady."

Marie rode silently, reviewing the jumble of events of the previous day in her mind. "He knew that our house would be destroyed?" she said finally.

"Yes, milady."

"He knew my mother would die in the flames?"

"Yes, milady."

Conflicting thoughts and emotions now churned within Marie's head, each striving to be examined and understood. The King knew and didn't stop it. A stranger died to save her. Her mother would have died to save her and did die to save her brother. Why then was she spared? The same King to whom she had trusted her heart had let her down. Why?

Words began to form in Marie's mind: "Trust me."

They were the same words Marie had heard once before. She sat up straight and looked around. *It is the same voice again.* Just to be sure, she asked Daniel, "Did you just say something?"

"No, milady."

It was the voice of the Prince again. She had trusted him once and he had delivered her. *He wants me to trust him in this, even though I do not understand it.* But Marie wanted to understand this time, because what had happened made no sense to her in a world supposedly ruled by a King who cared about his people. Did this King care about her? It seemed unlikely. But now that she knew of Daniel's relationship with the King, she needed to know more.

Marie exhaled, then let her thoughts flow: "Daniel, we are homeless now! I do not understand why the King would allow my home to be destroyed and my mother to die. We trusted him!" she cried. "My father was away because he trusted the King to help us. And now my mother is gone. How does any of this advance the King's Kingdom?" Marie paused, visualizing her mother's frightened face, begging her to surrender. "This morning, Sir Ralf told me that she performed the noblest action, yet I was the one spared. I do not understand why."

"It is not given to me to know the King's purposes in all things," Daniel answered, turning to engage Marie's eyes, "but I have observed that some are taken at the moment of their most loving act, while others are left to learn from it." Daniel's blue eyes pierced Marie's heart as he spoke. "Do you have any idea what your mother's last moments were like?"

Marie pictured herself outside the burning house, reaching arms up to take Edouard from a window that boiled black smoke. Then she had run with him in her arms into the woods.

"No," she replied. "I guess I never thought about it."

"Close your eyes," Daniel said, "and silence your thoughts."

Marie closed her eyes, seeing nothing but darkness. But then she heard shouts, the sound of feet, and screams—her screams! The darkness resolved into billowing smoke, which parted briefly to reveal a woman kneeling by a bed, her arms outstretched on top, her face buried in the cover, coughing, gasping. Marie looked on as if she were standing in the doorway. The woman raised her soot-covered, tear-streaked face, her gaze piercing Marie as if searching for something beyond. *Mother!* Coughing, the woman cried out, "O my King! Take me, but let them live!" Smoke obscured her face again as another voice cut through the thickening smoke.

"Do you know what she was talking about?" Daniel asked.

Still startled by the vision of her mother's ash-smeared face, tears glistening in the light of the fire that would consume her, Marie's mind was blank, her only reaction one of shock.

"No ... what?" she answered.

"Your mother heard your screams as you were being carried out of the house. She had no idea what had happened to you but feared the worst. She had just released Edouard to a stranger, hoping she had made the right decision, knowing the smoke was soon to overcome her. But her thoughts were not about herself. Her only desire was that you and Edouard be saved."

Marie had never seen this side of her mother, or perhaps had never noticed. So this was what sacrifice looked like. Was it also the face of love? She thought of what her father had said about love and what Lady Anne had said. Was this a love stronger than death? Then she attempted to conjure the vision in her mind again to learn more from it—to no avail. There was nothing but darkness and the sound of horses' hoofs until she reopened her eyes. But she was now certain of one thing: her father, Lady Anne, and Daniel knew something she did not. Love must be a complex thing, much more than a feeling, something deep and inscrutable—something so powerful it could move one to forgo life itself to secure the object of its love.

Sir Bailys's house soon came into view. Two of his men-at-arms who had escaped were lounging on the steps.

Marie watched as Daniel trotted his horse forward, sword drawn. "Your master is a prisoner of the true King and this house is now the property of the King. You may either leave of your own accord or become my prisoner," Daniel said.

The two rose and slouched toward their horses, eyeing Marie. "We almost had you, milady," one said, grinning.

A chill crept up Marie's back; she did not respond, her mind reliving her panic the previous night while in the suffocating grip of one of Sir Bailys's men, maybe even the one who was speaking, as he hustled her down the stairs of her burning home. Reining her horse a few steps back as Daniel gave the two a nudge with his sword, she looked away until they were mounted and gone. The rest of the party dismounted and entered the house. Although it was a knight's manor house, Marie found no other similarities to her former home. The floor of the hall was filthy, an odor of rotting food hanging in the air above food scraps and animal bones strewn around the room. A half-empty barrel of ale rested in one corner.

"This will require some work if we are to live here," Marie muttered.

"Yes, milady," Richard said, pinching his nose. "We will enlist a party of peasants to clean it. I do not even want Ginette or Henriette to have to deal with this."

In an attempt to avoid dwelling on what she had lost, Marie threw herself into tidying up the place, but it was no use. This was not her home. Even with Henriette, Ginette, and Edouard, it would never be home, and now the responsibility of running the household weighed upon her. True, she was glad to be alive and not captive or worse, but she could not dismiss a resurgence of the helpless feeling of having been abandoned by both her father and her King.

A few days later Sir Guy returned. An anxious Marie awaited him, her raw emotions tossing like an angry sea, threatening to break through at any moment. She was seated alone at the table in the hall when she heard the neigh of a horse from the stable, and waited breathlessly until the tread of her father's feet sounded on the doorstep and the door flew open to reveal him, his arms outstretched, an expression of immense relief on his face. Marie flung herself into his arms, burying her head in his shoulder, unable to speak, her pent-up frustration and sadness venting itself with deep moans. Her father held her silently as her body shook with sobs, gently stroking her hair until her outburst began to ebb.

"I am so grateful to find you alive and unharmed, Marie," he whispered.

Marie did not move, continuing to rest her head on his shoulder, dampening his surcoat with her tears. "Father, we have lost everything—EVERYTHING! And Mother is dead. Where was the King in all this?"

"Yes, I know," he replied softly. "I learned of our loss when I stayed the night at Bartscastle on my return. I have thought of nothing else between there and here. Lady Clare was a good mother to the two of you, and a good wife to me. Things will never be the same."

Marie lifted her head to wipe her eyes dry. She could not look her father in the eye, unable to give voice to her thoughts; she could only vent her anguish over her loss. Her journey to this point had seemed as if she had been writing a hopeful book of her life, one that would be filled with adventure and love and service to her King, but then she had opened it one day to find that someone had ripped out the first fifteen pages and thrown them into the fire. She was faced now with only a blank page and did not know what words to write next.

"Father, my whole life has been torn from me! I do not know what comes next, and I feel I cannot trust the King. This cannot be what the Kingdom is about!"

Sir Guy lifted a finger to brush a tear from her cheek and caught her eyes with his. "Marie, the Kingdom does not promise us freedom from pain. What it does promise is that we are on the side of what is right, and the side of victory."

"This was not a victory, Father." Marie sniffled. "On the way here Daniel told me that the King knew what would happen and did not stop it. You have told me that the King loves us. Why didn't he stop it?"

Sir Guy slipped his arm around Marie's waist and led her to the table to sit. "I have had time to think about how all of this fits into the King's purpose, Marie." He took a deep breath and sighed. "I have to confess to you that I do not know. Sometimes we just don't. What I do know is the *Chronicle* tells me that in all things the King works for good—his good and our good."

"Our home is a ruin and Mother is dead, Father! How can there be good in that?"

Sir Guy was silent, then said, "Sir Ralf told me that Mother gave her life that Edouard might be saved, and I know she would have done the same for you, Marie."

Marie's thoughts went again to her conversation with Daniel, and she replied, "Daniel said that sometimes people are taken at the moment of their greatest act of love while others are left to learn from it. I don't understand. What am I supposed to learn?"

Sir Guy reached out to place his hand on hers and give it a squeeze. "The deepest love may carry the highest cost." He caught her eyes with his. "It was the same for the King and the Prince, was it not?"

Marie turned her head away, trying to compare and make sense of the two examples.

Sir Guy continued, "I understand that losing your mother and our home has all been a terrible shock for you, and I do not expect you to be the cheerful, dreamy girl you once were before you knew the real world beyond your little world. But consider this: we have a roof over our heads until the new owner of this fief and manor comes to claim what is his. And I will ask the King to send a builder to supervise rebuilding our house. We may have to live in my traveling pavilion until the work is finished. But we are still a family. We must trust the King and persevere."

In Marie's mind she had endured enough already; she wasn't sure if she *could* persevere. What was the point now?

Hugh and Brian had dismounted at the Loynton fork, Brian turning his horse back over to Daniel.

Now, as they reached the outskirts of their village on foot, Brian said, "I never thought we would see Sir Ralf again."

Leading his horse, Hugh agreed, "Nor did I."

As they walked on, their attention was diverted to a crowd in the village center. There the bailiff addressed the villagers. Hugh and Brian pressed up to the crowd's outer limit to listen.

"...and then we turned on Sir Bailys's men and surrounded them, bows drawn. They dropped their swords like cowards and we delivered them over to the King's men."

Brian snickered. "That wasn't what I remember! When those arrows came flying over us, I'm pretty sure I saw his backside hurrying in the other direction."

Hugh laughed. "Let him have his moment. The truth will come out. Let's go."

They headed out of the square toward the smithy, but then Hugh stopped and sniffed the air. "The bakers are making bread. I'm hungry!"

When they poked their heads into the shop, Alis, the baker's wife, was arranging freshly baked loaves on a table. Brian plopped a coin down and ripped a loaf in half, giving the other half to Hugh.

"Do you have a moment?" Alis asked, wiping her hands on her apron. "There are many stories circulating about last night. Some of the men came back and told of an attack in the darkness and burning buildings."

Hugh nodded. "Sir Bailys led an attack on another knight's manor while he was away. The bailiff is in the town square right now claiming credit for foiling the attack." He smirked.

"When it was actually the King's men who rescued the knight's children and captured Sir Bailys," Brian said.

"Captured?" Alis said.

"He is being taken back a prisoner by Sir Ralf," Hugh said, "and his lands given to another."

"Oh! So we will have a new lord?"

"One of the King's knights," Brian said.

The baker burst in from tending the ovens in the back, his hands covered with flour. "We should put on a feast to welcome him!"

"I'm sure he eats better than we can feed him," Hugh said.

"That is not the point," Brian said. "You hunt rabbit, do you not, Hugh?"

"Yes," Hugh answered. "I am fortunate to find a few from time to time."

"I am sure he would be glad to know there is a group of Servants in Loynton," Brian said. "We have a vegetable plot. When he comes, I will make a stew of vegetables and rabbit, and we'll ask him to come to our Servants meeting."

Hugh nodded, swallowing his last piece of bread. "You are right. That would be the proper thing to do."

There was much to share at the next meeting of the Servants. William led as usual.

"Friends, this past week has been filled with things both good and terrible. For the past few days my mind has been on one of our own—Gerald. Some of you may not have heard—he made the ultimate sacrifice for the King. You also may not know that it was his plan to notch the horse's girth strap that proved Sir Bailys's undoing. Sir Bailys's saddle came loose just as Gerald predicted, and he was captured by the King's men. But before that happened, he tried to help Sir Guy's children escape, and was slain."

Murmuring ensued among the group, then a farmer said, "He did what we should all be willing to do."

"Exactly," William replied. "The *Chronicle* tells us that a true servant of the King should be willing to give all for the Kingdom, even his life."

Brian cleared his throat and said, "I am ashamed to say that I ran from the battle."

"As did I," Hugh added.

"Well, it wasn't that simple," Thomas said. "I ran too, but don't forget that we were receiving arrows from the King's men because we were with Sir Bailys."

"We all have our reasons for what we did," William said, "and we will have to answer to ourselves and perhaps to the King someday whether we served him well. Gerald was given an opportunity to decide whether he would stand for the King or run. He chose to stand."

"And what were the good things?" a youth asked.

"Most importantly Sir Bailys is gone. Our lands will be governed by a knight of the King."

"Is that really better?" the youth asked. "Surely the Dragon has heard of this and is greatly enraged. He will send retribution upon us, will he not?"

"But our new lord will be backed by the power of the King, won't he, William?" Charis asked.

"A lot of good that did Sir Guy!" Thomas said, stifling a chuckle.

"Look," William said. "This is useless bickering. We all believe that the King is aware of what is happening in his Kingdom, do we not? And that he has a plan for those in his Kingdom?"

"I am not so sure of the second part," Thomas said. "How could he allow the home of one of his knights to be attacked and burned? Why didn't the King's men get there beforehand?"

Hugh spoke up: "Did you know that the King's men were led by Sir Ralf? He captured Brian and me. I asked him the same question."

Thomas looked at him. "And...?"

"His answer was as William said: the King has purposes we do not know, and that when evil lords have power, terrible things can happen even to those who are loyal to the King."

Thomas shook his head. "That is just what I meant. The King could have stopped it and either did not or wasn't powerful enough to stop it. Either way we are not protected. It was the same with his son the Prince."

"That is a bold statement for someone who has never met the King, Thomas!" William said. "When the Prince spoke to Henry and me before he was taken, he told us that he followed his father's wishes. Do you not remember that he came not as a conqueror, but in humility and meekness so that the true nature of the Kingdom could be understood?"

"Yes," Charis added, "as a kingdom ruled through the loyalty of the hearts of its subjects rather than the strength of arms or fear of its lord."

"Well," Thomas said, "it is difficult to remain loyal and trust him when you see the things we just saw."

Hugh continued, "What Sir Ralf told me was that he reasoned that he was to catch Sir Bailys in the act of attacking Sir Guy so that he would have the opportunity to reflect on what he had done and perhaps seek forgiveness and become loyal to the King."

Thomas rolled his eyes. "So Sir Guy had to lose his home and his wife, so that Sir Bailys might change sides? A likely story."

"Maybe," Hugh mused. "But I have had to learn something about forgiveness myself, and I can say it is not something easy to ask for, nor easy to offer, until one understands what he has been forgiven."

"And," William said, "if Sir Bailys were to ask for forgiveness and change allegiance, I believe Sir Guy would offer it gladly and consider his loss necessary to the King's purpose."

"Speaking of Sir Guy," Hugh said. "I have some news. His family will be living in Sir Bailys's manor house. The King may be sending one of his builders in the spring to help Sir Guy rebuild his house and stable. There will be a need for those who are skilled at carpentry as well as for laborers to help him."

"Now that you mention Sir Bailys's manor house, did you learn who would be our next lord?" Charis asked.

"No," Hugh replied. "Sir Ralf did not say. Perhaps he has not been chosen yet."

"In the meantime we are unprotected," Thomas reminded everyone. "What if the Dragon sends his own replacement?"

"That is what I said to Sir Ralf, and he gave me no answer," Hugh noted. "We must be watchful. Perhaps we should place ourselves at the mercy of Sir Guy for now."

"You mean the knight who could not prevent his own home being torched?" Thomas said. "That sounds like the same as no protection."

Chapter 26

BARTSCASTLE BESIEGED

AFTER RECEIVING HIS knighthood Stephen returned to Bartscastle to remain for an indefinite time. It was not long before the first snow heralded the arrival of winter. Stephen often rode now with Sir Bart on his rounds to inspect the welfare of his peasants. Returning to Bartscastle from such a ride, they cantered through slushy snow to find Michael awaiting them at the outer gate, a grim expression on his face.

"Sire," Michael said gravely, "there are rumors that the Dragon has raised a larger army than we have yet faced … and his target is Bartscastle."

Sir Bart raised an eyebrow. "Surely he will not attack in winter. Spring is the usual time for campaigns … but if we must fight him again, we shall. See to our defenses, Michael."

They trotted across the drawbridge, Sir Bart seeming unconcerned, Stephen remembering with alarm his conclusion the last time they had played chess and Sir Bart had proudly pointed out how his castle was protecting his king.

"Now, I am hungry," Sir Bart said, showing no anxiety over the news he had just received.

Sir Bart dismounted by the keep and headed up the steps to the great hall, leaving Stephen wondering at his apparent disregard for the danger they were certainly facing. Even Michael had seemed concerned this time.

Shortly, Sir Bart and Stephen sat down for supper, Stephen now sitting at his right hand, both attended by a new squire. The meal was hearty as usual

– slabs of venison with vegetables, which they washed down with ale. Stephen waited patiently for Sir Bart to bring up Michael's news, but no mention was made of impending conflict.

"You will live here until the King grants you a fief, Sir Stephen," Sir Bart said. "I am sorry that I do not have quarters befitting a knight, but Sir Giles has also taken refuge here. You both will take all of your meals with me when he is not supping with Lady Margaret in the ladies' quarters. Whatever is available to me in the castle will be available to you."

Stephen nodded, then said, "Sire, might I make a request?"

"Anything, son."

"Might my mother come to live in the castle?"

"Of course," Sir Bart replied, smiling. "You anticipate me. I have already instructed my chamberlain to prepare quarters for her. She will live with Lady Anne, as does Lady Margaret. We will send for her as soon as her quarters are ready. Do you have any other requests?"

"Thank you, and, yes, I do. Might I work with Michael in training the new squire? I am sure there is more I can learn from Michael, and I can pass on some of my hard-earned experience to the squire."

"Well spoken, my boy! I had hoped you would volunteer. Your training was difficult and exasperating, I am sure, but you persevered. Michael is one of the best there is, and even he is proud of you."

Michael? Proud of him? Why didn't he show it? Stephen allowed himself a subtle smile, then frowned as he thought again of Michael's news. "Sire, on the way back today I was thinking about the battle earlier this year. We were almost overwhelmed and you were almost killed. If it had not been for Sir John, we would have been finished. And now the Dragon grows stronger?"

"The King certainly knows this," Sir Bart answered without changing his expression. "He sent us Sir John's forces. He will give us whatever we need to fulfill his purposes."

"I hope so," Stephen muttered, still not convinced by Sir Bart's seemingly blind trust in a King who, as far as Stephen knew, never ventured beyond his castles, much less leading an army.

The next day Stephen found Michael in the courtyard instructing the new squire in sword-and-shield combat.

"Michael, I would like to be in charge of the stone pile," Stephen said, glancing in its direction. It seemed like a perverse desire, given his struggle with it, but he knew that it had made him stronger, and he knew that moving it back every day would keep him strong.

"And that you shall be, sire," Michael said, resting from the thrust-and-parry. "This is Mark, Sir Bart's new squire. He is from Southwick."

"I guessed as much. He was with us at breakfast." Addressing Mark, Stephen said, "Trust this man. What he teaches you can save your life. I will wait for you by the stone pile."

In addition to helping with the stone pile, Stephen continued to run his circuit around the castle, even in the snow. In the fall he had gone hunting frequently with Sir Bart, using his archery skills to bring back game for their supper table. He examined the *Chronicle* daily and discussed his reading with Sir Bart. There always seemed more to learn, even from passages he had already read before, and he routinely wished he could fling the fog from his brain and understand it as Sir Bart apparently did.

The next few weeks flew by, but now Stephen grew restless. He had still not been granted a fief. Surprisingly, the life of a knight seemed to be less exciting than his life as a squire had been. There had been so much to learn and so many skills to master, and there had always been the distant goal of knighthood. There had also been the thrill of safe combat with Michael, and the high anxiety of actual combat. Knighthood had conferred on him no badge of bravery or aura of confidence. In some way he missed all of the turmoil of striving to become a knight. His goal having been reached, he had become bored and dissatisfied. Was this all there was?

He and Sir Bart continued to converse over supper about the duties of knighthood, especially concerning care for the peasants and the townsfolk. But what troubled Stephen most was the news that one castle and fief after another were falling to the Dragon. Even the manor of Sir Giles, closest to Bartscastle, had been looted and burned. Stephen envisioned a noose of doom being slowly tightened around Bartscastle. Why couldn't Sir Bart see the same thing?

Sir Bart had not been idle, however. The castle now contained stores to withstand three months of siege, and a stone outer gate with towers had been built in front of the drawbridge during the fall. The moat had been re-dug and made deeper. Barrels of pitch had been placed on the walls. But when the manor of Mark's family was taken and his family captured, Stephen could not contain his growing concern.

One night at supper, with Sir Giles at the table as well, Stephen asked, "Sir Bart, this young squire next to us has lost his home and family. The King's lands shrink year by year. Why have we done nothing to prevent it?"

"Surely you have been listening to the same news I have," Sir Bart replied, "and you have heard of the large army and mighty siege machines built by the Dragon. Do you think our small force can stand up to him on a field of battle?"

The answer sounded like defeatism to Stephen. He pressed his case: "But could we not combine forces with other knights like Sir John and defeat him as we did before?"

"Mm…, that was an unusual assignment," Sir Bart said. "We were defending against an assault to cut the main road to the closest of the King's castles. You forget that it is the King's desire that we each take responsibility for our own domain. In the last two years we have added ten more well-trained men-at-arms to Bartscastle and many more peasants to the kingdom. But we are still far stronger inside the castle than outside it. This castle has never been attacked, much less fallen to the Dragon, and no one campaigns in the winter."

"That may not always be the case," Stephen said. "You remember when I was a squire, a spy was gathering information, do you not?"

"And nothing came of it. What is your meaning?"

"Maybe our enemy knows of a weakness."

"Perhaps. Perhaps not."

Sir Bart's nonchalance now tested Stephen's patience for reasons he could not explain, other than he wanted the man he looked up to and admired to take control of the situation, as his father would have, and as his father would have expected him to.

Silent until now, Sir Giles said, "Sir Stephen, we must trust the King. He will defeat the Dragon, but the King's knowledge is greater than ours and his timing is different from ours."

"Well, I would feel more confident if he would share that knowledge with us!" Stephen said, bristling with impatience.

"He tells us what we need to know," Sir Bart replied. "Our responsibility is only to do what he desires."

Stephen fell silent, brooding over Sir Bart's fatalistic attitude and the imagined dangers that seemed to be encompassing him, realizing finally that there was nothing he could do about them on his own. He was not in a position to take charge, and he was not sure what he would be able to accomplish anyway. Perhaps the King would show up before the Dragon did. Perhaps….

Just days after the turn of the year, a horseman rode into the courtyard with dire news: the Dragon himself was on the march toward Bartscastle—in winter! Sir Bart called Sir Giles, Stephen, Michael, and Mark to an urgent meeting in the great hall.

Sir Bart handed out the tasks: "Michael, you will see to the defenses with Sir Giles. Prepare the men-at-arms. Call in the archers and any swordsmen and spearmen from Bartstown. Ready the courtyard to receive the townsfolk. Sir Stephen, you will be in charge of their feeding and care. Mark, you will dispatch a messenger to the King requesting a relief force should we become besieged."

The next day peasants and merchants began filtering into the castle, whose courtyard had been strewn with straw for them to sleep on. Part of the courtyard was roped off for peasants' sheep and cattle, which would be used for food if the need arose. The granaries were opened and the castle kitchen began to bake bread continually. The dungeon was unlocked and fresh straw spread so that all available space could be used for sleeping. Prisoners were put to work in the kitchen and making repairs. Produce brought in by the peasants was delivered to the kitchen and put into large iron cauldrons to be made into soup and stew.

Within three days the great army of the Dragon had been sighted; stragglers who had been captured by scouting parties confirmed that Bartscastle was its target. Soon thereafter the vanguard arrived. Under gray skies and intermittent snow flurries, the Dragon's army began to make its encampment below the castle. Tents sprang up, trees were felled, and soon cooking fires littered the former jousting grounds outside the castle like fireflies on a summer night.

Snow began to fall in earnest the next day. Stephen had been assigned to supervise defense of the gate towers and was at his assigned position on the wall above the drawbridge when he noticed a solitary rider approaching through the blowing snow, holding a flag of truce. The rider was admitted through the gate towers and came to a halt at the edge of the moat.

"I would speak with Sir Bart," he said. "Lower the drawbridge."

Seeing no visible threat from the enemy army, Stephen ordered the outer gate guard to bolt the gate and then had the drawbridge lowered. He tramped through the accumulating snow to the great hall to fetch Sir Bart. They both met the horseman at the inner gate.

"I bring a message from my lord, the king," the rider said. "No castle has yet withstood his attack. He bids you surrender the castle and pledge loyalty to him before he unleashes his machines of war."

Sir Bart was not cowed. "Tell the Dragon that this castle can withstand siege long enough for the true King to bring relief. We will not pledge loyalty to your imposter."

"As you wish," the horseman replied. "You are trusting in a power you do not see. You will now feel the might of a power you can see. Prepare yourselves to be buried beneath the force of our might!" He spurred his horse back across the drawbridge.

Stephen climbed back up to his post and commanded the drawbridge be raised and the outer gate reopened for the messenger.

In his role as commander of the gate towers, Stephen supervised the gate guard, who operated the portcullis and drawbridge and who were responsible for defending the gate should it be breached. He watched with awe as the enemy army began to stir itself in the gusting snow. Archers began to gather themselves in ranks on the wintry field below the castle, as did armored swordsmen behind them. Still farther back were arrayed the infernal machines of which the rider had spoken. Stephen had never seen them before but he knew their names. Just the sight of them and knowing what they could do took his breath away.

In front he saw an array of ballistas, which, like giant crossbows, would throw steel-tipped arrow-shaped bolts at the wooden door of the gatehouse to weaken it or, if elevated on blocks of stone, at the soldiers on the wall to impale them. Behind them sat a row of catapults, beside them piles of great rocks, each of which would be lifted into the cup-shaped end of the throwing arm and flung through the air to break down the battlements on the towers and maim anyone standing in its path. Those that cleared the wall could equally crush any unsuspecting soul laboring in the courtyard.

Behind the catapults stood several giant trebuchets, whose arms were like tree trunks, with hanging rope baskets that could sling stones large enough and with sufficient force to reduce a wall to rubble. Last came a row of battering rams, concealed inside wooden shacks on wheels. These iron-tipped beams, suspended horizontally under the protection of the roof, would be pulled back and slammed forward repeatedly against the wooden gate by a team of the strongest soldiers until the gate gave way.

Behind all of that loomed the black pavilion of the Dragon, his red dragon banner rippling above. His dark hair topped by a crown, he sat wrapped in his cloak on a throne in front of the pavilion, gnawing a lamb shank, as if he had no doubt about the outcome.

Having sized up the force now facing him, Stephen glanced back at the courtyard, where many peasants were gathered, sitting in the snow or tending to their animals. His eyes opened wide. *We must get the people out of the courtyard!*

He dashed down the steps and found the chamberlain. "You must crowd everyone into the keep," Stephen ordered. "They will be crushed by the stones if they stay in the courtyard."

Even as the chamberlain began to usher the refugees into the keep, the first arrows came flying over the wall, a few finding their mark in screaming peasants. The *thunk* of rock on stone told Stephen the catapults and trebuchets were already at work. He climbed back up to the towers above the drawbridge.

The siege machines concentrated on the outer gatehouse, large rocks caroming off the battlements, sending showers of stone with them as they pitted the walls. The few archers defending the gate towers proved largely ineffective because of the steady rain of rocks. They descended inside and shot from arrow slits in the towers. Stephen watched as the Dragon's forces trundled a battering ram up to the outer gate. With each dull thud he could hear the hinges of the gate squeak as they slowly weakened. But Stephen knew there was a defense against that and turned to observe two soldiers on the wall above the outer gate grab their torches, touch them to a barrel of pitch, and lift the barrel to the battlement. Although Stephen could not see it, he knew from the screams below that the stream of flaming pitch had found its target—the battering ram and the men within. The thuds ceased as a wisp of smoke rose from the burning ram.

The catapults continued their emotionless toil, some of their rocks ricocheting off the gatehouse and striking the castle walls proper. The *thoing* of ballista missiles resumed, but to no avail, their steel tips ineffective against the stone walls. Only a few struck the heavy wooden gate doors. The enemy slowly pushed another battering ram to the gate and the process began again. The beam holding the gate shut was strong but Stephen knew it could not last forever against the iron battering tip.

The day ended without a decision. Under cover of darkness, Stephen lowered the drawbridge to allow more barrels of pitch to be taken to the gatehouse. He stayed at his post all night, shivering in his armor and a wool cloak. Even the flaming brazier on the tower did not keep him warm as the snow blew in gusts and formed a rime on his cloak and face. Dawn brought more snow and a resumption of the assault. Two more battering rams were sent up in flames by burning pitch.

Ladders were brought up. The Dragon had apparently seen enough. His men would now scale the towers and try to conquer the gate from the inside. Stephen knew that would spell the end of the gatehouse. Even though the castle's men had poles to engage the ladders and topple them backward, the half-dozen defenders would be insufficient to force all of the ladders away or to engage the enemy soldiers as they swarmed up and over the battlements. Nevertheless Stephen gathered all available archers above the inside gate overlooking the moat.

As enemy soldiers jumped off their ladders onto the two outer gate towers, they were met with a hail of arrows from the inner gate towers. Many fell where they stood or careened backward to the ground, but some disappeared into the towers. The few defenders left were soon flushed out, standing now with their backs to the moat, ready to die. Not willing to lose any, Stephen had the drawbridge lowered before the enemy soldiers could open the outer gate.

Seeing the lowering drawbridge, the enemy swordsmen froze with indecision, unsure whether to follow the defenders into the castle or remove the crossbeam and open the outer gate tower for the rest of the army. By the time they decided to lift the beam and open the gate for more of the army to enter, the defenders had leaped onto the now rising drawbridge and were rolling down it into the courtyard. A crowd of enemy swordsmen soon stood on the lip of the moat, looking up at Stephen and the inner gate guard. A cloud of arrows from Stephen's archers sent them on a hasty retreat beyond the gate towers. Just as suddenly, the siege machines stopped their destructive work while the Dragon no doubt pondered his next assault.

That night Sir Bart met with Stephen, Sir Giles, Michael, and Mark in the great hall, now burgeoning with murmuring refugees sleeping on the floor.

Dismayed by the progress made by the enemy, Stephen slapped his hands on the table and said, "Only two days and the outer gate towers have fallen! What good were they? The same will soon happen to the castle!"

But Sir Bart remained calm as always. "The castle is much stronger than the gate tower, the walls taller and thicker. Though the catapult and trebuchet stones are no doubt cut from my quarry, they will not be able to bring down these walls quickly. The enemy has already lost three battering rams; one remains. We have large stocks of pitch. Soon that ram will be gone and it will take time to build more."

"And by now," Mark said, "perhaps the King has heard of our plight."

"But the towers were taken by ladder," Stephen said. "They do not need rams if they are willing to waste enough men."

"It only takes two or three men to push away a ladder before it is laden with soldiers," Sir Bart replied. "Each pair of men on the inner wall has a strong, forked limb or a billhook to engage a rung and force the ladder away, and, again, we have plenty of barrels of pitch along the walls to pour down on them. Moreover, you have more men at the inner gate than there were on the outer gate tower. You must have confidence in our preparations, Sir Stephen."

Stephen doubted now that even the inner gate could be held. "I wish the Prince was with us in person," he said with a sigh.

Sir Bart engaged Stephen's eyes with his. "The King is aware of what is happening and the spirit of the Prince is always with us, Sir Stephen. Whether the King sends help soon or not, we know that he has a plan and it will be fulfilled." Sir Bart then motioned toward the gate. "Sir Stephen, your position tomorrow will again be at the gate, to pour burning pitch on the ram and to push away ladders. Sir Giles, you will command the walls with Michael. Mark, you will oversee the townsfolk and peasants; determine which are willing to take up arms to defend the castle should the enemy succeed in entering, and supervise the supply of pitch and arrows to those on the walls. I will rotate among the various positions to supervise the overall defense."

Stephen was back at his post by dawn, more anxious than the previous day. To his astonishment the Dragon's army had seemingly grown overnight. Instead of just the group facing the west gate and south wall, soldiers now arrayed themselves on the north side of the castle as well, ladders resting on the snow. Archers stood in rows behind them. Once again great piles of rock were heaped by the catapults and trebuchets. And at their rear, sitting calmly on his black horse, only visible through the falling snow by his red surcoat, the Dragon surveyed the scene. As Stephen looked on, the Dragon slowly raised his arm and brought it down with a flourish. The creaking of catapult and trebuchet winches commenced, lowering their arms to receive their deadly loads. Ballistas were drawn to receive their murderous spears as scores of soldiers hoisted ladders and raced for the moat on three sides of the castle. The final assault had begun!

"Shoot at the ladder bearers, archers!" Stephen shouted. "Ready the pitch, men!"

All fire on his side of the castle seemed directed at the gate. Arrows skipped off the stone of the towers or sailed over into the courtyard. A large trebuchet boulder smashed into the battlements of a tower, sending an explosion of stone in all directions. Even the ballistas were targeting the inner gate towers in the hope of impaling its defenders. No one could stand under such a storm of projectiles. Stephen and his men hunched behind the stone parapet for protection. Two groups of enemy soldiers manhandled ladders into the moat while another group rushed forward with bundles of branches and then tossed them into the moat in front of the gate. Stephen discerned their strategy. *They are going to fill the moat for the battering ram.* The tower shook as another boulder crashed just below the battlements and broke apart. Things were not going as Stephen hoped.

Attempting to disregard a growing fear that the castle would fall to this onslaught, Stephen's mind raced searching for a solution. The rain of projectiles had mostly neutralized his archers. Sporadically they would rise to shoot, but their aim and rate of fire had been drastically reduced. Thus he directed most of the archers down into the tower to fire from arrow slits. And now he saw ladders begin to rise against each tower.

"Ladders!" he cried. "Push them away!"

He observed as two men on his tower took their forked limb and, with an agonized grunt, heaved the ladder away from the wall until it went vertical, then ever so slowly began to tip away. A chorus of groans sounded below as it dumped its contents into the moat. Stephen glanced to the ladder rising against the other tower. The men strained to push it back, to no avail.

"Use the pitch!" he bellowed.

The men gave up their fruitless task, stepped back, touched a torch to the barrel, and with great effort lifted the barrel to the top of the ladder to release its contents. Agonized screams confirmed that it had found its target. The men took up the forked limb again and easily pushed the ladder away. The gate was safe … for a while.

Stephen took a moment to glance along the walls. To his left he could see Michael patrolling the south wall, where burning pitch eliminated another ladder and its contents. No enemy had gained his wall. On the north wall he saw Sir Giles. His wall was clear of enemies as well. The latest attack had failed. A lull ensued, save for the relentless toil of the siege machines. And still the arrows came like a sleet of steel. Along the walls ran peasants recruited from the refugees, removing the fallen to the chapel, most having been felled by arrows, one impaled by a ballista bolt. Others struggled up the stone stairs with fresh barrels of pitch. Stephen looked down. The moat had already been filled to a width of ten feet with bundles of branches; now men were running forward with bags of dirt to throw over the branches.

"Archers! Fire as you can at the moat workers," Stephen called out.

In the distance he could see new battering rams already being constructed, though not as solidly, using the retrieved heads from the burned ones. *Another day and they will have a road built to our gate.*

"Sire!"

Stephen turned to find a breathless soldier struggling up the steps to the top of the tower.

"Sir Bart has fallen!"

Chapter 27

BARTSCASTLE BREACHED

S TEPHEN STOOD MOTIONLESS, stunned by the unexpected news. He glanced to the steps and then the courtyard, his heart racing. There knelt Michael, cradling Sir Bart's head in his arms, his hands covered in blood. Leaving his post, Stephen bounded down the steps, denying the evidence his eyes presented. *No! This cannot be!* Gasping for breath, he arrived at Sir Bart's side, his chest heaving, to find the knight already lifeless, his face pale, his lips blue, his surcoat soaked with blood from a neck wound.

Suppressing conflicting urges to rage his anger or burst into tears, Stephen tore into Michael. "We have turned back the assaults. How could you let this happen, Michael?"

Michael lifted a sweat-streaked, anguish-filled face. "I was not with him, sire. He was in the courtyard directing supplies to the walls. They said an arrow grazed his neck. He did not think it a mortal wound. He stayed to direct the defense until he collapsed. Furthermore Sir Giles is wounded. You must continue without them."

Continue without them? Me? The weight of Michael's words felt as if they would crush Stephen. He stood there, speechless, gazing down at the body of the man who more than any other had guided him from childhood to knighthood, the man he had looked to as a father. The enormity of the castle and forces arrayed around Stephen seemed to magnify; he envisioned himself diminishing to the size of the page who had come years ago, unsure of what lay in store for him. And now he was in charge of the entire defense? Without knowing Sir Bart's overall strategy? How could Sir Bart leave him like this? How could the King allow it?

He looked back at Michael for encouragement, finding nothing but sorrowful, expectant eyes awaiting an order. Stephen was alone, like the six-year-old who was told his father would never come home—now thrust into command without a plan.

"Take him to the chapel," he ordered. "The men must know only that he is wounded."

"Yes, sire."

Michael lifted the lifeless Sir Bart and turned to go as Stephen struggled to untangle the possible outcomes and solutions that swirled in his mind, and then to prioritize his actions. Their only hope now was the arrival of the King and his army. Somehow Stephen had to organize the defense to resist until then. Stephen versus the Dragon. It was an unequal contest.

"We have to send another messenger to the King to inform him about Sir Bart and request urgent relief!" Stephen shouted at Michael's back.

"There is only one way out of here now, sire," Michael said, turning to face Stephen, "and it is a filthy one. The messenger will certainly not be presentable to the King. Moreover we are surrounded on three sides now; what if he is discovered?"

"I am in command now!" Stephen yelled. "It is my duty to hold this castle for the King. The east wall is not yet guarded because of its rocky face. We will send him by night through the flow of the latrine and he can cleanse himself in the river."

"It is your decision, then, sire," Michael said, cradling Sir Bart's limp body and starting back toward the chapel, leaving Stephen feeling as a solitary figure in the courtyard, blind to all around him, deaf to the chaos surging against the castle walls.

Stephen sank to his knees, oblivious to the *whish* of arrows and the occasional catapult boulder clearing the walls and thudding into the courtyard. He had never imagined this moment coming—when he would have to stand on his own without his mentor next to him. What was the Dragon thinking now? Stephen attempted to devise a counterplan. Surely his foe would try to complete the road to the gate overnight and bring up battering rams; surely he would attempt to assault the walls again. But what else? How could he anticipate everything? He ran back to his position on the gate tower. The Dragon's men still rushed forward, dumping bags of earth on the bundles of branches; the road was halfway built, despite it being littered with bodies claimed by his archers. An idea sprang into Stephen's head.

"Men, bring a barrel of pitch above the gate and light it!"

Two soldiers muscled a barrel forward and torched it.

"Now lift it and heave it over."

Stephen watched as the flaming barrel crashed to the ground at the lip of the moat, split into pieces, and splashed burning pitch onto the bundles of branches nearest the gate. Within minutes they were aflame. The ant-like work of men hauling bags of dirt came to a halt as they gathered at the other end to watch their construction disappear in flames, before finally retreating under a barrage of arrows. Stephen glanced back to the Dragon's pavilion, where he sat motionless on his horse, as if unfazed by this new defeat.

After sundown Stephen met with Michael and Mark in the great hall again. "How many have we lost?" he asked Michael.

"Sire, we have lost fifteen, counting those lost in the outer gate towers: five dead, ten wounded. And Sir Bart—"

"Shhh!" Stephen exhaled. "There are ears!"

"And Sir Bart is in the chapel," Michael continued. "Moreover Sir Giles has succumbed to his wounds. But we have recruited five men who can handle a bow to replace some of the archers."

"Good," Stephen said. "Tomorrow you will command the north wall, Mark, and you the south wall, Michael. We do not know what the Dragon will attempt next, but no ladders must be allowed to remain against the walls. Enlist more peasants to push away the ladders. I will remain at the gate. The messenger has been dispatched and even now should be making his way out of the castle."

With a mixture of anxiety and sadness, Stephen took his place above the gate to wait out the night. A strip of glowing embers and flames marked the site of the would-be road to the drawbridge. They would be safe tonight. But what would the Dragon try next?

Near morning Stephen's fitful sleep on the tower was interrupted in the darkness by a shout from below.

"We are betrayed!"

The clash of steel on steel announced a struggle in progress near the gate—inside the castle! Stephen snatched a torch and hurried down the steps to find that he was too late. He saw at least a dozen enemy soldiers, strips of stinking wool hanging from their arms and mail tunics to muffle the noise of their stealthy crawl into the castle via the sewer. They had overcome the two gate guards and were hacking away at the drawbridge rope while others were cranking up the portcullis. Stephen watched in horror as the rope snapped and the drawbridge began to fall.

"Men! Defend the gate!" Stephen shouted, plunging into the mass of enemy soldiers, his blade slashing.

The walls cleared as defenders converged on the gate, but they would be too few. The drawbridge landed with a crash, sending sparks flying from the embers below, bringing the thunder of horses' hoofs.

"Sire, it is no use." Michael was next to him. "You must not waste your life. Give the Dragon what he has won."

"Never!" Stephen shouted.

He steadied himself to receive the onrush of armored horsemen in the dark. The collision was sudden and violent.

Stephen awoke to a splash of water in his face. Then he felt a firm grip on each arm as he was jerked to his feet, his head throbbing, his body aching. The morning had dawned; he did not know how long he had been unconscious. He was hustled to the center of the courtyard where Sir Bart's lord's chair from the great hall had been placed. A man sat on it, clad in black armor with a red surcoat, a golden dragon rampant emblazoned on his chest. Around his shoulders was the skin of a lion, its mane drawn around his neck to keep him warm, its paws clasped across his chest by a chain; his feet rested on a muddied lamb's fleece. Resting on his lap was his black helmet, adorned with the severed wings of a white dove, a coronet resting between them.

Stephen was brought to an abrupt halt, his eyes facing a pair of emotionless blue eyes framed by neatly groomed black hair topped by a golden crown; a carefully trimmed mustache above his mouth joined a closely cropped beard. Stephen knew whom he was facing. Were it not for the hatred stored in those eyes, it would be a handsome face. *Not at all what I would expect of one so evil.* Standing behind the Dragon was a large swordsman in black armor, perhaps his lieutenant, his face obscured by his lowered visor.

"This is the commander?" the Dragon asked, smirking. "He is only a boy! Where is Sir Bart?"

"You killed him!" Stephen shouted.

"Dead or alive, it matters little," the Dragon said. "One less to worry about." He leaned forward, his eyes burning. "So *I* am your master now. You will address me properly, boy!"

"As you wish—sire!" Stephen spat. "How fitting that the Dragon would enter under cover of darkness in winter—and through the sewer!"

"You will address me as 'your majesty!'" the Dragon said abruptly, then smiled. "It was your own doing, lad. If my men had not found your messenger bathing in the stream, we would not have known the flow from your latrine empties through a small hole at the base of your east wall."

"The stench of your men fits that of your methods," Stephen replied. "What you have done brings you no honor."

"Nor have you brought honor to your so-called King by losing his castle," the Dragon said. "You will kneel and address me as your king, or you have only one decision remaining—how you will die for your false King!"

Stephen considered the Dragon's demand. He would willingly have died defending the gate, but that was not granted him. *If this is where I am to make my stand, so be it.*

Stephen straightened to his full height and looked the Dragon in the eye. "I will not kneel before you, nor will I call you my king."

The Dragon, his blue eyes blazing, made a motion with his hand, where-upon Stephen felt a blow on the back of his legs, causing him to collapse to the ground on his knees.

"You *will* kneel," the Dragon said.

Stephen did not attempt to stand, his eyes remaining fixed on the ground in front of him, awaiting he knew not what. The tip of a sword nudged his chin and forced it up so that he could not avoid the gaze of the Dragon.

"Shall I execute you here and now, in front of your friends?" the Dragon said.

Stephen gave no reply.

"I-I have often seen him by the stone pile," someone said.

Stephen looked for the source of the obsequious voice, finally spotting his very own messenger, quivering behind the Dragon, held by two guards, his feet dangling.

"Hmm, different ... but sporting," the Dragon said, glancing toward the stone pile. "Strip him of his armor. Tie his hands with a length of rope twice his height to a stake in the ground so that he can move, and assemble my bodyguard for target practice."

As Stephen's guards jerked him to his feet and began to unfasten his armor, a familiar voice came from behind him: "Sire? I would speak a word with you."

The Dragon lifted his head and said, "Raise your visor and state your name, prisoner."

Stephen also turned, seeing both Michael and Mark, disarmed, held by guards.

Michael lifted his visor. "I am Michael, Guardian of Bartscastle."

"Michael..., yes," the Dragon said with a voice of recognition. "You didn't guard it very well, did you, Michael? But you may speak."

"You have taken one of the King's castles and killed one of his inner circle in battle," Michael said. "You have counterfeited the King's Rules with your own, as though they originated with you. The honorable procedure for captured knights is to offer them for ransom. Even the Dragon and his knights should be above executing other knights. This knight should be ransomed—and he will be."

"Do not deign to lecture me about honor and ransom!" the Dragon shouted. "You have dishonored your king by losing his castle. This castle and everyone in it is my spoil of war. You will be thankful if I allow you to be released to crawl back to your so-called King!"

Unfazed, Michael looked at the lieutenant behind the Dragon and addressed them both in a language Stephen did not understand. The lieutenant leaned down to whisper something in the Dragon's ear.

"I know what he means!" the Dragon said. "We speak the same language."

The Dragon cast a piercing gaze toward Michael, then broke into a smile. "Very well," he said to his lieutenant, his tone softening. "You will place the three in the dungeon for the time being. I will give it some thought. In the meantime release the refugees to their town and farms and declare them spared. I will not burn their town and farms this time. This will be my castle for a time and they will support me."

Once the keep and dungeon had been cleared of refugees, a group of the Dragon's soldiers led Stephen and the others down the steps and placed each of them in a dark cell. There was no outlet to the daylight. Stephen felt his way around the stone walls, determining that his cell was about six feet square, closed in by a thick wooden door with a small square window covered by a grate, the only way either light from a torch or semi-fresh air could enter. He could feel soiled straw scattered on the floor, along with a ragged blanket.

After exploring the cell, Stephen backed himself into a corner and sat, pondering what might lie in store for him. He deserved whatever happened next. He had lost Sir Bart's castle—the castle that Sir Bart said had never fallen. The King now probably regretted making Stephen a knight. Why couldn't he have died in battle? At least he would have done something praiseworthy for the King.

In the darkness, time had no meaning. Though Stephen had the threadbare blanket, he shivered in the cold. He did not know how much time had passed when he heard a soft knock on his cell door.

"Sir Stephen?" It was Michael's whispered voice.

Stephen stood and felt his way along the wall toward the voice. "Are you outside my door, Michael?"

"Yes, I am leaving. I must speak to you."

Stephen pressed his face to the grate. There was no light, and he did not hear a jailor. "How are you free, Michael?"

"I do not have time to explain everything. But here is what you must know. Guardians cannot be held within walls or behind locks. Nor are we mortal like you. I cannot remain here since the castle no longer belongs to the King. I am on my way back to the King's castle."

"What do you mean? Why did I not know this about you?" Stephen said. "All these years—"

"All fiefs of the King have a Guardian," Michael said. "Only the knight to whose fief we are assigned is afforded that knowledge. But though we possess powers you cannot imagine, we are still merely servants of the King, and for the most part we serve unknown among your kind, lest because of our powers we be accorded an esteem to which we are not entitled. Suffice it to say that I contended with the Dragon for three days over this castle. It was the King's desire to release it, for his own purposes. Now you must persevere. I will send you help from the King. Remember: persevere."

Stephen could hear him turning to leave. "Michael, wait! May I ask you a question?"

"Yes, but be quick!"

"I thought I was moments from death. What did you say to the Dragon?"

"I told him that it was the King's desire to give him the castle temporarily, but harming you would bring a swift response from the King, and I reminded him that he could not resist the King if the King wished to take it back."

Stephen shook his head in the darkness. "The King *wanted* him to take the castle? Michael, I don't understand."

But no reply came. Stephen was alone in the darkness again, pondering the meaning of Michael's parting words. From that moment he began to count what he thought were days by the frequency that a shallow bowl with thin soup and moldy bread was slid under the door by torchlight. He hoped he was being fed every day, but his constant hunger told him otherwise.

After some time he could tell that his chest and arm muscles, of which he had been so proud, were wasting away. He could feel his ribs and the tops of his hips. The blanket he had been given to ward off the cold was insufficient; he shivered continually. He knew he was weakening. He would not even survive until spring. What had been the purpose of all his training to be a knight if he was going to die of starvation?

Prisoners were not allowed to talk to each other. Any time an attempt was made, the jailor would come through and rap the doors with his sword, threatening a flogging or worse. Stephen wondered if Mark was still alive. He had seemed somewhat undernourished already.

Eventually Stephen resigned himself to die in the darkness before he was even eighteen, barely a knight. He thought of his time with Sir Bart. *All of the things he taught me—wasted.* He thought of how he had trained with Michael and become strong and skilled, of the victory at Pevensey Bridge. What he could have done as a knight of the King! Then he remembered his decision to send the messenger. Michael had not seemed in agreement. And that was how the castle had been lost. What had Michael said before he left? The King desired to let it go. But Stephen had listened to his own counsel and determined to hold it. He bore full responsibility for that decision. There had been no counsel from the spirit of the Prince. Why not? The King was certainly ashamed of him now. He deserved his fate. But Michael said to persevere. Why?

Stephen clung each day to Michael's last words—*"I will send you help."* He was too weak to stand now, having to crawl to the door to get the daily gruel.

Huddled in the corner, he awoke from a shallow sleep with a start at the sound of a voice, knowing not whether it was day or night, or how long he had been a prisoner. It was a strangely familiar voice, but it was not Michael's. Grasping the blanket around his shaking body, he groped his way to the cell door on unsteady hands and knees.

"Sir Stephen?"

"I...I am here. I think I have heard your voice before. But I cannot see you."

"I am the King's priest," the stranger whispered. "The King is aware of your plight. I have brought you sustenance."

"I remember now," Stephen said, unable to keep his body from trembling in the cold. "You...gave me my armor when I was knighted. I will never forget sharing the cup with you. But how did you get into the dungeon?"

"The dungeon guard is asleep. No one took note of me. Reach down under the door. There is a cloak to keep you warm, and two small bags—one with bread and the other water."

Stephen slid his hands to the bottom of the door where food was passed, and gathered the cloak and bags. He felt a loaf of bread in one and the other, a leather one, sloshed with water. He sampled both immediately, breaking the bread in half, biting off a mouthful and draining half of the water. The bread tasted fresh and sweet, and the water cool and pure.

"Thank you, father," he said. "I am grateful for your visit. This will give me a few more days if I conserve it."

Stephen considered it prideful to ask since he had scarcely been knighted, and he had already made a decision against the King's desires, as he saw it, but a flickering hope compelled him not to squander this opportunity. "Do you have news from the King? I know I have displeased him by my decisions. Will he yet ransom me?"

"He already has," the voice whispered again. "He does not hold your decision against you. But your freedom is not yet. What I have given you will sustain you until that day."

It would have to be soon. Stephen had already drunk half the water and eaten a quarter of the bread, and he was still hungry. Maybe it would last three days if he rationed it.

"Trust me. It will sustain you."

Stephen heard these words with disbelief. The priest knew his thoughts? "Father...?" he called out.

There was no answer.

Stephen remained by the cell door, trembling. There was something mysterious about this priest, walking into a locked dungeon without being seen, seeming to have no fear of being caught. Was he like Michael—a Guardian? Or was he something else? Stephen reviewed the event in his mind.

Did he say I had been ransomed? But now he was gone. Stephen had no answers. He drew the cloak around him and sank to the floor in despair, clutching the two bags to be sure he still had them. Denying what he felt, his hands groped at them again, one hand slipping inside the bread bag.

The loaf was whole again!

He lifted the water bag. It felt as heavy as it had been before he drank from it.

PERSEVERANCE

Chapter 28

FREEDOM

S TEPHEN CRAWLED BACK to the corner of the cell where he spent most of his time sitting, sometimes sleeping, uncertain if what he thought had just happened had really happened. Or, in his weakness and confusion, was it a hallucination? He drew the cloak around him, aware now that he was no longer shivering, as he had ever since he had been thrown into this darkness. His hands grasped two bags. There had been a man at his cell door who gave them to him. Why? And how had he avoided being seen? In his debilitated condition Stephen could not connect his thoughts to make sense of it.

As the warmth of the cloak began to flow over his body, his senses became sharper, his thoughts now piecing together the event that had just occurred, leading to more thoughts and questions. The priest said he had come from the King. *Did he really say the King had already ransomed me? Why would he after I lost his castle?* Stephen touched the bags again. The bread was still whole, as it had been the last time he felt it. How could it be? Still famished from his underfed weeks in the dungeon, Stephen was overcome by an urge to eat the whole loaf at once. *No, I have to ration it.* He paused and thought, *What were the priest's parting words? "Trust me."* Stephen had heard those words before. It was the same voice.

He forced himself to eat only a portion of the bread each day, but each morning the loaf was again whole and the water bag full. Try as he might, Stephen could not unravel the mystery of his visitor, but after a while he knew one thing:

as long as he wore the cloak, he never felt cold. And there was something else too: though he only ate part of the loaf each day and drank some of the water, he never grew hungry or thirsty. And even more surprisingly, he began to feel stronger as well. He no longer stumbled as he walked his cell, and after some time he no longer could feel his ribs. His body was regaining its strength and muscle as if he were eating a hearty fare of meat and vegetables. Clearly something was unusual about this bread and water ... and the "priest" who had brought it.

Though he sat in darkness and walked his cell periodically to stay active, Stephen no longer harbored thoughts of dying in the dungeon. He refused the gruel pushed under the door, eating only the visitor's bread and water.

After many more days had passed, he sensed a warming of the dungeon air. One day, or night, he knew not which, there came a voice at his cell door—a woman's voice: "Sir Stephen? Are you still alive?"

Stephen went to the small window in the door. There was a face he had seen before, now partially shrouded in darkness, half of it illuminated by a flickering torch.

"I know your face, milady," Stephen responded, "and your voice. Are you Lady Anne?"

"Yes. You are to be freed."

"How can it be?" Stephen asked. "How did you pass the guard?"

"The Dragon and his army departed the castle today. Your mother is with me as well."

"My son?" Lady Eloise cried. "You are alive! But are you well?"

Seeing her face press up against the grate, Stephen, not yet certain he could believe what he was hearing, said, "Mother! How did you—"

A key turned in the lock and the door swung open. Stephen's mother grasped him with open arms and held him, weeping, Stephen doing the same, incredulous at the sudden and unexpected turn of events.

"Am I really free?" he asked, studying the faces of his mother and Lady Anne. "I had almost despaired of it."

"They would not allow me to visit you," Lady Eloise said, sobbing. "Each day for the last three months I knew you were growing weaker. I thought you would die of the chill or of starvation, or both." She backed away, looking at him. "But, though in need of a bath and a shave, you seem no different than when I last saw you three months ago."

"Even I am surprised, Mother," Stephen said. "I did not know how many days had passed, but sometime during the three months, a man visited me. He said he was the King's priest. He gave me this cloak and a bag with bread and one with water. I have survived on it alone."

"You have more than survived," Lady Anne said. "You are the picture of health."

Stephen smiled. "He told me it would sustain me, and I doubted him at first, I but feel that it has not only sustained me but made me stronger."

"Come," Lady Anne said. "You must clean yourself and prepare to greet Sir Ralf when he arrives."

"Sir Ralf?" Stephen searched his memory.

"I do not know him either," Lady Anne answered, "but Owen said he stayed here briefly when fleeing the Dragon."

"Yes!" Stephen said. "The Rat. I remember now. He was one of the Dragon's top commanders. I faced him in battle once. He supped with Sir Bart one night. I was shocked to see him at the table that night as I served them, but I heard him say that he was now serving the King. He departed the next day."

"Perhaps that is why the Dragon abandoned the castle," Lady Anne said. "Sir Ralf is leading a contingent of the King's soldiers. Moreover, Michael is with him."

"Michael, too!" Stephen recalled his last conversation with Michael in the dungeon. "That must mean that the King is reclaiming his castle."

They climbed the steps from the dungeon to fresh air, Stephen's mother wrapping her arms around Stephen all the way. Stephen could sniff the scent of freedom before he stepped outside, but was unprepared for the blinding light that assaulted his eyes—eyes that had seen little or no light for three months. He stopped, covering his eyes with his hands, opening his fingers to form slits through which to see.

"From darkness to light," he said quietly. "I did not expect there to be such a difference. I had become so accustomed to living in darkness."

"We will take our leave of you now," Lady Anne said. "You may use Sir Bart's quarters to clean yourself, and you may wear his clothing as well if you have none in your former room. Owen has instructed the kitchen to prepare a meal for you in the great hall."

Stephen touched Lady Anne's arm. "Milady, you have lost your brother. I am sorry."

"As am I," Lady Anne replied. "But he died for his King. The Prince told his inner circle that they might be called upon to sacrifice their lives for the King as he himself was willing to do. My brother was prepared."

Stephen paused in silence, then continued, "He was as a father to me. I hope I will be prepared if the same is asked of me."

"He trained you well," Lady Anne answered, pulling away gently. "Now we must go. Owen is waiting for you. Please sup with me and your mother when you are able. We can share memories of my brother."

"I will."

After hugging his mother and bidding farewell to the ladies, Stephen entered the great hall and was escorted by Owen to Sir Bart's quarters. Befitting the man Stephen had known, they were functional but not elaborate. Once clean and shaven, Stephen could not bring himself to wear the clothes of the man who had mentored him. Instead he climbed to his old room in the tower, where he found his clothing piled in one corner, his room apparently having been used by one of the Dragon's soldiers. Returning to the great hall, he found Owen waiting by the table he had sat at so many times, Sir Bart's chair pulled out for him at the head.

"No, Owen," Stephen said. "I cannot sit in Sir Bart's place. He was a greater man than I. I will take my usual place to the right."

"Of course, milord."

Though the meal was a delicious one of roast goose with leeks and cabbage, Stephen ate alone, feeling very small, as if still in the shadow of one of the King's great knights. He glanced at the empty chair, remembering the unworthy imposter who had sat in it last, and began to ponder the course of his life. It had been a glorious upward journey of learning and maturing that had reached a peak when he was admitted to the Kingdom and knighted by the King. What had the King said? *"In you I am well pleased."*

And then Stephen had dropped from that peak like an errant arrow. He had lost the King's castle and been plunged into darkness, nearly starving to death. He deserved every bit of it. He would have and should have died, but then the priest brought him food and water that not only sustained him but essentially brought him back to life and health. Why? Was the man really the same priest? His voice had seemed the same.

Stephen's eyes wandered around the great hall, coming to rest on the Kingdom Rules, his mind recalling the very first time he saw them. *And I still have not kept them. Yet I am here … and Sir Bart is not. I should not be in this position.*

His self-examination halted at the entry of Owen. "Sire, our sentries have spotted the dust from Sir Ralf's column. He will be here soon."

Stephen hurried to finish his meal. "Tell me, Owen. What happened after the castle fell?"

"It was hard times, sire," Owen replied. "The Dragon released all of the townsfolk with the word that they all served him now. Then he lined up the surviving soldiers and ordered them to swear loyalty to him. Those who refused were executed."

"How then did you and Lady Anne survive?" Stephen asked, his heart burning at the brutality of the Dragon.

"He spared me to serve as his steward and likewise the castle staff to serve him and feed his men. I assume he saw the ladies as no threat."

"And where is Squire Mark?"

"Unfortunately he did not survive his imprisonment, sire."

Stephen lowered his head, thinking of the young life that had been extinguished, but then he heard a swell of cheers outside. He ran down the stairs to the courtyard where he saw the few remaining occupants now on the ramparts, observing the triumphant return of the King's men. Stephen hurried to the gate with Owen to see the portcullis lift and admit a column of horsemen and foot soldiers, led by Sir Ralf clad in the blue surcoat of the King's knights, with Michael at his side. Stephen ran to meet them as they dismounted.

"Welcome, Sir Ralf and Michael!" he said. "Your return has meant my freedom."

"Your freedom is a work of the King, Sir Stephen," Sir Ralf replied. "We are merely reclaiming what is his."

"Will you stay awhile?" Stephen asked.

"I will," Sir Ralf replied. "The castle and lands of Sir Bart have been granted to me by the King. Now I must visit the castle staff and inform them of the same. I hope you will sup with me and Michael tonight."

"Gladly," Stephen answered.

Envisioning himself at the beginning of a new and undeserved phase of his life, Stephen was encouraged by the return of Sir Ralf, and especially of Michael. He felt energized by a growing excitement at what might lie ahead for him now, an emotion similar to what he had experienced while waiting to sup with Sir Bart his first day as a squire. His first afternoon of freedom, he visited Jacky in the stables, then took a run around the castle, breathing the fresh aroma of the forest, and finally walked down into Bartstown to experience again the sensation of being part of something larger than himself, to be once again caught up in the unceasing flow of time and humanity with the promise, perhaps, of a part still to play in it.

As Stephen turned to make his way back to Bartscastle, his mind wandered to the upcoming supper with Sir Ralf and Michael. He especially wanted to speak more with Michael, who had left him with many questions to ponder that night in the dungeon. And they might ask about his imprisonment and how he seemed to have suffered no ill effects. He would tell them about the priest and—the bags! They were the proof. How could he have left them there?

As soon as Stephen reached the castle, he raced to the dungeon. His cell door was still open. Grabbing a torch he rushed in, kicking straw and searching each corner. The bags had vanished. But he still had the cloak. It was almost time to meet Sir Ralf and Michael in the great hall. He bounded up the spiral staircase two steps at a time to his old room, arriving breathlessly at the table where he had tossed the cloak. There was no cloak.

A sobered Stephen descended the steps to the great hall. Sir Ralf and Michael were already there, conversing. The kitchen staff was bringing out platters of steaming food. Stephen took his place to the right of Sir Ralf, who gave him a nod of welcome.

"You have endured quite an ordeal, Sir Stephen, yet you appear no different from when I last saw you," Sir Ralf said.

Stephen related the story of his imprisonment, the priest, the cloak, and the bags of food and water. "But I have no evidence to offer you of its veracity," he said. "All he gave me has disappeared."

Michael had been staring at Stephen somewhat pensively throughout. "It appears that you yourself are the evidence, sire. No one can withstand months in a dungeon without a serious decline in their well-being."

"But what I do not understand is why," Stephen said. "I ignored your counsel to refrain from sending a second messenger and, later, to surrender the castle. I was moments from execution and then I was plunged into a dark dungeon where I should have died. I dishonored the King. I deserved to die."

"As did I for slaughtering the King's subjects during my time as the Rat," Sir Ralf said. "We serve a merciful King, do we not?"

"It is not that I am ungrateful," Stephen replied. "I just want to understand. If my imprisonment was punishment, I can accept that. But why then was I saved from death? And why did I stay another month or two in the darkness after the King's priest came?"

Michael spoke again: "In my experience the King only punishes those who steadfastly reject his authority. Perhaps there was another reason." He seemed to be studying Stephen's face. "Perchance do you have your map with you?"

Stephen was aware that he was always to carry the map on his person, but he wore it more like an amulet. He had never studied it. He reached into his tunic and pulled up the small bag that hung around his neck. Producing the map, he unfolded it for Michael to see.

"Show me where your heart is on the map," Michael said.

Stephen felt a flush of embarrassment. "My heart? I have never examined the map closely. I can't tell you."

Michael leaned forward, placing a finger on the map, running it slowly toward the lower left corner. "It is here, just beyond the tower, is it not?"

There it was—a small green heart, on a road leading to the King's castle, just beyond a tower.

Stephen looked up at Michael in amazement. "How did you—"

"Do you see anything else?" Michael asked, his eyes still fixed on Stephen's.

Stephen looked back. As Michael lifted his finger, the forests on either side of the road began to form themselves into letters that spelled out the word *Perseverance*. Stephen was astonished, recalling the last conversation he'd had with Michael in the dungeon.

"That is what you told me when you left! You said to persevere." Stephen paused to consider the implication of what he had just said. "You knew then why I was imprisoned?"

Michael smiled a rare smile. "I did."

"When the priest came and I asked him if I would be ransomed, he said I already had been but my freedom was not yet. That was for the same purpose—so that I would learn to persevere?"

"I believe it was," Michael answered. "You have been restored to health and granted freedom for a purpose. You must discover it."

Stephen exhaled a breath of relief. "It makes sense finally."

"Undoubtedly the King allowed this to prepare you for something else," Sir Ralf said, "just as I was spared from my fall for the King's purpose."

Stephen's thoughts turned now to the questions he had stored up. "Michael, when you left me, you said you were going back to the King's castle. Is that what happened?"

"Yes," Michael said. "I returned to his court and served there for a time until I was to return to Bartscastle."

"I remember," Stephen continued, "that you told me the King decided to give up Bartscastle. How did he get it back without a fight? The Dragon left before you came."

"You may recall when we were brought before the Dragon after the castle fell, I said some words to him in a language that you did not understand."

"Yes," Stephen answered. "It seemed to change his mind about stoning me."

"I told him that you belonged to the King and he could not take your life without the King's permission. I also told him that it was the King's decision to allow him to have the castle for a time, but he would have to give it up when the King desired."

"Yes!" Stephen said. "Now I remember you telling me that in the dungeon. It sounds as if he has no power over the King, though he says otherwise."

"That is correct," Michael said. "Though he is more powerful than you, he cannot resist the power of the King."

"So when he learned that you and Sir Ralf were returning, he knew his time was up and he relinquished the castle?"

"Yes, rather than face the power of the King."

As Stephen slowly put together in his mind the pieces of the puzzle of the past three months, he found himself once again in a state of amazement. "So the Dragon's victory and his occupying the castle for three months had nothing to do with his power but rather with the King's purposes? And one of those purposes might have been for me to learn perseverance from my three months in the dungeon?"

"I think you understand now," Michael replied.

Stephen sighed. "What I understand is that the scope of the Kingdom and the King's purposes are so much larger than my small part in them. But I am grateful that I still have a part."

Stephen turned to Sir Ralf next and said, "Sir Ralf, the last time I saw you, you had just come back from your 'unfinished business.' You stayed the night and departed. Where did you go?"

Sir Ralf cleared his throat and turned to face Stephen. "I had returned from capturing a knight loyal to the Dragon after he had carried out a raid on one of the King's knights. My intention was to deposit him in the dungeon here, but the dungeon was full. I was instructed to continue on to one of the King's castles, leave him there, and wait for instructions from the King. During that time Bartscastle fell to the Dragon and I was summoned to the King's castle."

"Sir Bart told me that no one goes to the King's castle and returns."

"Few do, and it is not something I am at liberty to talk about in detail, but suffice it to say that I learned the time is short until the King rises up to reclaim all that is his and to bring all of his subjects under his protection. As a new follower I needed to learn much, and learn quickly, before I was to be granted the fief and castle of one of his inner circle."

"You said you are lord of Bartscastle now."

Sir Ralf nodded. "That is why I returned with Michael. And I have news from the King that concerns you."

"Me? Already?" Stephen queried. "I am only today out of the dungeon."

Sir Ralf continued, "You are to be granted the fief of Grandvil, which belonged to the knight I captured."

"And what happened to him?" Stephen asked.

"He also returned with me. He will occupy your cell until the King decides his fate. You will remain here another month until spring, to recover your skills and rehearse all that Sir Bart taught you. Then you may depart to claim your fief."

Stephen could not speak. In a matter of hours, he had gone from prisoner to landed knight. It took his breath away.

Chapter 29

SPRINGTIME

STEPHEN AWOKE BENEATH his lean-to of branches and boughs as the first light of dawn outlined the trees behind the field where he had stopped for the night. Birds already called their morning song as rays of soft sunlight filtered through branches sprouting new leaves. Rubbing the sleep from his eyes, he looked around at unfamiliar countryside. He had been traveling for two days since he departed Bartscastle to claim his new fief.

Stephen knew that his fief encompassed several villages, and was near the county seat, Grandvil. On the other side of Grandvil lay the fief of Sir Guy de Bonfrere, the burning of whose house and stable was the reason for the capture of the knight who had formerly been lord over Stephen's new fief. Stephen would now have his own manor house and stable. Sir Ralf had given him a manservant to begin his household and his mother would be lady of the house. She had abandoned the family house in Bartstown, and was at this moment still asleep in the knight's pavilion Sir Bart had given him after he was knighted. Nearby was a horse cart that held a few belongings and supplies.

Once underway, Stephen paused at the road to Grandvil where it forked and received a tributary from Loynton, one of his villages; he attempted to imagine what it would like to be lord of a fief. Would the peasants accept him willingly when they saw he was still a youth? He would have to visit all the villages to establish his authority and pay his respects to the mayor of Grandvil. All the responsibilities of managing a fief, as taught him by Sir Bart, began to march through his mind. How he missed his mentor already! He would have no one to ask when he encountered a problem he had not foreseen, and there were sure to be plenty of those. But he had seen enough while observing Sir Bart caring for his people that he thought he was ready. What he would truly miss were the deep conversations about the Kingdom, about which he still had much to learn.

Stephen was not prepared for the sight that met his eyes when he and his small entourage rode up to the manor house that would be his. Compared to the stately castle he had lived in while a page, then a squire, then a knight, the property seemed somewhat run-down. In places some of the plastering between the half-timbering had come loose, exposing the rubble that lay within. If it were not repaired soon, hard rains would erode a hole in the walls. The one bright spot was the stable, which looked clean and neat. The last lord must have had a good stable master.

Stephen was also not prepared for whom he found in the house, although Sir Ralf had told him the Bonfrere family would stay there until he arrived. As he rode up to the stable, a man ran from the house to hold his horse.

"Good morrow, sire. How may I serve you? Have you thirst or hunger?"

Stephen dismounted and handed the reins to his greeter, who was looking him over.

"I see that you are dressed in the livery of a knight of the King, sire. Have you come to see Sir Guy?"

"I am Sir Stephen, the new lord of this fief. This is … my manor house," Stephen replied, unable to hide his awkwardness in calling himself lord of anything. "And with me are my mother, Lady Eloise, and my manservant, Jacob."

"Yes, milord, and I am Richard, Sir Guy's steward. He has been expecting you. I will bring him to you."

After Stephen had waited a short time, Sir Guy soon appeared in the doorway in his blue jacket, smiling, and followed Richard from the house.

"Welcome, fellow Knight of the Blood," Sir Guy said, extending a hand. "We have been awaiting your arrival. We are grateful for the temporary roof to shelter us, but we are ready to return to Bonfrere whenever you wish. We will live in my pavilion until our house is rebuilt."

"How many are you?" Stephen asked, wondering about the size of the household he was about to evict.

"Come inside and I will introduce you," Sir Guy said.

Stephen and his mother entered the house and were seated at the table in the central hall, where someone had already placed mugs full of ale and baskets of bread and dried fruit. Sir Guy's family was already seated, seemingly in expectation of meeting the new owner.

Sir Guy motioned toward the table. "My son, Edouard, my daughter, Lady Marie, at the table; lady-in-waiting Henriette, and house servant Ginette, standing behind," he said, introducing each in turn.

Stephen's eyes did not progress past Marie. Confronted with a pair of large brown eyes framed by tumbling brown curls, and a quizzical smile, Stephen found his tongue suddenly glued to the roof of his mouth, his body flooded in hot prickles. He could only nod his head and swallow.

"And—And this is my mother, Lady Eloise," he said, aware his mouth had been agape.

From that moment Marie's face was not far from Stephen's thoughts. And from that day he would be on a quest. His first action was to assure the family that they could stay in the house until the rebuilding of their own house began. He noted that Marie and the servants had already taken the initiative to tidy up and clean the inside of the house. He pitched his pavilion near the stable. The family was kind enough to welcome his mother into the house, especially when she volunteered to supervise the housekeeping.

The arrangement only lasted two weeks, when word came that the King's builder would arrive at the ruins of Maison Bonfrere with a building team and cartloads of stone and tools. During that period Stephen had busied himself with repairs to the outside of his house, to which Sir Guy had lent his steward and a guard. Stephen otherwise kept to himself except at supper, when he was always welcomed to the family table, a most agonizing experience for him.

As the senior knight, and at Stephen's request, Sir Guy always sat at the head, with Stephen's mother on the left and Stephen on his right. Next to Stephen sat Edouard, and next to Lady Eloise, Marie. Something seemed familiar about her, but try as he might, Stephen could not guess what it was. Moreover he found it next to impossible to keep his eyes away from the lovely face seated across from him and even more difficult to attend to the conversation.

"Tomorrow we will load our cart and travel back to our house to rebuild," Sir Guy said. "This will be our last imposition on your kindness, Sir Stephen."

The words came as through a fog. *She will be gone. That is a relief. No—that will be unbearable!*

"Sir Stephen?" Sir Guy said.

"Oh, I-I—Yes, it has been my pleasure to be of service, sire."

"It was not necessary that you sleep in your pavilion, but I understand that you wished to allow my family as much comfort as possible. Your generosity will not be forgotten."

"Yes. Yes, you are quite welcome. Are you sure you will not stay until your house is nearly built?"

Sir Guy shook his head. "Thank you, but no. My pavilion is larger than yours. I will pitch it on the grounds and we will make do for a few weeks until the first floor is completed."

And idea struck Stephen and he blurted it out, "No! I mean, please take my pavilion for Lady Marie. And Edouard, of course," he added. He had almost given himself away. He dared not look at her now.

Sir Guy considered for a moment, then said, "That is kind of you, Sir Stephen. I think we will accept. Lady Marie can sleep in the larger one with Henriette and Ginette, and I will take Edouard in the smaller one."

The next day Stephen helped the family load onto a large four-wheeled cart the few possessions that had been salvaged from the ruins of their home. As Sir Guy mounted his horse, Stephen stepped forward, offering a trembling hand to Marie to help her onto her horse.

"Why, thank you, Sir Stephen," she said, taking his hand and tossing her curls with a mischievous smile.

Stephen was almost undone. He hoped she hadn't noticed his shaky hand as he steadied her step up. Again she had rendered him speechless. He only bowed and stepped away, watching with a churning stomach as the Bonfreres rode away, Marie's hair dancing in the sunlight.

As she guided her horse around puddles, Marie found herself in a quandary. She found something familiar about this young knight. But what? Was it the frightened look in his eyes? Where had she seen that look before? She thought back to her time at Bartscastle. What was the name of that squire? But that squire was much too young to be a knight already, and this knight had a neatly groomed mustache and beard. Yet Marie saw an indescribable earnestness in those eyes, and a sense of strength in the way he carried himself that appealed to her. Despite his awkwardness and seeming lack of self-confidence, she was inexplicably attracted to him. Try as she might to dismiss him from her mind, the suppers of the past two weeks fleeted before her. Sometimes she had caught him looking at her, and then he looked away, like the victorious squire at the joust. Why did he not talk to her? Did he find her undesirable? Was he too noble for her now that her family had lost their home?

She urged her horse forward to draw even with her father. "What do you think of Sir Stephen, Father?"

Sir Guy slowed his horse to keep pace with Marie. "He seems like an honorable young man. Why do you ask?"

Marie hesitated to ask the next question: "Is he the kind of knight you would choose for my husband?"

Sir Guy turned and smiled. "Well, your mother would have been the first to point out that he is not of noble blood and therefore not worthy of someone like you."

They rode along in silence, Marie wrestling with her thoughts. He was not worthy of *her*? Was that why he seemed unsure around her?

"Then how will you choose?" Marie continued. "And does it matter what I think?"

"I take many things into account," Sir Guy replied. "The King's desires, the character of the knight, the future of our family and his, and, yes, your desires."

Encouraged, Marie resumed, "Father, he was always kind to me. He offered his pavilion to me, and he offered his hand when I mounted my horse. He does not speak very much, but I feel as if he honors me when he is around me."

"Indeed. Yes, I have noticed. And I have also noticed how your eyes lingered on him over supper." Sir Guy chuckled.

The warmth of embarrassment flushing her cheeks, Marie did not answer. She was not sure how to describe the emotions tumbling within her as they distanced themselves from the house and she was struck by the realization that she might not see Sir Stephen again. By the time they reached the fork to Loynton, Marie's stomach grew uneasy. She could not dismiss from her thoughts the lively eyes, the gentle face, or the restrained strength of the young knight, nor could she understand the growing ache in her heart and the knot in her stomach.

"Father, I do not know what is happening to me," she half-cried, half-whispered. "My stomach is upset and there is an ache—an ache like I had when we last talked about me being a wife. I hated the thought then—but now I do not."

"You are thinking about him, aren't you?" Sir Guy asked, smiling.

She lowered her eyes, uncertain if she should admit the truth, but if anyone could understand, perhaps it would be her father. "Yes, I cannot dismiss the thoughts. Why?"

"You want to see him again, don't you?"

"Yes, I do."

Sir Guy reined in his horse beside her and reached his hand over to pull her into a hug. "Marie, I think you might be falling in love," he whispered, holding her tightly.

What does that mean? According to her father, love was not supposed to be a feeling, especially an unpleasant one. "Father, I do not understand," she said. "You told me love was not a feeling, but what I am feeling is like pain. Is love supposed to be painful?"

"No. Not this kind of love." He chuckled again. "But some kinds of love can be. What you are describing is the ache of separation after two weeks of having him near you."

This was love? How many kinds of love were there? Marie now faced a dilemma. If this was love, what difference did it make anyway? Her father was going to choose her mate, and she dared not try to manipulate him into making the choice she wanted. He already knew that game. But, as always, when she set her mind on something, she began to plot how to obtain it. How could she make herself more attractive to this handsome knight? What did she need to do? Was it even possible? She could not ask her father. What would he know about it? That was what mothers were for, she guessed. Her mother might have been able to advise her—but she was gone.

Marie began to consider her predicament. There were so many things she did not like about her appearance, yet, at times in Bartscastle, when dressed in the gowns Lady Anne gave her, Marie had felt attractive, especially the times the kindly Sir Bart took notice. But could she ever be attractive to someone younger than him? The champion squire at the tourney did not seem to think so. And those moments at the supper table when she had caught Sir Stephen looking at her face, her hair, her eyes, and then quickly looking away, what did it mean? Did he like what he saw? Or was he just regarding her as Sir Guy's child? Was that why he did not talk to her? She decided she had to find a way to see him again, to make him notice her, to talk to her, maybe to be attracted to her. Perhaps she could convince her father to invite him to sup with them once the new house was completed. But that was an unbearable month away, at least.

After watching Marie ride from sight, Stephen felt disgusted with himself. He could hardly speak in her presence. What must she think of him? In his own eyes he seemed a bumbling fool. And he had no idea how to change the impression he had made. If his father were alive, would he have counseled him how to court a lady? Perhaps he would have tried. But she was a noble lady, and no one, even his father, could have told him how to win the favor of a lady of such stature.

That night, supper in the manor house was a lonely affair, just Stephen and his mother, attended by their manservant.

"I am going to help Sir Guy with the rebuilding, Mother," Stephen said. "They will need all the strong hands they can find."

His mother gave a knowing nod, then smiled down at her food. "That wouldn't be the only reason, would it, son?"

"What do you mean? Of course it is!" Stephen said.

"I am not without eyes." She looked at him, her expression one of expectancy. "I have noticed where your eyes spent most of their time during suppers."

He sighed. "You are right, Mother. It is her. I don't think I can bear to be apart from her and I can hardly bear to be with her. She is constantly in my thoughts. I am most miserable."

"Then you must pursue her as a knight should. Did not Sir Bart educate you in those areas?"

"He was an old bachelor knight," Stephen replied, "but I think he tried. He arranged lessons in courtly dance and music, and encouraged me to write poetry. I don't think I was very successful at any of it. He told me that women desire honor, bravery, and strength in a man, but I was too focused on becoming a warrior to pay much attention. Women were far from my mind when I was being trained to fight for the King."

"Well, you must try to remember," his mother said softly. "What I know of courtship will not apply to a noble lady, but I can tell you one thing that applies to all women."

"Please, what is it?"

"You must pursue her heart."

"Pursue her heart?" Stephen repeated as if he had misunderstood. His mother might as well have been speaking a foreign language. "I know nothing about ladies' hearts. I cannot even look her in the eye. What do you mean?"

"I can only speak for myself," Lady Eloise said. "A woman wants to feel that she is being pursued because she is desirable. She wants to feel that there is nothing more important to you than her when you are with her and that you desire the best for her. She wants to know that you will fight for her if need be, and that if she gives you her heart, you will neither reject her nor abandon her.

And she wants to be your partner in whatever journey you undertake for the King. Your father did all those things."

His father did all those things. Of course he did. His father did everything right. But he was not his father. Stephen looked back at his mother, realizing that what she had said was probably true, though he did not fully comprehend what she meant. "I do want to do all of those things," he said. "But—" He shook his head and sighed again. "How can I get *her* to feel them? I can't even breathe normally around her."

Lady Eloise smiled. "You are your father's son, Stephen. I reared you to be like him—strong, gentle, and respectful of ladies. All you need is the courage to be who you are. Where did your courage come from in battle?"

"The spirit of the Prince," Stephen answered. "But that was in a battle, where life and death were at stake. I don't even know what this is."

"Then you must trust the spirit of the Prince in this matter. He rules her heart, not you."

"But it is her father who will choose whom she weds. I am like a child to him. How do I—"

"Do not assume he will look down on you because you are young, my son. You must trust the spirit of the Prince in that as well."

Chapter 30

AN INVITATION

A FEW DAYS LATER William was at the village square early with Brian and Thomas, Hugh being unable to free himself from the smithy. The baker's wife, Alis, joined them shortly, carrying a bag.

"Mmmmm!" Brian said. "I can smell it! Fresh bread!"

"Not for you, hungry Brian," Alis said, then laughed. "It's for our new lord, Sir Stephen. Perhaps he will break bread with us."

There were few travelers on the road as William and the others exited the path that led to Loynton and on to the main road to Grandvil. The early-morning sun cast long shadows over the waking countryside, the coolness of morning and the stillness of the air carrying a distant bleat of sheep. Where the road brushed against the forest of the knight, it was still in shadow. Soon enough the manor house came into view. A middle-aged woman, her sleeves rolled up, was sweeping the stone step at the entry.

"A good morning to you, mistress," William hailed as they approached the house.

The woman stopped sweeping, shadowing her eyes with her hand. "And a good morning to you, sir. What purpose have you visiting my lord?"

"We are members of the Servants of Loynton. We have come to pledge our loyalty to the knight. We would be indebted if you could show us to his steward."

The woman leaned on her broom. "He has no steward. He is a poor knight, without lands until now."

"Oh. How then does he pay you?" Thomas asked.

She laughed. "He does not pay me. I am his mother."

"I beg forgiveness, milady," Thomas said, his cheeks growing red. "I did not expect the knight's mother to be—"

"Doing manual labor? We were once villagers like you. Old habits do not die."

"We have brought fresh bread to share with you and him, then," Alis said, "if he will admit us."

The woman motioned to the side of the house, where rough scaffolding had been built. "He is there, patching holes. The previous lord of this fief must have been a pig." She huffed, then said, "If you will wait, I will fetch him."

William nodded, glancing at Thomas, who had assumed a dignified expression, as if attempting to recover from his gaffe. The woman walked slowly to the scaffolding and called down a youth with tousled dark brown hair, clad only in a sweat-soaked tunic and trousers, who appeared to be much younger than Brian and Thomas.

As they stepped forward at the woman's beckoning, Thomas whispered to William, "This cannot be the knight. He is no older than the farmer's youth in our group!"

Before William could reply, the young man called out from the scaffolding, "Welcome, men—and lady—of Loynton. I am Sir Stephen, and this is my mother, Lady Eloise." He climbed down and came to a halt before them. "A beautiful day in the Kingdom, is it not?"

"Good day, sire. I am William. This is Alis, Thomas, and my son, Brian." Not one to hide his thoughts, William said, "I confess, we expected someone much older. Are you really a—"

"Knight?" Stephen laughed. "Indeed, it is difficult even for me to believe, but, yes, it has been less than a year since I was made a Knight of the Blood by the King himself."

"We mean no disrespect, sire, but you appear still to be a youth," William said.

"To myself as well." Stephen smiled. "I am scarcely past my eighteenth birthday."

William looked to Alis as she held out her bag. "Sire," she said, "we would be honored if you would break bread with us, and we would like to invite you to our next Servants meeting. You know about them, do you not?"

He nodded. "I do. I knew of a group in Bartstown, although I could not frequent it on account of my duties in the castle. Please come inside."

Inside, William and his group looked on as Stephen and his mother drew a bench and some stools up to the table in the hall, then everyone sat. Alis placed the bread on the table while Stephen's mother ladled ale into mugs and brought out a bowl of dried fruit.

"You come from a castle, then?" William said. "Why did you not stay there? This is certainly a meaner position."

"I go where the King sends me," Stephen answered. "Bartscastle belongs to another."

"Bartscastle...that name is familiar," Brian said, his eyes half-closed as if he were trying to recall where he had heard it.

"It was the castle of one of the King's inner circle, Sir Bart, who died in the siege of the winter past. It is Sir Ralf's castle now," Stephen said.

"Sir Ralf is there? We heard it had been taken by the Dragon," William said.

"It was. And I was held in the dungeon for a time. Then, I have been told, the Dragon was informed that the King would reclaim it, so he and his forces abandoned it, and I was freed. When Sir Ralf returned to Bartstown with some of the King's soldiers to retake it as his grant from the King, the people there told him it had already been evacuated, so he re-occupied it without a fight. Now, what brings the four of you here?"

"We are all tradesmen—and women," William said, then took a swallow of ale. "I have a tannery with Brian to handle the leather needs of the village, and Thomas is a carpenter. We are also members of the Loynton Company of archers. Our hands and weapons are at your service. Oh—you probably figured Alis is our baker." He paused, then asked, "Might we render you aid in repairing your manor?"

"To know a baker is to be close to paradise." Sir Stephen smiled, tearing off a bite of fresh bread with his teeth. "Actually I could use your hands now, though not for myself. The next few weeks I will be with Sir Guy, helping him rebuild his house and stable. The King's builder will be arriving with a team of masons and carpenters to begin construction tomorrow."

"We have heard," Thomas said, "and already some from Loynton, including myself, have pledged to come."

"Excellent," Sir Stephen replied. "I hope I will see the three of you tomorrow, then. Now, if you will excuse me, the house walls still await me."

William and the others were in good spirits as they returned to Loynton, all of them relieved to be rid of their former master.

"He received us graciously," William said. "He will be a pleasure to serve as our new lord."

"I think he will take good care of us," Alis said.

"He seemed strong and healthy enough, but I don't see how he can protect us," Thomas said. "He is still a boy ... and he doesn't even have bodyguards like Sir Bailys did, or men-at-arms, like Sir Guy."

William did not share the concern, nor did Brian and Alis seem to either, choosing instead to enjoy the good feelings engendered by the short visit with their new lord.

The day following the visit from the villagers of Loynton, Stephen mounted his horse and rode to the construction site at Maison Bonfrere, arriving in the late afternoon. Work crews were already unloading stone from carts and dragging felled tree trunks to an area near the site of the burned stable, while others were finishing the clean-up of ashes and charred timbers. He noted two pavilions, one of them his, set up in the field at the edge of a forest across from the site, as well as a smaller tent and many lean-to shelters for the workers. He busied himself gathering some sturdy branches from a pile that had been cut for the purpose and fashioned himself a lean-to among the others, the opening facing the pavilions.

A small roped compound provisioned with hay and oats contained the few horses that had been brought. He led his horse through the gate and released it to graze, then walked over to the house and began unloading stones from a cart and carrying them to an area where stonecutters were already at work. It seemed like old times at the stone pile. The same muscles that had ached during his training as a squire now welcomed the chance to perform again. No one seemed to know who he was, shirtless and in trousers. He was enjoying his anonymity, and then he chanced to look toward the pavilions. There was Marie, seated outside doing something with a needle and thread. Was she watching him? He could not tell. He turned away and threw himself into his work, but it could not soothe the burning within his heart.

As workers scurried about the work site like bees on a hive, Marie sat outside her pavilion, attempting to keep her mind occupied by doing needlework, but repeatedly found her concentration interrupted by thoughts of Sir Stephen. How could she manage to see him again? Looking up to clear her mind, she froze. She was almost certain that she saw someone who looked like Sir Stephen, shirtless, by the ruined house carrying stones. She ran to find Henriette.

"Is that the knight whose house we lived in?" she asked, motioning toward the man.

"Yes, milady," Henriette said. "Perhaps he has come to help with the rebuilding."

Marie dashed into her tent, straightened the green and gold riding dress that Lady Anne had given her, for it was the only one she had left, fluffed her hair, and found several wildflowers behind her tent, placing them among her curls. She then ran out to find her father, who had just returned from conferring with the master mason.

"Father, he is here!" she said.

"Yes, I know," her father replied. "He was kind enough to offer his services to help us rebuild." Sir Guy took a step back. "And look at you! You look like the beautiful maiden I encountered at Bartscastle not long ago."

Marie smiled. But she was on a mission. "Father, could we invite him to sup with us tonight? He was so kind to allow us to live in his house."

"Of course," Sir Guy answered, "though we can offer only a meager meal."

"Oh, that doesn't matter." Marie paused, unsure whether to continue her petition, but she judged her father to be in a receptive mood. "Father?"

"Yes, Marie?"

"You know I love him, don't you?"

"Perhaps," Sir Guy answered cryptically.

"I know that you will choose whom I wed, but what if I could get him to fall in love with me?" she said, her eyes pleading. "Would that help?"

Sir Guy chuckled. "My daughter, you are always the schemer! And how do you propose to do that? Do you think love is something you can manipulate another person into?"

Marie's face fell, her eyes downcast. "I do not know, Father. I did not mean that." Her eyes began to glisten. "I just want to be loved." Marie's next thought surprised her: "I wish Mother were here to tell me what to do."

Sir Guy laughed. "Knowing her, she would have a detailed plan set out for you."

"But you say I am attractive, Father, and Sir Bart said so too. Maybe I could try to make myself attractive to him."

"Maybe." Sir Guy smiled again. "But I want you to be sure that you love him, and are not just attracted to a handsome knight. Remember our first conversation about love on the way to Bartscastle? Feelings are not love. Love is a process ... for you and for him. You must get to know him, and he you." Sir Guy lifted her chin with his finger. "You are attractive, Marie. And you are loved. Just be who you are."

Toward day's end a familiar voice interrupted Stephen as he carried stones to the house.

"Sir Stephen?"

Stephen turned to see Sir Guy's steward, Richard, waiting. "Yes, Richard?"

"My lord has sent me to ask if you would sup with him this evening. Will you accept?"

Stephen stole a glance at the pavilions. Marie was no longer there. "Uh, yes, of course. But I must first make myself presentable."

"Of course, sire. You will be expected at sundown."

Glancing at the western sky, Stephen could tell that would not be long. He hurried to the communal water barrel and began to wash himself down until he could no longer sniff the odor of sweat on his body. Fortunately he had removed his tunic before starting work. He donned it again and brushed a moistened hand through his hair before starting back to his lean-to to wait until sundown. They would be face to face again. *How do I pursue her heart?* He was a poor knight, without a noble family. What was the use? He sat watching the shadows lengthen, wishing someone were there to tell him what to do.

To pass the time he pulled his recorder out of his saddlebag and began to play. It had been awhile, to be sure, but after a few false starts, he was able to get through one of the tunes he had learned at Bartscastle, the music soothing his tortured heart. All too soon, though, it was time for supper.

Two torches had been set by the main pavilion. A crude table had been made by the workers splitting a log and placing the two halves side by side, resting them on crossed limbs. On either side was a bench made from each half of another split log. As before, Stephen was seated at the right hand of Sir Guy, but this time he was facing Marie! Beside Stephen sat Edouard. Ginette brought a kettle from a cooking fire behind the tent and ladled a portion onto each person's trencher.

"I regret that all we can offer you is peasant's stew," Sir Guy said, "but please be assured that we are grateful that you have chosen to come and aid us in rebuilding."

"It is the least that I could do for a knight of the King," Stephen replied, already aware that he was the center of attention, especially Marie's.

"You have already done so much," Marie said, her steady gaze on his face, "allowing us to live in your house and to use your pavilion here. You do us much honor."

Stephen glanced at Marie, then away. Those lovely eyes were all over him. "I...I—" He breathed deeply. "Yes, thank you," he said, staring at his stew.

"Sir Stephen?" Her voice touched his heart like the cool caress of a gentle breeze on a blazing summer day.

Stephen lifted his head to meet the intent gaze of Marie, her eyes inquisitive, her lips framing a half smile. "Yes?" he said.

"Was that you playing the flute?"

"A recorder, milady. Yes, it was I," Stephen answered.

"A recorder. Oh, yes, I should know that," Marie said, her smile widening. "I have heard that tune before. What is the name?"

Stephen could only shake his head. "I-I don't know, milady. I just learned it some time ago at Bartscastle."

Her eyes widened now, as though she had just realized something. She laughed. "I do not have to be 'milady' to you now," she said, glancing at her father. "After the time we have spent together at meals the past two weeks, you may call me Marie."

The warmth of his flushing face spreading down his neck, Stephen knew his cheeks had to be bright pink. He averted his eyes again, hoping it was not noticed in the failing light. "Yes ... Marie."

"Well, I liked your choice in music. There was a sweetness to it that touched my heart. I hope you will play it again sometime—for me."

Sir Guy's hearty laugh turned heads to him. "Did you two know it is a love song?" He leaned back, a broad smile on his face.

No! Stephen thought as he watched Marie blush, even as his own face got hotter, if that were possible.

"Mila—uh, Marie," Stephen said. "Upon my oath I did not know! I beg your forgiveness."

Marie smirked. Lowering her eyelashes, she glanced away. "Maybe that is why I like it," she said, lifting her eyes again to meet Stephen's.

Stephen was transfixed, feeling a mixture of confusion and misery, fighting an almost irresistible urge to either squirm violently or get up and run.

"Well," Sir Guy said, breaking the tension, placing his hands in his lap. "Tell us more about yourself, Sir Stephen. Marie did not hear everything you told me at your manor house. While we were staying there, you told me that you came from Bartscastle, that you were trained by Sir Bart, knighted at the young age of seventeen, and later imprisoned after the castle fell in a siege. Tell us about your family. Who is your father?"

Recovering his composure, Stephen answered, "Sire, I must tell you first that I am not of noble blood. My father was the bailiff of Bartstown. He died in battle defending Sir Bart. Thereafter Sir Bart chose me to become a page in his castle."

Sir Guy said, "You are too modest, sire. Your father saved Sir Bart's life, and I have heard that you did the same a decade later. That is why you were knighted at only seventeen, is it not?"

Stephen sat up, his eyebrows rising. "How-How did you know, milord? I have not told others—"

"I was in attendance when the King himself conferred your knighthood. Your bravery is well known among us." Sir Guy smiled.

"You were there!" Stephen said, temporarily forgetting where he was, his mind now in that great chapel, feeling the sword taps on his shoulders, hearing the kind voice of the King and the thunderous roar of the knights. "So you have seen the King!"

"As much as anyone sees him," Sir Guy replied. "You know that he sits on a high throne and that no one may look upon his face."

Stephen had noticed Marie's eyes getting wider and wider throughout this exchange.

"You were in the presence of the King, and knighted by him?" she said. "And you saved the life of Sir Bart in battle?"

Stephen returned his eyes to a now rapt Marie, her chin resting on her folded hands, her eyes fixed on him.

"Uh, yes, ...well, the spirit of the Prince was with me, and..." Stephen felt unbearably uncomfortable with all the attention focused on him, the tension of being once again in Marie's presence now totally unnerving him. Having finished the little that he was able to eat, he stood abruptly and said, "Sire, mil—Marie, thank you for inviting me. Would you excuse me?"

He dashed back to his lean-to and collapsed, breathing slowly and deeply until all his anxiety had drained away. Then self-recrimination flooded over him. The way he had behaved, Marie probably thought he could hardly stand to be around her. Should he go back and apologize for leaving so suddenly? Had he destroyed any chance he had with her?

All night he puzzled over the look Marie had given him before he left. What did it mean?

Marie was taken aback by Stephen's sudden exit. She wished she had another gown to wear besides the old green and gold one she had to live in every day until the new ones she had commissioned in Grandvil arrived. There had been no garlands to place in her hair—only wildflowers—and she had no scent with which to perfume herself. She probably had appeared too homely for the handsome knight. That must have been the reason he never smiled at her and seemed only willing to talk to her father. She had tried to be friendly and engaging, but he had showed no interest. And then he had just walked away without explanation.

Men were still a mystery. What was it going to take? She had no clue. Nevertheless, she determined that she could not allow this opportunity to slip away. She would have to try something else.

Chapter 31

REBUILDING

H**UGH WAS PUTTING** the finishing touches on a set of knives when the bailiff poked his head into the smithy. "Sir Stephen sent word that the King's builder has arrived and rebuilding will begin for Sir Guy. I am leading a contingent of laborers from Loynton. I understand that you are not going."

"I have too much to do here, but Brian and Thomas of the Company will be with you, Brian as a laborer and Thomas as a carpenter."

"Good. Since you are my lieutenant in the Company, I would like to ask you to act as bailiff while I am gone. It is a day's journey away, as you know. It will not be possible to return home at night."

"I will gladly serve," Hugh answered.

When the bailiff returned to the village square, Thomas and Brian were both there, and the three of them departed along with others who had volunteered, William remaining behind to manage the tannery. As they traveled to the building site, they passed the junction that led to Grandvil, where others fell in with them, so that by the time they reached Sir Guy's domain, they were a dozen men. It was afternoon, and already much work had been done. The charred remains of the stable had been cleared, the earth raked clean, and some laborers were digging postholes for upright beams. To the side lay felled trees that were being stripped of their branches in preparation for shaping into beams or sawn into boards. Thomas could tell already this would be a better and larger stable than had been there before.

The manor house had been cleared of debris as well, its stone base and a row of stone that outlined the walls marking its site. Next to it were piles of stone being shaped to extend the walls even higher than those of the original house. In the field facing the work site were two knights' battle pavilions, obviously those of Sir Stephen and Sir Guy, as well as some lean-to shelters for the workers made of brush and branches covered with woolen blankets. Thomas soon recognized the chiseled form of Sir Stephen, stripped to the waist, helping carry a beam to the stable. But who was in charge? A board balanced on two sawhorses stood next to the manor. A man beside it seemed to be pointing to the house and giving directions. *The builder,* Thomas reasoned. He tugged Brian in that direction.

"The foundation is stable enough that we can complete the entire first floor in stone," the builder said to one of the workers as Brian and Thomas arrived. "Complete the framing of the windows and we will build the walls up to receive the beams for the second floor."

Feeling eager to help, Thomas said, "I am a carpenter, sir. I can help with the framing of the windows."

The builder glanced at Thomas and Brian. "Please do," he said. "Where are you from?"

"I am Thomas, and this is Brian, a tanner. We are from Loynton."

"I am the King's builder," the man said, extending his hand. "You may call me Petra. The King will be pleased that you have chosen to serve him thus. Thomas, you may join the men working on the house. And, Brian, you may work anyplace there is a need."

Thomas judged Petra to be middle-aged, though shorter than he and sturdy of build. Perhaps in his younger years, he had carried the stones and shouldered the beams used in building. His bushy curls continued into a thick beard even longer than Thomas's beard. As they approached the house, Petra explained to Thomas how the new construction was to be different than the first. Masons were laying shaped stone in careful rows; already boards were in place to mark the site of future windows.

Thomas thought the whole operation beautifully and efficiently organized. Everyone seemed to know his function. Behind the house stood several wagons piled with stone; next to them stonecutters were at work shaping the stones to size. Over by the future stable there clamored a cacophony of shouts and woodcutting. From the stately oaks came logs that were being formed into beams with shaping axes. Overseeing it all was the builder, giving directions as needed to the master mason and master carpenter. Thomas hardly had time to pitch in to help shape some beams for the house before the light began to dim and work stopped. As men trickled away to their lean-tos, Brian rejoined Thomas by the house.

"What did you do today?" Thomas asked, drying his recently washed hands on his tunic.

"Just hauling rocks to the stonecutters," Brian replied. "While I was there, Sir Stephen came over to do the same. He said he had some prior experience carrying stones. I was surprised to see him working just like the laborers, quite able to carry the heavy stones himself."

Thomas nodded. "Yes, and I was watching him as he left the work site. He didn't go back to his pavilion. He seems to be sleeping under one of the lean-tos. It looks like Sir Guy and his household are using Sir Stephen's pavilion."

"And that reminds me," Brian said, "we don't have any place to sleep."

"I thought of that," Thomas answered, beginning to walk with Brian. "But it's getting too dark to build a lean-to. We can just find a place in the field and throw my cloak over us."

As they approached the encampment, small fires began to appear, interspersed among the lean-tos. Small groups of men were setting up branches to hold their pots over their fires.

"We should probably build a fire to stay warm after sundown, and eat some of our bread and dried game," Brian said.

They walked into the field toward the outer edge of the encampment, where they would be able to gather enough twigs to start a fire. Once they had enough, they took a handful to the nearest fire. Nearby was a small tent that they had not noticed. Three men sat around the fire in front. A pot hung from a crossbar set on two stakes.

Emerging into the light, Thomas asked, "Could we obtain some fire from you?"

"You're the new men from Loynton," a familiar voice said. "Come, sit with us."

Thomas recognized the builder, Petra, as the source of the voice. He surmised that the other two must be the master mason and the master carpenter.

"We don't want to interrupt your supper, sir," Thomas replied. "Just some fire will do."

"No, no," Petra said, "please sit down. Share our supper with us. We have plenty."

The savory aroma of venison stew was apparently more than Brian could bear. "With pleasure," he said, jerking away from Thomas's restraining hand, taking a seat immediately.

Thomas stepped forward. "I don't think we should—"

"It's all right," Petra said. "Please join us, Thomas."

Reluctantly Thomas took his place by the fire beside Brian, who had already assumed a relaxed position, leaning back on his elbows.

Petra motioned toward his companions. "This is Gregory, the master mason, and Patrick, the master carpenter. We have been discussing tomorrow's work."

Feeling welcomed now, Thomas also allowed himself to lean back and relax as well, finding his mind full of questions about the project. "Sir," he said, "it appears from the work so far that this will be a very fine house, much better than before."

"Well observed, Thomas," Petra replied. "I understand that the previous house was entirely half-timbered on a stone foundation. This one will have a ground floor of stone walls with a half-timbered second story. Moreover the hall will be built with a new fireplace and stone chimney, and the kitchen will be separate from the house. And the whole manor house will be enclosed by a stone wall now. Sir Guy will have the finest manor house in the area."

"The cost of rebuilding must be enormous. He must be quite wealthy to afford the King's builder," Brian said.

Petra shook his head. "Not so. As a gift, the King has bestowed upon him a grant of all of the stone for rebuilding, as well as the services of the three of us and funds to pay the laborers."

"That is a generous gift, indeed," Thomas said. "Who would have imagined that Sir Guy's misfortune would result in something so magnificent?"

"No one," Petra replied, "but we serve a generous King who loves to lavish gifts upon his loyal subjects."

Wondering how to best fit in as a worker, Thomas said, "In Loynton I primarily concern myself with fashioning tools and implements for the farmers, and I make furniture and household items for their homes and help my father frame small houses. But I do not know much about building on a scale like this."

"Tomorrow you shall work with me, then," Petra said. "We will be preparing beams for the house and putting up the beams to frame the stable. Now enjoy some of our stew." He ladled the stew into wooden bowls and gave one each to Thomas and Brian.

"May we share our bread with you?" Brian inquired, offering their only loaf in exchange.

"Yes, thank you," Petra said, breaking off a piece and passing it on to the others.

"Sir ... if I might ask," Thomas said, "how did you become the King's builder? It must be a highly favored and sought-after position."

"Actually no position at the King's court is sought after or more honored than any other. The King assigns positions to each according to his ability and the purpose the King has for him. We accept them with gratitude and obedience. In my case I began as a carpenter like you. When the king selected me to build larger buildings like castles, I had to learn masonry. Eventually he entrusted all of his building to me, so you could call me an architect, as I design the buildings and oversee their construction now, though I know how to do all of the tasks. I have trained both of the men who are beside me."

Thomas nodded, then finished his stew in silence, sensing that he had already been too inquisitive, and grateful that he would sleep with a full stomach. He and Brian took their leave and retired to the edge of the field, where they bedded down in the faint glow of a half-moon.

"Did you notice his hands?" Brian whispered. "He must have suffered a terrible accident."

"Maybe that is why he just supervises now," Thomas surmised.

Hugh had finished some knives and had begun to make some horseshoes when a breathless villager ran into the smithy, his eyes wide with fright.

"Hugh! There is an armored horseman in the village square who says he is looking for the bailiff. I told him the bailiff was away. He said he would not depart until he spoke to someone in authority. He is a large man, and heavily armed. I am afraid of what he might do!"

Hugh was puzzled. He knew that Sir Stephen would be at Maison Bonfrere for the rebuilding, and, unlike Sir Bailys, he had no armed bodyguards. There might be some men-at-arms in Grandvil who wore mail shirts, but why would they come to Loynton and demand to see the bailiff?

After setting down his hammer and tongs, and placing his leather apron on the bench, Hugh said, "Calm yourself, Jon. There is nothing to worry about. I will go and determine his purpose."

Hugh was not prepared for what awaited him. In the center of the square stood a solitary horseman of impressive size, clad in black armor, his visor down. His red shield clearly identified him as a soldier of the Dragon. Hugh felt apprehensive as he approached the silent figure, for he had come unarmed. He came to a halt, looking up at the horseman, who remained silent but menacing, his face unseen, heavy breathing audible through his visor.

"I am acting for the bailiff," Hugh said in as steady a voice as he could muster. "Who are you, and what is your purpose in our village?"

The horseman replied with a voice that was deep and ragged, "Who I am is of no importance, nor is this village of importance to me, but what has happened in this fief is."

A shiver ran down Hugh's spine as he recalled his last conversation with Sir Ralf. What if the Dragon sent someone worse than the Rat to exact retribution after Sir Bailys was taken? Sir Ralf had not answered his question. Was this horseman the answer? Was he the Dragon's replacement for Sir Bailys? Hugh determined not to show any weakness, though he felt certain he could not resist this emissary of the Dragon, having neither sword, nor bow, nor arrows.

"You must identify yourself if you would have any answers," Hugh stated.

The horseman drew his sword and pointed it at Hugh's neck. "Do not bicker with me, peasant! You are facing Gythreul!" he answered in a growling voice. "This fief has been taken from my king by a traitor knight and given to a knight of my enemy. I have come to take it back. I have just been at his manor house. He is not there. You will tell me what you know of his whereabouts."

Hugh's realization was immediate: this man had been sent to kill or capture Sir Stephen!

"Why should I know?" Hugh replied. "My lord does not inform me of his comings and goings."

Gythreul cocked his head as if to examine Hugh more closely. "You wouldn't be one of those loyal to the enemy King who bears a mark on his chest, would you?"

Knowing his inquisitor would not be able to see it anyway, Hugh responded, "Why would I tell you?"

The heavy breathing became more rapid as if Gythreul were becoming impatient. Suddenly he reached down with his sword and gave Hugh a slash across his chest. "Well, here's a mark from my king! And if you have hidden the truth from me, I will return and complete what I have started." Then he turned his horse and galloped away.

Stunned by the unexpected blow, Hugh staggered backward, gathering his tunic into a wad to put pressure on the bleeding gash, then ran back to the smithy to wash and examine his wound. Afterward he hurried down to the tannery, his wadded tunic pressed to his chest, to seek treatment from Charis. By the time he arrived, the bleeding had stopped.

"It is only a flesh wound," Charis said after examining the gash, "but you will bear a scar. And look! Though the enemy soldier may have intended to slash your mark, he could not."

The thought had not occurred to Hugh in his haste to stop the bleeding and have Charis treat him, but looking down, he was amazed to see that his wound stopped on one side of the dove and continued on the other. While Charis cleaned the wound and applied some salve, Hugh felt some relief at knowing the wound was not serious, but he was troubled by the violent and, in his mind, unprovoked act of the horseman.

"The man who did this is a soldier of the Dragon who was looking for Sir Stephen. I fear for him," he said to Charis. "I should go and tell him."

"Sir Stephen has scarcely become our new lord," Charis said. "Surely the King will protect him."

Brian and Thomas were awakened at dawn by the voice of Petra: "It is my privilege to share my food with you this morn," he said, placing a jug of water beside them with a loaf of bread and some dried fruit. "When you have eaten, join me at the house."

Thomas and Brian watched as Petra walked away toward the house, where men were already gathering in groups around logs or beams with saws and axes. Thomas and Brian each drank some water and tore the bread in half, eating it with the fruit before they followed. The work area was organized into two groups. Nearer the house was a team of men with various kinds of axes and saws, some shaping beams into the final square shapes, some sawing beams into thinner ones. By the stable a group was sawing logs, and shaping beams and posts for the stable. The corner posts had already been erected. They caught up to Petra as he was examining the work near the house.

Petra pointed at the beams. "The larger ones are cut to the dimension of the lower floor and will support the upper one on top of the stone walls. The men are shaping the ends so that one will fit into the other snugly. Likewise they are chiseling out the holes into which the wall struts will fit. We are making the upper story larger for the family's living space, so these crossbeams over here will cause the upper floor to jut out over the lower in order to create the extra space. One of our carpenters is carving supports that will be attached to each crossbeam to help support the forward horizontal beam. Perhaps you would like to help with that, Thomas?"

Thomas nodded, and with that Petra headed over to the stable. Brian followed, leaving Thomas to work on the manor house. Men were hauling beams to the stable and placing them on the ground on each side. The master carpenter seemed to be directing the crews. Surprisingly Petra did not take charge but joined a few men to shoulder a beam and take it to the stable where they dropped it in a cloud of dust. Brian followed suit, watching as the remaining post holes around the periphery were slowly filled with upright posts and then the horizontal beams were laboriously lifted and placed on top of the posts, the narrow tenon of the post fitting perfectly into the mortise hole on the beam to form the connection that joined them.

As the morning wore on, the men stripped to the waist in the heat of the sun, their muscles glistening in a glaze of sweat as they moved and placed the great pieces of wood. The whole experience was quite exhilarating for both Thomas and Brian; both were surprised at the fleet passage of time when word came to stop work for a rest to drink some water and eat some food.

As eager as ever to learn, Thomas sought out Petra, who sat with his master carpenter in the shade, gnawing some bread and a piece of cheese.

"I have never seen building on this scale," Thomas said, taking a seat. "It is so perfectly organized. Everyone seems to know exactly what to do."

"The ones who are skilled like I am," Petra said, shading his eyes, "and the other masters, know the overall plan. But it takes many willing laborers to accept our direction and work as a team."

"I am amazed that someone who builds castles would take the time to build something like a stable," Thomas said. "It seems so far beneath your abilities."

"Perhaps," Petra answered, "but even I am the King's servant, and regardless of what I am capable of, I still do what he desires. All that I build is a part of his Kingdom."

Another question had been nagging at Thomas all morning. It was probably inappropriate to ask, but his curiosity overcame him. "Forgive me if this question is out of line, sir, but Brian and I couldn't help but notice that you have some pretty nasty scars on your hands—a work injury perhaps?"

The builder held up his hands as if to examine them. His eyes met Thomas's eyes. "Yes, it was. It happened some time ago when the cornerstone was being set for one of the King's greatest edifices."

Chapter 32

A PROPOSITION

S TEPHEN AWOKE STILL berating himself for his oafish behavior the
night before. He had totally bungled his opportunity to pursue Marie's
heart. Not that he knew how. But his own ineptness had dashed his hopes.
There was nothing left except for him to apply himself to the work at hand and
try to forget the whole episode. He fell in with some of the men from Loynton,
lifting beams to frame the new stable, attempting to refrain from glancing toward
the two pavilions. The team had stopped for a water break when to his surprise,
he saw Edouard running up to him. Beyond, by his pavilion, he noticed Marie
seated out front looking his way, Henriette standing behind her.

"Sir Stephen! My family bids you come and break bread with them," Edouard
said as he came to a stop.

Although he could not see Sir Guy, Stephen was indeed hungry—and he
was still intrigued by Marie's parting look the previous evening. But how would
she receive him today? And why would Sir Guy invite him back after the way he
had fled their table? Regarding the invitation with a mixture of trepidation and
curiosity, he nodded and followed Edouard, his eyes on the ground, unwilling
to look toward Marie, anxious about what Sir Guy might say to him.

Arriving at the pavilion, Stephen could no longer avert his eyes. He stood
face to face with Marie, who, surprisingly, fixed him with expectant brown eyes
and smiled. Sir Guy was nowhere to be seen.

"Father is not here," Marie said. "He is eating with the master mason,
inspecting the house." The mischievous smile again.

"But Edouard said—"

"I told him to say that."

"Then I should not be here if your father is not in attendance," Stephen answered. Noting the puzzled look on Henriette's face, he turned to leave but stopped when Marie spoke.

"Henriette used to be my nurse," Marie said, nodding her head toward her. "Don't mind her. She knows she does not have authority over me anymore, and besides, my father said I could invite you." Marie turned to Henriette. "You are dismissed," she said with a wave of her hand. "We will remain in front of the pavilion."

Henriette backed away—reluctantly, Stephen noticed.

"And you too, Edouard," Marie said.

He smirked and skipped away to the main pavilion.

"There are bread and cheese in the basket," Marie said, motioning to the ground beside her. "And a jug of ale and two cups."

Stephen remained standing, perplexed. What was this about? Did her father really give her permission? Should he decline again? No! This was an opportunity for him to redeem himself. He must not squander it. Besides, he still did not know why she had invited him. He lowered himself to the ground facing Marie, his heart racing, trying to hide his anxiety, his eyes tracing every feature of her lovely face. "Um, why did you call for me?"

"You left so suddenly last night. Why?"

Stephen shrugged. It was exactly what he did not want to have to explain. Was this going to be an inquisition? He paused, struggling to find words. Should he tell the truth: that he felt like an idiot around her? Or should he invent some flowery phrase as he had been taught at Bartscastle? He was no poet. And his chances of impressing her were zero at this point anyway.

"Well, I—" He scratched his head. "I was embarrassed about the tune I played and—and I couldn't think of anything else to say. Forgive me for offending you, milady."

"Marie," she corrected, her lips parting in a sly smile. "I did not invite you to extract an apology, and I am not offended. I just wondered. There is something I have wanted to say to you, but the moment was never right."

Stephen raised an eyebrow. What could it be? She did not seem upset about anything.

"You said you were trained at Bartscastle."

"Yes, ... Marie." Stephen could hardly say the name. He had been taught to only use the first name of someone who was familiar and friendly. After the previous evening, how could he be either to her? "Ever since the age of seven. I was a page, then a squire."

Marie nodded. "When I was twelve, my parents sent me to Bartscastle to learn the ways of ladyhood. I returned to them just after my fifteenth birthday this summer past, to help my mother while my father looked for a match for me."

"That means—we were both there at the same time," Stephen guessed.

"Yes, we were. And do you remember that when you were taught how to dance by Lady Anne, your partner was a young girl?"

Stephen laughed. "It was a requirement, but I was just going through the motions so I could get out of there and do something worthwhile. I probably never even looked at her."

"That was obvious!" Marie laughed in turn. "*I* was that girl. I was four-teen then."

Stephen grew quiet, searching his memory for images of her face. Surely he would have remembered such a radiant face.

"I even dreamed about you a few times," Marie said, looking away and laughing again self-consciously, "after I saw you shirtless carrying those stones in the courtyard. In my fantasy you were carrying me instead of the stones."

Stephen remained silent, his fancy taking flight. *What is happening here?*

Marie continued, "I had forgotten your name by the time I left, but when you came to claim your manor near Grandvil, I had the strange impression of having seen you before … and the even stranger feeling of being attracted to you." She blushed. "I also knew that it would be unseemly for me to do anything to attract your attention."

Attracted to ME? Stephen hesitated, confused by the sight of Marie blushing. "You didn't need to do anything. I was already—"

"You were so earnest and sincere with me when we danced, even in your awkwardness, and now I also know that you are a man of honor and courage," Marie said.

Hot prickles spread up Stephen's neck again, just as they had the previous night. He looked down, studying the piece of bread in his hand, as if it could tell him how to respond to this unexpected revelation.

Marie grew silent, uncertain how or if to say what came next. She so wished Stephen would just talk to her. She took a deep breath and continued, "During the two weeks we supped at your manor house, I observed your humility and the way you honored your mother and me, and—" She stopped and looked away. She could not make her mouth form the words she knew came next. *I am about to give him my heart. What if he does not desire me?*

"I told—" *No! I cannot risk it.*

She took a deep breath and forced herself to continue, "I told my father—" The words would not come.

Instead different words formed themselves in her mind: "Trust me."

She closed her eyes and reopened them. *That voice again—the voice of the Prince.*

"I told my father last night that you are—the man I want to marry. There!" She exhaled. "I've said it."

She could not look at Stephen for a moment, though she yearned to see his reaction. "I know that it is his decision," she resumed, her eyes on the grass next to Stephen, "but I wanted you to know what I feel. I just hope you will consider what I have said if he asks you."

Stephen could hardly breathe. Those deep brown eyes were fixed on him now, no longer laughing, almost pleading. *Consider you? I would ride through flaming arrows for you! I would fight the Dragon for you!* But of course he said nothing of the sort.

"I don't know what to say," Stephen replied in disbelief.

Had she just given her heart to him? What was he supposed to do with it? He gazed back at her in stunned silence. He probably looked to her like a startled dog.

"You are a man of few words when you are with my family," Marie said, "and you likely think of me as just one of their children, but I am almost sixteen now, and ready to be a wife."

"No, no," Stephen said quickly. "I don't think that way at all."

He heaved a sigh. *A wife? Now is the time to pursue her, fool! What do I say?*

Still, no words came to his mind save two: "Trust me." He knew what they meant.

"I think…," Stephen said, "I think you're—"

Marie's eyes widened with obvious expectation. Then she looked away, lowering her eyelashes slowly, as if she could not bear the wait for Stephen to find his tongue.

"I think you're beautiful," Stephen half-whispered. "I-I mean, I will ... I will. You are in my thoughts—all the time."

Marie's eyes began to glisten, tears welling up, a single one escaping and coursing its fitful way down her cheek to her chin, where it hung suspended, like the rarest jewel. Stephen was transfixed, his own eyes brimming, lost in his own joy.

Their mutual trance was broken by Edouard's voice: "Marie, Father is coming!" Edouard came to a stop by them and said, "Did something sad happen?"

"No!" Marie said, hastily blotting her eyes on her sleeve. "Someday you will understand." She stood and darted into the pavilion behind her, poking her head out only to say to Stephen, "Will you speak to my father?"

Stephen was still trying to review in his mind what had just occurred when a shadow appeared on the grass next to him. He looked up to see Sir Guy peering down at him.

"Were you sitting here with my daughter, alone?" he asked.

Stephen jumped to his feet, straightening his tunic, still trying to assemble his thoughts. What was he to say? A bailiff's son could not ask a knight for his daughter's hand in marriage. "Yes, sire." *She invited me. No, I can't say that.* "Sire ... I thought ..."

Sir Guy's eyes were fixed on him. "You thought what? And where is the lady-in-waiting I left with her?"

Wide-eyed, Stephen could only blink. He had been caught alone with the knight's daughter, as if he had sneaked into their camp knowing Sir Guy was away. "I thought I was invited for dinner with the family. Edouard brought me the message. But when I arrived, it was just Marie, so I—"

"So you took advantage of the situation."

Stephen's cheeks began to burn. "No, sire! Upon my oath! I attempted to leave." He began to back away as if to return to the work site.

Sir Guy let loose a hearty laugh. "I know your character, Sir Stephen. In fact I gave her permission to invite you, and you have upheld her honor by declining to say that it was she who invited you."

"Yes, sire," Stephen replied, fidgeting with his tunic, attempting to compose himself.

"Do you know why I gave her permission?"

Stephen did not want to make any assumptions. "I am not sure, sire."

"It has not escaped your notice that she is of marriageable age?"

"No, sire," Stephen answered, now hoping for what he had once deemed impossible.

"For the past three years I have sought a deserving knight for her hand," Sir Guy said. "On my way back from visiting the King at one of his castles, I stopped at Bartscastle, where I heard of your misfortune from Sir Ralf. He told me then that you would be given the fief of Sir Bailys, where we were living temporarily. Naturally I was concerned about your lack of noble blood. But, as you know, I had been present when you were knighted and I knew of your bravery. When you arrived to claim your manor, I was impressed how you honored us by allowing us to remain in the manor house while you occupied your pavilion. Over the time that we stayed in your house, Marie believes she has fallen in love with you. I wanted her to have some time alone with you so that she could be sure."

"Sire, you are very kind," Stephen replied, trying mightily to suppress a grin.

"I don't know if you have even thought of marriage yet, but it would please me if you would consider the hand of my daughter. I believe that she has been well-educated, would be a good wife, and would loyally support you and your endeavors for the King," Sir Guy said. "Your lack of noble blood is no obstacle to me, in view of your demonstrated courage and commitment to the King. Would you give some thought to my request?"

"Would I!" Stephen exclaimed, releasing the emotion that had been mounting. "I-I was about to ask you—that is—if she will accept me."

"It is not her decision, lad."

"But I will!" Marie's radiant face appeared, framed by the flaps of the pavilion.

Sir Guy laughed. "I know you will, my daughter. I have heard nothing but that from you since last night!" He turned back to Stephen. "And that is what would make it special to me. So often we of noble families must marry our daughters for other considerations than love, but you are a landed knight now, and a man of proven honor and courage."

"You embarrass me, sire," Stephen said. "Were it not for the spirit and power of the Prince, you would find me a man of no courage."

"That is what guides us all, lad," Sir Guy said. "And you do well to remember it. Now I have made a proposal. Are you prepared to give me an answer?"

Everything had happened so quickly that Stephen had not been able to fully assimilate it. His most fervent wish had just been granted and, seemingly, he had had nothing to do with it. It had fallen into his lap like a ripe plum. He straightened to his full height and extended his hand. "Yes, sire. It would make me unspeakably happy to accept her hand in marriage." He glanced at Marie, her face bobbing up and down with excitement between the tent folds. "She already has my heart."

"Agreed, then," said Sir Guy, gripping Stephen's hand. "The first event in our new house will be a betrothal! You are welcome to visit Marie at her tent anytime now, son." He then walked by Stephen to his pavilion.

Marie burst out of her tent and grabbed Stephen's hands in hers. "Stephen! I am so happy!"

That lovely face— Those soft, deep eyes I could drown in— That lively spirit— beside me forever. Stephen grinned.

"So am I." His tongue no longer bound, his anxiety gone, Stephen pulled her gently to his side and sat with her on the grass, facing her, now holding her hands in his.

"After last night I was afraid you might not desire me," Marie said.

"And I thought I was not worthy of you, that you were too far above me."

"I almost could not tell you how I felt," she said, "but in my thoughts were the words 'Trust me,' as if someone was speaking to me. I have heard them before. I believe it was—"

"The voice of the Prince!" Stephen said. "I did not know how to pursue your heart. But I heard the same words when I was struggling to answer you. I too have heard them before." Stephen paused, considering the significance of what they both had said. "I think it means the spirit of the Prince has brought us together, Marie."

She looked away as if retrieving a thought. "For so long I was afraid I would never be loved, and would have to marry someone I did not love. My father once told me that if I would entrust myself to the King and his desires, he would give me the desires of my heart. And Lady Anne told me something as well - that the truest love must be awakened at the right time by the King's love. I did not know exactly what they meant, but I think it has happened just as they said."

Marie looked toward the wooden skeleton of her house. "With our house burned—and my mother gone—everything seems so uncertain now." She leaned in halfway, dropping her head, looking at their clasped hands. "Hold me, Stephen," she murmured. "Tell me our love is forever… that we will be together always."

Stephen drew her close, sliding an arm around her shoulder, placing a finger gently beneath her chin and turning it toward him, touching her lips softly with his. "Until the last beat of my heart—always."

They sat on the grass, side by side, Marie's head on Stephen's shoulder, Stephen's cheek on her hair, sharing their hopes and dreams, speaking of anything and everything, until the sun sank behind the trees to the west, swallowing the lengthening shadows in darkness. Even then they could not part, both lying back in the grass, lost in their reverie, watching the night come alive with the twinkle of stars and the evanescent glow of fireflies, as if the forest had become enchanted.

The rebuilding well in hand, Stephen returned to his manor the next day. His manservant, Jacob, met him at the stable to take his horse.

"Sire, there is a man here who says he comes from the King."

From the King? To speak with me? "Thank you," Stephen said, then hurried to the house.

A man clad in a mail hauberk sat at the table in the common room, a platter of Lady Eloise's barley cakes in front of him, slurping a cup of ale, his blue surcoat bearing the emblem of the King. Stephen's mother was busying herself with a kettle over the fire.

"Welcome, stranger," Stephen said, taking a seat opposite him. "I am told that you come from the King. What does the King wish of me?"

The man studied Stephen's face and spoke as if he were on a mission: "My name is Joel. I have been sent by the King to serve as Guardian of this fief."

It had been months, but Stephen recalled his conversation with Michael in the dungeon of Bartscastle when he had first learned about Guardians. It had not occurred to him then that it would someday apply to him.

"Excellent!" Stephen said. "You are indeed welcome. Just a few days ago while I was away, a large horseman clad in black armor came to the manor house, asking for me. He terrified my mother. You shall ride with me as my bodyguard."

Joel shook his head. "I would remind you, sire, that I am Guardian of that which belongs to the King. I am not your bodyguard."

Stephen raised an eyebrow. "But ... you are dressed as a man-at-arms. And with the arrival of this horseman in black, are you not here to help me? I have been in a battle where another Guardian, Michael, fought alongside his lord. And Sir Bart often spoke of Michael fighting alongside him."

"Yes, I know Michael," replied Joel, "and it is true that sometimes we fight to protect the lord of our fief, as the King desires. I will protect this fief for the King, and that protection will extend to you in the case of this Black Knight, whose name is Gythreul. Moreover, with my arrival, the King has placed a curtain of his protection around this fief. That is why Gythreul has not found you. And as a man-at-arms, I also can assume the responsibility of training your peasants and tradesmen to use weapons of war, should that be necessary. But be assured, I answer to the King first and I am pledged to carry out his wishes."

"Then perhaps you would be my steward, and help me manage the King's lands, as you say."

"Until you have your own steward, I will gladly fulfill that role," Joel answered.

"I have no dwelling to offer you at this time. You will eat at our table and sleep in this room if you desire."

"Thank you. I am a servant of the King. That will do. And when you visit your villages, I would like to accompany you."

Stephen thought back to his initial experience with Michael and the deep respect he had developed as he had learned the skills of a knight. "Michael was skilled in the art of combat," he said. "Will you also be able to help me keep my skills sharp?"

"Yes, sire. All Guardians are skilled in combat."

"Good. I would like to practice my swordsmanship with you daily. And there is a pile of stones by the stable, which I carry every day to strengthen myself. I would like you to time me as I carry them so that I may improve myself."

"Yes, milord," Joel said.

Stephen walked to the fireplace, where his mother stirred a pot, dodging the smoke that drifted up in wisps from the coals. He hesitated, then said, "Mother, I am to be married."

She dropped her ladle with a clang, lifting a sleeve to touch her eyes, then turned to embrace him. "My son," she cried, burying her face in his neck. "Now you will have a son as I do."

"And you will have a daughter," said Stephen, his hand tenderly stroking her hair.

"There is much to do," his mother said, stepping back, surveying the common room. "We must make this house suitable for a noblewoman."

Stephen laughed. "From tears to orders! You are a remarkable woman, Mother. But nothing we can do will equal the new house Sir Guy is building with help from the King. Marie has been living in my tent; she will adapt. But I hope to furnish a room for you soon since we will occupy the bedroom."

Stephen turned back to Joel, who was still munching barley cakes and draining his cup of ale. "Come, Joel. I would ride to Loynton today."

As they walked side by side out to the stable, Stephen could not help but smile. How his fortunes had changed! He was to be married, and now he had his own Guardian. Could things be any better? The two mounted and guided their horses toward the crossroads that led to Loynton, Stephen's head brimming with questions.

"Joel," he said, "There is much I do not know about Guardians. May I ask you some questions?"

"Much that I know and have seen is beyond your understanding, sire," Joel replied. "But I will tell you what I can."

"I understand now that each fief has a Guardian, provided by the King."

"That is true, sire."

"So Sir Guy has a Guardian?"

"Yes, his name is Daniel. He is Sir Guy's chief man-at-arms, as I am yours."

Stephen thought awhile as they rode and crested the rise before Loynton, then said, "There were some odd things about Michael. When I was captured by the Dragon and was about be stoned to death, he spoke to the Dragon and his bodyguard with words I did not understand. The bodyguard said something to the Dragon, who relented and imprisoned me instead."

"Undoubtedly that bodyguard was one of the Dragon's Immortals, which we call Companions, as was the Black Knight who visited your mother," Joel answered. "Michael spoke to them in the King's language, which they both know."

"Yes, Michael did mention the bodyguard was called a Companion. He was tall, like you, but did not speak except to the Dragon. Michael departed before we had time to speak of Companions or the King's language."

"This goes back to the earliest times, even before the time of the Prince and his knights," Joel said. "At that time all who served the King were called Guardians. The Dragon had a different name then and was our leader, but he attempted to usurp the throne, so he was cast out with his conspirators to roam the King's lands, forever banned from the King's castle. He subverted many of the nobles and still does to this day. The Dragon installed his own inner circle of rebels, his Black Knights, as powers over the fiefs that he gained; they are known to us as Companions. Because of our common origin, we speak a common language, the King's language, one that you do not know."

Stephen grew silent as he assimilated the new revelation.

"I understand now. Michael also said he contended with the Dragon and his Companions, for three days before the castle was lost. So then, do you and the Companions fight each other?"

"We serve different masters. Even now I am in contention with this Black Knight, Gythreul, as he seeks you out," Joel answered. "You will never witness us fighting, but there are struggles you do not know of and things you do not see."

Stephen felt both disturbed by Joel's answer and puzzled by his meaning, but he had one more unanswered question: "Michael said Guardians were not confined by walls and locks. You must have great powers, then?"

"Though we appear to be like you, both our powers and our limitations are not the same as yours. We use our powers as directed by the King."

Far from clarifying all of Stephen's questions, Joel's reply merely generated more. But he would have to come back to them another time.

The low, thatched houses of Loynton were coming into view, scattered like hay bales along the dusty path. The two cantered into the village square and out the other side.

"There are some loyal subjects of the King I wish to visit," Stephen said, pulling up before Hugh's smithy.

The clank of hammer on anvil announced that Hugh was busily at work. Upon entering, Stephen stopped, noticing Hugh bent over an axe blade, apparently unaware of their presence.

"Hugh Smith!" Stephen called between clanks of the hammer.

Hugh looked up and went to his knee. "Sire!" he said. "An unexpected honor!"

"You know me?" Stephen asked, for he knew he had not met Hugh before.

"You both wear the emblem of the King," Hugh said. "I know not which of you is Sir Stephen, yet I am sure that one of you is he. And I believe it is the one who has spoken."

"Well said," Stephen replied. "You did not refer to my obvious youth. Stand and face me."

Hugh rose to his full height, setting his hammer on the anvil.

"The taller man of seasoned appearance is my steward, Joel," Stephen said, motioning to Joel. "I have been told that a group of loyal subjects called Servants of the King meets here in your smithy. I have been invited by some of them."

"Every week, sire," Hugh replied. "It is led by William the tanner. How did you know about me?"

"A mutual acquaintance," Stephen said. "I came from Bartscastle, which is now the castle of Sir Ralf."

"Yes!" Hugh said. "Sir Ralf said a new lord was to come after I was captured in the service of our previous lord."

"I am told also that you are a skilled archer," Stephen continued.

"I am a member of the Loynton Company, sire, which is somewhat depleted since the raid on Sir Guy."

"I will need to know on whom I can depend if I am called to war," Stephen said.

"The Company is pledged to follow the lord of the fief," Hugh said. "However, not all are loyal subjects of the King, including the captain, as you may know."

Stephen nodded. "Yes. Though I inherited him as my bailiff and I understand he is not a member of the Servants, he is knowledgeable about the fief and I am inclined to allow him to remain in his position until he gives me a reason to remove him. In the meantime I would like your group of Servants to meet in my manor house once a month."

Hugh grinned. "We would be honored, sire. I will tell the others."

"Now, I have need of a carpenter to help me with some work in my house."

"You need Thomas, then," Hugh said, then explained the way to his house. "But, sire, might I have a word with you before you go?" Hugh lifted his tunic, displaying an angry, red, healing wound that spread from one side of his chest to the other. "An enormous knight in black armor came to our village a few days ago looking for you." Hugh pointed to his wound. "This was my reward for refusing to say where you were."

Stephen glanced at Joel, then back at Hugh's wound, wincing. "I am aware," he said, "and I am both indebted to you for your loyalty and dismayed by the price you have paid."

Dropping his tunic, Hugh said, "I believe he means you harm, sire. I only mention it because he appears to be much larger and more powerful than you. I hope you will be careful." Hugh glanced at Joel. "Though your steward is about his size and looks to be a worthy bodyguard."

Stephen knew he could not share what he knew about Joel, but the evidence of Gythreul's ferocity gave him no comfort, knowing what he now knew about Companions, despite what Joel had told him about the protection of the King. Who or what was this "protection" really protecting? Were the villagers of his fief protected or were they all at the mercy of Gythreul now? And what if he himself were caught by Gythreul without Joel next to him? Or if Joel declined to fight alongside him? What then? Stephen shuddered at the thought.

PART THREE

THE DRAGON AND THE LION

Chapter 33

THE DRAGON RISES

A S SUMMER GRACED the countryside, rumors began to trickle in from the coast of a great plague encroaching upon the King's lands. It seemed worse in cities and towns where people were in close contact with strangers. The afflicted developed ugly lumps on their bodies, took to bed coughing with high fevers, and were dead within days. When it reached Grandvil, some thought it a punishment for the raid on Sir Guy; others said it was due to indifference about the true King, the alignment of the celestial bodies, or just bad luck. But the plague struck followers of the true King and of the Dragon alike. Word quickly reached Stephen, who was at a loss what to do. His training had not encompassed how to deal with a calamity of such proportions. He rode throughout his fief advising his peasants not to congregate in groups and to avoid trips to Grandvil except when necessary. Even the Servants stopped meeting weekly. A feeling of watchful doom descended over the populace as they waited, avoiding each other in the streets and shunning strangers, hoping the mysterious merchant of death would pass over them.

But it was no use. Within weeks the plague had roared through Grandvil like a savage wildfire and spread its deadly fingers through the countryside, reaping its harvest indiscriminately. So rapidly did it spread that bodies soon lay unburied in the streets for lack of sufficient burial parties. One-third of the fields now lay untended, their farmers ill or dead. By the time what came to be called "The Great Dying" seemed to be diminishing, the fief was devastated. Stephen had remained in his manor house as much as possible, but his mother, who had gone to the market in Grandvil, returned with a fever and was dead within days. Now struggling with grief, Stephen felt even more at a loss what to do.

In Loynton the first sign of plague had appeared after a farmer returned from taking produce to Grandvil market. Brian's sisters both developed chills. Charis and William hovered over them doing their best until both succumbed. Then William developed fever and a cough, and took to bed. Exhausted from caring for her children, Charis sat by him as he became weaker, encouraging him to drink and eat. The next meeting of the Servants was cancelled until he could recover, but he grew worse.

On the night they should have met, Hugh took the risk to visit their cottage and breathe what some called "the foul air." He found Charis kneeling by William, who was covered with blankets, too weak to move. Brian sat behind on the floor, stone-faced, as if in a death watch. Hugh remembered the embrace William had given him on his return and his sorrow over his father, Henry's, death. Now it was Brian losing his father—for no apparent reason. Hugh took a seat beside Brian and extended an arm to draw him close. Brian did not resist.

Hugh sat silently, observing Charis dab beads of sweat from William's fevered brow, speaking to him soothingly as she held his hand. Hugh shook his head. It made no sense to him. How could the King grow his Kingdom when so many of its members, even leaders like William, were being taken by an ugly disease?

"Charis?" Hugh asked. "You seem to understand the ways of the King better than I. What does all this mean?"

Charis raised her head and sighed, looking at Hugh with tired eyes. "I do not know, Hugh. William said as he grew sicker today that we must accept what befalls us but never doubt that the King is good and that he has a purpose in it. I do not know that purpose. All we can do now is give comfort to those who need it."

"You have already lost two children, Charis. Isn't that enough? If we lose William, we might as well disband. Haven't you suffered enough?"

"No," Charis answered, her voice soft and trembling, her glistening eyes focused on Hugh, revealing in their depths the toll not only of her physical exhaustion caring for William but of the additional soul-weariness of one weighed down by a burden almost too heavy to bear. "One cannot suffer too much for the treasure that is promised those in the Kingdom—to be one day in the presence and love of our King. I must persevere in hope. You have lost your father and mother. You must do the same." She was looking beyond him, or through him, to something unseen, yet seemingly very real to her.

Hugh could not do that. He had experienced that defeat of loss when his father was murdered and his mother died, but he had replaced it with vengeance instead of hope. What was there to hope for if the Servants just dissolved from lack of leadership—if all those he cared about were taken away? Would Brian be next?

As if hearing his thoughts, William spoke, in a voice that was so soft it seemed to come from a great distance: "Hugh, I have … served my purpose as leader of the Servants. Perhaps it is time for you to take what you have learned … and carry on."

Hugh did not want to carry on. He wanted his King to act like a king and take care of his people.

William lingered awhile longer, but the residual weakness of a body ravaged by two years of imprisonment and malnourishment eventually allowed the disease to claim him as well, leaving only an emotionally drained Charis and Brian. Both of Thomas's parents and his siblings were swept away as well. In the Bonfrere household Henriette succumbed, leaving only Marie, Richard, and Ginette. Fortunately Edouard had been taken to Bartscastle by Sir Guy to be trained as a page. Both were staying there until it was safe to return.

Some blamed the King for not preventing the catastrophe; others claimed he was powerless to stop it. Some even murmured that perhaps the King himself was dead. Soon, as grain stores dwindled, the specter of famine began to raise its ugly head. There would not be enough workers to tend the fields, feed the livestock, or grow the food of the realm. Many of the survivors had no doubt that a cloak of evil had descended on the land.

After several days had passed with no deaths or new fevers, and after all the dead had been hastily buried, Hugh spread the word that the smithy was available if the Servants wished to meet again. The group was small—only five—and the mood somber. Charis, Brian, and Thomas were still stunned by the sudden loss of their families, though Thomas had been too busy making coffins to think much about his loss. Alis related that her husband, though alive, was still too weak to come. He had developed the lumps and still had a cough. She had nursed him through the fevers but was fearful that he too would not recover.

"I do not understand why I am the one left and not William," Charis said, tears streaking her cheeks. "He was the leader of the Servants and such a strong follower of the King."

Hugh thought the same: William had been the last link they had with the Prince; his loss was felt by all.

"We still have the *Chronicle* and each other," Brian said, "and with everyone's agreement, I suggest that Hugh should assume leadership."

"William was your father," Hugh answered. "It should pass to you."

Brian declined, saying, "It was your father who saw the Prince again after he was struck down, and you have spent time with Sir Ralf and Sir Stephen. We meet in your smithy. You must lead us."

"And your father received the mark before my husband, and you before Brian," Charis added. "It is right that you should now take the role of our leader. Remember, William passed the mantle of leadership to you just before he died."

Since Hugh had led the group briefly when William was gone—though he thought he had done so poorly—and to honor William's parting words to him, he reluctantly agreed. It would give him a purpose amidst the chaos, but, as before, he felt ill-prepared to lead anyone.

Alis spoke up, "We are nearly out of grain. How will we survive without flour and bread?"

Already viewed as their leader, Hugh now had to think of the welfare of all, not only himself. "Many of those who have passed had small stores of grain for baking their own bread," he said. "I will ask the bailiff to supervise distribution to those who remain. All of us may have to spend time in the fields at harvest time to collect the abandoned grain."

A knock on the door brought sudden silence. Hugh rose and opened the door a crack.

"Sire!" Hugh said. "An honor indeed! Please enter." He bowed and then opened the door wide to reveal Sir Stephen, clad in his green and gold tunic.

"Your group is small," Stephen noted, looking from face to face. "Many are missing."

"Yes, sire, we are the survivors," Hugh said as they all knelt before him.

"I bring news that will impact us all," Stephen said. "Some of you know about a black rider who has been seen from time to time. He is terrorizing villagers and now he is proclaiming the death of the King in the Great Dying!"

"No!" Charis said. "We thought that rider was looking for you and that the King was protecting you! How could this be? What will happen to you—and us?"

"It is a lie!" Hugh shouted.

But Thomas chuckled sarcastically. "That must be why the Great Dying took so many. Even the King could not resist it."

Stephen continued, "Hugh is correct. I believe it is a lie. The Dragon is attempting to take advantage of everyone's weakness to gain control of the rest of the King's lands. He has now proclaimed himself king over all of our King's lands and claims all fiefs as his."

Hugh had been busy riffling through sheets of the *Chronicle*. Running his finger along a sheet, he said, "Look! On this sheet it says clearly that the Prince predicted there would be those after he was gone who would rise up and pretend to be the true King!"

Thomas shook his head. "Surely the King would prevent this if he were alive. He sent Sir Ralf to rescue Sir Guy's children. He could certainly send his army against the Dragon now and stop him. That would remove all doubt."

"And I would be the first to join with him," Stephen said. "But he has not called us. Though I am young, I do not know of an instance yet where the King has been the aggressor. He desires peace in his lands and so far has only called on us to defend what is his when attacked."

"And I do recall that some called his son the 'Prince of peace," Charis said quietly.

"But the *Chronicle* also says that eventually there will be a battle in which he defeats the Dragon," Hugh said.

"I am aware of that," Stephen replied. "I believe he will call us together at that time and we must be ready. But now the risk of being his followers has greatly increased. I do not know what will happen." He scanned their faces. "Those who are not followers of the King have taken the news indifferently, but for us the lines will be clearly drawn. We who are loyal to the King will be in a struggle with the forces of the Dragon for the allegiance of the rest. There will be no middle ground. We all must be bold in our loyalty to the King."

"Bold? It wasn't easy before." Brian sighed. "We had to meet in secret when Sir Bailys was our lord. Are you saying it will be even worse with you as our lord?"

"Not by my hand," Stephen said. "But the Dragon is a powerful enemy. I believe he will use lies to turn the other villagers against you so that they will do his evil work. I have come just to tell you to be cautious, and to tell you, Hugh, to be ready to come with Brian and Thomas should I need archers. I must take my leave now to ride to other villages. Good-bye."

Hugh walked Sir Stephen out, looking on as the knight mounted his horse and rode away, followed by another horseman, whom Hugh recognized as Joel.

Stepping back into the smithy, Hugh met only stunned silence from the others.

Then Thomas murmured, "First the Great Dying, and now our King is replaced by an evil one. And our new lord cannot protect us. What will be next?"

"Starvation," Alis answered gloomily, bringing them back to their original subject.

"I will talk to the bailiff on the morrow," Hugh said. "Each of you must try to make your grain and flour last."

"Did I mention the miller has raised the price of milling our grain by a penny?" Alis said.

"No matter," Hugh said. "We must pool our resources and grain, and persevere as one."

"Well spoken, Hugh," Charis said. "That is the true spirit of the Kingdom."

"And we will bake bread for all of you as long as we have flour," Alis said.

The group exited individually into the evening coolness, each captive to his or her own thoughts and anxieties, uncertain how they would survive, but more determined than ever to stay together, work together, and support each other.

Hugh sought out the bailiff the next day to ask about distributing the excess grain.

"Ha!" the bailiff laughed. "Obviously you were not one of those who slipped into the vacant houses and emptied them of anything of value. I have had my hands full with the miscreants. There are three men in the gaol even now awaiting the king's justice. There is no 'excess grain.'" He paused and gave Hugh a quizzical look. "And have you not heard of the new king's announcement? He will be sending wagons through the villages to distribute grain to all those who declare allegiance to him. There will be no famine."

To all those who declare allegiance to him. Frowning, Hugh determined that he would not be one of those. As summer waned, he attempted to survive by rationing the bread provided by the bakers and by hunting rabbits and whatever else he could find, which he shared with those in the group who needed meat. There being only a month until harvest, he thought he could make it until then. Sir Stephen had declared his forest open for hunting, that all who were able should join in the harvest, and that all which was harvested, even from his fields, should be distributed to everyone as needed. He was still able to provide a weekly delivery from his and Sir Guy's stores to the miller to be milled into flour, some of which he had sent to the bakers to be made into bread for villagers who had none.

Not long after, the bailiff appeared again at the smithy. "Hugh, the king's grain wagon will arrive in Loynton tomorrow. I will need your help in distributing the grain. Each villager must sign a document of allegiance prior to receiving his bag of grain. I need you to write the names of those who do not know how to write as they come to the wagon. They will place their mark beside the name you write."

"And what if they do not declare allegiance?" Hugh asked.

"That would be foolish, wouldn't it? Who would refuse the generosity of the king?"

"The self-proclaimed king," Hugh muttered under his breath.

"I will set up a table and bench in the square. All villagers will form a line and sign before coming to the wagon for their grain."

"What does Sir Stephen say of this?" Hugh inquired.

"He has not forbidden it. Besides, he cannot supply everyone's needs, can he?"

Hugh was dubious. *I cannot believe he would approve it.* Nevertheless Hugh would do as requested, though he himself would not sign.

Brian and Thomas found him at the table the next morning as hungry villagers shuffled around in the square waiting for the wagon to arrive.

"What do you think of this?" Brian asked, surveying the crowd. "Will you sign?"

"Of course not!" Hugh spat.

"And when Sir Stephen runs out of grain to give us, what then?" Thomas asked.

"The harvest will be in a few weeks," Hugh said. "That will get us through the winter if we are careful, and then everyone will have to help with planting."

"By the way," Brian said, "did you notice that a fresh copy of the Kingdom Rules has been posted by the bailiff? They're a little different from the previous ones."

"No," Hugh said. "Different how?"

"Come take a look."

The three strolled over to the gaol, which stood next to the tavern on the square. Hugh began to read the parchment posted outside:

1. I am the king. There is no other lord but your king.

"It looks the same to me," Hugh said.

"Now look at the second and third ones," Brian said.

*2. No emblem may be displayed other than the emblem of
the king, which is the golden dragon on a sea of red.*

*3. No one shall dishonor the king by denying allegiance to his name,
for the king will not hold guiltless anyone who dishonors him.*

Hugh looked at Thomas and Brian, shaking his head.

"And the fourth," Thomas said.

*4. Six days shall you work as directed by the lord of your
fief, but the seventh you shall work for the king. The fruit of
all work on the seventh day shall be sent to the king.*

Hugh sighed. "Well, those are different, and there is no longer a day of rest from work."

"And allegiance to the Dragon is *not* optional," Thomas said.

"How can he do this?" Hugh said. "Many knights are still loyal to the true King. We must go to Sir Stephen. Surely he would not allow it if he knew. As soon as I am finished with this task, we will go."

Troubling thoughts distracted Hugh while he dutifully recorded names as they were spoken to him. It seemed as if the Dragon was doing whatever he wished. Would he just sweep away all the knights still loyal to the King? Would the King just sit in his castle and watch?

When the list was complete and the grain distributed, the names of Brian, Hugh, and Thomas were not on the list. Nor were those of Charis or Alis. He handed the list to the bailiff and gathered Brian and Thomas. They broke into a brisk walk to the crossroads that led to Grandvil and Sir Stephen's manor, no one speaking, all pondering the events of the morning. After a couple of hours, the stable and manor house came into view, a banner with the true King's emblem hanging over the entrance. They were intercepted by Joel as they approached the house.

"Greetings. What business have you with my lord?"

"Troubling events," Hugh said. "We desire to know his thoughts on the new king."

Joel smiled. "Well, 'king' would not be my word or my lord's word to describe him, but if you will wait, I will see if he can receive you."

Joel disappeared inside for a while as the three paused to look around. It seemed as if the morning's news had not reached Sir Stephen. Two horses grazed quietly in a paddock next to the stable. The King's emblem ruffled above them as puffs of a breeze came and went. The whole scene of peace and rest contrasted starkly with the turbulence engulfing Hugh's mind.

The door opened. "My lord will see you," Joel said.

The group filed in to find Sir Stephen seated at the head of a wooden table in the hall. A bench had been placed at the far end of the table so that everyone could face him.

"What troubles you, Hugh?" Stephen asked as the men took their seats.

Hugh did not know where to begin. "Much has happened since you last visited the Servants, sire," Hugh finally said.

"Yes," Stephen said, remaining silent, his eyes studying the three.

"It's the Dragon's grain wagon," Hugh said. "Sire, if I may be so bold, why did you not stop it? Do you not know that—"

"That the Dragon is requiring a signature of allegiance to receive grain?" Stephen said.

"And," Brian said, "the original Kingdom Rules—"

"Have been changed," Stephen continued.

"Yes! And where is our King in all this?" Thomas asked. "Is he truly dead?"

Stephen hesitated, his eyes regarding each of the faces opposite him, then said, "I will answer each of you in turn. First of all, the King is alive and well. Do not allow false rumors to weaken your loyalty to him. Nevertheless you will remember that I said the risk would increase for each of us. We are now learning what that entails. I hope that your presence here means that you did not sign the list."

"Of course not!" Hugh said. "But why did you not—"

"Careful, Hugh. Remember where you are," Stephen said. "Why did I not intercept the wagon and turn it around? Did you notice the four armed guards that accompanied it? I am but one—two if my steward is with me."

"No, sire," Hugh said, shaking his head. "I saw no armed guards."

"Cleverly hidden once they reached your village, then," Stephen replied. "Our enemy is using deception. He appears to be giving free grain while capturing the allegiance of the people."

"Then why doesn't our King send help, as he did for Sir Guy?" Thomas asked.

"That is not for me to answer," Stephen said. "He certainly knows that, alone, I am too weak to resist the Dragon's forces. But I also trust that if and when he chooses, he will provide the wherewithal to resist and resist successfully. It is my duty, and yours, to remain loyal."

"And what about the Kingdom Rules?" Brian asked.

Stephen nodded. "Yes, they have been changed. And we who do not take an oath of allegiance are now outlaws in the eyes of the Dragon."

Hugh exhaled and jumped to his feet. "So are we to just lay down our arms and be herded like sheep to the slaughter?" He began pacing the room.

"We will fight if and when our King desires," Stephen answered. "I am awaiting direction from Sir Ralf even now. Speaking of whom, he reminded me of something about the Kingdom Rules that I learned originally from Sir Bart. The Kingdom Rules were never intended to be a test of loyalty to the King, even in their original form, because no one could keep all of them at all times. The nobles who now do not follow the King have mistaken the King's intention and have been deceived by the Dragon into elevating loyalty to the rules above loyalty to the King. The Dragon has now been revealed as one who desires loyalty to himself through obedience to his false Kingdom Rules."

"So the Kingdom Rules are not to be obeyed?" Thomas said.

"Certainly not in their present form," Stephen answered. "But even in their original form, they were only intended to prepare us for the message of the Prince, which was that true loyalty to the King is measured by the state of the heart, not by words of mouth or adherence to rules. And the Prince condensed them into two rules, which are found in the *Chronicle*."

Hugh sat in silence, faced with a childhood image of his father and Brian's father bent over a map by candlelight. He could still hear their words clearly as they smoothed the edges and murmured to his mother and Brian's mother in the darkness of their common room. *The Kingdom is the hearts of those who have trusted and are loyal to the King. We are his. We will always be his.* They had said nothing about loyalty to the rules, only loyalty to the King.

"Then what should we do?" Hugh asked.

"Be wise, but not rash," Stephen said. "Look for opportunities to present the truth to your villagers if they are open to it. The truth will still turn to the King those who are prepared to hear it."

"But, sire," Hugh said, "the Black Knight, Gythreul, seems to be searching for those who bear the King's mark. What if he returns?"

"Joel has been assigned to take care of that," Stephen replied without further clarification.

"Also, milord," Hugh said, "the bakers have informed us that their supply of grain is dwindling. Those of us who do not declare allegiance to the Dragon will soon face starvation."

"Do not worry," Stephen answered. "I still have some of my 'lord's share' of grain, which I will distribute. If you use it sparingly, it will last a few more weeks."

"And then what?" Thomas asked.

"Then all will come together to harvest the ripe grain," Stephen said. "That will buy us more time."

With that the three bade farewell to Stephen and shuffled out. Hugh felt no better than before, uneasy that their lord would not, or could not, prevent the Dragon from doing what he wished, but he was still more determined than ever to find a way to survive while remaining loyal to the King. As much as he wished it were not so, it seemed that his only hope now was in his King—his absent King.

Stephen sat solemnly, watching the backs of his subjects as they filed out in silence, their heads bowed. He knew he had not served them well. Should he have given them false encouragement? He considered his own situation. He was being hunted by a Black Knight whose powers far exceeded his. He could not depend on Joel to protect him. Perhaps Joel was indeed out contending with Gythreul, but it did not make him feel safer. And what did "contending" mean anyway?

He thought back to Sir Bart and his confidence that his castle would protect him. How he wished to be behind walls like that now! But even the castle had not protected Sir Bart from the Dragon. Stephen felt he was at the mercy of the Dragon, who knew no mercy, and at the mercy of his King as well. He thought of his newly acquired fief. One third of its inhabitants were dead, the rest struggling to survive. Nothing he had learned at Bartscastle had prepared him for this. All who had shaped who he had become—his father, his mother, Sir Bart—were gone. The silence that engulfed him pressed in on him; even the air he breathed seemed heavy.

Never had he felt so alone.

Chapter 34

THE MARK OF THE DRAGON

SINCE THE COMPLETION of Maison Bonfrere and his betrothal to Marie a few months before, Stephen had made trips to see her as often as he could spare the time, especially when Sir Guy had to be away. Sir Guy had gone to meet with Sir Ralf at Bartscastle and to leave Edouard to be a page to Sir Ralf, while also waiting out the plague.

Stephen was in his stable grooming his horse when he heard the sound of galloping hoofs. The noise stopped in front of his house briefly, then resumed again, coming toward the stable. He walked to the entrance to see a horseman dismounting and running to him.

"Richard!" Stephen said, with a voice of recognition. "What brings you here in such haste?"

"I have an urgent message from Lady Marie! Her father has returned. He is ill. She bids you come quickly!"

Reading the look of desperation on Richard's face, Stephen answered, "You must return to her at once. I will follow shortly. Tell her I am just behind you."

Richard mounted his sweat-soaked horse and set off at a gallop. It would take the rest of the day to reach Maison Bonfrere, Stephen knew. He hurried to saddle Centaur, then armed himself, notified Joel of his departure, and finally spurred his horse onto the road. There was only one reason he could imagine for such distress—Sir Guy had returned with the plague.

Daylight was fading as he drew near Maison Bonfrere, now the finest manor house anywhere around, with its walls of stone, larger second floor, and separate outbuildings, all surrounded by a gated stone wall. He recalled with pride the part he had played in its construction and marveled at the skill of the team that had been led by the master builder.

A lonely light already shone from the upper floor. Stephen handed his horse to a manservant and knocked lightly on the door.

Richard greeted him. "She is upstairs, milord."

Stephen quietly began the climb to the upper floor, the flicker of candlelight from the wall casting shifting shadows across his steps as he mounted the stairs. A sad sight greeted his eyes—Marie sitting by a bed, leaning over it and dabbing the glistening brow of Sir Guy.

"Good evening, sire—and Marie," Stephen said, emerging into the candlelight that cast a solemn glow over the scene before him.

"He has been like this since he arrived from Bartscastle last night. He is feverish and will neither drink nor eat." Marie choked a sob. "What can I do, Stephen?"

Stephen dragged a chair to the bedside and scanned Sir Guy's face, dappled with beads of perspiration, his breathing rapid and shallow.

"Are you unwell, sire?" Stephen asked. "Was there disease at Bartscastle when you departed?"

Sir Guy's eyes flickered open, gazing at the ceiling. His voice was soft, his words uttered with grunts and heavy breaths: "It came first...to Bartstown... two weeks ago. Lady Anne and Sir Ralf...tried to limit entry...to the castle, but then...the fevers began inside." He stopped to take a deep breath. "I thought...I had escaped, but...on the way home I fell ill." He coughed raggedly.

Stephen had both heard and seen this story before when his mother fell ill. His worst fear materializing, Stephen turned to Marie. "Does he have the lumps?"

"Yes!" Marie moaned. "And they are already turning black. I am so frightened, Stephen!"

Stephen's thoughts drifted to his own ordeal just three weeks past, watching his mother suffer from the fever, coughing, and in her final moments gasping for air. It had been a time of utter helplessness and confusion for him, of questions unanswered. Why was this happening? What good could come from the loss of so many of the King's loyal subjects? He had even journeyed into Loynton to ask Charis what could be done. She had offered no answer while she herself nursed William until he was gone. Stephen struggled to reconcile the scale of human loss around him with the idea of a caring King.

Stephen took Marie's hand in his. "I do not know what can be done, Marie. We must stay with him so that he will not be alone. Perhaps he is strong enough to fight it. I will sleep here tonight. We will see this through together."

"Please don't let me lose him. Please," Marie whimpered, clutching Stephen's hand.

"All I can tell you is what Charis said to me about her husband," Stephen answered. "If the King desires that he live, he will live." But he knew his words offered little comfort to one watching her father die.

Ginette entered, bearing a pot of soup with bread. "Milady said she would sup in here," Ginette said to Stephen as she set the pot on a table next to Stephen. "There are two bowls."

Stephen sat sipping his soup in silence, his arm around Marie, watching Sir Guy's chest rise and fall, Marie grasping his hand, her eyes fixed on his face, dabbing his brow periodically with a cloth. He had never seen such an expression of fear on her face before. He longed to wipe it away with a word or a gesture, but he had none. He remained until Marie released him to sleep, gently kissing her hair and excusing himself quietly to the other bedroom, which Ginette had prepared for him. He departed, leaving Marie in the same position leaning over her father, watching every breath, hoping against hope.

Marie remained at her father's side throughout the night, her hand on his, as if to restrain him from slipping from her grasp. She had not seen her mother die; the possibility of her father dying was unthinkable. She had always been able to overcome obstacles in the past. Why not this one? Stephen had said something about the King. Did her King love her enough to bring her father through this? Was he even aware?

The room was dark save for the feeble light of the nearly spent candle, the only sound the rhythmic sighs of her father's labored breaths. As the sighs became softer, Marie lay her head on his chest to be sure he was still breathing. Exhausted, she was lulled into periods of sleep, her head rising and falling with Sir Guy's breaths as if bobbing on a vast ocean of desperation and despondency.

Stephen was awakened near dawn by an urgent conversation in the next room. The voices of Marie and Ginette drifted through the open doorway.

"Ginette, bring more covers! He is shaking. His skin feels cold!"

"Yes, milady." The sound of hurried footsteps echoed down the stairs.

Stephen rose and entered the bedroom, his eyes on Sir Guy, who was still clinging to life, his breathing now more labored and irregular, his body clearly shivering beneath the covers.

"Stephen, he is worse!" Marie said, bursting into tears. "I have tried all night. I can't keep him from—" Her voice broke into an anguished sob. "I just can't—"

A grunt drew the eyes of both to Sir Guy, his mouth moving as if to speak. His eyes remained closed, but a whisper escaped from his parched lips. "Is… Sir Stephen…still here?"

"Yes, I am here, sire," Stephen said, drawing closer to the bed.

Sir Guy took a deep breath. "You must take care…of her now. Love her." He gasped for another breath.

"Father!" Marie cried, clutching his body, pressing her tear-streaked face to his. "Please do not leave me! Please do not—"

Sir Guy heaved a labored breath and sighed, "You have St…"

There came neither more words nor breaths.

"Please," Marie groaned. "Please…" Her voice trailed off into a deep moan, her small body convulsing with sobs, her arms still gripping her father.

Stephen could only embrace her; he had no words.

Marie cried until she had no more tears, then she lay motionless on Sir Guy's still form, limp and empty. She felt as if she had been engaged in a struggle, holding a rope with both hands, straining against the tug of a boat in which her father sat, attempting to keep it from going out to sea. She had dug her heels in the sand, leaving furrows as she was pulled closer to the water, until finally her strength had failed and the rope had slipped through her clutching fingers, the boat beginning to drift away. Yet it wasn't the waves that bore him away; there had been someone else in the boat, paddling gently. Her father had been smiling at her, seemingly accepting the journey. Her father had spoken a soft *Au revoir,* as if he expected to see her again. But now the struggle was over. The boat was gone, the sea was motionless, the beach deserted but for her, prostrate in the sand, her empty hands outstretched.

Stephen remained crouched beside her and held her until she grew silent, each of her sobs piercing his heart like a sword thrust. He continued to hold her as she fell into a fatigued sleep, perhaps for the first time in two days, awakening only as night was falling, turning her head, which still rested on her father's unmoving chest, to face Stephen.

Her voice was faint, almost breathless, as if bearing a great burden. "I feel so lost now," she whispered. "He taught me so much." She took a deep breath and sighed again. "He understood me—better than I understood myself."

"He was a good man and a good father," Stephen said, caressing Marie's hair.

"And sometimes I did not appreciate how good," Marie murmured, her eyes again filling with tears. "I never told him. I thought he would always be here."

"I know," Stephen answered.

But he did not know. How could he? He was too young when his own father had been killed and he was not at his side, watching him go. He wished he could say more, something more appropriate, something more comforting, but no words came. What *can* you say to one who has just lost someone dear to them? He did only what he knew, holding Marie gently as she closed her eyes again and wept silently.

The next day, they buried Sir Guy next to Lady Clare, Stephen holding a solemn Marie in his arms, looking down at the freshly heaped earth. She seemed listless, as if all life had been drained from her in the past few days. Their previous times together had been ones of happiness and anticipation buoyed by young love, as they first lay on the grass holding hands watching the stars come out. Then came a joyous betrothal at Maison Bonfrere and visits when Stephen would come to see her, their hearts filled with devotion for each other, and they would converse into the night about their imminent wedding, how they would serve their King together, and raise their children to do the same.

"Today I am sixteen," Marie said, her voice tinged with plaintive resignation. "Birthdays were always times to celebrate, but—" Her voice quavered and she became quiet.

Stephen remained silent, continuing to hold her, pressing his lips to her hair, allowing her deep moans to pour out her grief over all that she had lost—her parents, the happiness and promise of childhood, and a future she expected to be filled with love, excitement, and adventure.

Marie shivered, imagining she were standing alone now, whipped by a chill wind, her future obscured by dark, rushing clouds. Finally she took a deep breath and exhaled. "I know it is not true because I have you, but I feel today as if my life is over. I thought he would give my hand to you at our wedding, and that I would share him with you as we raised a family." She shook her head. "I don't know how to begin again."

"There will still be a wedding," Stephen said softly. "We will begin again together."

Marie rested her head on Stephen's shoulder. It might as well have been a cold rock.

"I wish I could believe that," she said. But now she could not. She felt adrift, at the mercy of swirling currents that were bearing her away from all she knew— toward an imperceptible horizon with deepening shadows.

Stephen remained with Marie in his arms until a light rain began to fall, and she permitted him to return home. He rode back to his manor with a heavy heart, burdened by the knowledge that Marie would now have to manage Sir Guy's fief alone. He resolved that somehow he would visit her as often as he could and be involved in the oversight of both fiefs, whatever it required, though he was already overwhelmed by the requirements of managing his own devastated fief. He felt in control of nothing. Thus far, his life as a knight seemed like an autumn leaf, blown by whirling winds, at the mercy of forces he could neither see nor master.

Marie returned to a manor house that would be empty except for her and Ginette. Richard and Daniel would help of course. She sent off a message to

Bartscastle to inform Edouard of his father's death, knowing that Edouard would probably not return until he was a knight, if then. She wished that she did not have to carry on, but she was a landed lady now, and there were duties and responsibilities. She understood, perhaps for the first time, why her mother had been who she was.

Within a week the rain came again on a gentle breeze, throwing up puffs of dust as it speckled the parched roads, blowing a welcome dampness through open windows. Summer had been mostly hot and dry; the surviving villagers uncovered their cisterns to collect the life-giving moisture. By afternoon the winds had intensified, gusting through the nearly ripe wheat and rye, turning the fields into restless, waving seas. Pools formed in the roads and villagers scurried to the shelter of their cottages, peering out at the roiling clouds that brought the crack of lightning and the drum of thunder. The next day was like the first, the rain falling in large, powerful drops, sometimes mixed with hail that bounced on the window sills and into the cottages, caroming randomly across the floors. For a week the tempest raged, until fields were soaked and beaten down, streams overran their banks, and trees were overturned.

The force of the torrent at Loynton carried trees downstream, dislodging the water wheel at the mill, flooding the pits at the tannery, driving Charis and Brian to shelter with Hugh at the smithy. By the time the storm had passed, the fields of wheat, rye, and barley were sodden and flattened, as if an invisible ogre had trampled them underfoot. With the loss of many of the farmers in the Great Dying, it would now rot quickly in the fields. There would be no harvest, only a gleaning of what could be found on the ground before it spoiled.

Hugh had laid out pallets in his modest cottage that adjoined the smithy. He and Brian slept in the common room next to the fire pit, leaving the bed to Charis. Brian was able to bring as many hides and parchments as he could to safety before the tannery flooded, stacking them in the corners of the room, but he had had to leave his chemicals and lime to the mercy of the rising waters. He would have to start over again. They had brought their precious supply of bread, dried fruit, and game, which Hugh supplemented with cabbage, leeks, and onions from his small garden, and his own rabbit stew. No one had been prepared for or even expected this; it seemed to those loyal to the King as though one disaster after another were being visited upon them.

"What will you do when the waters recede?" Hugh asked Brian and Charis.

"I hope we will find that our house and its contents remain," Charis said. "As for the tannery—" She shrugged.

"I will bail as much water out of the pits as necessary to reformulate the mixtures," Brian said. "But then I must go to Sir Stephen and fall upon his mercy for more chemicals. We do not have the resources to restore everything. We are surely insignificant in the King's eyes, but perhaps he will send us aid as he did Sir Guy."

Hugh thought a moment, allowing his mind to wander. "I imagined life for us would improve when Sir Stephen came, but it seems to have worsened instead. The storm has taken away your livelihood. The Great Dying took William. Sir Stephen cannot protect us from the Dragon and we cannot accept the enemy's grain. With the wheat ruined, we face certain starvation. How can our King grow his Kingdom when the few subjects he has left face such hardship?" He sighed.

"I can only believe that the King has a plan for those who trust him," Charis said. "The *Chronicle* says that he will never leave nor forsake us."

"The *Chronicle* again!" Hugh huffed. Someone always brought it up at the most inopportune time. "It doesn't buy us new supplies, and we can't eat it!"

Brian grinned. "Well, there is some poetry in it that speaks about eating its words."

Hugh scowled. "How can you joke about it, Brian? We are facing death by starvation and you cannot even take our plight seriously!"

In her typical soothing voice, Charis spoke again: "Hugh, worry and anger will not make us whole. Brian is right. The words of the *Chronicle* cannot feed our stomachs but they can feed our hearts if we allow them to. It says that the King cares more about us than the birds and flowers in his Kingdom. I do not know what will come next, but I believe that the King is good to those who trust him."

Hugh had heard enough and was about to spew another tirade about the King when Thomas thrust his head into the doorway.

"I thought I might find you here," he said. "The bailiff sent me for you, Hugh. Another wagon has arrived from the Dragon. He apparently knows of our situation. He is distributing milled flour this time. The bailiff needs you to do the writing again."

Feeling even more deflated, Hugh made his way to the square through the sucking mud. The bailiff stood there, talking to the wagon guards, who stood in full view this time.

As Hugh strode up to the table, the bailiff said, "Ah, Hugh! There is a new order from our king. On the table are stamp and ink. Before each person receives a sack of flour, he must receive a stamp on his hand signifying his loyalty to the king. The guards are here to supervise. They will only give flour to those with the image on the stamp."

Hugh sat heavily and picked up the stamp. Carved in it was the emblem of the Dragon. *I will not take that image. Nor will I imprint it on others.* While he was examining the stamp, he overheard some of the peasants murmuring.

"We already signed our X. Why do we have to receive a stamp?" one said.

"Because we want to eat," another replied.

"The previous king did not require it," a third noted.

"You do not have to do this," Hugh whispered, looking to verify that the bailiff was not listening. "There is another way. If you would know more, come to the smithy tonight. Look, I am not taking the stamp."

His appeal fell mostly on deaf ears. A few peasants backed away from the group as Hugh stood and walked away.

"Hugh!" the bailiff called. "Where are you going?"

"I will not be part of this!" Hugh exclaimed. "Do it yourself!" He continued walking.

"You will regret this!" the bailiff called after him. "And if I recall correctly, you did not sign the roster of allegiance either."

Hugh did not reply. He found Brian and Thomas still at the smithy when he returned.

"We must go to Sir Stephen immediately," Hugh said. "There is a new development."

"What now?" Brian asked.

"All who wish to have the Dragon's flour must receive a stamped mark on their hands."

"Sort of like our mark?" Brian asked.

"Except it is the Dragon's emblem," Hugh replied. "It is as Sir Stephen said. There will soon be only two sides. It looks as if it will be those who have the mark of our King and those who have the stamp of the Dragon."

"Hmm," Thomas said. "So, since the enemy cannot tell us by our mark because he cannot see it, this is how he will discover who follows the true King."

"Exactly," Hugh said. "Our danger increases by the day. We must inform Sir Stephen."

The three plodded the muddy path to Sir Stephen's manor house once more. On higher ground, it had not suffered significantly from the effects of the storm. Sir Stephen and his manservant were both in the stable grooming his horse.

"The Loynton three," Stephen said as they approached. "How did you fare in the storm?"

"Not well, sire," Hugh replied. "Brian and his mother have lost the tannery. It is under water. The mill is damaged, and the wheat crop is ruined. The bakers were trying to ration their flour to feed us but now we cannot have more grain milled. We face starvation soon."

Stephen nodded. "Yes, I am aware of the grain problem, and I know the loss of the tannery is a terrible blow, Brian."

Despite what Hugh had just said, the knight did not appear saddened or concerned. Rather, he seemed preoccupied. *By what?* Hugh wondered.

"Sire," Hugh went on, "the Dragon is now requiring us to accept a stamp in the image of his dragon emblem in order to receive milled flour. Many of those who know the grain crop is ruined have already taken it. We fear the Dragon will use his stamp to ferret out all who are not loyal to him. Furthermore, your bailiff is working against you. He knows I did not take the stamp. We could be arrested as soon as we return to the village."

"Indeed," Stephen replied. "Joel has so informed me. There has been extensive crop damage throughout the fief, but I did not realize the seriousness of the flooding in Loynton. It was my intention to visit Loynton on the morrow to see how I could help. I had also decided to replace the bailiff, now that he is clearly against me. But—" Stephen paused, seeming to want to carefully select the right words. "Everything has changed now."

Hugh stared at him, wondering what could be so important that he would seemingly dismiss all he had just been told.

"I have received an important message from Sir Ralf this very day that the King has issued a call to all of his loyal subjects to gather under his protection," Stephen said.

"What good is that?" Hugh said, not even trying to hide his frustration. "Why doesn't he just come with his army and get us?"

"Right. That is no help at all," Thomas said, then paused. "Wait, is this the final gathering spoken of in the *Chronicle*? Are we to leave Loynton?"

"It may well be," Stephen answered. "I hope it is. Joel is making the circuit of my fief even now to inform the leaders of the loyal Servant groups. You are to bring only what you can carry. The bakers should bring whatever flour and bread they have left. I will provide a wagon to carry what stores we have. Wait for me at the Loynton crossroads tomorrow morning."

"Leave everything? Tomorrow?" Hugh said, his expression one of disbelief.

"This is so unexpected and sudden," Brian said. "Where are we going and how long will it take? Will our food last?"

"Those are questions I cannot yet answer," Stephen replied.

"A party such as ours on the roads will attract the attention of the Dragon's soldiers, not to mention hungry brigands," Thomas said. "Who will protect us?"

"I will," Stephen answered, "and you will."

Thomas laughed. "One knight and three archers? Not likely."

"Especially if Gythreul finds us," Hugh added, feeling himself shiver.

"There will be my steward, Joel, and other armed men from Grandvil and surrounding villages. I do not know how many. We must trust the King. He is our only hope now," Stephen said, looking each in the eye.

Hope? Is that all we have? Hugh did not feel it.

Stephen knew his reply did not inspire confidence, the three men's eyes expressing only doubt, a doubt that he shared. What was the "King's protection"? Where was it? How would they find it? Stephen knew only that he had now been thrust into the role of leading all the King's followers in both his and Marie's fiefs to safety, wherever that was.

As the three villagers took their leave, shoulders sagging, Stephen fought the impulse to allow the situation to overwhelm him. He recognized that a task of inestimable difficulty and danger loomed before him—protecting a band of fugitives journeying they knew not where through lands roamed by the enemy. The words of Sir Bart formed themselves in his mind—*"A knight is a leader."* Stephen must lead, then, as best as he knew how. He hoped he could do what he had just asked his people to do. And he hoped they would not meet Gythreul along the way.

Chapter 35

FORSAKING ALL

T HE THREE RETURNED to Loynton, discouraged and full of questions, stopping by the bakery to notify Alis of the plan for the morrow. As night fell, Hugh, Brian, and Thomas sat in the smithy by the light of the coals, discussing the events of the day and what they should do.

"Should we really meet Sir Stephen at the crossroads tomorrow?" Thomas asked. "He doesn't even know where we are going."

"Well, it is unsafe for us here," Brian said. "Only arrest or starvation await us if we stay."

Himself dismayed by the parting words of Sir Stephen, Hugh was in a quandary. Either choice presented clear danger. It seemed as if the power of the Dragon was surging around them like a raging flood and they would be swept away regardless of what course of action they took. But he was curious about Sir Stephen's admission that the invitation to follow him might represent the call of the King foretold in the *Chronicle*, the call so anticipated and hoped for by his departed parents.

"My father and yours spoke of a time when the King would gather his people, Brian," Hugh said. "And it would happen during a time of distress. What if this is it?"

"Somehow I imagined it would be him coming to us, not we to him, because we do not know where he is," Brian replied.

Hugh shrugged. "I think our chances are better in a group that has some armed men. We should go, though if we must bring only what we can carry, I can bring nothing from the smithy. It will be the same as if I had lost everything in the flood like you did, Brian."

"And I must leave the hides I worked so hard to rescue," Brian said.

"We must take our bows and arrows," Hugh said. "Sir Stephen will be counting on us. And I will bring my sword." He stood to remove it from the wall. "This is not my idea of what being soldiers of the King would resemble. I imagined myself as part of a great army led by someone like Sir Ralf."

"Wait! What about the map and key, and the *Chronicle*?" Thomas asked. "Are they still of value if this is the final gathering of the King's subjects?"

Hugh nodded. "Of course we must take them: they are to be with us until we see the King, are they not? What if we are called upon to present them? And we will also need to bring as much food and water as we can carry too."

"We will be beasts of burden, then," Thomas said, his brow furrowed. "We will not go far, especially as our food runs out."

"My horse will be our packhorse," Hugh said. "We should each prepare a sack with our belongings and the horse will bear them."

"A-humm," a voice interrupted from the darkness of the road outside the smithy.

Hugh looked up. In the glow of the embers of the forge, Hugh recognized the miller's face. "Come in, friend," he said.

The miller shuffled in, head hung, looking abashed. "This morning in the square, you said, um, something about an alternative to accepting the new king's stamp."

"Yes, I did," Hugh said.

"I would like to know more. With the damage to the mill wheel and the flooding, I have no livelihood now. I am lost without the ability to mill grain." He kept his eyes on the floor. "To be truthful, I am not exactly certain why I am here."

Thomas could not hide his disdain. "Perhaps you are afraid of the villagers, who dislike you because they think you cheat them."

"Yes, I know that," the miller answered, still gazing down.

"Enough, Thomas," Hugh said, then looked at the miller. "You are here to learn about the alternative to following the Dragon, are you not?"

The miller looked up at Hugh. "Dragon? I just do not want to accept the stamp. I feel there is something sinister about it. I am not sure the new king will save us from our misfortune. He is good to provide us with flour but he is not like the previous king. That one did not try to control us like this one. I wish he were still alive."

"Actually he is," Hugh stated, standing. "Come, sit with us. We will tell you the truth."

"Truth?" the miller asked as he sat down. "What is the truth?"

"The true King has a plan that will save us," Brian said.

"The true King? The Dragon?" The miller sighed. "I am confused. Who is really king?"

"The Dragon is a usurper, taking advantage of the disaster that has befallen us," Hugh said.

The miller shook his head. "But how can I know who the rightful king is?"

"Consider this," Hugh said. "You never saw the previous king, did you?"

"Nor have I seen the new king."

"Yet you believed he was alive, did you not?"

"Yes. I would like to believe it even now."

"I want to show you something." Hugh stood and retrieved his copy of the *Chronicle*. "This is something sent by the true King to all who are his followers. It contains the truth that he wants everyone to know about him, including how to become his follower."

"It is of no use to me. I cannot read," the miller said.

"It sounds like in your heart you want to believe the true King, as we call him, is still king," Brian said.

The miller paused, seeming to consider Brian's comment. "Yes, I think so."

"Then trust your heart," Hugh said. "It says here in the *Chronicle* that if you believe in your heart that the true King is your ruler, and are willing to tell others to whom you are loyal, you will be his follower and he will be your King."

"And," Brian said, "no matter what you have done, even if you have not obeyed his Kingdom Rules, he will save you from the Dragon, who wants to possess you with his mark."

"No matter what I have done? Kingdom Rules?" The miller became silent. An expression of embarrassment formed on his face. He looked at Brian. "I am ashamed to tell you that I used to keep for myself a small portion of the grain that I milled, sometimes I mixed chalk in with the flour, and I raised the price of milling to line my own pockets. What if this true King knew that?"

"Many of the villagers already suspect you are dishonest," Brian replied. "That is why they do not like you. But that is not true of our King. The *Chronicle* says that anyone who trusts him will not be put to shame."

"Even after what I have done—stealing grain from the villagers and over-charging for milling—the king you call the true King would be good to me?"

"Yes," Hugh said, "if you believe he is who he says he is and profess loyalty to him and only him."

"But I thought I was loyal to him before there was a new king. Now I am more confused than ever. I must give it some thought. What do I gain by trusting this King the way you say?"

Hugh and Brian exchanged a glance. "You will be on the right side," Hugh said, then confided, "Some of us are leaving Loynton to seek his protection from the Dragon. If you would be one of us, come to the crossroads that leads to Grandvil in the morning with whatever belongings you can carry."

The miller's eyes widened. "And leave Loynton?" He pursed his lips for a moment, as if surprised by the revelation, then said, "This is a difficult choice. But I am not sure I can trust the new king." He paused again, apparently struggling with his decision. "And I can see no clear future for me here now." He looked back at Hugh and Brian as if he had made up his mind. "On the upper floor of the mill, I have a few sacks of milled flour that I kept for myself. Should I bring them?"

Hugh nodded. "There is no time to bake bread before we leave, but the bakers are part of the group. I will come by with my horse in the morning. We will take it in case we find an abandoned oven along the way."

Before dawn Hugh led his horse to the mill. Sacks containing the belongings of Charis, Brian, and Thomas were already draped over the horse's back along with his own. Hugh wore his sword and a quiver of arrows slung over his shoulder, carrying his bow. The ground felt soggy near the mill; water was still overflowing the millrace. A glow in the upper window of the mill indicated the miller was up. Hugh waded through the knee-deep water swirling around the mill and climbed the stairs to the upper room.

The miller sat alone on a stool, a sack in his hand. "I am coming," he said. "There is no life for me here. Now, if you will help me, I have two bags of milled flour to take."

Hugh and the miller each shouldered a bag and carried it to the horse, securing them with rope. Then they plodded uphill to the road where it passed the last of the village houses and turned toward the crossroads. A group had already assembled, sitting in the drying grass next to the signs that pointed three ways: to Loynton, Grandvil, and Purdyton. Hugh noted Charis, Brian, and Thomas talking to two peasants Hugh had seen step away from the group receiving the stamp the day before. Alis was standing beside a two-wheeled cart containing bread and her belongings, which they must have helped her pull from the village. As the rising orange disc of the sun to the east chased away night's lingering shadows, Hugh and the miller joined Alis.

"We have two sacks of milled flour to give you," Hugh said, looking toward her cart. "If we can rig a harness for my horse, we can carry them in your cart along with our belongings."

"Thank you," Alis replied. "I could not bring all of our flour, believing it possibly spoiled. My husband found a dead rat in some of it. I wonder if that is what caused him to take ill and die?"

"There was a rumor during the Great Dying," said Charis, approaching, "that it was worst where there were many rats."

"You said you needed a harness, Hugh," Brian said. "When Mother and I went by the tannery on the way here, we found the water only calf-deep in the house. I had fashioned a harness for one of the farmers that might work, and it stayed dry, as it was hanging on the wall. I can go and get it while we wait."

"Hopefully we will not wait long," Hugh replied, glancing up the road toward Grandvil, "but, yes, bring it."

The sun had climbed half-way to its zenith by the time Brian returned, accompanied by a horseman. As they neared the group, Hugh recognized the bailiff. His expression looked both stern and troubled as he reined in his horse.

"You should not leave the village, Hugh. By taking with you some of our tradesmen, you will cause us much hardship," the bailiff said, his voice laden with exasperation and anger.

Hugh stood and faced him. "You know that both Thomas and I leave our smithy and carpentry intact. You must find someone to take our places. The tannery is ruined, the mill is destroyed, and many peasants make their own rye bread anyway. In any case they can use the baker's ovens for the flour they receive from the Dragon."

The bailiff grunted. "I do not have the necessary men to arrest all of you, nor could I count on the support of Sir Stephen. But rest assured, I know that you do not support the new king, and he shall certainly hear of this." The bailiff pointed a finger at Hugh. "You and those with you will be hunted by the king's men and brought back bound at the hands—or worse!"

"You are correct that we will not serve a false king!" Hugh retorted. "At this very moment we are waiting for Sir Stephen to lead us to the banner of the true King, who is alive and still our ruler. I invite you to come with us."

The bailiff snorted a laugh. "And give up my position as bailiff? I will be the law around here now with Sir Stephen gone. You do not know what danger you face. Even if you avoid the king's men, there are other vicious men who lie in wait for travelers. You will not find food along the way. Why would I expose myself to such hardship?"

Hugh looked back through slit eyes. "And you do not know what danger awaits you when the rightful King reclaims his lands!"

"Bah! I will take what I know rather than throw it away for a future I cannot see," the bailiff said, jabbing a finger at Hugh as he turned his horse. "Mark my words. You will come back with yokes on your necks—if you come back at all!"

As the bailiff rode out of sight, Hugh could see the miller trembling. "This sounds much more dangerous than I thought," the miller muttered.

"Look!" Thomas said. "It must be Sir Stephen!"

All looked up the road toward Grandvil. Cresting the rise where Hugh had first seen the Rat were the silhouettes of two horsemen. The group watched as more figures appeared. There followed a crowd of figures on foot, bags slung over their shoulders, and a wagon flanked by several archers on foot, bows in hand.

Now Hugh saw clearly that Sir Stephen rode in front, Joel beside him. As they drew near, Hugh recognized the archers as ones who had taken part in the raid on Sir Guy. Some members of the Grandvil Servants followed, surrounding a bumping cart. But there were many faces Hugh did not recognize.

Sir Stephen came to halt before the small Loynton contingent. "There are fewer than I hoped," he said, surveying the group. Then he backed up his horse and faced the combined crowd. "Servants of the King," he said. "The journey that lies ahead may be arduous. There will be dangers that we cannot foresee. Even I do not know our final destination. But I am trusting the King to provide what we need. Today we will continue to the junction that leads to Maison Bonfrere, where their household plus others will join us."

"That is not reassuring," Thomas whispered to Hugh. "We are to follow a lad who still knows not where he is going?"

"I will lead," Stephen said. "Joel will be rearguard. Archers, there are six of you. You will guard the flanks of the group. Men with swords and spears should intersperse themselves within the group close to the wagons. Now let us depart."

Hugh watched as Stephen spurred his horse to a slow walk and headed up the road away from Loynton, splattering mud with each hoof strike. The mass of perhaps fifty people fell in behind, archers spreading to the flanks as if they were herding sheep, the few men with swords and spears walking by the wagons. Hugh was alone with his thoughts as he trudged through the grass to the side of the road, beside his horse and its cart, his sword slapping his leg as he moved.

This was not what he envisioned the Kingdom to be. In the beginning he believed he served a great King who was powerful and able to defeat his enemies. He remembered how excited he had been after he had received his mark, but then came disillusionment upon disillusionment. His father had been taken and died at the hand of the Dragon. Then his mother had died of sorrow. Where had the King been? Next he'd had to serve Sir Bailys in a cowardly raid. Then came the Great Dying. The storm. The lord of their fief a mere boy who did not know his way. What would be next? Starvation? A vicious attack by brigands or the Dragon's soldiers led by Gythreul? How could Sir Stephen know the King would provide? It seemed that hope was all that led them on now—in Hugh's mind an empty hope at best.

After an hour the group stopped at a dry grassy area to rest those who carried heavy burdens. Stephen dismounted to let his horse graze.

Hugh approached him cautiously. "Sire, I was not encouraged by your words. Do you know more than you are telling us?"

Stephen had been alone with his thoughts as well. He knew that he and his men were no match for the Companions, even one of them, so he had not shared his fears with anyone. Hope could be a powerful motivation for those who were desperate. Even he was hopeful that the "King's protection" mentioned by Joel would materialize, and do so soon. He smiled at Hugh though, considering carefully how much information to reveal.

"I can tell you a little more," he said. "Our first goal is to arrive at Bartscastle where Sir Ralf awaits us. It is yet two or three days hence. We must keep the group safe until then."

"Safe from what?" Hugh asked.

"There are rumors that the Dragon has unleashed his Black Knights to terrorize and disrupt all who are journeying to the King's protection. At least one has been roaming our lands, as you know very well. We must be watchful."

Stephen watched as Hugh shook his head in dismay. "What can one knight and a few soldiers do against the likes of these Black Knights? He could have cut me in half the day he slashed me! Why doesn't the King bring his 'protection' to us? And what is his 'protection' anyway?"

That was a question Stephen had already asked himself. He could not reveal that he had no answer. He assumed as confident an expression as he could muster. "Yes, we are few, Hugh, but sometimes the King shows his strength in our weakness. I have experienced it myself on the battlefield. There have been things I could not do myself that I have done with the spirit of the Prince."

"The spirit of the Prince?" repeated Hugh. "How can a mere spirit protect us? My father spoke of it and even I have said those words, yet I do not understand exactly what I have said."

It was admittedly a difficult thing to comprehend. Stephen himself had struggled with it during his time with Sir Bart, but he went on, "The Prince was equally as powerful as the King. His spirit is endowed with the same power. Perhaps you have not faced the necessity to be guided by the spirit of the Prince, but you may be sure of this: when you received your mark, with it came the promise that the spirit of the Prince would be there to guide you thereafter."

Hugh's face was blank; he still seemed puzzled by the idea of the "spirit of the Prince" helping anyone. "I don't remember being told that. How does it happen?" he asked.

Stephen paused for a moment. *How do I explain this?* Then he said, "I know only my own experience and feel unqualified to speak for anyone else." He stopped. But, realizing this was an opportunity to declare what he knew about his King and his Prince, as bizarre as it might sound, he continued, "For me it has been like a voice in my thoughts. At first I did not know what it was, but over time the voice becomes familiar, one that you recognize the more you trust it."

"What? You hear voices?" Hugh said, shaking his head.

Stephen nodded. "I admit the idea of hearing something like a voice in your thoughts sounds daft, but I know what I heard and what happened afterward. During our journey maybe it will happen to you and you will believe me." Stephen straightened to his full height, looking Hugh in the eye. "That spirit is the difference between you being led by a mere youth and being led by a youth who is led by a lion."

Stephen believed what he had said was true, yet he also knew he had said it just to inspire confidence and sustain hope. Considering the unknown dangers they might yet have to face, he still was not sure about the lion.

Chapter 36

TRIALS

MARIE HAD BEEN notified by Daniel about the news of the King's gathering of his subjects. Initially she received it as just another burden heaped on those she was already attempting to bear since her father's death. But as she thought about it, she came to view it in some ways as a relief from the impending weight of having to manage her lands and the people on them. And there was something else positive too. She had been struggling with episodes of tearful sadness when she was alone at night. Though she had been grateful for the new manor house she now called home, she would be leaving behind many sorrowful memories when she departed to join Stephen on the way to the King. Instead of seeing Stephen only when he had time to come, she would now be beside him where she belonged. He had promised they would always be together; she desperately needed that assurance now.

Dispatching Daniel and Richard to inform those in her fief loyal to the King, Marie threw herself into organizing the departure of her people. Surprised at the urgency of the message to assemble her group, she scarcely managed, as instructed, to equip a cart with some clothing and all the food she could find. It seemed wrong to be leaving the house to whoever wanted it. If the King knew he was going to gather his subjects so soon, why did he bother to send his builder to rebuild it? With all that had happened she had scarcely had time to enjoy it. But she was going to obey her King.

When the day they were to meet Stephen dawned, a handful of peasants, some with bows and spears, had assembled outside her manor in silent obedience to her summons. As she took the lead with Daniel and Richard on horseback, she cast a parting glance at the manor house. She felt no emotion. It was no longer a family home now; it was only a building. She watched her pitiful band of followers fall into line behind, knowing only what she had told them—that they were to join a larger force led by Sir Stephen. Where they were going she knew not, but she trusted Stephen to get them there.

Soon after his company was underway again, Stephen halted his horse, Joel doing the same. Ahead in the road was a group of perhaps twenty people, three of them on horseback, with a cart.

"Halt the others," said Stephen. "I believe I know them."

Coming closer, he recognized Marie in her leather jerkin, bow at her side, and Richard, in a mail hauberk. He guessed the third taller one must be Daniel, Guardian of Bonfrere, and the rest loyal subjects from the fief.

"Good day, Marie. You have received the message?" Stephen asked, approaching her.

"Good day, Stephen. Yes, we were advised that you would be coming from the direction of Loynton with your party and that we should join you, there being safety in numbers."

"The more swords and bows the better," Stephen said, "though I do not know what dangers we will face." Shading his eyes from the westward sun, he added, "The day is waning. We should make camp soon while it is light."

"There is a grassy meadow up the road about an hour," Marie said.

He nodded and smiled, his mood buoyed just having her by his side.

The groups mingled, and before long the autumn air was filled with the sound of leaves being spread to cover grass and mud, and swords and axes hacking limbs from nearby trees to fashion lean-tos. As Stephen supervised the placement of sleeping areas, Alis approached.

"Sire, I have counted the loaves we brought with us, and Lady Marie has said that she brought all she had, as well as some dried fish, dried game, and fruit. I believe we have enough bread and perhaps a small bit of fish and meat to feed everyone tonight, but that is all. Though I have yeast and flour, we will not be able to bake more bread unless we find an oven. We could perhaps make fry bread from the miller's flour tomorrow."

"That will do," Stephen answered. "I will send some hunting parties into the forest for small game and berries to supplement our food. It is only three days at most to Bartscastle. If we must go hungry, we shall, but we should still be able to arrive without loss."

By the time shadows were lengthening and night falling, fires flickered to welcome hunters returning with rabbits and squirrels to skewer and roast. Stephen marked the perimeter of the camp and set guards at intervals, plus one to guard the carts and one the horses. He erected his pavilion in the center, Marie's beside his. They took their place at a crackling fire with Richard, Daniel, and Joel, sharing a loaf of bread and two fish.

"Daniel...Joel," Stephen said, "you seem to know more about the King's plans than we. Will we reach Bartscastle unharmed?"

"It is not given to us to know all future events," Daniel said, "though we answer to the King's wishes. At the present time it is his desire that you bring as many of your group as you can to Bartscastle."

It was not the answer Stephen expected. "As many as I can? Are you not here to provide sure protection?"

Joel shook his head. "As I once told you, we fight when the King bids us fight, and there are battles that you do not know of, but sometimes you must fight your own battles, trusting in the spirit of the Prince."

Marie spoke up. "That happened to me in the forest with Sir Bailys. My father told me it was the spirit of the Prince that gave me strength to resist him."

Stephen's thoughts went back to his first battle alongside Sir Bart. "It has happened with me too, in my first battle, but why does it have to be so difficult? I almost ran away."

Daniel answered, "I do not presume to know the mind of the King, but I believe that he allows us to be in struggles that threaten to overwhelm us because he wants us to trust him, not ourselves, for the outcome. He delights in showing his strength in our weakness."

"That is exactly what the voice said to me!" Marie said.

"Really? You heard a voice too?" Stephen asked.

"Yes," Marie answered. "At first it seemed like a thought, but it was speaking to me."

"And I thought I was the only one hearing voices," Stephen said. "But it did come like a thought."

"Remember what you said to me the night my father asked you to accept my hand in betrothal?" said Marie. "It was the same then too, wasn't it?"

"The spirit of the Prince guides us in many ways," Joel said. "If it is not a voice in our thoughts, it may be through the voice of another. Or it may be a conviction that one way is the right way to proceed or that another way is not."

"So," Stephen said, "you are saying that it is the spirit of the Prince I must trust to bring us safely to Bartscastle, not the two of you?"

"Yes," Joel and Daniel responded in unison.

Though he had certainly experienced the guidance of which Daniel and Joel spoke, Stephen felt no comfort in their answer. It sounded more like they were telling him he was on his own. Maybe they would not encounter any problems, but if they did, how could he know the spirit of the Prince would show up?

Stephen's thoughts were interrupted by the sound of running feet, and Hugh emerged into the dancing firelight.

"Sire, a stranger has asked to join our party. Should we feed him?"

"I will have words with him," Stephen replied. "Take me to him."

As Hugh led Stephen past glowing campfires toward the back of the encampment, the sound of a voice accompanied by a musical instrument wafted over the smoke curling from the fires. They came to a stop before a fire surrounded by a crowd of listeners. Next to the fire a man played a small harp as he sang:

> "Happy is he who delights in his King
> And heeds his ways both day and night.
> Like a tree by water is he,
> Bearing fine fruit in season."

"A minstrel!" Stephen exclaimed.

"Or a spy," Hugh whispered.

The man laid down his harp as they approached. Stephen judged him somewhat older than many of those listening, his scarred, brown face weathered by much traveling, or cares, or worse. His beard was somewhat unkempt, though he had a ready smile as he rose and bowed before Stephen.

"Good eve, sire," he said, then motioned to Hugh. "Your bowman told me he was going to tell his leader about me."

"I am Sir Stephen, leader of our group. And you are—?"

"Fitzroy - a minstrel, as you say. Might I pass the night with you and trade song for food?"

Heeding Hugh's words, Stephen asked, "Whence have you come and where are you going?"

"Throughout the Kingdom and throughout the Kingdom."

"That answer is no answer," Stephen said. "We have little food and we have eaten most of it tonight."

"Yes, you seem to have a troubled band, but I have a small stomach. Perhaps some song would help fill everyone." The minstrel took his harp and began to strum, then sang again:

"How sweet are the King's ways
To my tongue.
Sweeter than honey
To my mouth."

Stephen could not deny that he was troubled about the journey he was undertaking with this large group for which he bore sole responsibility, nor could he deny the peace that came upon him as he listened to the minstrel sing.

"Did you notice the scars?" Hugh whispered. "This man may be a warrior in disguise, and a servant of the Dragon. Moreover his skin is darker than ours; he cannot be one of us!"

Stephen could clearly see the reasons for Hugh's concern, yet inwardly he sensed neither the fear nor the suspicion he expected if he were in the presence of one sent by the Dragon. "I believe he sings of our King," he answered. "Feed him and allow him to rest with us."

"Thank you, milord," Fitzroy answered, taking his seat by the fire again.

Walking back to his fire in the darkness, Stephen sat with the others until only coals remained, pondering what the next day would bring. He hoped he had made the right decision about the minstrel. Hugh had been concerned for a reason. Was Stephen missing something? He did not wish to be the one who admitted a spy into their camp. How did the minstrel receive his wounds? Why did he come at night? Had he been shadowing the group? What were his intentions?

Stephen was no closer to an answer when the light of morning filtered into his tent and he rose to greet the new day. Marie was already by the re-stoked fire munching on some dried fruit in the damp chill of the foggy morning, Daniel sitting beside her.

"A minstrel joined us last night," Stephen said to Marie as he took his place by the fire. "Although I do not know why, I am inclined to allow him to accompany us."

"Perhaps if the people become disheartened, his songs will encourage them," Marie said.

Stephen nodded. "Yes, they do seem to have a peaceful effect."

The camp reverberated with noise and murmuring as people awoke and gathered around fires to eat the last of the bread and what few scraps remained from the previous night.

"We must make it to the inn by Roaring Fork by nightfall," Stephen said. "Perhaps we can buy food and drink for our people there."

"Sire!"

The voice sounded urgent, so Stephen turned and saw Hugh running to him, breathless.

"The people are becoming frightened. Two peasants are missing. They disappeared in the night. No bodies have been found. Some thought they heard wolves during the night!"

"Wolves?" Stephen said. "There are no wolves in this area. Perhaps wild boars, but brigands are more likely. What have you found?"

"Nothing, sire. We have searched the perimeter. They just vanished."

Stephen remained skeptical, but he knew that a fearful group would be much more difficult to lead than a confident one. "Get everyone on the road and moving. Tell them there are no wolves."

Resuming his place at the front of the column, Stephen silently took counsel of his fears, trying not to show anyone the struggle raging in his mind. Did the peasants just walk away? Or were they taken? Was it the Black Knights? Gythreul?

The sound of a harp came from behind him; then he heard, "Good morrow, sire." Fitzroy trotted up beside him. "Where do we go today?"

"To Roaring Fork, and across if we have time," Stephen replied, concerned about the possible effect of the recent rains on the boisterous river. "Sing me a song now that you are here."

"Gladly, milord."

The dulcet sound of the harp flowed over Stephen's tormented mind like cool water over a parched tongue. Then came the minstrel's words:

"My King is my refuge
In him will I trust.
I make him my dwelling;
He is my fortress.

413

"My King says,
'Because he loves me
I will rescue him.'

'I will be with him in trouble;
I will deliver him
And honor him.'"

Stephen could not explain why, but the song seemed directed specifically to him. No longer able to ruminate on his worries, he felt his muscles relax. His tension drained, and he allowed himself to entertain hope for an uneventful day.

The crowd fell into column behind Stephen, Marie, and Fitzroy, with Daniel and Joel serving as flank guards, the archers and swordsmen walking beside the carts. Hugh, having delivered the news about the peasants, was particularly wary, keeping his bow in hand. Brian walked with him on the other side of the bakers' cart.

"Why so vigilant, Hugh? We have flank guards," Brian said.

"I cannot escape the feeling that the Dragon is behind the disappearances," Hugh answered. "I think the peasants were captured in the night. Our enemy does his nefarious work in darkness, remember? It was growing dark when we attacked Maison Bonfrere."

"We are fortunate that we have not been attacked thus far," said Thomas, walking behind Hugh.

The still-anxious crowd plodded onward, some in the muddy ruts of the road, others fanning out onto the grass, still others heaving the carts forward through the muck, a spirit of uneasiness tugging at them. It was a time-consuming process, and the day was nearly spent by the time rushing water was heard ahead. The people already seemed unhappy that there had been no food to eat since they had struck camp. Low clouds hinted of more rain, and a steady wind blew a chill through the dejected mass as Stephen halted their progress to reconnoiter.

When Stephen rode into view of the inn, his worst fears were realized. Water swirled around its base, the sign declaring the Wolf's Den swinging with each gust of wind. The inn appeared deserted, water undoubtedly a foot deep now over the rush-covered dirt of the first floor.

And worse still, the bridge was gone—swept away by the swift current! Stephen's hope of bringing his people safely to Bartscastle was crushed. He knew the river was shallow in normal times and could actually be forded when water was low, but observing the skeletal remains of the bridge—the wooden posts that held the entrance to the bridge—he judged the water to be at least two feet higher than normal. The entire center, perhaps three-quarters of the bridge, had vanished, though the plankway leading to the bridge on either side remained, the surging flow now less than a foot from the top of the planking.

Defeated, Stephen rode slowly back to the waiting crowd, unsure what to say, or even what to do next. Hugh, Brian, and Thomas had come forward to see what was happening. Daniel and Joel were already there, conferring.

"Bid the people make camp," Stephen said. "We must send parties up and down the river to look for a place to cross. Daniel, you take a group upstream, and, Joel, you a group downstream. Hugh, Brian, Thomas, search the inn for food."

As the groups departed and the crowd dissolved into murmuring knots to find firewood and prepare places to sleep, Stephen trudged to a grassy spot off the road and collapsed, gazing vacantly at the river that had defeated him, his mind blank, unable to conjure a solution.

Marie soon appeared, taking a seat beside him. She grasped his hand. "It seems hopeless, doesn't it?"

Stephen did not look at her. "There has to be a way, but I do not know what to do," he said finally, his eyes fixed on the rushing water. "The water is chest deep. Many cannot swim and would be swept away if we attempt to ford here."

"Perhaps the spirit of the Prince will guide you," Marie said.

Stephen exhaled a heavy sigh. "I have listened for that voice, Marie, but I am hearing nothing—no one! He spoke to me before when I did not expect it. Now that I need him, he does not. I just do not understand how I am supposed to trust him." Stephen knew Marie was attempting to encourage him, but he was not Marie. She seemed to have retained a simple trust in the King and the Prince despite the loss of her mother and father. Stephen wished he could have the same trust.

"May I join you?" a cheerful voice spoke from behind Stephen.

"No, I do not need a song, Fitzroy," Stephen replied. "You cannot sing us across this."

"Perhaps not, milord. But might I ask if you have your map in your possession?"

"Of course I do!" Stephen snapped. "Why are you asking about trivial matters? A piece of parchment will not float us across this torrent either!"

"If you examine it now, I think you will find something that will," Fitzroy replied.

"What can a minstrel know about my parchment?" Stephen said, his irritation mounting.

"More than you allow yourself to believe," Fitzroy replied, taking a seat on the grass.

"All right, if it will still your tongue, I will show it to you!" Stephen wrestled with his surcoat and mail hauberk to find the small bag in which he kept his map and key. "Here!" he said, handing the map to Fitzroy.

"Open it."

Stephen unfolded his map. "So?" he huffed.

"Have you ever looked at your map since you received it?"

"Only once or twice," Stephen answered. "It was just something I was supposed to keep with me. No one told me why. What is your point?"

"I am sure someone told you. Perhaps you do not remember. Do you not know what the map represents?" Fitzroy asked.

"Why are you asking me all these questions? What I need are answers!" Stephen said.

"Wait, I know," Marie said. "It is a map of the Kingdom, with the King's castle at the center. It shows the characteristics of the Kingdom and represents the hearts of those who belong to him."

"So what does that have to do with crossing the river?" Stephen questioned.

"On your map is a heart that represents you. Show me where it is," Fitzroy said.

Stephen recalled now his supper with Sir Ralf and Michael, when the answer to the reason for his imprisonment had appeared on the map. He had not examined his map since then, nor did he remember where the heart representing him had been. He scanned the map with his eyes, glancing at the hills, pastures, roads, and rivers. Some had names, some did not. Distracted by the roar of the river and his anxiety, he could not find it.

Apparently sensing Stephen's frustration, Fitzroy pointed. "Middle left."

And there it was on one of the roads, the same small heart in green, the colors of Sir Bart, now of Stephen. How could he have missed it? He placed his finger on it. "All right. So?"

"Describe the features of the map associated with it," Fitzroy said.

Stephen looked closely. "There is a river just in front of it. And a building, maybe a house, beside it."

"An inn," Fitzroy said. "Look at the river on the map. What do you see?"

Stephen focused his eyes on the river, which began to move—ripples, then waves beginning to appear, the froth rising to form into letters. To his astonished eyes, the word *Patience* now overlay the river.

"Now look at the inn."

The smoke rising from the chimney began to curl and writhe, writing the word *Trust* over the inn. Stephen understood that these words were somehow meant for him, but how? And why?

"Patience—and trust?" Stephen said. "What does it mean?"

"Oh! The same happened to me!" Marie exclaimed. "When I was at Bartscastle being educated by Lady Anne, a man came to look at my tapestry of the map and showed me where I was on my road. Words appeared to me just like they did for you. Lady Anne said the map speaks to us when we need it."

"And that is your answer," Fitzroy said.

Stephen looked at him, his brow furrowed. "Patience and trust will get us across the river?"

"Exactly," Fitzroy said. "If the spirit of the Prince is not giving you the answer to this now, perhaps you must be patient, trust him, and believe he will provide a way. In fact, if you look farther back on your road, you will find another time the map spoke even though you did not then possess it. It preserves a record of your progress in the Kingdom, which begins even before you enter." With that Fitzroy stood and silently walked away.

Sliding his finger down, Stephen traced his road back to the bottom of the map. It passed a tower with the word *Perseverance* next to it. He followed the road all the way to the bottom of the map. His heart jumped. At the very bottom was a gate. Outside the gate was a bridge, beside it a field. The bridge bore the name *Pevensey.* On the field was the word *Courage.*

"What did you find?" Marie asked.

"I will never forget," Stephen answered, gazing into the distance. "In my first battle I was scared. I wanted to run. It was the first time the spirit of the Prince spoke to me and gave me the courage to stand firm. And it is on my map, though it happened even before I received my map and was knighted."

"So, that must mean the spirit of the Prince is with us even before we are aware of what the Kingdom is about," Marie said. "It happened to me too. Just before I entered the Kingdom on my thirteenth birthday, I think his spirit was telling me I needed to trust the King."

Stephen nodded. "After that battle I expected to hear the voice whenever I needed it." Then he frowned. "But I did not hear it when Bartscastle was besieged, nor do I hear it now."

Marie seemed lost in thought for a moment. "You know, when the words appeared on my tapestry, I did not hear a voice either, yet I knew there was something I needed to do. Perhaps it will be the same for you. Didn't Joel say you don't always hear a voice?"

Stephen sat pensively, his eyes still fixed on the roaring, splashing water of the obstacle before him, pondering the words of Fitzroy and of Marie until the light began to fail. He still did not know what to do.

The search parties returned. Joel reported first: "Milord, there is a ford about a mile downstream where the river pools. It is covered by water, but I know where it is. The water is perhaps shallower but it is twice as wide. The current is still rapid and I am not sure even a horseman could safely cross."

Daniel said, "Sire, we went upstream as far as Sir Andrew's manor house. There was no ford, but we searched his abandoned manor and outbuildings and brought back a bit of food and some ropes. If a rope could be strung across the ford, perhaps we could cross holding onto it."

Hugh reported last: "We sloshed through the inn and its outbuildings. There was no food to be found, sire. Even the ale has been taken."

After pondering the reports Stephen took Joel and Daniel aside. "I know that Guardians have powers beyond my comprehension. Cannot one of you take the rope and swim across to the other side to secure it?"

Joel shook his head. "I would remind you again, sire, that we serve the King, not you. What the King desires, that we do. But his plan involves all of us, each performing as the King desires, and even we Guardians sometimes are left to look upon and seek to understand the mysteries of his ways with you and your kind."

With Joel's refusal Stephen became despondent. There was still no solution. He did not have time to be patient! What purpose could the King have that he would not help him now? What if Gythreul had detected their departure and was preparing to attack them now with no way of escape? There seemed to be nothing else Stephen could do but try to trust the absent spirit of the Prince, who seemed unwilling to speak to him.

"I guess I will *have* to be patient," he muttered. "I will sleep on it. Tomorrow, Daniel and Joel, you must go farther up and down the stream. Look for a narrower place to cross."

But he could not sleep. He tried to envision how the next day would unfold, but his mind was blank. There seemed to be no hope. Surely Gythreul would find him on the morrow.

The next morning a light rain had returned on the chill breeze. Stephen awoke with a sense of impending doom, crushed by his responsibility for the lives of those who looked to him for their safety, disheartened by Joel's and Daniel's refusal to help him. Couldn't they see that he had no solution? Didn't they appreciate the danger everyone was in?

As Stephen conferred with Daniel and Joel, Hugh and Brian ran up to Stephen's tent. "Sire," Hugh said, "three more peasants vanished during the night. No cries were heard, nor were there any traces of their bodies. The people grow fearful, saying you cannot protect them."

Stephen struggled to conceal his alarm. *They are right. I cannot. We soon will be attacked with our backs to the river and perish to the man.*

Seeing to sense Stephen's fear, Joel spoke: "Sire, do not lose heart. It is the beginning of the winnowing."

"Winnowing?" Stephen said. "What do you mean?"

"It is spoken of in the *Chronicle*," Daniel said. "During the gathering there will be a winnowing of those who do not belong to the King from those who do."

"Wait, doesn't everyone on this journey belong to the King?" Stephen asked. "Why else would they leave home and come on this journey?"

"There are many reasons," Joel said. "Some have come in the expectation of safety, some in hope of food and provision. Others think in their minds that they follow the King, but he does not have their hearts."

"Then should we bring everyone together and check for their marks?" Stephen asked, wondering if had had omitted an important step at the beginning.

Joel shook his head. "That is not your purpose, sire. Your purpose is to lead and inspire. The King knows who belongs to him; he allows the Dragon and his Companions to take in the darkness those who are theirs."

"Then we *are* being pursued by the Dragon, as I feared!" Stephen said. "And this is the perfect place for him to attack and capture us all."

"Perhaps. Perhaps not," Daniel said. "I do not know what the Dragon intends. But you are aware that the Dragon prefers to do his deeds in darkness rather than light. He also targets leaders, because if he can remove them, their followers are easy prey. He is more likely to attack *your* heart and mind with fear and doubt in the night than to attack your people in daylight."

Stephen took a moment to reflect. *Is that why I am so troubled? Is that why I am impatient and why I lashed out at Fitzroy? Is the Dragon attacking even my thoughts?* Stephen had no answer, but now he was aware of a real danger—a Black Knight, perhaps Gythreul, must be shadowing his party and entering his encampment by night to snatch his people. Not only that, but some of his people apparently were not loyal to the King. Were they somehow involved in the disappearances? Was Hugh right? Were there spies among them? Stephen sensed he was losing his grasp over those he was supposed to protect.

Joel and Daniel departed up and down the river, and Stephen guessed, based on the previous night's conversation, they would not provide the answer he needed.

"Sire, we may have a solution to crossing the river," Hugh said once they were gone.

"Tell me." Stephen sighed, desperate for any hope. "I will listen to any possibility."

Brian said, "Sire, I am a strong swimmer. Hugh told me about the ropes that were found. I can fasten one to myself and swim to the other side, then tie it to a tree for people to hold to as they cross."

Stephen was skeptical. "I am a strong swimmer as well, and I would not attempt it. The current will sweep you away. What does a tanner know about swimming anyway?"

"My father's tannery was located by a river," Brian said. "For years I have swum in the river at the end of the day—" he chuckled self-consciously, "to remove from my body the stench of the animal hides and the dyeing vats. I have come to enjoy it and have covered great distances just for the strength it provides me."

Despite Daniel's counsel about the methods of the Dragon, Stephen could not shake the disturbing revelation that the Dragon's forces were indeed lurking around him unseen, nor his fear that they might decide to attack in daylight. Something needed to be done, and quickly. He considered Brian's solution.

"I am reluctant to give you permission because I judge it a dangerous undertaking," Stephen replied. "But we dare not stay here any longer. We must not let the people know, lest they become discouraged if you fail. Fetch the rope and go with me to the ford, where it is shallower. Hugh, set up a perimeter watch with the other archers and swordsmen."

The two walked to the ford, Brian with the ropes coiled over his shoulder. The river was much wider there than Stephen had expected, water pooling and swirling in the depressions that led down to the ford. He judged the distance to be about fifty yards, twice the distance at the site of the bridge.

"You will be swept downstream as you swim," Stephen said. "Let us walk that direction and look for a likely exit point that does not exceed the length of the rope where you can make it ashore on the other side."

After a short walk along the flooded shoreline, Brian pointed at a fallen tree on the opposite bank, its trunk partially in the water, its limbs projecting out of the water. "I will aim for that tree, as it will give me something to grab onto."

Stephen nodded, as it appeared to be a good exit point. "Go, then, and once you have gained land, run upstream to the fording point and tie the rope to a sturdy tree there." As he finished saying it, Stephen feared that he had made a foolish decision, but he was desperate. He hoped that Brian would prove him wrong. He could only wait anxiously. *Patience and trust.*

Once back at the ford with Stephen, Brian tied two ropes together to make one long enough to span the river. Then he tied one end around his waist and the other to a tree. Stepping into the water, he found it colder than he expected. He waded, careful of his footing until the water was thigh deep and he was near the main channel where he could see rapidly flowing water. After locating his goal twenty yards downstream, he plunged in. For a moment he could not move, his muscles shocked by the frigid water. He began slowly to swim, reaching midstream with much effort. This was the critical point, he knew. He could hardly feel his arms now, but he had to stroke harder to get out of the rapid current.

Looking up, he saw the fallen tree quickly approaching. He would not be there in time. He stroked harder, a sudden wave splashing his head underwater. When he came up, he was disoriented and being swept downriver, his strength draining. But he thought he was closer to the shore. He went under again, his arms and legs still propelling him forward, his hands grasping for something, anything, to hold to. His head bobbed back up, his blurred vision seeing the shore race by. He knew he was close, but his strength was gone, his throat choking on swallowed water, his frigid muscles refusing to follow his command. Out of the corner of his eye, he could see another downed tree partially in the water as he hurtled toward it. Summoning his last effort, he lunged desperately at the oncoming branches.

Chapter 37

THE CROSSING

W HEN BRIAN OPENED his eyes, he was flat on his back. Absentmindedly he reached for the rope. He could not find it. His vision still blurred, he could make out the shape of branches above him. The rushing sound of the river filled his ears. The form of a face appeared in his field of vision. He jerked to the side. He did not recognize the face.

"Wh-Who are you?" Brian gasped.

"I am the King's healer," the face said. "You have fulfilled the King's purpose." He took Brian's hand. "Come and receive your reward."

Stephen watched in horror as Brian was swept past the fallen tree, just as he had feared. A few moments later the movement of the rope stopped. Stephen gave it a tug; it remained taut. *He is across! We will be safe.* Stephen took a seat by the tree, waiting for the rope to begin moving again as Brian brought his end back upstream to the ford. But it did not move. Why not? Stephen gave the rope another tug. It still seemed to be secure, but there was no tug back as he expected.

"Brian!" he called over the roar of the torrent.

There was no answer.

A fist of nausea formed in Stephen's throat as myriad possible outcomes fleeted through his racing mind. There was only one way to dismiss the worst possibility that reared before him. He stripped to his tunic, took hold of the rope, and waded into the chill water. The rope held as he inched his way out into the current. Then he was swept off his feet. Gripping the wet rope, he pulled himself along, kicking with his feet, the river clawing with icy fingers to rip him away. Finally the clasp of the current released him. As his eyes followed the line of the rope to the shore where another downed tree touched the water, his heart dropped a beat. The rope led to a still body tangled in the branches. Stephen hurried to pull himself to the motionless form—Brian. Suppressing hot tears of anguish, he grabbed Brian's face to shake him, but his lifeless visage was already cold and pale.

Stephen realized now that he was also very cold and becoming stiffer the longer he remained in the water. He heaved his body onto the tree trunk, shivering. Moving in a sitting position backward up the trunk, he slowly hauled the heavy burden onto the shore, and sat, numbed by the confirmation of his greatest fear. He'd had reservations, but his determination to find a way across the river had caused him to brush those reservations aside.

He had sent Brian to his death. The fault lay with him. How could he face Brian's mother now? He wished he could just stay on that side of river, separated from all the cares and worries on the other side, but he knew he could not. He was still their leader. His shivering body nudged him to action. After untying the rope, he made his way back to the ford and tied it to a tree so that it now spanned the river. Wading and kicking his way back across, he collapsed, totally exhausted physically and emotionally.

He was still huddled on the ground shivering when he felt a hand on his shoulder. "Sire, much time has passed. What has happened? Where is Brian?"

Stephen looked up at Hugh. He could not say the words. He lifted his arm and pointed downstream. "He—He is there." Then Stephen wept aloud.

Sensing the truth, Hugh gasped, "No!" Then he grabbed the rope, splashed into the water and pulled himself to the other side. Dripping wet and chilled, he raced down the bank, hoping he would not find what he feared. But there at his feet lay his lifelong friend, stiff and cold. Hugh fell to the ground and sat, lifting Brian's head, cradling it in his lap, giving full vent to his grief, and then to his rage.

"Why have you allowed this? Why?" he shouted above the emotionless roar of the water, his anguish swallowed by the ceaseless rushing of the river.

There was no answer.

Hugh sat bent over Brian's body, unmoving, his head touching Brian's. His body convulsed with agonized moans, oblivious to passing time. Memories of shared experiences never to be repeated burning in his mind, he remained there until the sound of excited voices on the far bank broke through his tangled thoughts.

Walking reluctantly back upstream, Hugh could see that Stephen had roused the camp and brought the people to the ford. As he trudged back to his side of the ford, Hugh caught a glimpse of Brian's mother, Charis, seated alone near the tree to which the rope was tied, head in hands, weeping. Hugh pulled himself back across the rope. Dripping wet and shivering, he plopped down beside Charis.

"My son—my firstborn," she groaned, her face covered by her hands, her body slowly rocking back and forth.

Hugh's anger was long gone, replaced by a feeling he was not accustomed to—compassion. He had met the deaths of his father and mother, even of Brian, with anger and frustration. Scarcely able to deal with his own sorrow over losing his friend, he could not imagine what it was like for a mother to lose her son. No words came to him that would ease Charis's pain. Like him she was now alone, bereft of family. He placed his arm around her and held her, his thoughts again taking flight. He remembered how proud she had been when Brian received his mark, how she had nursed Sir Ralf back to health when he was still their enemy, her simple trust in the goodness of the King. How could the King permit this to happen to a faithful and trusting servant like Charis? But as angry as he had been over his loss, Hugh felt only sadness for Charis's loss—and bafflement about the King to whom he had once sworn loyalty.

" I thought the King had marked him for great things," Charis said, her voice interrupted by an occasional sniffle. "When he began to make parchments for the map, I was so proud. I dreamed that someday he would bow before the King and be honored in his court."

"And he will," Hugh said, surprised to hear the words coming from his mouth, unsure if he even believed them. "He gave his life to save us. Look, people are already crossing the river."

Charis looked up as the first brave souls edged out into the river holding to the rope. "I know what you say is true, Hugh. It is the kind of thing I would have said to you, but far more do I wish that I had been taken in his place."

A shout and commotion interrupted them. People were now rushing toward the river, crowding around the rope.

"Hurry! Before they slaughter us all!"

"Out of the way! Let the women cross first!"

No one seemed to be in charge. Hugh could not see Sir Stephen anywhere. Sensing an unseen danger, he jumped up and grabbed his bow and arrows, which he had deposited by the tree before crossing. He ran through the crowd toward the wagons. There stood Sir Stephen, sword in hand, and Marie, an arrow nocked, facing a group of armored horsemen, obviously outnumbered even with Richard, sword at the ready, and four archers including Thomas, bows drawn, behind them.

A single knight in black armor was speaking. "The wagons are mine. You and your lady can spare your people by coming with us also, or you can die with them!"

Still panting from crossing the river, Hugh sized up the situation. It was one of the Black Knights, perhaps the same one that had wounded him, and he counted nine horsemen besides the knight. Clearly Stephen and the others would be overcome and would not be able to hold their adversary at bay long enough for the rest to cross the river. He crept behind a tree, nocking an arrow, his mind racing. *I am as yet unseen. Should I shoot? Will I risk their lives?* There was no time to debate the questions.

He emerged and shouted, "For Brian!" letting his arrow fly.

The horsemen all glanced in his direction, seeking the source of the voice. Hugh's arrow was followed by the four other archers' arrows, finding their marks among the momentarily distracted enemies. Four men dropped from their horses. The other five horsemen looked from Hugh back to their fallen compatriots in confusion, and spurred their mounts away, leaving only the Black Knight. With a great blow, he struck Sir Stephen's sword, sending it flying. Hugh's next arrow was for the Black Knight's horse, which reared, sending the knight crashing to the ground. The four archers immediately surrounded him, bows redrawn. Before they could release, the knight rolled and sprang to his feet, swinging his sword in a great arc, knocking their bows from their hands. Marie's arrow ricocheted off his armor.

Galloping hoofs sounded to Hugh's left. As he loosed another arrow toward the knight, Daniel and Joel rode past him in a blur, swords drawn. The Black Knight paused to see who the two oncoming horsemen were as Hugh's next arrow struck the knight's helmet and bounced off. As if he recognized them, the Black Knight turned to face Daniel and Joel, sword at the ready, while Stephen retrieved his sword and the archers their bows. Words were exchanged between the Black Knight and the two Guardians, after which the Black Knight sheathed his sword and led his wounded horse away with a departing growl to Stephen.

"Good fortune has saved you today," the Black Knight said. "There will be more of us next time."

Hugh dashed to the wagons.

Stephen greeted him with an unusually stern look. "You made a very risky decision, Hugh. That was Gythreul. He could have killed us all single-handedly after that."

His dander up, Hugh responded, "It looked like he was going to anyway. You should trust your archers. We eliminated half his force." Hugh pointed toward the four wounded horsemen who had been felled by arrows. "They are our prisoners now."

Stephen's jaw clenched, then he said, "Do not praise yourself! The Dragon's Black Knights cannot be overcome by such as us. It was not you who saved us but the spirit of the Prince. Only he has the power."

"He is right, Hugh," Marie said. "Isn't he, Daniel?"

"He is, milady. We were both returning from our scouting assignments when we were urged to come to the ford immediately. Gythreul saw that he was over-matched by two of us." He looked at Hugh. "But Hugh may have played a part."

It had all happened so quickly in Hugh's mind—sensing the danger, needing to act, hesitating because of the risk, then the strong feeling that he should go ahead.

"I don't know," Hugh said. "I did know it was risky, but I experienced the strongest confidence that I should proceed."

"The spirit of the Prince," said Stephen and Marie in unison, then Stephen continued, "Perhaps your diversion allowed time for Daniel and Joel to reach us."

Hugh thought back to his conversation with Sir Stephen about the spirit of the Prince at the beginning of their journey and how Sir Stephen had explained the way it had guided him. "It wasn't a voice like you told me, sire," Hugh said. "It was a strong and confident impulse to act, like I usually have. And I did." He thought a moment. "But there was a small difference. Usually I am more tense and anxious when I follow the impulse; this time there was a focus and a peace unlike I have experienced before."

"That is an astute observation, Hugh."

At the sound of the voice, Hugh turned to see Fitzroy approaching.

"The Prince's spirit may guide us in different ways," Fitzroy said, "aligning itself with our underlying nature. Perhaps that is how it will be for you. Now, I suggest you all attend to the ford crossing. There is a need for leadership."

"Right!" Stephen said. "I totally forgot."

He raced toward the ford, Hugh right behind him, wondering what they would face next.

Upon arriving back at the ford, Stephen found the scene chaotic; people were crowded at the water's edge and no one was in charge. Two peasants had managed to get themselves across and were standing in shallower water holding the rope ready to lend a hand to the next one. Then someone told Stephen that already a man had lost his grip and been swept downstream. A well-meaning peasant was attempting to coax a frightened woman into the water. Shouts and shrieks came from the panicky crowd as they jostled around the rope.

Stephen ran to the water's edge and raised his arms. "Stop! We are safe now! Everyone will cross. Have a seat and be calm. Let us develop a plan."

It was clear to Stephen and the others that the weaker members of the party would not be able to get themselves across the rushing waters even holding onto the rope.

"Sire," Hugh said, "when we searched the inn, the beds still had blankets. Perhaps we could cut them into strips and tie them together and use them as a tether to the rope."

"It is worth a try," Stephen said. "Take some men and bring back all you can find."

Stephen waited until Hugh and his men returned with armfuls of blankets, which they began to cut into strips. Several blanket strips would be knotted together, one end to be tied around a person, the other tied around the rope so that the blanket tether could be slipped along the rope. The critical point would be at the center where the two ropes that made the crossing rope were knotted together and where the current was the swiftest. Another tether would have to be made on the other side of that knot and in turn tied to the person crossing before the first tether was untied. Stephen had several of the stronger peasants cross using this method so that all could see that it would work. The stronger ones would then have to take turns in the middle of the river attending to the tying and untying of knots while they themselves were tethered to the rope to prevent them being swept away. Those waiting still sounded fearful as they waited, but as more successfully went across, encouraging their followers from the other side, progress was made. Most of the day was spent by the time the last had crossed. Then it was time to bring the wagons across.

Stephen had been thinking about how to do this. He knew the current was swift enough to undercut the footing of the horses and he wasn't sure how well they could swim the crucial part. The most rapid current was contained within the central ten yards of the river. If there was a man riding the wagon, whipping the horses to move faster and one leading along the rope with their bridles, it might work.

"Tie three horses to each wagon. If one slips, the others can keep going," Stephen said. "Then we will rest them and bring them back for the next one."

Marie's wagon, the lightest, went first. It was a painstaking and tedious process but it was successful. By the time the second wagon—Stephen's, the contents of the bakers' cart having been unloaded into it—was across, the sun had sunk behind the trees, shadows obscured the crossing, and dusk was upon them. Last to come was the Grandvil wagon, which contained the remaining scraps of food from the previous night, little though it was. The horses were tiring and shivering from the repeated passages and were moving more slowly. As the wagon approached the center of the river, a shout went up from the opposite bank.

"Stop! A tree!"

Stephen looked upstream. Hurtling toward the wagon was an uprooted tree, its root-faced trunk aimed like a missile at the struggling horses. A groan went up from the helpless onlookers as the roots snapped the rope and struck the hind wheel of the wagon, then the other one, breaking them both off, causing the wagon to collapse and twist in the water, pouring its contents into the onrushing torrent. There was nothing to do but keep going, or lose the horses as well.

The straining beasts yanked the empty wagon into shallower water and onto the bank, leaving a furrow where the wheel-less back of the wagon plowed through the mud. Without pause, next came the men with horses, Stephen leading Marie's horse quickly, her clinging to the horse's mane, knees locked against the saddle, surrounded by Hugh, Fitzroy, Daniel, and Joel on their horses, all gaining the other side successfully. Though darkness was falling, Stephen knew the day was not yet over. Those on the bank formed an exhausted and dispirited group, still shocked at watching the loss of what little food they had, some dangerously chilled by the frigid water and their wet clothing. For a few minutes there was stunned silence, then the murmuring began.

"What will we do now?" one asked.

"We will starve before we reach Bartscastle," another said. "We have already lost six. How many more?"

Stephen was certain they could reach Bartscastle now if not attacked again. He was less sure that he could keep the group together and maintain their hope. Physically and emotionally spent from all of the events of the day, he could hardly keep his spirits up, much less sustain hope. Again he felt like collapsing on the bank and resting his head on his knees. But he knew he needed to get everyone moving to a place open enough to make camp. First he found Charis to offer his condolences and give her a promise to return and bury Brian once they'd made camp upstream, saying that she and Hugh could remain with his body until then. It seemed an inadequate response to Brian's sacrifice, but night was falling and Stephen needed to get everyone into camp quickly where they could recover from their ordeal.

He addressed the shivering survivors above the roar of the torrent. "It is only a mile back to the main road. We will continue along the shore until we arrive there and make camp, build fires, and dry out. Yes, we have lost our food, but we will not starve. We are only two or at most three days from Bartscastle. Those who can hunt must do so. The strong must help the weak. Some of us may go hungry. I will send someone ahead to the castle to ask them to bring us food. Now we must move. Stay in view of, or touching, the person in front of you and no one will get lost in the darkness."

The sodden group formed into a straggling serpentine column, each person attempting to remain in contact with another as it made its way back along the shore to the main road where the bridge was washed out—Stephen leading, Thomas bringing up the rear, with Joel and Daniel in the woods on the flank. Once they'd stopped, wood-gathering parties slipped into the woods to gather twigs and branches, and soon fires sprang up, attended by clusters of cold, damp peasants warming themselves and drying out. Stephen erected his pavilion and declared it a hospital where the weak and tired could take refuge. Then, leaving Thomas and Daniel to set up a tent for Marie and manage the camp, Stephen and Joel headed back downstream to join Charis and Hugh.

They found a shivering Charis stretched out on top of Brian's body, cradling his head, her cheek pressed to his. Hugh was to the side picking at the ground with his sword to dig a grave. Leaving Charis in her silent embrace of Brian, Stephen and Joel joined Hugh to complete the digging. When they had finished, Charis allowed them to slide Brian's body from beneath her and lower it into the grave while she sat on her knees, head in her hands, sobbing with low moans.

Stephen and Hugh crouched beside her, holding her close as Joel heaped up the earth. They remained, unspeaking, until finally Charis rose and began to trudge aimlessly along the river bank as if lost.

Joel leading the way, they returned to the camp, where Charis volunteered to stay at the makeshift hospital pavilion and do what she could to ease the suffering of the others. Stephen joined Marie and Daniel, who had started a fire in front of Marie's tent, taking his place next to Marie and then sinking to the ground, exhausted.

Marie put her arm around Stephen's shoulder and gave it a squeeze. "We are safely across now, Stephen. You can relax."

"But we lost two more, and one was my fault," Stephen lamented. "And we lost our food. Any more trials like this and I am undone."

"The King surely knows of your troubles," Daniel said. "Perhaps they provided an opportunity for you to trust him more?"

"An opportunity to trust him?" Stephen said. "Hmpf! I would not call it that. It seemed more like an opportunity to fail him." He exhaled a heavy sigh. "He could have made it much easier, and with less suffering. He could have sent an armed guard to escort us and food wagons to accompany us."

"And maybe someone to rebuild the bridge?" Marie added.

Stephen was not comforted by Marie's comment, perhaps intended gently to point out his unrealistic expectations. He was responsible for the loss of two lives, perhaps more, and Gythreul had finally caught up to him as he had feared. He was at his wits' end, wishing he could just walk away from everything, to drop the burden he was carrying and leave it to someone else. What would come next? He wanted to trust his King and his Prince. He looked at Daniel. Yes, Daniel and Joel had rescued him from Gythreul just when he was feeling the situation was totally beyond his control. Both he and Marie had agreed it was the spirit of the Prince at work, voice or no voice. Why then didn't he have the peace Hugh spoke of having or the trust that Marie seemed to have?

Marie sensed Stephen's struggle. Since the trauma of losing her home and her parents, she too had wrestled with what form her life would take next and what purpose the King might have for her. Stephen was her anchor now. He seemed to need encouragement. Perhaps that was her purpose.

"Remember the words on your map?" Marie said. "You waited patiently for a solution, which the King gave you, and you trusted the solution to keep us safe and get us across the river. Perhaps you were trusting the King even while you were so absorbed with leading us."

"I wanted to," Stephen said, "but what I was feeling was more like panic. I know that it has fallen on me to lead, and I am trying to, but I was not prepared for all these trials, especially the loss of life. Each trial is almost more than I can master."

"Great trials are sometimes given to build great trust," Daniel said.

"Judging from the trials, I must be in great need of building trust, then." Stephen sighed. "I just wish it was not so difficult."

Marie also wished it were not so, because it was painful watching Stephen struggle as he did, but she began to sense that in such a struggle lay a purpose for her.

Stephen lifted his head to the sound of a harp, announcing the arrival of Fitzroy, whom Stephen had seen strolling among the people, attempting to improve the spirits of those grouped around the fires.

"Sit with us, Fitzroy," Stephen said. "I could use a song now."

"Of course, milord." Fitzroy began to strum and sing:

"My trust is in my King.
I will be glad and full of joy."

"For he saw my affliction
And knew the anguish of my soul."

"He has not handed me over to my enemy,
But has set my feet in a spacious place."

As the words touched Stephen's ears, the tension and worry of the past two days drained from his tortured heart and mind. In its place came the peace he so longed for. *How is it that he can speak so to my heart?*

"Fitzroy," Stephen asked, "where did you find these songs? Who wrote them?"

"I write them, milord. There are songs for all occasions."

Indeed there were. Stephen was surprised at the spark of encouragement that arose from hearing this one song, setting his mind not on what had just transpired but on planning the next day, a burgeoning confidence building that, although he did not understand exactly how, somehow he was safe in the King's hands.

Marie's eyes had wandered to the nearby campfire in front of Stephen's tent, where a solitary woman sat, unmoving, gazing into the fire. In the flickering light, through curling smoke, Marie recognized the face of Charis, her face glistening where tears rolled silently as they were formed.

Excusing herself, Marie walked over and took a seat opposite Charis, uncertain whether or how to speak to her.

Finally Marie said, "You have lost your husband and son. I have lost my father and mother. How do you make sense of it?"

Charis did not look up. "I am sorry for your loss, milady," she said quietly.

"As I am for yours," Marie replied. She paused, seeking words. "I thought the Kingdom would not be one of sadness, but one of joy."

Charis lifted her head, her eyes searching the darkness as if for something lost. "It was," she answered wistfully. "I remember how proud William and I were when we first held our baby son. I was proud of William when he led the meetings of the Loynton Servants, and of the man Brian had become. Perhaps I loved them too dearly, for it hurts beyond words that they are gone."

Marie's throat tightened as scenes of her father passed before her—his hearty laugh at supper when he would ask her what she had learned, his pride at the lady she had become, the conversations they'd had when they rode together, the agony of watching him die.

"William and my father were taken by an ugly disease. How does that advance the Kingdom?" Marie said.

Charis lowered her eyes, searching Marie's, her eyes filled no longer with tears but with compassion. "It is my struggle too. No one knows what difficult times await them, but the *Chronicle* assures us they will come and that, as we trust the King for his purpose in them, he will be with us through them. Even after what has happened, and though my sorrow seems as if it will crush me, I believe this."

Charis's words were devoid of comfort for Marie. She still trusted her King too, but she could not understand why he would allow her mother and father to be taken from her—or a child to be taken from his mother.

"I do not see the King's purpose when one is lost through a random event," Marie said, allowing her bitterness to color her voice.

"I did not mean the King purposes the events, but that he makes something purposeful of them," Charis said. "The purpose may be for one who is left behind. It is my hope."

Marie remained silent, contemplating Charis's reply, her eyes fixed on a glowing coal. Shifting her body, she continued, "I do not see any purpose for me in my father's death, for it brings me only sadness and grief." She paused to think. "But I have come to understand that my mother gave her life to save her children and I was told that it was the highest act of love … though I did not appreciate it at the time."

"And though I would gladly have taken the place of my son," Charis responded, "I understand that he gave his life in an act of love as well."

"What do you mean? How can you say that?" Marie asked. "Was it not just a tragic accident? A risk taken that went wrong?"

"No… No, it was not," Charis replied, her voice scarcely audible. "We reared him to love his King. Today we were facing a hopeless situation with the swollen river before us and enemy soldiers behind us. He did not speak of it to me, but I believe he understood the possible consequences and was willing to lay down his life for his King if necessary so that the King's people could be saved, just as your mother did so that you might be saved. There is no greater love than this."

"Dying for the King? That is love?"

"It is what the Kingdom is about, milady—loving the King more than self, his purposes above ours, his people above ourselves," Charis said, "even when the pain seems unbearable."

To Marie, the pain did seem unbearable. What kind of love could bring such pain to those who were left?

Chapter 38

FOOD

S TEPHEN FELL INTO a fatigued slumber inhabited by dreams in which his mind revisited and reassessed the previous day. He had not trusted enough. But the spirit of the Prince had been present anyway. How else would Joel and Daniel have known to come to his rescue? Even Hugh had seemed to play a role. Was it possible that the whole event, the crossing and the rescue, had somehow been guided by the unseen hand of the King?

Sanguine that the new day would be better than the previous, he sat up from the pallet he occupied outside his tent, a cool, gray dawn greeting him and his collection of hungry refugees as they stoked their fires and listened to their stomachs rumble. Surveying the makeshift camp, he hoped there would be no news of more people gone missing in the night. The greatest barrier had been overcome; they were perhaps two days from Bartscastle if they could begin moving in a timely manner. Ahead lay a dense forest, a likely place for an ambush. He sent Daniel and Joel ahead to scout. By the time the people had formed up, the two returned with their report.

"Sire," Joel said, "we rode the entire length of the forest and saw nothing. We should move quickly, however. News of our encounter with Gythreul yesterday will have reached Draignytha. The Dragon may attempt again to prevent our reaching Bartscastle."

"Then let us proceed at once," Stephen said, spurring his horse. "Daniel and Joel, you will ride flank guard through the woods. Tell the archers and swordsmen to walk by the wagons."

Stephen led the way into the dark gloom of the forest. His last memory of it had been different—a sun-dappled pathway chorused by birds as he rode to his new fief near Loynton. But now he was responsible for a group of people he did not fully know. He felt as if he was attempting to herd a group of sheep with Joel and Daniel on the flanks to keep them together.

Marie took her place beside him, her thoughts apparently full of memories as well: "This is where the spirit of the Prince first spoke to me after Sir Bailys tried to take me," she said as they entered the leafy tunnel, now beginning to show colors of yellow and red. "It was the first time I ever felt helpless and alone."

"You are not alone now," Stephen replied, feeling unaccountably tense, his eyes shifting from side to side attempting to penetrate the shadowy forest.

"I wasn't totally alone then either, but my father was lured away from me," Marie said. "I was so frightened."

"I will not leave you, Marie," Stephen said, but his mind was still preoccupied with the road ahead.

Stephen's words were not reassuring to Marie, seeming as though they were just cursory replies ignoring the reality of a major trauma in her young life. True, she believed she was safer beside Stephen, but her thoughts and eyes were also drawn warily to the darkness of the forest. No birds were singing, the clip-clop of the horses' hoofs echoing hollowly off the tree trunks, punctuated by the drip-drip-drip from the moisture-laden boughs. Marie's hand instinctively clutched her bow, as if to be prepared for any unpleasant surprise. She knew there were no fire-breathing dragons in the forest as she had once feared, and that she was in the company of many armed men, but she was aware it might harbor a different sort of Dragon.

Near midday a lighter gray began to show at the end of the forest. Soon they were clear of the woods and approaching the crossroads to Purdyton—only there was no longer a crossroads. In a curve of the road where the former signpost once stood was merely a post with the red dragon shield and a sign pointing to Purdyton. The road to Bartscastle was no longer easily visible, bushes apparently having been planted to obscure it. The road only took a right turn toward Purdyton. By the shield a solitary horseman stood beside a wagon.

Stephen reined in his horse and motioned the column to halt.

The horseman led his wagon to the now stationary and curious rabble. "Good day, milord," said the smiling horseman, clad in shiny armor beneath a white surcoat. "I bring succor to your hungry masses."

Stephen eyed him with suspicion. "Who are you and where are you from?"

"The king has heard of your difficulty and has sent provision. There is enough bread, cheese, and ale in the wagon for all."

The effect was immediate. Word rippled down the line, which quickly became a crowd jostling around the wagon. Stephen could not deny that this met a need. Even he was attempting to suppress his own gnawing hunger.

"Very well," he answered. "You may distribute the food."

Grateful hands snatched the bread and cheese as it was handed out, and people sat in groups to satiate their hunger. Stephen was pleased that everyone would be fed as he watched the horseman pass out the food with a smile while he spoke in a reassuring tone to the recipients.

"Sire, might I speak with you?"

Stephen turned to find Daniel behind him, surveying the scene. "Yes, Daniel. What is it?"

"Sire, what did this man say to you?"

"He said he had brought provision for us from the King. You told me yesterday that the King knows our troubles. Today I have been trying to trust him more. And look!" Stephen motioned to the small groups consuming their bread, cheese, and drink. "He has supplied our needs."

Daniel did not seem to share Stephen's pleasure. "You are aware, sire, that the Dragon calls himself 'king,' are you not?"

"Of course," Stephen answered. "But this man does not wear the colors of the Dragon."

"Neither does he wear the colors of our King," Daniel said.

Stephen was not going to have his mood darkened by Daniel. "So what is your meaning? Be clear about it!" he snapped.

"Milord, the Dragon is a deceiver. His servants may appear as doers of good, even as servants of our King." Daniel looked Stephen in the eye. "Most assuredly this man has come to steal your sheep."

Stephen's chest tightened, constricting his pounding heart. *I have been made a fool!* He spurred his horse to the wagon.

"Stop!" he shouted to the horseman. "Begone!"

The peasants, who had been garrulously enjoying their repast, drew back in disbelief as if witnessing the tirade of a madman. The white-clad horseman wore an expression of shock.

"Take your food and go!" Stephen exclaimed. "You are not from our King!"

The horseman smiled, his blue eyes sparkling. "Sir Stephen, I have fed your hungry people and you treat me like this?"

"You are taking our food away?" a peasant asked, looking at Stephen.

A chorus of protesters joined in:

"How can you do this?"

"Do you want us to starve?"

"Why should we follow you?"

Stephen now faced an angry crowd, growing more hostile by the minute. "This man is an imposter! He is not from the King," Stephen said.

"But he has fed us. And you have not!" one of the protesters cried.

The horseman faced the mass of angry faces. "I will depart as your so-called leader desires, but—" He surveyed the watching eyes. "If you desire full stomachs and freedom from want, you will follow me." He spurred his horse toward Purdyton, the wagon following.

"I am coming," a peasant said, hoisting his cup of ale.

"Me too!" another cried.

"It is more of a sure thing than following you," the miller said as he passed Stephen.

"No!" Stephen shouted. "Do not go with him! That is the way to bondage. I am leading you to freedom and safety."

"You are leading us to danger and starvation," another said, joining the growing queue.

Stephen looked on helplessly as ten of their number, men and women alike, followed the white knight, joking and laughing without even looking back.

"Let them go," Daniel said, having rejoined Stephen. "They never belonged to the King."

"Why then were they with us?" Stephen said. "Is this more of the winnowing?"

"It is," Daniel said. "Many homes and livelihoods were destroyed by the flooding and disease. Some were attracted by the idea of a King who would provide for them, though they had not professed loyalty to him. Others perhaps thought you were leading them to a safer place."

"I am," Stephen replied uncertainly. "Am I not?"

"You are, but the *Chronicle* says that anyone who would be saved from the power of the Dragon must trust the King even in times of difficulty, and that there will be those who fall away in difficult times because they do not trust him."

"Tonight," Stephen said after a moment of reflection, "perhaps I should bring everyone together to make sure all are acquainted with the words of the *Chronicle*, then."

Daniel bowed his head. "A splendid idea, milord."

Stephen dismounted and addressed the remaining members of the party, some still registering doubt on their faces about whether to stay. "I understand that some of you may question the ability of a youth to lead you, but the mantle of leadership has fallen on me because of my title and I have accepted it," he said. "I am led by a King who loves his subjects and desires that all be loyal to him. If you trust your King, you must trust the leader he sets over you." Stephen stopped, aware that he was saying words which he had not even thought before.

Hugh stood up and spoke to the crowd. "His words are true. They come from the *Chronicle*. I have led a group in my village that studies the *Chronicle*."

"Read it to us, then," a voice said.

"Milord?" It was Charis's voice. "May I?"

Stephen turned to see Charis standing behind him with the *Chronicle* in hand. "By all means," Stephen said, then gestured to Charis, still somewhat astonished that he had uttered words from the *Chronicle*.

Charis shuffled through the parchment pages and read the appropriate passages to the listeners.

Then Stephen heard Marie's whispered voice in his ear: "Why are you acting so surprised at your words? Lady Anne taught me that the spirit of the Prince will give us the right words when we need them, even if we do not remember reading them."

Stephen recalled then that he had read from the *Chronicle* many times, both on his own and with Sir Bart, even some with Marie, but it had always seemed like a chore. There were very few of its words he could repeat upon demand, yet he had just done so. Was this the spirit of the Prince again?

When Charis stopped reading, Hugh said, "Sir Stephen is our leader. I, for one, will follow him wherever he leads us." Hugh walked forward to stand beside Stephen.

"As will I," Charis said, "because he follows the true King." She took her place beside him as well.

One by one, others came and stood with Stephen, until only a handful were left sitting. They looked at each other and, as a group, stood and followed those who had preceded them.

"Thank you," Stephen said, humbled by the whole event. "I will do my best, trusting in our King, to deliver us all to the safety of Bartscastle. Now we must continue on."

The ragged but depleted band fell back into column as Stephen picked his way through the brush and downed trees to find the abandoned road to Bartscastle. A way for the wagons was found and soon they were following the grass-overgrown ruts of the old road.

Marie came up alongside Stephen. "The worst is behind us now," she said, "don't you think? This road goes straight to Bartscastle."

Though Stephen was hopeful, he was unwilling to totally relax until his flock was safe. "I would like to think that, Marie," he replied, "but we must not let our guard down."

The journey thereafter was indeed uneventful, passing through patches of woods and beside fallow fields until a grim reminder of the war between kingdoms appeared before them. Stephen reined in his horse before the charred remains of Sir Giles's manor house.

Marie stifled a sob. "I was a guest here twice—such warm hospitality from Lady Margaret," she said, her voice quavering. "And now it is gone. I hope they escaped."

"They did, but this is indeed a sad sight," Stephen answered. "Sir Giles was with me in the castle when the Dragon besieged us. He was fatally wounded; I never knew what happened to his wife." He spurred his horse. "We must not tarry, lest the people become discouraged. There is a field a mile farther where we can make camp."

The specter of war behind them, Stephen led the way out into a field where groups formed to build fires and hunt for food. As before, Stephen designated his tent to be the place for the weakest to sleep and for Charis to tend to sore feet and other ailments. Stephen was gratified that, though they had no food other than a few squirrels and rabbits caught by hunting parties, there was no grumbling this time. A day had passed with no severe challenges or loss of life. As night fell and the fires became small beacons around which several peasants clustered for warmth in the autumn coolness, Stephen allowed himself to envision gaining safety at Bartscastle on the morrow.

Pounding footsteps attracted his attention. Hugh and Thomas appeared, breathless from running.

"Sire!" Hugh puffed. "You must come and see what Thomas has found!"

Fatigued mentally from the tension of being alert for more threats throughout the day, Stephen wanted to relax by the fire; he definitely did not want to take a walk around the encampment in the darkness. "Just tell me," he said.

"No! You must see it!" Hugh said.

Stephen roused his weary body and followed Hugh and Thomas, striding down the road they had just traveled, puzzled by their seeming excitement. They stopped by a dark object.

"This is one of our carts," Stephen said. "You brought me out here for this?"

"It is not ours. The others are accounted for," Hugh said. "And what do you smell?"

Stephen sniffed the night air. "The scent of fresh bread."

"Look!" Hugh said, drawing back the covering.

Inside were baskets filled with bread, cheese, and dried fish, along with a barrel of ale.

"But where did it come from?" Stephen asked. "There is no animal to pull it."

"I was making a circuit of the camp after dark, and I came upon it," Thomas said. "Maybe it is from the white knight?"

"Where is the white knight then?" Stephen said. "You know as well as I that he was sent by the Dragon. And he had no fish. Perhaps it has come from someone else. Look inside again."

Hugh climbed into the wagon and rummaged around. Soon he hopped out, brandishing a piece of parchment. "Look at this!" he said.

"It is the emblem of the King," Stephen said. "Call the people and let us sup."

Stephen passed out the food as one by one each person came for their share. There was more than enough. In fact it seemed as if there was as much after the food was handed out as there had been when Stephen began.

He returned to Marie's tent with hands full of bread, cheese, and fish, taking a seat next to her by the fire.

"What do you make of it?" Marie asked, gladly nibbling a piece of bread with some cheese.

There was something about it that Stephen could not dismiss from his mind. He searched his memory for the particulars. "Something similar happened to me when I was in prison after the Dragon took Bartscastle," he recalled. "A man visited me in prison and left a bag with bread and a skin with water. I never saw who he was, but each day thereafter the bag contained as much bread as the day before and the skin as much water."

"The King was looking after you," Marie said.

"Yes, he said he was from the King," Stephen answered. "And I believe it is the same with this wagon."

"Stephen, do you remember in the *Chronicle*," Marie said, "it says that if the King cares about even the birds and flowers in his kingdom, he cares for us much more?"

"No, you know I don't remember what I read," Stephen said. "But I do know what I have experienced. I asked Hugh to set a guard on the wagon for the night. It will sustain us until we reach Bartscastle."

Stephen and Marie sat by the glowing fire pit in front of her tent, their stomachs full, Stephen feeling both grateful and amazed at the King's provision. Perhaps he should be more trusting. But then, he had been earlier and the white knight had taken advantage of it. How could he always trust his King? As the hour grew late, he lay down in front of Marie's tent, covering himself with his cloak, while Marie went inside. It seemed as if he had hardly gone to sleep when he was awakened by a firm hand on his shoulder.

Hugh's face materialized in the darkness. "Sire!" he whispered.

Stephen sat up, disoriented in the blackness of the night. "What now, Hugh?"

"I want to show you something. Stand up and look behind you."

Stephen turned and peered into the darkness. His heart froze. "When did this happen?" he whispered.

"I was by the wagon. For the past hour or more I have watched it. And still it grows."

In the distance, arranged around in the fields bordering their position, was a semicircle of campfires.

"We are in grave danger," Stephen looked up. "By the look of the sky, morning must be near. Quickly, go and wake everyone. Assemble them and lead them by the wagon to pick up some food. Leave the fires smoldering. Then we must start for Bartscastle without delay. There must be the utmost silence."

Stephen poked his head in the tent to wake Marie.

A few moments later Hugh appeared again, out of breath. "Sire, the food wagon is gone!" he said. "It is my fault. I should never have left it to come to you earlier."

"No matter," Stephen replied. "We must depart immediately! Leave the wagons. We are only a day from Bartscastle."

Stephen rode to find Daniel and Joel. "Daniel, go to Bartscastle and tell them we are near but in danger. Joel, ride rearguard and keep me informed about what you see. It is probably Gythreul again. We must try to make it to Bartscastle before we are attacked!"

Stephen waited as Hugh and Thomas circulated among the sleeping forms to rouse them. Gythreul had promised to return. Stephen had hoped he could get to Bartscastle first, but the agonizingly slow pace of a mostly unarmed rabble on foot accompanying wagons had made it impossible. There was always the chance that the force behind him was only to keep him under observation. He was closer to Bartscastle now. Perhaps that would restrain whoever it was from attacking.

Or perhaps not.

Chapter 39

CORNERED

L OW MURMURS SPREAD among the weary fugitives as they fell into column, once again without full stomachs, and trudged obediently behind Stephen, uncertain why they had been awakened from their rest while it was still night. Stephen led, hoping they would be able to distance themselves from their pursuers in the darkness.

But when the eastern horizon began to display a rosy glow, Joel rode forward with a disturbing message: "Sire, we are being followed by horsemen and men-at-arms. Moreover, some of them are wearing the colors of the Dragon."

Stephen knew they were still too far from Bartscastle to make a run for it. His people were fatigued. Lack of sleep and lack of food had left them weakened. *It is just as I feared. The lot of us will be overwhelmed before Daniel can return with help.*

"What should I do?" Stephen asked, turning to Joel. "Most of our people are unarmed and helpless. Is there a Companion with those behind us?"

"Our pursuers are not threatening us at the moment, and there is no Companion. I would suggest you continue to Bartscastle," Joel said.

Stephen knew that Daniel would not even have reached Bartscastle yet. No help was on the way. But each minute that he could lead his band onward toward their goal would bring them closer to safety. Attempting to suppress a growing unease, he nudged his horse forward, glancing over his shoulder from time to time to see if his enemies had gained on him. They were advancing steadily and inexorably but drawing no closer, as if toying with their prey.

Stephen paused on his way up a small hill, looking back to assess the size of the opposing force behind; he counted perhaps five armored horsemen and twenty archers and swordsmen. *Why are they not attacking? We are certainly unable to resist them.* It did not make sense why they were just following, keeping their distance. But if Stephen's group could reach the outskirts of Bartstown, surely they would not attack.

Stephen crested the hill—and stopped. Now the answer was clear. Three hulking knights in black armor sat on enormous chargers astride the road, their red shields bearing the golden dragon, their closed visors obscuring their faces.

"Companions," Stephen muttered to himself.

He sat on his horse in silence as those behind him came to a stop and began to murmur again. Hugh and Thomas joined him, along with Joel and Marie. No outcome Stephen could imagine was favorable. He was certain the Black Knights would not allow passage, but he would hear them out nevertheless.

He rode forward, Hugh and Thomas following with their bows, then Marie and Joel.

"Marie, you should not risk yourself," Stephen said.

"My place is with you, Stephen," she answered, clearly not to be denied.

The small party came to a halt before the knights. Stephen glanced behind, noting that the pursuers had split into two groups, now moving slowly around each flank.

"Good morrow, Sir Stephen," one of the knights said in a deep throaty voice that echoed inside his helmet.

"Who am I addressing?" Stephen asked, attempting to show no fear.

The center knight raised his visor to reveal two emotionless, startlingly blue eyes that pierced Stephen from within the shadows of the helmet. "You know who I am. I am Gythreul, and you have fallen into my hands again. This time there will be no escape."

Now recognizing the voice of the same knight who had accosted him at the river crossing, Stephen felt already defeated, but he was still the leader of those behind him. Summoning his failing courage he said, "Stand aside and allow us to pass. These people have done nothing to anger you."

Gythreul gave a booming laugh laden with derision. "I am not angry. I offered you a choice before and I offer you one again. You may turn your people around and follow us to Purdyton or be slaughtered where you stand. I place before you life or death—which do you choose?"

The force that had been following Stephen was now assembling behind the knights, all three of whom, visors up, now stared Stephen down as if he were an insect about to be squashed. It was like the event at the river all over again, only there were three Black Knights and many more soldiers. Stephen thought of the lives that trembled behind him. How could he allow them to perish? How could the King allow them to be extinguished? Was this the time for him to lay down his life for the King, as Brian had done? If he surrendered himself, perhaps he could escape or be ransomed again. He made his decision.

"I will go with you if you spare the others," Stephen replied.

"No, Stephen!" Marie gasped. "Do not do this. We need you!"

"Hah! Do you think you can bargain with me?" Gythreul answered. "That was my previous offer. This time it is all of you or none!"

Stephen watched as Gythreul eyed Marie, then he laughed again, a deep hoarse laugh that betokened both immense confidence and utter disdain. "You come against us with women? You are all women! Put down your puny weapons, come with us, and there will be no bloodshed."

Stephen did not know how to answer this threat, his false bravado having been quenched. He was well aware that even with Joel they were no match for three Companions, not to mention the rest of the force behind them. He searched the faces of those with him. He saw no sign of fear. Hugh and Thomas wore an expression of quiet determination, as if they had trust in whatever Stephen's decision would be. Even Marie sat calmly on her horse, an arrow nocked, regarding him with silent confidence. But they also did not know just how overwhelming was the force they faced. Stephen knew that even one Companion could strike all of them down.

"Milord," Joel said quietly, "perhaps we could ride back and have a parley before you make a decision?"

"You are overmatched this time, Joel," Gythreul shouted. "I told you I would return with more. Even *you* cannot overcome three of us."

"Yes," Stephen said. "Give us a short time to consider your proposal."

"Time will not help you," Gythreul said. "It will be hours before Daniel can return with help, if he does at all."

Stephen knew this was true. He took his group aside. It would still buy time. He searched Joel's eyes for a sign of hope. "Do you have something to say, Joel? Is he not correct that we are outnumbered and overmatched?"

"He is not," Joel said, "for you have a power behind you that he does not, if you claim it. He does not want you to realize that you do; therefore he is trying to intimidate you into believing your only strength is what you possess yourself. There is power that you cannot see."

"The power of the King?" Stephen asked. "Where is it, then?"

"You must call on it," Joel answered. "If you call on the power of the King, neither your adversary nor his force, overwhelming though it may seem, can resist you."

"I wish I could trust in that now," Stephen said, looking back at the army arrayed against him. "I want to. But how?"

"You *can*, Stephen," Marie said, grasping his hand. "Look at the faces of your followers. They believe in you. They trust in the King. I trust in the King. You must trust him also."

"I-I don't hear the voice like I did before," Stephen said, swallowing audibly to keep his pounding heart from jumping into his throat. "I am just—not—sure."

The sound of a harp announced the approach of Fitzroy.

"Allow me to go with you, sire. I will sing you a song for the occasion."

"A song? When we are faced with certain death?" Stephen sighed, astonished at Fitzroy's apparent failure to appreciate the gravity of the situation. "A song will not overcome these knights. Do not risk yourself too, Fitzroy."

"My life has been placed at risk before, milord. I am familiar with danger," Fitzroy said.

The heavy burden of expectation threatening to crush him, a cold sweat on his brow, Stephen could not decide what to do. All eyes were on him. They trusted him. He could not fail them. As hopeless as his situation appeared, he did not know how it could turn out otherwise, but he decided that he would not turn his people over to the Dragon. This was not the way or the time he thought his life would end, but voice or no voice, he would die trusting his King.

"All right," he said finally. "We are going to stand for our King. Fitzroy, you may come. And, Joel, you and Daniel rescued us at the river crossing; would you fight by Marie's side and protect her?"

"No, sire," Joel answered. "You do not need me this time."

"What?" Stephen shook his head. "But you alone are worth one or two of the Black Knights! I am not asking you to protect me, but are you just going to sit there and watch us all be cut down?"

"Remember in whom you have placed your trust, milord. If you do not stand firm in your trust, you will not stand at all."

Stephen gaped in dismay while Joel spurred his horse away, turning his back on the suddenly weaker group of defenders. As they turned around to retrace the short distance to the waiting Black Knights, Stephen was certain that he was experiencing his last moments alive. He reached out to draw Marie close.

"I die loving you," he whispered.

"And I will be at your side—always," Marie responded quietly.

Fitzroy began to sing:

> "My King is my rock,
> In whom I take refuge.
> I call to my King
> And I am saved from my enemies.
>
> "The King thunders
> From his castle.
> The voice of the Most High
> Resounds.
>
> "He shoots his arrows
> And scatters the enemies,
> Great bolts of lightning
> And routs them.
>
> "It is my King who
> Arms me with strength
> He trains my hands for battle.
>
> "He gives me
> His shield of victory.
> His right hand sustains me.
>
> "The battle belongs to the King!"

By the time Fitzroy finished his song, they had stopped before the Black Knights, whose horses had begun to stamp and become skittish. A brisk wind had stirred up, whipping through the trees on either side of the road, cracking branches and releasing bursts of autumn leaves into the air. The knights took no notice of Stephen's pitiful force; their faces were now turned upward, their eyes focused on the sky as low, dark clouds roiled in.

"We will fight you!" Stephen shouted in the strongest voice he could muster. "We come against you with the power of the King!" He raised his sword.

A peal of thunder drowned out his voice as lightning flashed, a bolt smashing into a nearby tree, splitting it in half. The enemy soldiers began to shift their feet; a horse reared, almost throwing off one of the Black Knights.

"Steady, men," Gythreul roared, his pale eyes blazing defiance. "They cannot resist us. Strike them down!"

Three arrows flew: from Hugh, Thomas, and Marie, each knocking a sword from the hand of a Black Knight. The two Black Knights flanking Gythreul exchanged glances as the wind strengthened, now moaning palpably around those standing, causing them to brace themselves so that they would not be blown off their feet. The helpless peasants had all dropped to the ground, covering their heads. Another peal of thunder rumbled, followed by a bolt of lightning that struck a bush by the road next to the Black Knights, bursting it into flame. The soldiers behind the knights began to melt away.

Each of the Black Knights had dismounted and retrieved his sword, but their attention now was fixed on Fitzroy, as was Stephen's—seeing the minstrel's hands outstretched toward the sky. Lightning flashed again, revealing an expression of terror on the faces of the Black Knights.

Stephen stood his ground, his sword held high. Recalling Fitzroy's song, he shouted, "The battle belongs to the King!"

He nudged his horse forward, whereupon the Black Knights hurried to remount, then turned their horses and galloped away, as if they could not put distance between themselves and Fitzroy fast enough. In moments the entire enemy force had vanished.

Stephen watched them go, then realized he was spent, his body so tensed that he had neither moved nor scarcely breathed. He leaned over his horse, limp with fatigue, his sword sliding from his hand to the ground as he attempted to comprehend what he had just witnessed.

He heard Hugh and Thomas already trading comments.

"Did you see that?" Hugh asked excitedly.

"What just happened?" Thomas replied.

"I do not know, but somehow we were saved," Hugh said.

Then Stephen felt Marie's arm around his now trembling body. He looked at her. "I almost did not trust him," he choked. "I am so sorry."

"But you did. Even when our trust fails, he is trustworthy," Marie said. "Lady Anne taught me that."

"I need to talk to Fitzroy," Stephen blurted, his mind still attempting to understand what had just occurred.

Already the wind was dying down; thunder and lightning had ceased. The peasants, most of whom were still on the ground in fright, were slowly, anxiously, beginning to stir. Stephen found Fitzroy talking to Joel.

"Your song," Stephen said. "It was as if you knew what would happen."

Fitzroy smiled. "It is a good song for such an occasion, is it not?"

Stephen still felt confused. "But what actually happened?"

Joel spoke. "What you saw was the power of the King, which no one can resist. That is why you did not need me."

"Many things in the Kingdom are unseen," Fitzroy added, "but no less real."

Stephen sensed that there was something about Fitzroy he did not fully perceive, yet he could not figure what it could be. This brown-skinned minstrel had joined their party uninvited, he sang songs that comforted, even encouraged Stephen, he knew what was on Stephen's map, and somehow he had been involved in vanquishing Gythreul and his army. Had he been sent by the King? He did not have the appearance of a Guardian. Who was he?

Feeling his strength returning, Stephen rode back to Hugh and Thomas, who were helping some of the weaker peasants to their feet.

"Hugh," Stephen said, "we will take a moment to rest and recover. There is still time to reach Bartscastle by nightfall."

While everyone gathered into small groups to share their impressions of the remarkable event they had experienced, Marie dismounted to inspect the smoking bush, its coals still glowing. As she peered at it, she noticed Hugh and Thomas approaching.

"That was an impressive shot, milady," Hugh said, "with such a tiny bow."

"Yes indeed," agreed Thomas.

Marie looked from Hugh to Thomas. *Are they complimenting me? Or mocking me?*

"I do not possess a bow like yours, but with it I could do the same," she said.

Hugh laughed, then covered his mouth. "No offense, milady, but I do not think so. My bow is taller than you are."

So they are mocking me.

"Give me the bow and an arrow," Marie demanded.

As she took them from Hugh, she thought, *He might be right.*

But she was undeterred. The bow was so long it felt unwieldy in her hands. She nocked an arrow and lifted the bow off the ground, straining to draw the string to her ear. Try as she might, she could not.

She could see Hugh and Thomas watching, hands over their mouths, surely hiding grins.

Finally Marie turned and shoved the bow into Hugh's hands. "All right!" she said. "You have succeeded in embarrassing me!"

"Milady," Hugh said, "that was not my inten—"

"But I assure you that I can place three arrows in a target with my bow as well as you can with yours!" Marie said.

Hugh shook his head. "Please, milady. There is no need for that. Your accuracy with the Black Knights was as good as ours. We did not know you overheard us discussing what to do nor did we expect you to succeed with the third knight. We were both surprised and pleased. We came to compliment you."

Marie had already nocked an arrow in her shortbow as if to prove her statement in an immediate competition. She slowly relaxed her draw. "Very well," she said, but still smarting from her rather public humiliation. "I accept your words. But I am still willing to prove mine."

"No, no, milady," Hugh said. "We will gladly count you as one of us without the demonstration."

Marie forced a thin smile. "I accept your compliment, then."

The sun was approaching noonday by the time Stephen had his charges rested, on their feet, and ready to move. They had no wagons to slow them down, having left them behind in the camp, and although he believed they were safe now, Stephen did not think it advisable to go back to their camp to retrieve them. It would be near sundown when they reached Bartscastle anyway.

The hungry, unsettled group fell into column as Stephen led, but he heard no grumbling, awed as they were by the recent events. The sun was halfway to the horizon when Stephen spotted a crowd coming from the opposite direction, led by three horsemen. As they were backlit, he could not make out faces, though they did not appear threatening. Eventually they were close enough that he recognized Sir Ralf, Michael, and Daniel as the horsemen, followed by a number of men-at-arms and archers.

"We came as fast as we could," Sir Ralf said, "though Daniel surmised correctly, it seems, that you would not need us."

"Thankfully that is the case," Stephen said. "But I am still heartened that you came."

Sir Ralf then nodded to Marie. "Good day, milady."

"It seems I only see you when you come to rescue me, Sir Ralf," Marie said, smiling.

"You appear prepared to rescue yourself, milady," said Sir Ralf, nodding downward at Marie's bow, which she still had in hand.

"Oh," she said, "a habit now." She slid the bow back into its case.

Stephen noticed Michael's eyes on him; they had not seen each other in almost a year.

"Good day, sire," Michael said. "You have perhaps learned something about the King today— and about yourself?"

Aware now that he had brought his followers to safety, Stephen allowed himself to relax. "Yes," he said. "I have seen that it is better to depend on the King than on myself." He glanced at Marie. "And that he is trustworthy." He looked back at Michael and sighed. "But I wish I were not repeatedly given situations such as this in which to trust him."

Michael's face broke into a rare smile. "You are perhaps aware that he promises he will not forsake us when we face more than we think we can bear, milord?"

Stephen exhaled. "Apparently he knows me better than I know myself." Turning to Sir Ralf, Stephen said, "We should keep moving, sire. My people have not eaten today and some have fallen ill."

"Yes," Sir Ralf replied. "I alerted Lady Anne before we left to expect sick and wounded." Looking at Marie, he said, "She asked if you were in the group, milady. Daniel said you were."

"It will be good to see her again, and I will gladly help her care for our sick," Marie said.

Stephen's flock fell in line behind Sir Ralf's soldiers as they began their trek back to Bartscastle, coming into view of the houses of Bartstown as the sun touched the western horizon. Curious onlookers stopped to watch the strangers move through their streets down to the bridge over the river. Seeing the familiar towers of Bartscastle in the distance, Stephen was flooded with a sense of relief and peace. His people were safe, his burden lifted; he was safely home.

"I spent ten years of my life here at Bartscastle," he said to Marie, "and seven years before that in Bartstown. It is my home, yet so much has happened since I left."

"Only two years for me," Marie said, "and I have no home now."

As they rode across the drawbridge, Stephen noted that the gate tower had been repaired and the gate now bore the banner of Sir Ralf—royal blue and white with a gold helmet surmounted by a scarlet crest. They rode into the courtyard and Stephen dismounted. The castle looked the same, yet it felt different. Not long past, he had been a freshly created knight, eager to serve his King. His eyes went to the keep, where he had been educated by Sir Bart, to the place in the courtyard where Sir Bart fell, to the place where he was forced to kneel to the Dragon, and to the keep again, in whose dungeon he almost died. How many had lost their lives in that siege and its aftermath? Would Bartscastle ever feel the same again? How many lives had been lost in his fief and on the journey? Would he ever be the same again?

Waiting in the courtyard was Lady Anne, almost in the same place she had stood when Marie first arrived at Bartscastle. Marie dismounted and ran to her, holding her in a silent embrace, fighting tears. Marie realized she was home too.

Chapter 40

BARTSCASTLE ASTIR

S TEPPING BACK FROM their embrace, Lady Anne eyed Marie's leather jerkin. "Welcome back, Lady Marie. And you are dressed just as you were when you left."

"It is so good to see you," Marie said, then once again embraced her—this time as a mother—for she had seemed as one during Marie's two years there.

"You will share my quarters as you did before," Lady Anne said.

"Thank you," Marie answered, "and I long to see how Edouard is."

Lady Anne's face saddened. "I am sorry to tell you that shortly after your father left, Edouard became ill. I nursed him as best as I could, but he did not survive."

"No!" Marie gasped. "Edouard too?"

"We sent word to your father," Lady Marie said. "But perhaps the message did not reach you?"

Feeling the prick of tears as her eyes welled up, Marie faced the awareness now that she alone was the last. "Father is gone as well." She sighed. "I have no family left."

Marie watched as Lady Anne's eyes went to Stephen, who stood conversing with Sir Ralf.

"But are you not wife to Sir Stephen?" Lady Anne asked. "We heard—"

"Betrothed. We are handfast," Marie replied, looking down. "A wedding in one of the King's castles was envisioned, but after all that has happened—"

"I am sorry," Lady Anne said. "Come, I will prepare some tea and we can talk further while the others are being shown the quarters they will occupy, and the sick are given shelter in the chapel."

Marie entered the common room where she had spent many hours before, a crackling fire welcoming her, musical instruments and a hand loom positioned as if ready for her to resume her education. Lady Anne brought cups and steaming tea to the table, where each pulled up a chair, Marie's spirits dampened by the news that another piece of her life had been torn from her. *Why Edouard?* The room that had appeared warm and inviting when she walked in now seemed cold and austere. Her eyes explored the contents again. She saw dust on the loom and musical instruments.

"Do you not have a lady-in-training?" Marie asked.

"No, I do not," Lady Anne said. "We have had difficult times here too. After you and your father left, the castle came under siege by the Dragon himself. Sir Bart and Sir Giles lost their lives in that siege, and the Dragon took over the castle. It was a terrible time. Some were imprisoned, including Sir Stephen and Squire Mark, who died of starvation and cold. I was forced to care for the Dragon's wounded, which I gladly would have done voluntarily. But I was not allowed to mention the true King in their presence, though I believed I was serving my King in caring for them."

"I am sorry to hear about Sir Bart and Sir Giles," Marie said. "We passed the ruins of Sir Giles's manor house on the way. I enjoyed two nights of their hospitality journeying to and from Bartscastle. Is Lady Margaret well?"

"Alas, milady, she was also taken in the Great Dying."

Marie slumped. "I will miss her. And how did the castle come back into the King's hands?"

"I do not know," Lady Anne replied, then took a sip of her tea. "One day, after his men had recovered from their wounds, I saw the Dragon assemble many soldiers in the courtyard, and then they marched out, perhaps to capture another castle?"

"So you were left alone?"

"Almost. The kitchen staff had remained to serve the Dragon, and our steward, Owen, took charge of all castle staff. You remember him, don't you? Later the same day Sir Ralf and Michael returned with some soldiers, and Sir Ralf claimed the castle as his."

Marie sipped her tea. "I would ask a favor of you, milady. There is someone I would like you to meet."

"Gladly," Lady Anne replied.

"I hope you will learn to appreciate her as I have," Marie said.

She hurried out into the courtyard, returning with an arm around her newest friend.

"This is Charis of Loynton," Marie said, observing Charis as she introduced her. Charis stood quietly in her soiled clothing, her weathered face bearing lines of sorrow and loss. "Along the way she has lost everything, but she has cared for everyone. It would be a happiness for me if she could stay here with us."

Lady Anne needed no prompting, holding both hands out to Charis. "You are the one who nursed Sir Ralf back to health, are you not?"

Charis lifted eyes that seemed old and tired, as if dimmed by sadness, yet Marie knew that within them were deep springs feeding luminous pools which could not be dimmed, pools of compassion and love.

"I am, milady," Charis answered, lowering her head deferentially.

"Sir Ralf has told many, including me, that you saved his life in more ways than one," Lady Anne said.

"I merely cared for him as I would my own, milady," Charis replied softly.

"And in so doing," Lady Anne said, "you loved your King by loving one who was your enemy. He was your enemy then, was he not?"

"I am told he was, milady" Charis answered, "but I did not think him so. To me he was a wounded man placed in my care to be nursed to health and told about the King."

"And thereby he was rescued from the kingdom of darkness and brought into the true Kingdom," Lady Anne said. "It would be my privilege to have you live with us. There is another room next to Marie's. And you will sup with us as well after you both have had time to rest. I will find you some fresh clothing."

"Milady?" Charis spoke in a voice that was scarcely audible.

"Yes, Charis?" Lady Anne said.

"Forgive my presumption, but I feel as if I have been given special treatment compared to those still in the courtyard, some of whom are injured and unwell. What will happen to them?"

Marie watched, blinking back a tear as Lady Anne took Charis's hands again, smiling empathetically. "We have already prepared places for them in the keep and in the chapel. They will be fed by the castle kitchen tonight. You may accompany me when I visit them tomorrow to supervise the care of the sick and the weakened."

It was dark when Lady Anne knocked on Marie's door. Both she and Charis had fallen asleep immediately upon reaching their rooms. The irresistible aroma of roast pheasant with carrots and onions wafted into Marie's nose as she descended to the common room. Charis followed soon after, looking somewhat embarrassed in the simple but fine gown Lady Anne had provided. Conversation resumed as they eagerly partook of the repast with some fresh bread and wine.

"I have had only one other young lady since you departed, Lady Marie," Lady Anne said, "and we had to smuggle her out to her family after the fall of the castle. Then, shortly after Sir Ralf came, he said there would be no more young ladies."

"Why?" Marie asked.

"He had been back to see the King. I think he knew something was going to change. He sometimes spoke of the last days of Bartscastle, though I do not know what he meant. There have been preparations in the castle as if someone was going on a journey. Carts and supplies are being brought in. There is a rumor that it is the gathering of the King's loyal subjects spoken of in the *Chronicle*."

Marie sighed. "That is what I was told when I was advised to leave Maison Bonfrere. I suppose I should feel excited about it. But I have lost so much, I just want to be still for a while and feel safe." She realized that she had just been pushing her food around her plate, unable to take a bite. "I hoped our journey was over and that I would stay here awhile. I feel so tired."

"We are not departing soon," Lady Anne said softly. "You will have time to rest."

Rest. That was what Marie needed—time to assimilate and ponder the events of the past few months. Her world had been overturned and she had lost her moorings, swept by the flow of fugitives from tragedy at home through the trials of the journey. She had tried to maintain trust in her King and be an encouragement to Stephen, but it had drained her. Soon there would be more striving again, more fleeing from the Dragon. How different—and unexpected—her life seemed now compared to when she had departed Bartscastle just over a year ago.

"When I left here before," she reminisced without emotion, "I was full of excitement about the Kingdom and serving the King. But since then it seems like there has been nothing but trouble and loss, as if the King is not in control of his Kingdom."

Lady Anne offered a sympathetic smile. "I know it does seem that way. The King has displayed immeasurable patience with the rebellion of the Dragon, and though I trust he will be victorious, I must remember that he does not promise we will be free of trouble."

"Look at what has happened, though!" Marie said. "You have lost your brother, Charis her husband and children, and I have lost my entire family. These are not trivial losses. I would not term it 'trouble.'" Marie bit her lip, lest even darker thoughts escape.

Charis, who had been silently enjoying the meal and listening, now spoke: "What comes after the loss is peace, if you can receive it." Her voice was quiet, tinged with resignation but still firm with conviction.

Marie shook her head. "When everything is taken from you, how can you have peace? It hurts beyond words."

"Charis is right," Lady Anne said. "When you are focused only on your loss, there is no peace. The peace comes in knowing the King is fulfilling his purpose in that loss."

"As he did with the sacrifice of my son," Charis said. "And his son."

Marie did not want to think about "sacrifice." Her losses were real, personal—and painful. "But what about your husband and my father and brother, Charis? Where is the King's purpose in the Great Dying?"

"There were two daughters as well." Charis was silent for a moment, thoughtful as always. "I cannot presume to speak for the King," she said finally, "but I cannot allow bitterness to stain my trust in his goodness. I must believe that William had fulfilled his purpose for the King, and perhaps your father and brother had too. William poured himself and his love for the King into me and all our children. Perhaps before he was taken, your father did the same for you?"

Marie felt deflated now, as if all breath and energy had been sucked out of her. She lowered her head, scenes of her father's earnest face and his heartfelt words fleeting before her mind's eye: "There are many things in life we do not desire, yet we must do them... What do you know about love? We learn how to love... Our role is to serve the King however he wishes. The Kingdom does not promise us freedom from pain... When you truly desire what the King desires, he will give you the desires of your heart."

All those conversations would never happen again. *That is what he was doing—pouring himself into me.* Tears began to well up, sliding unimpeded down Marie's cheeks. *I miss him so.*

Momentarily swallowing her sorrow and frustration, Marie blotted her cheeks and sighed. "Yes, maybe he did. But I thought it would last so much longer—I wanted it to. I do not feel prepared to go on without him."

"But you still have something we all have, something which can never be taken from us," Lady Anne said.

Marie knew what Lady Anne meant. She could see her father's mouth forming the words, "The spirit of the Prince."

The next morning Stephen received a message that Sir Ralf was convening a council of leaders in the great hall. As he descended the stairs, Stephen was surprised to see Fitzroy coming down as well.

"Are you joining us, Fitzroy?" Stephen questioned.

"Yes. Sir Ralf wished that I play some music for his guests."

They entered the hall together. Michael, Daniel, and Joel were already leaning over the lord's table, where Sir Ralf, his arms outstretched, examined a map. He looked up in acknowledgement as they entered, Stephen experiencing the odd sensation of remembering many meals with Sir Bart at this same table in this same room. He glanced around. Seemingly nothing had changed. The Kingdom Rules still adorned the back wall. The Dragon apparently had not taken the time to remove them. A fire crackled in the fireplace behind Sir Ralf.

"Welcome," Sir Ralf said, looking up from the table. "Please play a song for us, Fitzroy."

Fitzroy took a seat in a corner and began to tune his harp while Stephen advanced to the table. Before him was a map, not like the one he possessed, but one of the actual countryside. He noted the names of *Bartscastle* and *Bartstown*. His eyes strayed around the edges, coming to rest on *Grandvil*, then *Maison Bonfrere* and *Loynton*. He had never seen such a map before.

Sir Ralf seemed to take note of Stephen's expression of amazement. He said, "Sir Stephen, this is a copy of the map that is drawn on a wall of the great hall in the Dragon's castle. On it he displays his conquests and his goals for new ones as he grows his kingdom." Sir Ralf rested his hand to the north of Bartscastle. "These lands are all his." He swept his hand to the east and down past Loynton and Grandvil. "These he has recently taken." He rested his hand south of Bartscastle. "He is moving now to besiege the castle of Sir John here. Soon our only route of escape will be to the west."

Stephen was taken aback. "Sire, this is discouraging news indeed. I do not understand why the King does not send his army now, especially to help one of his inner circle."

"Do you forget the reason for your recent journey here?" Sir Ralf said. "Property and possessions have no importance when the King gathers his subjects. All those who followed you here gave up everything but what they could carry. And you have lost your fief, have you not?"

Stephen slumped into a chair. He had been a landed knight for less than a year and now he was a fugitive. "I thought we were coming here to safety." He sighed. "But there is only more danger. I am tired of running from the Dragon. I would rather die in battle for my King than continue to run."

Sir Ralf looked up with pursed lips. "Mmm... You may well have that opportunity...as may I. Tomorrow Daniel and Joel will be returning to the King, as the fiefs under their watch have been abandoned to the Dragon. We will continue preparations to journey westward ourselves."

"What are you saying?" Stephen said, jumping to his feet. "And abandon Bartscastle without a fight? Sir Bart shed his blood to defend this castle, and I—"

"And you gave it up," Sir Ralf interrupted.

"At least I fought for it!" Stephen retorted.

"Careful, Sir Stephen," Sir Ralf said. "I am lord of Bartscastle now. Do not presume to know what the King desires of me!"

Stephen bit his lip. "Then what does the King desire of you? And how do you know?"

Sir Ralf paused as if retrieving a recent memory. "Do you remember the supper you had with Michael and me after you were released from prison upon our arrival?"

"Yes, vaguely," Stephen answered.

"After my escape from the Dragon's castle, I did not know where to go. We rode for a day until our horses were exhausted. We were a day from Bartscastle, but I feared to approach because I was a sworn enemy. Michael found me and the few who were with me, and brought us to Sir Bart, who welcomed us. While there I received a message that the King wished to see me."

"And did you go the King's castle?" Stephen asked.

"Not then," Sir Ralf replied. "Although I did later."

"So you have seen the King's castle? The one where he lives?"

"Few are invited to see it, but yes, I did. It is immense and beyond description."

"Did you actually see the King?" Stephen asked.

"It is said that no one can look upon the King's face and live, but I was brought into his court and into his presence. He was high on a throne, but his face was in shadow. He told me many things, some of which I cannot repeat, but the main reason he summoned me was to give me a mission."

"Part of which you were carrying out by rescuing me?"

Sir Ralf nodded. "Yes. Just as I was a trusted subordinate of the Dragon, I now serve as a trusted subordinate of the King, as a member of his inner circle. Just as I once seized domains for the Dragon's kingdom, my mission was to enlarge the King's Kingdom, traveling throughout his lands, encouraging the knights who serve him, seeking new ones who would come to his banner, even spreading the news about him as Charis did while I remained in my stupor."

"That would sound odd coming from the mouth of the Rat," Stephen said.

"It would indeed." Sir Ralf chuckled. "But I am not responsible for how they respond to it. The King knows who is ready to hear it. I am just the messenger, as you are—are you not?"

"Yes, I am supposed to be," Stephen said, looking down as if embarrassed, "but you have caught me being a poor example, distrusting the King and questioning his purpose."

"One thing he revealed to me was the imminence of the gathering of his people and the assembling of his army for a final battle with the Dragon. The call came first to his inner circle. That is why you received a message to come here. But there is farther still to go, and that is why we must leave Bartscastle to the Dragon."

"It seems odd to me that the King is giving up his lands just to retake them. And you just told me you were given a mission to enlarge his Kingdom. How do those relate to each other?"

"First, you must remember that lands and castles do not constitute his Kingdom," Sir Ralf said. "Your mission and mine—to find hearts prepared for his Kingdom—still stands. Second you may recall from the *Chronicle* that notice of the gathering would come without warning to those who are ready, and replace any plans we might have regarding defense of lands and castles."

"Yes," Stephen said, remembering the message from Sir Ralf. "It came so suddenly, in the midst of the turmoil of the Great Dying and a flood. I hardly had time to know my fief before I had to leave it." Stephen paused to reflect. "But in a way it was a relief at the time, as I was faced with so many troubles."

"It should be a relief," Sir Ralf said, "because it means the King is stirring his forces to put an end to the Dragon's rebellion. He is gathering his people from all over his realm, so we must journey west to meet him. There is no time to waste."

"The rest of the King's lands are unknown to me," Stephen said. "How will we know where to go?"

Sir Ralf turned back to the map. "A road leads west over the Stony Mountains to a place called High Rock." He placed a finger on the edge of the map. "The King's army will assemble here, and here we will come under his protection. You will follow me as rearguard."

"When will we depart?" Stephen asked, hoping it would not be soon, longing for time to rest and recover from his harrowing journey.

"As soon as possible. If we can be on our way before Sir John's castle falls, we may avoid being trapped as the pincers close."

"The pincers?" Stephen cringed. "It is that serious?" The vision of icy fingers closing around Stephen's heart sent a chill through his body.

As Sir Ralf shared his thoughts while pointing here and there at the map, the sound of Fitzroy's voice rose above them:

"My King is my stronghold.
Of whom shall I be afraid?

"When evil men advance against me,
When my enemies and my foes attack me,
Though an army besiege me,
My heart will not fear.

"One thing I ask of my King,
That I may dwell in his castle.
For in the day of trouble,
He will keep me safe
And set me high upon a rock."

"Well sung, Fitzroy," Sir Ralf said. He turned back to those at the table. "Good travels, Joel and Daniel."

Everyone bade their farewells to the two Guardians, and then Sir Ralf said, "Michael and Sir Stephen, I would be honored if you would sup with me tonight."

Michael nodded and said, "Of course, milord."

"Yes, certainly," Stephen said. "What about Fitzroy?"

"I am departing also, milord," Fitzroy replied. "Another mission."

"Mission?" Stephen asked.

"I serve the King. I go where he desires and do what he wishes."

"Allow me to walk with you, then," Stephen said, nodding to Sir Ralf and then Michael.

As Stephen and Fitzroy descended the spiral staircase to the courtyard, Stephen's curiosity overcame his reticence. This might be the last time he saw Fitzroy, after all. So he asked, "You serve the King? Have you ever sung for the King?"

"I have," Fitzroy answered.

"In his court?"

"In his court."

"Was joining my group one of your missions?"

"It was."

They reached the exit to the courtyard. Stephen still felt intrigued by this man, his songs and the reaction of the Companions in his presence—and there was something else.

"Your voice reminds me of someone I met before," Stephen said, "but he said he was a priest, and I doubt he could sing and play a harp like you."

Stephen's eyes lingered on Fitzroy's face. He was reluctant to see Fitzroy leave. He would miss the songs, which always seemed to fit the occasion. He wanted to spend more time with him, to learn more about who he was.

"Could I ask you one last question?" Stephen said.

"Yes, milord?"

"More than once you have caught me gazing at your face—actually your forehead. There is a jagged row of scars there. I can't help but wonder how..."

Fitzroy ran his fingers over his forehead. "Oh, those." He smiled. "One of my missions. My brow became entangled in thorns while I was retrieving something of inestimable value to the King."

Chapter 41

TRANSFORMATION

HUGH, LIKE THE others, was relieved to have reached the safety of a castle, but after a few days with no smithy of his own, he volunteered to help in the castle smithy, forging arms of war. Even that was not enough to calm his restlessness, so, determined to use the rest of his time maintaining his skills of war, he and Thomas set up straw targets in the former jousting field to practice their archery, inviting any who were interested to join them. One of the first to notice was Sir Ralf, who appeared at the archery butts one afternoon.

"Your initiative has not gone unnoticed, Hugh," the knight said. "We will need to train every able-bodied man to use a weapon, because the Dragon will attempt to draw us into battle if he catches us. Michael is training some in swordsmanship and use of the spear. I would like you to train men in the use of both the longbow and shortbow. All will be given a choice to learn swordsmanship, spearcraft, or archery. You will work with those who choose the latter."

"You honor me, sire," Hugh answered. "But mastering the longbow may require more time than we have, not to mention the time it would take Thomas to make more longbows."

"I am aware of that," Sir Ralf replied. "We have a few longbows in the armory, but every man who chooses archery must be able to shoot a bow even if it is a shortbow. You must do what you can."

"Gladly, sire. I will work in the smithy each morning and gather the men for archery instruction each afternoon."

"You will have a week or two at most," Sir Ralf said, then walked away.

After the call had been issued for weapons instruction, Hugh divided his archery volunteers into two groups. Those who had used a bow before, he assigned to Thomas to improve their skills. Those who had never handled a bow, he took himself. Eventually they had a total of twenty: eight working with Thomas, twelve novices with Hugh. Toward the end of the first week, an unexpected visitor surprised Hugh.

"May I practice with you?" Marie asked, shortbow in hand, a quiver of arrows over her shoulder. "Otherwise I will have to sit with Lady Anne and weave all day."

Hugh stifled a chuckle. How should he answer the request of a noble lady who wished to be among the men? He had forgotten neither her humiliating failure with the longbow nor her expert shot with her shortbow. "Of course, milady," Hugh answered. "You have certainly earned a place with us. In fact you may help me teach these men the shortbow."

Marie took a group of six archers aside, all of them noticeably reluctant to be instructed by a lady—especially a noble lady, no doubt. Their truculence disappeared after she placed three arrows in a tight pattern first at twenty-five paces and then fifty paces.

"I do not expect you to do this after only a few days' practice," she said, "but you must develop a steady arm, a steady draw, and measured breathing if your shot is to be true. When many arrows are shot by many men, some will find their mark."

Marie watched as her pupils shot their arrows, giving individual instruction to correct angle of fire and aim. She caught Hugh stealing a glance from time to time.

At day's end he strode over to her as she was practicing on her own. "Watching you and listening to your instructions," he said, "I believe your men may perform as well as mine."

"They will perform better," she answered without looking at him, then released an arrow.

"Those are careless words, milady," Hugh replied, "if you will forgive my presumption. I have used a bow to hunt game since I was a child."

"The question is not how well you can shoot *your* bow, but how well you can instruct others to shoot *their* bows," Marie said, smiling politely. "I will pit my men against yours in two days to prove it."

"Agreed!" Hugh said.

Over the next two days Marie used all her focused energy and encouragement to keep the attention of her pupils and mold them into a group anxious to please her and perform well, noting that Hugh tended to become frustrated with his men, frequently berating them for not trying hard enough.

At the end of the second day, two targets were set up at fifty paces. Hugh and Marie agreed that whichever team had the most arrows in the target after two rounds would be the winner.

Marie took her men aside and looked them in the eye. "Remember what I have taught you." She smiled. "And that you want me to be proud of you."

She listened as Hugh gathered his men and pointed at her group. "Those men have been trained by a lady," he said, laughing. "You are not going to let a lady beat you, are you?"

Marie was disappointed after the first round. Only two of her six had put arrows in the target. Three of Hugh's men had done the same. One of her men—though clearly the oldest—seemed to have learned the technique quite well, however.

She took him aside. "What is your name, sir?" she asked.

"Piers—my name is Piers," he said.

Marie gathered the others around her. "Watch carefully how Piers shoots his arrow and try to do the same. Take your time, aim carefully, and correct what did not work the first time. Make me proud of you."

The second round began. Piers placed his arrow in the center of the target again. After five shots, each group had placed three arrows. The last of each group took aim. Marie's archer hit the top of the target. She looked to Hugh's target. There was no arrow in it. They were tied at six arrows apiece. Hugh appeared to be disappointed.

Marie approached Hugh. "To break the tie, I suggest that you and I place an arrow in our targets and select one of our men. The man who places his arrow closest to ours is the winner."

"Agreed," Hugh responded. Clearly, he was not going to be shown up by a lady.

Both Marie and Hugh placed their arrows in the center of their targets. "Piers," Marie called. "Can you place an arrow next to mine?"

"I will do my best for you, milady," he replied.

Both men stepped to the line; both hit their targets. But Piers's arrow hit the bull's eye again, coming to rest an inch from Marie's.

Hugh, though obviously surprised by the outcome, proved a gracious loser. "Once again I have underestimated you, milady. It is most unusual to find a lady who understands and is skilled in the arts of war. I must learn not to doubt you. I am grateful for the instruction you gave my archers, though I hope they are not called upon to use it."

"As do I," Marie said, though from what she had heard from Stephen and others, it seemed that would not be the case.

As the castle prepared for the departure of its occupants, one of Stephen's assignments was to decide what to do with the prisoners. Sir Ralf had tasked him with determining whether to execute them, leave them in prison, or release them. There was no question of taking them along. They would be extra mouths to feed and would have to be guarded lest they escape. He descended to the dungeon under the keep to find out who was there and why. Arriving at the heavy door and grasping a torch to enter, he was reminded of one of his most desperate times, during which he had despaired even of life. Had it not been for that unseen priest and his gift, Stephen would almost certainly have died there. He knew he could not execute anyone and was surprised that Sir Ralf even mentioned it. Perhaps vestiges of the Rat still remained. But Stephen decided he would still use the threat as a tool.

His torch illuminating the rows of wooden doors with their small grated openings, Stephen called out, "Ho there! The castle is to be vacated as we journey to the King. I have the authority to release you or execute you. As I stop at your door, call out your name and the reason you are here."

One after another, names and offenses were given:

"Jonathan. Stealing food."

"Marcus. Cattle thief."

"Matthew. Overcharging."

"Sir Bailys. No reason."

Bailys? The name sounded oddly familiar. Stephen stopped at the door of the last cell and held the torch near. "Come to your window, Sir Bailys."

Some shuffling ensued, and a grimy, bearded face appeared behind the grate. Stephen asked, "You are a knight, and in prison? How did that happen?"

"The Rat put me in here."

"His name is Sir Ralf," Stephen said. "Why did he imprison you?"

"He said it was to think about what I had done. He will not let me out until I change my mind."

"Change your mind?" Stephen asked. "About what?"

"He says it is because I supported the wrong lord and attacked a knight of what he calls the true king. But it was he who told me to do it. Frankly I do not care who is king, as long as they leave me alone."

Stephen considered Sir Bailys's answer. "That is part of the problem, then. If you have not declared loyalty to the true King, you are his enemy, regardless of whom else you support or do not support."

Sir Bailys shook his head. "I bear no ill will against any king. I just want to get out of here and return to my fief."

"Where is your fief?"

"It included Loynton and Grandvil."

Stephen realized he was looking into the eyes of the knight who had preceded him.

"That also was my fief briefly," Stephen replied. Then a thought occurred to him: "I was told that the previous knight was captured while raiding nearby Maison Bonfrere."

Sir Bailys scowled. "I was just following orders, doing the bidding of the Rat. He said there would be a reward, and then he came back while I was doing it and said he had changed sides. It was most unfair."

Stephen felt his face burn as a wave of anger surged over him. "Unfair?" he shouted. "You burned down the house of my betrothed and killed her mother! Do not speak to me of unfair. You can rot here forever!"

Stephen turned and stalked back toward the entry.

"Sire?" Sir Bailys called in an obsequious voice.

"What!" Stephen stopped without turning, his teeth clenched.

"Perhaps if she would come, I could ask for her forgiveness."

Stephen walked on, slamming the dungeon door shut and jamming the torch back in its holder, then finally leaping up the steps to fresh air. *Forgiveness? Not likely!* He had no intention of telling Marie of this encounter—until the next evening when he was invited to sup with the ladies in Lady Anne's quarters.

Entering through the door into the common room, Stephen was flooded with long-past memories of a gawky youth who had stumbled through dancing lessons with a patient partner and who could hardly wait to get out of his misery.

And there that same partner was at the table, now his beautiful betrothed, sitting with Lady Anne and Charis.

"Thank you for coming, Sir Stephen," Lady Anne said. "We are honored by your presence, and of course Lady Marie has asked many times if we could invite you." She smiled at Marie.

"Milord," Charis said, rising from her chair and bowing.

"And thank you for the invitation, milady," Stephen said, taking his seat by Marie, trying his best to retrieve all he had been taught about manners when in the company of ladies.

"I'm sure you are busy with preparations to depart the castle," Lady Anne said. "We are grateful for your time. I fear it will be a bitter parting for me."

"Bitter?" Stephen repeated, looking at both Marie and Charis as if there were something he did not know.

"Oh—No, not for them," Lady Anne said. "I have spent my life here and poured it out into young girls like Marie once was. But I am old now and, I fear, too infirm for the journey ahead. It will be for me like pulling an aged tree up by the roots to replant it elsewhere. I am afraid this old tree may not survive the process."

"Of course we will provide you a horse, milady," Stephen said.

"Alas, I am no longer able to ride a horse without pain now." Lady Anne sighed.

"Then we will provide a cart with a straw pallet," Stephen said. "You must not worry, for you will be traveling to see the King."

She nodded. "Yes, and that is the only thing that gives me the courage to attempt the journey."

After they had finished dinner, Marie turned to Stephen and asked, "How are the preparations going? Do you know when we will depart?"

Stephen hesitated, uncertain how much information to give in answering the question. "Sir Ralf has put me in charge of what to do with the prisoners," he said finally. "I cannot bring myself to recommend execution, but that leaves only release or continued incarceration until the castle is reclaimed by the Dragon."

"Are they dangerous, then?" Marie inquired.

"I think not—except for one." He fixed his eyes on Marie.

"I know of whom you speak," Lady Anne said. "The knight, Sir Bailys."

Stephen watched as both Marie and Charis straightened in their chairs, their eyes wide with surprise—or was it alarm?

"Sir Bailys? Here?" Charis said.

"He was captured after the raid on my family's house," Marie said. "I remember seeing him tied to a stake. So he lives, and he is here?"

"Yes," Lady Anne said. "It was Sir Ralf's desire that he be given time to reflect on his actions. I myself have visited him in the dungeon to tell him about the Kingdom, hoping he would change."

"He seems not to care which kingdom he is in," Stephen said, his eyes focused on Marie, "but he did say something interesting that I guess I should pass on to you, Marie."

Stephen thought Marie tensed, likely remembering the encounter in the forest on her way home from Bartscastle, which she had told Stephen about.

"He said if you came to him, he wished to ask your forgiveness." Stephen quickly added, "I think it inadvisable to go."

"Forgiveness?" Marie repeated.

"Well, that would certainly be a change," Lady Anne said, raising an eyebrow.

"We should always be ready to forgive, as the King forgives us," Charis said quietly. "Forgiveness is a powerful weapon in the hand of the wronged. It frees the forgiven of a debt they cannot repay."

"I know in my heart that I have forgiven him and put all of that behind me," Marie replied. "But—if it would help him turn to the King, then I should go."

"I will accompany her," Lady Anne said. "Perhaps two will be more effective than one."

"Again, I would not advise it," Stephen said. "He has done you great harm."

"Perhaps you have not forgiven him yourself, Sir Stephen?" Charis asked.

"Me?" Stephen replied, but then he thought on it. "Perhaps," he said, "or perhaps I did not want Marie to."

"Charis has suffered as much as I due to the actions of Sir Bailys," Marie said. "After he sent Hugh's father, Henry, to the Dragon, her husband, William, followed to seek Henry's release. Years of imprisonment and mistreatment rendered William too weak to survive the Great Dying. She has told me she has forgiven him too. Perhaps Sir Bailys must hear me say it to him in order to turn to the King."

"I see your point," Stephen replied. "I cannot imagine the anguish you experienced over the loss of your mother and your home; I just wished to save you from having to re-experience those wounds when you saw him again."

Marie gave a pained smile. "Those wounds never go away, Stephen. They just become less of a burden to bear. Charis has helped me understand that we all experience loss and pain, even the King, but we cannot allow it to cause us to doubt the King's goodness or keep us from following the second Kingdom Rule—loving others. It is how we respond to the loss and pain that molds who we become. I want to be the person who inspires others to be who they can be. I must go to him."

"Those are sentiments of a true member of the Kingdom, milady," Lady Anne said. "You have learned well."

Indeed she had, Stephen thought. He himself was a beneficiary.

The next afternoon Marie and Lady Anne descended to the dungeon, rose-petal-filled kerchiefs held to their noses to guard against the stench, to seek out the cell of the imprisoned knight.

"Sir Bailys," called Lady Anne at the cell door. "I have brought you a visitor."

"Who is it this time?" a gruff voice spoke from within.

"Lady Marie de Bonfrere," Lady Anne said.

Marie heard the voice immediately change tone, becoming sweet and welcoming: "Lady Marie." A bearded face appeared at the grate. "Forgive my appearance, milady. Thank you for coming."

"I understand you have something to tell me," Marie said.

"Yes, yes," he replied. "It is so good to see you and to hear your voice. I have had many months to consider my ways. I have decided to ask your forgiveness and follow your King."

Marie exchanged a shocked glance with Lady Anne.

Marie forced herself to look him in the eye. "What prompted this decision?"

"I was visited by a knight named Sir Stephen and the idea just came into my head."

Marie looked away. An idea came into his head. That was how she first felt the movement of the spirit of the Prince in her life the night she entered the Kingdom. Maybe it was the same for him. Anything was possible with the King.

"I have already forgiven you, Sir Bailys," Marie replied, then had a thought. "But have you received your key and map?"

There was a pause. "Not yet ... but I think Sir Stephen may be bringing them. Would you inform Sir Ralf of my decision?"

"Of course," Marie answered. "Sir Ralf will be very pleased and I believe the King will be as well."

"I hope so," Sir Bailys said. "It is my desire to accompany you to see the King."

"All of my visits were not in vain," Lady Anne whispered to Marie.

Both women left the dungeon in high spirits, astonished by the transformation they had witnessed.

"Another addition to the Kingdom!" Lady Anne said. "And a knight at that!"

"We must tell Sir Ralf immediately," Marie said.

Lady Anne nodded. "I will send word. Let us go and tell Charis now."

They found Charis sweeping the common room, removing cobwebs and dust. She was wearing her own clothes again, doing what she always did—serving others.

Marie was ebullient. "Charis! He has turned to the King," she said. "All it took was my visit."

"And perhaps a few visits from Lady Anne?" Charis said, smiling.

"But he seemed to genuinely want forgiveness and to serve the King," Marie said. "I never thought such a change was possible—just from my offering forgiveness."

"Is it not true that all such transformations are the work of the King, though we may be the ones who receive the news?" Charis asked, nudging a pile of dust out the doorway. "I, too, am happy for every new person admitted to the Kingdom. I hope for all our sakes it was genuine."

"I will admit that it was quite an unexpected change of heart, considering his reactions to my previous visits," Lady Anne said, "but with our King all things are possible, even that which we think is impossible."

Marie smiled. That was typical Lady Anne.

Chapter 42

BARTSCASTLE ABANDONED

T HE TWO WEEKS of preparation passed quickly, and the day of departure had arrived. Stephen watched as a large crowd filled the castle courtyard, Sir Ralf organizing the procession. He would lead with some men-at-arms and archers, both mounted and on foot. The mass of townspeople and peasants from the region, interspersed with wagons of food and supplies, would follow, flanked by men-at-arms on horseback. Stephen was to lead the rearguard with his Loynton, Bonfrere, and Grandvil fugitives. In addition to Richard, steward of Bonfrere, and Hugh, Sir Ralf had posted two more horsemen with them and had assigned five archers to accompany Thomas on foot, as well as some men with spears. Lady Anne's wagon was at the rear of Sir Ralf's contingent. She had asked Charis to accompany her in the wagon, and then Marie had wished to ride alongside them. Stephen had agreed, desiring that Lady Anne have the utmost attention during the journey.

The procession wound out of Bartscastle quietly and solemnly, without the pomp and fanfare Stephen remembered when he and Sir Bart rode out to battle over a year before. Sir Ralf had addressed the assembled mass outside the castle, assuring them that they were soon to see the King, but the mood had been far from jubilant. Most were mourning what they were leaving behind—homes, livelihoods, and families—nudged onward only by hope in a long-held promise.

After passing the gatehouse with his rearguard, Stephen cast a farewell glance over his shoulder at the place he had come to call home. The castle now represented merely a lonely sentinel of times past, a lifeless heap of stones like the ones he had once labored to carry in its courtyard. It seemed wrong to abandon such a fortress, but Sir Ralf had rightly reminded his charges that buildings and castles were not what the true Kingdom was about.

The long column passed through Bartstown unheralded, heading west toward a destination unknown to all but Sir Ralf, the townspeople who had decided to stay seemingly indifferent to their departure. The Dragon had been their lord a short time; he would be again, though a few came out to watch and jeer, shouting "Cowards!" at the slowly moving procession. There having been no rain for over a week, Marie noted that the road had dried into its usual dusty, rutted state.

With each bump and rattle, Lady Anne, lying on a straw mattress in the back of her cart, issued a muffled groan, Charis sitting beside her on some scattered straw, Marie walking her horse slowly beside the cart. An archer walked alongside as guard.

"I have never felt so many pains in so many places," Lady Anne said. "Perhaps it would have been better if I had stayed at Bartscastle and ended my days there." She closed her eyes, allowing her body to be rolled and pitched back and forth, Charis attempting to hold her steady.

"Have hope, milady," Charis murmured. "Sir Ralf said this will only be for a few days."

"I do have hope," Lady Anne replied between groans. "One cannot trust in the King and follow him without having hope. But it is waiting for the hope to be fulfilled that is testing me."

Marie couldn't agree more. The period of rest in the castle had been much too short before she had had to mount up again to 'run from the Dragon,' as she saw it.

A shadow cast over Marie as a horseman rode up beside her. Clean-shaven, with closely cropped hair, he wore the blue surcoat of the King's knights, but neither mail nor a helmet.

"Good morrow, ladies! It is a good day to meet the King, is it not?" he said, then spurred his horse ahead of them.

"Who was that pleasant young man?" Lady Anne asked. "I thought I knew most of Sir Ralf's knights, but I do not know him."

"It is a face I cannot forget," Marie replied, "though it has changed. It was Sir Bailys."

"Then his change of heart must be genuine," Lady Anne said. "That alone makes my pains easier to bear."

Stephen managed to keep his rearguard within sight of the dust stirred by the main group until nightfall when they camped together near the road. Stephen joined Sir Ralf by his campfire, hoping to learn more about their journey. Moments earlier a horseman had galloped into their midst, asking for the group's leader. The same breathless rider now spoke animatedly to Sir Ralf.

"The castle has fallen and Sir John has been captured leading his people to the King! The Dragon knows of your departure. He has divided his forces into two, one to go before you and one to pursue you from behind."

Sir Ralf winced. "I had hoped the Dragon's focus on Sir John would afford us more time. We must rise early and end our day beyond the Stony Mountains tomorrow if it is possible."

"Our pace has been very slow with the wagons and the elderly, milord," Stephen said. "How can we hope to move faster?"

"We will move as quickly as we can to Stony Pass," Sir Ralf said, "after which it will become easier. But you may have to fight a rearguard action there to give us time. I will assign more of my soldiers to you."

"Might I also have Michael?" Stephen asked.

Sir Ralf shook his head. "Unfortunately, no. Since we have abandoned Bartscastle and he no longer has a domain, he has returned to the King, just as Daniel and Joel did."

"I noticed that you released the prisoners and gave Sir Bailys the colors of the King," Stephen said.

"Upon your recommendation."

"Except for Sir Bailys," Stephen said. "I did not—"

"Lady Anne notified me that he had asked for forgiveness and said he wished to follow the King."

"I would remind you, sire, I did not think it was genuine. Did you check for his mark?"

"Sir Stephen," Sir Ralf said, a tinge of exasperation coloring his voice, "with all that I have had on my mind to ready this caravan for its departure, I did not have time to go around checking marks. However, as a precaution, I told him that he could not wear mail and could carry only a sword to defend the old and the weak until I could observe his actions. He agreed gladly."

"I think he would do anything gladly to be released from prison," Stephen muttered, taking his leave.

The entourage was assembled before dawn and the long column began to snake forward toward the jagged ridge before them. The so-called Stony Mountains were not high mountains, rising only one or two thousand feet from the valley floor, but Stephen had passed this way once before. He knew there were steep and rocky passages with drops of hundreds of feet if one made a misstep. To complicate matters, a light dusting of late-autumn snow now covered the upper slopes. He posted Hugh at the front of his rearguard to keep the main body in sight. He chose to ride at the back to be watchful for enemies.

Marie joined him briefly before riding forward to accompany Lady Anne. "Well, we are up before sunrise and running from the Dragon again," she said with a facetious smirk. "But it must be a little easier on you, with Sir Ralf shouldering the responsibility."

Stephen nodded, having been thinking the same himself. The previous day was uneventful; he had even been able to relax and enjoy the sunshine and surrounding countryside. Though Sir Ralf's warning that he might have to fight a rearguard action cast a shadow over his mood, he was buoyed by knowing that Sir Ralf was in charge and knew what he was doing.

"Yes," he said. "I am hopeful that the worst is behind us now. Every step brings us closer to the King."

"It is easier to trust the King when things are going well, is it not?" Marie said, reaching out to give Stephen's hand a squeeze.

Recalling his recent episodes of panic and desperation, Stephen allowed himself a smile. "That goes without saying. But when you are in the midst of a storm, it is difficult to imagine there will ever come a time of calm. I will not soon forget your steadiness and trust, Marie. You were my anchor through it all."

"When I left Bartscastle, Lady Anne told me I must find my purpose," Marie said, looking ahead as if in thought. "Perhaps that is it. I don't know."

"Hugh told me how you bested his men," Stephen said, smiling. "Maybe I should put you in charge of the archers."

Marie smiled as well. "It was fortuitous. I had one man who was a very good shot."

"Just the fact that you challenged him endears you to me." Stephen chuckled. "Someday I will have a warrior wife."

"I do not want anyone to make assumptions about me based on my appearance," Marie said, drawing herself to her full height and encouraging her horse forward.

"And I will not, but you understand that a knight's duty is to protect his lady."

"Then your duty will be a small worry," Marie said before galloping ahead, leaving Stephen to breathe the dust.

Alone to focus on his mission, Stephen glanced behind him periodically for pursuers. He could see no one following. The Dragon's forces surely could not move fast enough to catch them now. Ahead he could see Sir Ralf's column disappearing among the boulders, winding their way upward toward the pass. As he had advised, progress was slow. The path was rocky, negotiated slowly by the infirm and the carts. There were frequent halts to help those who had lost their balance or to lead reluctant horses over uneven ground. As they gained altitude, Stephen was able to see farther behind. As best he could tell, still no one was on their tail.

By noonday Stephen guessed Sir Ralf might have reached the pass, though the rearguard was still an hour or more away. Stephen allowed himself to bask in the warming sun and enjoy the stark beauty of the mountain landscape. They were in an area of thinning trees where views were expansive. Contouring a hillside, he noted a small tarn below, its surface sparkling in the sunlight. Ahead were rocky snow-streaked crests outlined against a deep blue sky. His thoughts were transported. He envisioned the grand spectacle of joining the King's army. There would be a grand procession to the King's castle. Then there could be a wedding, and then—

"Sire!"

Stephen looked up to see Hugh winding his horse among the slow-moving peasants, finally coming to a stop before him.

"Milord, there has been an accident!" Hugh said, catching his breath.

"Calm yourself, Hugh," Stephen replied, reining his horse. "Tell me more."

"I heard a rumbling ahead. I did not see what happened, but soon several witnesses hurried back to me, saying there was a rockslide. At least two were crushed and a wagon tumbled over the side. The path is blocked!"

Stephen paused to look around. "That is unusual. The ground here does not seem steep enough for a rockslide. Was it steeper where you were?"

"I did not go to the site of the slide, sire. I thought I should tell you immediately because we are cut off from Sir Ralf now."

Stephen glanced behind him. Seeing no one following in the distance, he replied, "Have everyone rest. You and I will ride forward and investigate what has happened."

Marie and the cart with Lady Anne had been much closer to the tragedy. They had just passed the snow line where footing for both people and animals was becoming difficult. Only moments after they passed a wide area in the path, Marie heard a rumbling noise high on the slope behind and to her right, followed by screams and shouts and the sound of something tumbling down the steep slope to her left.

A pale, breathless peasant came running, slipping and sliding up the path. "Milady! There has been a terrible accident! Rocks have come down and pushed a cart over the edge. And people are injured."

Charis climbed out of the cart. "I must go to them and do what I can, milady."

Nodding to Charis, Marie felt torn. Should she continue with Lady Anne or go back to help? She rode forward to tell the cart driver to continue on. Before she could make a decision about her own course of action, she saw Sir Bailys trotting down from higher up.

Carefully passing the cart, he asked Marie, "I heard noise. What has happened?"

"A rockslide," Marie answered. "I—"

Sir Bailys took charge: "Archer," he called, "stay with the cart. Lady Marie, you and I will go and help the victims."

Her decision made for her, Marie nudged her horse down the path, Sir Bailys following behind her. Most of the peasants between them and the accident had returned to help as well. They had almost reached the site of the slide when she heard Sir Bailys call, "Wait!"

Marie halted her horse and turned it around. "What is it?" she asked.

Sir Bailys was sitting on his horse, grinning at her. She had seen that grin before.

"You will come with me, milady." He nudged his horse forward toward her. "We are going quietly up this hill. This time, it will end differently."

Long-submerged fears gripping her, Marie looked behind her, as if expecting to see her father galloping to her rescue. Though she could hear excited voices around the bend, no one was in sight. Those at the accident scene would surely be too preoccupied to come to her aid.

"You are truly without help this time, milady," Sir Bailys said. "No one will hear you."

Stephen is on the other side of the slide, Marie realized. *I am indeed alone— again.* "You cannot do this!" she said, backing her horse away, grabbing for her bow.

As Sir Bailys reached for the bridle, her horse reared, tossing Marie backward onto the snow with a thump, leaving her holding the bow but no arrow. Sir Bailys slowly dismounted and began to approach her, a sick grin on his face. Scrambling, Marie tried to edge herself up the slope on her back but kept slipping down in the snow. Suddenly a shadow came between her and Sir Bailys. She recognized the back of the archer who had accompanied the cart, bow slung over his shoulder, sword in hand, now facing Sir Bailys.

"You must come through me to get to the lady!" he said, raising his sword.

"Get out of the way, old man!" the knight barked.

Seizing the respite, Marie rolled to her side, climbing to her feet amidst the sound of steel clashing with steel. When she reached her horse to pull an arrow for her bow, she heard a moan and the horrible sound of a sword plunging through flesh, followed by a heavy thud. Reacting instinctively, she drew her bow and whirled, pointing her arrow at whoever had been left standing.

Sir Bailys was pulling his sword from the unfortunate archer, looking at her with an expression of triumph. "Now you are mine."

Without further thought Marie adjusted her aim and let her arrow fly, striking her assailant mid chest. He stopped, a stunned expression on his face, looking down with disbelief at the spreading crimson stain on his surcoat. Dropping his sword and grabbing the arrow as if to pull it out, he coughed and began to sway.

"You have slain me, wench!" he gasped, his voice mixed with both fury and surprise as he staggered backward, coughing up a mouthful of blood-tinged froth, before toppling into the snow.

"As you said," Marie replied, her face registering no emotion, "this time it will end differently."

Marie dropped her bow and rushed to the wounded archer. The blood-soaked tear in his side gave evidence the wound soon would be fatal. She looked at his face, and her breath caught.

"Piers!" she said. "It is you! You have saved my life! I cannot repay you."

"You already have," Piers answered between labored breaths. Searching her eyes, he said, "You do not remember, do you?"

She paused to think, then shook her head. "No. I do not. How?"

The man struggled to lift his head. "When you were a girl, you came upon me by the road. I was almost dead from hunger. You gave me your meat pie, and said to me, 'Live another day.' And because of your kindness then, I did."

Marie's eyes widened as she recalled the dirty, pleading face of the beggar on the road to Grandvil. It seemed so long ago now.

Her eyes began to fill. "It was such a small gesture, compared to—this," she said, choking back a sob, cradling his head in her hands, tears beginning to creep down her cheeks.

"You gave me my life that day, and it is my privilege to give it back—for yours." He closed his eyes, lay back, and, taking a final breath, murmured, "I lived my entire life a poor man, but I die...a rich man."

Stephen and Hugh picked their way forward among the rocks until they came upon a scene of chaos and dismay. Two dead peasants' bodies had been covered, though each lay partly beneath a boulder, several of which now stood in the path. Stephen looked up the slope above. It was steeper than where he had come from, but there was no rock face from which the boulders seemed to have broken off. The furrows made by them were clearly visible in the snow. He decided to ascend the slope to investigate further.

"Sire," Hugh said, "this man says he saw a figure above running away after the boulders came down."

Stephen nodded. He had been thinking the rock fall looked unnatural. Following a furrow to its source, he discovered the origin of one of the boulders, a large earthen depression. Behind it were small holes, as if something small, like a spear, had been used to budge the boulder from its resting place. He continued searching the slope, locating the sites of other upended boulders, and finally, the proof of his suspicion: a discarded iron bar. This had been the work of men, intended to cut the party in two! He hurried down the slope, his calm shattered, preparing himself for action.

"We have been isolated for a reason!" he shouted. "Richard, begin helping everyone over the boulders to join Sir Ralf. We will have to abandon our wagons. Have everyone take as much food as they can carry. Hugh, station your archers in the rocks to repel an attack. All armed men are to remain with me."

Stephen crouched behind a rock, prepared for imminent combat, his eyes shifting from the slope above to the path behind, searching for movement. Nothing happened. Minutes passed, heralded only by the sound of feet scraping on rock as the remaining peasants clambered to safety. Stephen had turned to join the archers when a flash of light caught his eye in the valley they had passed through hours before. Could it be the glint of sunlight on armor? He strained to focus on the area. For a few minutes he saw nothing, then came another flash. His heart jumped. He could see no troops, but he was certain now that an enemy force must be pursuing him.

Shortly, Richard returned with grave news. "Sire, the people on the other side of the boulders are not moving. They are disheartened. They say Sir Ralf has been captured."

Stephen's legs almost gave way. *Captured? I have been made a fool again! Did the enemy know Sir Ralf had weakened his force to strengthen mine?* And then he realized: *Their target was not the rearguard, but Sir Ralf.* The pincers were closing already!

He motioned to his men. "Quickly, everyone over the barrier! Lead your horses if you can. We must discover the truth."

Stephen began to wind his way among the boulders, leading his horse, followed by the foot soldiers, the archers coming last. Once safely through the boulders, Stephen encountered a scene of discouragement and bewilderment. People were seated on rocks or beside the path, seemingly unwilling to move. Farther up he came upon Marie sitting quietly beside two more bodies, weeping.

After dismounting, Stephen hurried to Marie's side. "What happened?"

"This archer saved my life," Marie said, sniffling.

"How?" Stephen asked, then looked at the other body. "Sir Bailys? He is dead?"

Marie looked up at Stephen, her face still glistening with the trace of tears. "You were right. It was not genuine. He attempted to take me again."

Stephen clenched his jaw, remembering his doubts. He looked back at the archer's body. "And the archer killed him?"

"No!" She broke down in loud sobs. "I did. Piers tried to protect me while I was down." She leaned over to Stephen and embraced him, her tears moistening both of their cheeks. "I never wanted to kill anyone, Stephen. Not even Sir Bailys. I just reacted."

"As you were trained to do," Stephen said, holding her firmly.

"But I was not trained to kill. I only wanted to be able to defend myself," Marie sobbed.

"And you did," Stephen said with a voice that was almost angry.

Marie dabbed her eyes and took a deep breath, suddenly appearing introspective. "When I wanted to learn how to shoot a bow, I never thought it would come to this, Stephen. I was a headstrong girl then, and I did not know the possible consequences of my childhood whim."

Stephen looked up, noticing Charis approaching Marie from behind. She laid a hand on Marie's back, causing Marie to look up as well.

Charis said softly, "Sometimes the King gives us the desires of our hearts, knowing the consequences for us and for others. But all things he uses for good."

"I don't feel very good right now," Marie responded, wiping her face and nose.

"I meant for *his* good," Charis said, "even if we do not see it. Sir Bailys served no one but himself, and the King has given him his rightful reward for disloyalty. You and your family suffered much harm from him; it seems just that he received his reward by your hand."

"I wish I could see things as you do, Charis," Marie said, "but I have just killed a man and caused another to die for me. I do not see any good here."

"But you could have been harmed or even killed by Sir Bailys," Stephen said. "Perhaps you have been spared for a reason."

Marie sighed at Stephen's comment. "This is the second time I have been spared." She lapsed back into introspection. "The burden of wondering why is almost too much to bear. Surely I am unimportant in the eyes of the King."

Charis spoke again. "Small acts of encouragement, kindness, and mercy, which seem inconsequential to us at the time and are quickly forgotten, may be of great value to the King. I have noticed how you offer encouragement to Sir Stephen. Perhaps you have been spared for another opportunity to do this."

It seemed like an insignificant reason for Piers to die, because he, like her mother, would not have known its purpose for Marie beforehand. But they had not done it for her; they had done it for their King. Marie thought back to the event with Piers on her trip to and from Grandvil when she was twelve. She had forgotten about it until Piers reminded her. At the time, her heart had been moved. It was an act of kindness that had consequences far beyond her imagination. She thought of times when Stephen's confidence seemed to fail and how she would bring up something she had read in the *Chronicle* or something Lady Anne had taught her, and how Stephen seemed to take heart afterward. She had always been like that. Perhaps Charis was right.

Leaving Marie with Charis, Stephen remounted and rode slowly to the front of the column, where he found a group of disconsolate archers and men-at-arms seated on the snow. Apparently no one had been wounded in the fight with the Dragon's soldiers.

Stephen stopped, his soldiers closing up behind him, weapons ready. "Who will tell me what has happened?"

A bearded swordsman stood. "Sire, Sir Ralf has been taken. We were almost to the pass. You can see it ahead. There was a report of a rockslide at the end of the column. He sent some of the soldiers back to investigate. Then a knight in black armor rode down from the pass with a mounted column and foot archers. Sir Ralf rode forward to learn their intent. When he returned, he did not tell us to prepare to fight. He said they only wanted him and he was going with them to spare a slaughter of the rest of us. He said Sir Stephen would lead us now."

Stephen frowned and exhaled a heavy breath. *The Rat would not have given up so easily!* He paused to review the recent events in his mind, realizing that he had again been thrust unprepared into the role of leader of a disorganized group—a much larger one this time. *Or perhaps Sir Ralf has betrayed us and gone back to his former master.* He caught himself. *That is impossible! Is the Dragon attacking my thoughts again?*

"When will it end?" Stephen muttered aloud.

"Pardon, sire?"

"Nothing," Stephen replied. "A useless thought. I am Sir Stephen. I will lead you now. Stir the people and follow me."

Stephen cast nervous eyes toward the pass from whence the enemies had come. He had done his part bringing his people to Bartscastle, hadn't he? And now he was responsible for everyone? He did not even know where they were going or how to get there. That information had vanished with Sir Ralf. This time he had no Guardians to advise him, and no Fitzroy to comfort him. He could hardly think or even breathe, nearly incapacitated by the responsibility of extricating and leading everyone to safety, wherever that was. Pursuers were gaining on him, and who knew what lay ahead of him? Maybe it was Gythreul again. They would all be captured if they remained still, though. The only way was ahead.

"The Dragon and his men are unabashed liars," Stephen said. "What Sir Ralf told you may be untrue. They may yet intend to ambush us; keep your weapons ready. Send word to the back of the column to move as quickly as possible."

He took his place at the front of the column, Marie rejoining him, bow in hand.

"I do not understand why they did not capture or kill the lot of us," Stephen said. "We were easy prey, strung out along the path. They even left us our food wagons."

"Perhaps they believe we will stay here until they come back with a larger force," Marie replied.

"Well, we won't," Stephen said. "Though I do not know where this road leads, we are going to follow it until we meet the King, or die trying."

"Spoken like the leader I will follow anywhere," Marie said, touching his arm.

A glance at Marie's face reminded Stephen that her comments were always intended to encourage, regardless of the inner struggle he was having. Acutely aware of the mounting pressure to keep his courage up and inspire confidence in his new role as leader of all who remained, but knowing what they did not—that the Dragon's forces were both before them and behind them—he said nothing. But he noticed Marie's eyes did not leave him.

"Look, Stephen," she said, "I am as aware as you that we are in danger and that a great burden has been placed on your shoulders again. Worrying about whys and wherefores will only increase your burden. My comment to you after that event with the storm would do well for this occasion as well."

"When our trust fails, he is trustworthy," Stephen said, recalling the event.

"Yes. Do you think the King is unaware of our situation?" Marie asked.

"Right now I wonder. Who could have foreseen all of this?" Stephen said. He stopped as he reached the pass to look for movement or signs of the Dragon's troops. Seeing none, he allowed himself a moment for self-examination. "But I have to confess that he has never failed me, even when I have failed myself."

Marie nodded. "That is the kind of man I want to spend the rest of my life beside—one who believes that statement and acts upon it."

Stephen's eyes met Marie's. "You are too good for me, Marie," he said, "but I need you."

"And I need you," Marie replied, "—to lead us." She nudged her horse ahead.

Stephen spurred his horse on, and downward, his confidence growing again thanks to Marie's encouragement. They progressed over the pass without finding the aforementioned Black Knight and his troops blocking their way. Had he really left them alone? It did not seem like something Gythreul would do. But Stephen figured he had several hours' lead over those following him. He looked back over the slow-moving column; he had nearly three hundred people to deliver safely to the King at an unknown place. How would he find it? The only clue he had was a mental picture of Sir Ralf's finger at the edge of a map and his words, "High Rock."

Perhaps the road they were on went straight to the rock. He could only hope the King would be there with his army and that somehow the spirit of the Prince would see him through this new trial. But would Gythreul find him first? Would the pincers close before they arrived?

Chapter 43

DECEPTION

THE TREK DOWN from Stony Pass took the rest of the day. Darkness was near when the column came to a wide meadow and made camp. Stragglers kept stumbling in for several hours thereafter. Stephen assigned Hugh to scout the perimeter on horseback while others set up camp and built fires to huddle around, waiting for food to be distributed.

Not long after, Hugh returned, shoving a man to the ground before Stephen. "This man was in the woods spying on our camp," Hugh said.

"P-Please do not kill me," the man said. "My farm is near here. I have a family."

Stephen crouched in front of him. "What is your purpose? Are you a spy?"

The man hesitated, then nodded. "They paid me, sire. I am a poor man."

"Who paid you?"

"The soldiers who are following you. They wanted to know who was leading the people now."

"How many are they? And who is leading them?"

"I-I did not see them all, sire. But it is a large force. And they spoke of a king."

"That would be the Dragon himself," Hugh muttered.

"And we are in the middle of nowhere, following a path to an uncertain location," Stephen said, rising. "You will stay with us tonight," he said to the prisoner. "We will release you tomorrow after we depart. You will tell the Dragon that he faces Sir Stephen, Knight of the Blood, Defender of the Kingdom, and that my people are under the protection of the true King."

"That is a bold statement, milord," Hugh replied, "given what we have just experienced."

Stephen stood and looked Hugh in the eye. "He had a chance to capture us all yesterday and did not. Why do you think we escaped?"

"The protection of the King, I suppose?" Hugh answered. "But I did not see anything."

"Nor did I," Stephen said, "but I must believe he will protect his people. I cannot get us out of this alone. Now set up a perimeter guard. We break camp at dawn."

"And go where, milord?" Hugh asked.

"Where I lead!" Stephen said, fully aware that without Sir Ralf, he did not know exactly where he was leading anyone.

As a chill dawn broke over the meadow and smoke curled from extinguished fires, the shivering masses formed into a column, slapping themselves to stay warm. Stephen rode ahead with Hugh to scout the way, which eventually led up a hill. Cresting the hill, Stephen stopped.

"I know this place!" he said. "Yonder is Pevensey Bridge. I fought my first battle here." He turned to Hugh. "Our backs are to the stream with only the bridge as an escape. Tell Richard, the Bonfreres' steward, to start the column over the bridge immediately. Down the hill behind us, you should find some sharpened boughs stuck in the ground. Reposition any that are down and station the archers behind them. Send all other armed men to me. We will fight a delaying action here if necessary so that the others may be saved."

As Richard passed leading the column, Stephen told him, "Once everyone is over the bridge, continue on the path. The King's army will meet you. We will follow as soon as we can."

Richard nodded, asking no questions, though Stephen had no idea where the King's army was, or if the King even had an army, given that he seemed to be allowing his subjects to do all the fighting for him. The sleepy fugitives straggled past as Stephen rode down to inspect Hugh's line and assess the force at his disposal. Hugh had spread his two score archers behind the sharpened stakes as Stephen had advised. A group of fifty or sixty men stood in a group behind them, some brandishing spears, others grasping swords. Stephen separated out about forty spearmen and placed them behind the archers, as he had seen Sir Bart do before.

"Hugh, you will command the archers and spearmen. As soon as the enemy advances, your archers will fire arrows until the enemy is near, then they will retreat behind the spear wall and continue firing until their arrows are spent. I will stand behind you on the hill with the swordsmen to deal with any enemies who get through."

After Hugh nodded his understanding, Stephen trotted back to the top of the hill where Marie awaited him. The column had begun its descent on the other side, Richard leading them on horseback.

"I know you will not accept me asking you to go with Richard for your safety," Stephen said to Marie, who sat astride her horse holding her bow. "But I would like you to stay here out of danger and wait. If we are facing the Dragon's entire army and are overcome, you must ride and inform Richard."

"My place is beside you, Stephen," Marie said, her voice firm. "But I will stay here until you come. There can be no 'ifs.' Remember who stands with you."

Stephen gave a terse acknowledgement, wishing he could have the unwavering trust Marie seemed to have, then turned his horse to ride back to the swordsmen. He had done all he could do. He was about to face the Dragon again. He pictured the entire force once arrayed against Bartscastle soon drawing up to engage him in battle. Silently he placed all his hope in the spirit of the Prince ... or the King. Maybe one would show up. But there was no voice in his thoughts, and no Guardian standing beside him to reassure him this time. Strangely, instead of the panic that had nearly undone him before, a peace settled on him. He had sent his people on toward the King; they were his responsibility now. If he were to die on this hill, so be it.

The neighing of horses interrupted his thoughts. Across the meadow a line of archers was forming; behind them a mass of swordsmen. He did not see any horsemen, but he knew they must be in the woods behind. Both sides waited. Stephen knew from before that he held the better position, but so far he was outnumbered at least two to one, and who knew how many hid in the woods. Moreover he had no Sir John to strike them from the flank this time. Mindful that his force was the only obstacle between the Dragon and the rest, he resolved that voice or no voice, he would not run; he would give his life for his King, as Sir Bart had, as Brian had.

Eventually the swordsmen parted to reveal two horsemen in black armor, followed by another who was partially obscured. They stopped and parted, revealing the third horseman. Stephen strained his eyes to examine the central figure. A gold dragon was emblazoned on his red surcoat, over his shoulders and arms hung the skin of a lion, beneath him on the saddle lay a lamb's fleece, and on his helmet he bore a crown nestled between two sundered dove's wings. He had seen this before. *The Dragon! And the same trick the Rat used. He can think of nothing original. I will not go down there as Sir Bart did.*

Stephen felt troubled, though, about something in the Dragon's posture, and his armor. He seemed stiff in his armor, his arms hanging rigidly at his side, his legs straight, as if he could not bend them. Furthermore his helmet did not seem to fit correctly, leaving a gap above his breastplate. *The Dragon is a deceiver,* Stephen reminded himself. *He would not expose himself like this. Perhaps the armor is filled with straw?*

Farther down the slope, Hugh observed the advancing horsemen. They stopped in the middle of the field and sat awhile, one of the two Black Knights bearing a white flag.

"The Dragon makes himself a target!" Hugh shouted to his men. "And he has even put on his armor carelessly. Do you see that gap between his helmet and his breastplate? I will fell him with one shot to the neck."

Hearing Hugh's boast, Stephen looked down the hill, his eyes drifting to his line of archers and spearmen, coming to rest on Hugh as he drew his bow and aimed. "No, Hugh!" he cried. "You cannot—"

Stephen's cry came too late. He watched Hugh's arrow fly true, threading the gap, striking the center figure in the neck. He suddenly seemed to go limp, sliding off the horse, hitting the ground with a thud.

"Hah! I have killed your king!" Hugh shouted, jabbing the air with his bow.

The two Black Knights spurred their horses back to the forest edge, dropping the white flag, as enemy swordsmen began to retire into the woods, their archers following.

Stephen galloped down to Hugh, his mind racing. "That is not him!" he shouted. "The Dragon cannot be killed by an arrow. Who have you killed, Hugh?"

Stephen spurred his horse to the center of the field, Hugh running behind. The red-garbed knight lay on his side, unmoving, moaning. Stephen scanned the enemy lines with his eyes. They were still retiring. *Why?* He crouched and snapped open the knight's visor, revealing not a face but a glimpse of auburn hair. The helmet was on backward! His heart pounding, Stephen began to remove the wounded knight's helmet, a mountainous fear gripping his heart. Lifting off the helmet, he faced the terrible truth and the face of a gasping Sir Ralf.

Turning brimming eyes to Hugh, Stephen cried, "What have you done, Hugh?"

Hugh looked ashen, his eyes wide with shock, his bow slipping from his hand. He collapsed to his knees, brushing a strand of hair from Sir Ralf's face, clearly crushed by the consequences of his brash action.

"Sir Ralf! I have slain you!" Hugh rocked back and forth, his body convulsing with loud moans, inconsolable in his remorse. "Forgive me, milord! Forgive me. Please, forgive me!"

Sir Ralf's breathing was already labored, causing him to speak in short disjointed phrases as he struggled for air. "It is not—your fault. It was a ruse—gone wrong."

"What do you mean?" Stephen asked, beginning to unbuckle Sir Ralf's armor. "I sensed something was wrong. I should have—"

"No!" Sir Ralf took another agonized breath. "The Dragon was after me and me alone… after I embarrassed him by releasing his prisoners." He paused and strained for another breath. "I went with his men—to avoid a massacre of the others. He did not remember—you were also with us." There came another pause and another gasp. "He thought they would scatter without me—but when he learned you were leading them now—" Another gulp of air. "He thought of a ruse to trick you into killing me—and maybe even lure you out where his archers could wound or capture you."

"That is an old trick," Stephen said. "You used it yourself to lure Sir Bart. And it worked that time."

"It did. It was the Dragon…who told me to use it the first time."

"But I did not fall for it."

"No. He did not know you were in that battle. I told him it would not work." Sir Ralf's chest heaved as he continued to struggle for air. "When you did not come forth, his two Companions began to discuss killing me themselves. I could not move with the armor on backward—I hoped you could see my feet pointing the wrong way."

"But you wore his crown!" Hugh blurted. "How was I to know?"

"I did not know I wore the crown," Sir Ralf sighed. "It is not your fault, Hugh. He would have executed me anyway. You must leave me to die. You are in great danger here beside me." Sir Ralf turned his eyes to Stephen and breathed a shallow breath. "Lead the people onward, Sir Stephen."

Stephen stood. "They have retreated. I will not leave you alone on this field! We will take you with us."

"Sir Stephen," Sir Ralf rasped. "Look at me—I can neither feel nor move the rest of my body." The effort of taking a simple breath was clearly draining his strength. "I am a dead man. You must lead them to safety—before the Dragon comes back for you."

"I will not!" Stephen cried, motioning for Marie to come. "We will bring you to the King. Perhaps his physicians can heal you."

"No!" Sir Ralf said weakly. "I am paralyzed, Sir Stephen. If I do not die today, I will die tomorrow."

Stephen turned to Marie, who had come to a halt behind them, an expression of horror contorting her face. "Marie, you must ride to Richard and bring back a wagon. We will stay with Sir Ralf until you return. And bring Charis."

Marie galloped away in a cloud of dust.

"Hugh, take the rest of the men and join Richard," Stephen said. "I will remain with Sir Ralf."

"And leave you alone, sire?" Hugh said. "What are you thinking? We can ill afford to lose both of you. Sir Ralf said they were after you now."

Stephen shook his head as if to remove a cloud of bafflement, recognizing that indeed he was not thinking clearly, the shock of seeing Sir Ralf gravely wounded having scattered his thoughts and thrown a fog over his brain. He needed to focus. Why had the Dragon's forces retreated? Were they preparing even now to burst out of the woods and capture him? What was he supposed to do?

"You are right," Stephen replied, remembering now the ruse he had been determined to avoid, yet puzzled why the enemy had not attacked, now that he was a target in the middle of the field with Sir Ralf.

"I was distracted by Sir Ralf's condition. Help me get Sir Ralf out of this armor and drag him to the shade of a tree and form a perimeter with those who are armed at the base of the rise. Send some men for water."

Once under the tree Stephen now focused his attention on the arrow in the back of Sir Ralf's neck. "I am going to pull this arrow out. Hugh, bring some leaves and grass to press on the wound to stanch the bleeding." Stephen watched Sir Ralf wince as he eased the arrow out, then he pressed a handful of grass on the wound to slow the seep of blood. Apparently it had entered only far enough to sever his spinal cord, but Stephen knew there already had been blood loss, perhaps too much for Sir Ralf to withstand. He sat in the coolness of the tree's shadow beside Sir Ralf, his hand firmly pressing leaves and grass to the wound, eyeing the fringe of the forest on the other side of the field for movement. The enemy troops had seemingly melted away, their opportunity squandered.

Sir Ralf lay quietly as if awaiting the end, while Stephen periodically dripped water from a goatskin onto his tongue. The day wore on, Stephen baffled why the Dragon did not return and overpower them, Sir Ralf lying in the shade taking shallow, labored breaths. Finally a trail of dust announced the return of Marie with a wagon, Charis seated in the back. Charis bandaged Sir Ralf's neck and helped load him into the wagon while steadying his head, where he was placed on a bed of straw. She then took a seat beside him with a skin full of water.

Stephen leaned over the side. "Sire, we are resuming the journey, but I do not know where to go. I told Richard to stop when he found the King's army, but in fact I do not know where the King is."

Sir Ralf's eyes fluttered open as he gulped a breath. "This path leads to High Rock. You will reach it in a day or two. Then you will be safe."

Any large rock could be that rock. "There are many rocks in the Stony Mountains," Stephen replied. "How will I know it is the right one?"

"It is a large and jagged rock—with a cleft in it," Sir Ralf said. "You will know. You must lead now."

Stephen touched Sir Ralf's arm, then spurred his horse to find Richard and the head of the column, leaving a small force of archers and swordsmen to accompany the cart. He did not have far to go. Richard had stopped the column upon Marie's arrival. Everyone was scattered about in the grass resting, as if waiting for someone to take charge.

The cart slowly bumped along the path behind, Charis dripping water on Sir Ralf's tongue, Sir Ralf settling into a dream-like state, feeling as though he were naught but a head rolling back and forth when the wagon wheels jumped over ruts. His eyes opened periodically, revealing to him a face long stored in memory—a face that had launched his life in an unexpected direction.

"Gentle Charis," he rasped following a strained breath. "How is it that now you are with me in death—when once you nursed me from death back to life?"

"It is my purpose, milord. I know nothing else," Charis said, dabbing water on his lips. "No one should die alone."

Sir Ralf lapsed into silence, his eyes closed, then he began to laugh softly, ending with a spasm of coughing.

He felt Charis lay her hand on his forehead. "Why do you laugh, milord? Do not exert yourself so."

He opened his eyes again, searching for her face. "I was just reviewing my life—as those who are dying do. The ironies are many—besides your presence both in my rebirth—and my dying."

"Do not trouble yourself, milord." Charis answered, smoothing his hair. "Conserve your strength."

"In my country, I was known as the red knight—for my hair.' He coughed again. "I served the Dragon in his red colors, yet I die his enemy as a red knight—dressed in his colors."

"Yes, milord," Charis replied, dripping more water on his tongue.

"I survived a fall—which should have paralyzed me, and I die paralyzed all the same." Sir Ralf groaned as the cart bumped over a large stone. "And the greatest irony—"

"Yes, milord?"

"The greatest irony...is that he who would have slain me as an enemy, has slain me even so—as a brother."

"Yes, milord. The King's ways are a mystery, but surely you have fulfilled his purpose."

Sir Ralf grew silent again, images and thoughts drifting in and out of his consciousness, spoken as he thought them.

"My life for the King was a short one, but I am grateful he appointed me to his service ... and made me trustworthy." He grunted and gasped. "I was a merciless man, though I acted in ignorance—but I was shown mercy nonetheless."

"You must rest, milord," Charis said. "Do not struggle so with your thoughts."

"And you, dear Charis—are the face of that mercy." Sir Ralf coughed, then closed his eyes.

Surveying the scattered crowd, Stephen was alarmed. He had hoped Richard would have led the column much farther than he had. Time was slipping away.

"Why is everyone sitting about like lost sheep?" Stephen shouted. "Why are you not leading them forward?" He stared at Richard. "The enemy is on our heels!"

"Sire, I was not sure—"

"There is only one way to go. Forward!" Stephen said. "Form them into a column!"

Stephen took his place at the head of the column with Marie, sending Richard to the back to act as rearguard. Feeling the ominous presence of the unseen army of the Dragon pressing into the diminishing space behind him, reliving the horror of watching Sir Ralf struck down by one of his own men, Stephen's peace had vanished, his mind now filled with myriad unpleasant outcomes. He thought he had sent the people to safety, yet here they were in danger again.

Once again he mobilized his flock and headed west. He could not imagine why the Dragon did not end it all immediately, for if he were in the Dragon's place, he would certainly have surrounded and captured the entire column by now. Perhaps Gythreul was ahead of him blocking the road even now.

"You are worrying again, aren't you?" Marie's soft voice came from his left as she rode up beside him.

"How can I not worry?" Stephen said. "I am responsible for the life of everyone in this column, and I do not even know where I am going!"

"No, that is not exactly true," Marie answered evenly. "The King is responsible for those who are his. Perhaps you are assuming more responsibility than you are intended to have."

"Well, he isn't here right now, and I am," Stephen said, his voice rising. "How am I supposed to lead them without even a plan?"

"Have you forgotten what you said to me at the top of the pass yesterday?" Marie asked.

"What did I say? My mind is totally jumbled right now, Marie."

"You said, 'He has never failed me, even when I have failed myself.' Whom were you referring to?"

Stephen knew what Marie meant, remembering what had happened at the siege of Bartscastle when he had taken matters into his own hands, and before the storm when his courage had failed him. He wished he did not have to wait until the last moment for the spirit of the Prince to show up. He wanted to have everything under control ahead of time, every eventuality thought through and addressed. He hated the feeling of helplessness as he waited on the spirit of the Prince or the power of the King. He hated listening for voices in his thoughts. Why couldn't he just receive help when he saw the need for it?

They rode until the sun was low in the sky. No attack materialized. Marie had again been the voice of truth. Stephen needed to trust the King, not himself.

A grassy meadow surrounded by forest came into view. He stopped, the others following and separating into groups.

"We will camp here," he said. Mustering his own faltering confidence, he announced to all, "Have heart. Tomorrow we join the King." He hoped he had spoken with veracity.

Foraging parties having entered the woods to search for firewood and edible berries, Stephen busied himself erecting Sir Ralf's pavilion in which to house Marie for the night.

Richard approached and said, "Sire, Charis has informed me that Sir Ralf has succumbed to his wound."

Nodding, Stephen breathed a sigh, and then sat heavily. His last connection with the King's plan for the group under his command was gone. There was no map; it had been in Sir Ralf's head. Stephen knew only a name: High Rock.

"The people must be wondering why they have not seen Sir Ralf," Stephen said. "We must tell them. I hope they will accept me as their new leader."

The next voice belonged to Thomas, who arrived just after Richard: "Sire, a local shepherd has offered some of his sheep and lambs to sustain us for the night."

"Thank him, Thomas, and divide them among the groups. Where is Hugh?"

Thomas was silent for a moment, then responded, "I have not seen him, sire. After the, um, incident, he seemed dispirited. I heard him say something about being worthless to you and the King now, and that maybe he should just go the Dragon's camp and try—"

"What?" Stephen shouted. "Hugh, a deserter?"

"Sire, I do not think—"

"Do not think, Thomas! Just find him!"

Chapter 44

NIGHT VISITORS

A LEG OF ROAST lamb had assuaged Stephen's hunger, but he was still troubled, his mind swirling with disturbing possibilities as he hunched over his campfire wondering what the next day would bring. *What is the Dragon planning? Is his army surrounding us even now? Surely Hugh would not desert to the Dragon. But where is he?*

Approaching footsteps alerted him to a visitor. Richard emerged from the shadows.

"Sire, a traveler has asked to speak with you."

A caped, hooded figure stepped into the flickering light of the fire.

"Identify yourself and your purpose, stranger, and be quick about it," Stephen said.

The man drew back his hood, revealing a handsome face, carefully cropped beard, and piercing blue eyes.

"You!" Stephen shouted, jumping to his feet. "How did you get through our guards?"

"Sir Stephen, this is *my* kingdom." He smiled. "I roam to and fro as I wish. And you know they cannot harm me anyway."

Stephen knew he was right. "So, have you come to take me, as you took Sir Ralf?" he asked.

The Dragon smiled again, not maliciously, but as to a companion. "Perhaps I should have had you stoned when I captured you before, but, no, I have come with a proposition."

"Like the one you gave Sir Ralf?" Stephen asked, his voice colored with sarcasm.

"Better," the Dragon replied. "He got what he deserved. You can have much more."

"Speak your mind, then," Stephen said, curious why the Dragon would come alone with no bodyguard.

The Dragon's smile became broader, as firelight danced in his eyes. "You care very much about the people you are leading, do you not?"

"Of course I do. They are my responsibility now," Stephen answered.

"Yet you are leading them you know not where, to a supposed King whom you do not know, whose face you have never seen," the Dragon said.

Stephen paused to think. The Dragon's statement contained a kernel of truth. Stephen did not truly know the King, nor had he seen the King's face, and he still was not sure about their supposed destination—High Rock. Was the Dragon toying with his mind? Stephen had been deceived once; he resolved that he would not be deceived again.

"I do know where I am going," Stephen said, "and I have seen my King. Furthermore, I believe he is very near."

"'Believe?" the Dragon spat. "What is your belief but a hopeless wish?"

"There is more to my belief than that." Stephen folded his arms, forcing himself not to blink as he stared into the Dragon's now icy cold eyes.

"So be it," the Dragon said with disdain. "I thought I had cut off the head of the serpent yesterday, but apparently it has grown another!"

"Curious words, coming from the Dragon himself," Stephen said sourly.

"No one is allowed to call me by that name!" the Dragon said, his eyes suddenly blazing. But immediately his countenance changed to a disarming smile again. "Here is my proposition: you and your lady join me and I will allow the rest to go free. It is a better offer than Gythreul gave you."

"Perhaps, but that is what your Companions told Sir Ralf," Stephen replied. "And the others do not belong to you anyway."

"I know who you are!" Marie's voice came from behind Stephen.

Stephen turned to see her come to his side, an expression of determination on her face.

"And I will not go with you!" she continued, placing her hand on Stephen's shoulder.

The Dragon's eyes shifted to Marie, giving her a condescending glare. "You must control your lady, Sir Stephen. She is neither obedient nor submissive."

Then his face resolved into a smile again. "But perhaps she will like this: you and she will be lord and lady of Bartscastle if you join me. It will be my gracious gift to you. You will live out your lives in honor and peace."

Stephen was taken aback, fond memories of his years at Bartscastle flooding his senses—the beauty of dawn in the east from the castle walls, the warmth of a crackling fire in the great hall, the aroma of savory meals at the table with Sir Bart, the exhilaration of conversations about life as a knight. What would it be like to be lord of Bartscastle with no more fear or anxiety? For Marie to be lady of Bartscastle? To rear their children there in peace and safety?

"It is not yours to give!" Marie exclaimed. "It was taken from the true King, and he will have it again."

"That remains to be seen," the Dragon replied, ignoring Marie. "What say you, Sir Stephen? Are you going to allow a willful girl to trample your manhood and decide for you?"

Stephen continued to stare back at the Dragon, his mouth half-open. No words came.

"When I was a girl, I was terrified of you," Marie said, slipping her arm around Stephen, "but I know now that you have no power over those who belong to the King!"

Nonetheless, Stephen knew at the moment he had no power over the Dragon, who stood over a head taller than him, looking down at him from what seemed a great height. He stood motionless for a while, his mind blank, as if shackled and confined in a dark cell like the one he had experienced in Bartscastle. *Has the Dragon chained even my thoughts?* Then the words of Marie coursed through his tormented mind, untangling each knot as he struggled with how to respond.

The thoughts he spoke next were not his, though they came from his mouth: "We both belong to the true King! We will not go with you, whatever you offer us. And if you attack us, we will resist you with the full power of the King!"

"An empty threat!" the Dragon sneered, scowling. "The Prince is long dead and your King is nowhere to be seen! You have grievously miscalculated. Tomorrow you will watch all your people die at my hand—and then I will kill you." He glanced at Marie. "Oh, and your lady will be next to last, so that you can watch her cry out in her agony!" The Dragon jerked his hood back over his head, turned, and stalked into the shadows.

Stephen's heart pounded, his body so tense he could not move for a moment, his only reaction to think, *I do not know what to do. Help me!* He knew that the Dragon's army could wipe away his small force like a stain on the ground. He had no idea where the King was. The lives of those depending on him could be snuffed out tonight or tomorrow if he could not find the King. He collapsed to the ground holding his head, his thoughts as devoid of a solution as darkness is of light. He felt Marie's hand rest softly on his shoulder.

"Your words were well spoken, Stephen," Marie said quietly.

"I wish they were my words," he said, pushing himself up to a sitting position, gazing at the dying fire, attempting to compose himself. "What do I know about the full power of the King?" I feel helpless. How can I and a few soldiers guide these people to the King tomorrow and fend off an attack by the Dragon?" He nudged a coal back into the fire with his foot.

"Consider whose words they were, then," Marie replied. "And you do know something about the full power of the King. I do not know how, but I cannot help but believe that the King has protected us to this point and he will be faithful to protect us tomorrow. Is not that what the Kingdom is about? When we are weak and helpless, he is strong, and when we trust in his strength, we are victorious. Is not that what happened in the storm?"

Stephen realized Marie was right—as always. He just needed to hear it again. He placed his hand on hers. "You always know the right thing to say, Marie. I only wish it was not so difficult to trust in a strength I do not see and a power I do not control."

"Stephen," Marie said, tugging him close to her, "your strength and courage were what first attracted me to you, but what endears you to me now is your heart. You seek only the best, not for yourself, but for your people ... and for me. Lady Margaret told me once that our possessions and even our lives are not to be held dear, but the King will guard our hearts. He will guard yours against the threats of the Dragon."

Stephen looked up at Marie, encouraged by the unwavering look of confidence on her face. "I hope he will—and I do want the best for my people and for you." He pressed his lips to her cheek. "I love you, more than I can express in words. If the Dragon tries to lay a hand on you tomorrow, I will fight for you until my last breath."

"I know that, Stephen. You have shown me by your actions. And I will draw my last breath at your side. I just don't want it to happen tomorrow." She took his hands in hers. "Stephen, do you have your map with you?"

Nodding, Stephen reached up under his mail shirt to the pocket in his tunic, drawing out the sweat-stained parchment. "Why do you ask?"

Marie unfolded her map. "Look at your map, then show me on my map where your heart is."

Stephen opened his map and traced his road to the green heart representing him. Then he took Marie's map and traced his route on hers, leaving his finger in the same spot.

"And mine is here," Marie said, placing her finger beside his, touching it. "If our maps were one, our hearts would be touching now. Our roads have brought us side by side where they join just outside the King's castle. We will enter on the same road—together. This is all that matters to me."

"And to me as well," Stephen murmured, drawing her close.

Since leaving the battlefield, Hugh had told Richard he would ride at the back of the column as rearguard. He kept his distance, consumed by thoughts too dark to deserve being counted among the followers of the King. It was clear to him that he had done the unthinkable and was no longer worthy to be a soldier of the King. He could not even face Sir Stephen now, much less the King. It would be best if he did not accompany the column on the morrow. Perhaps he should just go to the Dragon's camp, attempt to do what he thought he had done earlier—kill the Dragon—and end his own life in the process. No one who belonged to the King would want him near them once they knew what he had done, and no one would miss him if he did not return.

When the column stopped for the night, he hung back farther and slipped into the forest to be alone. Even a growing hunger could not bring him out, though he could see campfires and hear the voices of people enjoying a meal. Darkness had fallen when he heard footsteps. For a moment he tensed, then drooped his shoulders in resignation, reasoning he might as well let someone end it now, since he was of no use to anyone at this point. The man stopped and stood before him in the darkness.

"Go ahead, whoever you are. You have found me," Hugh said. "Kill me now. Get it over with."

"I did not come for that," said the stranger, pulling his hood back. "You deserve better."

The stranger was bearded, but Hugh could not make out the face. "Who are you? I do not know your voice."

"I am your king, Hugh," the voice declared.

Hugh's eyes widened, his knees giving way as he fell to his hands and knees, sobbing. "Milord! I cannot be in your presence. I am not worthy, for I have killed one of your knights." He prostrated himself, overcome by his anguish and the memory of what he had done. "Please, sire, depart from me. Forgive me if you can—or kill me at once!"

"No, Hugh," the soothing voice said. "You have done just as I wished."

"How is that possible, milord?" Hugh asked, peering up at the stranger, the moonlight revealing a glint of blue in his eyes. Something did not feel right, as if the darkness around Hugh had become embodied in this figure standing over him. But one thing was now clear to him: "My King would not speak like that! You are not my King!" He sat up.

"I can be, Hugh. The so-called King you follow has no use for you now. You have disappointed him beyond measure. How can he trust you now?"

"Who are you?" Hugh said again, this time as a forceful demand, feeling the presence of the one standing above him enveloping him and pressing him down like a heavy shroud.

The stranger crouched in front of him and fixed him in his gaze. "You are a master marksman, Hugh. No one could have made that shot today but you. Come with me now. I will make you chief over my archers."

Hugh's breath caught. "The Dragon! You are the Dragon!" He jumped to his feet. "Get away from me!"

"Hugh, I am not here to harm you," the Dragon said, remaining in a crouch. "Come, follow a king you can see and trust, not one who takes from you for no reason."

Hugh became silent, the faces of his father, mother, and Brian passing before him, the anger over his loss beginning to rise again. "You killed my father! Go away!"

"No—No, Hugh, I did not," the Dragon replied. "The Rat killed your father. I have only helped you obtain what you wanted—revenge. What has *your* King done for you? He could not save your father, he allowed your mother to die of grief, and he took away your best friend. I can give you what you want. You really belong to me."

The struggle that raged within Hugh took away his words. He had been angry at the King for every one of those wounds. Why should he trust a King who allowed them to happen?

Finally he said weakly, "My mind tells me I should listen to you, but—" He shook his head. "But my heart is not willing."

"Do not listen to your inconstant heart, Hugh." The Dragon's voice became irresistibly persuasive—its sibilant sounds silky soft, soothingly smooth, slithering like a snake. "You must do what your mind tells you is right for you."

"I need more time," Hugh said, battling the almost overwhelming impulse to step forward and go with the Dragon. "There is—something wrong with this. I no longer want revenge. What I want is—I still hope—the King is who I believe him to be. I hope he can forgive me. I need to think it through."

"Forgive? Hope?" The Dragon's voice was filled with derision. "There is no forgiveness for what you have done. And you have no hope, other than the hope of being a great warrior in my army. You are confused, Hugh. Now is the time. Come." The Dragon stood and held out his hand. "You know you want to."

The enticement to go to the Dragon and be led away was nearly overpowering. Hugh leaned in to it, and then jerked away, as if extracting himself from a deadly grasp. "No! I do not want to!" Hugh said. Then, almost involuntarily, he began to lean in again. "But—maybe it is all that is left for me, after what I have done." He sighed.

"It is your destiny, Hugh. Come."

Hugh could sense his breaths becoming shallower and more labored, beads of sweat glistening on his forehead as if he were struggling to lift a crushing burden. "But I can't—I can't right now. Something inside will not allow me. Just go!" he shouted.

"Very well," the Dragon replied. "Be sure you are on the right side come morning. The wrong side will be exterminated. I am counting on you."

Hugh watched the Dragon dissolve into the darkness, suddenly aware that he was shaking uncontrollably and totally exhausted. He lay back, alone, each breath an effort; he could hear animated voices around the campfires in the distance. How he wished to be among them! But he dared not approach them. Word of how Sir Ralf was killed would have spread through the camp by now. There would be questions; he would be shunned, perhaps even assaulted. He continued to lie in the darkness, pondering his choices, longing for the brotherhood of friendly voices, food, and a warm fire. What was he to do? Had the King already disowned him? Did he really belong to the Dragon now, or would he always belong to the King, as his father had taught him and as he himself had said in meetings of the Servants? Could he aim an arrow at Sir Stephen, or at Thomas? No, he could not. He could not be a part of either side now.

He felt lost.

Footsteps crackled again. *He's back.*

"Go away! I haven't decided," Hugh called out.

"Hugh!" Thomas said. "Where have you been? Sir Stephen told me I must find you. He thinks you have deserted to the Dragon."

"I almost did," Hugh said. "I cannot go back with you, Thomas. I cannot face Sir Stephen or the King after what I have done."

"Hello?" another voice called from the darkness.

"Who is that, Thomas?" Hugh asked in a low voice. "Were you followed?"

"By the smell preceding him, it must be the shepherd who fed us," Thomas whispered.

The snap of twigs and trampling of leaves announced the appearance of the shepherd, carrying an object wrapped in cloth. "You must be hungry," he said. He un-wrapped his parcel and offered a steaming shank of lamb to Hugh. Hugh looked up with an expression of confusion, but accepted it with a nod of thanks.

"Everyone seems to know where I am when I want no one to know," Hugh said. "But I thank you for your kindness, sir."

"Yes, the gift you offered all of us was costly for a poor shepherd," Thomas said.

"It was my pleasure," the shepherd said. "I have many flocks, so I am not as poor as I might appear."

"But—why did you look for me and bring food to me? You don't even know me," Hugh asked.

The shepherd laughed. "I will admit it was like looking for a lost sheep, but I have found you, Hugh."

"How do you know my name?" Hugh asked, his skin beginning to prickle. "Who are you?"

"I heard Thomas say your name," the shepherd answered. "Hugh, do you remember a story your father used to tell about a shepherd he met once?"

Hugh thought for a moment, his eyes meeting those of the shepherd. "That was a long time ago. When I was a child, he would tell the story. It seems odd that you would know about it. But that shepherd was really not who he appeared to be. Why do you ask?"

"I am the same," the shepherd answered.

"The same?" Hugh gasped, his eyes widening. "How can it be? Then, you are—the Prince?"

"You have spoken truly."

Hugh fell to his knees, his face on the ground. "Milord! I have dishonored you!" he cried. "Can you possibly forgive—"

"No, you are not the Prince!" Thomas interrupted, turning to face the shepherd. "The Prince would not disguise himself as a shepherd! And he was killed years ago. What are you trying to do, fooling us like this? Who are you?"

The Prince looked toward Thomas and shook his head slowly. "Thomas..., Thomas, what proof do you require? Why would I claim to be the Prince if I am not? You have already seen me once and you did not know me."

"Nonsense! The Prince died of a sword wound in the side," Thomas said. "Show me!"

"So that you know I am not tricking you, tell me which side," the Prince replied.

"According to the *Chronicle*, it was the right side," Thomas said.

"You cannot see in the darkness, but place your hand on my right side. You will feel the scar of that wound."

Hugh could just see Thomas put his hand slowly into the shepherd's cloak, drawing it back with a jerk, then dropping to his knees.

"Milord, forgive me!" he cried. "I did not—"

"You are forgiven, and happy are those who trust me without the proof I have given you, Thomas. What you both have asked for is what I have come to speak to you about," the Prince answered. "Hugh, do you remember a time when Clyffe brought you a message that burned itself into your map? What was it about?"

"It was about forgiveness," Hugh recalled, sitting on his heels, still in disbelief that he was talking to the Prince. "It was the hardest thing I have ever done, forgiving Sir Ralf for killing my father." He looked at the Prince with brimming eyes. "And I really did forgive him, milord." Hugh began to sob. "Why then did I have to kill him? Everything has gone wrong!" Hugh put his head in his hands, rocking back and forth, reliving in his memory the horror of seeing the gasping face of Sir Ralf, an arrow in his neck.

"The King has purposes in our lives that we do not fully understand, Hugh. You have just been severely tested."

"You do not know the full truth of what you say," Hugh said. "I was just visited by—"

"The Dragon," the Prince said. "I do know. And there is a purpose in all of it."

"There can be no purpose but to make me feel like a worm that should be squashed underfoot," Hugh said, his head drooping.

"That is perhaps one purpose," the Prince said, "for you have always been possessed of an impetuous pride in your own ability. That has been taken from you. But another purpose has to do with forgiveness. It has been difficult for you to both forgive and to ask for forgiveness. The King has forgiven you, but you have not forgiven yourself, have you?"

"I have killed one of the King's best knights. How can I? I am worthless to him and to you now." Feeling totally broken, Hugh sobbed with great groans.

"Your King is a merciful king, Hugh. You are worth more to him than you can imagine. Nothing you can do or have done is so shameful that it is beyond his forgiveness. I willingly took this wound in my side so that he could forgive the prideful wounds you and others have given him by trusting in your own strength and not his. You must now forgive yourself. You will have an important role to play for the King tomorrow. You must be ready."

"What do you mean?" Hugh lifted his head. "The King has forgiven me—of this? You want me back?"

"You belong to us, Hugh. We never forsook you; you turned away from us. Go back to Sir Stephen and tell him you are ready to serve him and the King tomorrow, whatever comes."

Hugh fell to the ground prostrate and grasped the Prince's ankles, tears of relief and gratitude bathing the shepherd's dust-covered feet. "Thank you, milord, thank you! You have restored my life to me. I will gladly lay it down again for you tomorrow."

With a comforting touch on Hugh's head, the Prince backed into the shadows and disappeared.

Marie having already entered her tent to sleep, Stephen sat by his dying fire, nudging embers with his sword, trying to imagine what his last moments before the Dragon would be like. He was not afraid to die. His mind was on the innocent people who trusted him to lead them to the King. They had not chosen to die. It tore at his heart to contemplate they would all be mercilessly slaughtered because he could not protect them. There seemed to be no way out of his dilemma. No one sleeping quietly in the field knew what he knew, yet they had heard him say they would see the King on the morrow. Even if he was willing to give up his life defending the rear of the column, they still had an unknown distance to go. The Dragon's forces could be encircling them even now. And though he had just claimed the power of the King in the presence of the Dragon, he felt none of it now. Despite the warmth of the coals, he shivered; though the night was cool, great drops of perspiration plopped from his brow, sizzling when they struck the coals.

A figure emerged from the darkness and crouched facing him across the glowing coals.

"We are grateful for you feeding us," Stephen said, recognizing the shepherd. "Everyone has gone to sleep with a stomach full of delicious lamb tonight."

"Except you," the shepherd said. "You are not asleep yet."

"You have done us a service. My problems need not concern you," Stephen said.

"Perhaps not," the shepherd answered. "But you appear to be troubled. I understand you are leading your people to join the King."

Stephen sighed. "If we can find him."

"He is very near," the shepherd said, "and I know the land around here very well. Perhaps I can help."

Stephen sat up. "I don't know. We must find a rock called High Rock."

"It is about two miles from here, across a creek," the shepherd replied. "I know it well."

"But tomorrow we will almost certainly be attacked and my people slaughtered by an enemy army before we can reach it," Stephen said, giving little heed to the shepherd's offer.

"You seem to care more about the people than yourself. Do you think the King will not protect his people?"

Stephen shrugged. "I confess that I have my doubts. If we are so close, where is he when we need him?"

"Nearer than you think," the shepherd answered. "If you are willing to leave your wagons and depart now in the moonlight, there is a sheep path leading over the hills; it comes out near the ridge on which High Rock stands. You must leave your fires burning and make no noise and you must leave at once."

"We tried that once before and we were caught," Stephen mumbled.

"Oh? But you are here now. How did you get away?"

"A storm came up and chased them away," Stephen said.

"And what did you attribute that to?"

Stephen felt his hair stand on end. This shepherd seemed to know more than he was telling. He was leading Stephen to a particular answer he had been dismissing.

"Afterward, I realized it must have been the spirit of the Prince and the power of the King," Stephen said. "There was a minstrel in our party. He had just sung a song to encourage me, and then the storm arose. It seemed as if he himself had called down the storm. I almost could not believe it."

"So the protection of the King was there when you needed it to be."

Stephen nodded. "Yes. I guess it was."

"And why do you think the Dragon has not attacked you with his full army since you left Bartscastle, especially when you were a target in the middle of the battlefield today?"

"I have asked myself that many times and I do not know." Stephen paused, scrutinizing the weathered face across from him. "Wait! What did you say? How do you know all of this about me?"

Though he felt intrigued by the questions the shepherd was asking, at the same time Stephen was beginning to feel uncomfortable under this man's gaze, as if he needed to stand up and walk away from this inquisitor who appeared to know too many details about him.

"That is not important," the shepherd said, "but you must understand that the King works in unseen ways and that his protection has surrounded you since you left Bartscastle. Now gather your people and move quickly. The path begins on the south side of the field by a large pale stone." The shepherd stood, turned, and vanished into the darkness.

"Depart in the night?" Stephen called out. "But how do I know this will succeed?"

"Safety is within your reach," came the shepherd's voice from the darkness. "Be strong and have courage. Trust me."

Stephen's heart skipped a beat at those words. He jumped up and started after the shepherd, but he had disappeared. Trembling, Stephen repeated to himself the shepherd's last words. Why did they give him gooseflesh and why was he shaking? It was the voice—the same voice he had heard before, twice in his thoughts and once from a man he could not see. It was the voice of the Prince. But this man was a shepherd. How could it be?

With a resolve he could not muster moments earlier, he hurried around to the smoldering fires and began to wake everyone, telling them to gather quietly at the south end of the field with only the clothes on their backs.

"Hurry! We must leave now. Today we will see the King!"

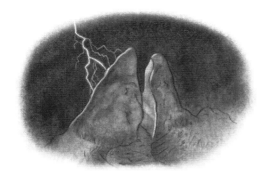

Chapter 45

RUNNING FROM THE DRAGON

B Y THE TIME Stephen had gathered everyone, the moon had vanished behind rushing clouds, and cold drops of rain were beginning to fall. He took a last look at his pavilion, the wagons, and the glowing camp-fires, all to be left behind. He surveyed the faces of his trusting followers, who, rousted from their sleep once again, possessed nothing, yet trusted in him now for everything. He was still wearing his mail shirt. Should he take his shield and helmet? If the shepherd was correct, he would not need them. If the Dragon was correct, it would not matter. He grabbed both. As he turned to mount his horse, he was stopped by a tug on his shoulder.

"Sire, I am with you. I have not deserted."

Stephen turned to face a beaming Hugh.

"I am forgiven!" Hugh said. "The shepherd—"

"You have returned, Hugh! I feared—" Stephen cut his words short. "You'll have to tell me about it later. We must move quickly before the rain puts out the fires and the Dragon suspects we are gone."

He studied Hugh's earnest face. It seemed to be the old Hugh he knew he could depend on. He clasped Hugh's shoulder and told him, "I want you to lead and find the path for everyone. I have sent Richard ahead to look for High Rock. I will take the rear. Safety is within our grasp!"

Marie had slept briefly after she left the campfire, lying awake thereafter ruminating on the ramifications of the Dragon's visit. She knew they had done the right thing in rebuffing the Dragon, but was his threat real? Was it possible she and Stephen and everyone else, even Charis and Lady Anne, could be dead by the end of the coming day? Would her King really allow this?

She was surprised to see Stephen poke his head into her tent while it was still dark to tell her they must depart immediately. She had not shown it at the time, but the more she had thought about the Dragon's parting comment, the more she had come to consider that it may not have been an idle threat. Though she did not want to suffer any more than anyone else, she sensed this day would be a critical test for Stephen.

"Stephen," she said after they mounted their horses and began to ride slowly up the sheep path, "I do not know how this day will end, so I want to say now that I love you and I will always be at your side."

"And I love you too, Marie," Stephen replied. "Why talk about that now?"

"I have been thinking about what love is since last night when we looked at our maps together. When I was twelve, I did not understand love. My father told me it was not a feeling but an attitude—toward the King and toward others. He told me I needed to learn about love and how to love. I think he was right."

"So why are you telling me this?" Stephen asked, guiding his horse around a rock.

"I just wondered what you thought," Marie replied. "Is love something we learn?"

It was an inconvenient question to have to answer on a day sure to be filled with uncertainty and possible loss of life. But it seemed important to Marie, so Stephen attempted to flush from his mind the flurry of thoughts about how to find the King while avoiding the Dragon. What did he know about love? It was just something that happened, wasn't it? Then he grew quiet, his thoughts transported back to his first day with Sir Bart and the two rules he had read on the wall of the great hall. No, maybe it wasn't a chance occurrence. Maybe it *was* an attitude and a decision made based on that attitude.

"I haven't told you this before, Marie, but when I became a squire to Sir Bart, he had me read the writing on the wall of his great hall. He said there were two Kingdom Rules, summarized by the Prince."

"I know. I saw them, too," Marie replied. "My father taught them to me—and from the time I left home for Bartscastle, I have been trying to understand what they really mean."

"You shall love the King with all your heart and you shall love others as you love the King," recalled Stephen. "It was a mystery to me then, too."

"And now?"

"It still is, but the rules seem to speak of something we must decide to do. Loving the King does not come naturally. It seems like over and over I have had to learn to trust the King," Stephen said. "So, if it is something we learn, I think loving the King means learning to trust him. I have also had to learn that trust is not based on how I feel about myself, but on the reliability of the one I trust. You have helped me see that."

"And for me, it has been obedience," Marie said. "When I was a child, I was willful. I thought only of my desires. I have had to learn that to love the King is to obey him, to be willing to seek what he desires instead of what I desire."

Though at first it seemed like an odd topic for conversation amidst the growing danger, Stephen now became fully engaged, his anxiety about the Dragon pushed aside. "Sir Bart told me something else. He said to love the King, I must first understand what it means that he loves me. That was the true mystery."

"My father had something to say about that, too," Marie said. "He told me that to love someone was to want the best for them, so for the King to love us would be for him to want the best for us and to love the King would be to want what is best for him. Isn't that right?"

"I guess," Stephen said. "It sounds simple, but how can you know what is best for the King?"

"Lady Anne showed it to me in the *Chronicle*. You and I just talked about it. I think the King wants to be honored, trusted, and obeyed. That is what is best for the King, what he desires."

"So what does that have to do with you and me?" Stephen asked, spurring his horse to keep up with Marie, just able to see her next to him in the darkness.

"It is the other part of the King's rules, isn't it? To love others as we love the King."

"You mean things like honor and trust?"

"Yes. I do honor and trust you, but I want to love you with a love like the King's love, to want for you what the King desires as best for you, even if I cannot see it. Whatever happens today, I want to be at your side forever, being a part of his purpose for you and helping you attain it."

"That is what I want for you too, Marie," Stephen said, "the King's best."

They rode together side by side, unconscious of the growing storm and rolling thunder, oblivious to the chilling rain that now began to turn the path into a rivulet of mud. Stephen attempted to assimilate what he had heard, still wondering why Marie had brought it up. He had been trying to trust the King; would the King see that as love? And who could know what purpose the King had for each of them? Was it something they had already done, or did it lie in the future? Time after time Marie had been beside him with an encouraging word. Had she been fulfilling her purpose—doing what the King desired? And what was Stephen's purpose?

Wrapping her cloak tighter to ward off the rain, Marie pondered their conversation as well. She thought that her purpose might be to nurture and encourage; she felt most fulfilled when doing so. Would obedience to that purpose be loving the King? It seemed to have a salutary effect on Stephen. She had witnessed him emerge from trial after trial to lead them to safety. But how could she be a part of the King's purpose for Stephen today? Had he been fulfilling his purpose in leading the people to the King? And where did her love for Stephen fit into loving the King? Her mind told her she must love her King, but in her heart she loved Stephen more. Was there a way these two loves were linked? She didn't know. But then the words of Lady Anne came to her: "It was a love like the King's that was given to my beloved and me." What was a love like the King's? Was she missing something? What had Daniel told her about her mother?

"There is something else," Marie spoke again. "I did not honor my mother when I was a child, yet it was from her and others that I learned the other dimension of love."

"The other dimension? What we just talked about summed it up, didn't it?" Stephen replied.

She shook her head. "No, that was about us loving the King. You said Sir Bart told you that you needed to understand what it means that the King loves you and that it was a mystery to you."

"It was," Stephen said, "and it still is."

"I was thinking about my mother—and the archer, Piers," Marie said. "I have come to understand that my mother gave her life to save my brother and would have done the same to save me. And yesterday Piers gave his life to save me. The Prince did the same for the Kingdom, did he not?"

Stephen was silent, as if pondering Marie's last comment. "Mmm...Sir Bart did say the Prince died intentionally so that the King could grow his Kingdom. I found it hard to accept," Stephen said, "but how does that relate to us?"

"I think the other dimension of love must involve sacrifice," Marie said. "The Prince loved his father the King so much that he wanted what was best for the King, so he was willing to sacrifice his life for it, just as my mother and the archer did for me."

Again Stephen did not reply, so Marie kept quiet, giving him time to assimilate her words. Marie was certain she must be right. She felt an unexplainable compulsion to speak about it. The dimensions of love and loving possessed her now with such clarity and urgency she could not restrain herself.

Finally Stephen said, "I was asked if I would agree to die for the King when I was knighted. It seemed an unlikely possibility at the time, but today it seems very real. Do you think it applies to everyone? Are you saying dying for the King is a way of loving him?"

"That is what I concluded last night, when I was pondering the Dragon's threat," Marie said, looking over at Stephen. "I think the true meaning of love is not only to desire the King's best for the one you love but to be willing to sacrifice everything, to give all you have to give—even your life—for it. That is what my mother did. She loved the King so much that she gave her life for her children. And Piers loved his King so much that he gave his life for mine. I could not understand why someone would do that, but then I thought of something my father told me."

"Right," Stephen said. "Come to think of it, my father probably did the same when he was killed defending Sir Bart. What did your father say?"

"He said, 'The deepest love may carry the highest cost.' There is no higher cost than our lives, is there?"

"No, I guess not," Stephen said. "So if we love the King with all our heart, it may cost us our lives? Sir Bart told me there would be costs along the way, which I would willingly pay for the treasure that is the Kingdom. It did not occur to me then that the cost might include my life."

"And it applies to the King and the Prince, too. Look at what it cost them."

Marie felt Stephen grasp her hand, and then he said, "Are you asking if I would die for you, Marie?"

"No," Marie said. "I know you would. I—"

"Then is it about what the Dragon threatened to do to us?"

Marie paused to choose her words. "That is what led me to think about it, but I've been thinking about something else Lady Anne said about love. I think it is about whether love would ask me to die for you—or with you. I have decided I am not afraid to die with you. "

"I would never ask you to do that, Marie," Stephen replied. "What did Lady Anne say?"

"She said the truest love is stronger than death." She grabbed Stephen's arm to pull him close. "Tell me we have a love like that, Stephen," she said, her voice almost pleading.

Stephen gave Marie's hand a squeeze and leaned in to give her a gentle kiss. "We do, Marie—a forever love."

Having said what was on her heart, Marie felt she was prepared now for whatever might come. She thought her King loved her, because in Stephen he had given her the desire of her heart. And she wanted to love her King. But what would that love require of her today? She rode with Stephen hand in hand, soaked to the skin by gusting rain, until Stephen spoke again.

"I decided last night that I am also not afraid to lay down my life for the King, or for you, Marie. What tugs at my heart now is the hundreds ahead of us who have not consciously made that choice and do not know that they may have their lives snuffed out today. I told them we are going to meet the King today. I still hope that is true and that this conversation will be irrelevant." Stephen paused and gave Marie a sidelong glance. "After you went into the tent last night, I had another visitor—the shepherd—who assured me the King was very near."

"Yes, I know," Marie answered. "I could not sleep and I heard you talking. I had the strangest feeling—"

"It was his voice, wasn't it?" Stephen said. "After he told me of this way to High Rock and advised me to leave immediately he said, 'Trust me." It was the same two words and the same voice I have heard in my thoughts! It was like the spirit of the Prince, but it was a person this time. I called after him to learn more, but he had vanished."

"It *was* the voice!" Marie said. "I recognized it too. Stephen, if we just trust that voice, we can know that the King is in control no matter what happens."

"I know you do, Marie, and I wish I had the same confidence," Stephen answered, "but a part of me is worried that the Dragon may be right. We have just seen him in person; we know he is hunting us. We have not yet seen the King. At this point all we are relying on is a promise from a shepherd whose voice sounds like the spirit of the Prince. We both know the Prince is long dead. Could we just be imagining it was him? Do we have a false hope?"

"No, Stephen. Our hope is not based on what we see but on what he has already done." Marie's voice was firm, rooted in confidence.

Stephen shrugged. "I hope the King is in control and he that will bring us through this together, Marie. I want you beside me forever. I want to be your husband and father to your children." He reached out to squeeze Marie's hand again.

"Stephen, remember the last page of the *Chronicle* where the Prince appeared to his followers after his death? He did it once. He could do it again. What if it was the Prince? Who else has the same voice? We must trust it."

Stephen had read that passage and dismissed it. The focus did not seem to be on the appearance of the Prince himself after his death, but on the spirit of the Prince. That was how Stephen had experienced him. He would not return again in person, would he? But he had appeared then as a shepherd too. Maybe Marie was right. If only he could be certain....

The entourage slogged on in darkness through the steady rain, Stephen and Marie lapsing into silence at the back accompanied by a few men-at-arms and Thomas with the archers. Once again Stephen was in a familiar position, doubting his King, while Marie was encouraging him to trust a power he could not see and a simple voice he could not question further. The reality of a present and menacing Dragon seemed to be crowding it out. Yes, he had just confessed to Marie that he had learned to trust his King, but the looming danger to his desperate band and their pitiful ability to resist were gnawing away at that tenuous trust. They needed to find the High Rock of which Sir Ralf had spoken. It was their best hope, perhaps their only hope now.

Eventually, in the dim light of dawn, Stephen could tell that they were coming to the top of a rise. The sodden band of fugitives was shivering and dejected in the cold rain, their heads down, their weakened bodies faltering, following the muddy track they knew not where. A horseman splashed past the soldiers and reined in next to Stephen. As Marie rode ahead to find Lady Anne, Stephen turned and recognized Richard, whom he had sent ahead in the darkness that morning to scout. He looked excited.

"Sire, I believe I have seen it!"

"Seen what?" Stephen said.

"There is a ridge, maybe a mile or more ahead beyond this rise. At its highest point a jagged rock pierces the sky."

"The High Rock!" Stephen exclaimed. He stole a glance behind to determine if he could see any pursuers. "How can you be sure it is the one?"

"Sire, there is a great cleft in it, as Sir Ralf said."

"At last!" Stephen's tension began to drain from him. *The shepherd was right. The King is near. We are saved.*

"We are nearly safe, then," Stephen said to Richard. "Is the King's army visible beside it on the ridge?"

"No, sire. I saw no one."

Stephen's spirits crashed as quickly as they had risen. If it was High Rock, as it seemed to be, how could the King's army not be there?

"Then it cannot be High Rock," Stephen replied, feeling doubt take root again. "The King's order was to gather to meet him and his army at High Rock. Nevertheless, take the lead again and encourage the others to push on. Give them hope. Tell them it is our destination. Perhaps we can see something from the ridge. Send Hugh back to me."

Looking ahead for Marie, Stephen found Hugh waiting as he crested the rise. "Hugh, take some of your archers and scout behind us for the enemy. There is a ridge ahead where we may have to make our last stand if we can reach it."

"No need, sire," Hugh answered. "They are not behind us. Look."

Stephen followed Hugh's gaze through the slanting rain. Perhaps a mile away to the north, he could see movement and a fluttering red banner.

Sighing, Stephen shook his head. "We should never have left on this path. It has taken too much time. I fear the King may not be near enough, if he is here at all. We are done, Hugh."

"Maybe not, sire. They are on the main road. I do not think they have seen us."

"But they must have discovered our camp. They will know we are on the move. Once we return to the main road near the rock, they will be upon us."

"Sire, remember what you said to me once. A power is with us that is stronger than the enemy. Last night I spoke with the—"

"Tell me later, Hugh. Now we must try to get all our people to safety—and quickly," Stephen said. "Perhaps it is only a small advance guard that searches for us. We will form a line with all the swordsmen and archers on top of the ridge by the rock if we can reach it unscathed. Hurry the noncombatants ahead of us to the ridge top. Perhaps we can save them if we get them over it in time."

"I once pledged to die for the King, and I will do so again," Hugh said, his voice jubilant. "There was never a promise that following him would be easy."

For all Hugh's enthusiasm, it seemed to Stephen at the moment like a forlorn hope. His people would be targets scrambling up the ridge in view of the Dragon's men. There would be certain loss of life. But if he and the other armed men were the last over the ridge, perhaps they could take the target off the poor souls who were struggling ahead of them.

"So many of the King's followers have already been lost," Stephen said, "but perhaps we can save some by forming a line of battle to attract the Dragon's attention. Go, Hugh! Lead the soldiers to the ridge and push the rest!"

Stephen watched as Hugh rode off. Then he looked down the hill in front of him. Encouraged by Richard, the peasants were struggling faster down the other side of the rise and toward an intervening ridge, among them a horse bearing the slumped, shivering, cloaked figure of Lady Anne, Charis plodding beside her and holding her steady, straining up the slope in the mud.

Marie had joined the two out of concern for Lady Anne. Lady Anne had said riding horseback was painful, yet here she was, with no other choice, barely holding on with Charis's help, an occasional soft moan escaping her bent body beneath her drenched cloak.

"Lady Anne, we are almost there," Marie called out. "You are going to see the King."

Lady Anne did not move, her head resting on the horse's neck. "With each step and pain, I am telling myself the same," she replied with an exhausted voice. "But I am so weak and cold. I don't think I can remain on this horse any longer. I just want to lie down and rest."

Marie knew stopping would mean certain death from exposure. "Charis will stay beside you to hold you up," Marie said, looking at Charis, who now had both hands on Lady Anne trying to keep her in the saddle. Charis was clearly tiring too, and she was shivering. Would she even have enough strength to get them both to the Rock?

"I will ride beside you for a while," Marie said, slowing to keep pace. She looked around in the low light. People were both ahead and behind, slipping in the mud, struggling to stand and walk, saying nothing. Only grunts and groans could be heard as they labored up to the top of the ridge before them. The last time Marie had ridden with Lady Anne she was in a cart climbing a path in the Stony Mountains. And then the accident happened, and Sir Bailys came, and Piers had died for her. She had just been talking to Stephen about that. She had been spared from death twice now. For what? The entire group could be caught by the Dragon and exterminated today. Had Piers's sacrifice been in vain? No, she could not entertain the thought. She had been spared for a reason. What was it? Her thoughts turned to Stephen, who was riding rearguard. His mind would be undoubtedly occupied with the Dragon. Was he losing hope without her beside him? She turned her horse to go back.

As soon as she was within earshot, Marie called out, "We are almost there. Do not lose heart, Stephen. Remember who has brought you safely this far and whose purpose you serve. Persevere!"

"I am trying, Marie," Stephen called back, still hoping for what he now thought impossible. "We will be able to see the rock when we reach the top of the next ridge. Maybe the King will be there."

They rode in silence, Stephen's mind turning over all the possibilities, finding none that allowed him to resist the Dragon unless somehow the King were to appear with his army. Nor was there any voice in his head to give him direction or comfort. He was now fully conscious of the chill in the autumn rain, icy drops from his hair rolling down his back beneath his mail, triggering fits of shaking that further impaired his ability to concentrate.

Viewing the struggling mass in front of him, he had compassion on the simple souls as they slipped and fell in the mud, stood up shivering and tried again, ignorant of the danger they faced, knowing only to do what the young knight asked, trusting him with their lives. He knew that some would die of cold and exhaustion on that very ridge if they did not find the King today. Or perhaps they would all die trying at the hand of the Dragon.

Chapter 46

THE LAST ACT

A SPONTANEOUS CHEER PIERCED Stephen's gloom, and he lifted his gaze to the next ridge, where some of the peasants clumped in a group at the top, their fists in the air. Richard must have shown them the rock. Stephen hurried his horse up the slope to the top. Cresting the rise, he could see in the distance through sheets of rain the faint outline of the rock Sir Ralf had spoken of. It was the height of three men, its top pointing like a finger to the sky. A flash of lightning outlined the rock into a jagged silhouette with a certain cleft in the center where the road went through. But there was something else beside it. Stephen wiped the rain from his face and strained his eyes to see more clearly as thunder rolled over him. There seemed to be a shadow with a light in the center. Another flash of lightning revealed more: the shadow was in the shape of a solitary horseman who appeared to be holding a something like a beacon close to his chest.

Stephen felt both heartened and puzzled. It could not be the King. He certainly would not risk himself alone. But who else would? Stephen galloped to the front of the jostling group as it began its descent. Whoever or whatever it was, he could use it to rally his people for a final push up the slope.

"Fix your eyes on the horseman by the rock and run to him. There you will be safe," Stephen shouted to all, feeling certain he was giving them false hope, since the army of the King was nowhere to be seen. One extra man was not an army, but was he a harbinger?

Stephen stopped at the bottom of the ridge to await Marie, Thomas, and the archers where a small stream rushed over smooth stones. Hugh soon rode up, his face dripping with rivulets of water from the driving rain.

"The enemy force at the stream where the road crosses grows," Hugh said, "and it is closer to the rock than we. I have told the soldiers ahead of us to stop at the top of the ridge and form up until we can speak to the horseman."

Stephen nodded, having already noticed the same. "As soon as they see us climbing the ridge, they may attack, Hugh. We must hurry everyone and close up behind them to form a defensive line."

The ragged band had dissolved, everyone slipping and sliding down the ridge, path or no, to the stream, splashing across and up the slope diagonally toward the horseman. Stephen glanced toward the growing enemy force; several armored knights had reined in at the stream crossing, now about a half-mile away, enemy archers running quickly to form a firing line. Behind them sat a flag bearer, the sodden red banner of the Dragon flapping fitfully on its standard. But there were no Black Knights yet.

Stephen focused back upon the rock as he nudged his horse across the stream. If everyone would just hurry, they might make it over the ridge before the enemy force was organized for an attack. The horseman had not moved. He wore no helmet. Gusts of wind whipped through his surcoat and rippled through his hair. A soft light seemed to gleam steadily from his chest level. He stood as motionless as the rock he was beside, apparently undismayed by the red tide lapping about the base of the ridge. Lightning crackled behind the rock, outlining his solitary silhouette.

"Look! He is holding up a great longsword!" Hugh shouted. "Maybe it is a signal."

"But he is holding it by the blade, with its hilt upward," Stephen said. "What kind of signal is that?"

"Maybe he is lifting it up for us to come to him," Marie said.

The surging crowd now had been noticed by the enemy; already arrows were beginning to skim past Stephen and his men. The main mass of fleeing fugitives was halfway up the ridge, the few peasants with enough remaining strength helping others to keep going. A dozen enemy knights, some clad in black, had now paused at the stream's edge, their visors down, lances ready, forming a line. Stephen and Hugh turned their backs on the menacing enemy and began to make their way upward through the muddy morass made by the struggling peasants, keeping their eyes on the horseman.

"Stay ahead of us, Marie!" Stephen called above rolling thunder. "Wait for us on the other side!"

Arrows brought down several of the peasants as they fled upward amidst growing panic and chaos. No one stopped for the fallen, all struggling toward safety from the arrows. Now halfway up the ridge, Stephen watched as peasants reached the ridge top and began to slip and slide safely to the other side. Now he could concentrate on forming a line of defense at the top, and perhaps inquire further of the horseman. Why was he there by himself? What did the beacon mean? Did he know where the King was? The lonely horseman did not seem to be alarmed by the oncoming enemy army, but sat motionless astride his mount, his sword still held high, hilt in the air. Stephen could make out the blue color of the horseman's surcoat now. A knight of the King—a brave but foolish one.

Arrows glanced off Stephen's shield and helmet as he drew closer to the horseman.

"Make a firing line below the ridge crest near the horseman, Hugh, until all are over," Stephen commanded, "and form the spearmen and swordsmen in front of them. I am going to speak to the horseman."

Suddenly a burning stab jolted Stephen's back. He dropped his shield and reached for the arrow that had struck him, falling from his horse like a stone. Gritting his teeth against the pain, he slowly pushed himself up to his hands and knees and began to crawl toward the horseman. *Must reach him. Perhaps he knows—if the King is near.* Another arrow thudded into his hip, causing him to collapse to the ground with a muffled groan, his head in the mud. Straining to keep his eyes on the horseman, he lifted his mud-smeared face and struggled to drag himself closer, tugging mightily at tufts of grass to pull himself forward. *Cannot—give up. I must persevere.* Each inch was won with desperate effort, but he knew he was weakening, his lower body having become a dead weight. Finally, exhausted and defeated, he could do no more, releasing his grasp and lying still, allowing the rain to pelt his body, waiting for the arrows to complete their deadly mission, knowing not whether he had led his people to the safety of the King.

Hugh had arranged Thomas, the other archers, and some other armed men in a line below the ridge crest, Richard commanding the men at arms and spearmen. He glanced behind him to make sure all the rest were over. Marie was nearing the top on her horse but had stopped to dismount. Why? Near her lay two bodies. He thought he recognized one. Running to them he found Charis lying on her side in the mud embracing an older lady; Marie was cradling the lady's head in her arms.

"Charis! Get up!" Hugh exclaimed. "You are only feet from safety. And you must go with them, Lady Marie."

"I cannot," Charis said weakly, lifting her head to regard Hugh with a mud-spattered face that was drained of emotion. "Lady Anne slipped from her horse. I do not have the strength to lift her. She is still breathing. I must stay with her to keep her warm." Charis dropped her head and went limp.

Without hesitation Hugh bundled Lady Anne up in his arms and headed to the ridge crest, meeting Richard coming up behind him. Handing her carefully to Richard, Hugh said, "Take her to the other side. Maybe the King is there. Get help." Next he went back for Charis. Marie had sat her up and was holding her close to warm her and protect her from the rain.

"She is failing," Marie said in an anguished voice. "She has poured herself out. Her strength is gone."

As Hugh lifted her in his arms, her eyelids fluttered open. "What is happening? Lady Anne—"

"She is safe," Hugh said. "Are you able to walk?"

"No. Lay me down, Hugh," Charis murmured, closing her eyes again. "It is my time... I have nothing more to give."

"Then we will carry you to the King," Hugh said—to give her hope, though there was no sign of the King.

"To see the King?" Charis sighed. "It is my fondest wish, but it is more than I could ask."

Richard had not returned. Hugh called to Thomas, who stood with the archers. He carefully placed Charis in Thomas's arms with the same instructions he had given Richard, and watched Marie go with them, holding her cloak up to shelter Charis's head. Then Hugh turned back to attend to his defensive line. He looked down the hill for Sir Stephen. There was his horse—without him on it! Hugh scanned the area anxiously, spotting him lying on the ground nearby, his arms outstretched, an arrow in his back. Hugh raced down the hill and was beside him immediately, carefully removing his helmet. Stephen lay on his side, his hand on the arrow in his hip, attempting to crawl again, finding that his legs had neither sensation nor the ability to move.

"I am slain," Stephen coughed. "I thought my mail would protect me. You must leave me here and continue on. Find—Find the King, Hugh."

"Never!" Hugh shouted above the growling thunder. "We are nearly at the top. I will carry you!"

Stephen lay still. He had done all he could.

Marie had said farewell to Charis near the top of the ridge, squeezing her hand gently, and had gone back to her horse to remount when Stephen's horse appeared beside her, the saddle empty. Her heart pounding, she looked down the slope and saw Stephen lying in the mud, Hugh bent over him. Giving no thought to the *whish* of arrows around her, she galloped back to him, dismounted, and ran to his side.

"Stephen!" she cried, suppressing the impulse to collapse and weep as she viewed the arrows piercing his body. "We will take you to safety," she said, lending a hand as Hugh lifted Stephen's legs from the mud. Marie winced as Stephen struggled to breathe, his chest heaving with great efforts.

"Put me down," Stephen said. "Hugh, you must take Lady Marie—and make sure all are safe on the other side. You are their leader now."

"Go, Hugh!" Marie yelled. "I will stay."

"No, Marie!" Stephen cried. "You must go too. This is not your time to die. You are almost to safety. Please save yourself and go with Hugh!"

Marie did not move. "I will not leave you," she said, kneeling by Stephen, smoothing his drenched hair. "Look at me!" she said, her voice unwavering, her face determined. "I love you."

Stephen's eyes engaged Marie's. His voice choked with anguish, Stephen spoke with short breaths, "Marie, for the sake of love,—please do not do this!"

"It is for love that I *am* doing this," Marie replied, moving to a position on the grass behind him.

It was not how she had imagined their life together. They were supposed to enjoy sunrises and sunsets in their country manor, dandle babies in their arms, and serve the King together. But instead she sat in the mud in a blinding rainstorm, helplessly watching Stephen suffer. She thought about their conversation just hours before. Was this what love was asking of her? When she was twelve, she had thought love was like her bubbly brook—a froliscome stream that tugged two hearts into camaraderie. But now it seemed much more profound, like a deep current that hugged two hearts into eternity.

She slid her arms under Stephen's and clasped her hands around his chest. "I am staying with you."

"No—please, no," Stephen moaned.

"The deepest love bears the highest cost," she said calmly, her eyes filling with tears. "I understand what it means now." She leaned over to block the rain from his face. "Last night I told you that I would draw my last breath at your side. I am where I want to be."

"Please—, don't," Stephen exhaled, lifting a hand to caress Marie's cheek.

Gathering some strands of her damp hair, Marie wiped her tears and carefully blotted the moisture from Stephen's face, touching her lips to his. "Shhh," she said, placing a finger on his lips. "We will enter on the same road."

Cradling Stephen's head in her lap, Marie raised herself to a crouch and began to pull. It was no use. Stephen's body was too heavy, hers too small. She could do nothing more.

Through eyes blurred by rain, Stephen beheld her resolute face, her brow furrowed, her lips pursed, attempting to will her body to do what it could not.

He heard a sickly thud and a pained cry, and then Marie released her hold and fell backward into the rain-soaked grass. She struggled to stand and regain her position, only to stumble and fall to the ground beside him, her head coming to rest at Stephen's feet.

Stephen turned his head to gaze down at her, finding her arm reaching up toward him. "Stephen, look at me," she called breathlessly.

His eyes seeking hers, he found an expression not of fear, but of peace, despite the fatal arrow in her heart.

"Take—my hand," she gasped.

Immobilized by his leaden legs, Stephen desperately stretched out his hand to take hers, but only his fingertips came to rest on hers. He wanted to take her in his arms and hold her, to kiss again the lips that had just pressed against his, to comfort her, but he could not. He opened his mouth to answer; no words came. His eyes remained fixed on her angelic face and the steadfast brown eyes that held his in thrall, watching drops of rain form like shining jewels on her eyelashes and the lips that had just kissed him good-bye. He could only mouth, "I love you, Marie," as he watched life ebb irretrievably away and her face became still.

An evanescent smile crept slowly across her pallid lips. "The same road—" Her voice was soft like a sigh. "Together."

Hugh arranged his archers behind the men at arms, taking command in the absence of Richard, and then turned back to check on Stephen and Marie, only to see Marie fall. Heedless of the storm of arrows, Hugh hurried down the slope again, finding Marie already lifeless, her cold fingers touching Stephen's—Stephen lying motionless, blinking water out of his eyes, waiting for the inevitable end himself. Stephen's eyes met Hugh's as if he wanted to speak; Hugh leaned over him.

"Hugh, I thought I would see the King today—I wanted to, but it is not to be. Please, go to the horseman—and ask him where the King is. If you find him, tell him that—though I was an ordinary and imperfect knight—I died loving the King as best as I could. Will you?"

"Sire, you made yourself a target so that all could reach safety. Surely the King will hear of this. But I will not leave you," Hugh replied, carefully lifting Stephen's head.

Cradling the head of his dying lord in his arms, Hugh sat helplessly as Stephen's chest jerked with its final breaths, his dark eyes growing dull, his head becoming limp. Hugh cried deep within. *It should have been me, not this humble knight!*

Gently lowering Stephen's head, Hugh glanced down the slope. The enemy army, now more than he could count, had massed at the foot of the ridge; at its front stood ten mounted knights clad in black armor. More horsemen crowded forward to join those at the bottom of the ridge. A massive army was assembling. And there by the flapping standard, astride his charger in his black armor and red, dragon-emblazoned surcoat, wearing his lion-hide cape, sat the Dragon himself, a false crown atop his winged helmet.

Suppressing hot tears, Hugh tramped his slippery way up to the horseman, who had neither changed position nor been touched by an arrow since they first had seen him.

"Sire, my master has fallen!" he shouted above the thunder. "Please, do you know where the King is?"

The horseman looked down at Hugh, his eyes showing neither fear nor anxiety about the horde assembling below him.

"Send your soldiers over the ridge and go to the top of the ridge to wait, Hugh," he said. "I will look after your master."

Knowing he had done all he could, Hugh returned to his defense line, dismissed his pitiful force and started for the ridge crest himself, but he could not go over; he could not will himself to abandon Sir Stephen's body. He collapsed heavily just below the top, his head in his hands. How had it come to this? A parade of faces passed before his mind's eye—his father making the key that ushered him into the Kingdom, his mother proudly unwrapping the box with the map, even-tempered Brian smiling at him, William consoling him over his father's death, Sir Ralf thanking him for the box and key—they were all gone now. Sir Stephen and Marie lay lifeless below him. He was the only one left.

It seemed unfair.

Stephen opened his eyes with a start. He had been moved and now was lying in shadow. A face bent over him. The beating rain jabbed at his eyes, rendering him unable to make out the identity of the face.

"I am a dead man," Stephen said. "Leave me and save yourself!"

"I have come to save *you*," the face said. "The King is waiting for you."

"Alas, you are wasting your time, sire," Stephen said. "But—I would make a request. I thought I would live to do great things for the King, and even now I would ask him—" He fought back tears of disappointment, unable to voice the thought that tugged at his heart. "Instead—it seems I am destined to die alone in the mud on a rain-swept ridge. Sire, would you please tell the King that I died loving him as best as I knew?" Stephen closed his eyes again, awaiting his last breath.

"You are not alone, Stephen," the voice answered. "You have never been alone. And your unspoken question is on the lips of many when they draw their last breath."

Forcing his eyes open again, Stephen blurted, "How do you know—"

"So many think they must do some great deed for the King before they die. If they do not, they die wondering if their life mattered at all to the King. But it is much simpler than that."

"*Yes!*" Hearing his thought stated was too much for Stephen to bear, years of self-doubt and feelings of falling short welling up in a surge of regret. "I failed him in so many ways. But I just want to know," he said, his voice breaking with anguish, "did it matter?"

"You persevered through trials, overcame obstacles, and brought your people to safety," the face replied. "Perhaps the King raised you up to be a knight for such a time as this."

"But that was all done by the spirit of the Prince," Stephen said. "I know it was."

"Yes, it was."

"Then what did I do that would please the King?"

"You will receive that answer from the King himself."

Blinking rain from his eyes, Stephen strained to recognize the face before him. "Forgive me, sire, I believe I know your voice. And I think I have seen your face before, but in my weakness I do not know who you are."

"I am the King's healer, Stephen."

Stephen rubbed his eyes and squinted. The face became clearer, but he had not seen it in the livery of a knight before. The figure wore the king's emblem on his surcoat, the lamb glowing white as if lit from within. *The beacon.* Stephen fought the fog that gripped his brain, his mind fitfully assembling images that floated in and out of his consciousness.

"Your voice—It is the voice that led me in battle and visited me in prison, the voice of the minstrel and of the shepherd. —But your face is that of the priest who gave me my armor, and you are also—?"

"The Prince."

Through the haze of confusion that clouded his mind, Stephen thought he had heard the answer correctly, but he could not respond. He was conscious of a strong arm sliding beneath his legs and another under his back as he was gently lifted and placed on his feet.

"You are healed. Go, and join Hugh on the other side."

Clarity returning to his mind, Stephen said, "Marie! Where is Marie? She—"

"She is ahead of you. Now go to her."

Stephen stood, his legs now supporting him and following his command as he moved them to walk. He touched his back and hip. There were no longer arrows sticking out. He was aware now of arrows hurtling by his head, but none touched him. Looking to the top of the ridge, he saw Marie taking a seat beside Hugh. Glancing down, he could see below him ranks of armored knights in red, fronted by the ten in black and the Dragon himself, behind them stood lines of archers and men at arms, all waiting as if for an order to charge. Why had they not charged him or the horseman?

"Milord," Stephen said, "I do not understand. The Dragon's army is almost upon us. We are but two. Why do they not overwhelm us?"

"This ground belongs to the King," the Prince said. "Look again."

Stephen blinked and wiped the rain from his eyes. His senses were suddenly heightened and sharpened. At the bottom of the hill on his side of the stream, spaced twenty paces apart, stood a row of mounted knights, each robed in a white surcoat, holding a flaming sword in the air. Stephen could hear the crackle of the flames and feel the heat on his face even as far away as he stood. The glowing blades sizzled as rain struck them but the flames were not extinguished. Stephen turned to ask more, but the horseman had disappeared, leaving Stephen standing in shadow. He was in the cleft of the Rock.

Stephen climbed to the top of the ridge, his mind brimming with confusing questions. *Where did the horseman go? Did he really say he was the Prince? But the Prince was killed, wasn't he? And so was I, wasn't I?*

Marie was smiling, her hand outstretched to Stephen as he reached the top of the ridge.

Glancing to his other side, Stephen thought Hugh seemed awestruck.

"Look!" Marie said, motioning behind the ridge.

Stephen turned, and at the sight his legs nearly gave way. He collapsed beside Marie, almost in disbelief. Drawn up in line of battle behind the brow of the ridge were row upon row of knights clad in white surcoats, their visors up, their shields bearing the emblem of the King, with one addition—above the dove on their shields there was also a pair of outstretched white wings. Stephen's jaw dropped as he recognized some of the faces. There were Michael, Joel, and Daniel, sitting in readiness, lances in hand, their eyes on the solitary horseman in front of them, a different one than the sentinel by the rock.

The horseman sat motionless on his white charger, his white tunic covered by a royal blue surcoat with the King's emblem. He wore no armor save a helmet, his blue shield bearing the image of a lion rampant, his visor down as if prepared for battle, a crown encircling his helmet. Stephen watched in awe as the Prince trotted over and took his place on the right side of the King, his shield clearly showing the emblem of a recumbent lamb, his helmet bearing a diadem. Then, as if from nowhere, a white dove glided soundlessly above the waiting host and hovered briefly over the two horsemen before floating softly down onto the shoulder of the Prince.

As Stephen sat transfixed by the spectacle, the King raised his visor and looked Stephen's way. Immediately Stephen felt enveloped in light and warmth, all seemingly radiating from the unseen face of the King as if it were the source. It was the same beacon-like glow as that from the lamb on the Prince's surcoat, and the same that emanated from the body of the dove as it now perched on the Prince's shoulder.

Stephen realized that his wish had been granted. He was looking into the face of the King. It was not as he had imagined. He had been dead; now he was alive. There were no eyes to look into, yet he was somehow experiencing an unbreakable bond with the King, as if entrained by love from the figure that regarded him. He sat, bathed in the warm glow, imagining he was being held safely in a strong but gentle hand, yet the question he would have asked still tugged at his heart: *Did my life matter to you? Did I do enough?*

The Prince turned his head toward Stephen and raised his visor. What had the Prince said? "It is much simpler than that." No words were spoken. In Stephen's mind the answer began to form in a voice that was kind and good, like the one he had heard in the King's chapel when he was knighted.

"Stephen—you trusted my son. That is all I ask."

Stephen was overcome, his eyes brimming. And that—trusting his son— was the simple answer to his question. He thought of Sir Bart, and of Michael. It had nothing to do with becoming a knight or with him making the King proud by doing great things in his service. He thought of the trajectory of his life—the upward climb to knighthood, the fall to the bottom during the siege of Bartscastle and thereafter, the angst-filled journey from his fief to his final breath on the slope below him. An image of his map appeared before him, the words 'trust' and 'perseverance' standing out. He had tried to trust his King, but so often he felt had not; he had tried to persevere, but felt he had fallen short. Yet the Prince, in person or in spirit, had always been there when he needed him. And then he thought of the inscription on his key—'Trust is the key to the Kingdom.' The answer had been there all along.

Initially, Marie had been unwilling to look at the solitary horseman in front. He was the King!—the same King she had been scared to meet as a lady-in-training, the same King whose benevolence she had doubted, the same King who had seemingly allowed her life to unravel. She thought about her journey to this moment. At its heart it had been about love. She had wanted desperately to be loved, yet she had felt unloved, even by her King. She longed to understand love.

Marie thought of those along the way who had given her pieces of the puzzle—her father, Lady Anne, Gerald, Sir Ralf, Daniel, Piers, Stephen, and, yes, even her mother. But the puzzle never seemed complete. Then she thought of her last conversation with Stephen. It had been about the King—loving the King and being loved by the King. And she thought of her map and the words it had spoken to her: 'trust' and 'obedience.' She thought she had tried to trust her King and love him by being obedient to the purpose she thought he had laid before her—to nurture and encourage. An image fleeted before her of Lady Anne holding the queen over the chess board explaining her role in sacrifice. Like the queen, she had sacrificed herself for her King—in obedience to her calling. Had the King seen it as love?

Now that she was so near him, Marie felt a gentle beckoning to finally look. The former fear and disappointment were gone; rather, she felt as if she were being drawn into an embrace she could not resist. Hesitantly, she lifted her eyes. There were no features to regard, yet she felt enveloped in the warmth of the King's presence. But more than that, she sensed that she was somehow face to face with the King, and words began to form in her mind:

"You gave what was most precious to you, Marie. That is love. And I have always loved you. In your mother's womb, I chose you; from your first step I have led you, with bonds of love. Through all your pain and heartbreak I have walked beside you, holding you close when you doubted, taking your hand when you faltered. You are my beloved daughter."

Tears rolled silently down Marie's cheeks as she sat, unmoving—gazing into the face of love. Now the puzzle was complete.

Hugh had been awed by the vast array of the army of the King, but then he saw the King on his charger. A mixture of emotions began to rise as he beheld the person who had been central to his journey. He had raged against this King, he had been disappointed by this King, and he had nearly abandoned this King. He had stored up so many questions to ask, yet he realized now his journey had been about none of them—it had been about trust and forgiveness, the word on his key and the word his map had revealed to him.

Out of respect for his parents' belief, Hugh had tried to maintain trust through all his loss and disappointment, but just hours before this moment he had come to a point with the Dragon where he was certain his King could not trust him; he was ready to sunder the final thread that joined him to his King. And he could not. Why? What had the Prince said to him? "We never forsook you; you turned away from us." He understood now that the filamentous thread of trust by which he had been suspended was incapable of being broken—because it was held firmly in the hand of the King, and because it was secured by bonds of forgiveness and love. He thought about what he had been unable to forgive, and then he thought about what he had been forgiven.

As Hugh looked back at the King, he no longer had any questions. He thought of his father, his mother, and Brian; they had all been taken from him, but they had died trusting their King. He felt no anger, no disappointment over his loss—only gratitude that he was found. The King had lifted him up when he had fallen; the King had forgiven what he could not; the King had loved him when he could not. This King was no longer his parents' King; this King was forever his King.

Marie turned to Stephen and slipped her arm around him. He did the same, and turning to Hugh, who appeared deep in thought, reached out his other arm and tugged him in. The three were at peace; they each had found what they needed. Marie's longing for a forever love had been granted, but not in Stephen. It was a gift, from her King, as Lady Anne had said. As he studied the inscription on his key, Stephen understood that he too had been granted not what he wanted but what he needed. *Fides*, faith some might call it, was not something he could conjure up when he wanted it; it was also a gift from the King. Hugh looked at Marie, and then at Stephen, and grinned. After tracing a course that had been tumultuous both inside and out, he had found peace, and that was likewise a gift from the King. Though they were now complete, each instinctively knew that they were on the verge of another journey—one that would last forever with their King.

As they looked on, the King turned back, lowered his visor, and raised his arm. At either end of the line, heralds raised golden trumpets bearing the standard of the King and sounded a mighty blast. Then the King motioned forward, and rows of Guardians snapped down their visors in reply, raising their lances with a shout, a flicker of flame licking along each lance as it was seated for the charge.

The army surged forward as one, topping the ridge and thundering down the other side, the whole ridge shaking as if from an earthquake as the host swept down, throwing great clods of mud into the air. Over the advancing army, the white dove circled, causing a great wind to spring up, a wind that moaned through the treetops as if all nature was breathing its last, then rushed downward ahead of the quickening host.

The Dragon's army drew back from the weight of the wind and stinging rain. Many began to melt away in fright when they saw the great force descending upon them, but the Black Knights stood firm and defiant, trusting in their leader. At the bottom of the ridge the cordon of Guardians parted to allow the onrushing tide to flow across the stream and crash into the enemy army. Flaming swords slashed. The stream ran red as the King's host plunged like an avenging blade into the enemy, dealing death to all they touched. It was over in moments, the enemy army routed or dead, save the ten Companions in black and the Dragon.

The ten Companions were brought before the King and forced to kneel to the Prince before being chained and shackled at the neck and led away. Then the Dragon was dragged to the front and stripped of his lion cape. His helmet was thrust in his face as the false crown and dove's wings were ripped off and thrown in the mud.

He would not bow and he refused to kneel, holding his head high in defiance until he was approached by the Prince. The Prince, the hem of his surcoat drenched with the blood of the vanquished, struck him behind the knees with his sword, sending him head first to the ground, splattering his face with mud. The Prince then walked in front of him and, with a nod from the King, placed his mailed foot on the Dragon's head, crushing it into the mud.

The Guardians, dismounted and clustered around the King, kneeled with a great shout, proclaiming the name written on the surcoat of the Prince, "King of kings! Lord of lords!"

The lion roared.

The King had come.

Soli Deo Gloria.

ACKNOWLEDGEMENT

I am deeply indebted to Diana Moore, not only for her amazing illustrations, but also for her skilled content and copy editing. Without her thoughtful suggestions through many drafts, the final version you are holding would not have been possible. Linda Moore gave me the personal space and time to sit with my office door closed and just imagine. Draft readers Dana Buck, Sarah Park, Kelly Crowdis, Carrie Erickson and Elaine Bedlion offered encouragement and valuable feedback which made the story better. J.D. Kudrick provided expert writing insights and content editing to this first time author. And last, I would be remiss if I did not acknowledge my personal God, author of all creativity, who enabled me to turn a simple idea into the story you have just read.

Printed in Great Britain
by Amazon

61331448R00324